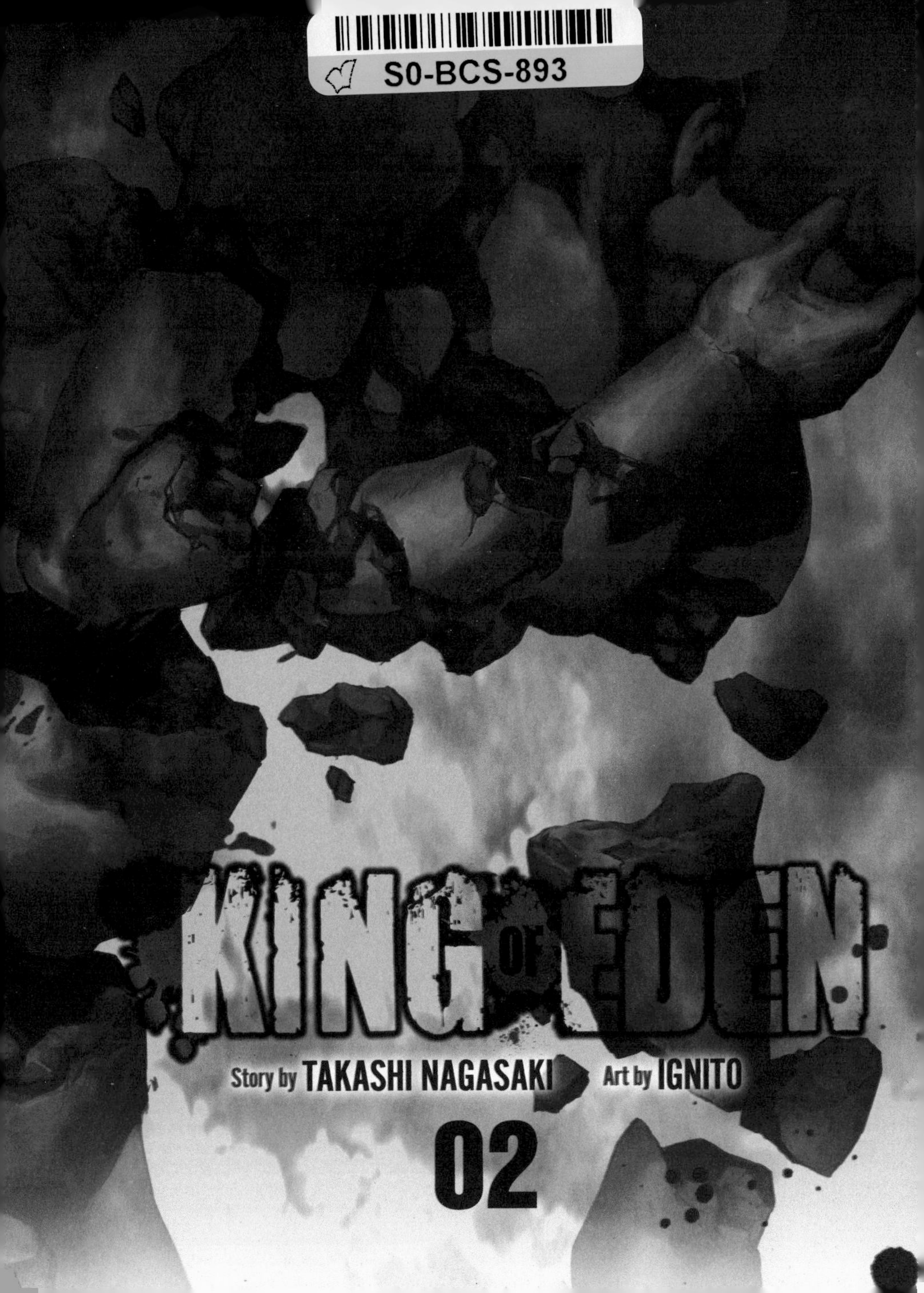
KING OF EDEN
Story by TAKASHI NAGASAKI Art by IGNITO
02

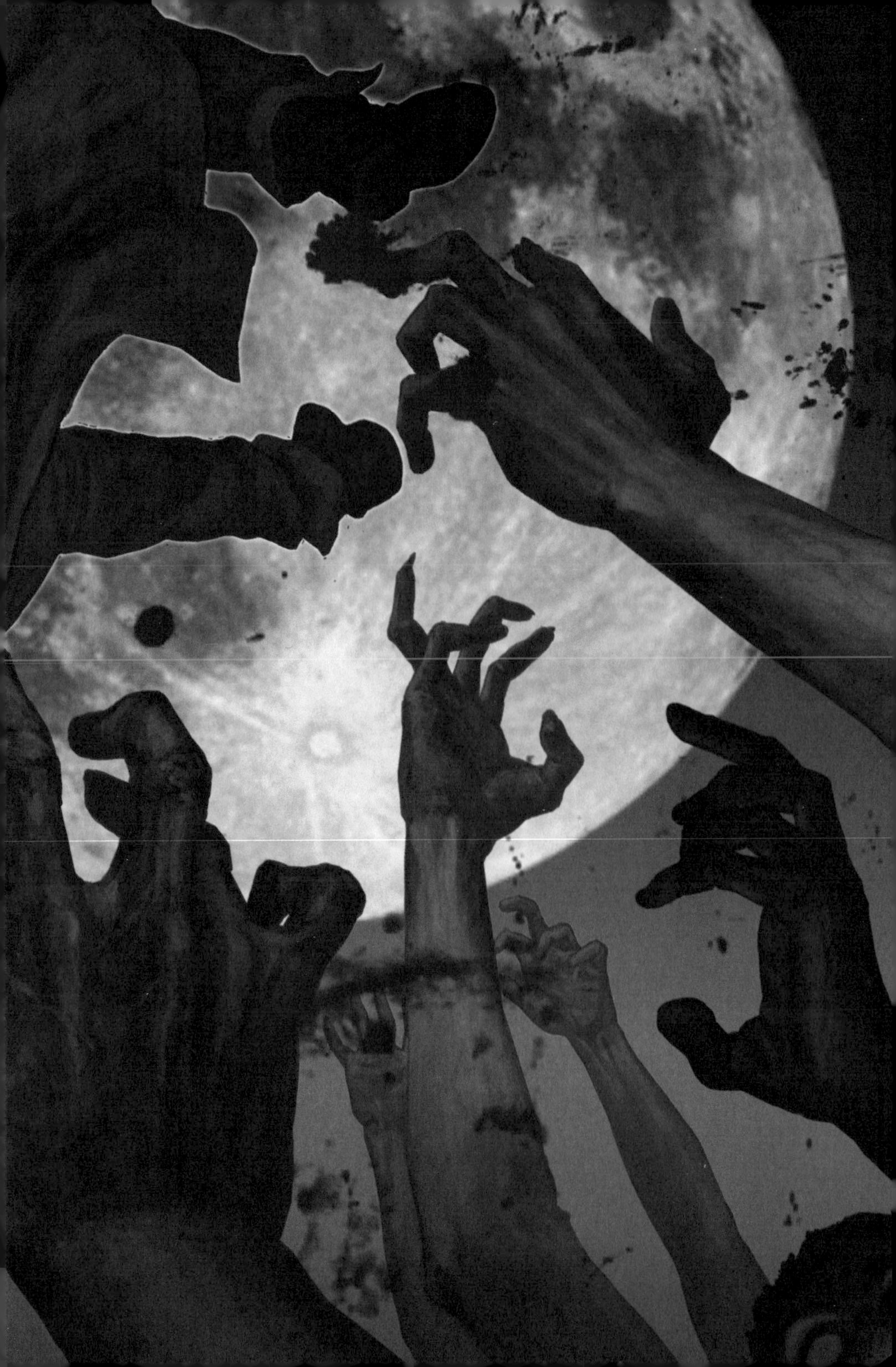

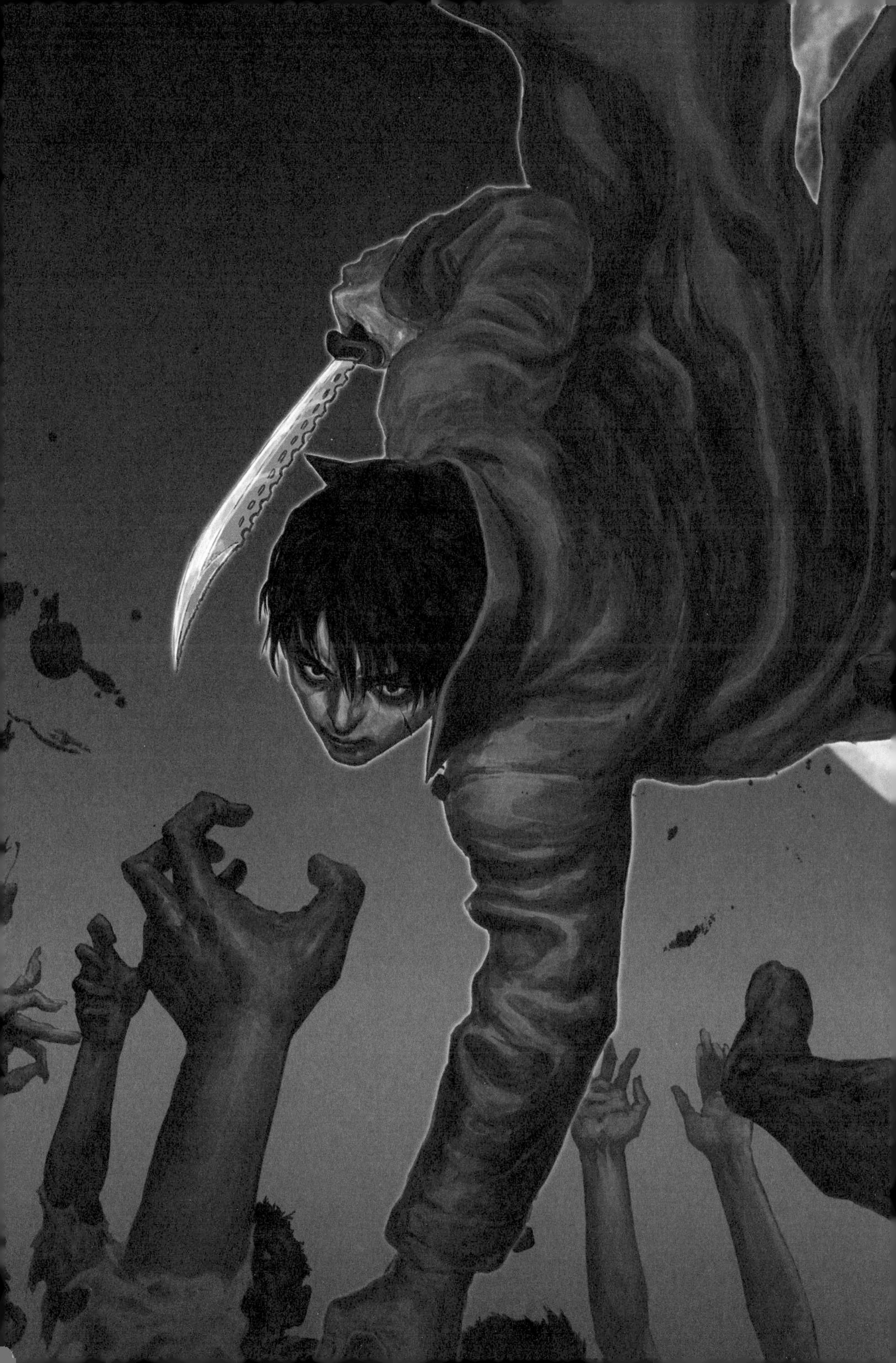

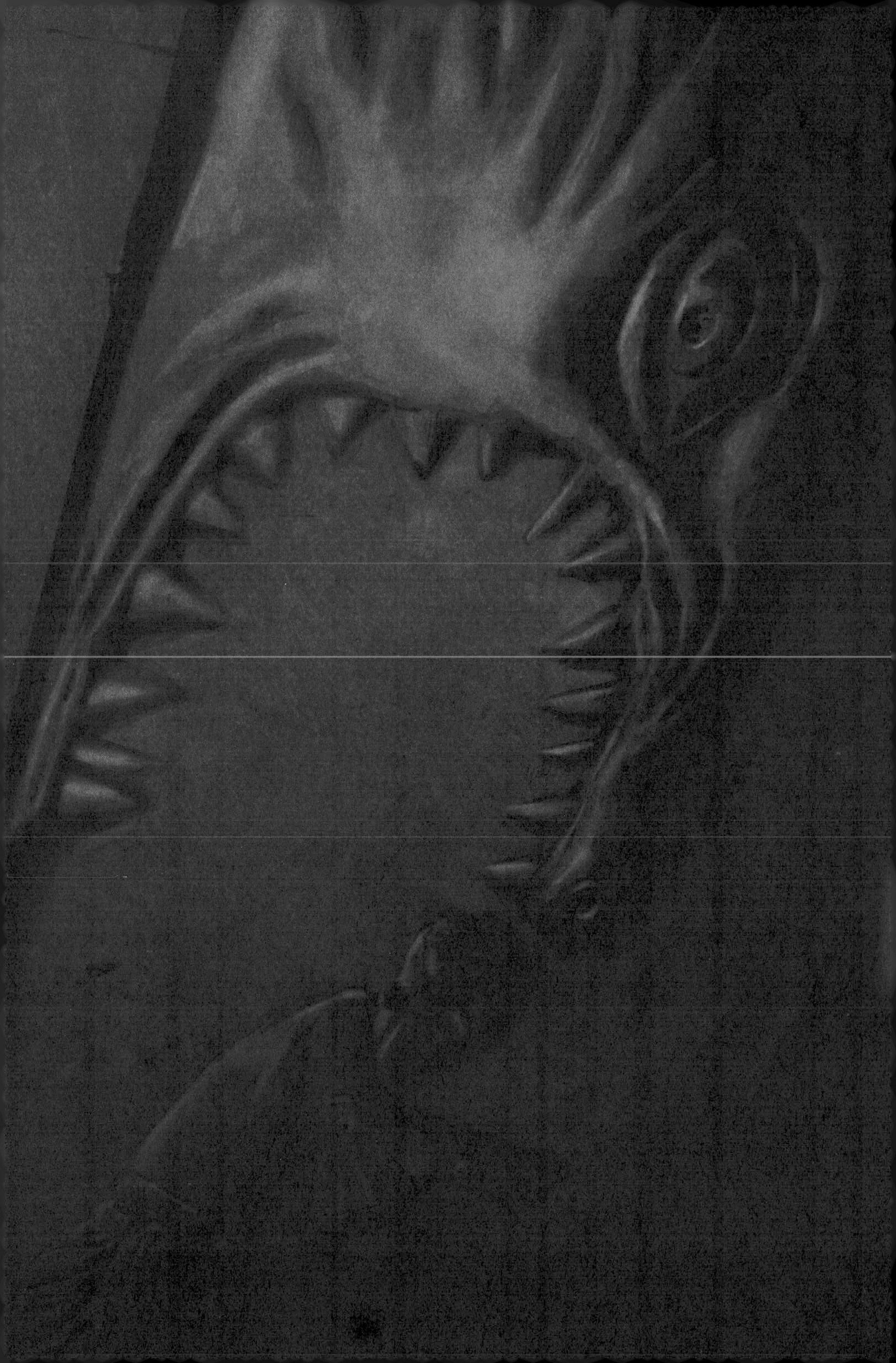

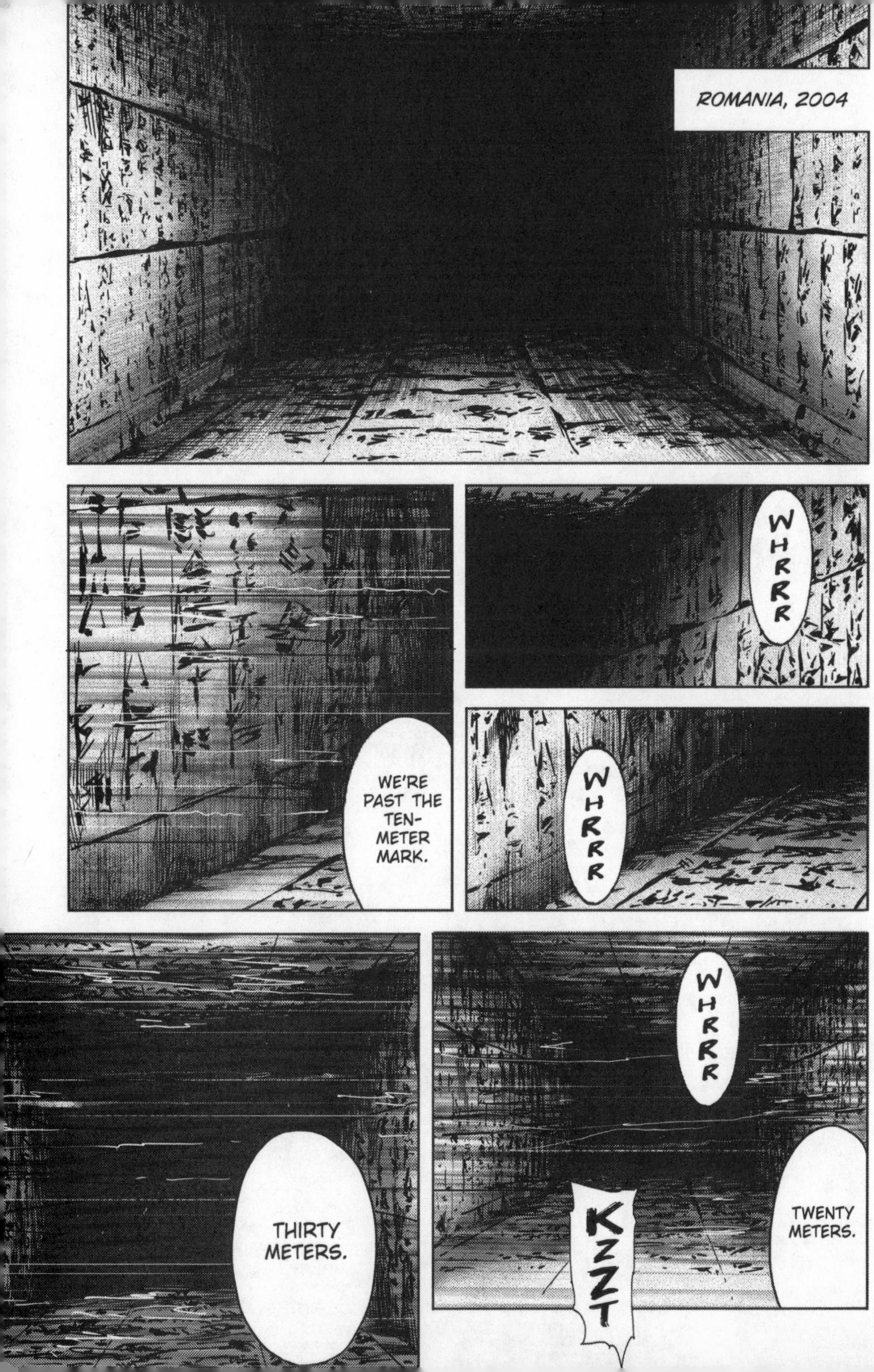
ROMANIA, 2004
WHRRR
WHRRR
WE'RE PAST THE TEN-METER MARK.
WHRRR
TWENTY METERS.
KZZT
THIRTY METERS.

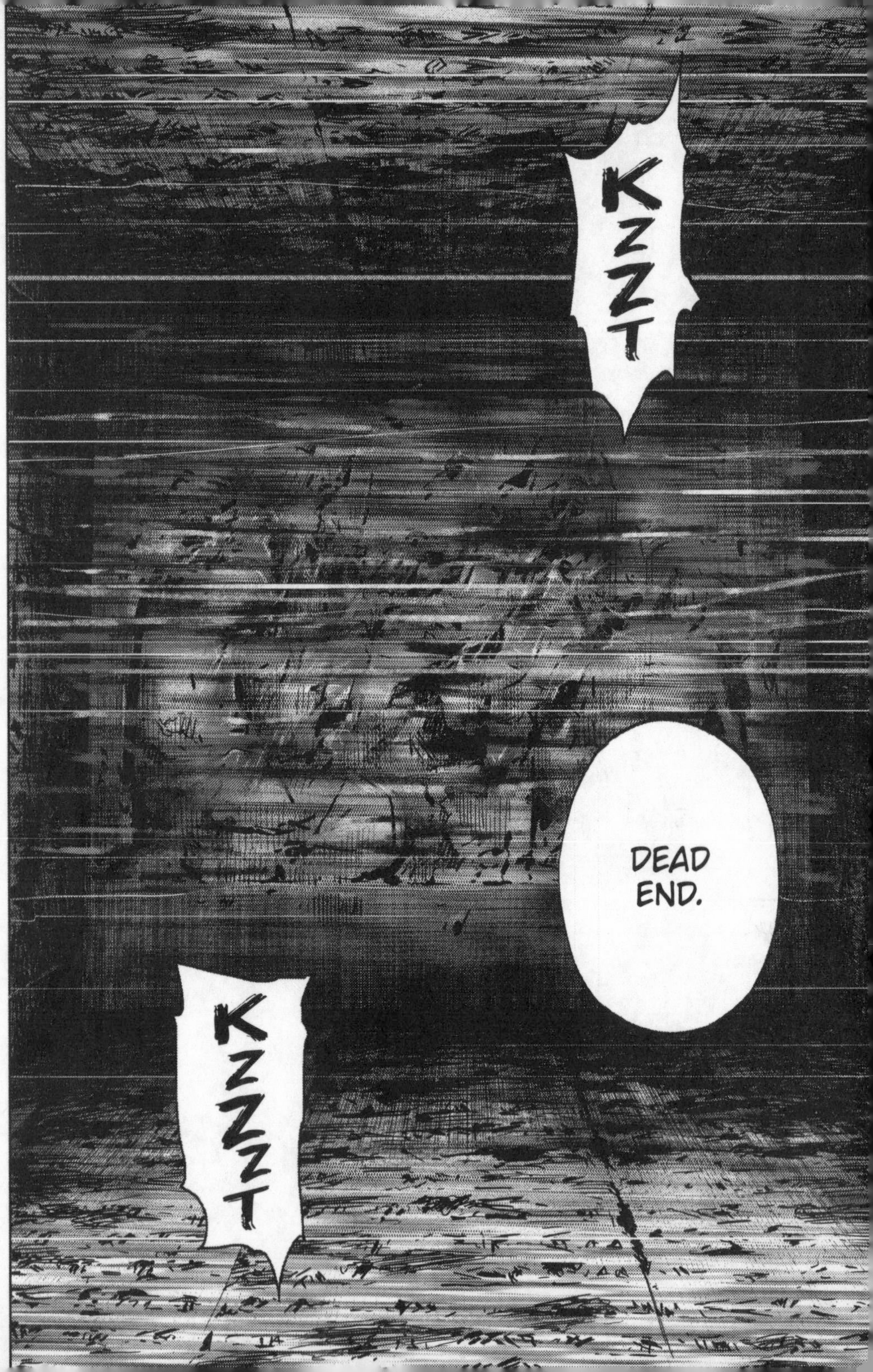
KZZT
DEAD END.
KZZZT

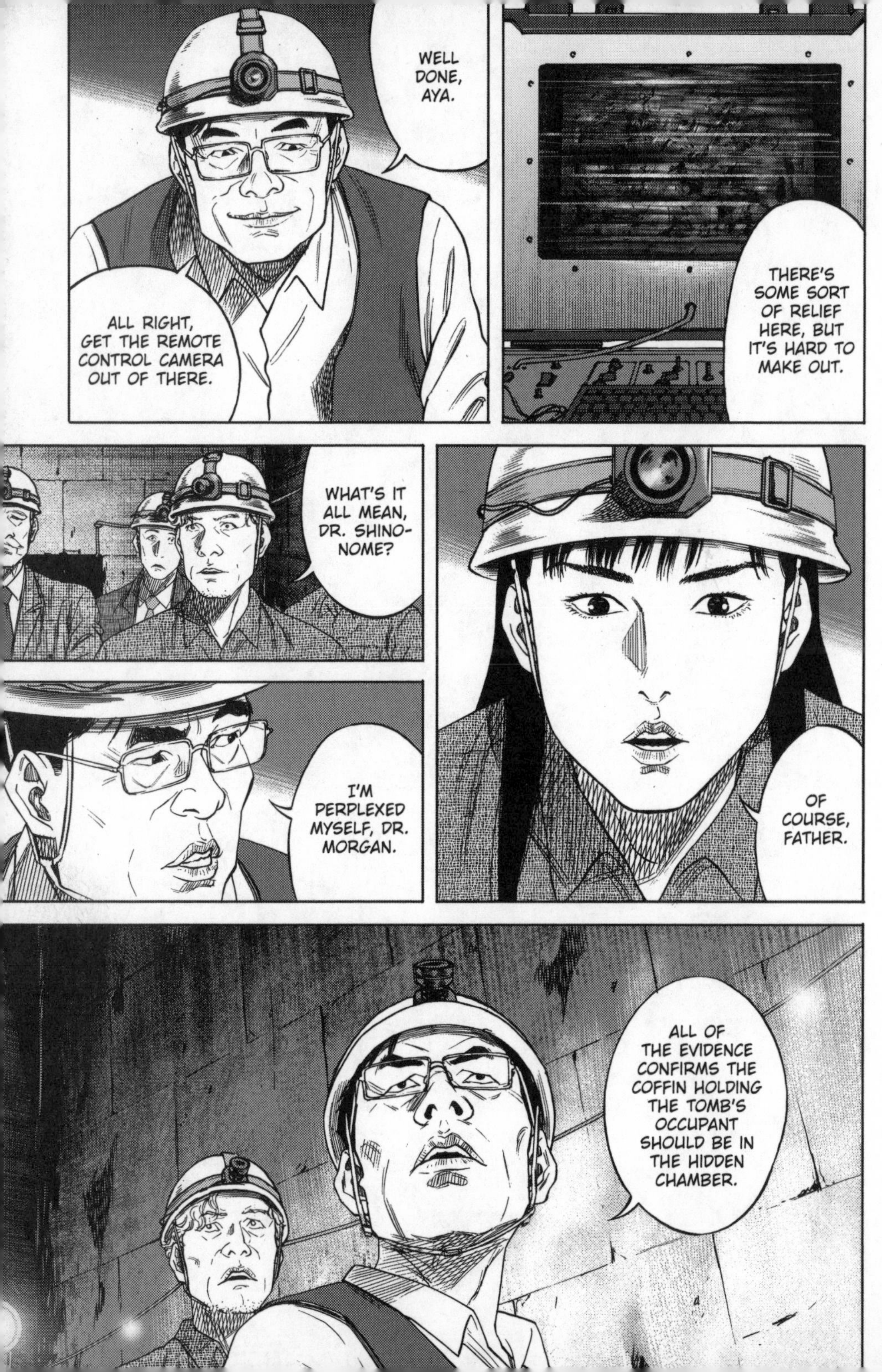
THERE'S SOME SORT OF RELIEF HERE, BUT IT'S HARD TO MAKE OUT.
WELL DONE, AYA.
ALL RIGHT, GET THE REMOTE CONTROL CAMERA OUT OF THERE.
OF COURSE, FATHER.
WHAT'S IT ALL MEAN, DR. SHINO-NOME?
I'M PERPLEXED MYSELF, DR. MORGAN.
ALL OF THE EVIDENCE CONFIRMS THE COFFIN HOLDING THE TOMB'S OCCUPANT SHOULD BE IN THE HIDDEN CHAMBER.

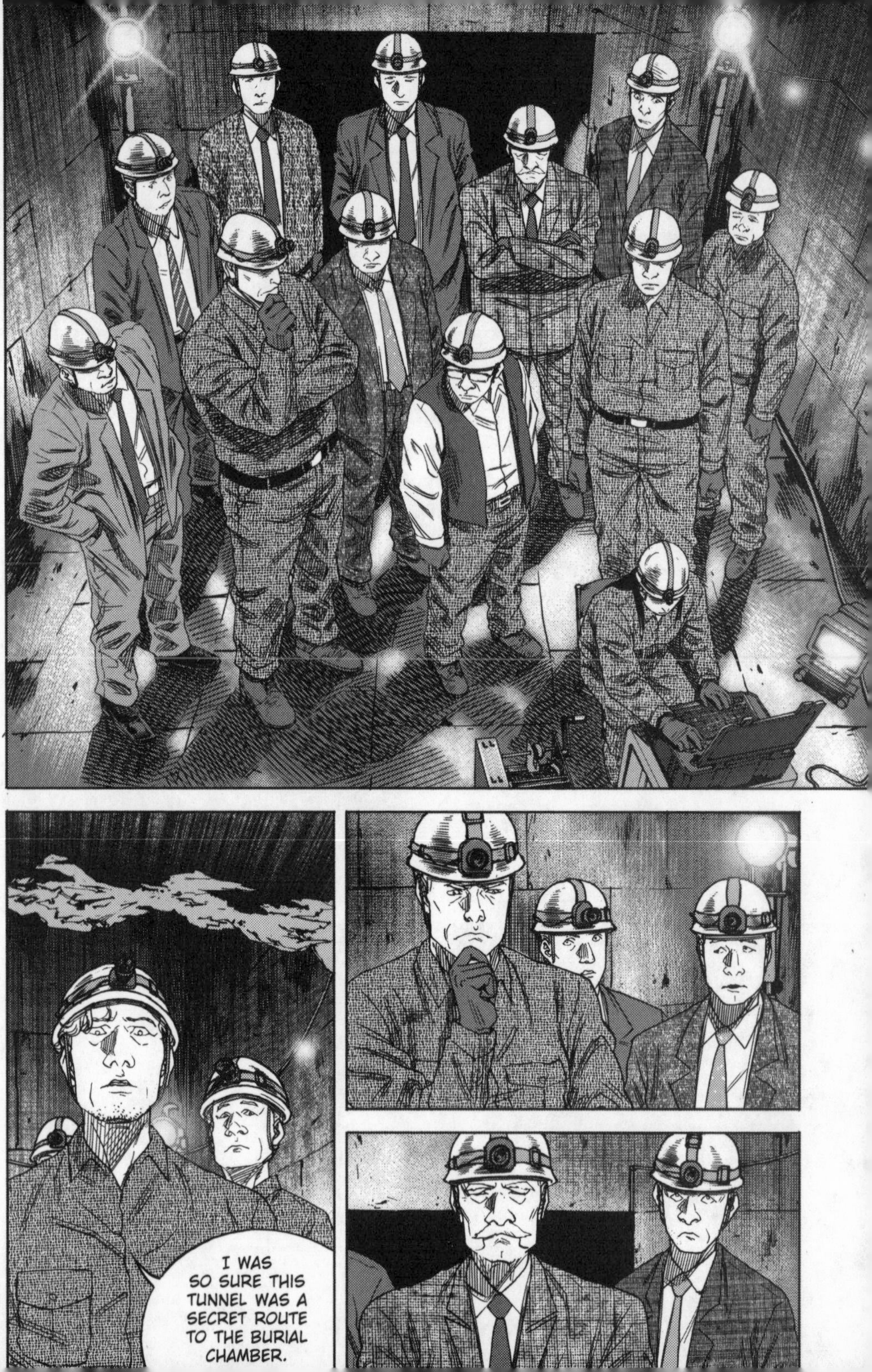
I WAS SO SURE THIS TUNNEL WAS A SECRET ROUTE TO THE BURIAL CHAMBER.

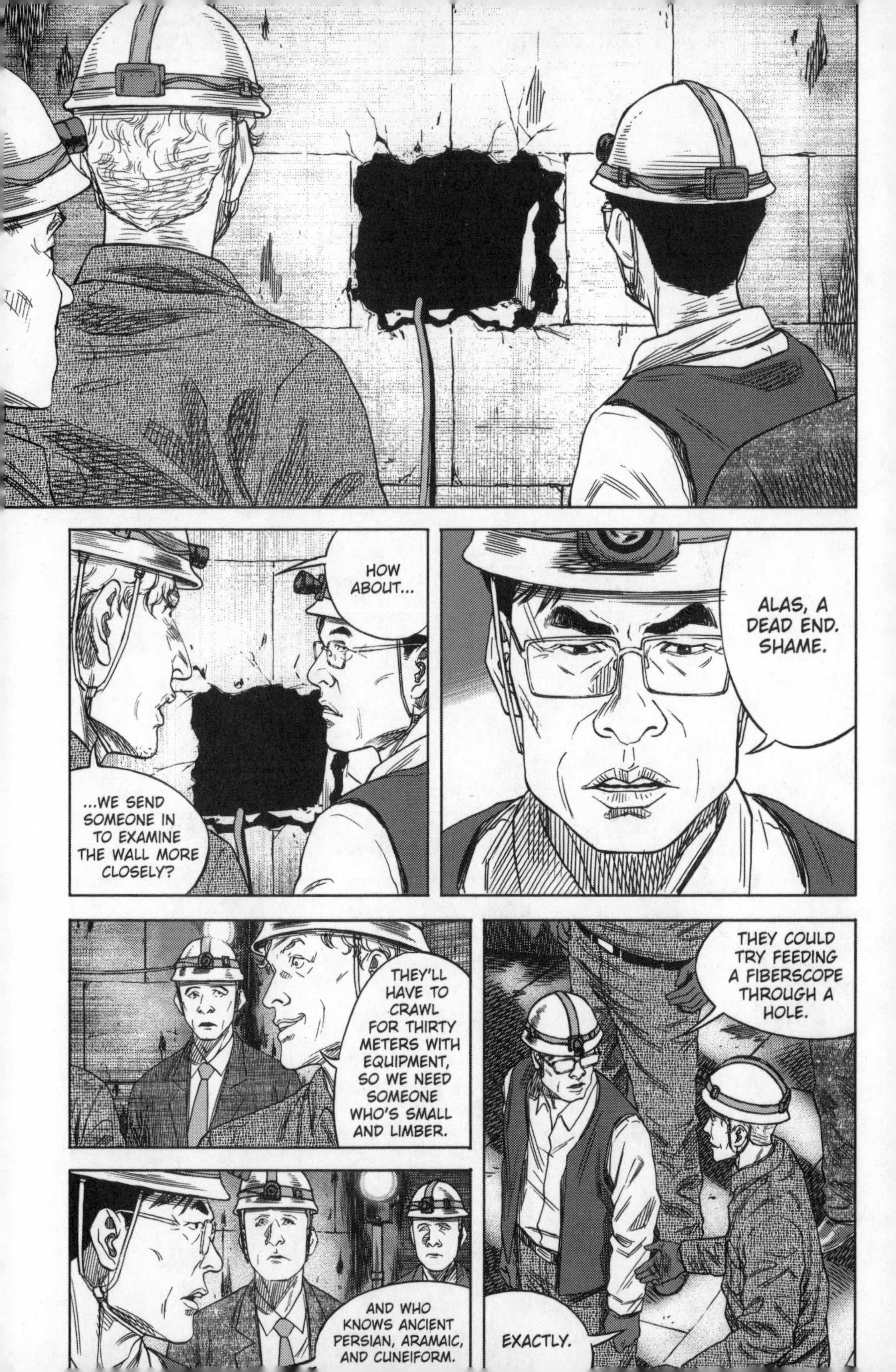
ALAS, A DEAD END. SHAME.
HOW ABOUT...
...WE SEND SOMEONE IN TO EXAMINE THE WALL MORE CLOSELY?
THEY COULD TRY FEEDING A FIBERSCOPE THROUGH A HOLE.
EXACTLY.
THEY'LL HAVE TO CRAWL FOR THIRTY METERS WITH EQUIPMENT, SO WE NEED SOMEONE WHO'S SMALL AND LIMBER.
AND WHO KNOWS ANCIENT PERSIAN, ARAMAIC, AND CUNEIFORM.

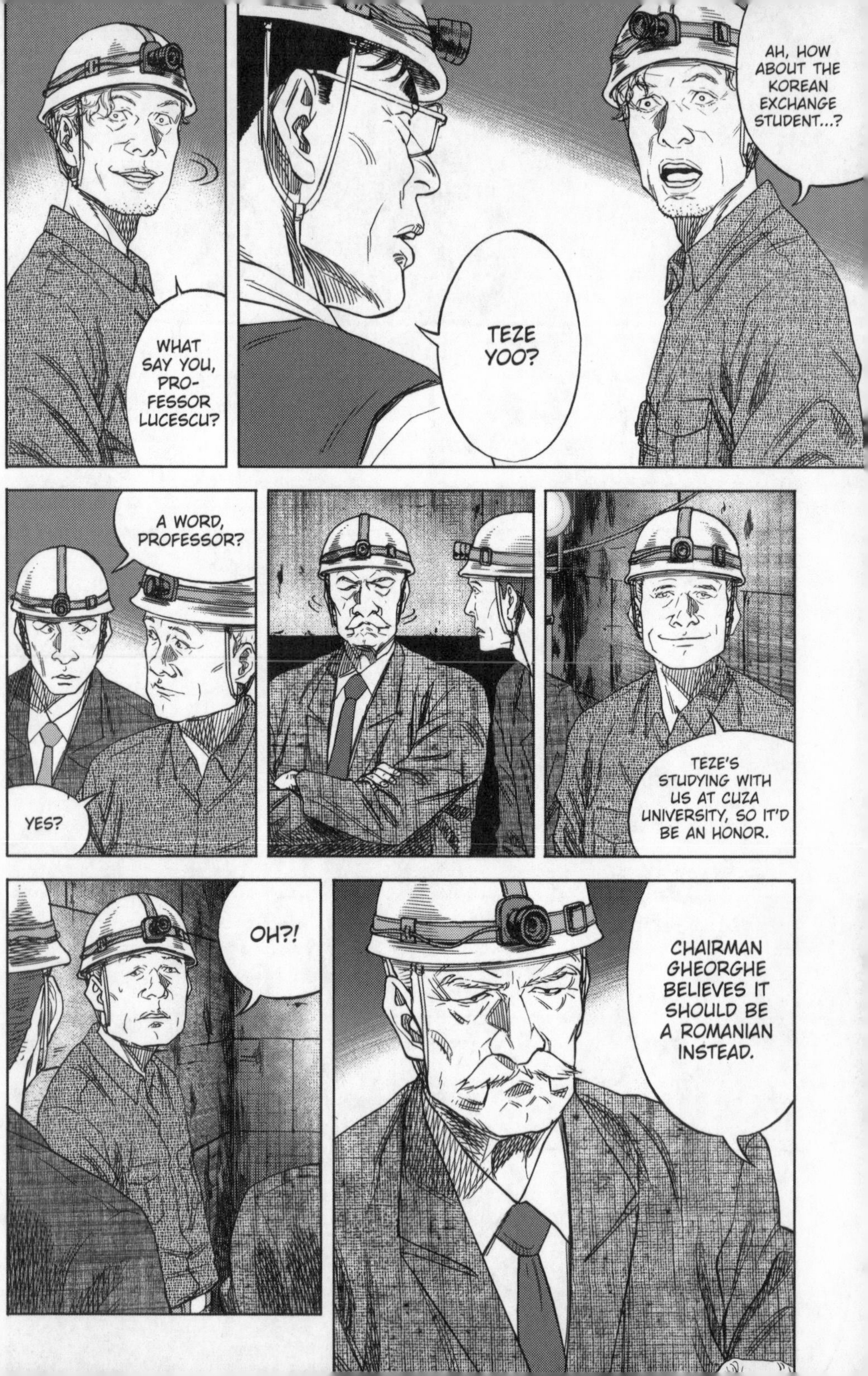
AH, HOW ABOUT THE KOREAN EXCHANGE STUDENT...?
TEZE YOO?
WHAT SAY YOU, PRO-FESSOR LUCESCU?
TEZE'S STUDYING WITH US AT CUZA UNIVERSITY, SO IT'D BE AN HONOR.
A WORD, PROFESSOR?
YES?
CHAIRMAN GHEORGHE BELIEVES IT SHOULD BE A ROMANIAN INSTEAD.
OH?!

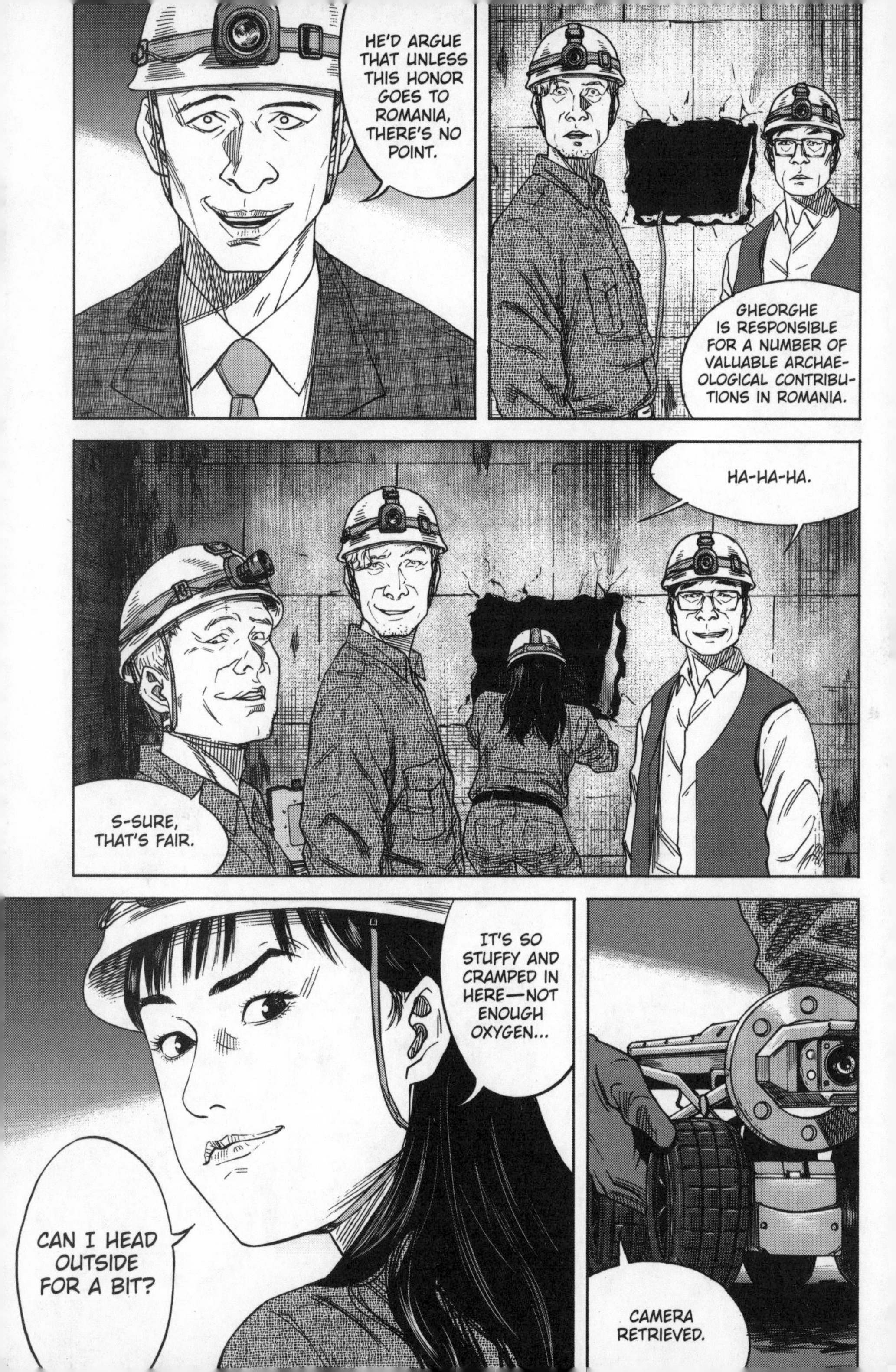
GHEORGHE IS RESPONSIBLE FOR A NUMBER OF VALUABLE ARCHAE-OLOGICAL CONTRIBU-TIONS IN ROMANIA.
HE'D ARGUE THAT UNLESS THIS HONOR GOES TO ROMANIA, THERE'S NO POINT.
HA-HA-HA.
S-SURE, THAT'S FAIR.
CAMERA RETRIEVED.
IT'S SO STUFFY AND CRAMPED IN HERE—NOT ENOUGH OXYGEN...
CAN I HEAD OUTSIDE FOR A BIT?

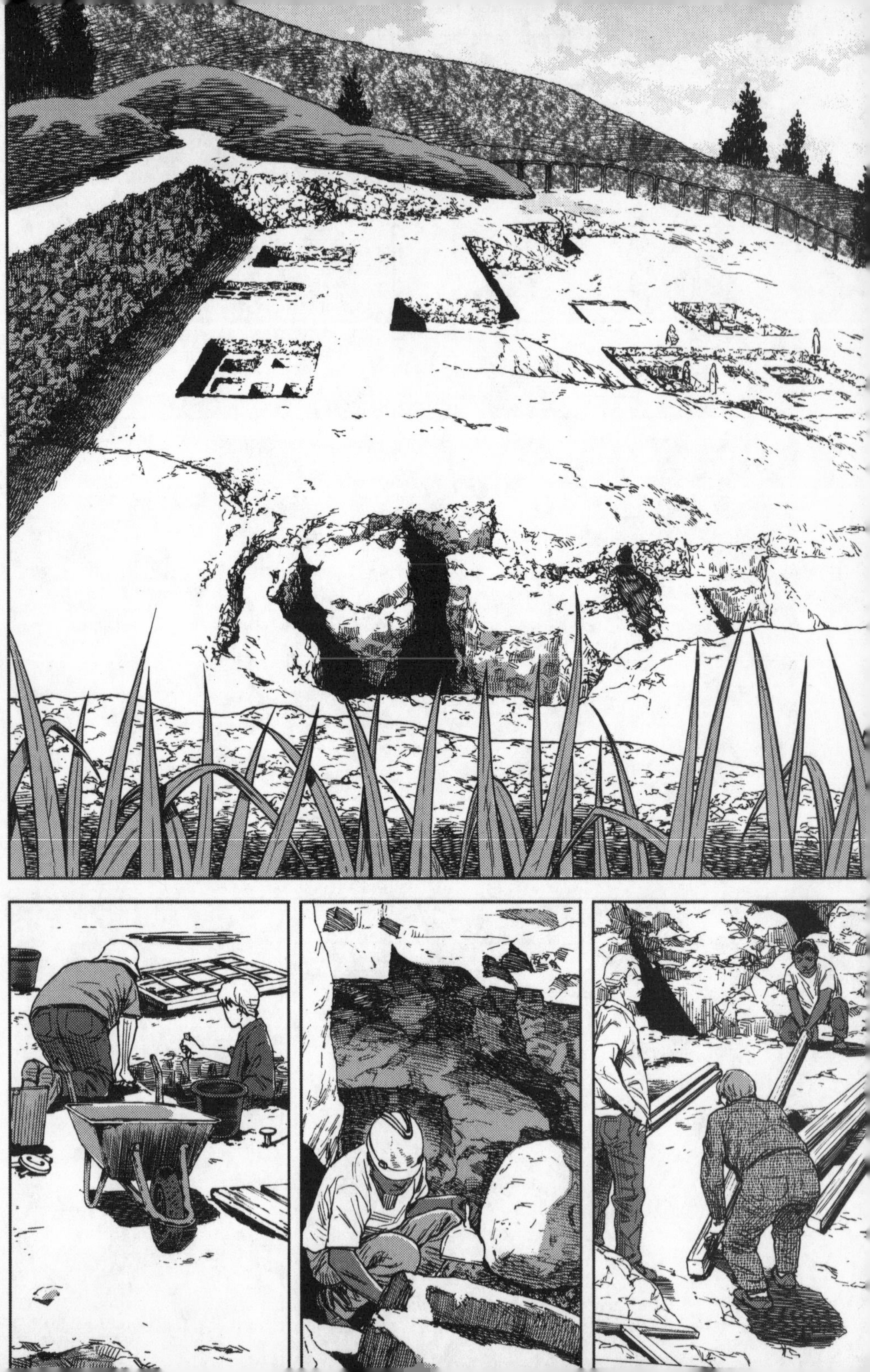

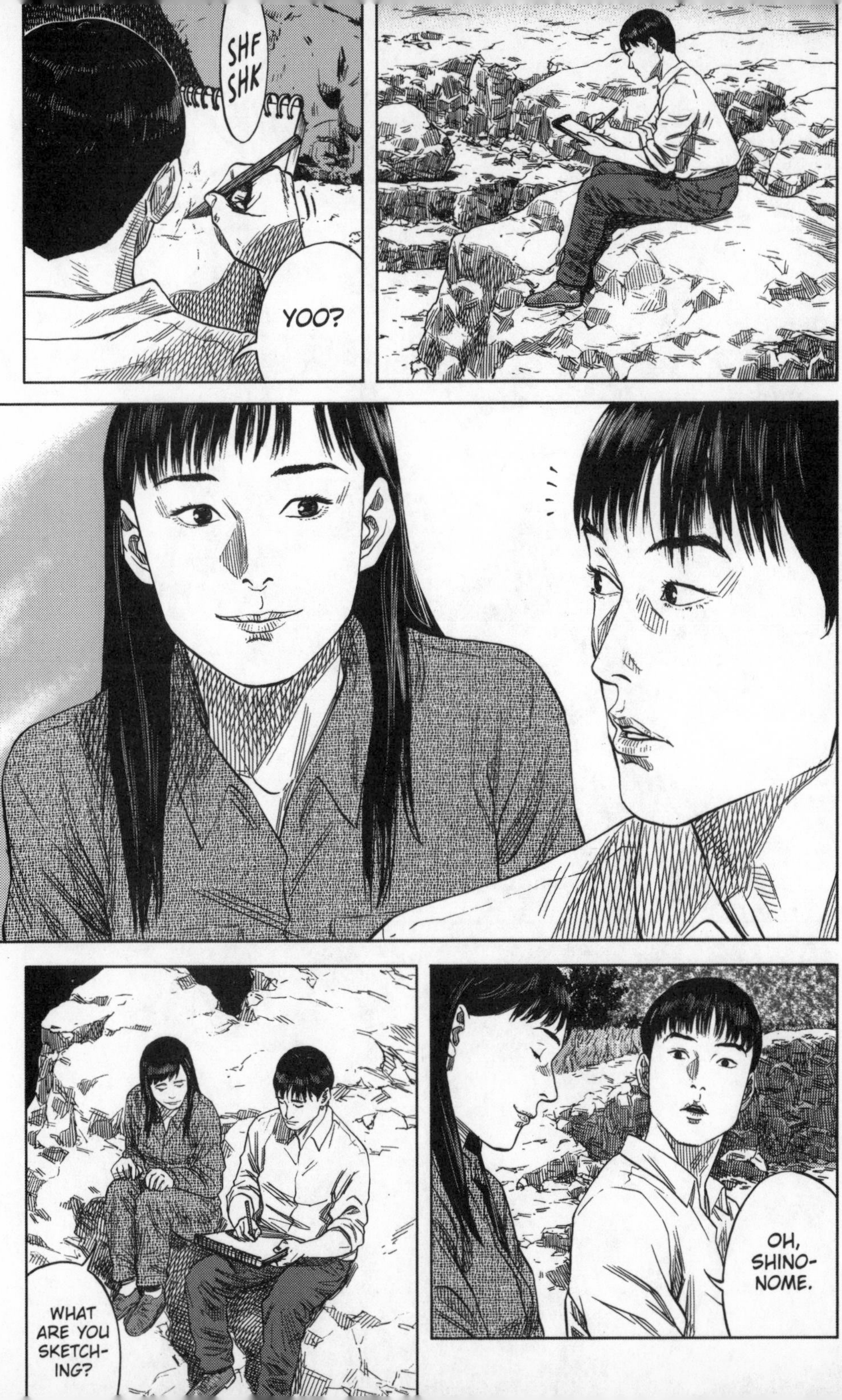
SHF SHK
YOO?
OH, SHINO-NOME.
WHAT ARE YOU SKETCH-ING?

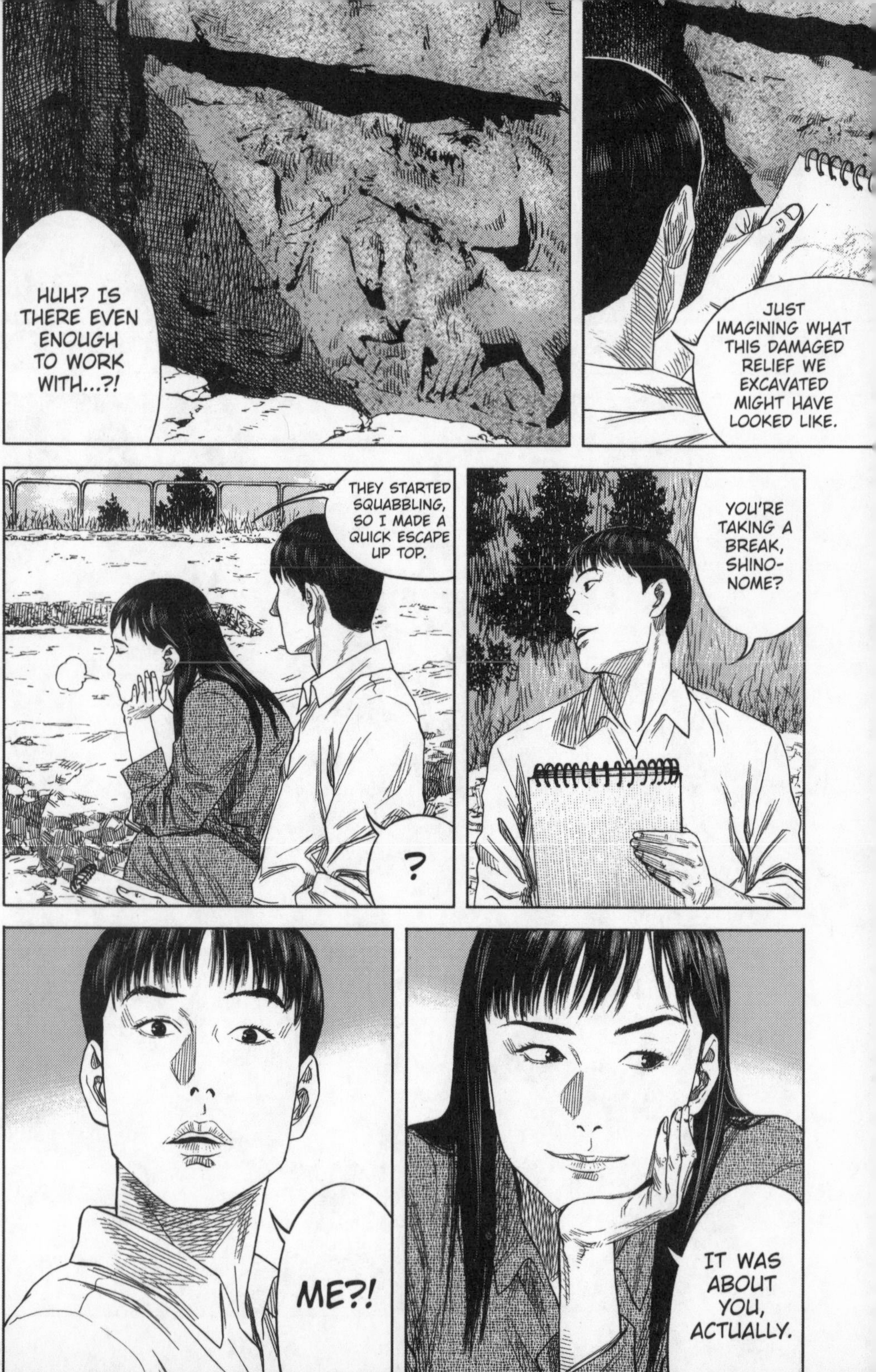
JUST IMAGINING WHAT THIS DAMAGED RELIEF WE EXCAVATED MIGHT HAVE LOOKED LIKE.
HUH? IS THERE EVEN ENOUGH TO WORK WITH...?!
YOU'RE TAKING A BREAK, SHINO-NOME?
THEY STARTED SQUABBLING, SO I MADE A QUICK ESCAPE UP TOP.
?
IT WAS ABOUT YOU, ACTUALLY.
ME?!

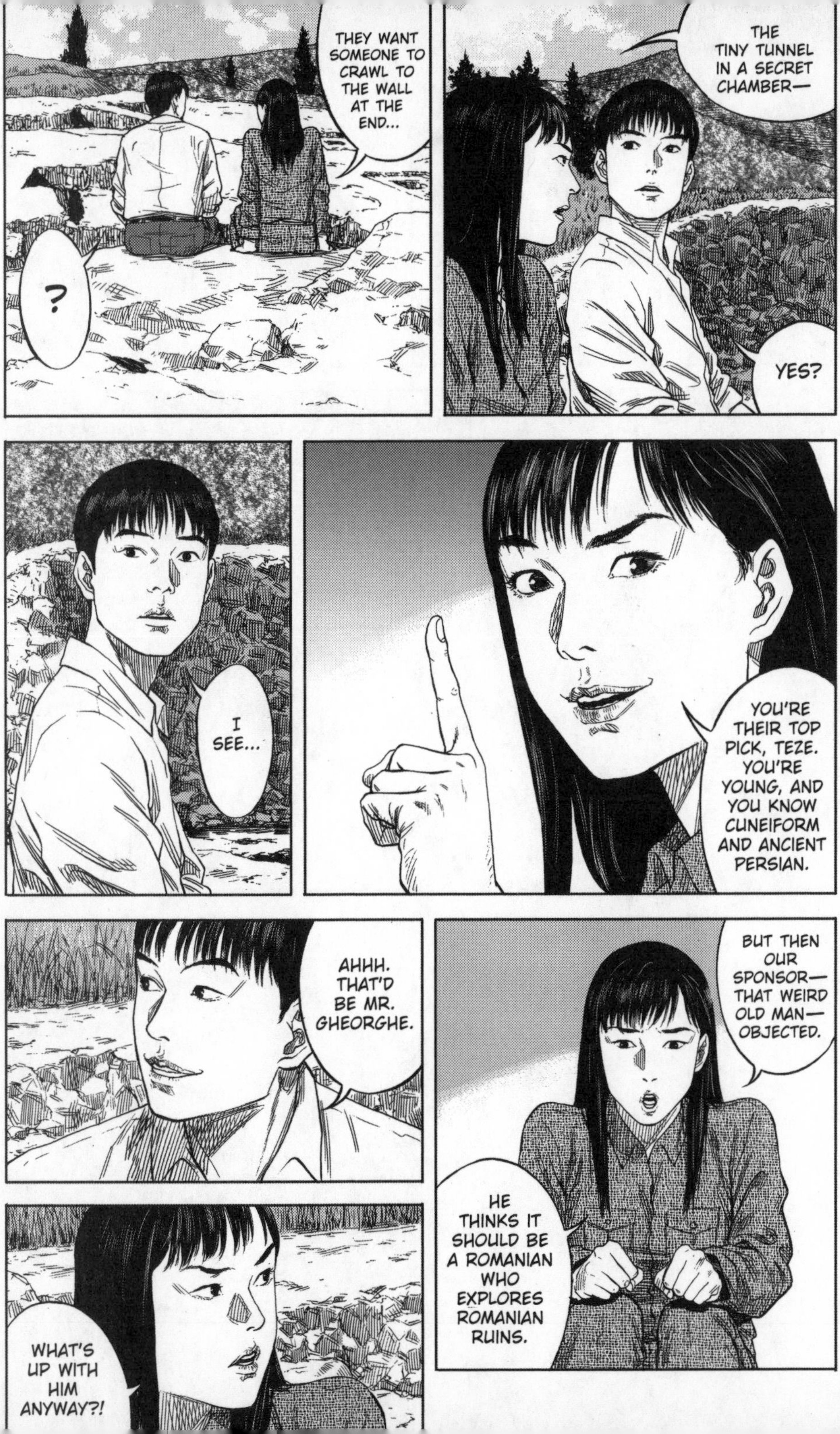
THE TINY TUNNEL IN A SECRET CHAMBER—
YES?
THEY WANT SOMEONE TO CRAWL TO THE WALL AT THE END...
?
YOU'RE THEIR TOP PICK, TEZE. YOU'RE YOUNG, AND YOU KNOW CUNEIFORM AND ANCIENT PERSIAN.
I SEE...
BUT THEN OUR SPONSOR—THAT WEIRD OLD MAN—OBJECTED.
HE THINKS IT SHOULD BE A ROMANIAN WHO EXPLORES ROMANIAN RUINS.
AHHH. THAT'D BE MR. GHEORGHE.
WHAT'S UP WITH HIM ANYWAY?!

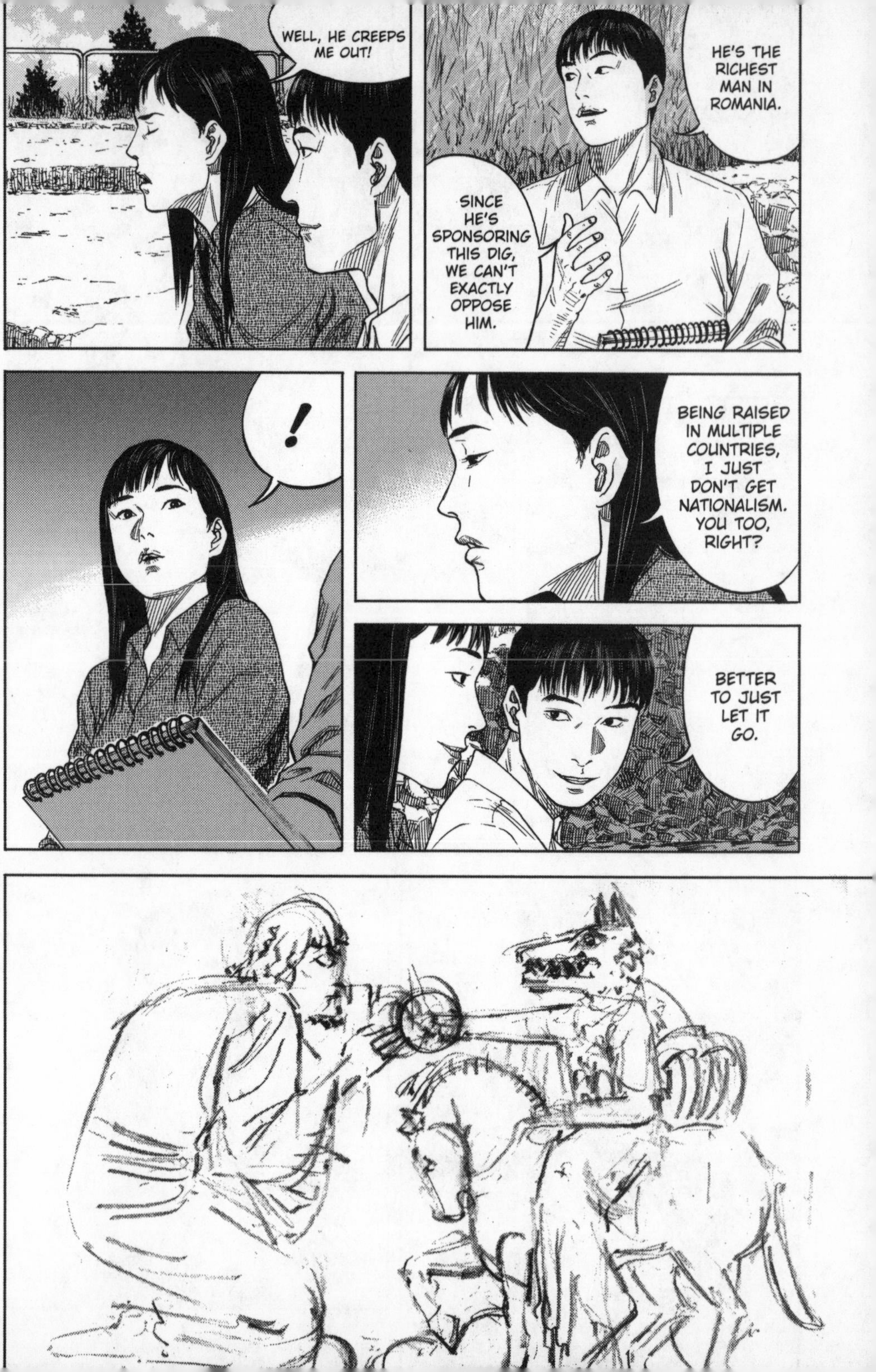
HE'S THE RICHEST MAN IN ROMANIA.
SINCE HE'S SPONSORING THIS DIG, WE CAN'T EXACTLY OPPOSE HIM.
WELL, HE CREEPS ME OUT!
BEING RAISED IN MULTIPLE COUNTRIES, I JUST DON'T GET NATIONALISM. YOU TOO, RIGHT?
BETTER TO JUST LET IT GO.
!

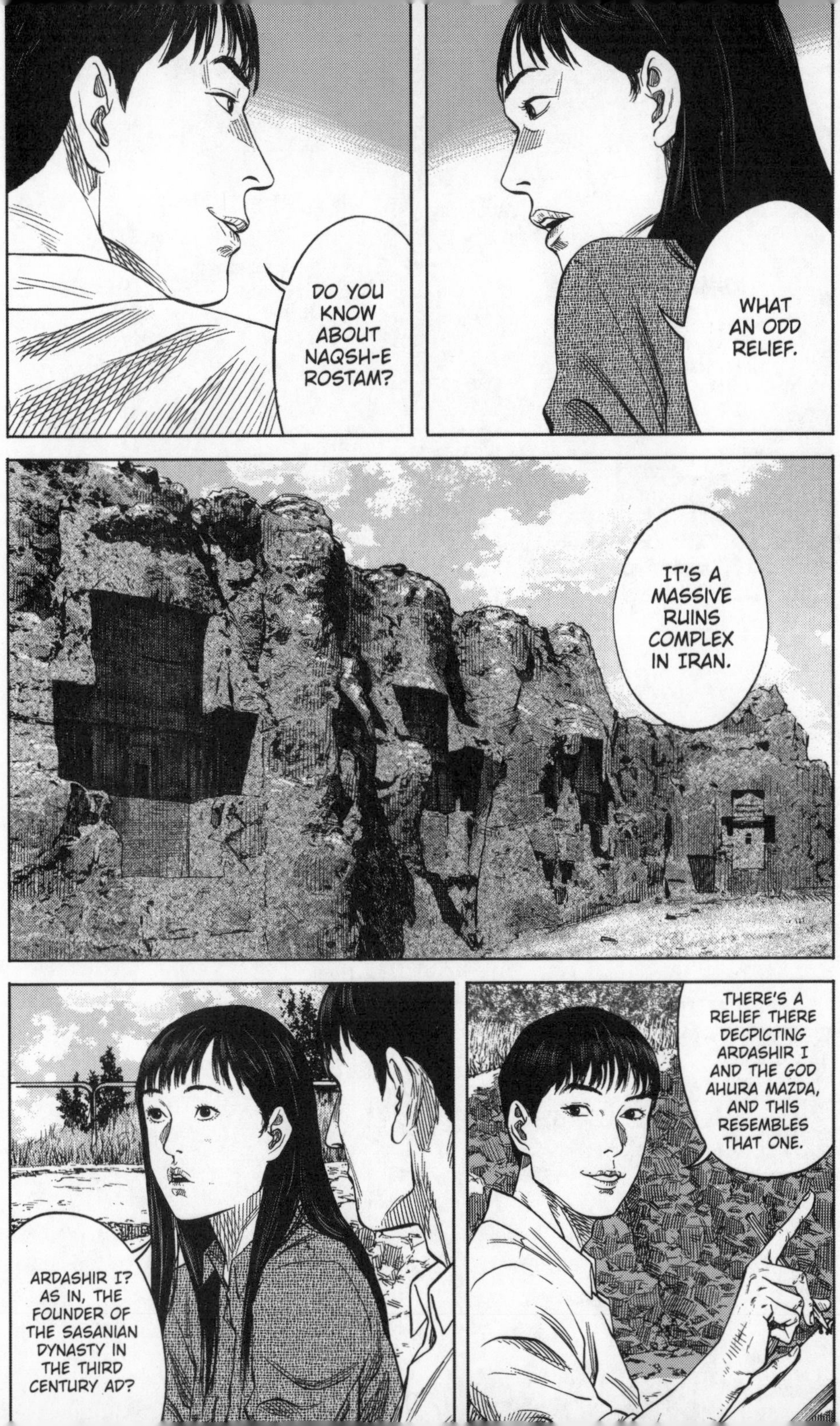
WHAT AN ODD RELIEF.
DO YOU KNOW ABOUT NAQSH-E ROSTAM?
IT'S A MASSIVE RUINS COMPLEX IN IRAN.
THERE'S A RELIEF THERE DECPICTING ARDASHIR I AND THE GOD AHURA MAZDA, AND THIS RESEMBLES THAT ONE.
ARDASHIR I? AS IN, THE FOUNDER OF THE SASANIAN DYNASTY IN THE THIRD CENTURY AD?

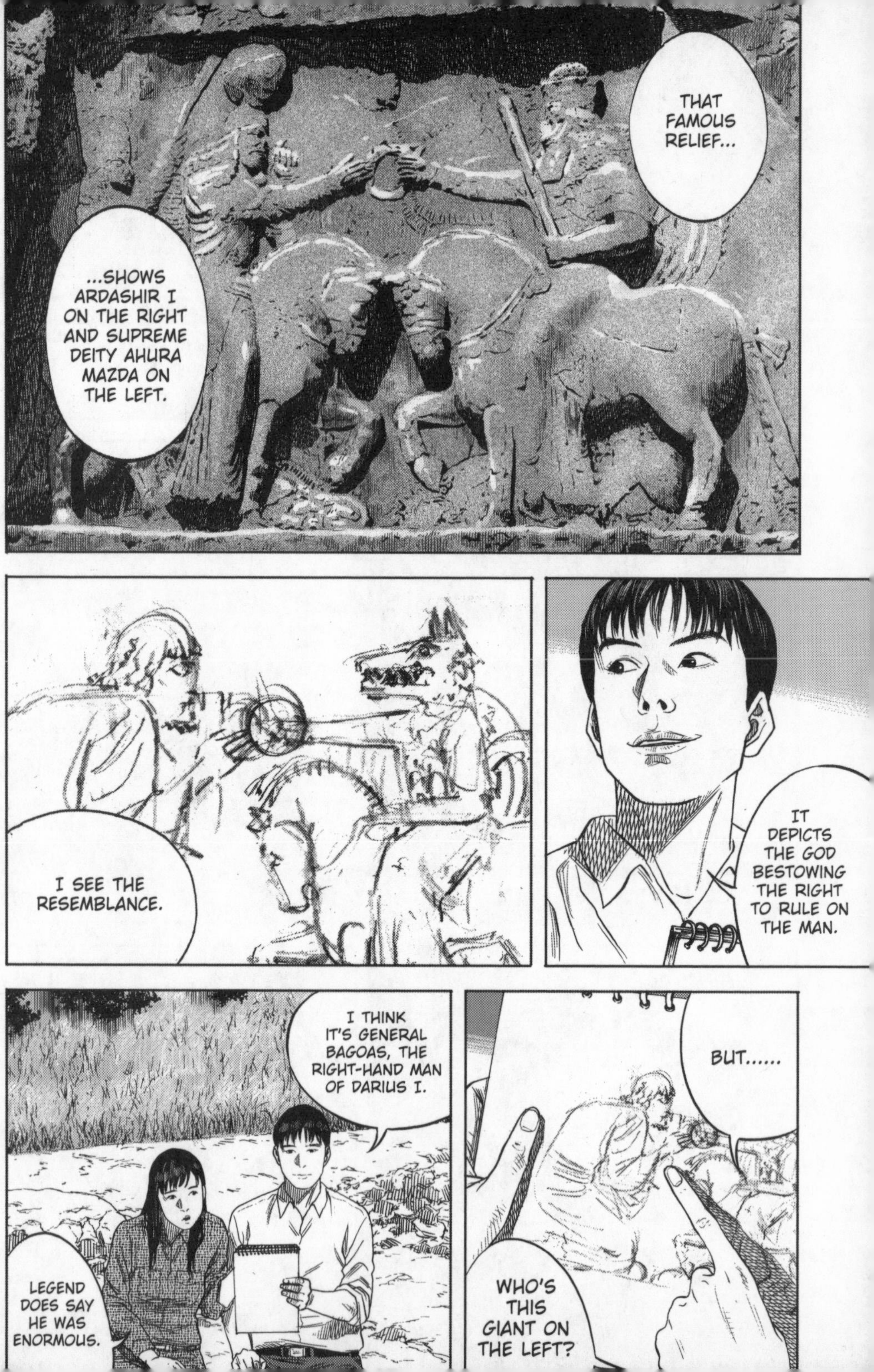
THAT FAMOUS RELIEF...
...SHOWS ARDASHIR I ON THE RIGHT AND SUPREME DEITY AHURA MAZDA ON THE LEFT.
IT DEPICTS THE GOD BESTOWING THE RIGHT TO RULE ON THE MAN.
I SEE THE RESEMBLANCE.
BUT......
WHO'S THIS GIANT ON THE LEFT?
I THINK IT'S GENERAL BAGOAS, THE RIGHT-HAND MAN OF DARIUS I.
LEGEND DOES SAY HE WAS ENORMOUS.

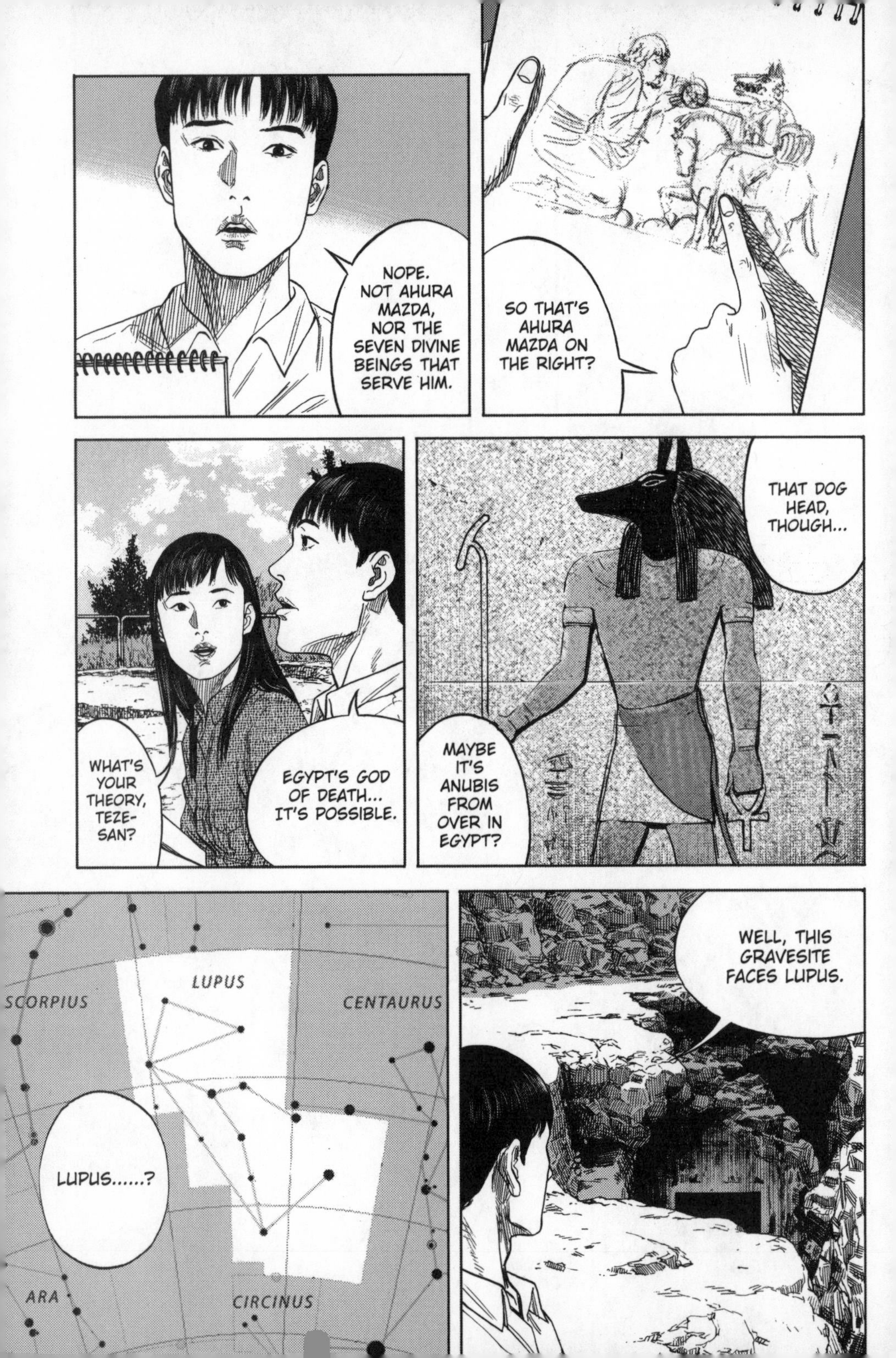
SO THAT'S AHURA MAZDA ON THE RIGHT?
NOPE. NOT AHURA MAZDA, NOR THE SEVEN DIVINE BEINGS THAT SERVE HIM.
THAT DOG HEAD, THOUGH...
MAYBE IT'S ANUBIS FROM OVER IN EGYPT?
EGYPT'S GOD OF DEATH... IT'S POSSIBLE.
WHAT'S YOUR THEORY, TEZE-SAN?
WELL, THIS GRAVESITE FACES LUPUS.
LUPUS
SCORPIUS
CENTAURUS
ARA
CIRCINUS
LUPUS......?

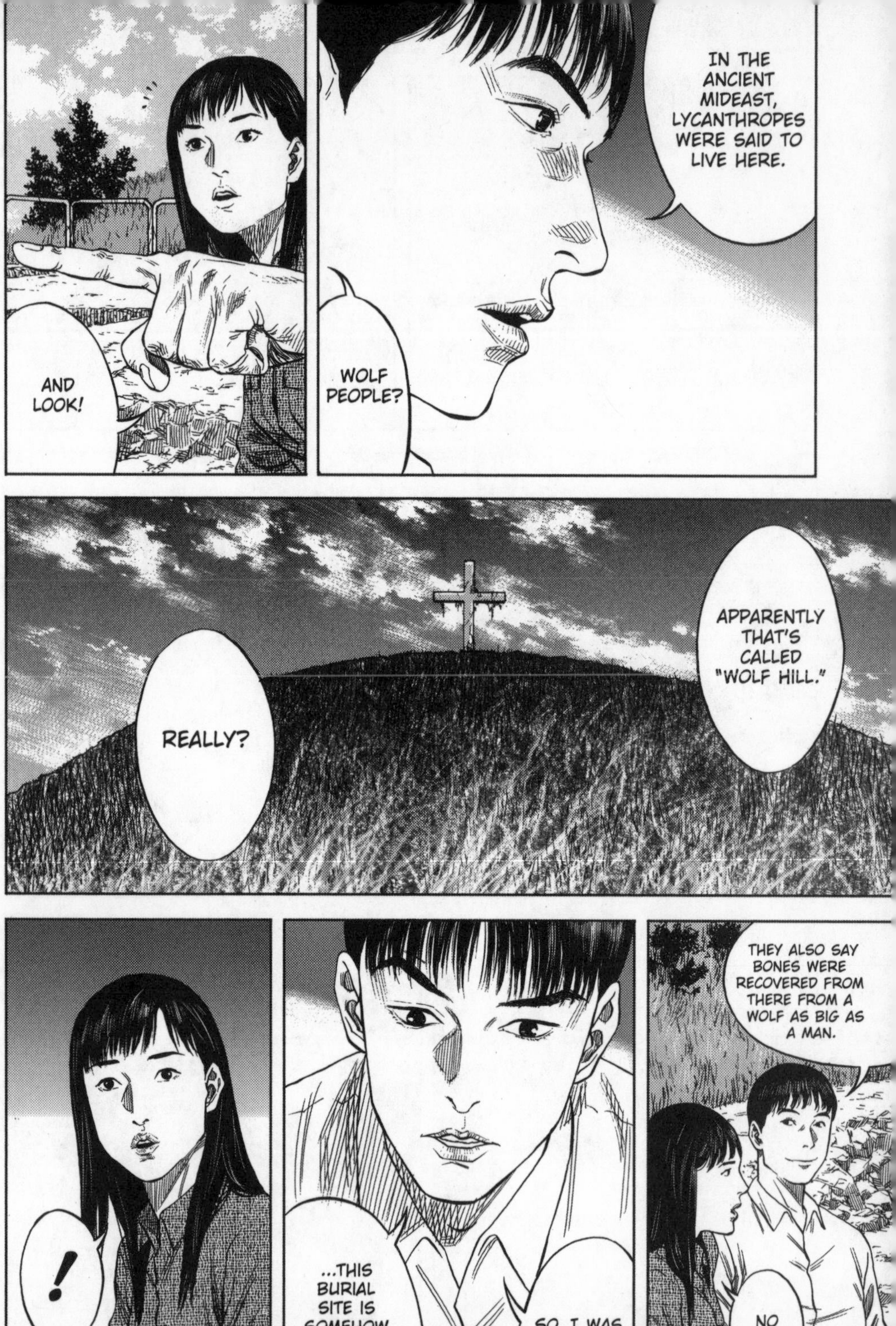
IN THE ANCIENT MIDEAST, LYCANTHROPES WERE SAID TO LIVE HERE.
WOLF PEOPLE?
AND LOOK!
APPARENTLY THAT'S CALLED "WOLF HILL."
REALLY?
THEY ALSO SAY BONES WERE RECOVERED FROM THERE FROM A WOLF AS BIG AS A MAN.
NO WAY?!
SO, I WAS THINKING...
...THIS BURIAL SITE IS SOMEHOW CURSED.
!

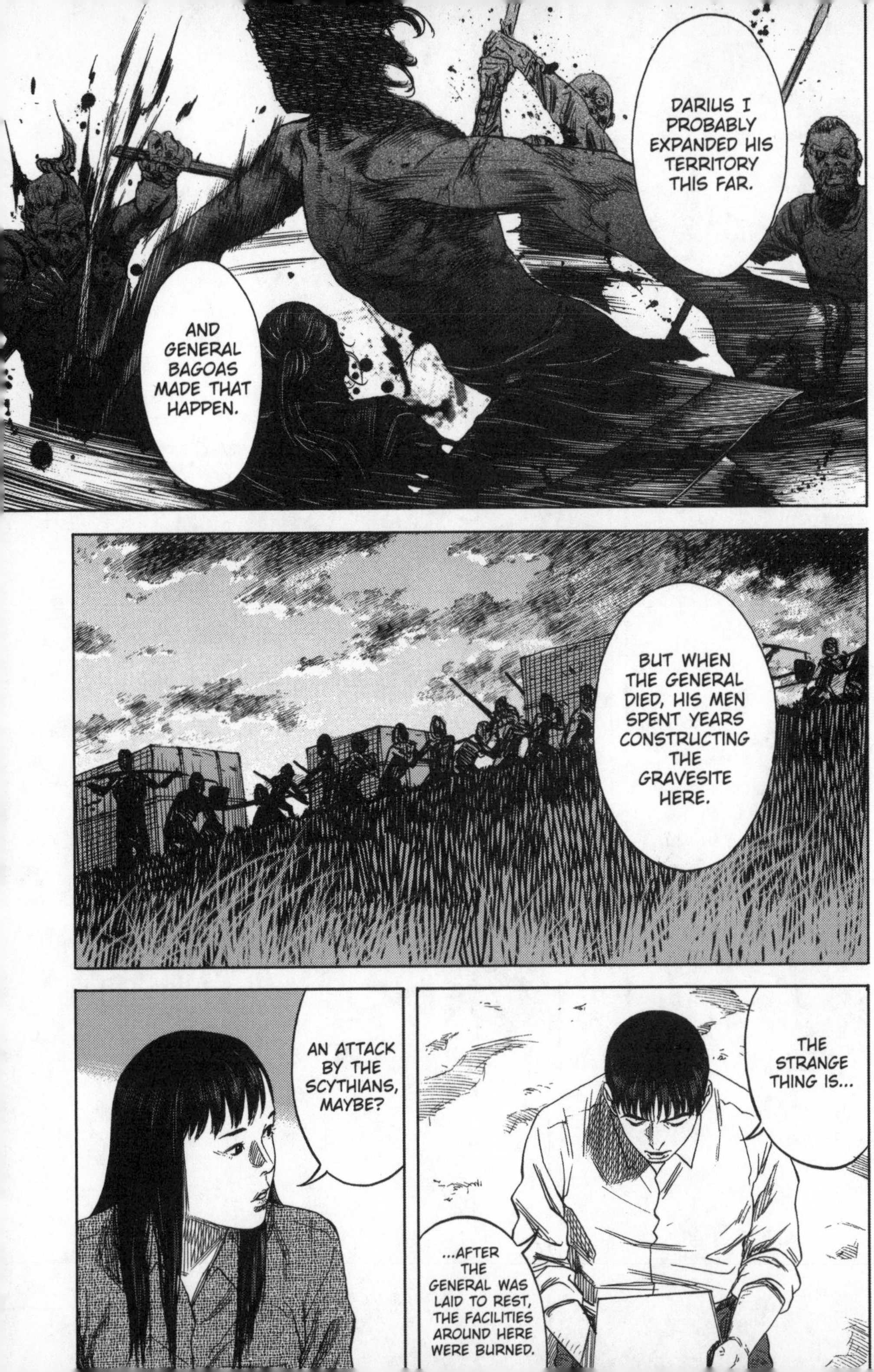
DARIUS I PROBABLY EXPANDED HIS TERRITORY THIS FAR.
AND GENERAL BAGOAS MADE THAT HAPPEN.
BUT WHEN THE GENERAL DIED, HIS MEN SPENT YEARS CONSTRUCTING THE GRAVESITE HERE.
THE STRANGE THING IS...
...AFTER THE GENERAL WAS LAID TO REST, THE FACILITIES AROUND HERE WERE BURNED.
AN ATTACK BY THE SCYTHIANS, MAYBE?

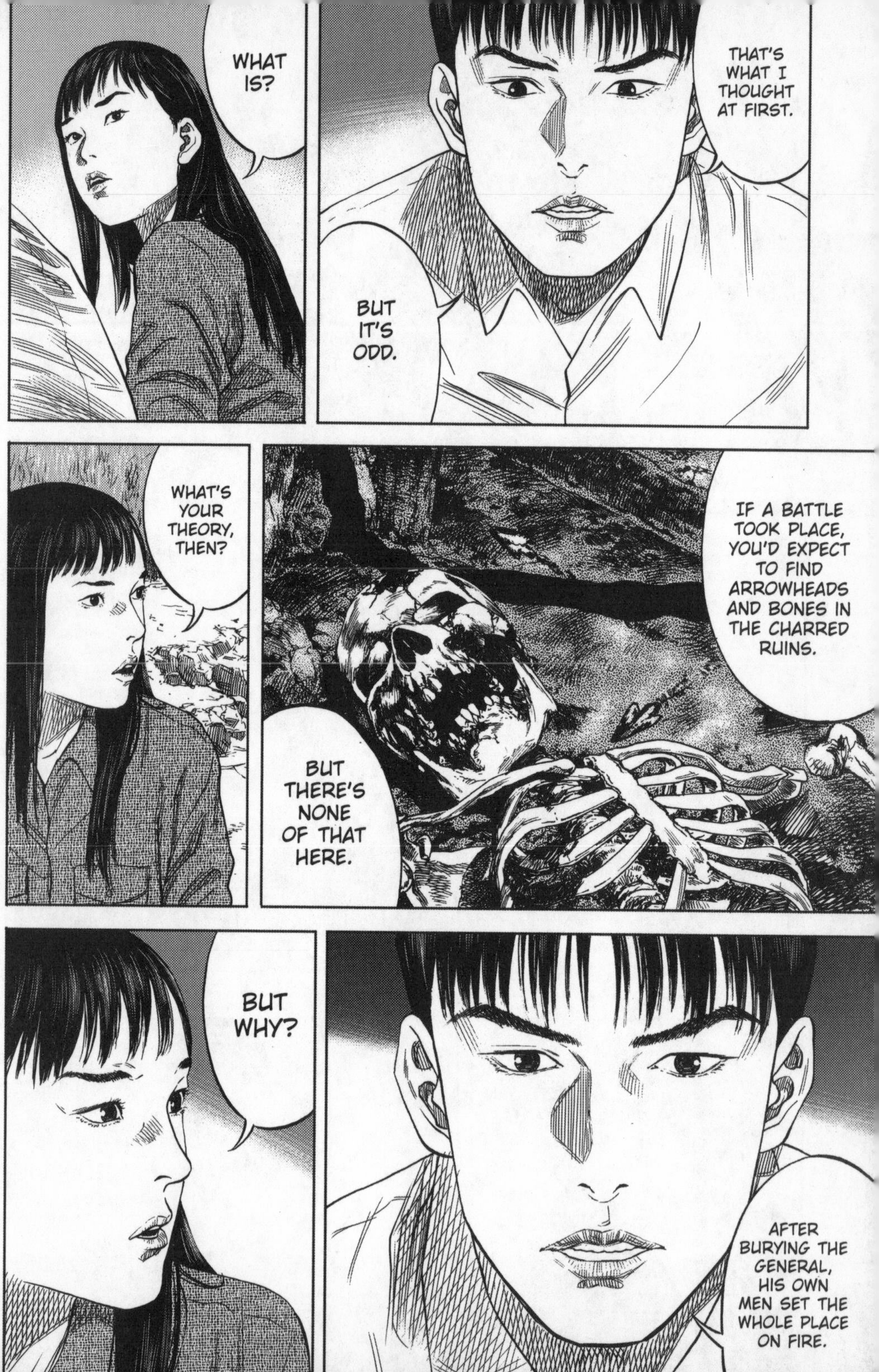
THAT'S WHAT I THOUGHT AT FIRST.
BUT IT'S ODD.
WHAT IS?
IF A BATTLE TOOK PLACE, YOU'D EXPECT TO FIND ARROWHEADS AND BONES IN THE CHARRED RUINS.
BUT THERE'S NONE OF THAT HERE.
WHAT'S YOUR THEORY, THEN?
AFTER BURYING THE GENERAL, HIS OWN MEN SET THE WHOLE PLACE ON FIRE.
BUT WHY?

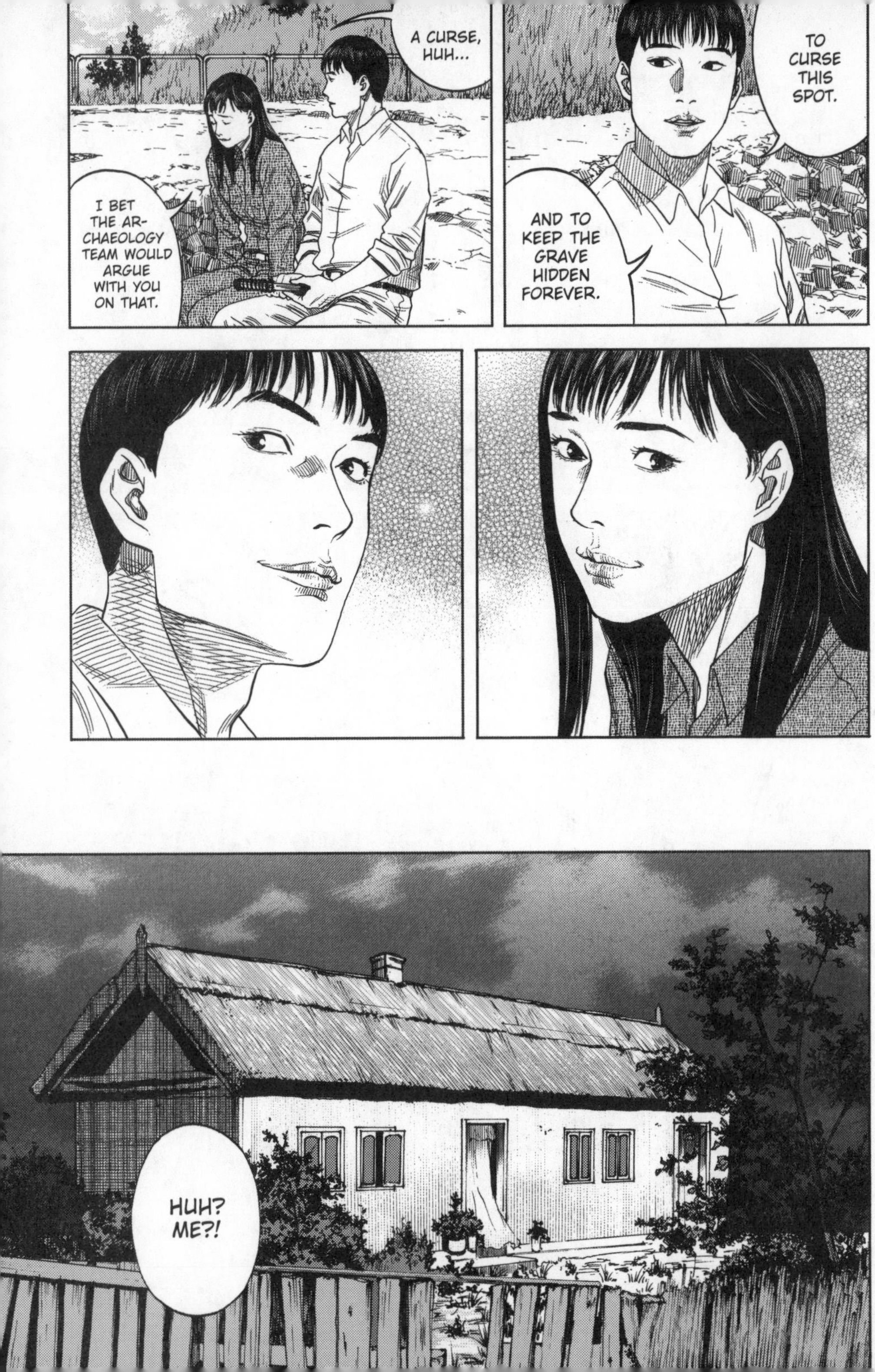
TO CURSE THIS SPOT.
AND TO KEEP THE GRAVE HIDDEN FOREVER.
A CURSE, HUH...
I BET THE ARCHAEOLOGY TEAM WOULD ARGUE WITH YOU ON THAT.
HUH? ME?!

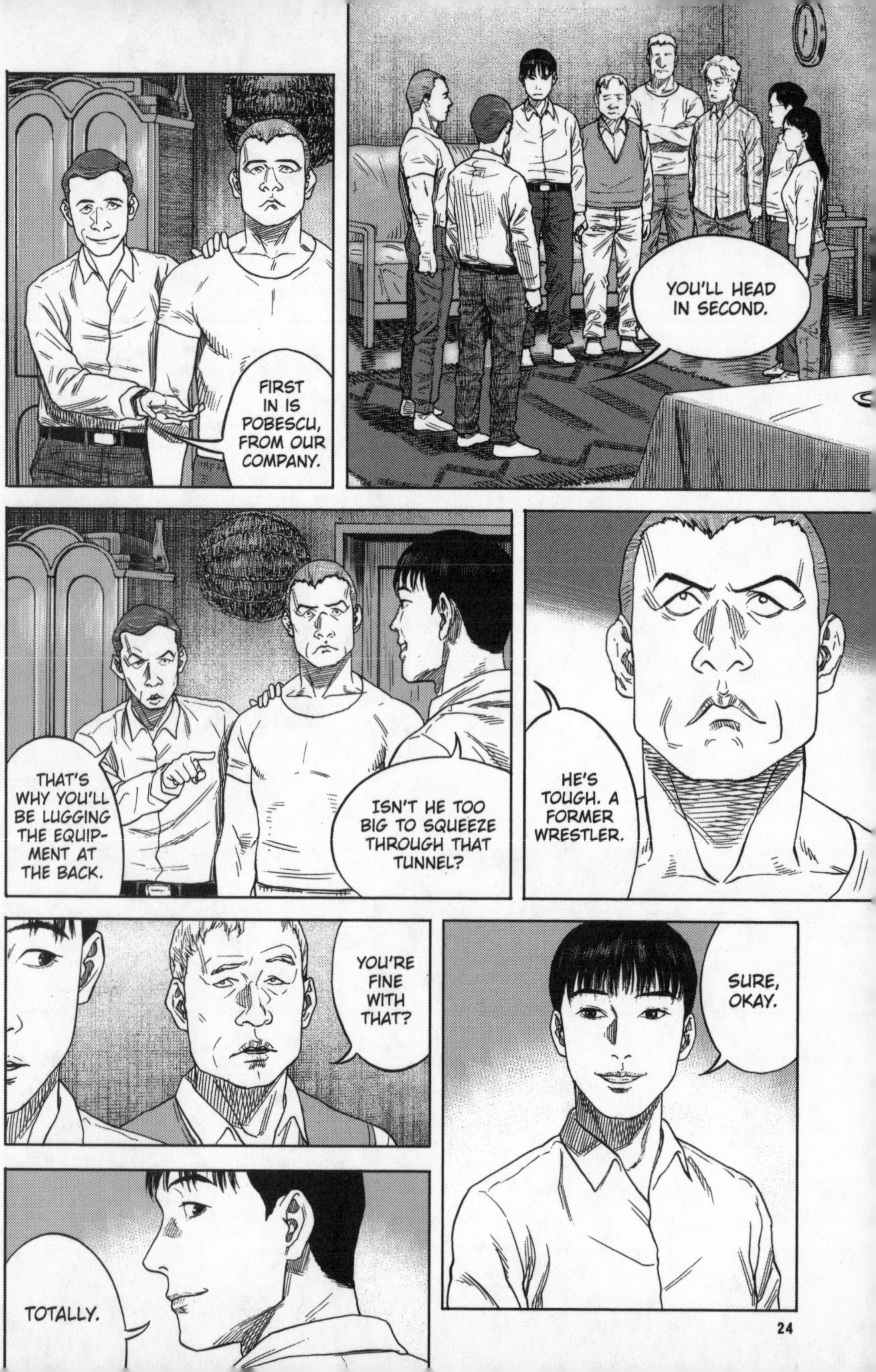
YOU'LL HEAD IN SECOND.
FIRST IN IS POBESCU, FROM OUR COMPANY.
HE'S TOUGH. A FORMER WRESTLER.
ISN'T HE TOO BIG TO SQUEEZE THROUGH THAT TUNNEL?
THAT'S WHY YOU'LL BE LUGGING THE EQUIPMENT AT THE BACK.
SURE, OKAY.
YOU'RE FINE WITH THAT?
TOTALLY.

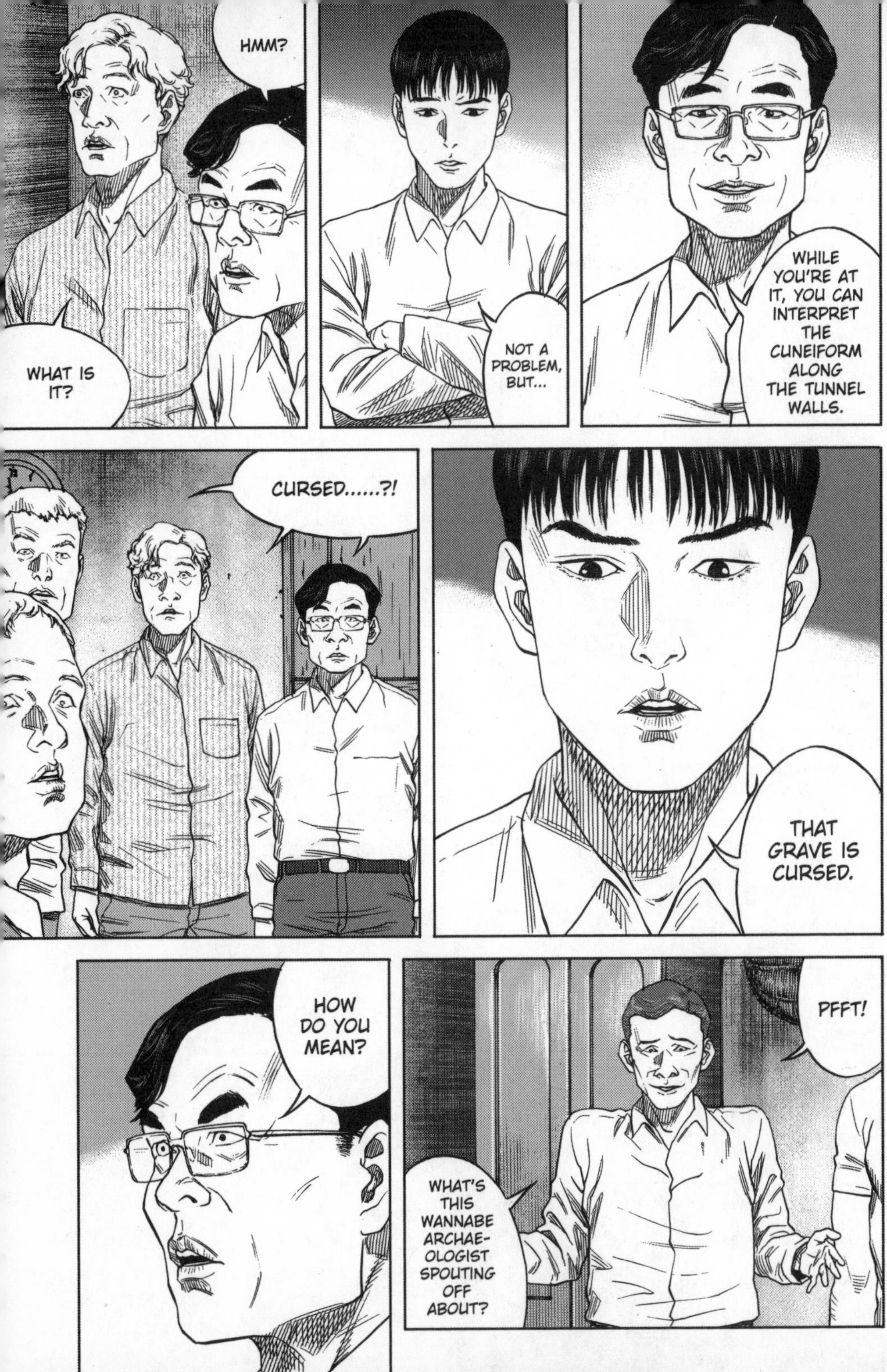
WHILE YOU'RE AT IT, YOU CAN INTERPRET THE CUNEIFORM ALONG THE TUNNEL WALLS.
NOT A PROBLEM, BUT...
HMM?
WHAT IS IT?
THAT GRAVE IS CURSED.
CURSED......?!
PFFT!
WHAT'S THIS WANNABE ARCHAEOLOGIST SPOUTING OFF ABOUT?
HOW DO YOU MEAN?

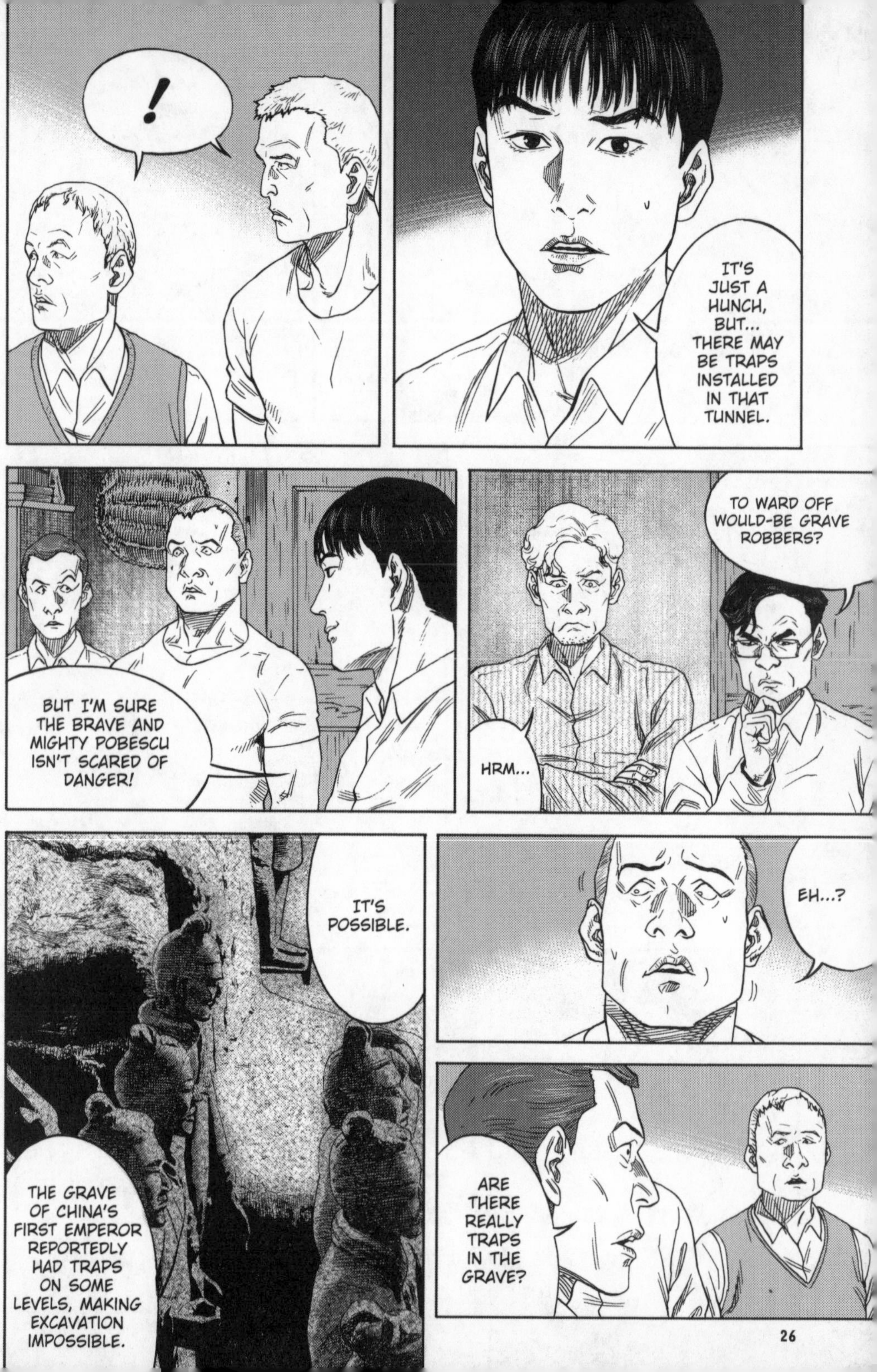
IT'S JUST A HUNCH, BUT... THERE MAY BE TRAPS INSTALLED IN THAT TUNNEL.
!
TO WARD OFF WOULD-BE GRAVE ROBBERS?
HRM...
BUT I'M SURE THE BRAVE AND MIGHTY POBESCU ISN'T SCARED OF DANGER!
EH...?
ARE THERE REALLY TRAPS IN THE GRAVE?
IT'S POSSIBLE.
THE GRAVE OF CHINA'S FIRST EMPEROR REPORTEDLY HAD TRAPS ON SOME LEVELS, MAKING EXCAVATION IMPOSSIBLE.

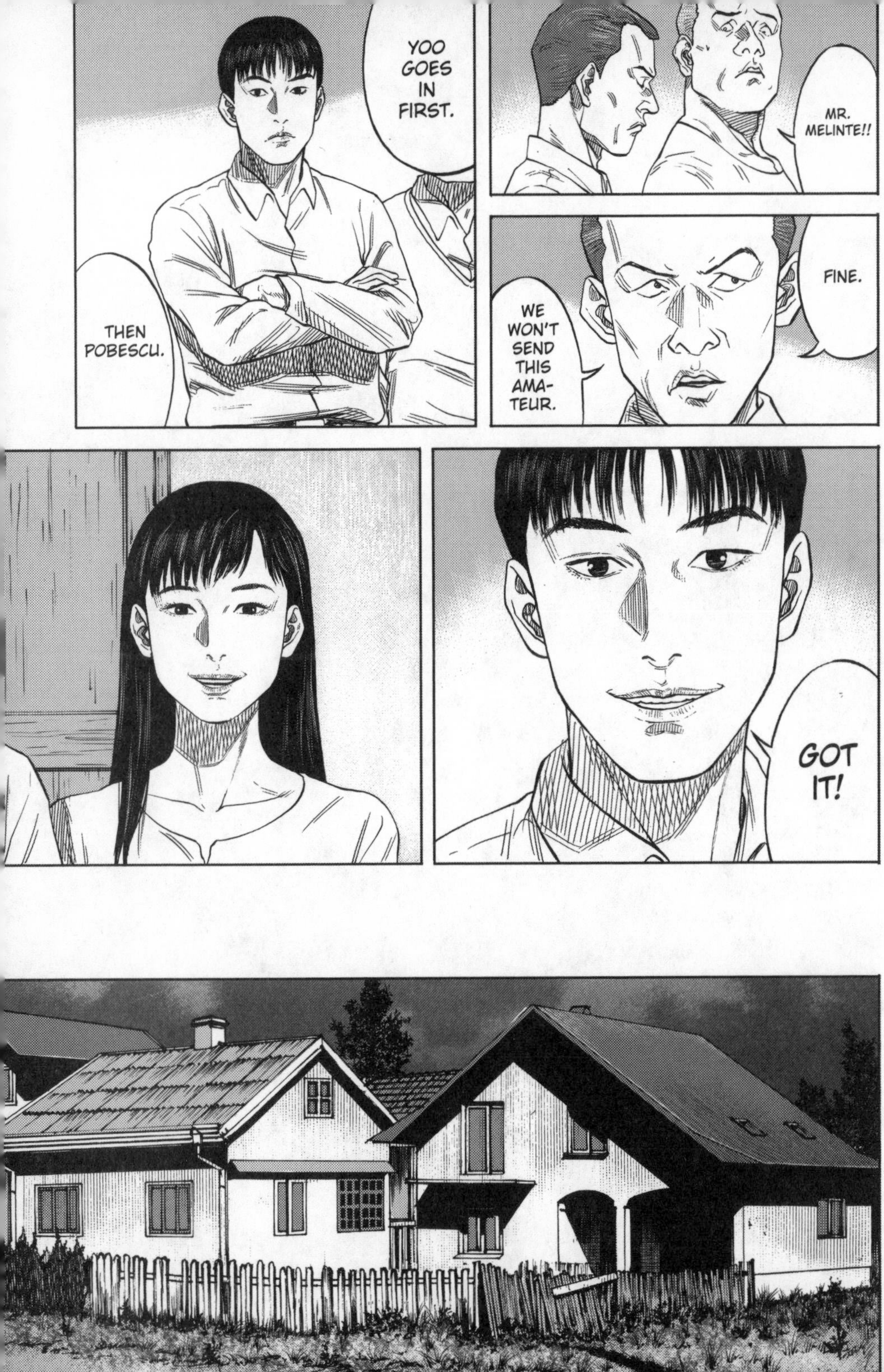
MR. MELINTE!!
FINE.
WE WON'T SEND THIS AMATEUR.
YOO GOES IN FIRST.
THEN POBESCU.
GOT IT!

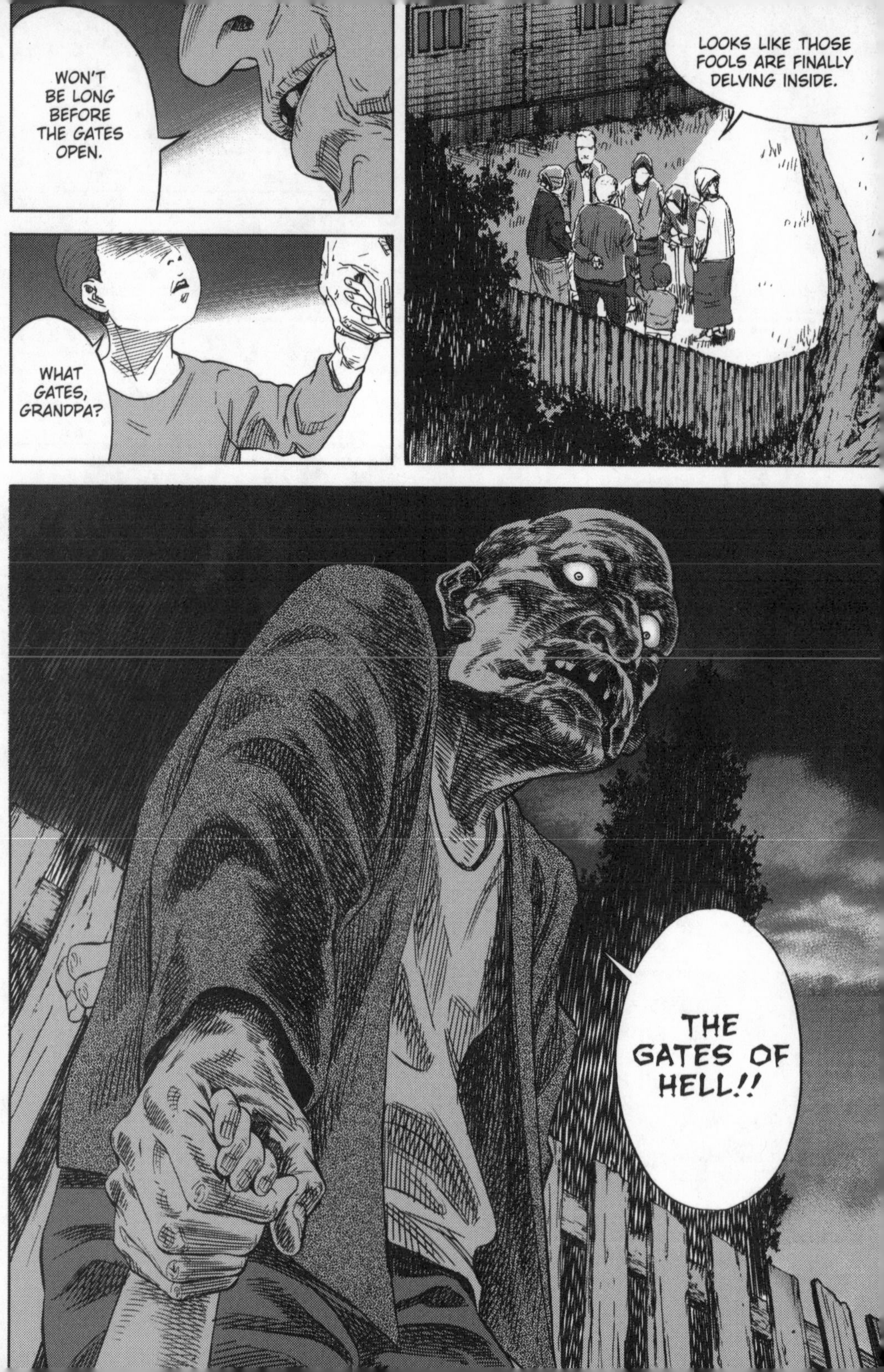
LOOKS LIKE THOSE FOOLS ARE FINALLY DELVING INSIDE.
WON'T BE LONG BEFORE THE GATES OPEN.
WHAT GATES, GRANDPA?
THE GATES OF HELL!!

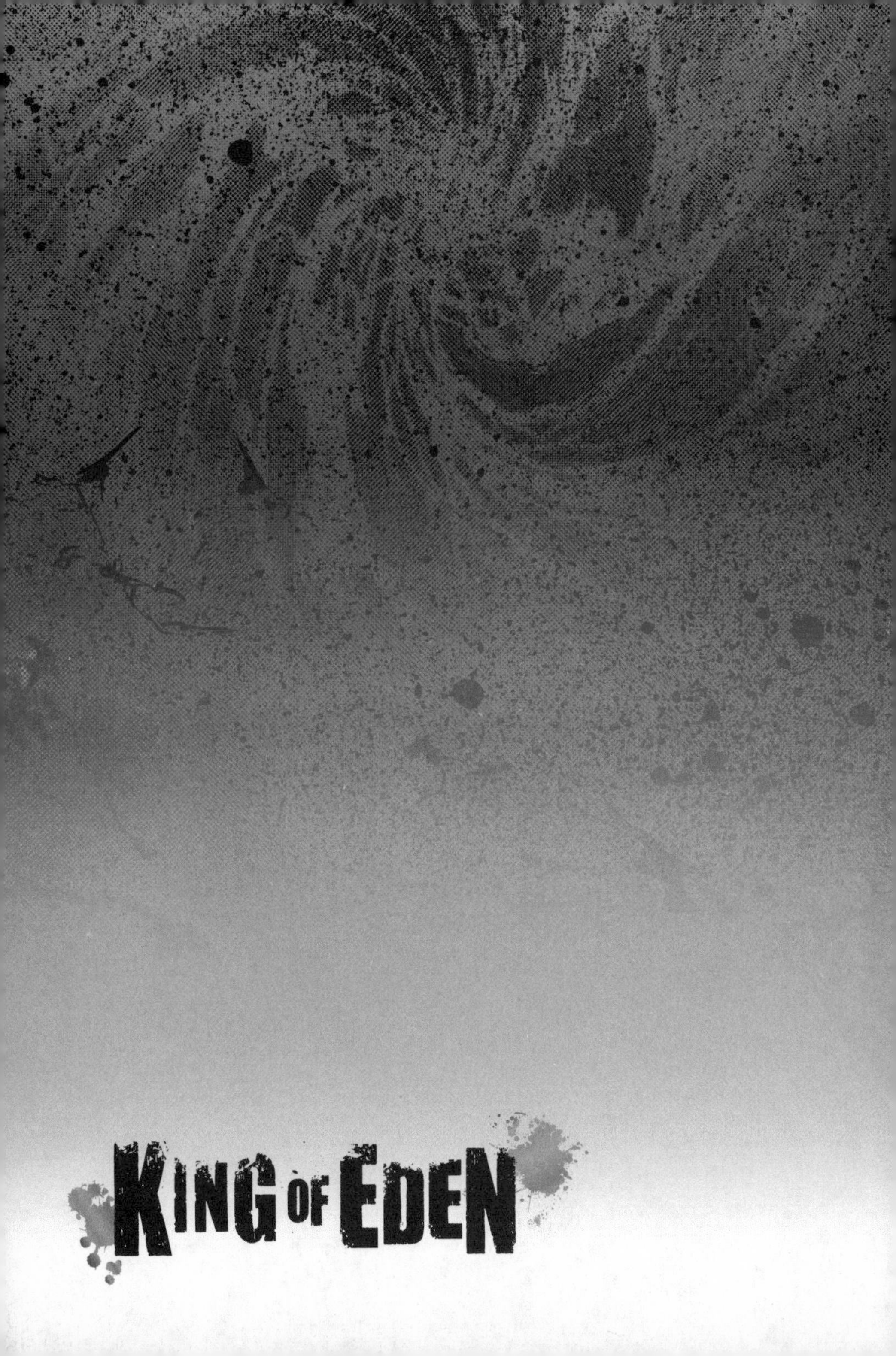
KING OF EDEN

KING OF EDEN

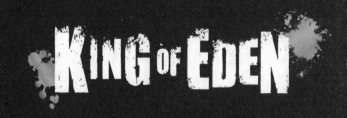

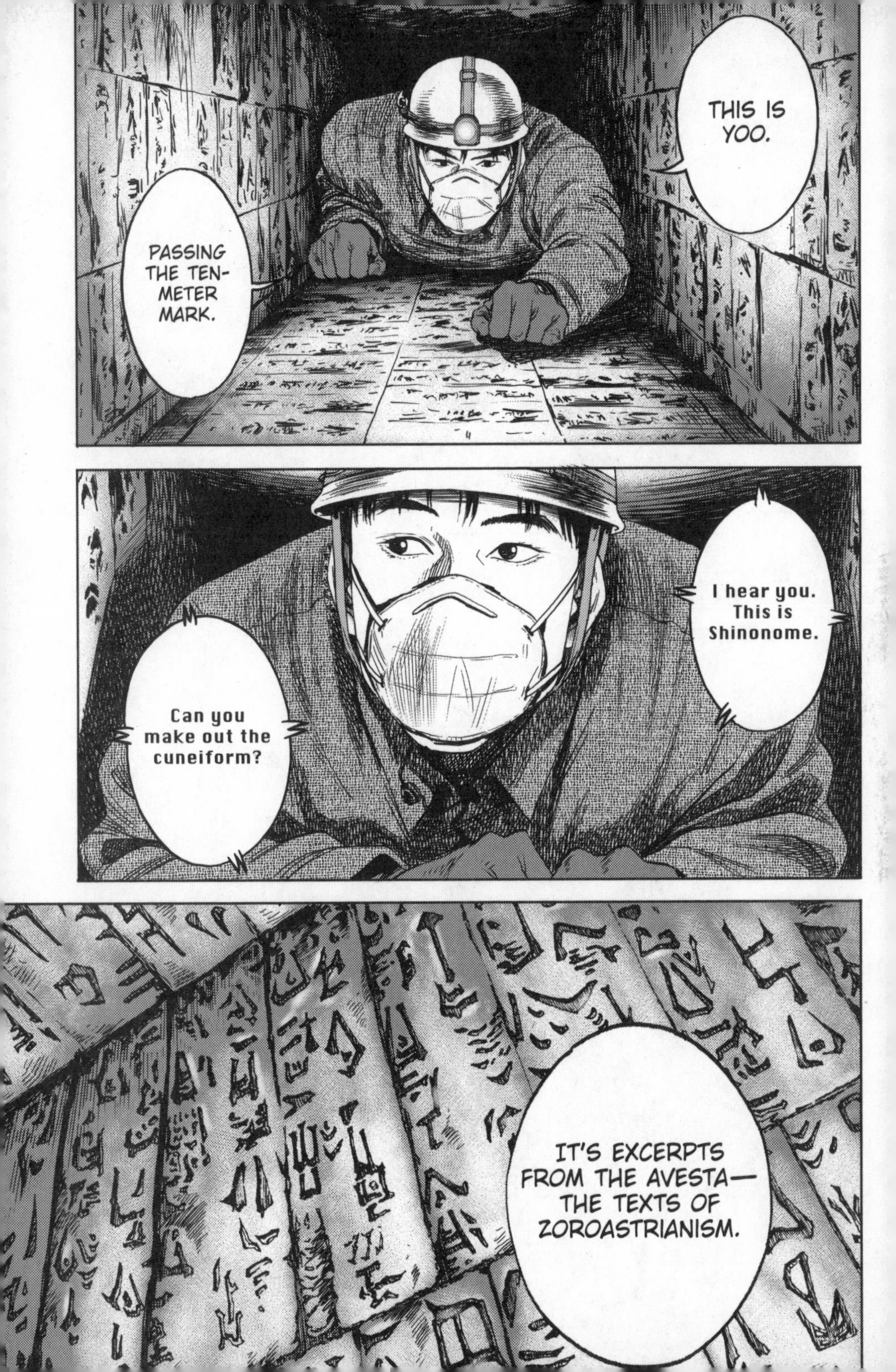
THIS IS YOO.
PASSING THE TEN-METER MARK.
I hear you. This is Shinonome.
Can you make out the cuneiform?
IT'S EXCERPTS FROM THE AVESTA—THE TEXTS OF ZOROASTRIANISM.

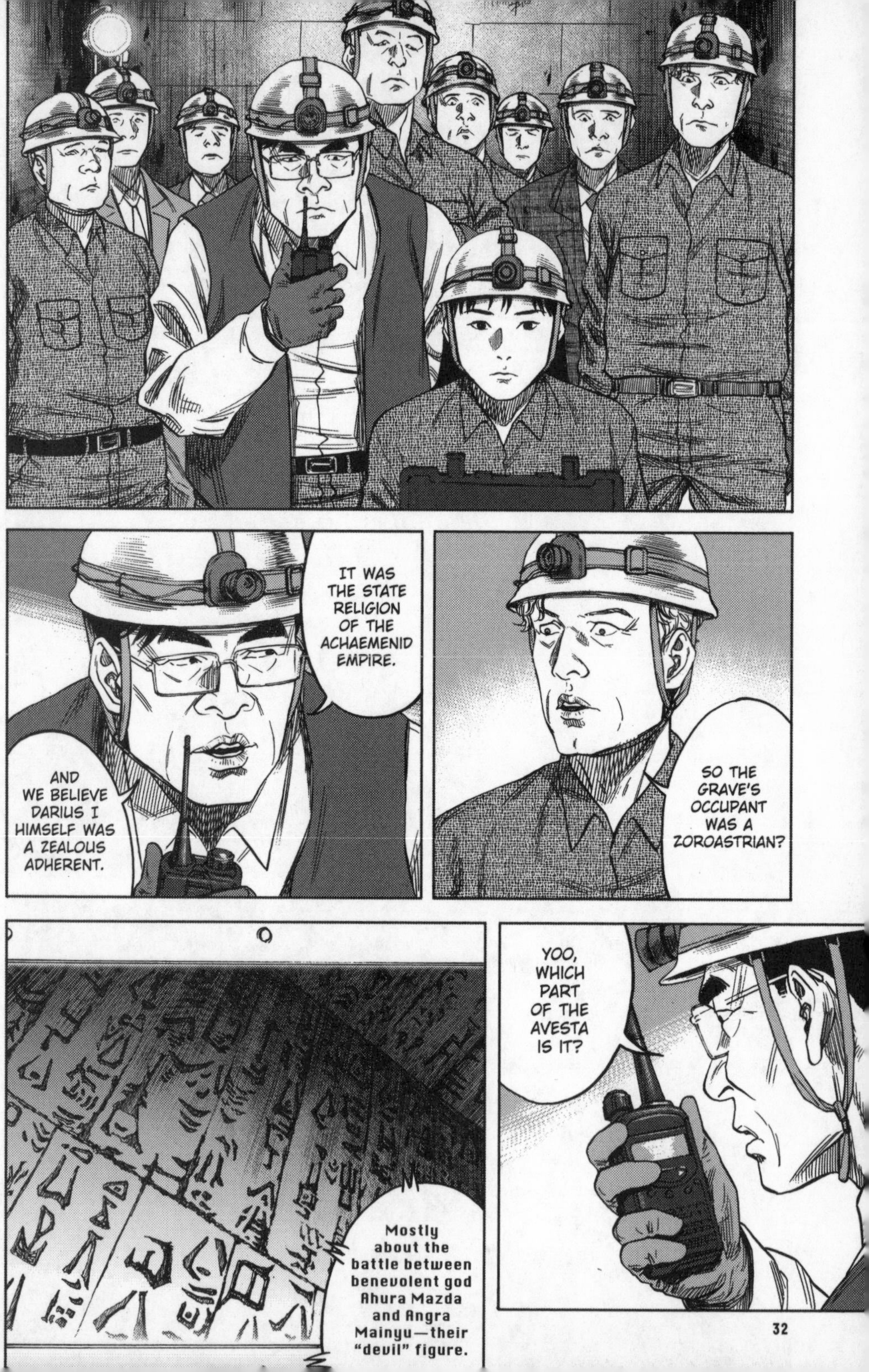
SO THE GRAVE'S OCCUPANT WAS A ZOROASTRIAN?
IT WAS THE STATE RELIGION OF THE ACHAEMENID EMPIRE.
AND WE BELIEVE DARIUS I HIMSELF WAS A ZEALOUS ADHERENT.
YOO, WHICH PART OF THE AVESTA IS IT?
Mostly about the battle between benevolent god Ahura Mazda and Angra Mainyu—their "devil" figure.

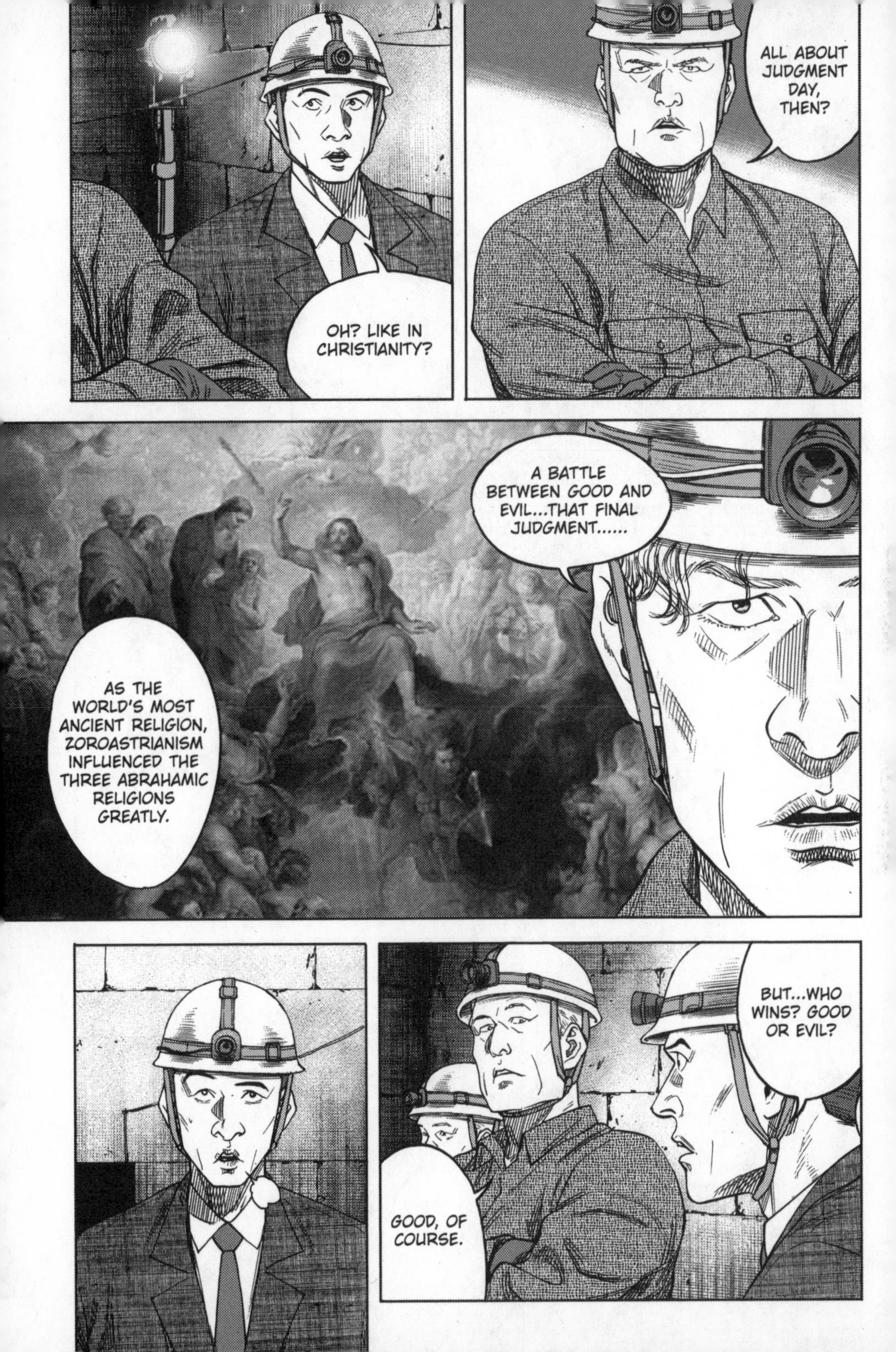
ALL ABOUT JUDGMENT DAY, THEN?
OH? LIKE IN CHRISTIANITY?
A BATTLE BETWEEN GOOD AND EVIL...THAT FINAL JUDGMENT......
AS THE WORLD'S MOST ANCIENT RELIGION, ZOROASTRIANISM INFLUENCED THE THREE ABRAHAMIC RELIGIONS GREATLY.
BUT...WHO WINS? GOOD OR EVIL?
GOOD, OF COURSE.

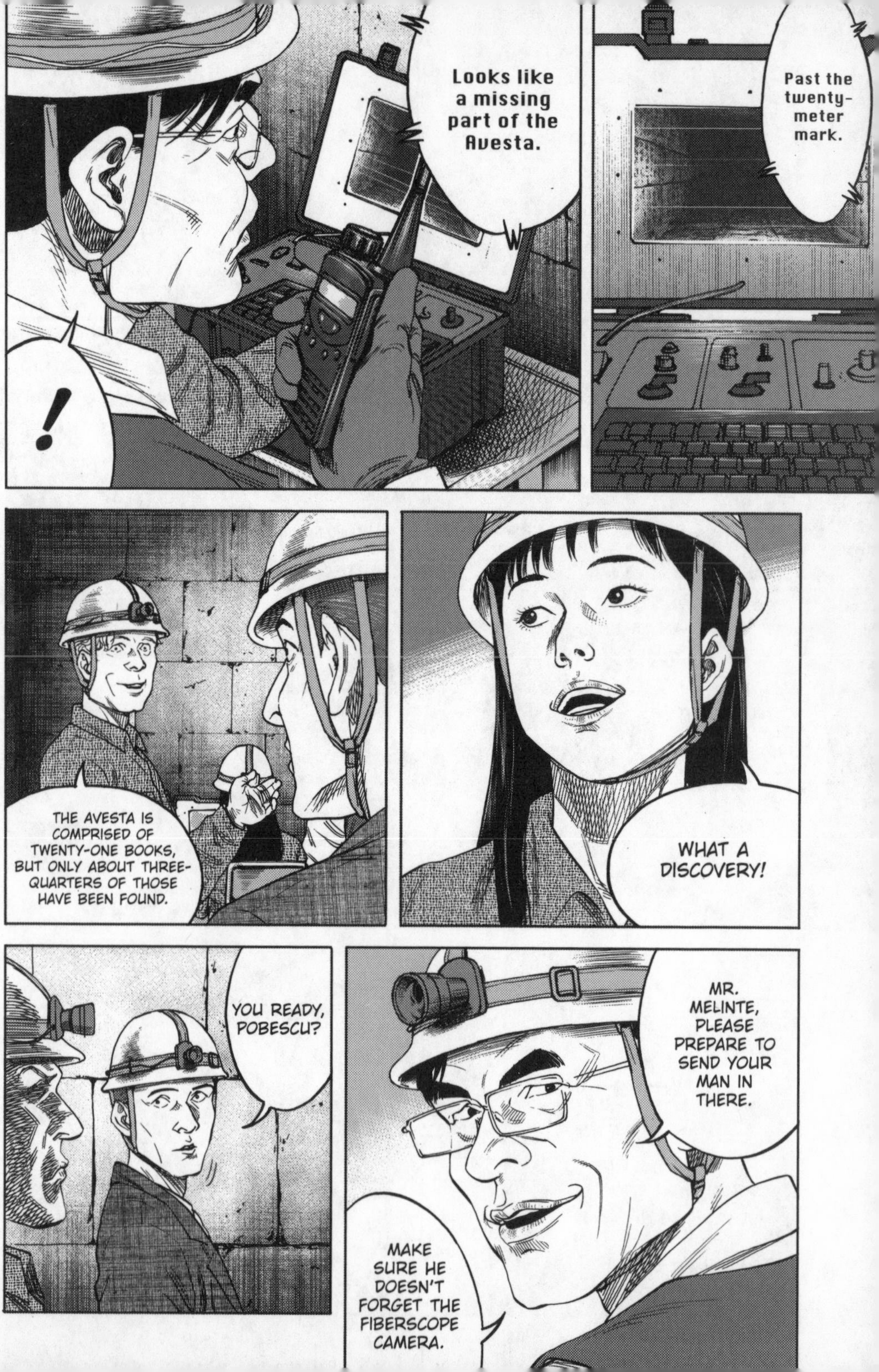
Past the twenty-meter mark.
Looks like a missing part of the Avesta.
!
WHAT A DISCOVERY!
THE AVESTA IS COMPRISED OF TWENTY-ONE BOOKS, BUT ONLY ABOUT THREE-QUARTERS OF THOSE HAVE BEEN FOUND.
MR. MELINTE, PLEASE PREPARE TO SEND YOUR MAN IN THERE.
MAKE SURE HE DOESN'T FORGET THE FIBERSCOPE CAMERA.
YOU READY, POBESCU?

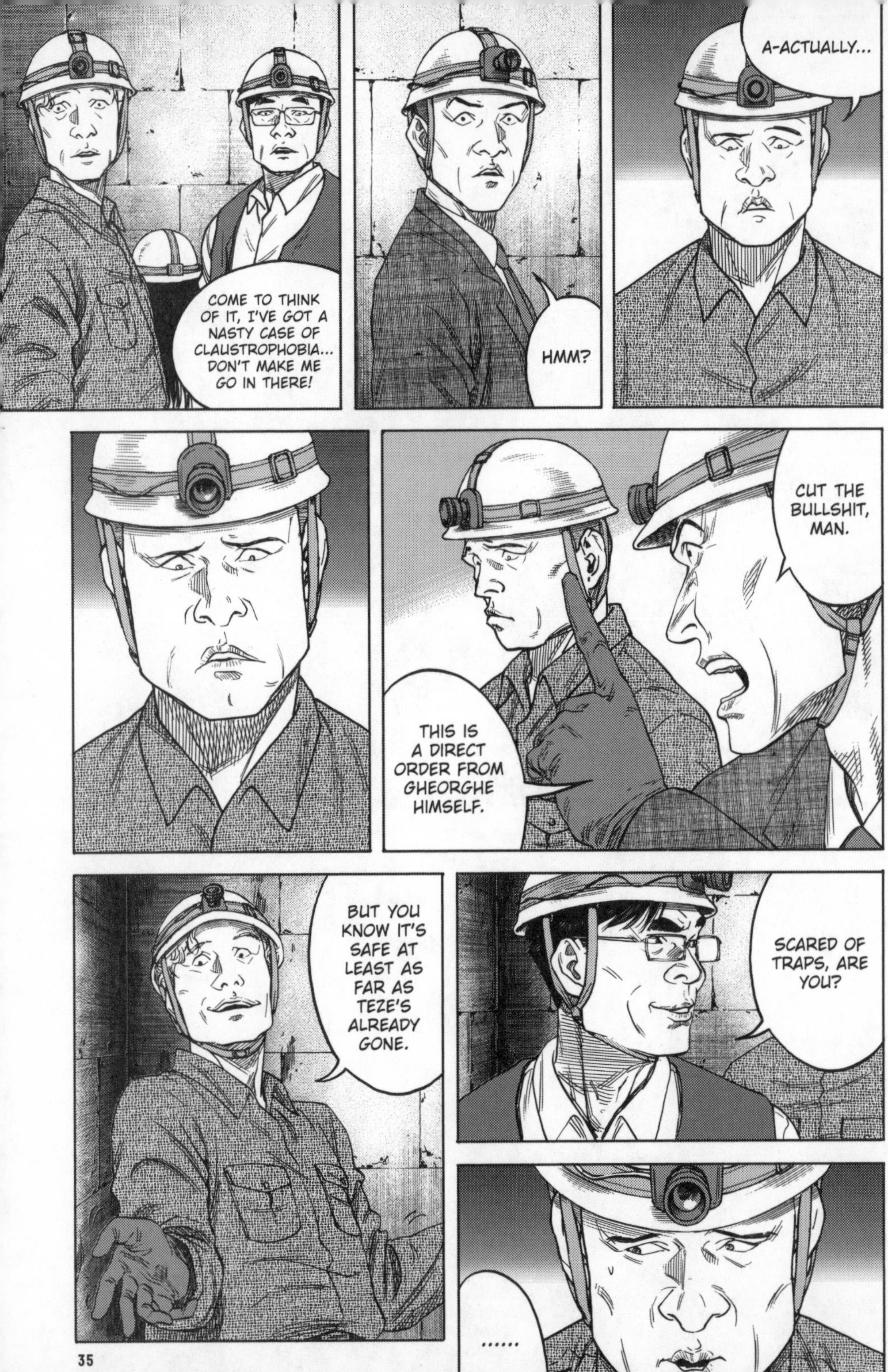
A-ACTUALLY...
HMM?
COME TO THINK OF IT, I'VE GOT A NASTY CASE OF CLAUSTROPHOBIA... DON'T MAKE ME GO IN THERE!
CUT THE BULLSHIT, MAN.
THIS IS A DIRECT ORDER FROM GHEORGHE HIMSELF.
SCARED OF TRAPS, ARE YOU?
......
BUT YOU KNOW IT'S SAFE AT LEAST AS FAR AS TEZE'S ALREADY GONE.

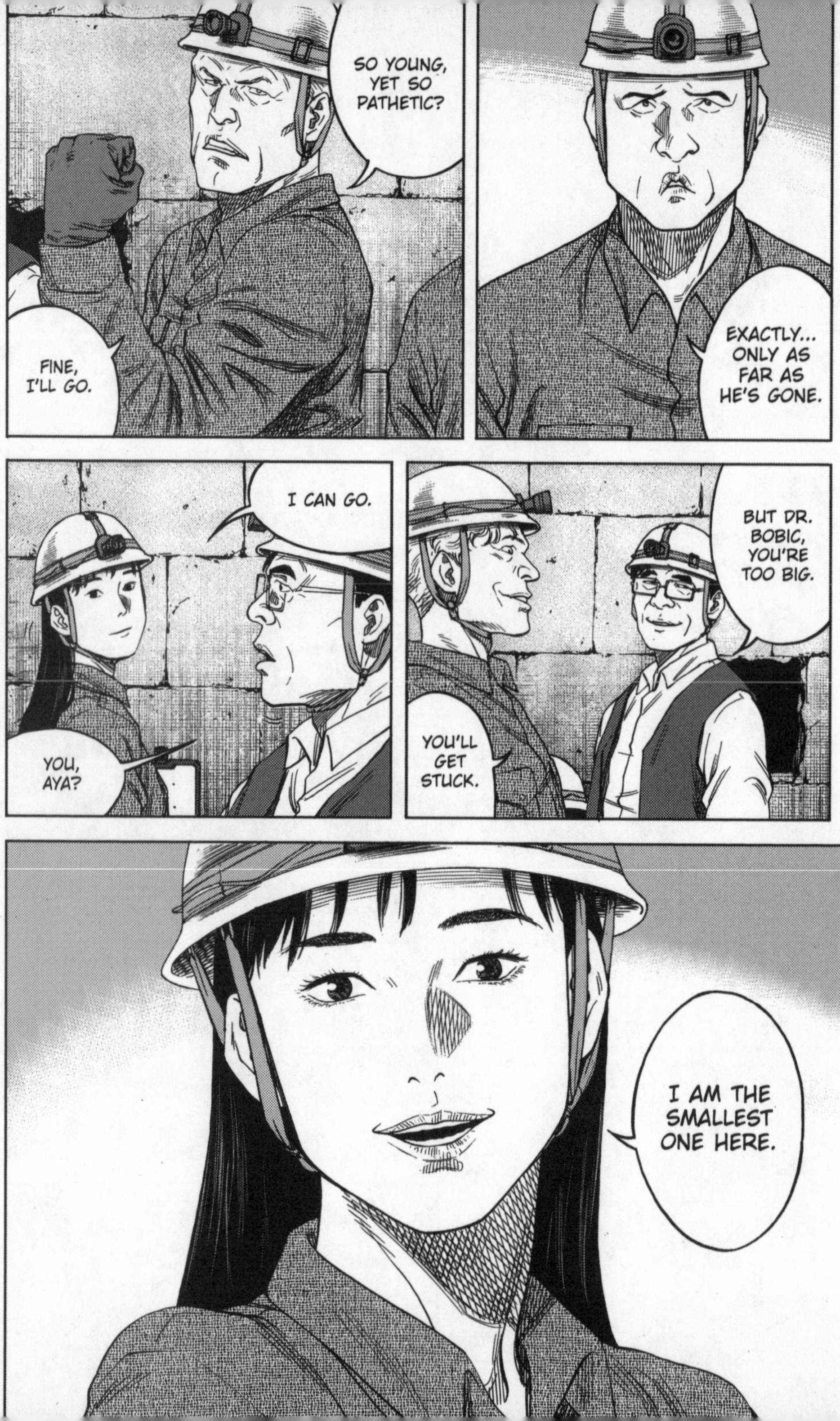
EXACTLY... ONLY AS FAR AS HE'S GONE.
SO YOUNG, YET SO PATHETIC?
FINE, I'LL GO.
BUT DR. BOBIC, YOU'RE TOO BIG.
YOU'LL GET STUCK.
I CAN GO.
YOU, AYA?
I AM THE SMALLEST ONE HERE.

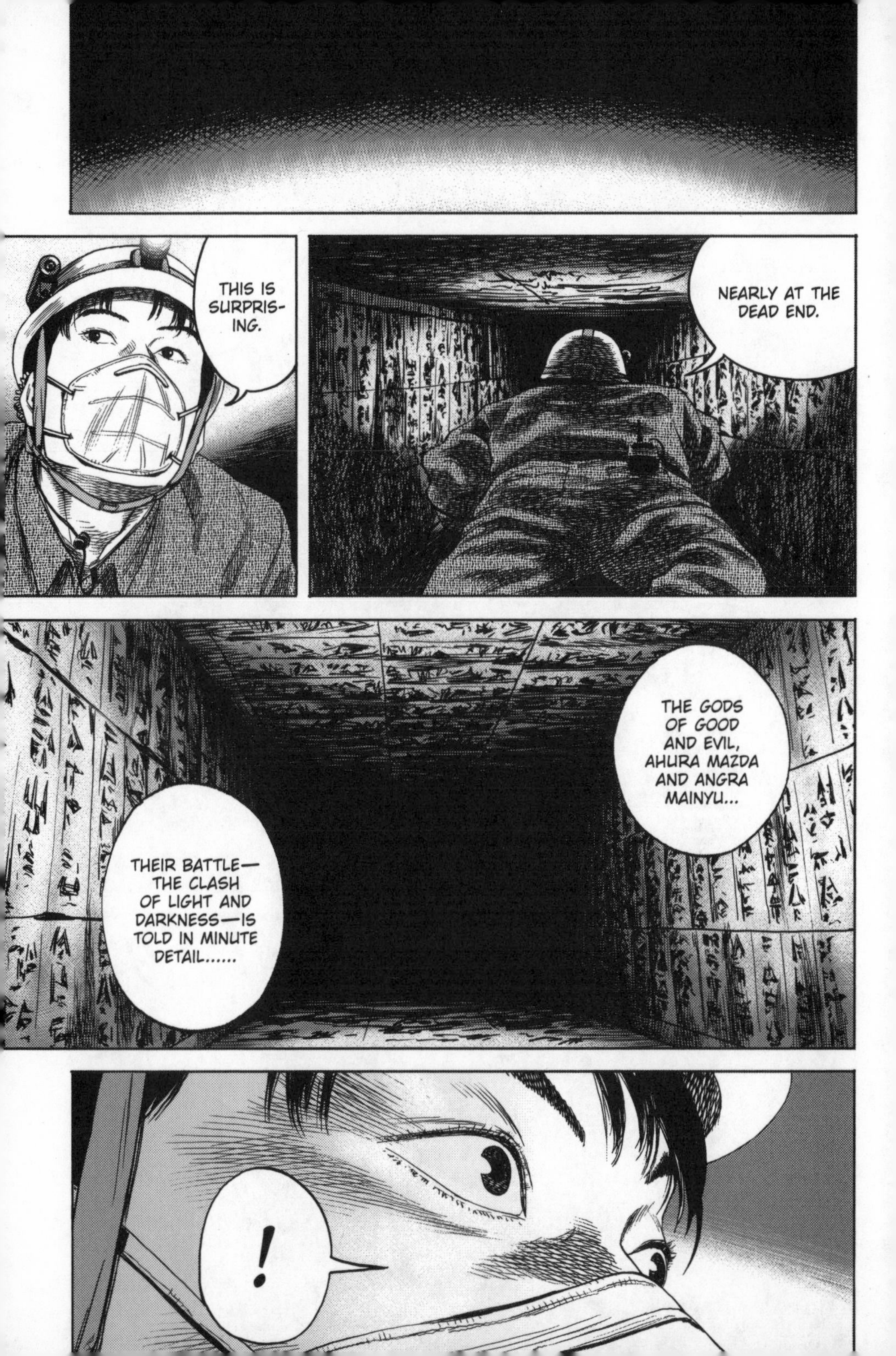
NEARLY AT THE DEAD END.
THIS IS SURPRIS-ING.
THE GODS OF GOOD AND EVIL, AHURA MAZDA AND ANGRA MAINYU...
THEIR BATTLE—THE CLASH OF LIGHT AND DARKNESS—IS TOLD IN MINUTE DETAIL......
!

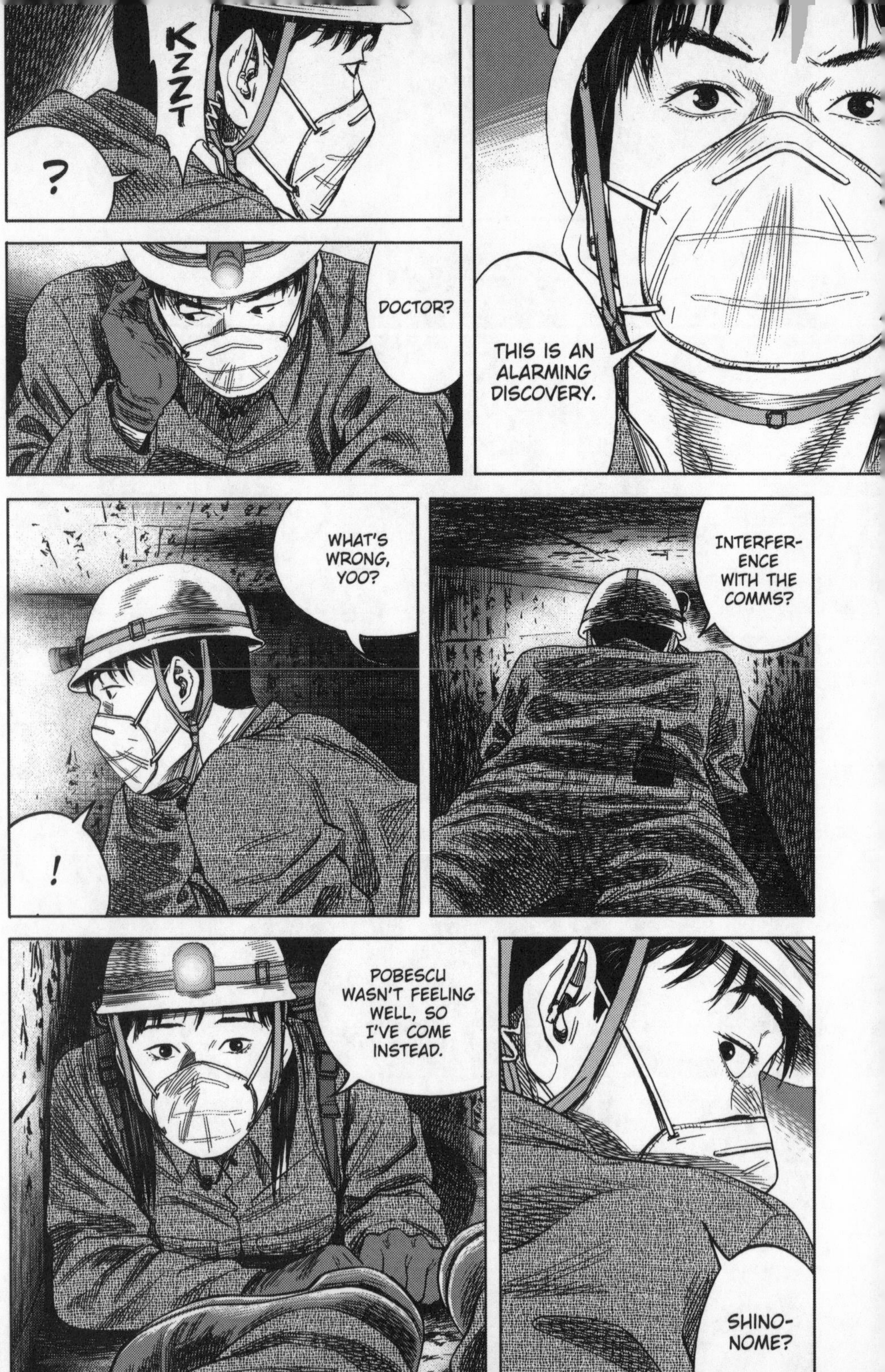
THIS IS AN ALARMING DISCOVERY.
KZZT
?
DOCTOR?
INTERFER-ENCE WITH THE COMMS?
WHAT'S WRONG, YOO?
!
SHINO-NOME?
POBESCU WASN'T FEELING WELL, SO I'VE COME INSTEAD.

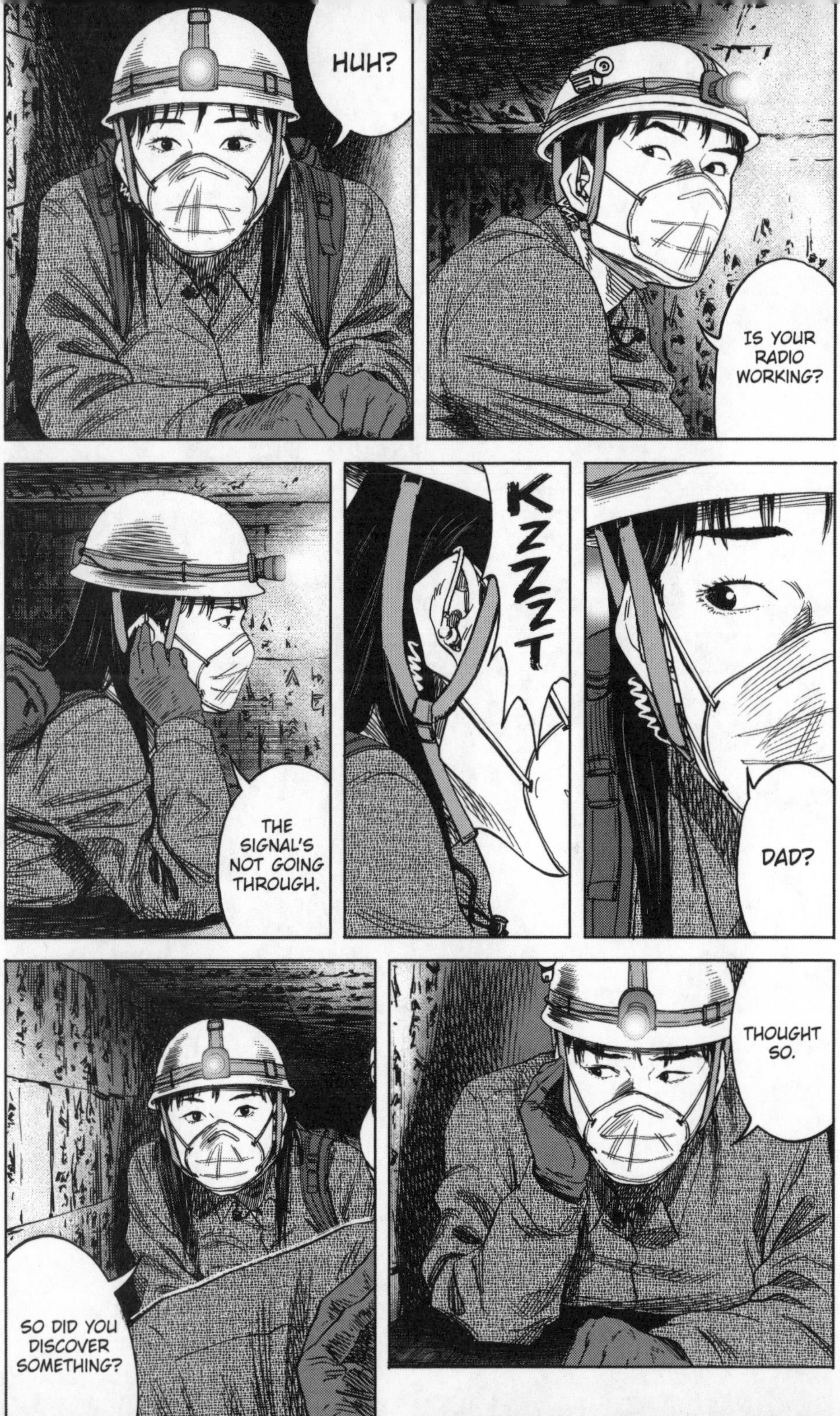
IS YOUR RADIO WORKING?
HUH?
DAD?
KZZZT
THE SIGNAL'S NOT GOING THROUGH.
THOUGHT SO.
SO DID YOU DISCOVER SOMETHING?

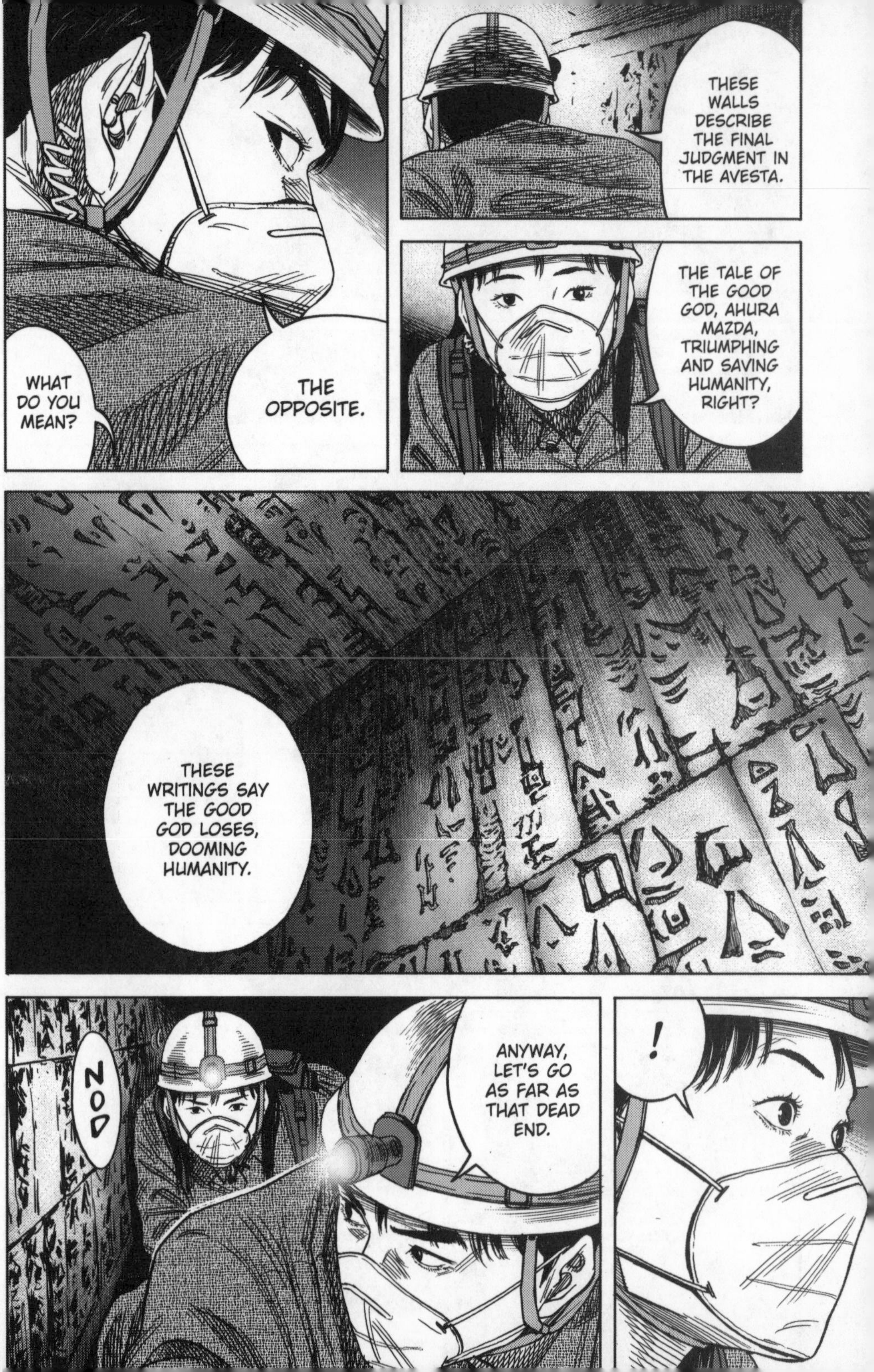
THESE WALLS DESCRIBE THE FINAL JUDGMENT IN THE AVESTA.
THE TALE OF THE GOOD GOD, AHURA MAZDA, TRIUMPHING AND SAVING HUMANITY, RIGHT?
THE OPPOSITE.
WHAT DO YOU MEAN?
THESE WRITINGS SAY THE GOOD GOD LOSES, DOOMING HUMANITY.
!
ANYWAY, LET'S GO AS FAR AS THAT DEAD END.
NOD

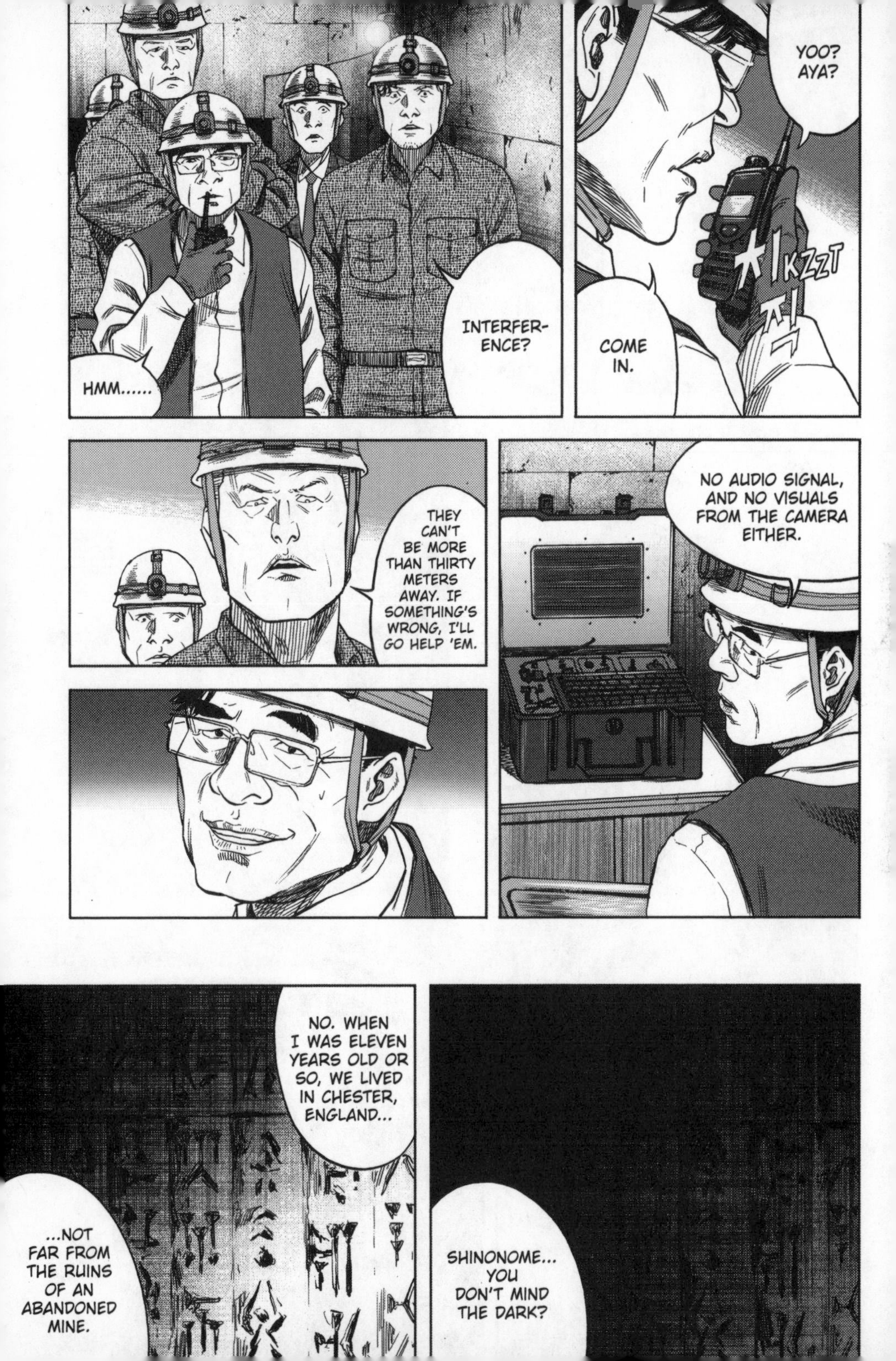
YOO? AYA?
KZZT
COME IN.
INTERFER-
ENCE?
HMM......
NO AUDIO SIGNAL, AND NO VISUALS FROM THE CAMERA EITHER.
THEY CAN'T BE MORE THAN THIRTY METERS AWAY. IF SOMETHING'S WRONG, I'LL GO HELP 'EM.
SHINONOME... YOU DON'T MIND THE DARK?
NO. WHEN I WAS ELEVEN YEARS OLD OR SO, WE LIVED IN CHESTER, ENGLAND...
...NOT FAR FROM THE RUINS OF AN ABANDONED MINE.

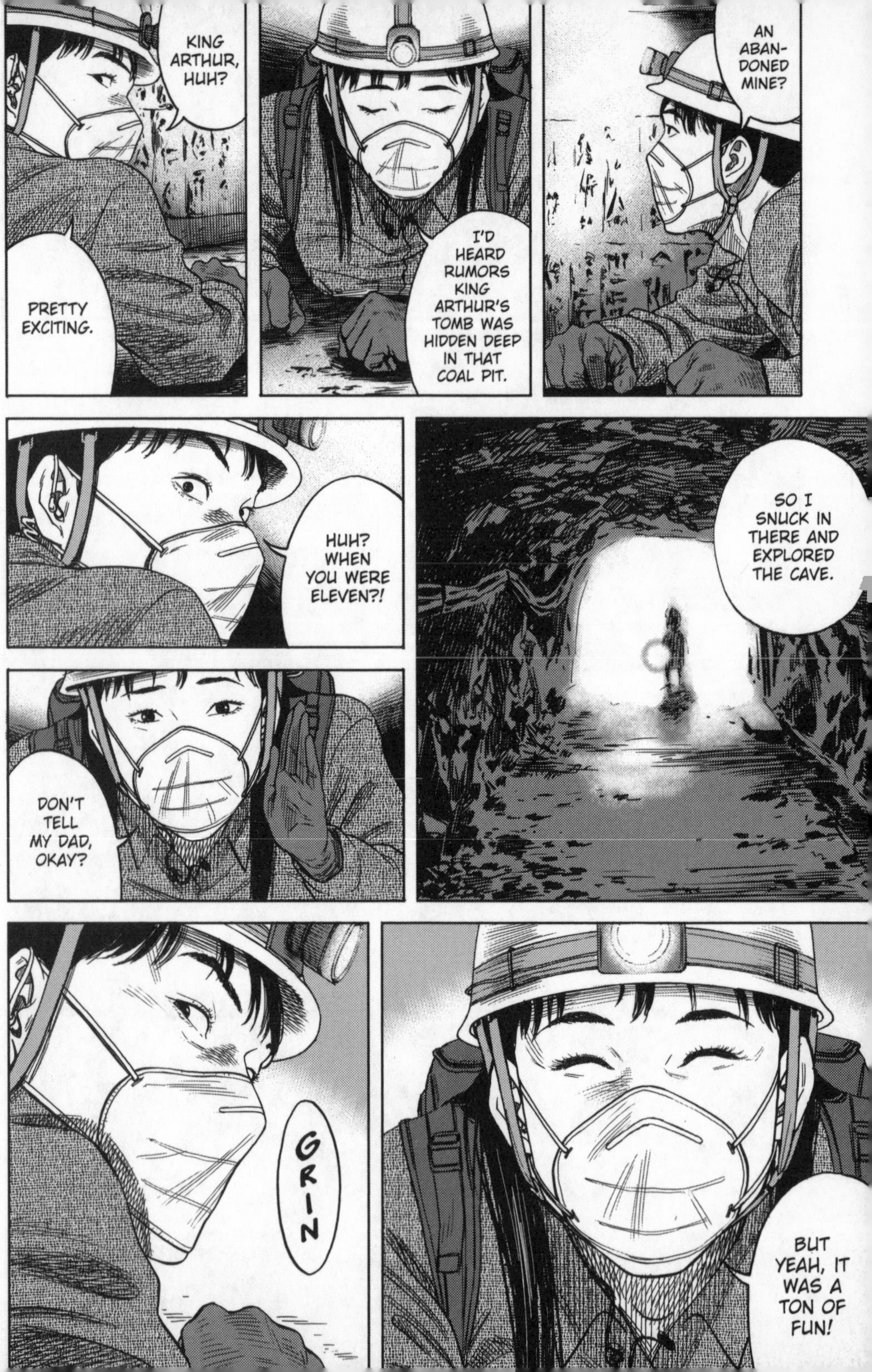
AN ABAN-DONED MINE?
I'D HEARD RUMORS KING ARTHUR'S TOMB WAS HIDDEN DEEP IN THAT COAL PIT.
KING ARTHUR, HUH?
PRETTY EXCITING.
SO I SNUCK IN THERE AND EXPLORED THE CAVE.
HUH? WHEN YOU WERE ELEVEN?!
DON'T TELL MY DAD, OKAY?
BUT YEAH, IT WAS A TON OF FUN!
GRIN

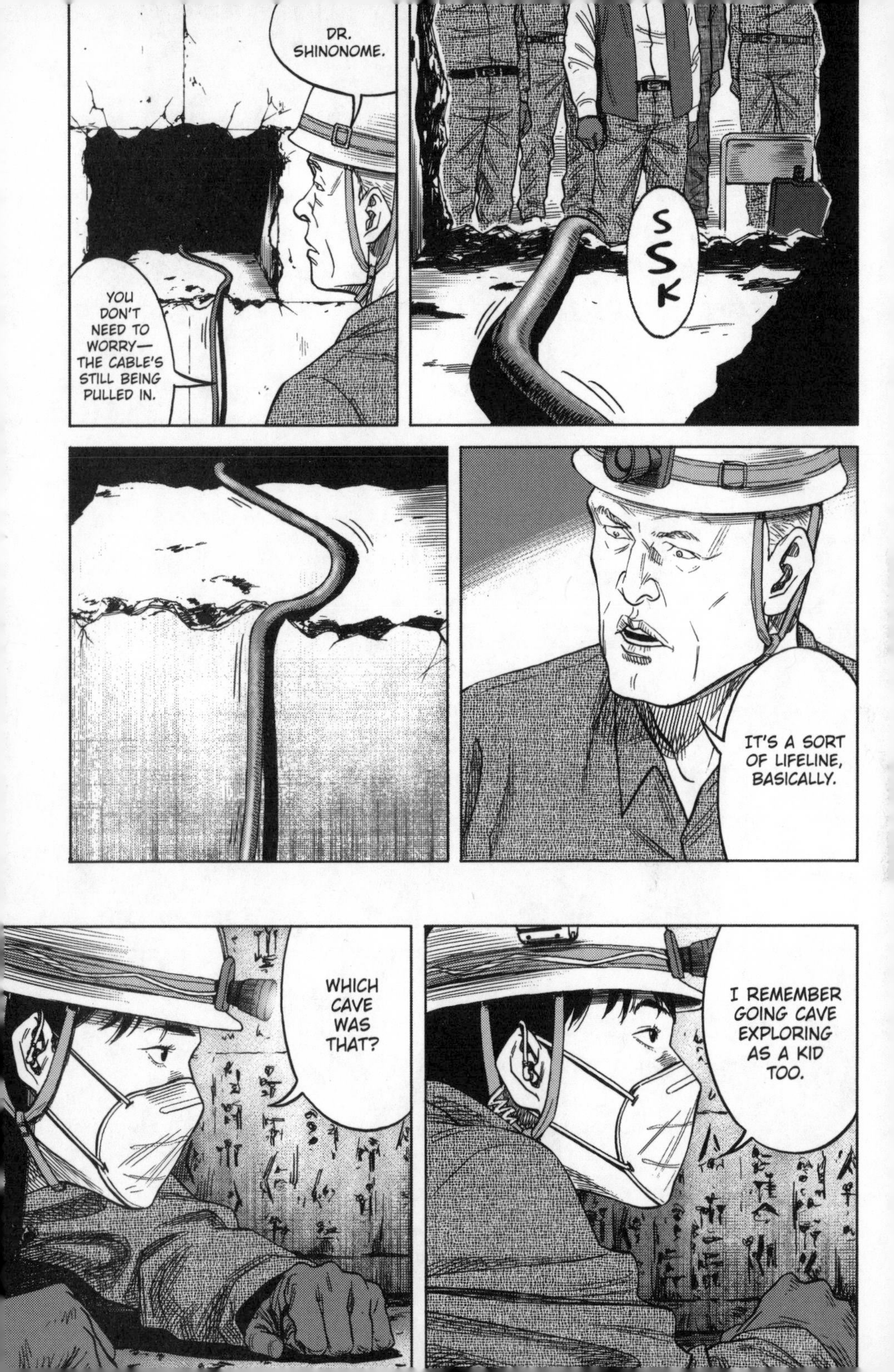
SSK
DR. SHINONOME.
YOU DON'T NEED TO WORRY— THE CABLE'S STILL BEING PULLED IN.
IT'S A SORT OF LIFELINE, BASICALLY.
I REMEMBER GOING CAVE EXPLORING AS A KID TOO.
WHICH CAVE WAS THAT?

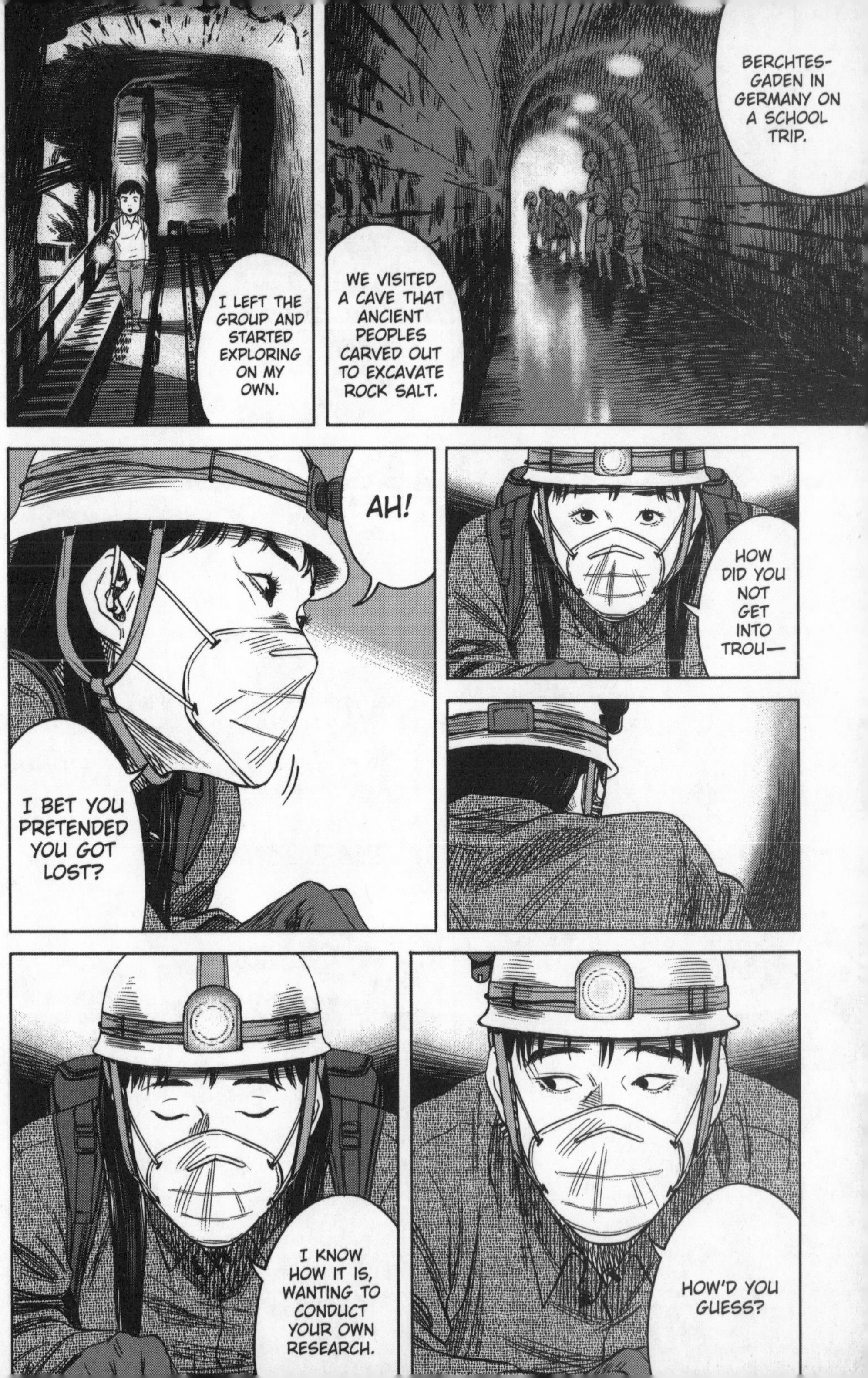
BERCHTES-GADEN IN GERMANY ON A SCHOOL TRIP.
WE VISITED A CAVE THAT ANCIENT PEOPLES CARVED OUT TO EXCAVATE ROCK SALT.
I LEFT THE GROUP AND STARTED EXPLORING ON MY OWN.
HOW DID YOU NOT GET INTO TROU—
AH!
I BET YOU PRETENDED YOU GOT LOST?
HOW'D YOU GUESS?
I KNOW HOW IT IS, WANTING TO CONDUCT YOUR OWN RESEARCH.

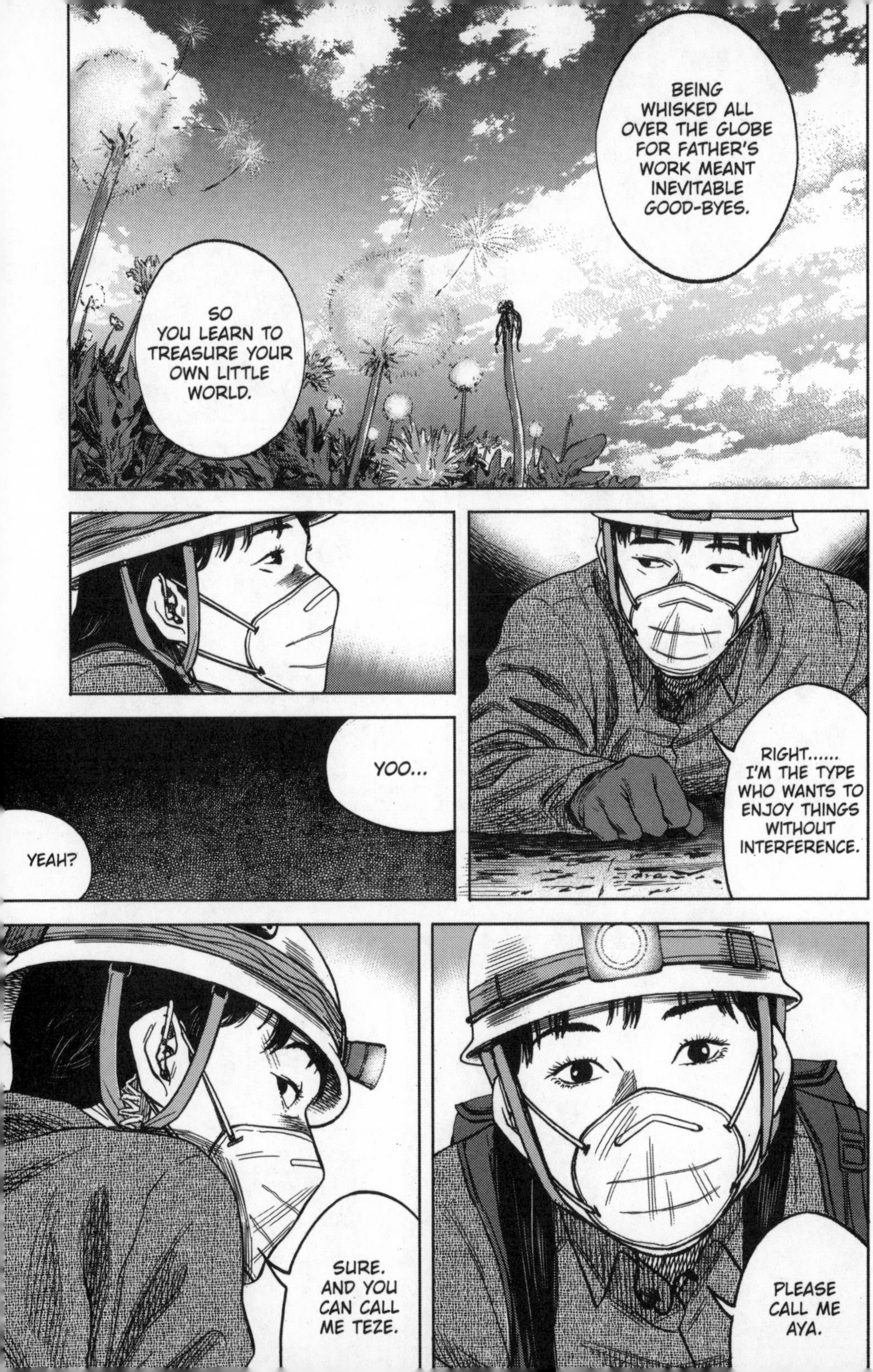
BEING WHISKED ALL OVER THE GLOBE FOR FATHER'S WORK MEANT INEVITABLE GOOD-BYES.
SO YOU LEARN TO TREASURE YOUR OWN LITTLE WORLD.
RIGHT...... I'M THE TYPE WHO WANTS TO ENJOY THINGS WITHOUT INTERFERENCE.
YOO...
YEAH?
PLEASE CALL ME AYA.
SURE. AND YOU CAN CALL ME TEZE.

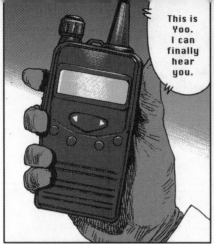

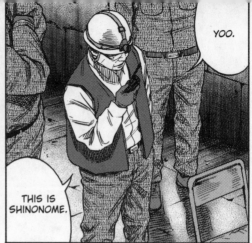

YOO.
THIS IS SHINONOME.
This is Yoo. I can finally hear you.
DID AYA FIND YOU IN THERE?
Shinonome is...Erm, Aya is right behind me, yes.
AH, WE'VE GOT THE CAMERA FEED BACK TOO.
Nearly at the end.
KZZT

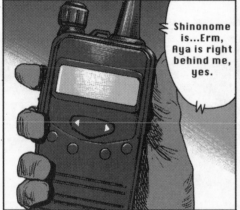

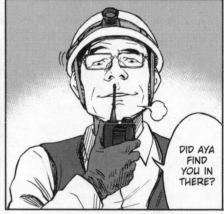

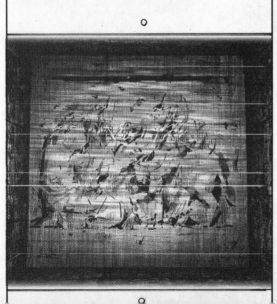

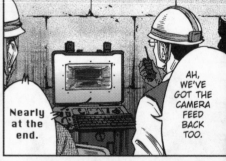

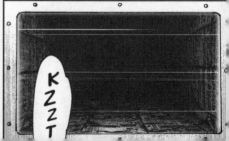

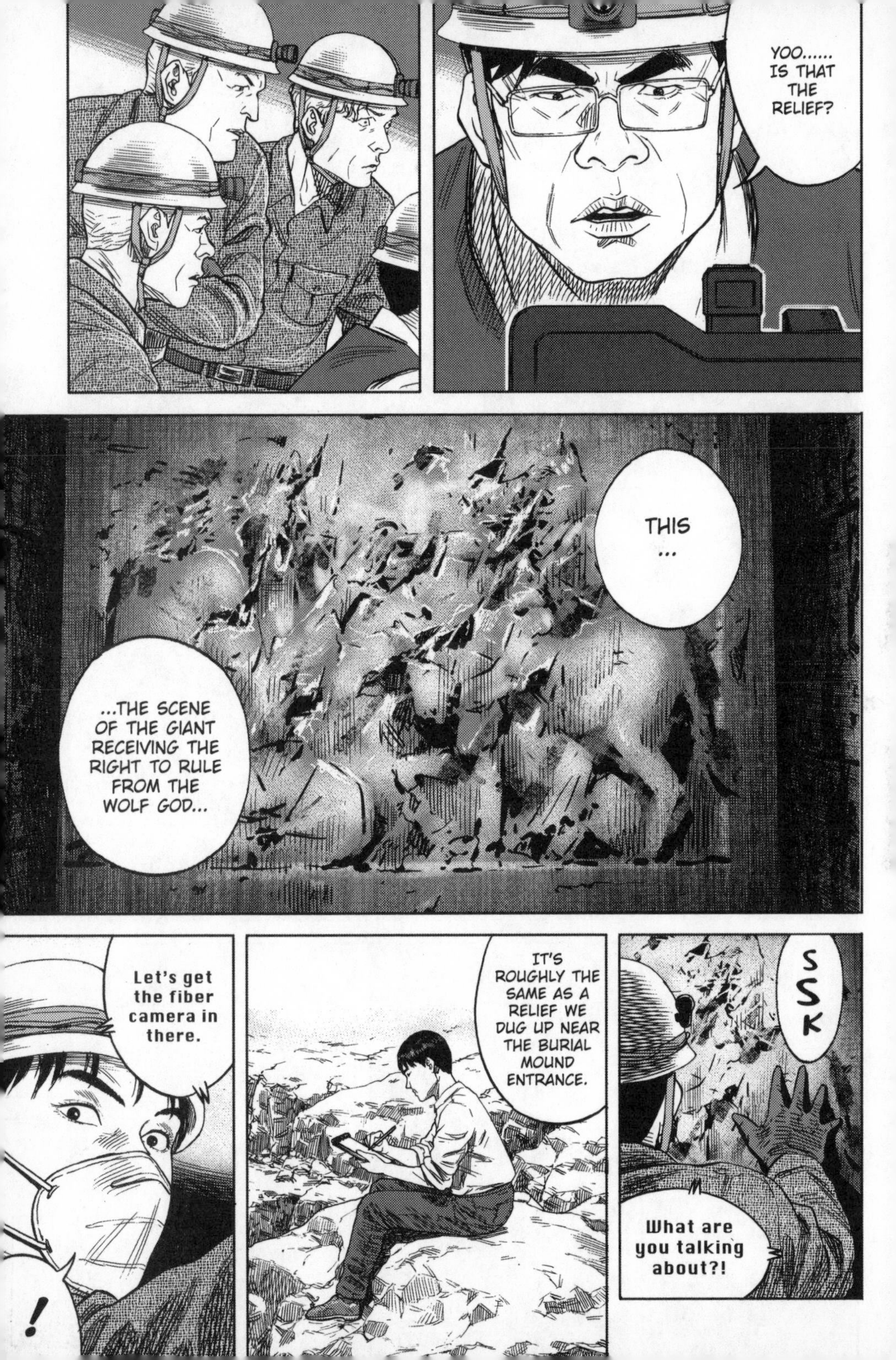
YOO...... IS THAT THE RELIEF?
THIS ...
...THE SCENE OF THE GIANT RECEIVING THE RIGHT TO RULE FROM THE WOLF GOD...
SSK
What are you talking about?!
IT'S ROUGHLY THE SAME AS A RELIEF WE DUG UP NEAR THE BURIAL MOUND ENTRANCE.
Let's get the fiber camera in there.
!

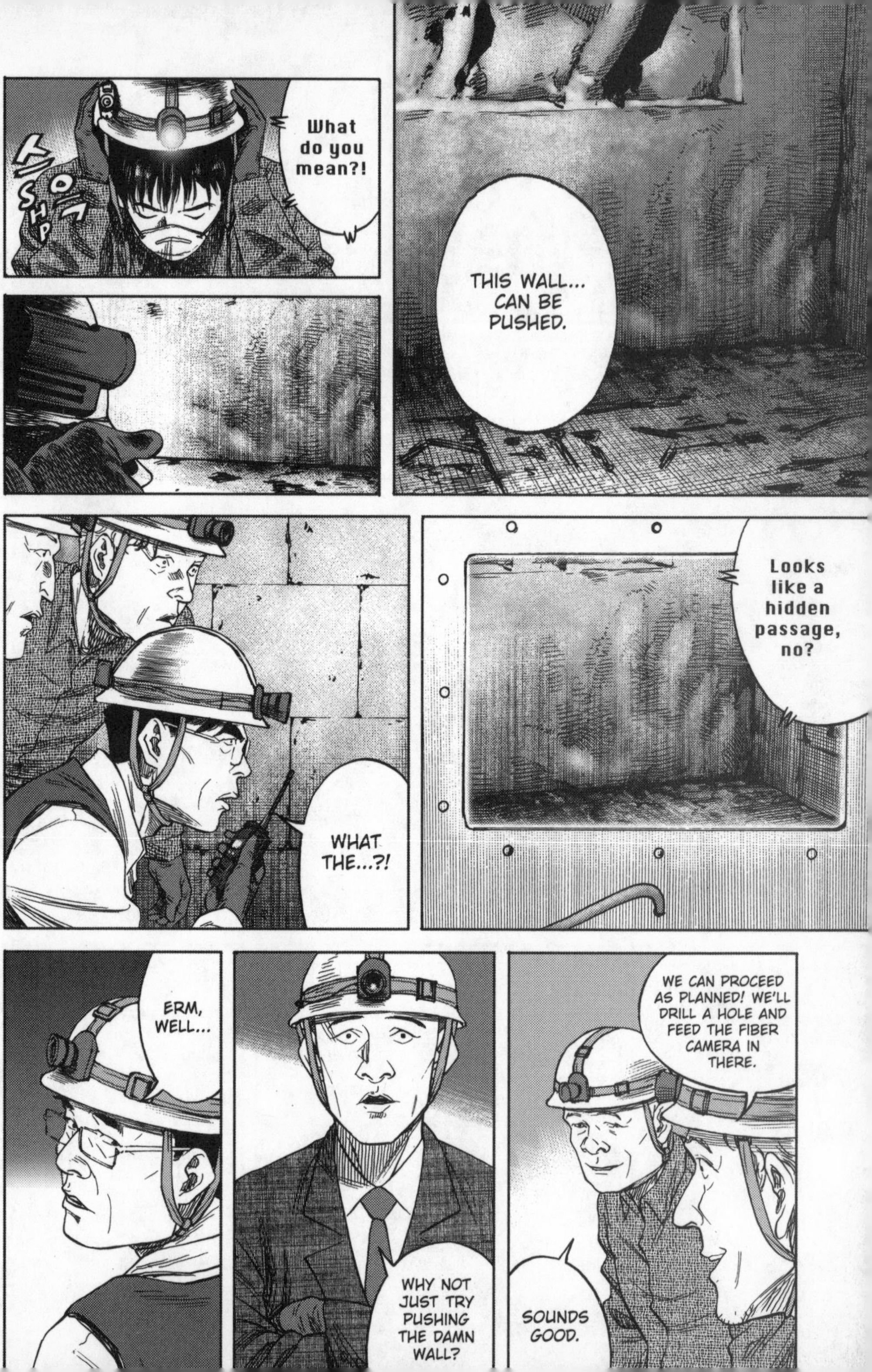
THIS WALL... CAN BE PUSHED.
What do you mean?!
KSHP
Looks like a hidden passage, no?
WHAT THE...?!
WE CAN PROCEED AS PLANNED! WE'LL DRILL A HOLE AND FEED THE FIBER CAMERA IN THERE.
SOUNDS GOOD.
WHY NOT JUST TRY PUSHING THE DAMN WALL?
ERM, WELL...

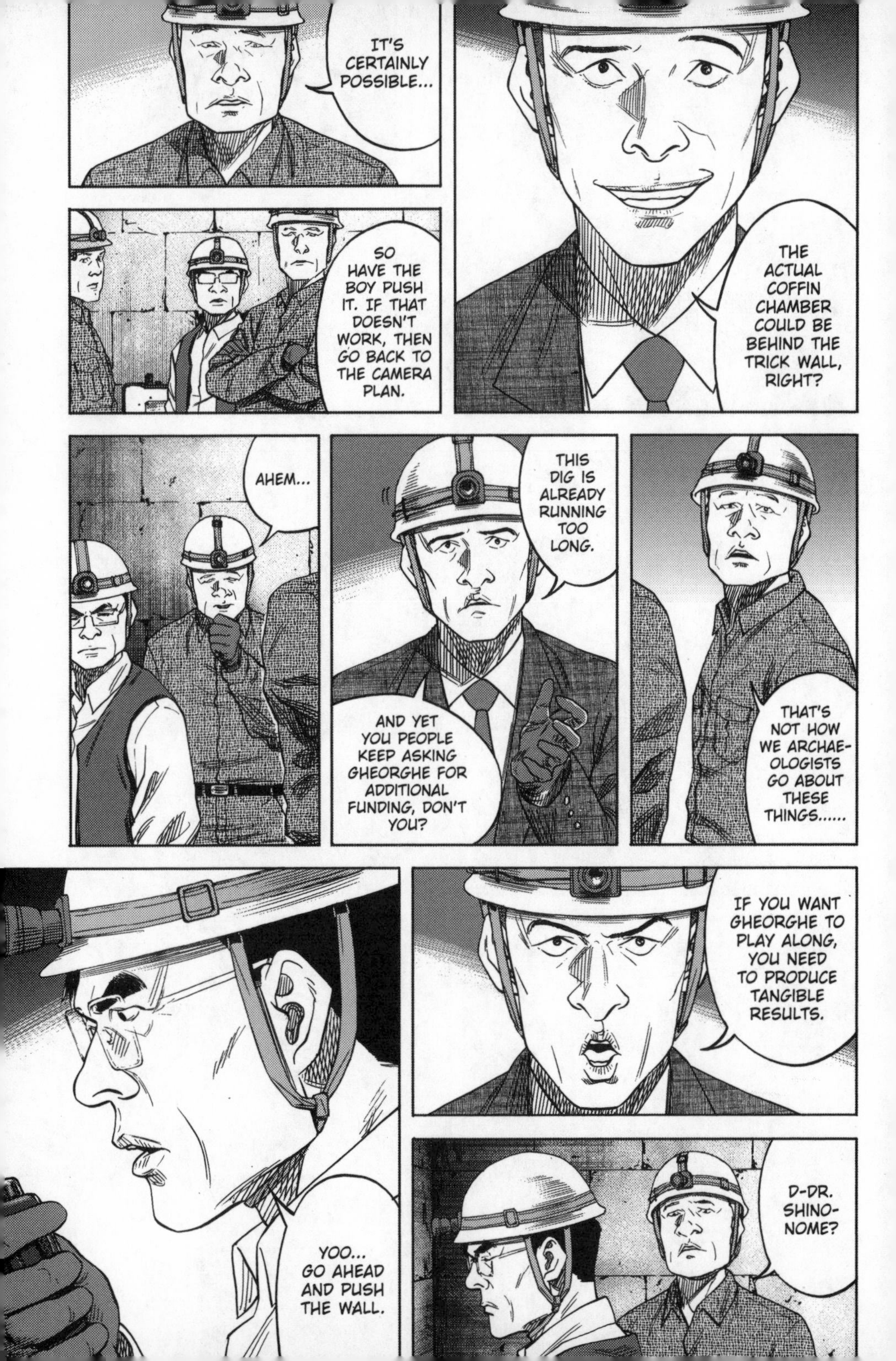
THE ACTUAL COFFIN CHAMBER COULD BE BEHIND THE TRICK WALL, RIGHT?
IT'S CERTAINLY POSSIBLE...
SO HAVE THE BOY PUSH IT. IF THAT DOESN'T WORK, THEN GO BACK TO THE CAMERA PLAN.
THAT'S NOT HOW WE ARCHAE-OLOGISTS GO ABOUT THESE THINGS......
THIS DIG IS ALREADY RUNNING TOO LONG.
AND YET YOU PEOPLE KEEP ASKING GHEORGHE FOR ADDITIONAL FUNDING, DON'T YOU?
AHEM...
IF YOU WANT GHEORGHE TO PLAY ALONG, YOU NEED TO PRODUCE TANGIBLE RESULTS.
D-DR. SHINO-NOME?
YOO... GO AHEAD AND PUSH THE WALL.

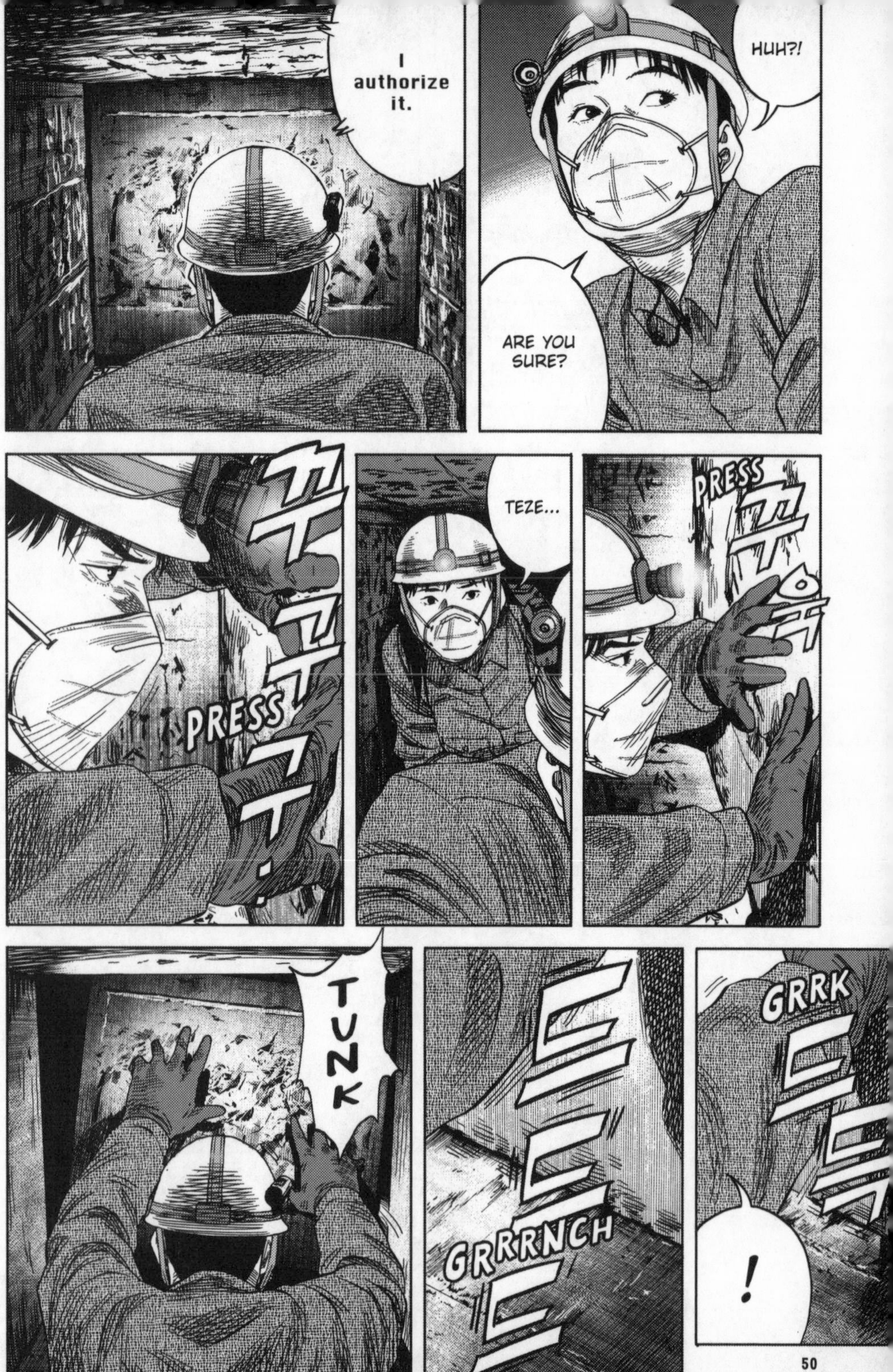
HUH?!
ARE YOU SURE?
I authorize it.
PRESS
TEZE...
PRESS
GRRK
!
GRRRNCH
TUNK

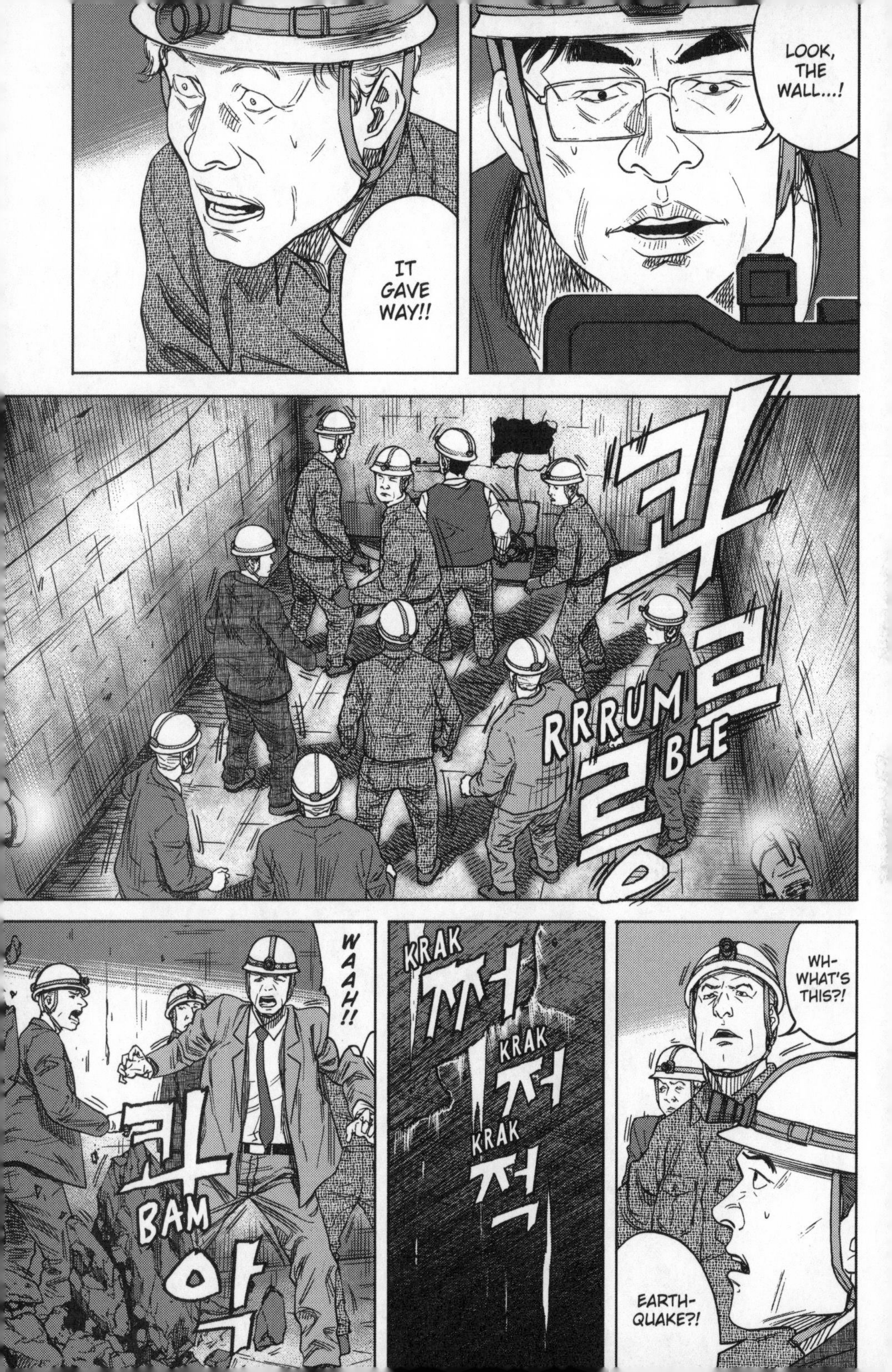
LOOK, THE WALL...!
IT GAVE WAY!!
RRRUMBLE
WH- WHAT'S THIS?!
EARTH- QUAKE?!
KRAK
KRAK
KRAK
WAAAH!!
BAM

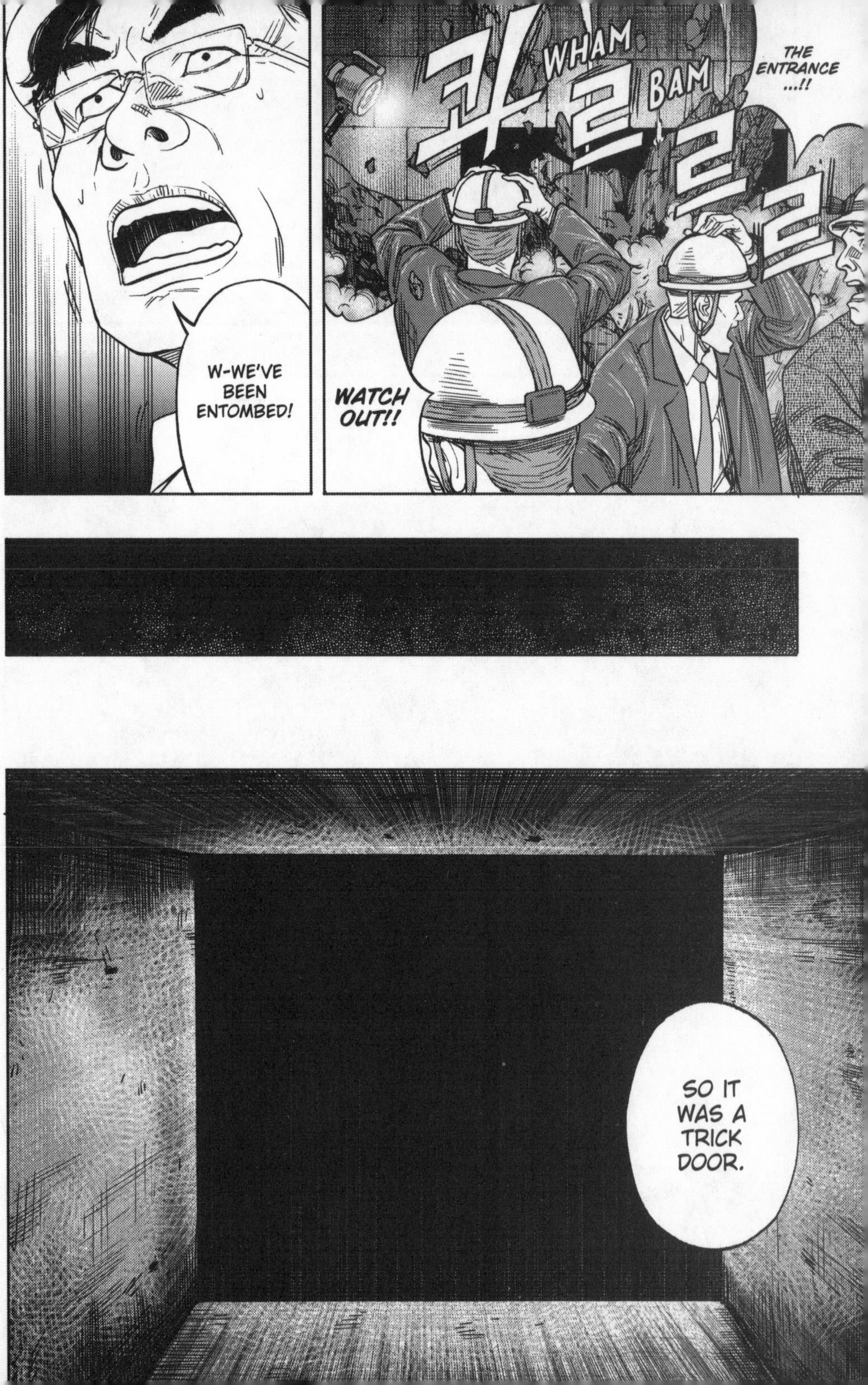
WHAM
BAM
THE ENTRANCE ...!!
WATCH OUT!!
W-WE'VE BEEN ENTOMBED!
SO IT WAS A TRICK DOOR.

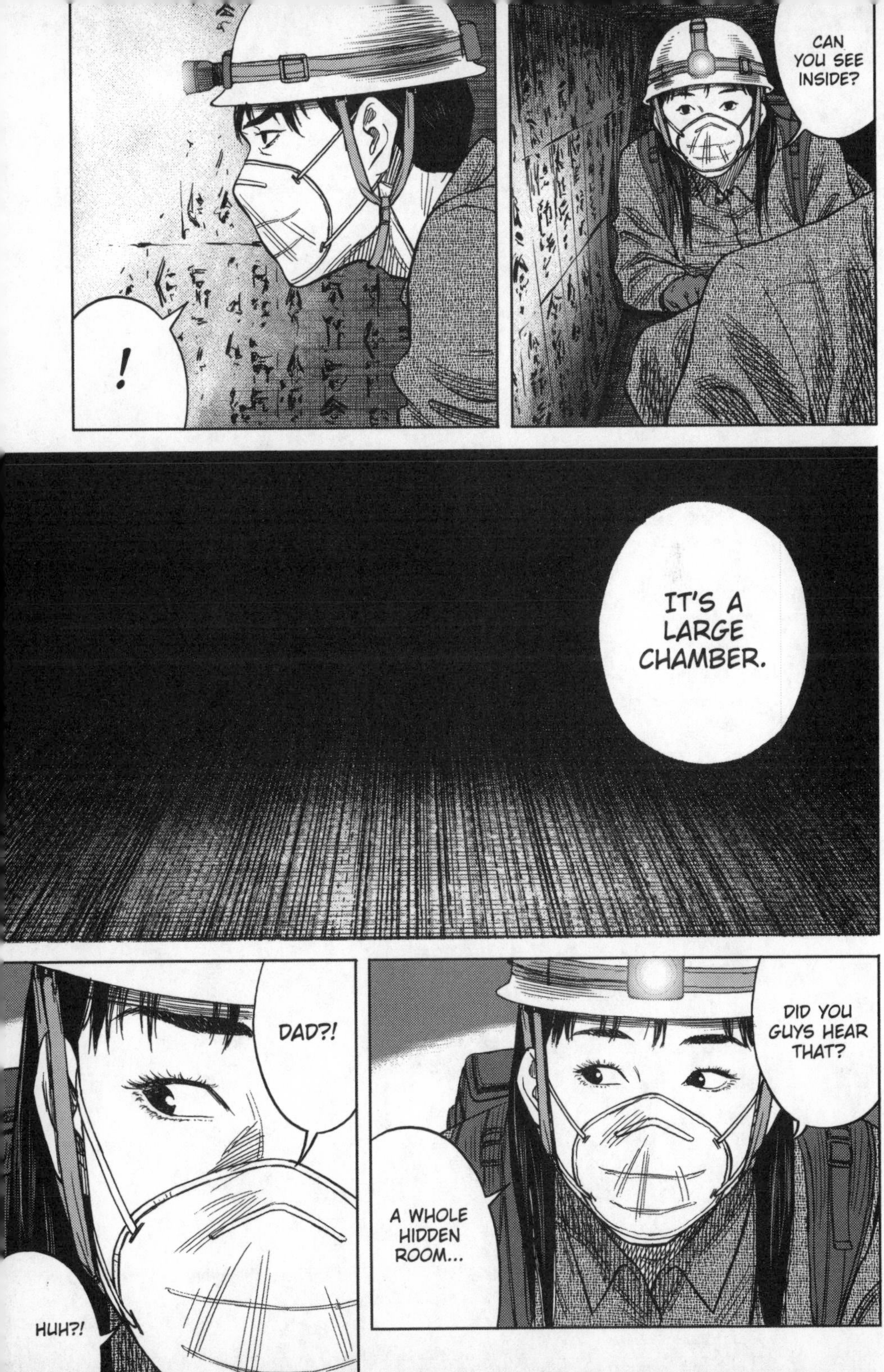
CAN YOU SEE INSIDE?
!
IT'S A LARGE CHAMBER.
DID YOU GUYS HEAR THAT?
A WHOLE HIDDEN ROOM...
DAD?!
HUH?!

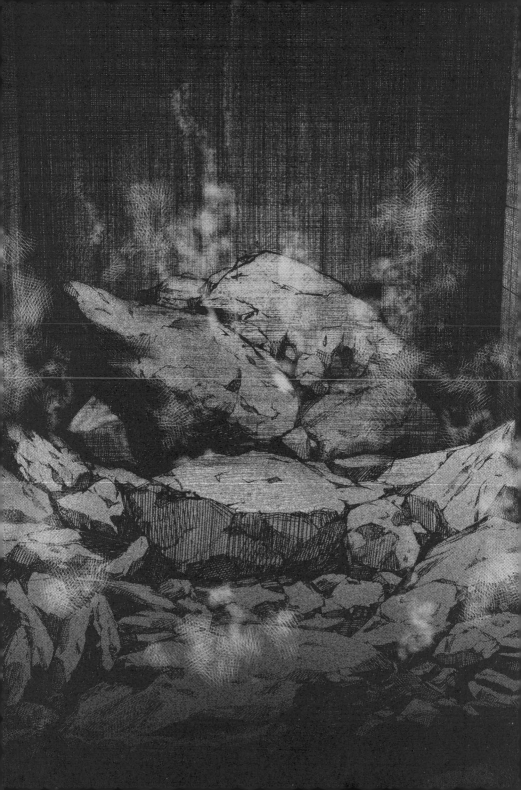

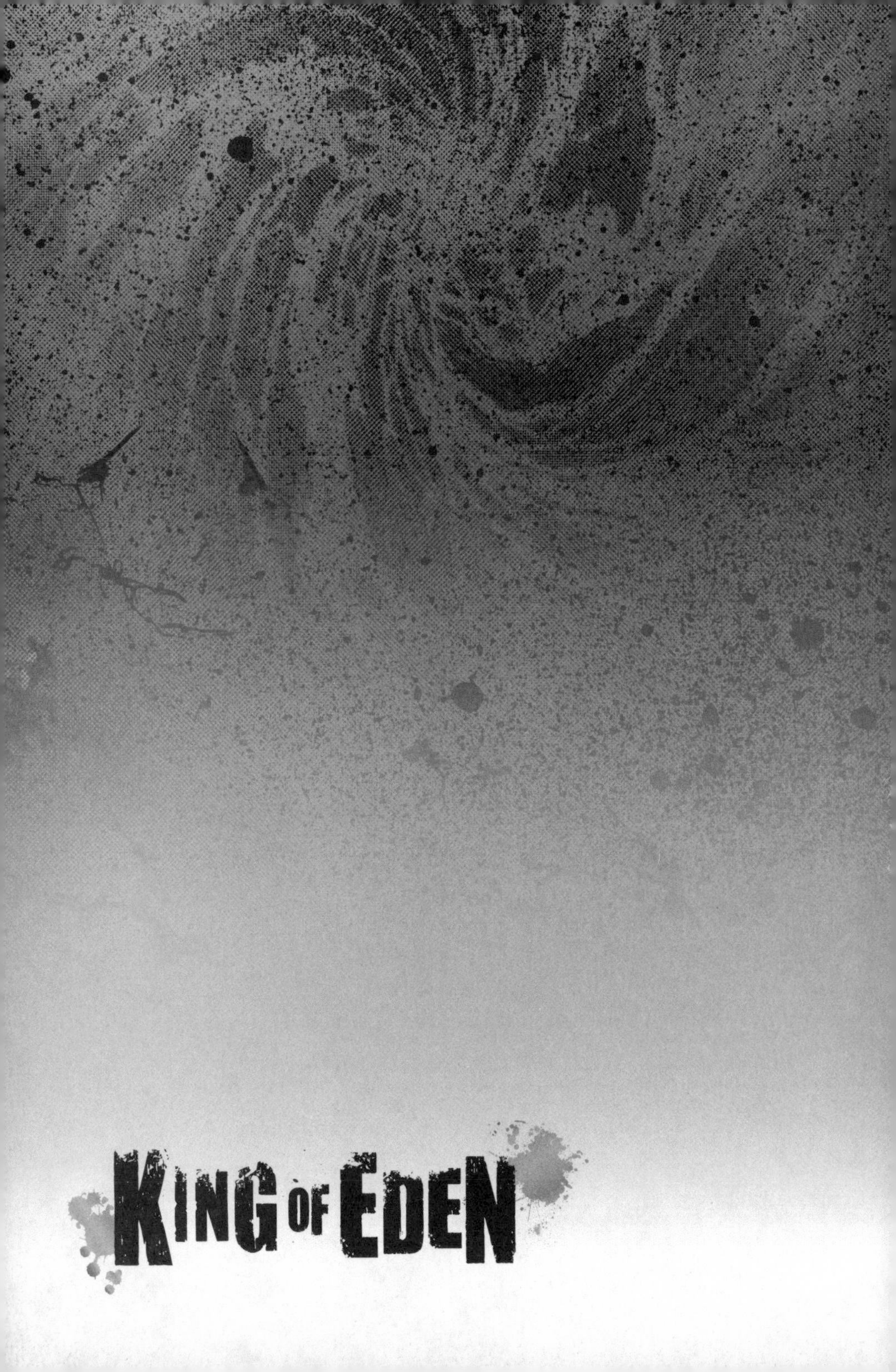
KING OF EDEN

KING OF EDEN

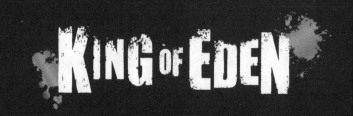

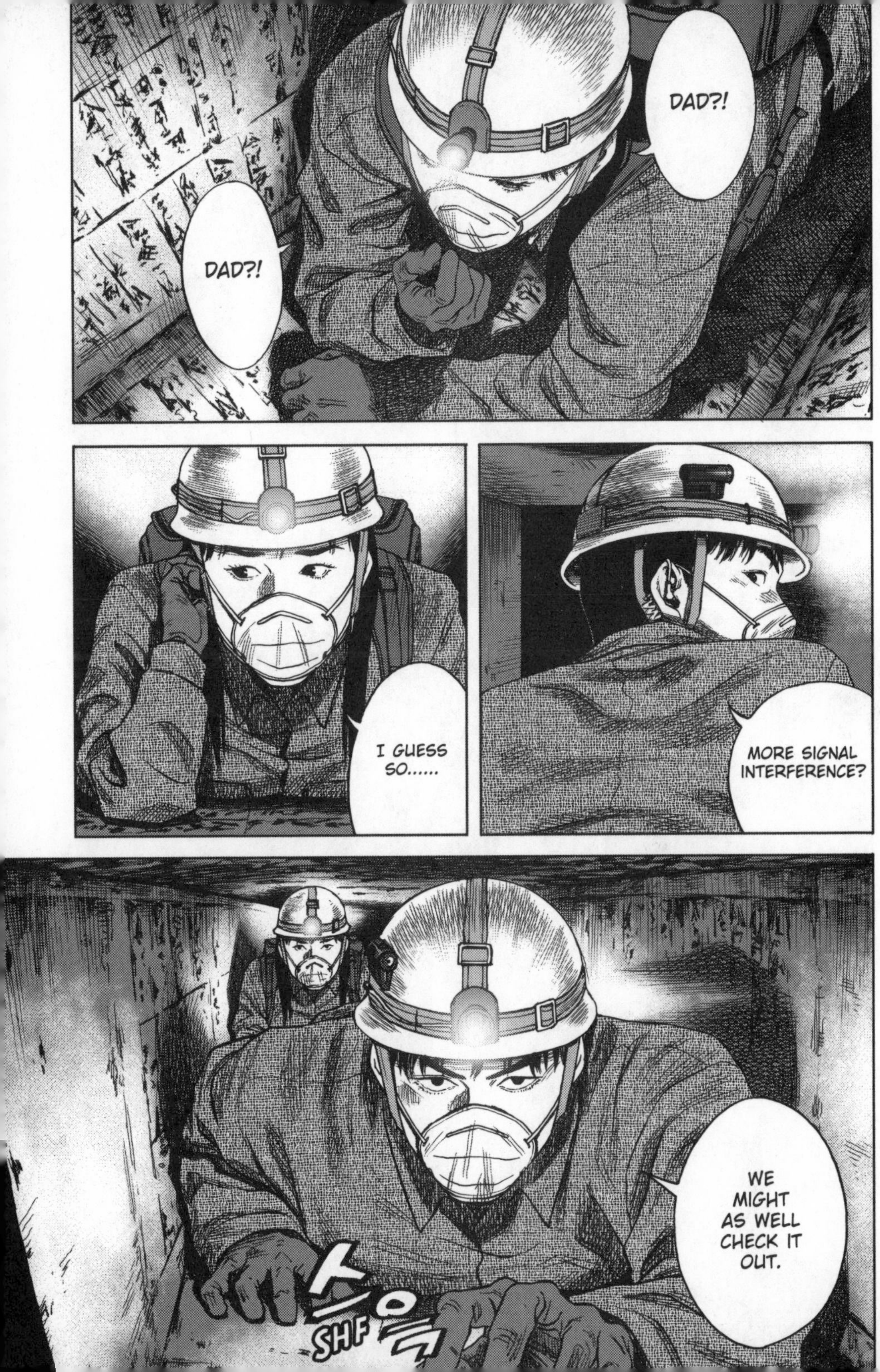
DAD?!
DAD?!
MORE SIGNAL INTERFERENCE?
I GUESS SO......
WE MIGHT AS WELL CHECK IT OUT.
SHF

BIG ROOM, HUH.

FWP

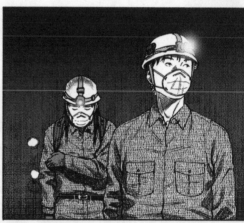

ABOUT TEN METERS SQUARE.

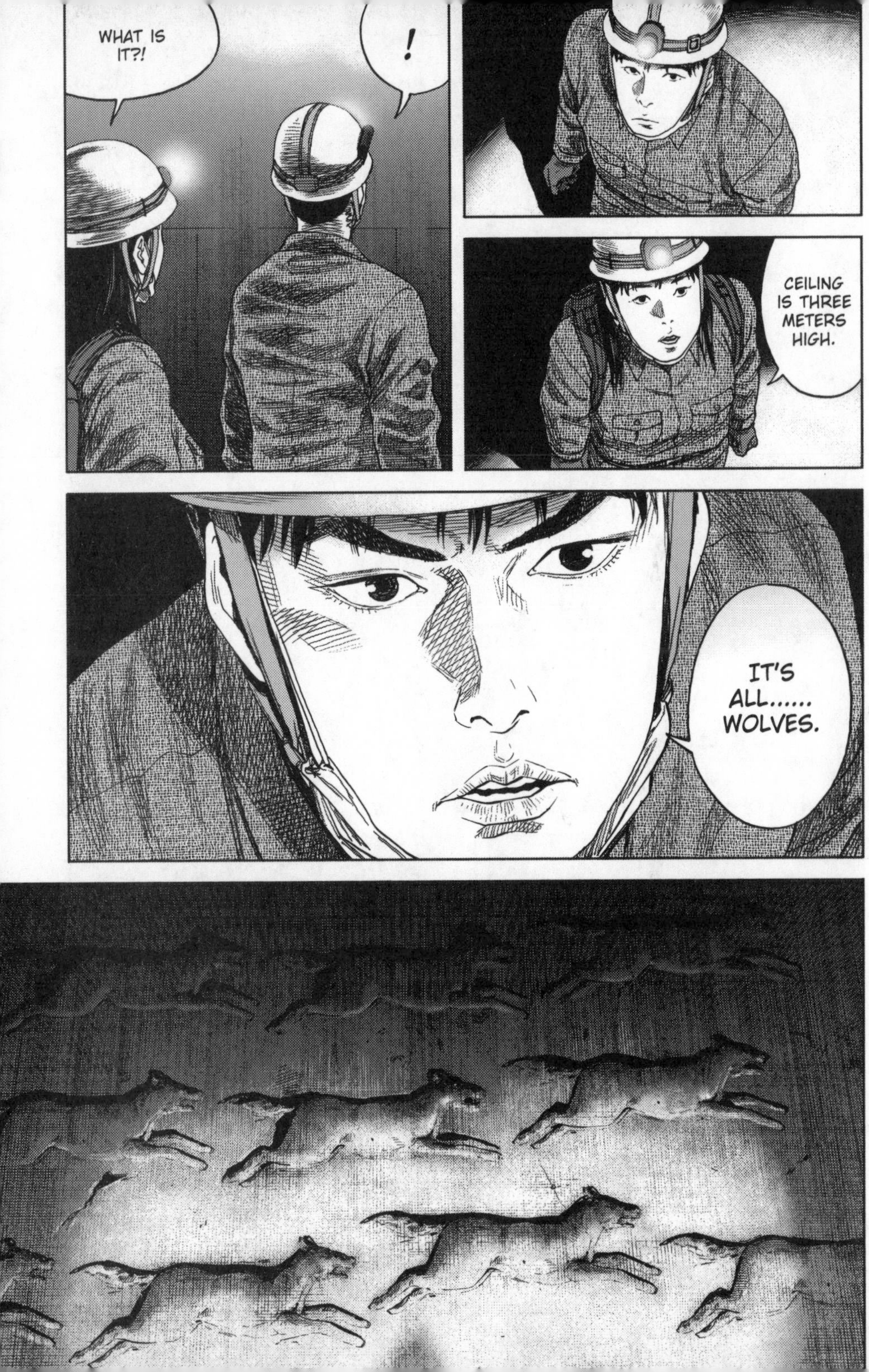
CEILING IS THREE METERS HIGH.
!
WHAT IS IT?!
IT'S ALL...... WOLVES.

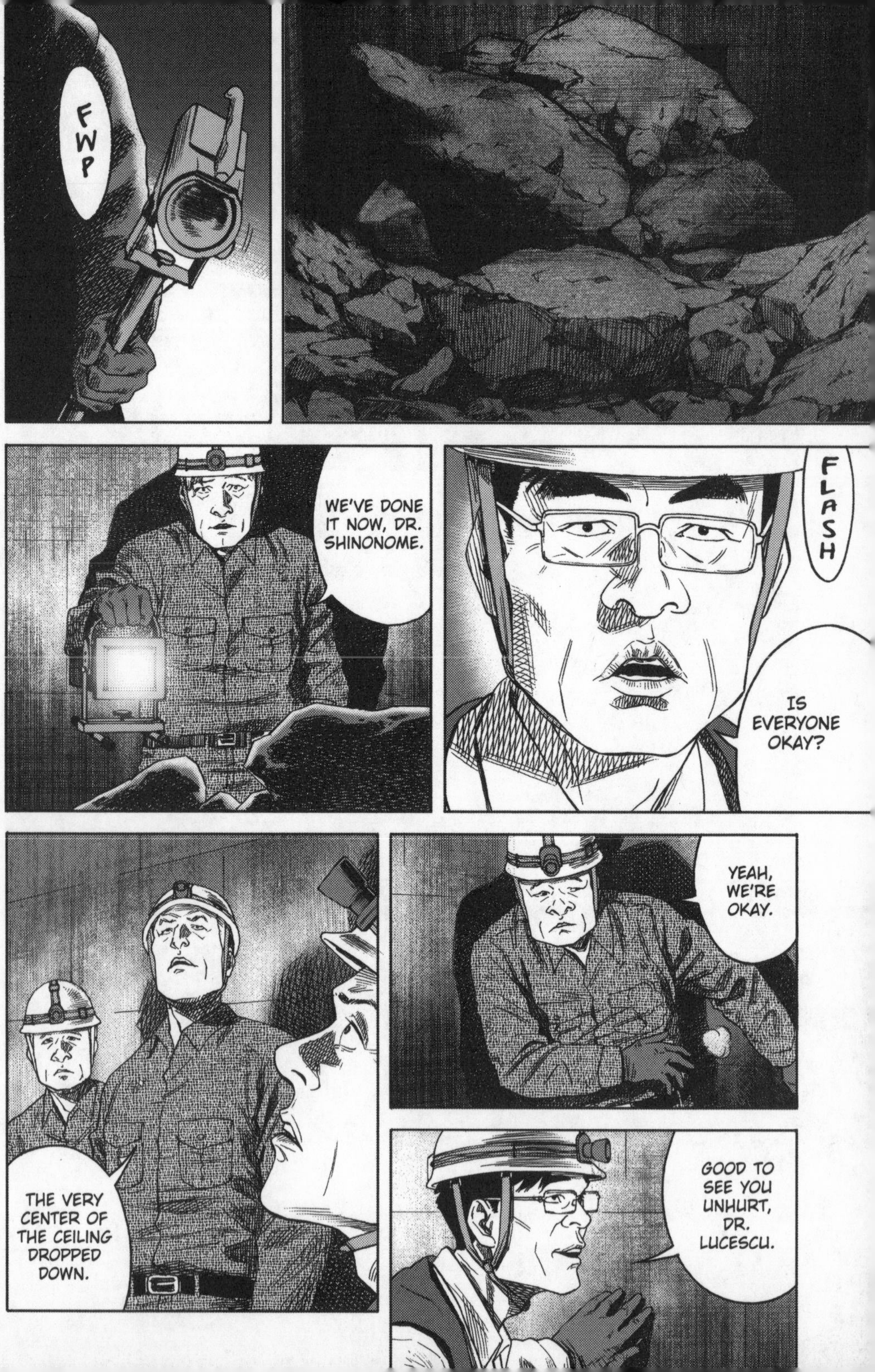
FWP
FLASH
IS EVERYONE OKAY?
WE'VE DONE IT NOW, DR. SHINONOME.
YEAH, WE'RE OKAY.
GOOD TO SEE YOU UNHURT, DR. LUCESCU.
THE VERY CENTER OF THE CEILING DROPPED DOWN.

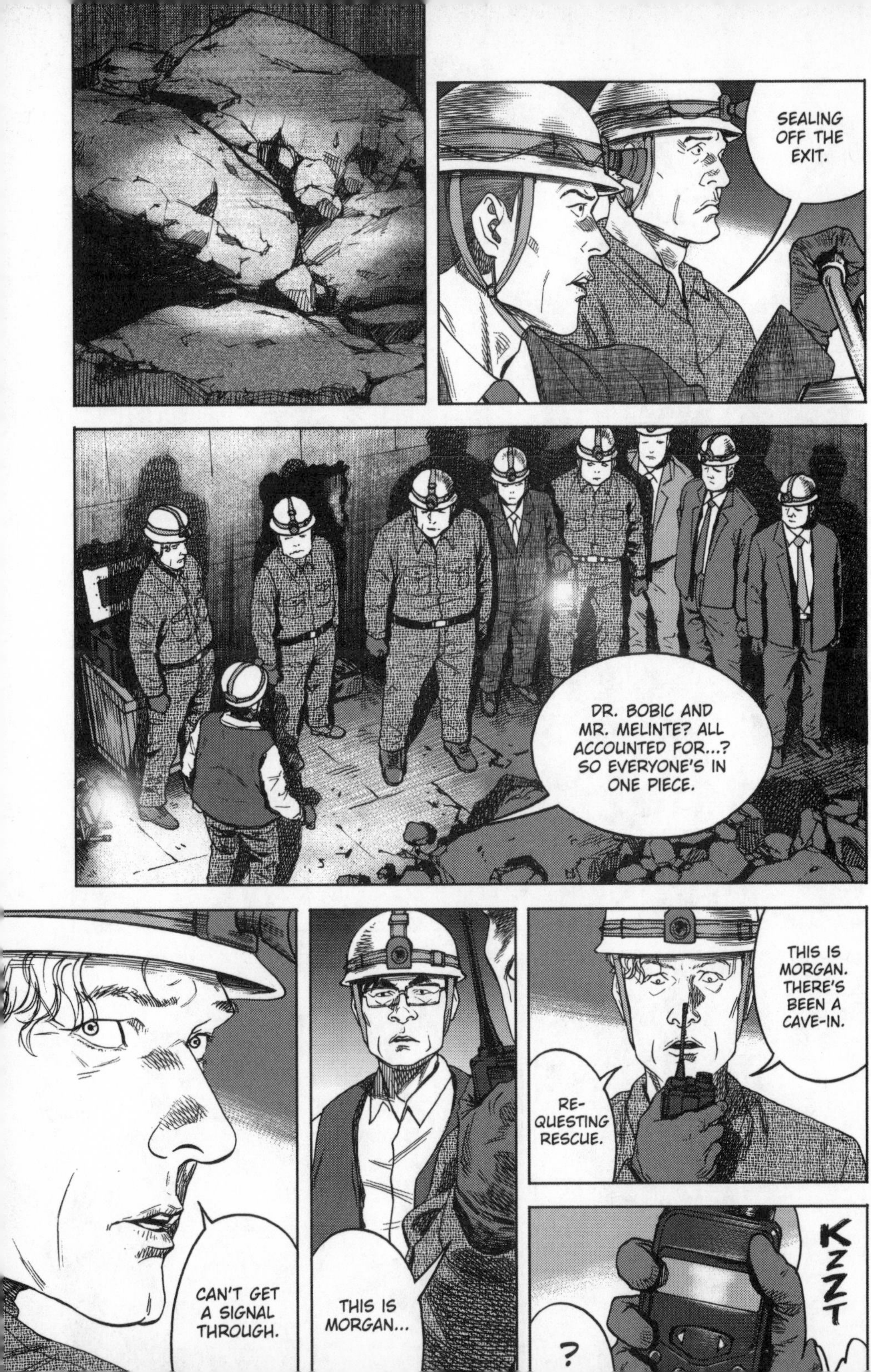
SEALING OFF THE EXIT.
DR. BOBIC AND MR. MELINTE? ALL ACCOUNTED FOR...? SO EVERYONE'S IN ONE PIECE.
THIS IS MORGAN. THERE'S BEEN A CAVE-IN.
RE-QUESTING RESCUE.
KZZT
?
THIS IS MORGAN...
CAN'T GET A SIGNAL THROUGH.

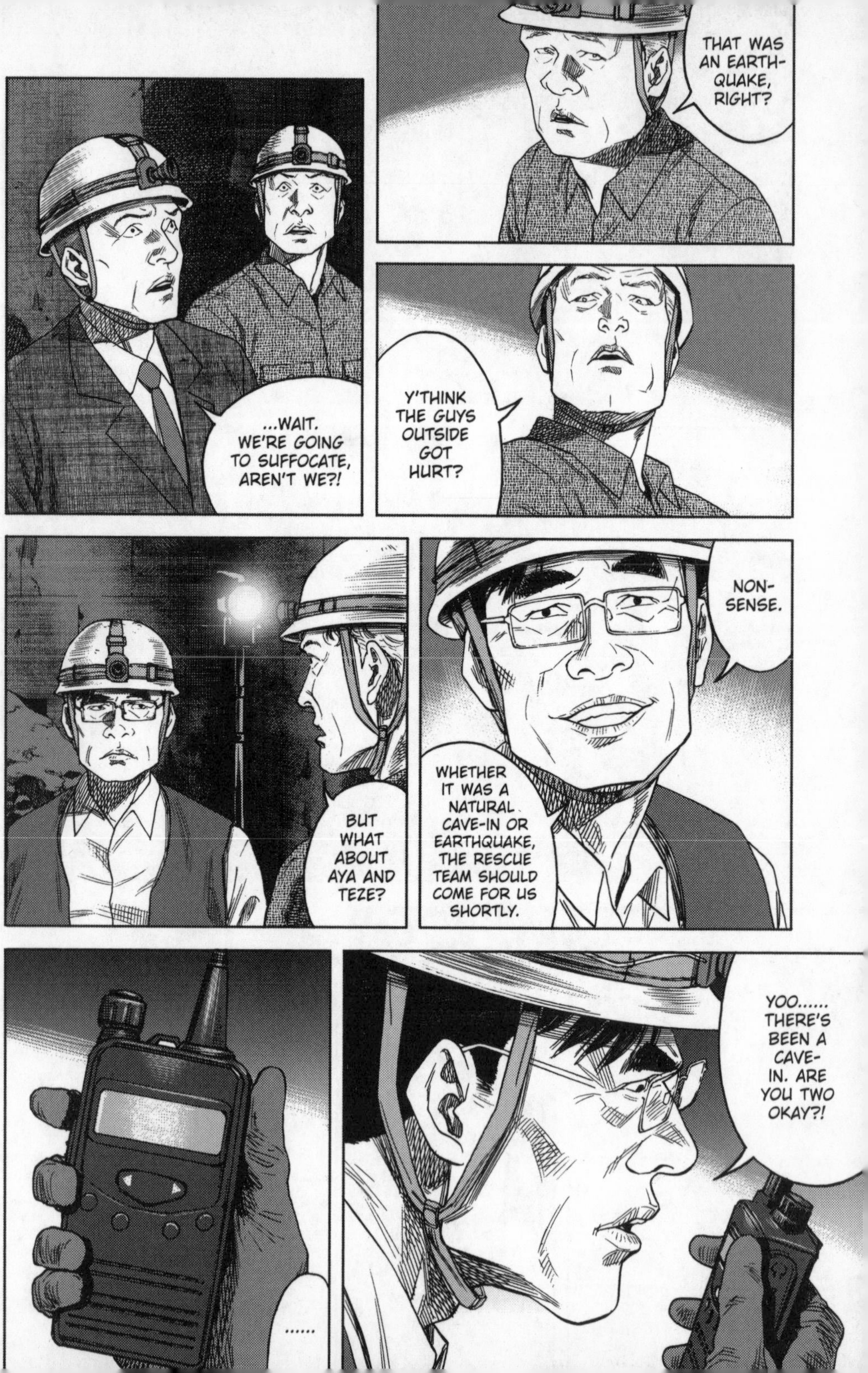
THAT WAS AN EARTH-QUAKE, RIGHT?
Y'THINK THE GUYS OUTSIDE GOT HURT?
...WAIT. WE'RE GOING TO SUFFOCATE, AREN'T WE?!
NON-SENSE.
WHETHER IT WAS A NATURAL CAVE-IN OR EARTHQUAKE, THE RESCUE TEAM SHOULD COME FOR US SHORTLY.
BUT WHAT ABOUT AYA AND TEZE?
YOO...... THERE'S BEEN A CAVE-IN. ARE YOU TWO OKAY?!
......

DO WE HAVE VISUAL, DR. SHINONOME?

NO SIGNAL.

OY, TEZE!

AYA!!

OY!

NO ANSWER...

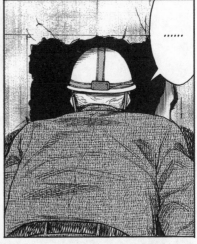

....

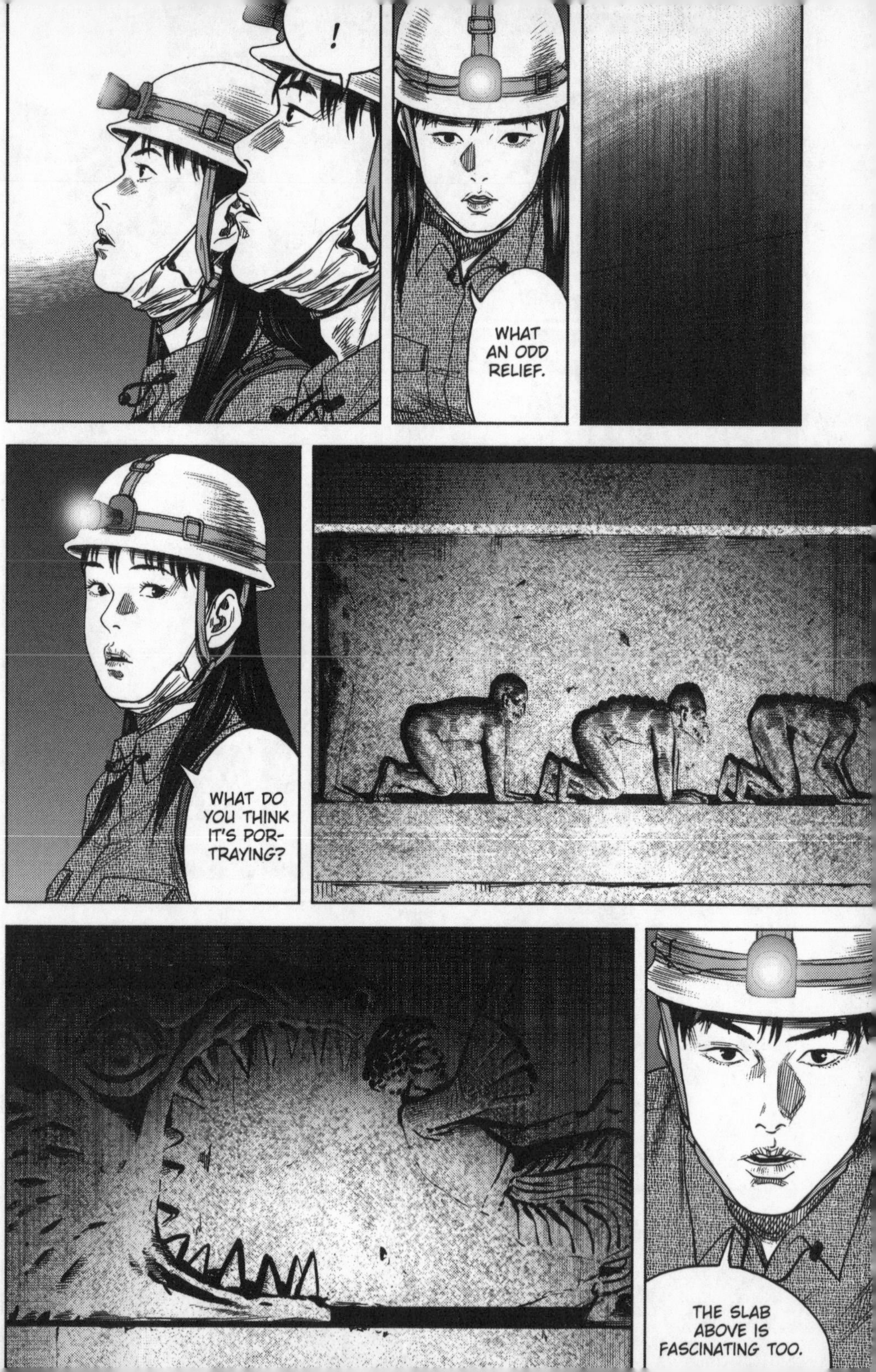
WHAT AN ODD RELIEF.
!
WHAT DO YOU THINK IT'S POR-TRAYING?
THE SLAB ABOVE IS FASCINATING TOO.

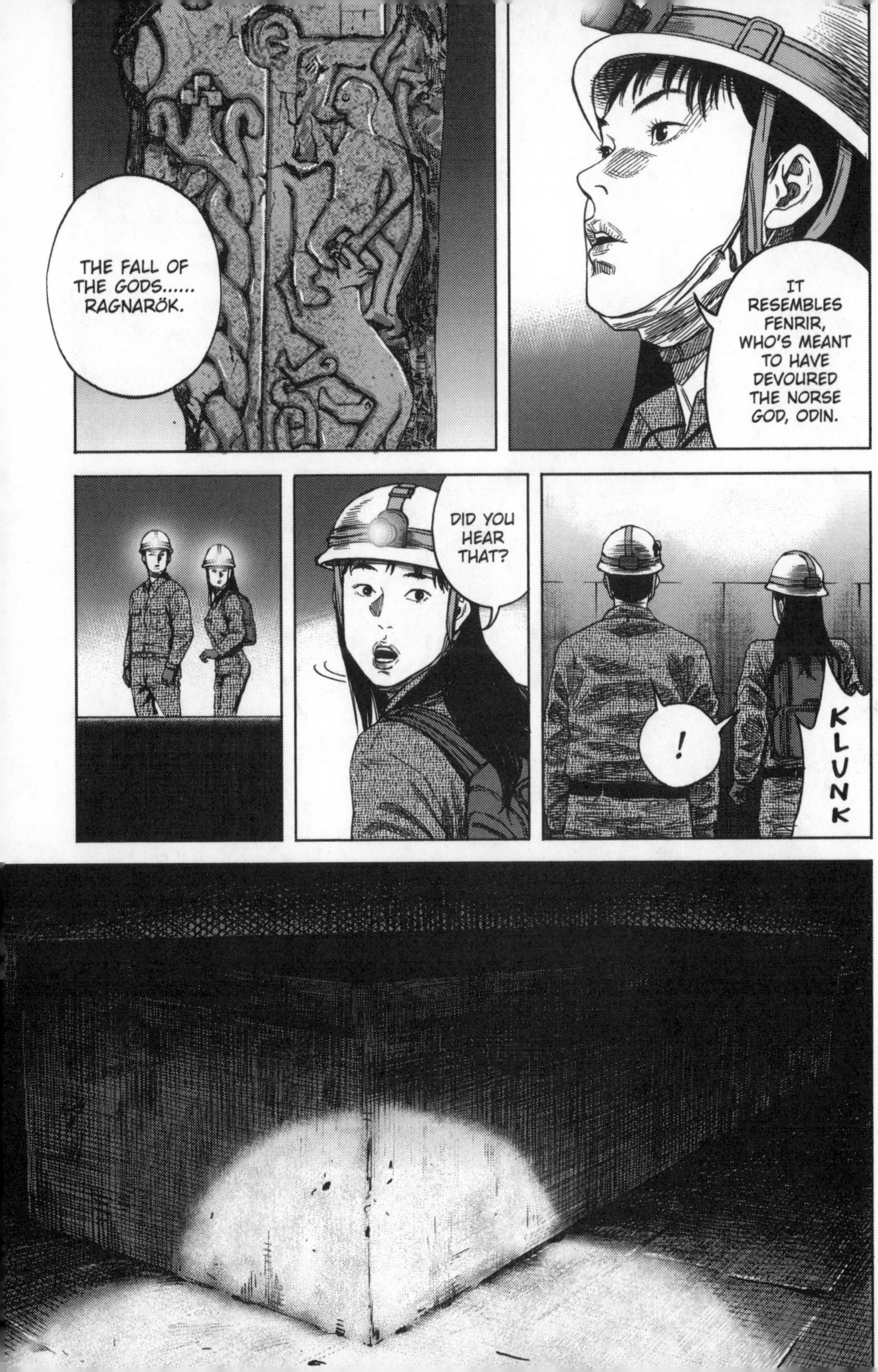
IT RESEMBLES FENRIR, WHO'S MEANT TO HAVE DEVOURED THE NORSE GOD, ODIN.
THE FALL OF THE GODS...... RAGNARÖK.
KLUNK
!
DID YOU HEAR THAT?

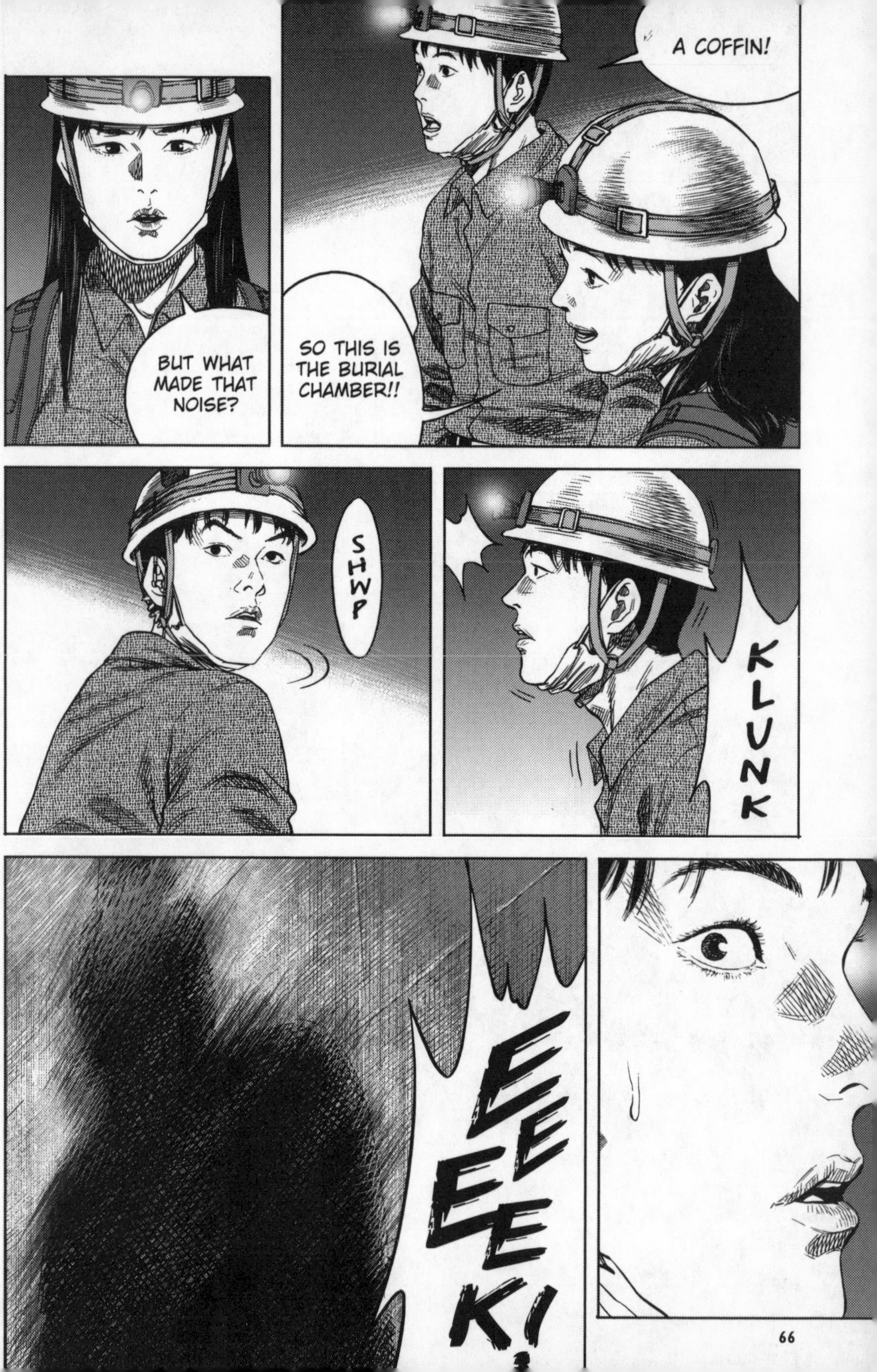
A COFFIN!
SO THIS IS THE BURIAL CHAMBER!!
BUT WHAT MADE THAT NOISE?
KLUNK
SHWP
EEEEEK!

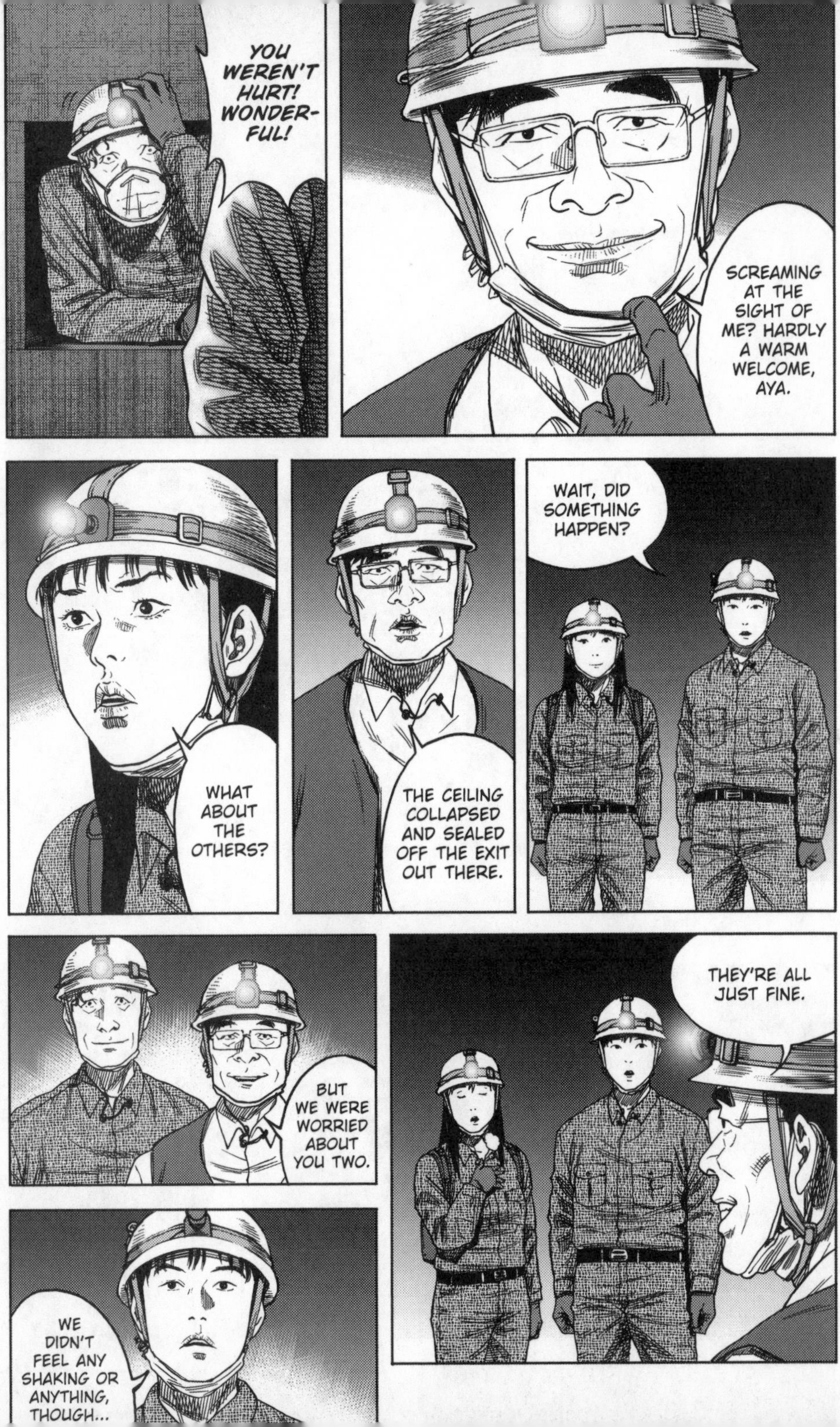
SCREAMING AT THE SIGHT OF ME? HARDLY A WARM WELCOME, AYA.
YOU WEREN'T HURT! WONDER-FUL!
WAIT, DID SOMETHING HAPPEN?
THE CEILING COLLAPSED AND SEALED OFF THE EXIT OUT THERE.
WHAT ABOUT THE OTHERS?
THEY'RE ALL JUST FINE.
BUT WE WERE WORRIED ABOUT YOU TWO.
WE DIDN'T FEEL ANY SHAKING OR ANYTHING, THOUGH...

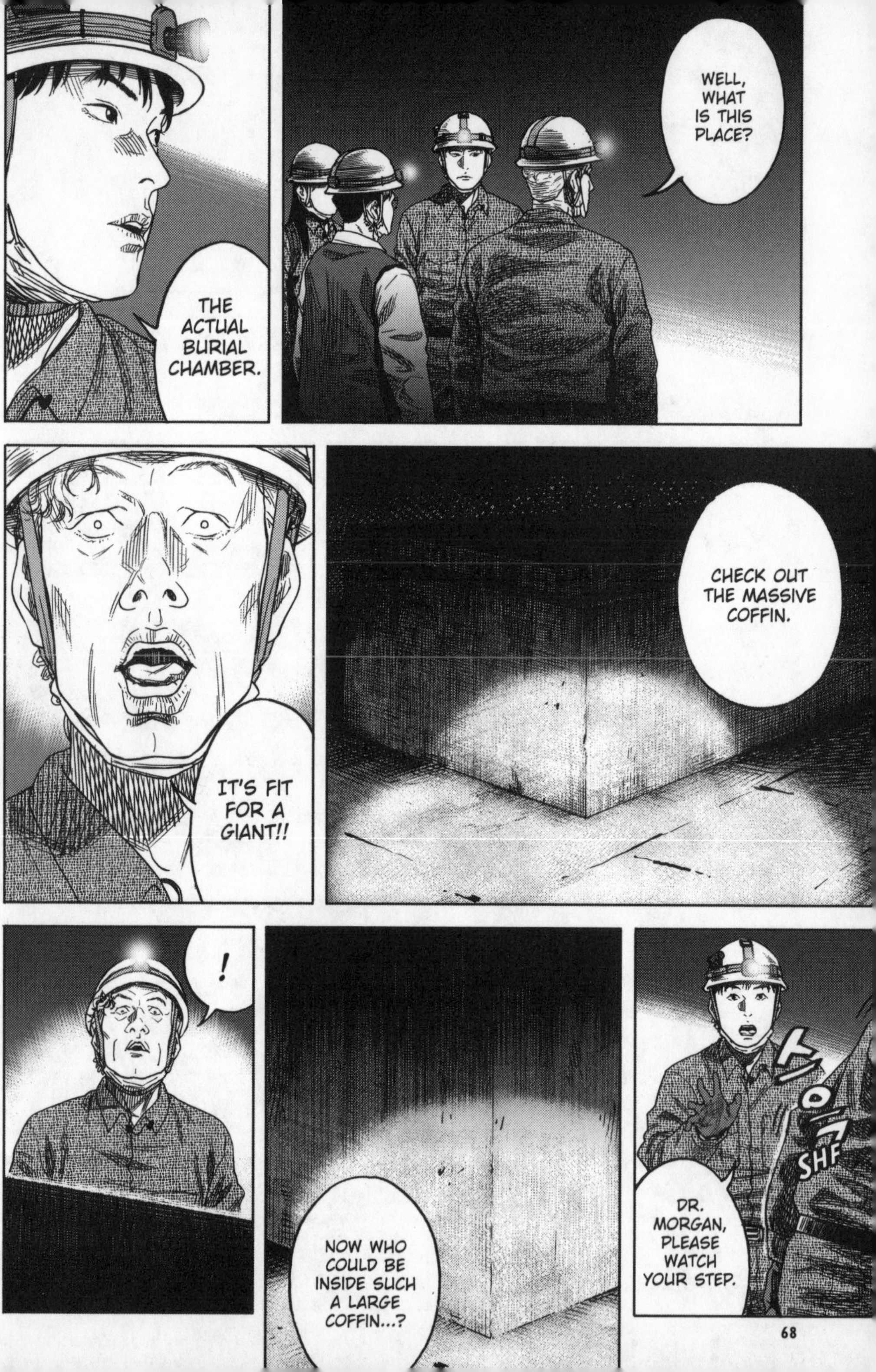
WELL, WHAT IS THIS PLACE?
THE ACTUAL BURIAL CHAMBER.
CHECK OUT THE MASSIVE COFFIN.
IT'S FIT FOR A GIANT!!
SHF
DR. MORGAN, PLEASE WATCH YOUR STEP.
NOW WHO COULD BE INSIDE SUCH A LARGE COFFIN...?
!

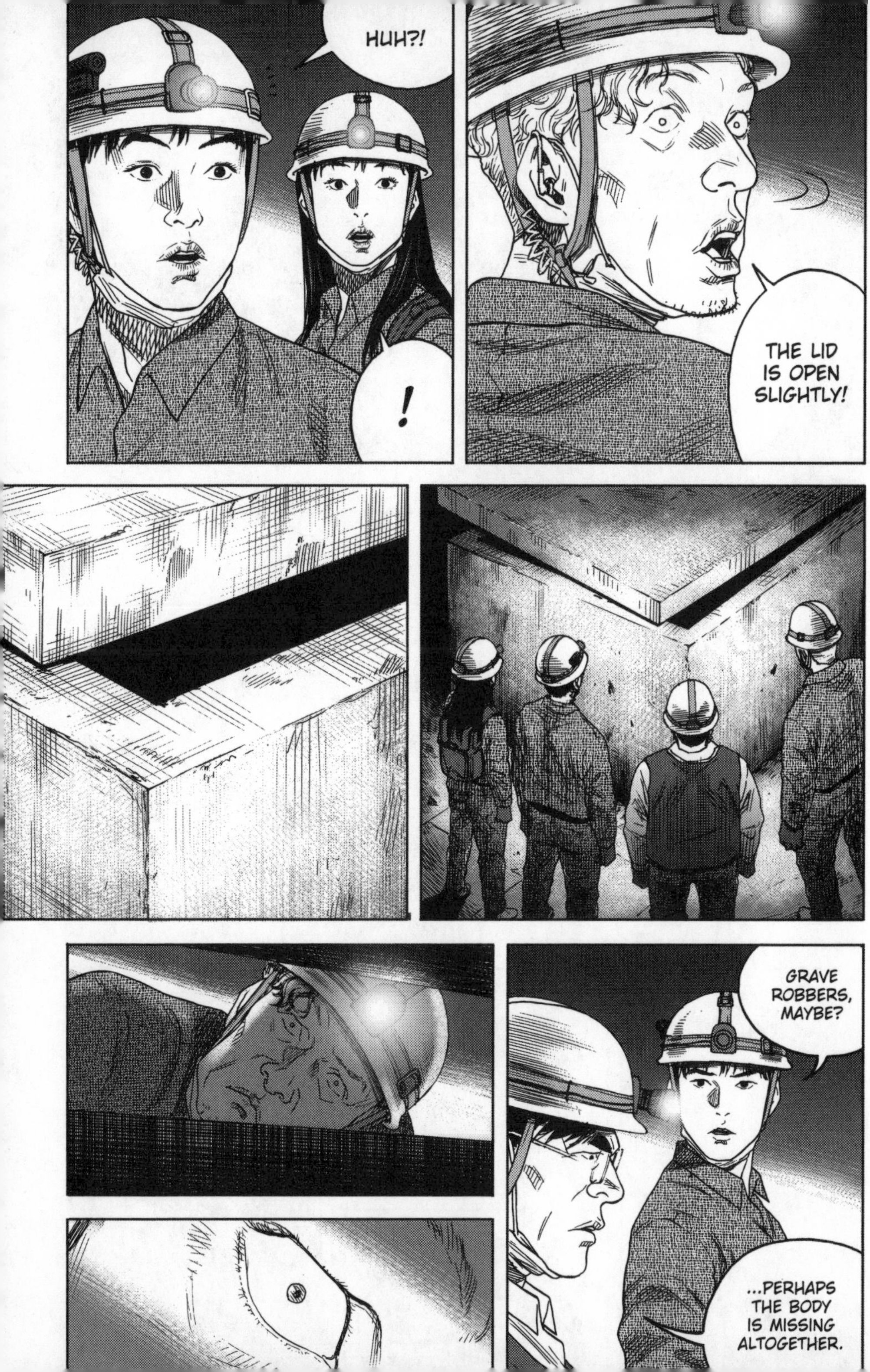
THE LID IS OPEN SLIGHTLY!
HUH?!
!
GRAVE ROBBERS, MAYBE?
...PERHAPS THE BODY IS MISSING ALTOGETHER.

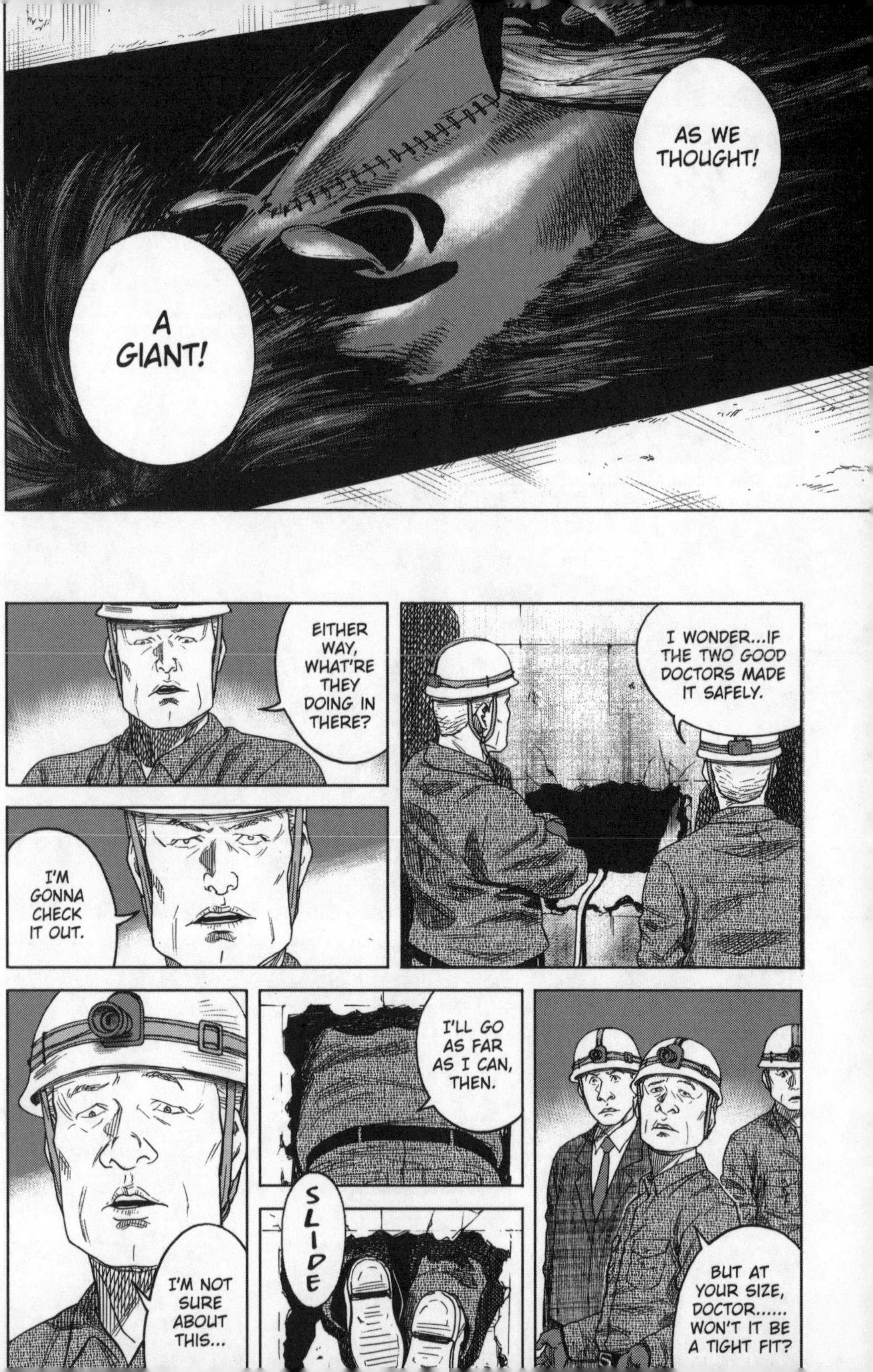
AS WE THOUGHT!
A GIANT!
I WONDER...IF THE TWO GOOD DOCTORS MADE IT SAFELY.
EITHER WAY, WHAT'RE THEY DOING IN THERE?
I'M GONNA CHECK IT OUT.
BUT AT YOUR SIZE, DOCTOR...... WON'T IT BE A TIGHT FIT?
I'LL GO AS FAR AS I CAN, THEN.
SLIDE
I'M NOT SURE ABOUT THIS...

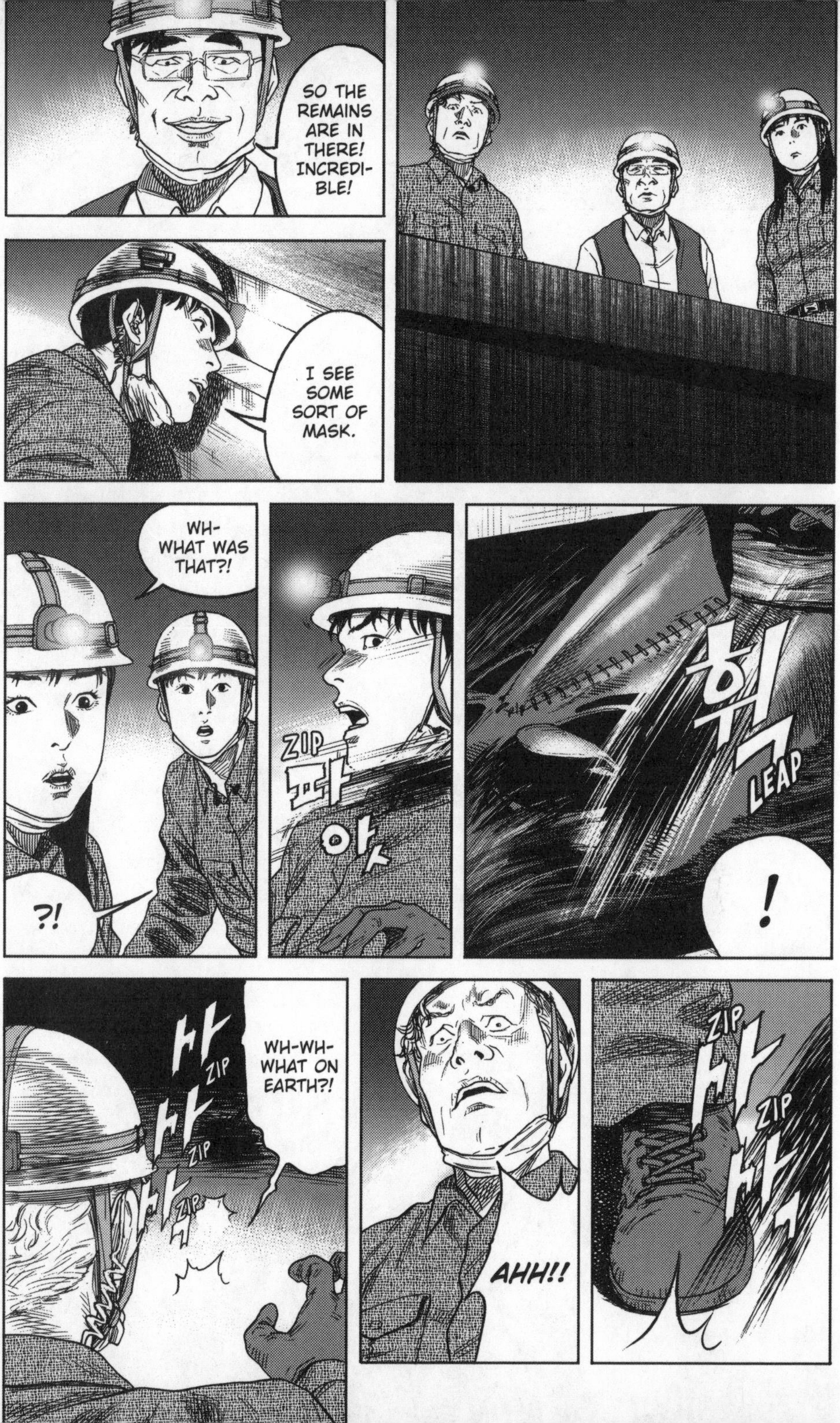
SO THE REMAINS ARE IN THERE! INCREDIBLE!
I SEE SOME SORT OF MASK.
LEAP
!
ZIP
WH-WHAT WAS THAT?!
?!
ZIP
ZIP
AHH!!
ZIP
ZIP
ZIP
WH-WH-WHAT ON EARTH?!

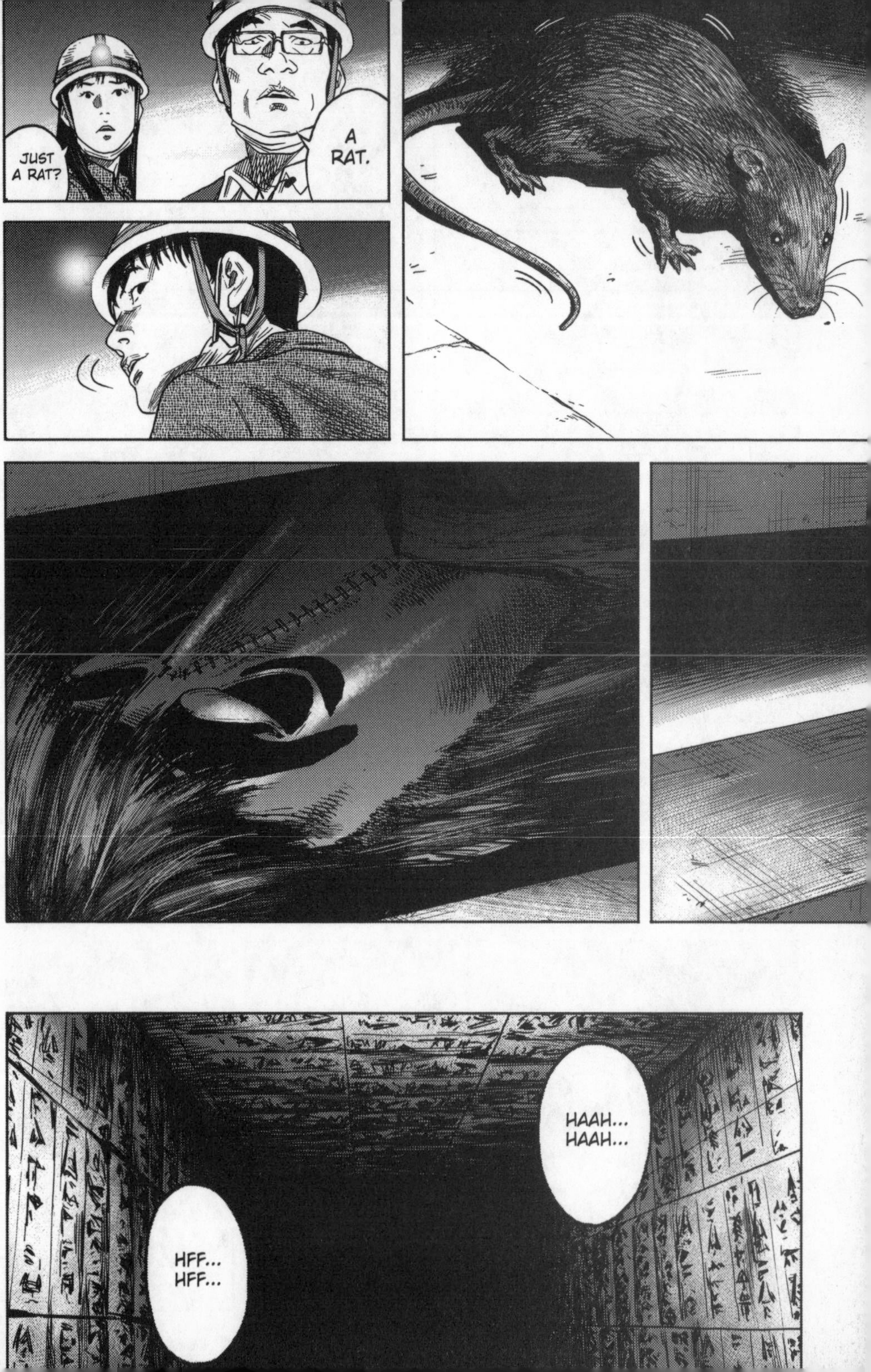
A RAT.
JUST A RAT?
HAAH... HAAH...
HFF... HFF...

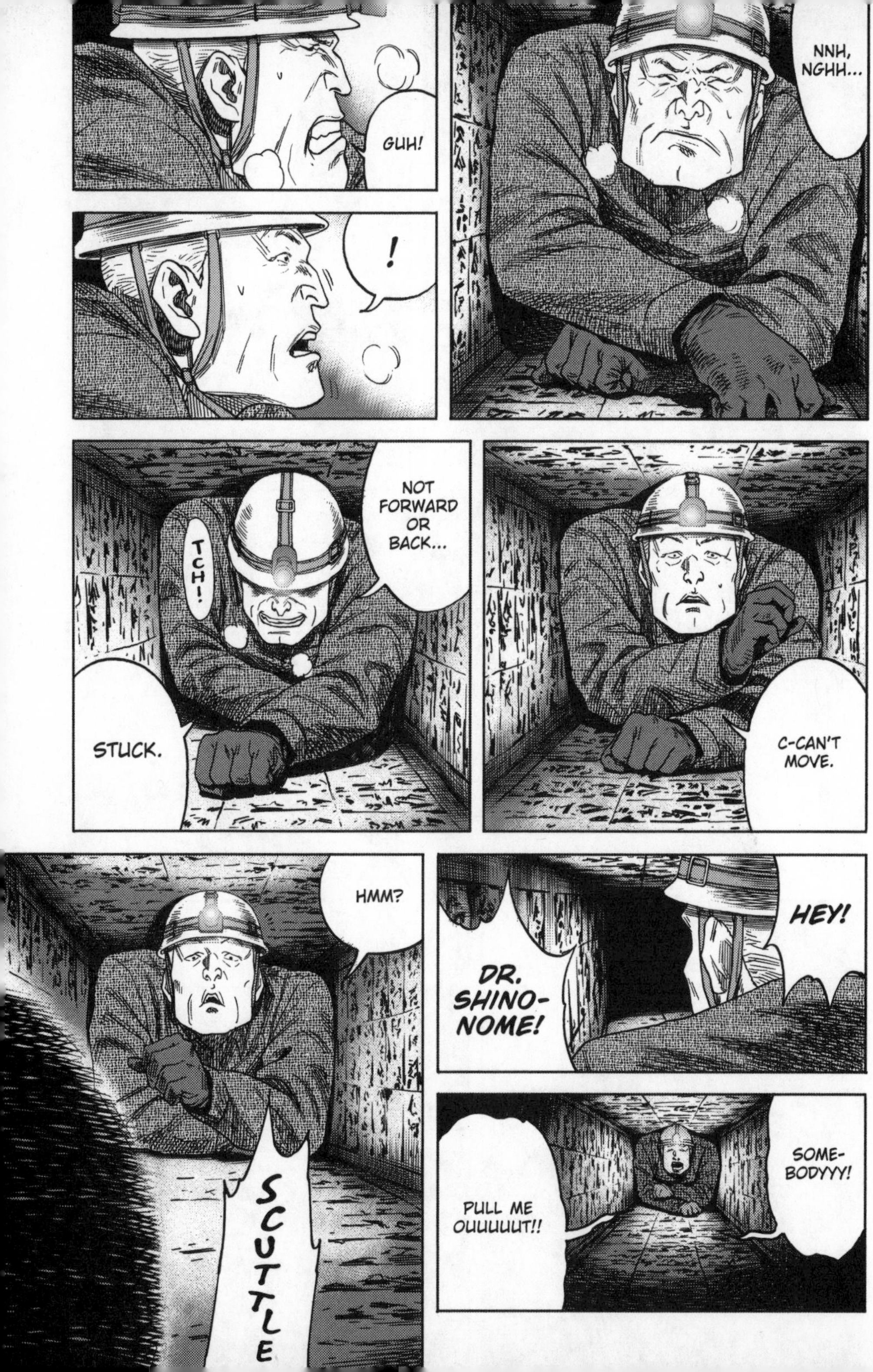
NNH, NGHH...
GUH!
!
C-CAN'T MOVE.
NOT FORWARD OR BACK...
TCH!
STUCK.
HEY!
DR. SHINO-NOME!
SOME-BODYYY!
PULL ME OUUUUUT!!
HMM?
SCUTTLE

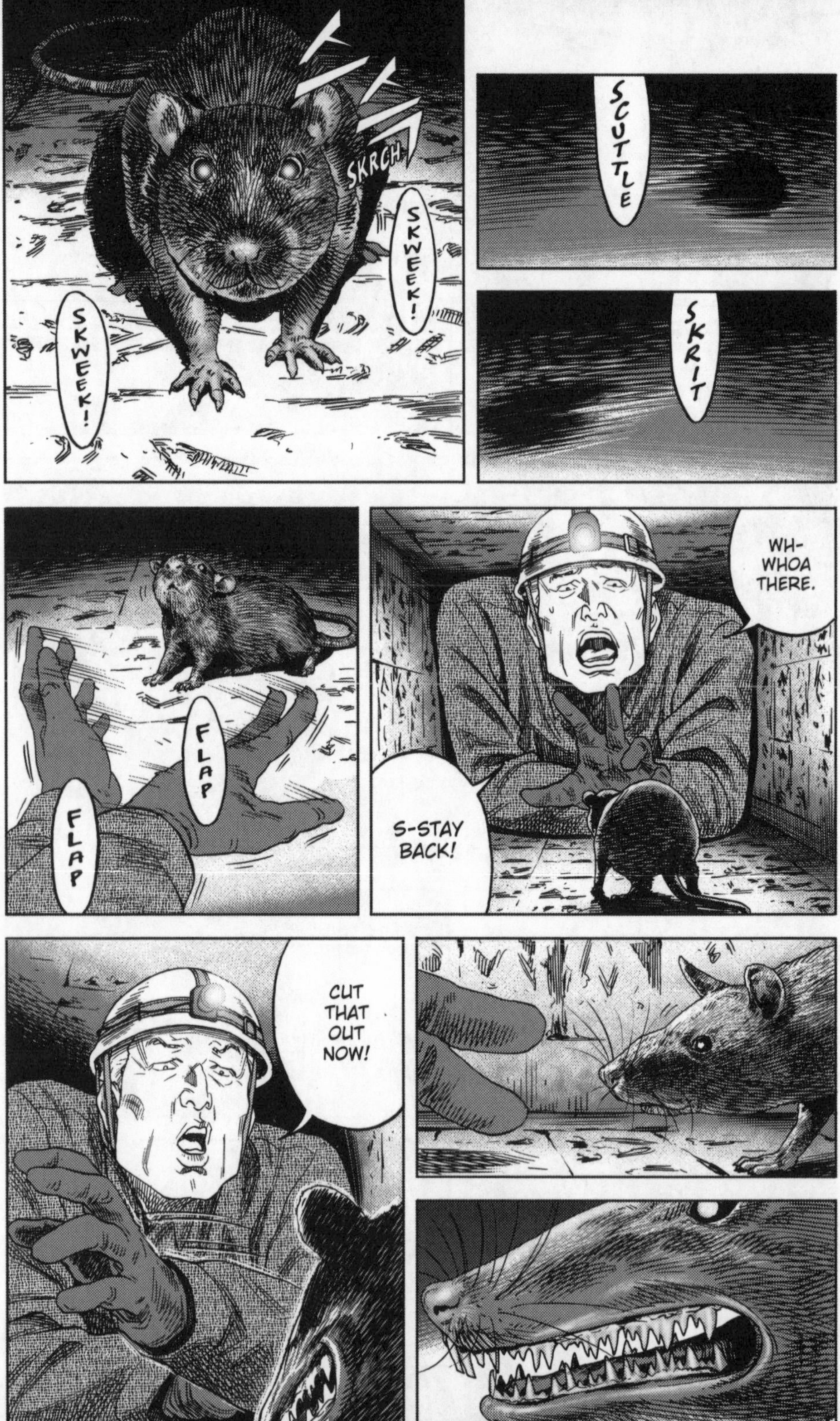
SCUTTLE
SKRIT
SKRCH
SKWEEK!
SKWEEK!
WH-WHOA THERE.
S-STAY BACK!
FLAP
FLAP
CUT THAT OUT NOW!

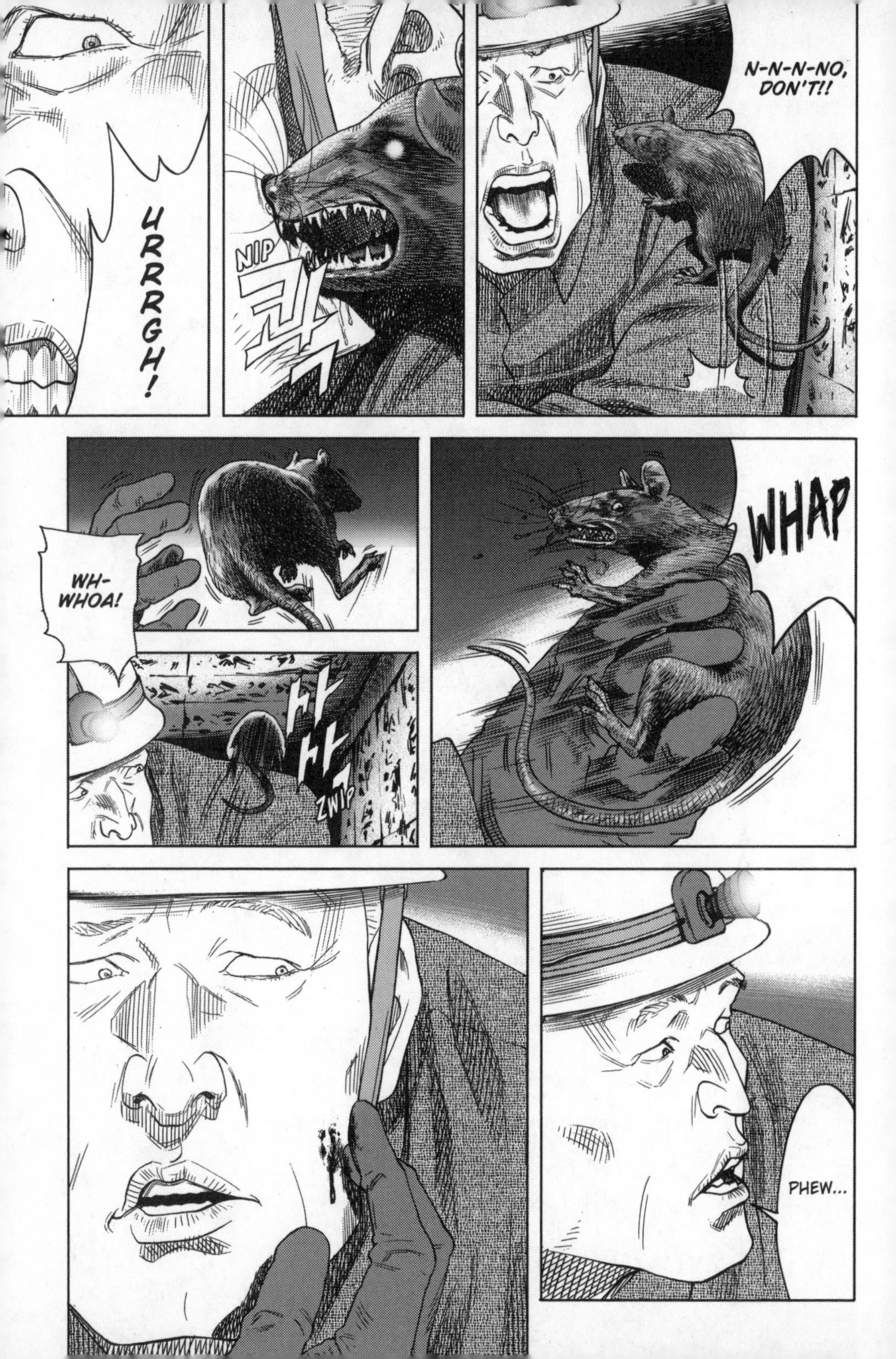
N-N-N-NO, DON'T!!
NIP
URRRGH!
WHAP
WH-WHOA!
ZWIP
PHEW...

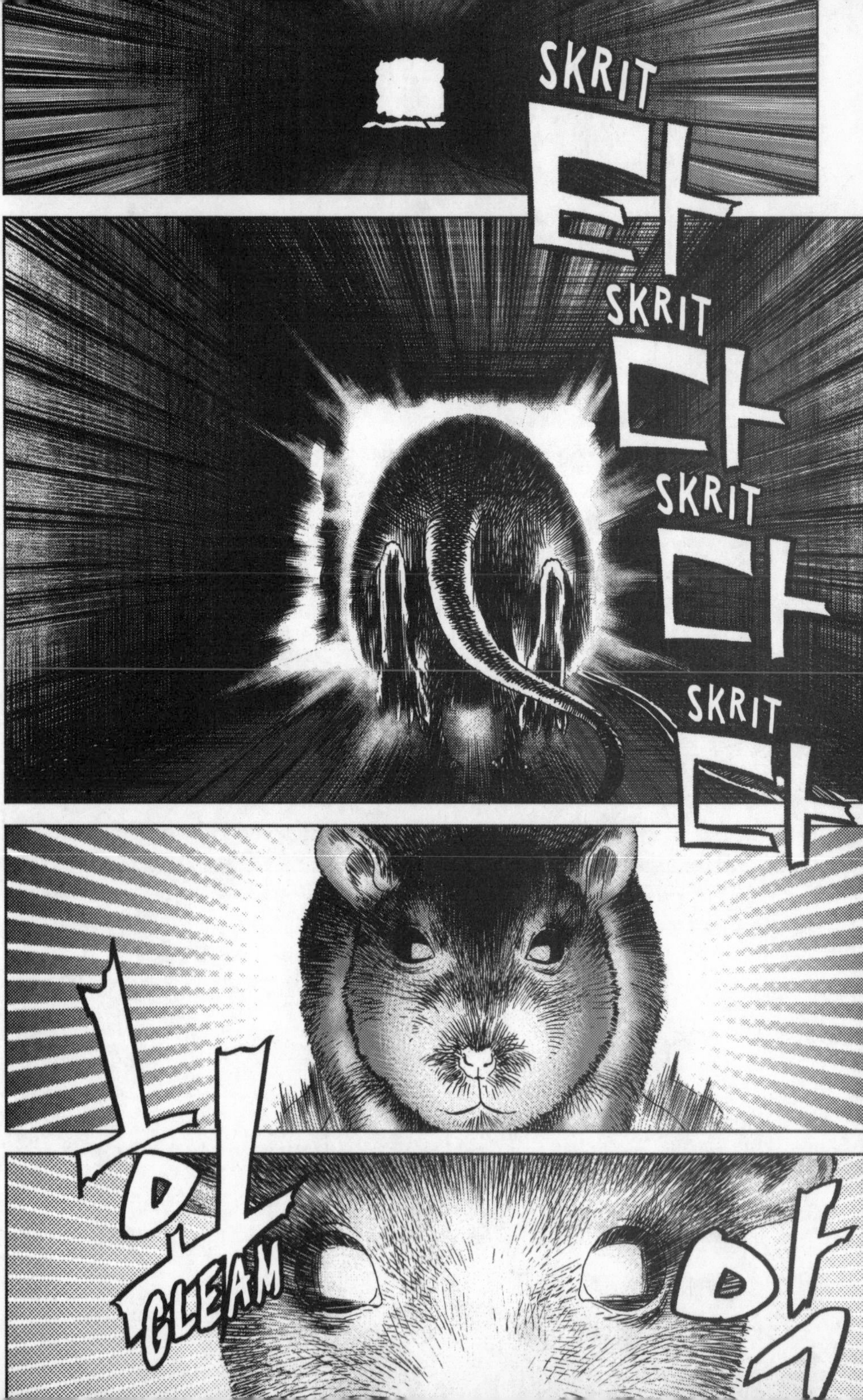
SKRIT
타
SKRIT
다
SKRIT
다
SKRIT
다
GLEAM

ZIP ZIP

HM?

SKRIT SKRIT SKRIT

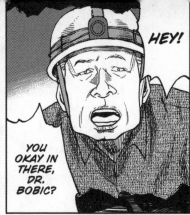

HEY!

YOU OKAY IN THERE, DR. BOBIC?

BITE

Y-YOWCH!

AAAH, GET OFFA ME!

SHP

SHP

EEEEE!

A RAT?

SKWEEK!

GUH!

UWAH!

ZIP

SKRT

AAH!

SHOO! SHOO!

FWAP

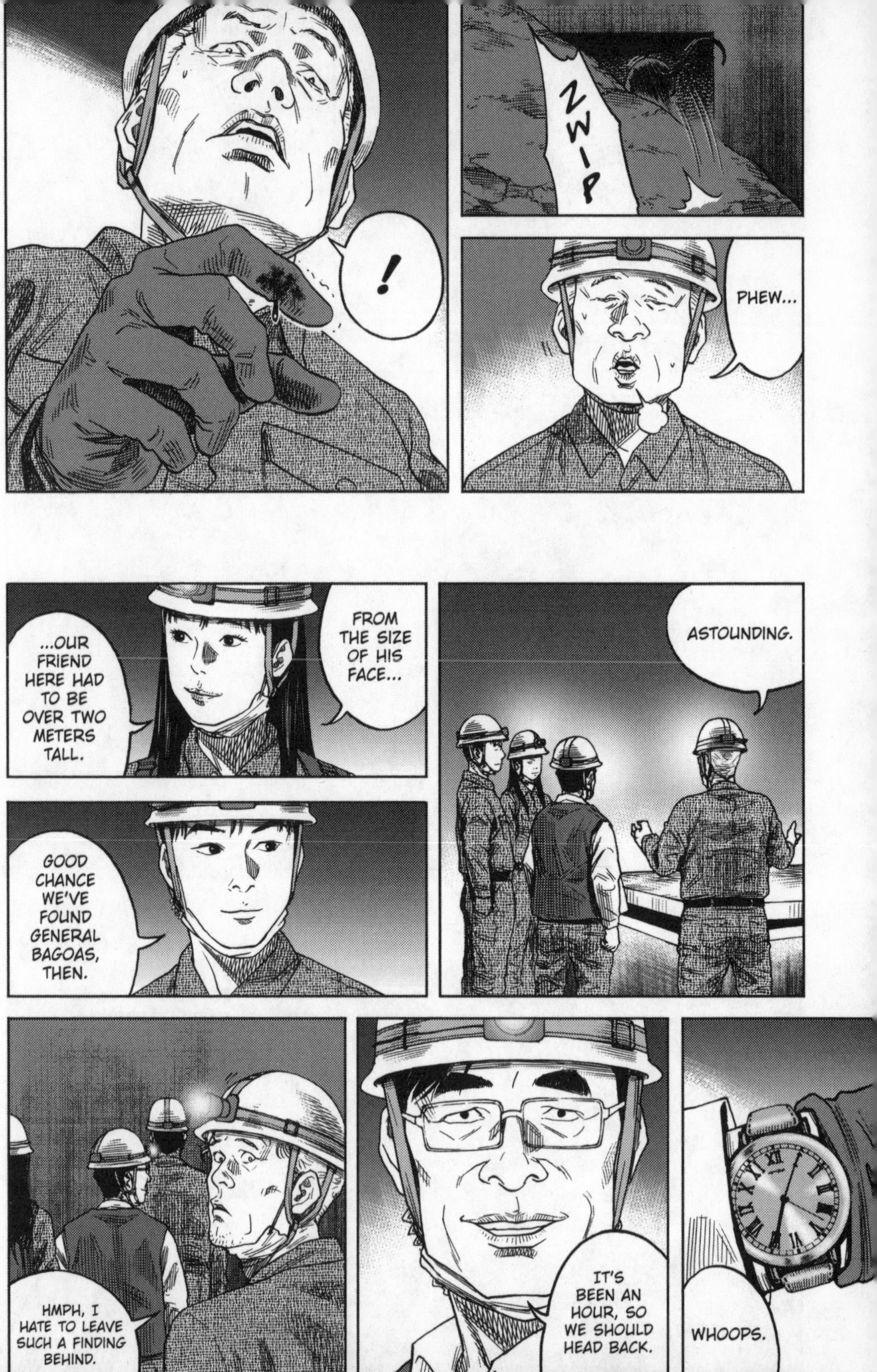
ZWIP
PHEW...
!
ASTOUNDING.
FROM THE SIZE OF HIS FACE...
...OUR FRIEND HERE HAD TO BE OVER TWO METERS TALL.
GOOD CHANCE WE'VE FOUND GENERAL BAGOAS, THEN.
WHOOPS.
IT'S BEEN AN HOUR, SO WE SHOULD HEAD BACK.
HMPH, I HATE TO LEAVE SUCH A FINDING BEHIND.

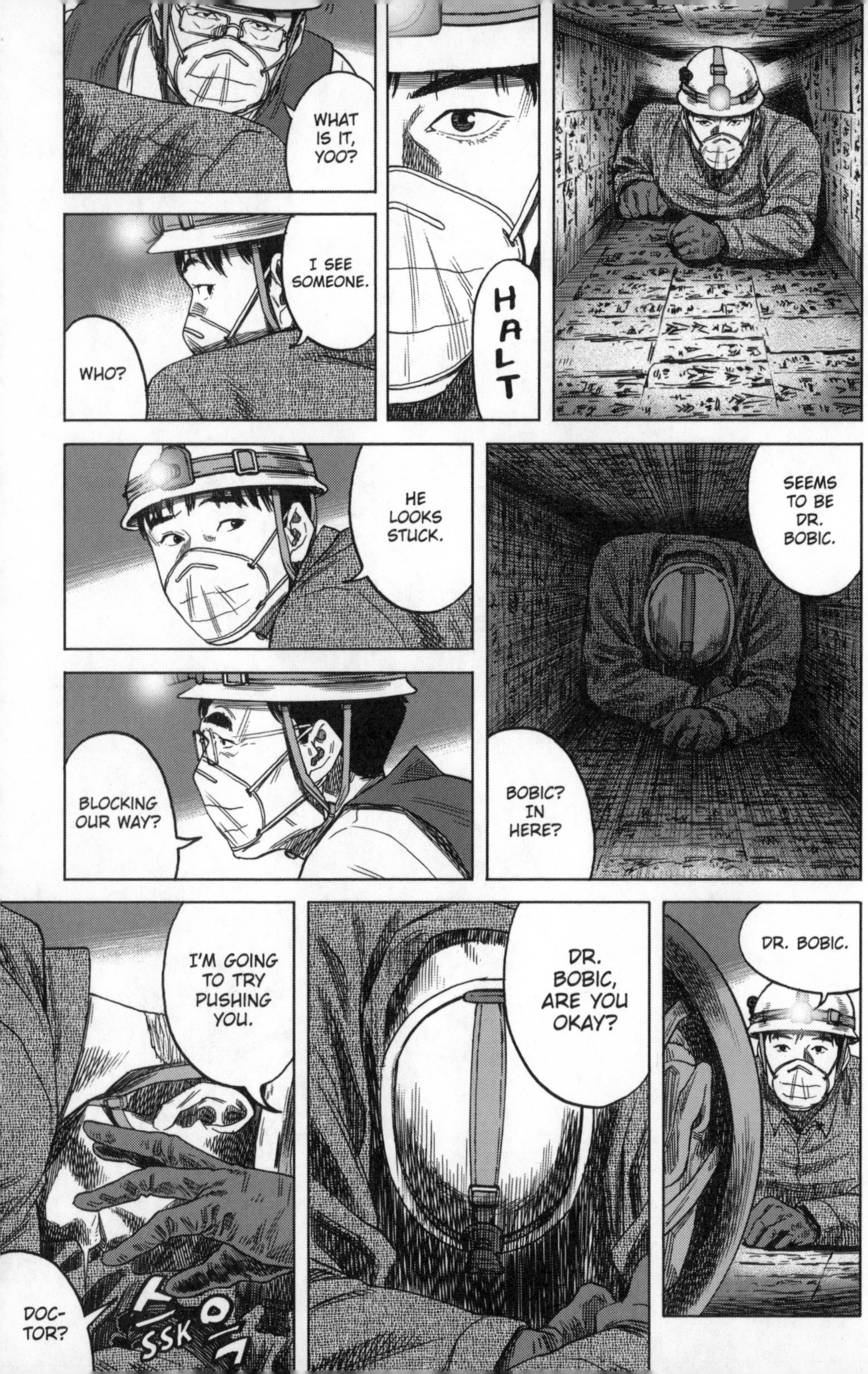
HALT
WHAT IS IT, YOO?
I SEE SOMEONE.
WHO?
SEEMS TO BE DR. BOBIC.
BOBIC? IN HERE?
HE LOOKS STUCK.
BLOCKING OUR WAY?
DR. BOBIC.
DR. BOBIC, ARE YOU OKAY?
I'M GOING TO TRY PUSHING YOU.
DOCTOR?
SSK

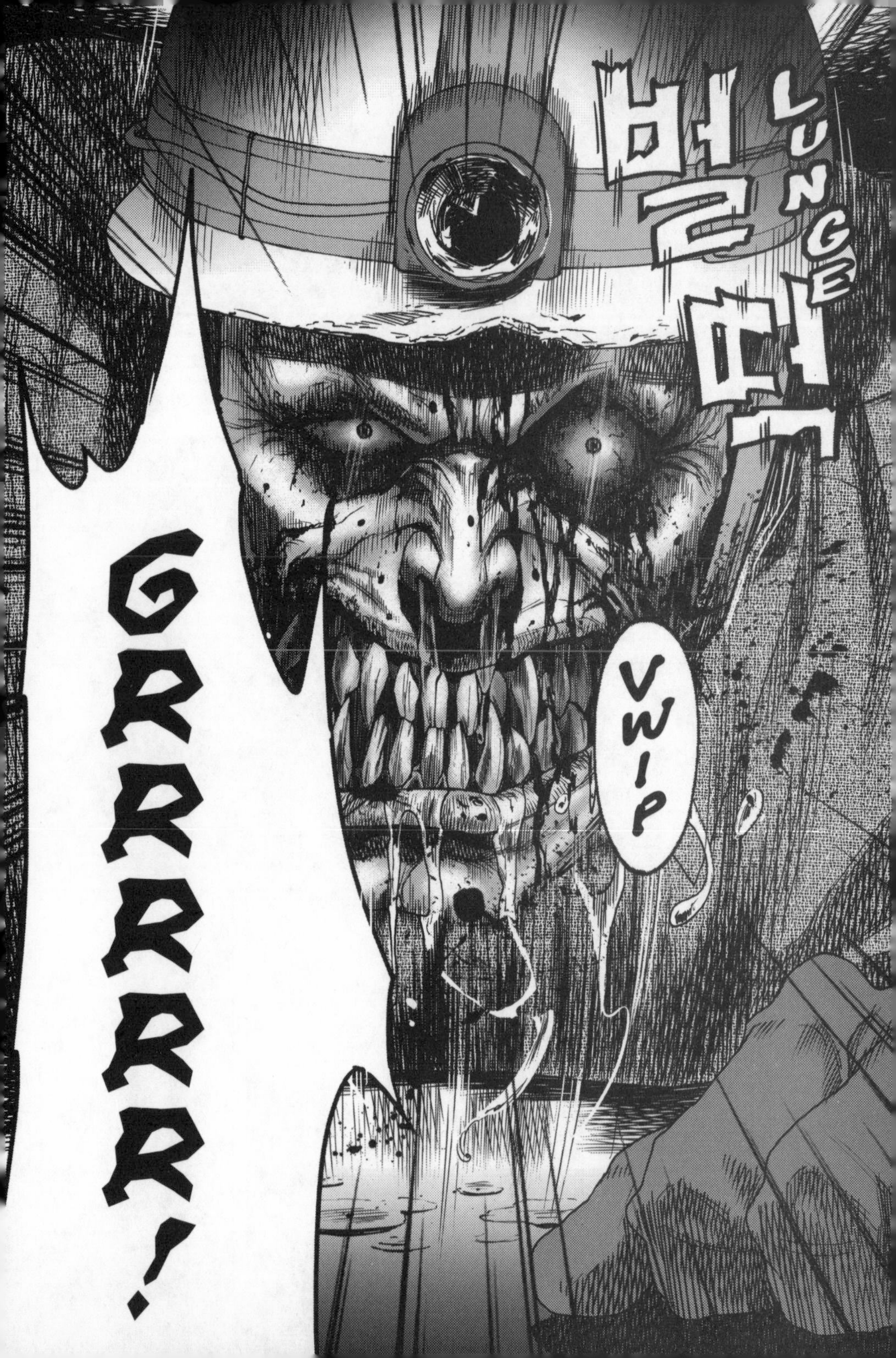
LUNGE
VWIP
GRARRR!

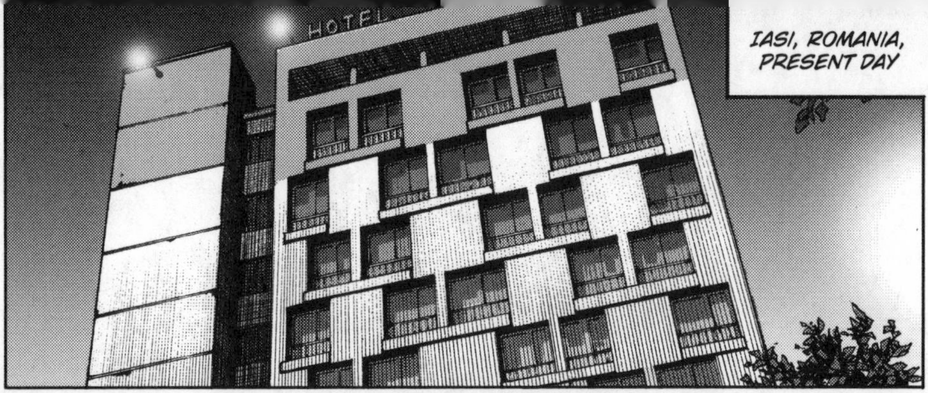
IASI, ROMANIA, PRESENT DAY

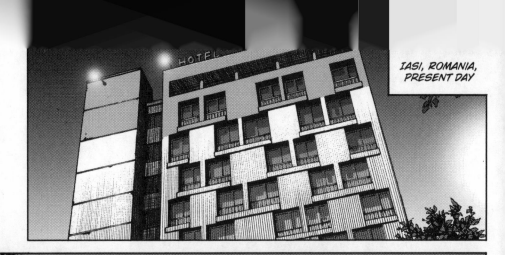

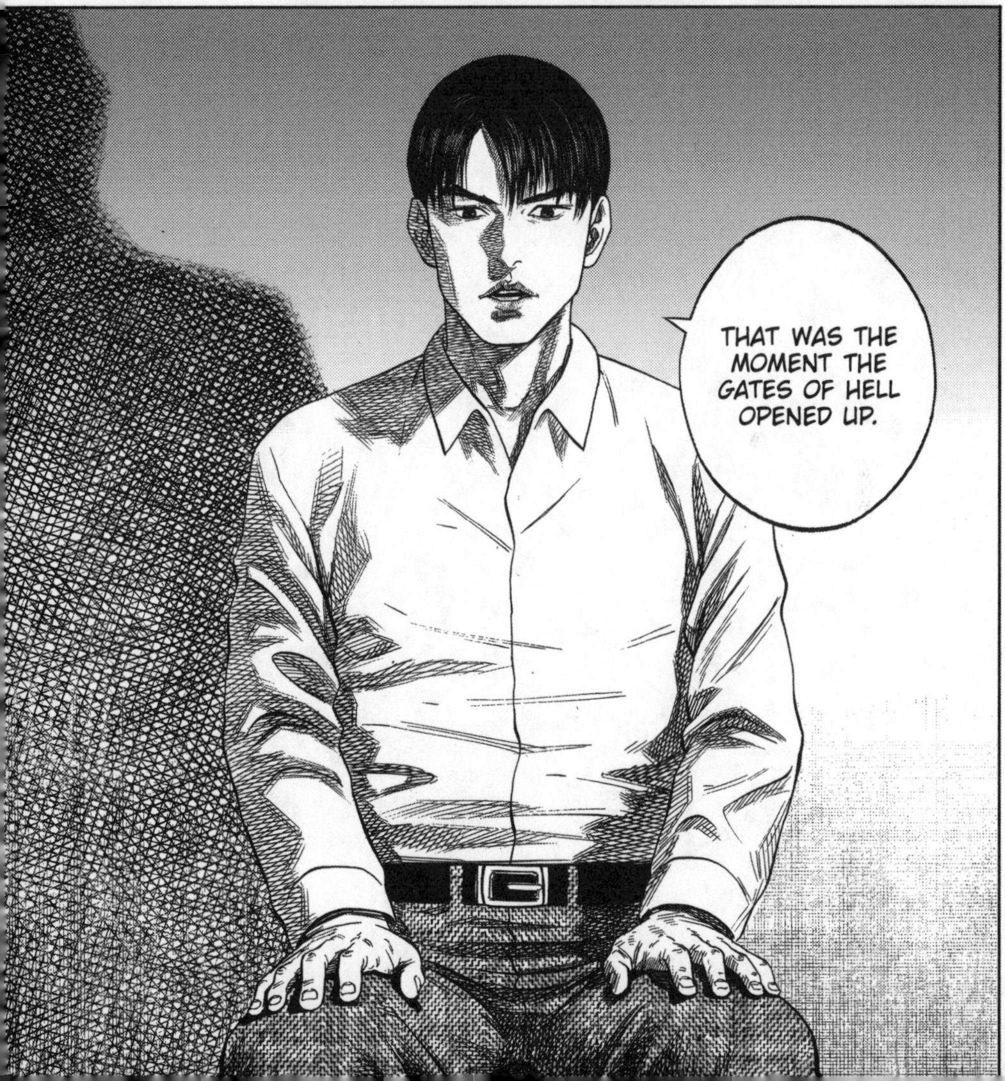
THAT WAS THE MOMENT THE GATES OF HELL OPENED UP.

KING OF EDEN

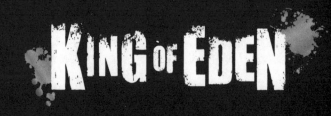

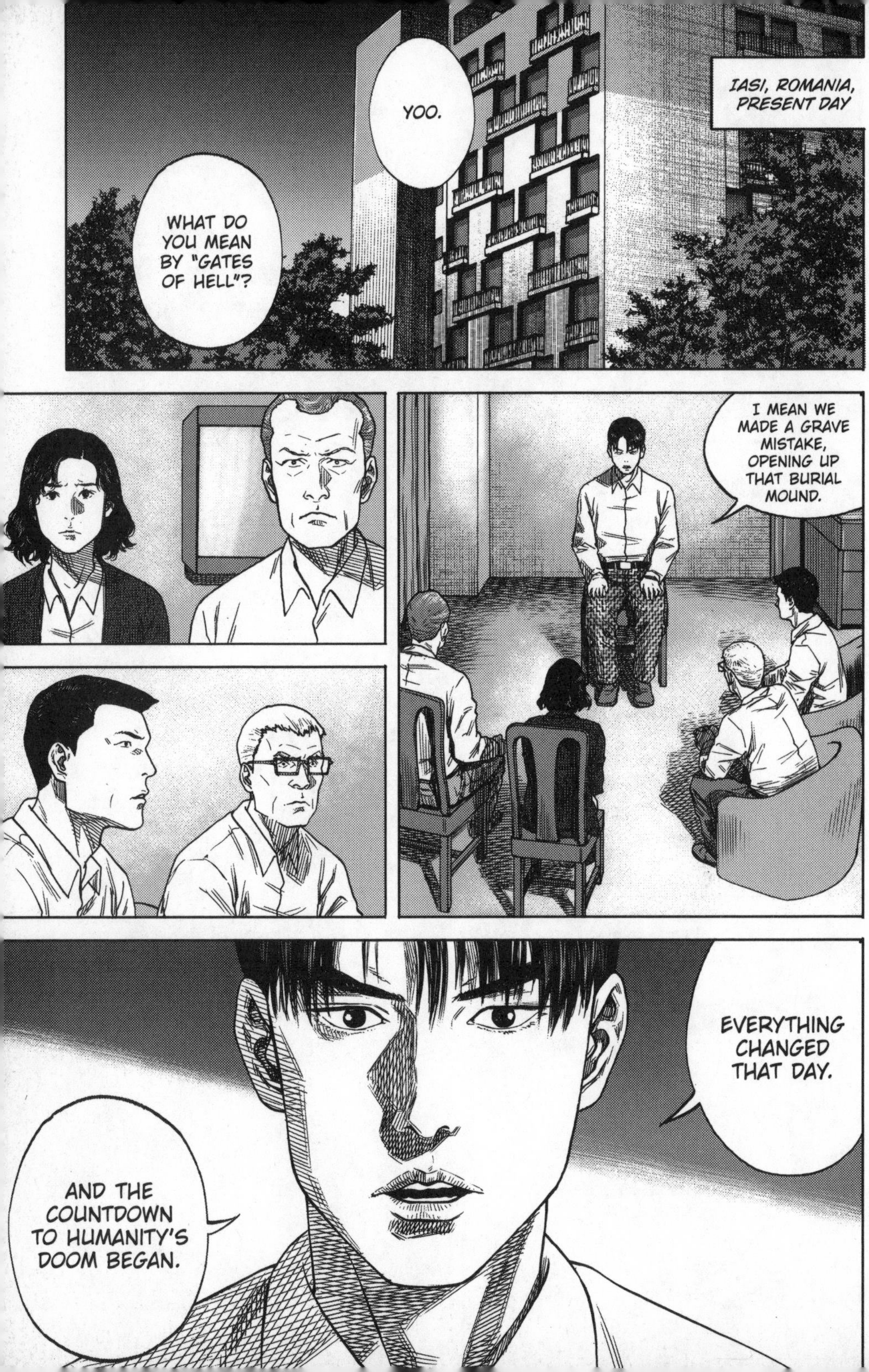
IASI, ROMANIA, PRESENT DAY
YOO.
WHAT DO YOU MEAN BY "GATES OF HELL"?
I MEAN WE MADE A GRAVE MISTAKE, OPENING UP THAT BURIAL MOUND.
EVERYTHING CHANGED THAT DAY.
AND THE COUNTDOWN TO HUMANITY'S DOOM BEGAN.

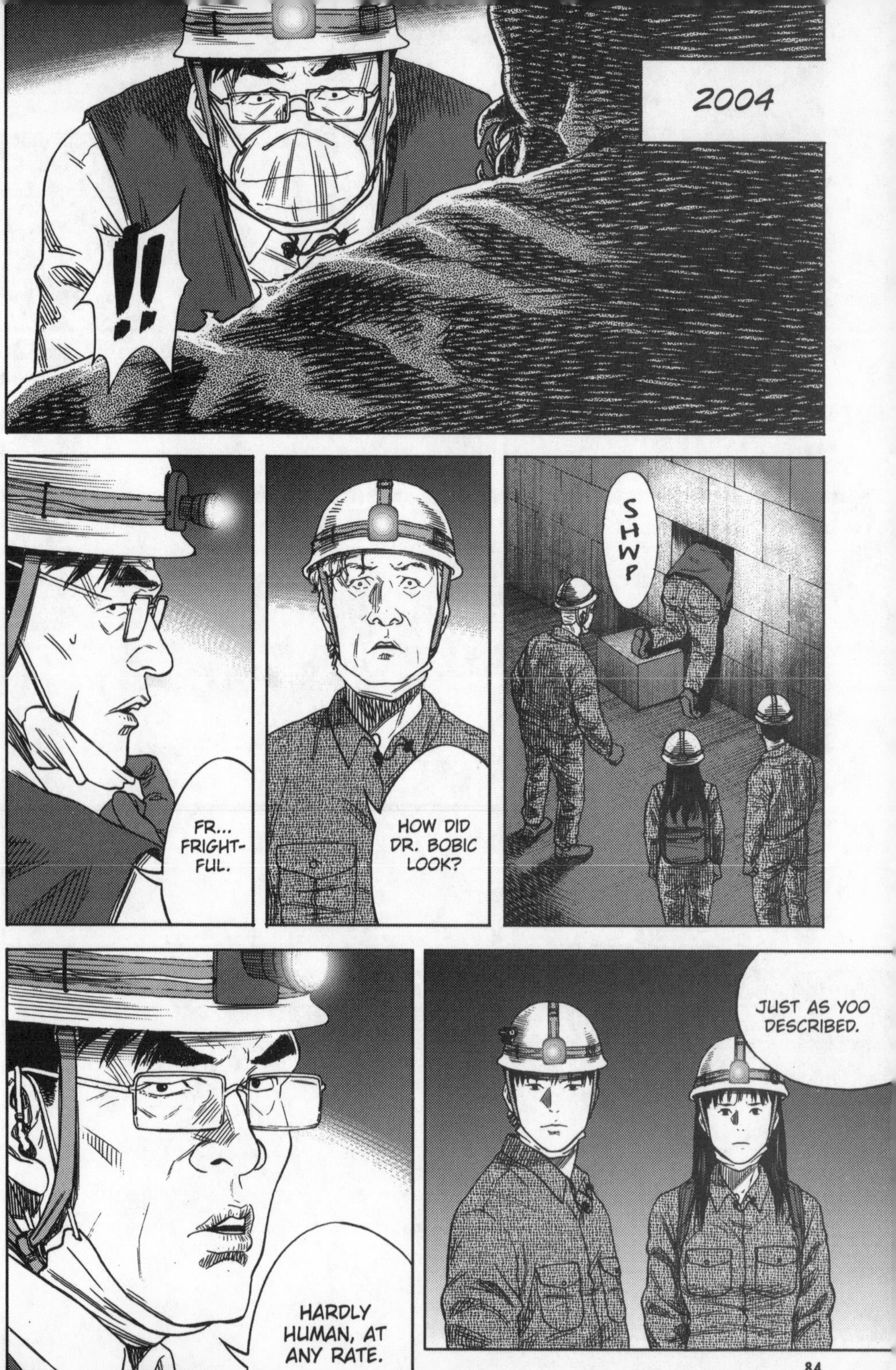
2004
!!
SHWP
HOW DID DR. BOBIC LOOK?
FR... FRIGHT-FUL.
JUST AS YOO DESCRIBED.
HARDLY HUMAN, AT ANY RATE.

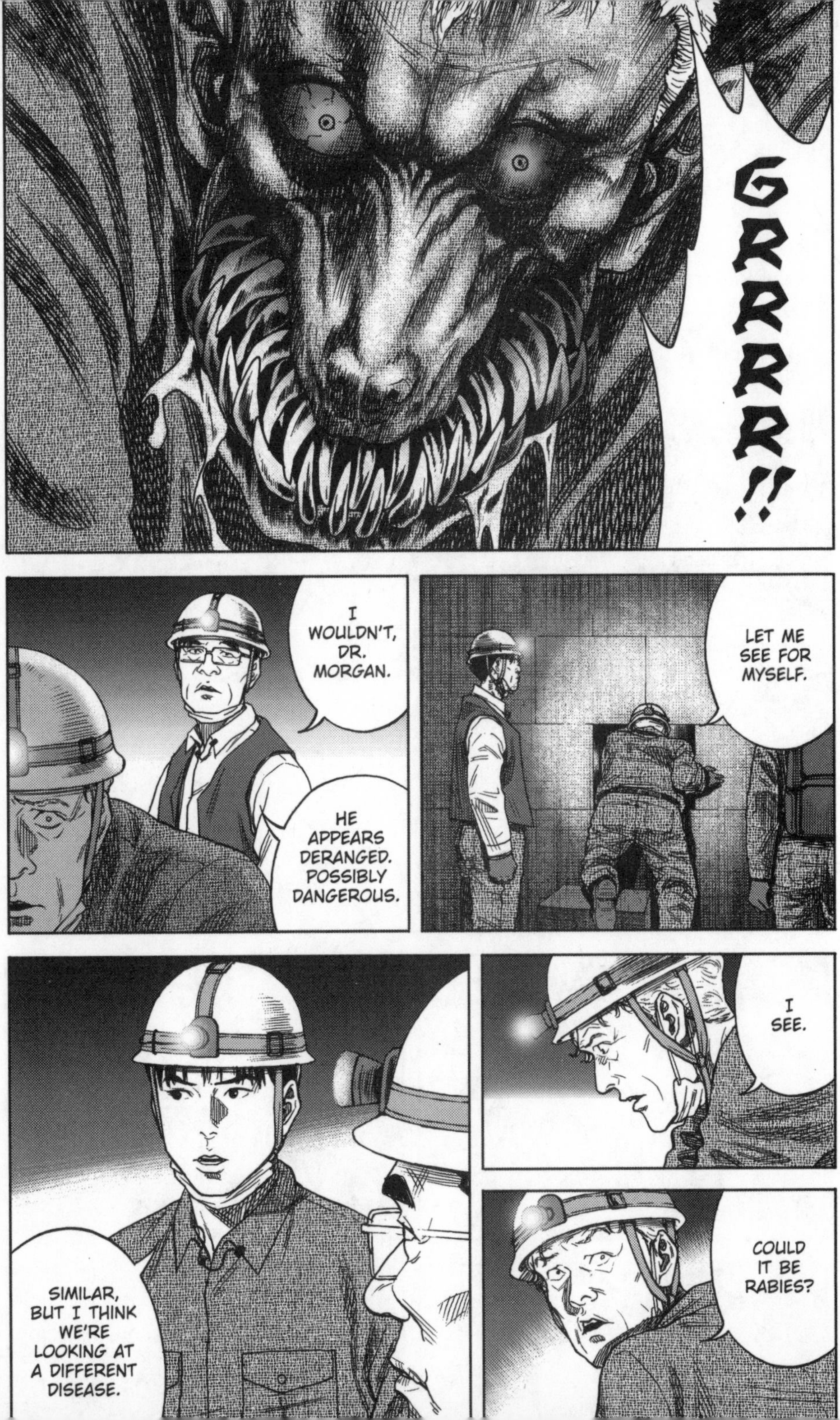
GRRRR!!
LET ME SEE FOR MYSELF.
I WOULDN'T, DR. MORGAN.
HE APPEARS DERANGED. POSSIBLY DANGEROUS.
I SEE.
COULD IT BE RABIES?
SIMILAR, BUT I THINK WE'RE LOOKING AT A DIFFERENT DISEASE.

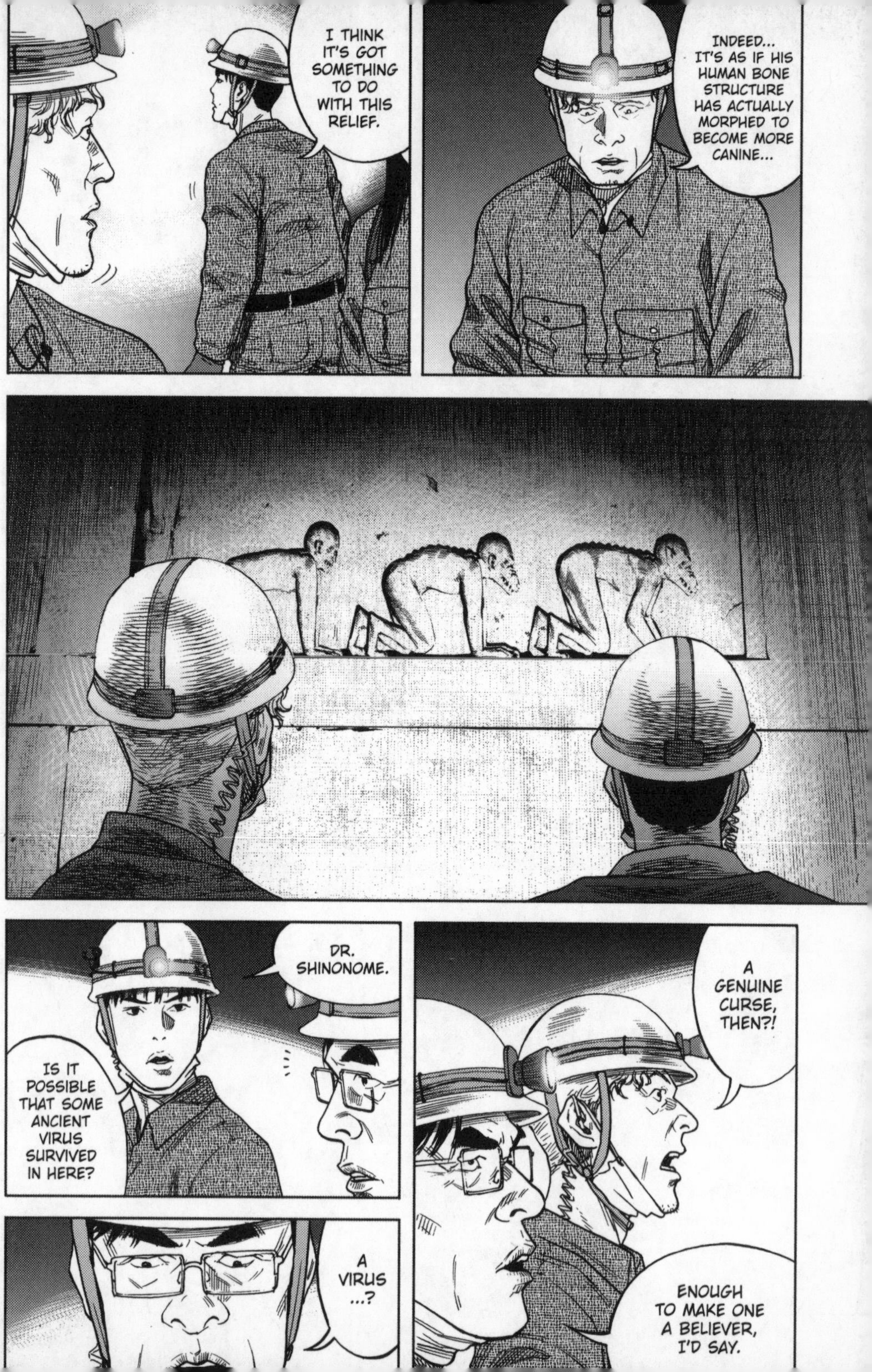
INDEED... IT'S AS IF HIS HUMAN BONE STRUCTURE HAS ACTUALLY MORPHED TO BECOME MORE CANINE...
I THINK IT'S GOT SOMETHING TO DO WITH THIS RELIEF.
A GENUINE CURSE, THEN?!
ENOUGH TO MAKE ONE A BELIEVER, I'D SAY.
DR. SHINONOME.
IS IT POSSIBLE THAT SOME ANCIENT VIRUS SURVIVED IN HERE?
A VIRUS ...?

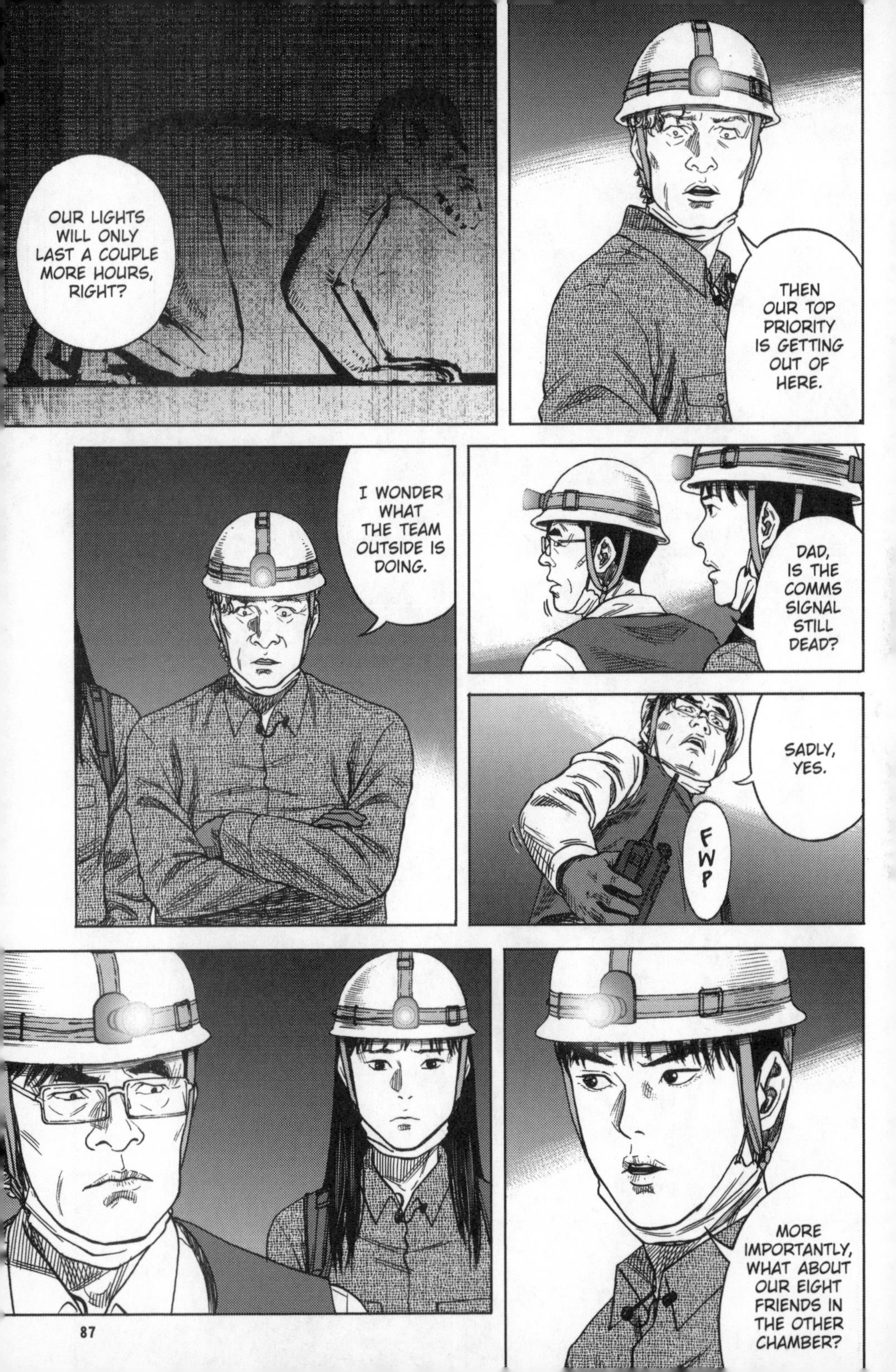
THEN OUR TOP PRIORITY IS GETTING OUT OF HERE.
OUR LIGHTS WILL ONLY LAST A COUPLE MORE HOURS, RIGHT?
DAD, IS THE COMMS SIGNAL STILL DEAD?
SADLY, YES.
FWP
I WONDER WHAT THE TEAM OUTSIDE IS DOING.
MORE IMPORTANTLY, WHAT ABOUT OUR EIGHT FRIENDS IN THE OTHER CHAMBER?

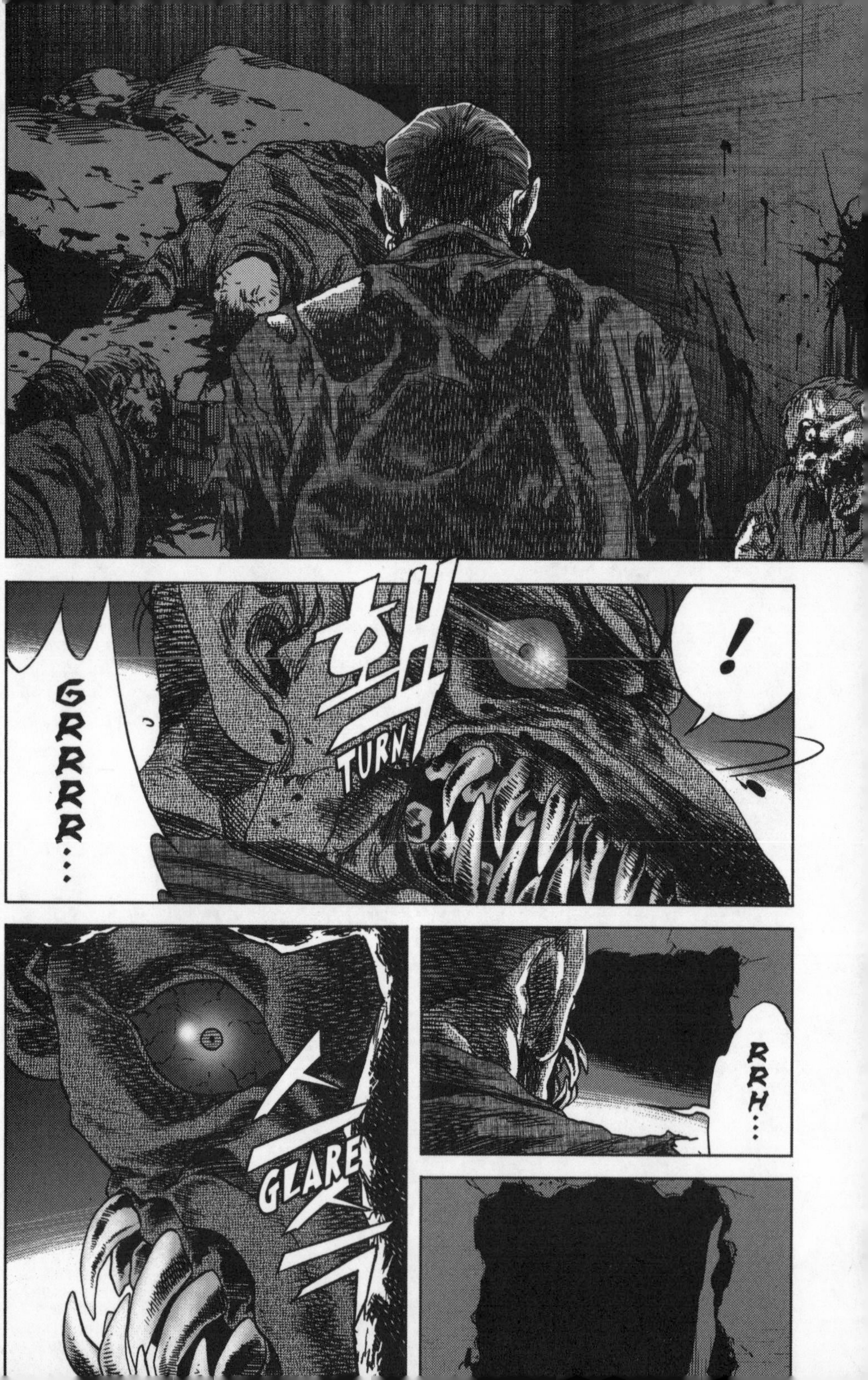
!
홱
TURN
GRRRR...
RRH...
GLARE

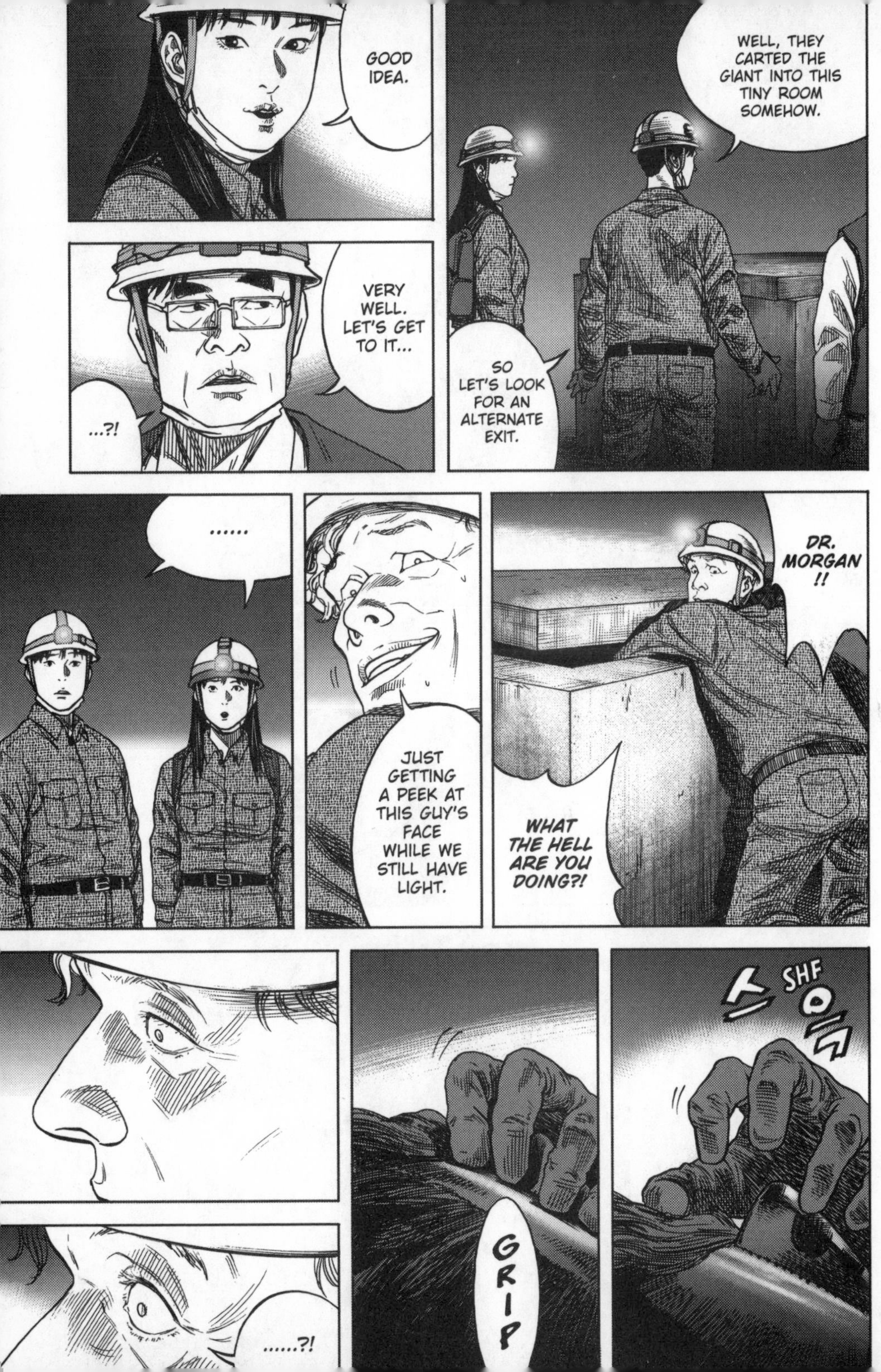
WELL, THEY CARTED THE GIANT INTO THIS TINY ROOM SOMEHOW.
SO LET'S LOOK FOR AN ALTERNATE EXIT.
GOOD IDEA.
VERY WELL. LET'S GET TO IT...
...?!
DR. MORGAN!!
WHAT THE HELL ARE YOU DOING?!
JUST GETTING A PEEK AT THIS GUY'S FACE WHILE WE STILL HAVE LIGHT.
......
SHF
GRIP
......?!

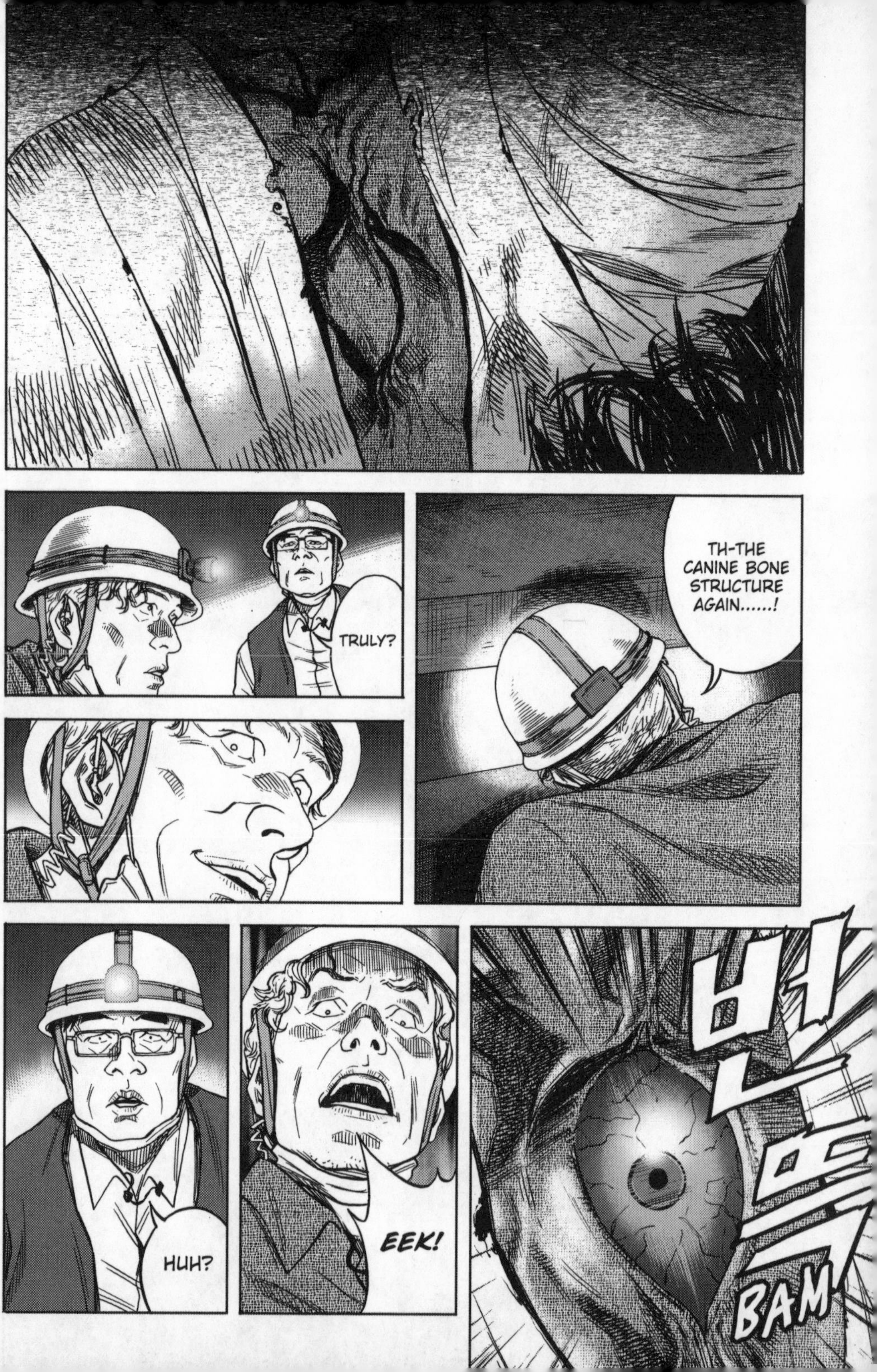
TH-THE CANINE BONE STRUCTURE AGAIN......!
TRULY?
BAM
EEK!
HUH?

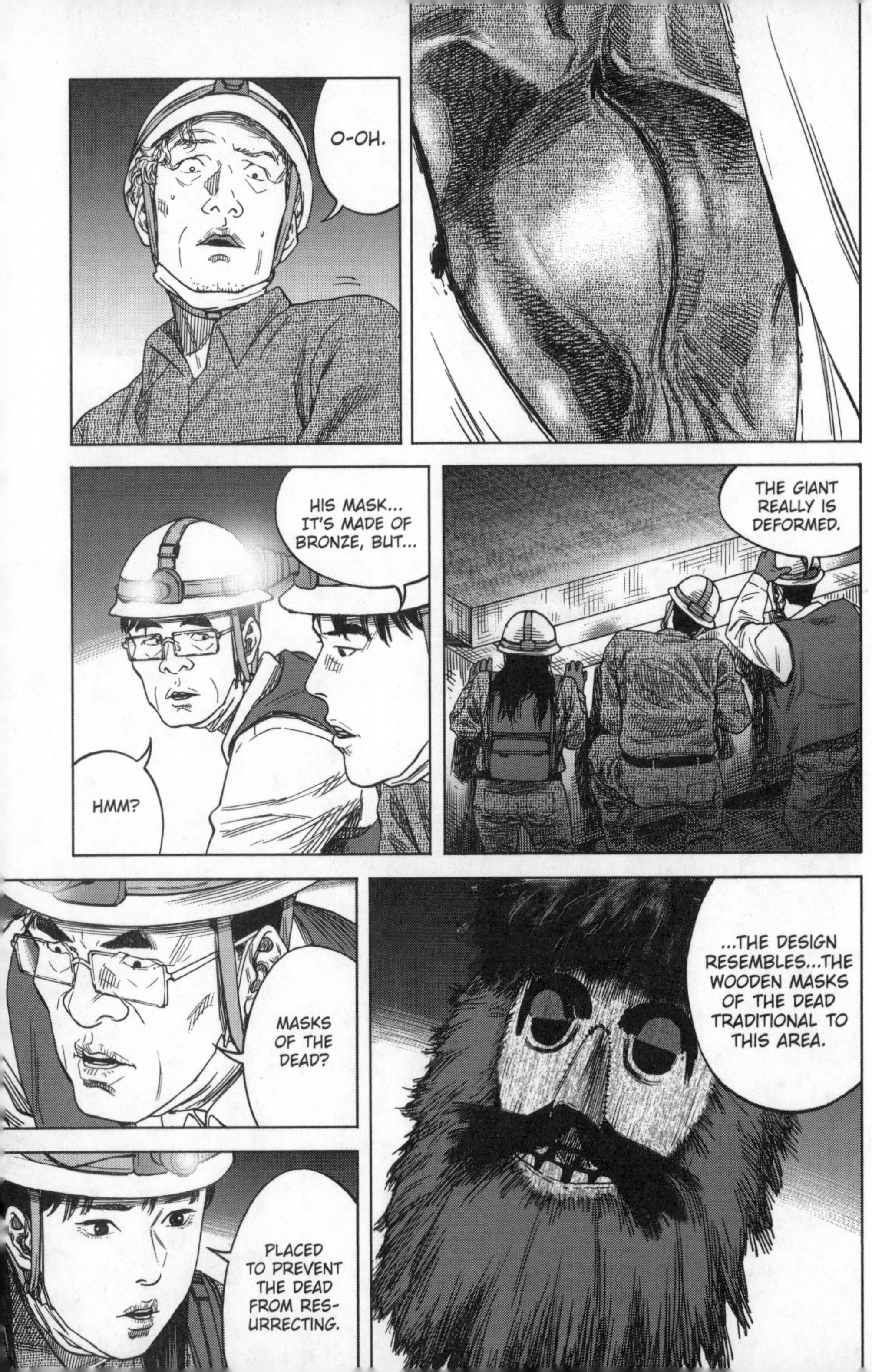
O-OH.
THE GIANT REALLY IS DEFORMED.
HIS MASK... IT'S MADE OF BRONZE, BUT...
HMM?
...THE DESIGN RESEMBLES...THE WOODEN MASKS OF THE DEAD TRADITIONAL TO THIS AREA.
MASKS OF THE DEAD?
PLACED TO PREVENT THE DEAD FROM RES-URRECTING.

IT'S FROM THE LEGENDS ABOUT VAMPIRES.

SHF

GRNCH

SLAM

HFF! HFF! HAH! HFF!

DRAAAG

GRRRH!

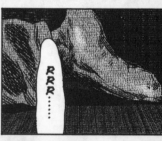

RRR......

DRAG

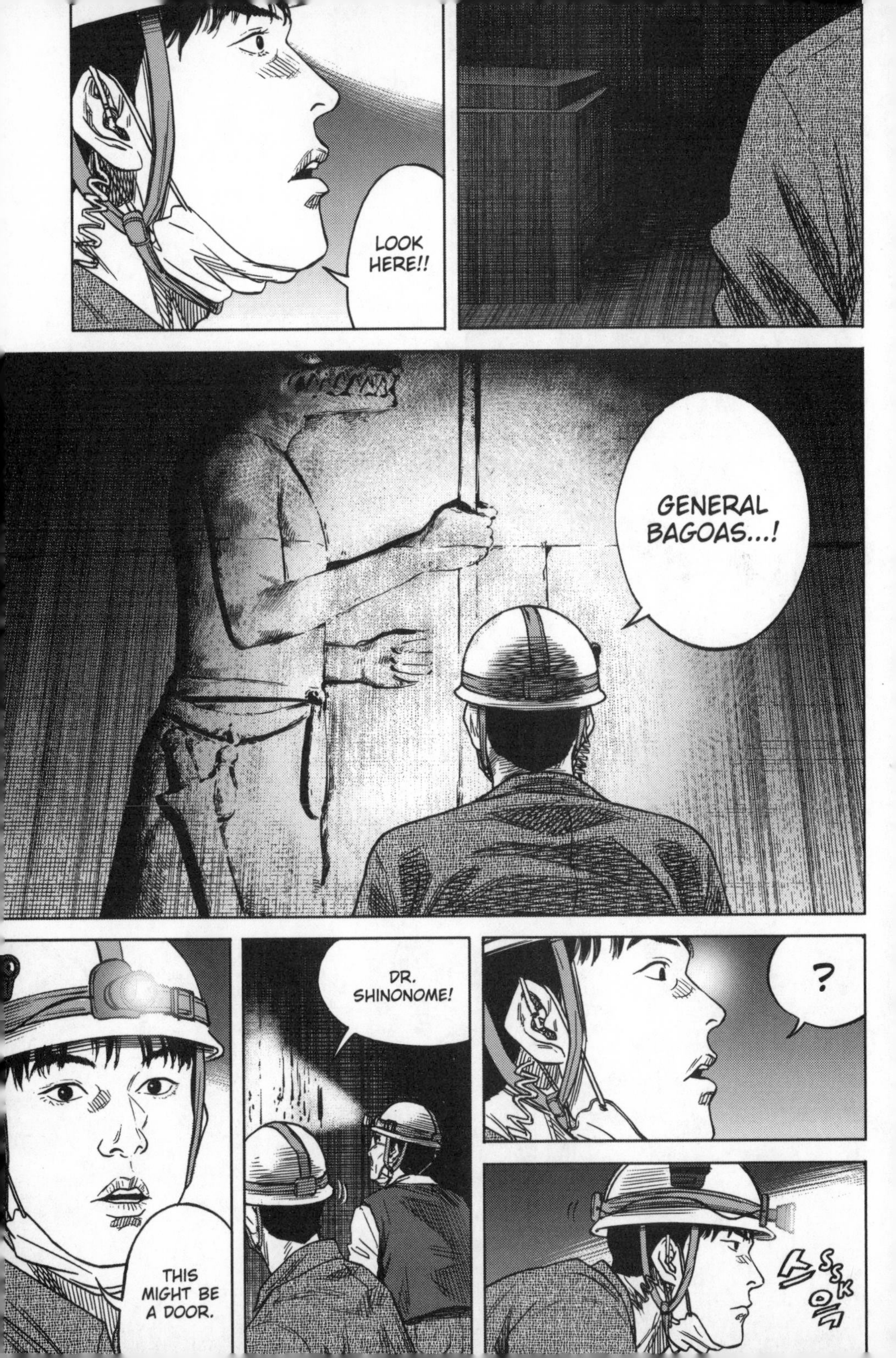
LOOK HERE!!
GENERAL BAGOAS...!
?
SSK
DR. SHINONOME!
THIS MIGHT BE A DOOR.

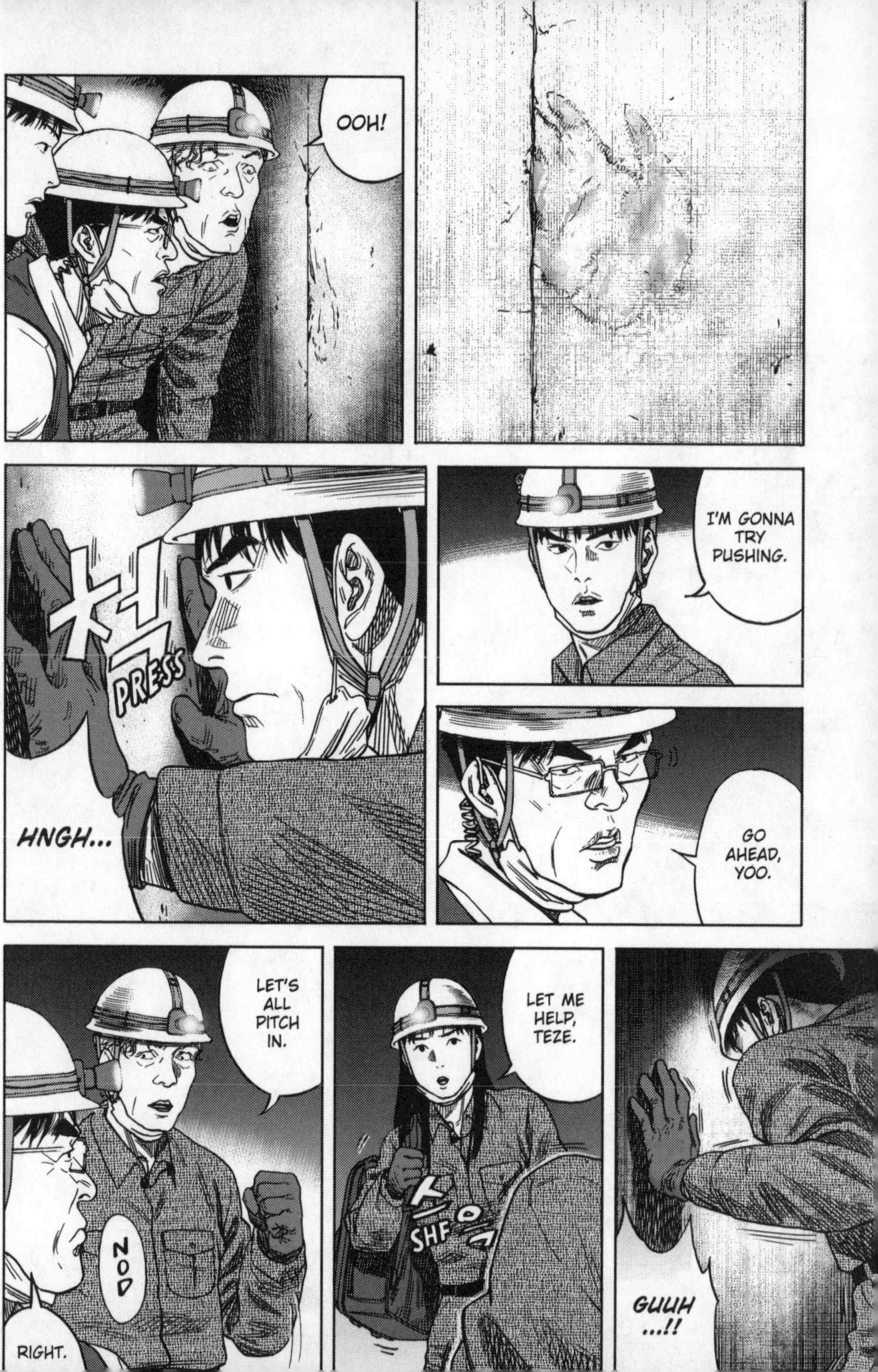
OOH!
I'M GONNA TRY PUSHING.
GO AHEAD, YOO.
PRESS
HNGH...
GUUH ...!!
LET ME HELP, TEZE.
SHF
LET'S ALL PITCH IN.
NOD
RIGHT.

GUUH!!

RAAAH!!

NGH!!

SLIP

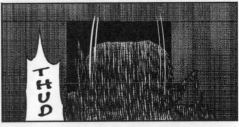

THUD

TMP

TMP

GRRR...

GRRH!!

!

RRRH!

SSSK

DAMN!

IT WON'T BUDGE.

TURN

GRRRRR...

......?

HUH?

SHFF

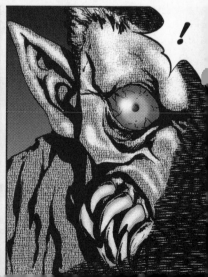

!

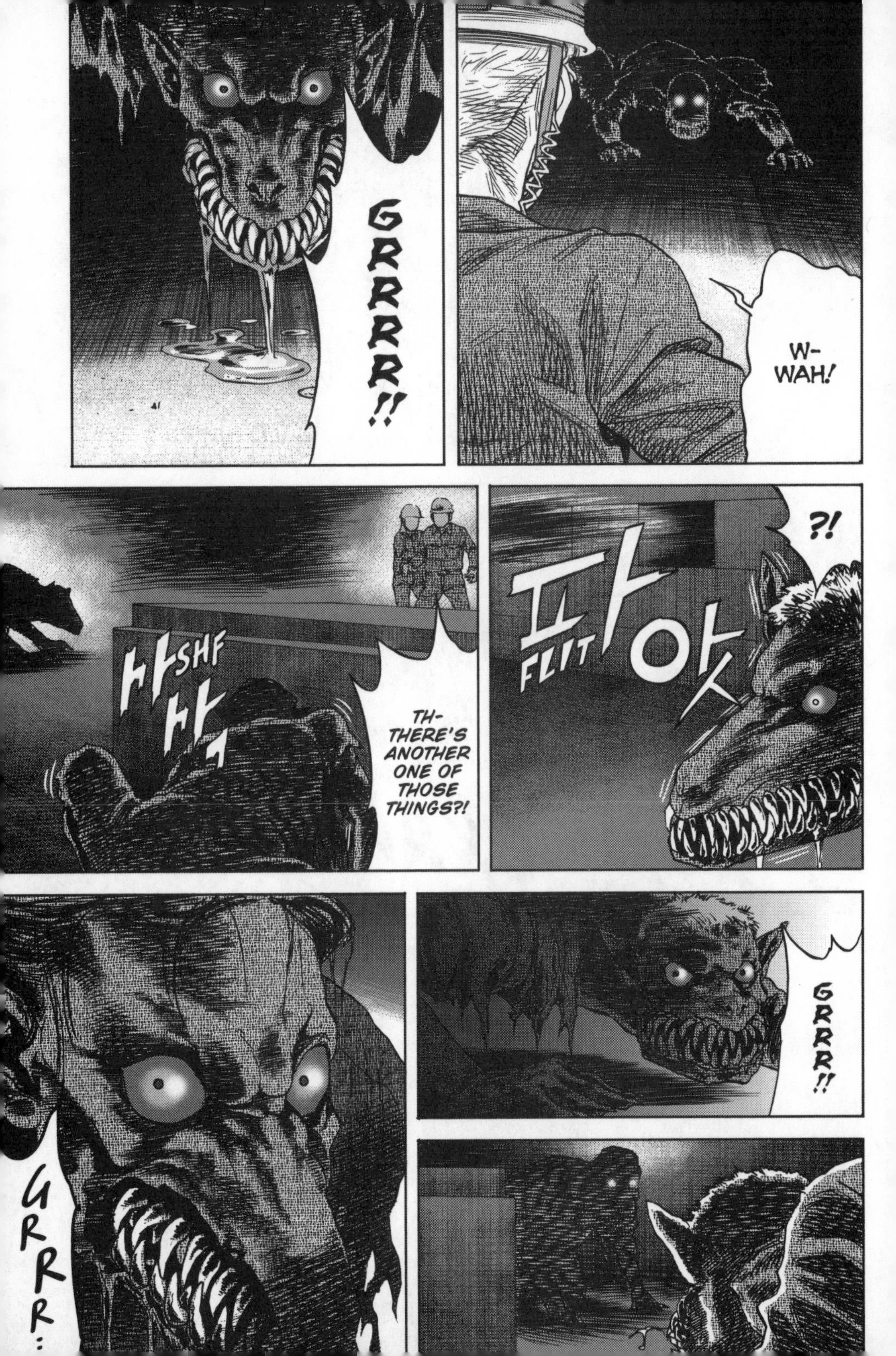
GRRRRR!!
W-
WAH!
?!
파앗
FLIT
TH-
THERE'S
ANOTHER
ONE OF
THOSE
THINGS?!
SHF
GRRRR!!
GRRR...

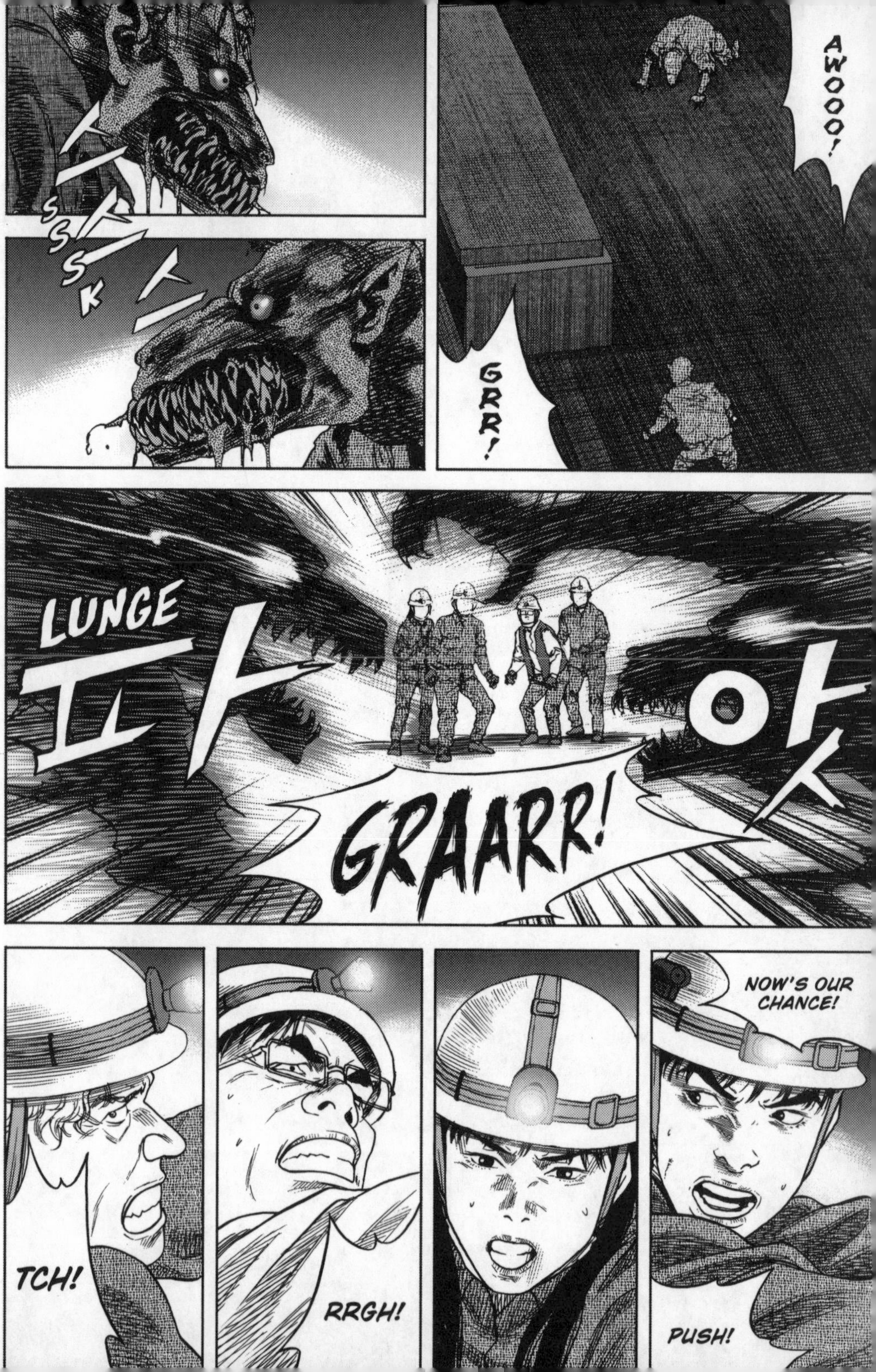
AWOOO!
GRR!
SSSK
LUNGE
GRAARR!
NOW'S OUR CHANCE!
PUSH!
RRGH!
TCH!

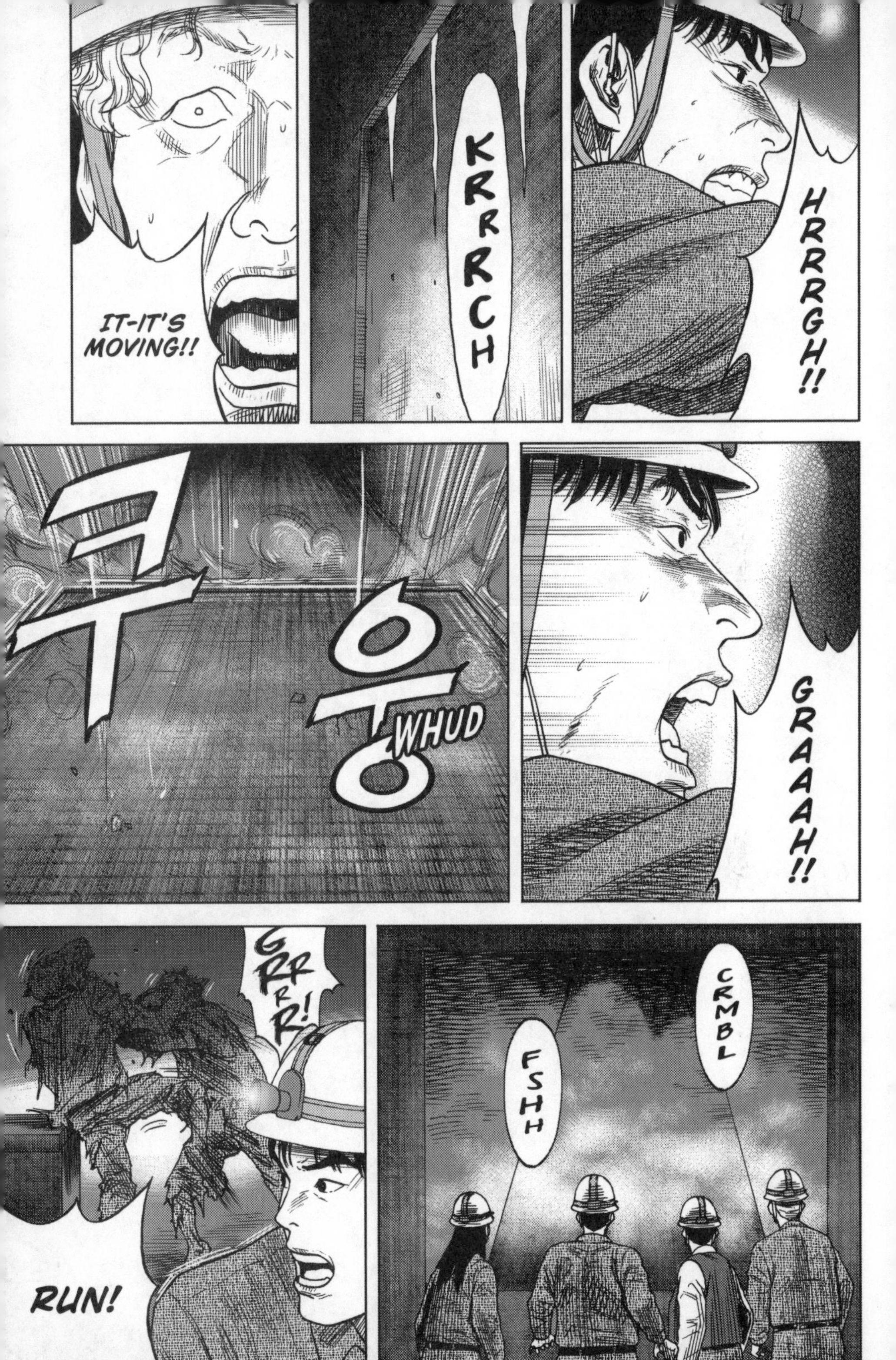
HRRRGH!!
KRRRCH
IT-IT'S MOVING!!
GRAAAH!!
쿠웅
WHUD
CRMBL
FSHH
GRRRR!
RUN!

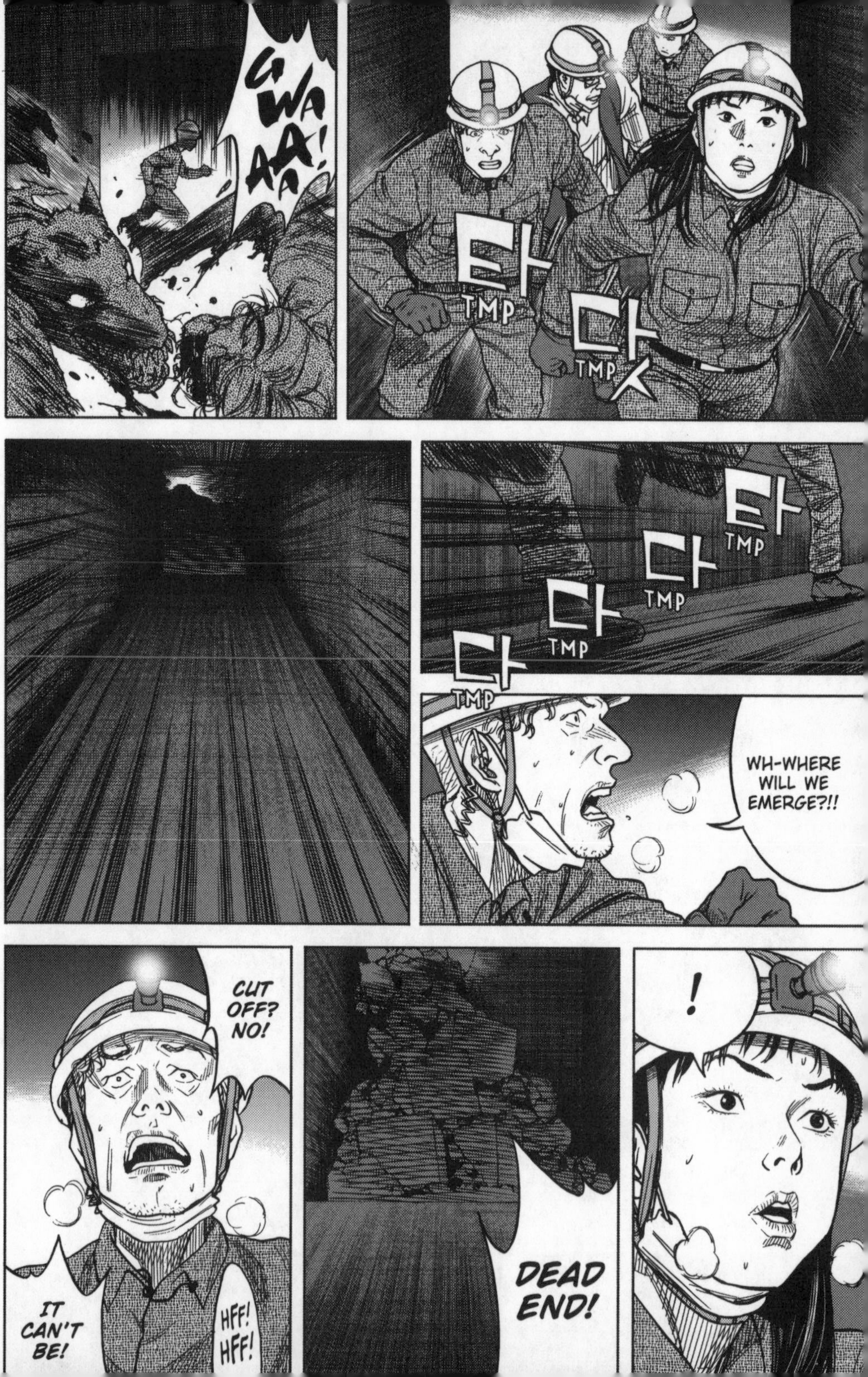
타
TMP
다
TMP
닷
GWAAAA!
타
TMP
다
TMP
다
TMP
다
TMP
WH-WHERE WILL WE EMERGE?!!
!
DEAD END!
CUT OFF? NO!
IT CAN'T BE!
HFF! HFF!

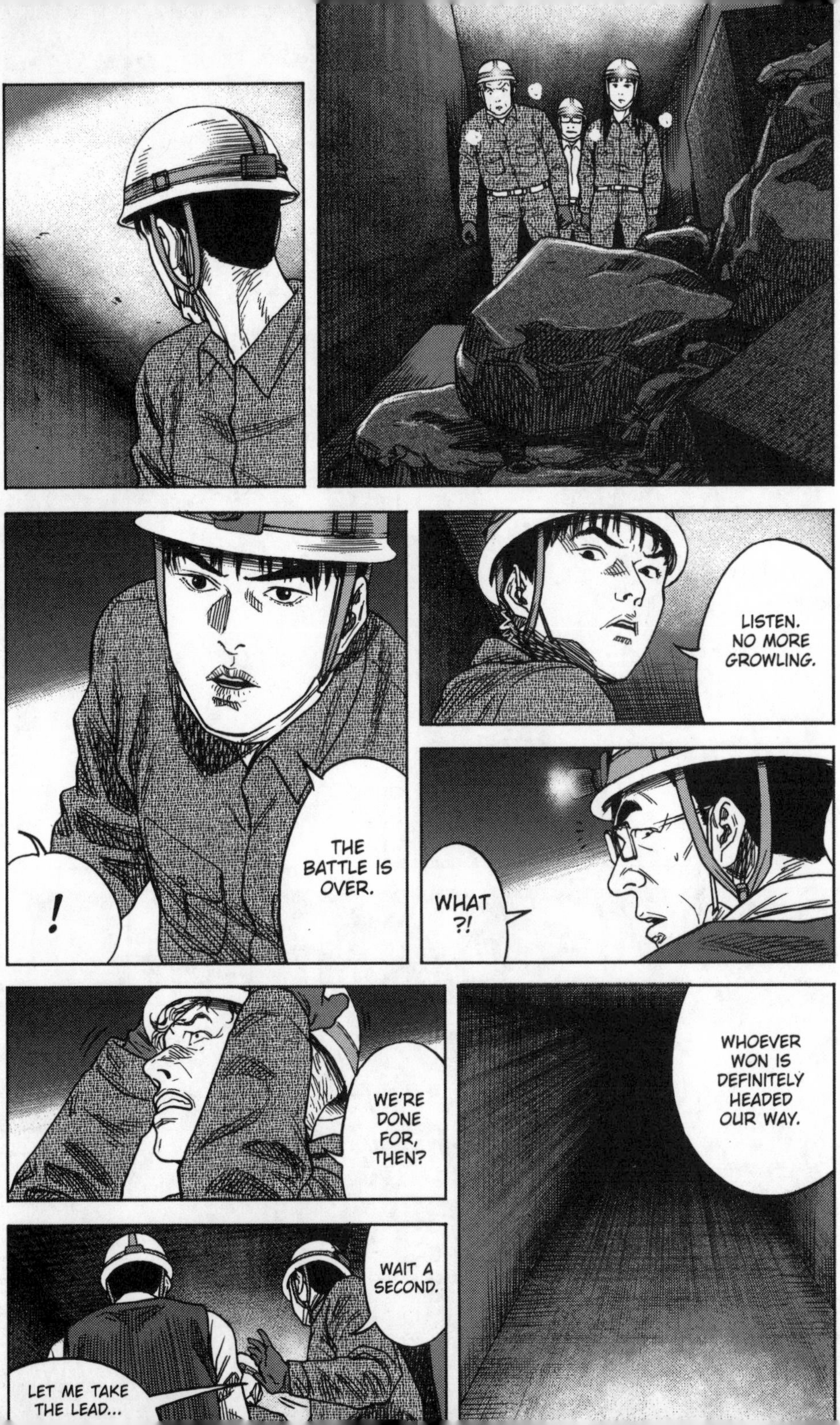
LISTEN. NO MORE GROWLING.
WHAT ?!
THE BATTLE IS OVER.
!
WHOEVER WON IS DEFINITELY HEADED OUR WAY.
WE'RE DONE FOR, THEN?
WAIT A SECOND.
LET ME TAKE THE LEAD...

......

THERE'S NO WAY WE CAN CLEAR THE RUBBLE WITH JUST THE FOUR OF US.

KRAK
KRAK

KRAK

!

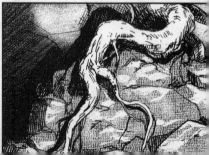

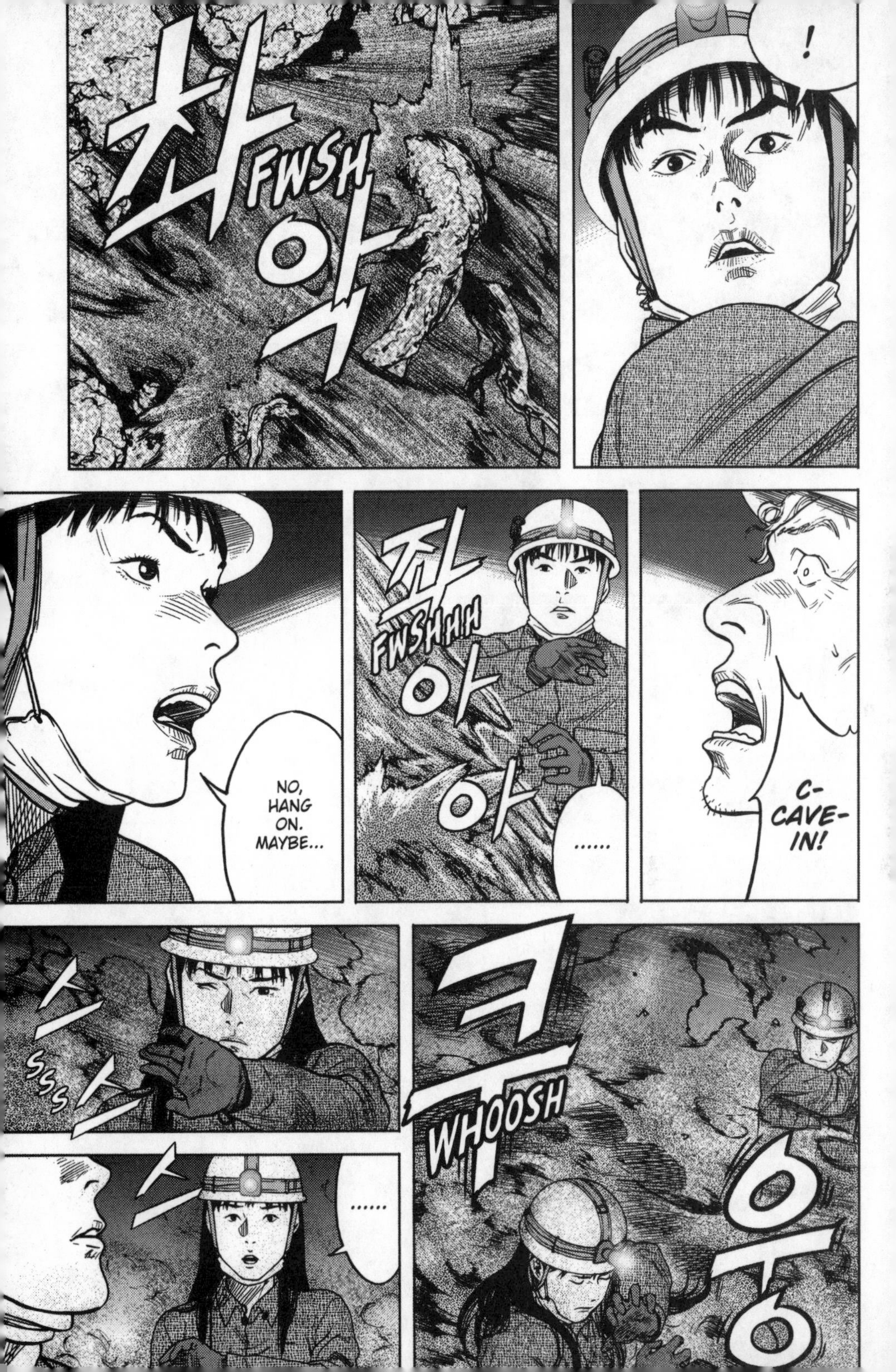
!
FWSH
C-CAVE-IN!
......
FWSHHH
NO, HANG ON. MAYBE...
WHOOSH
SSS
......

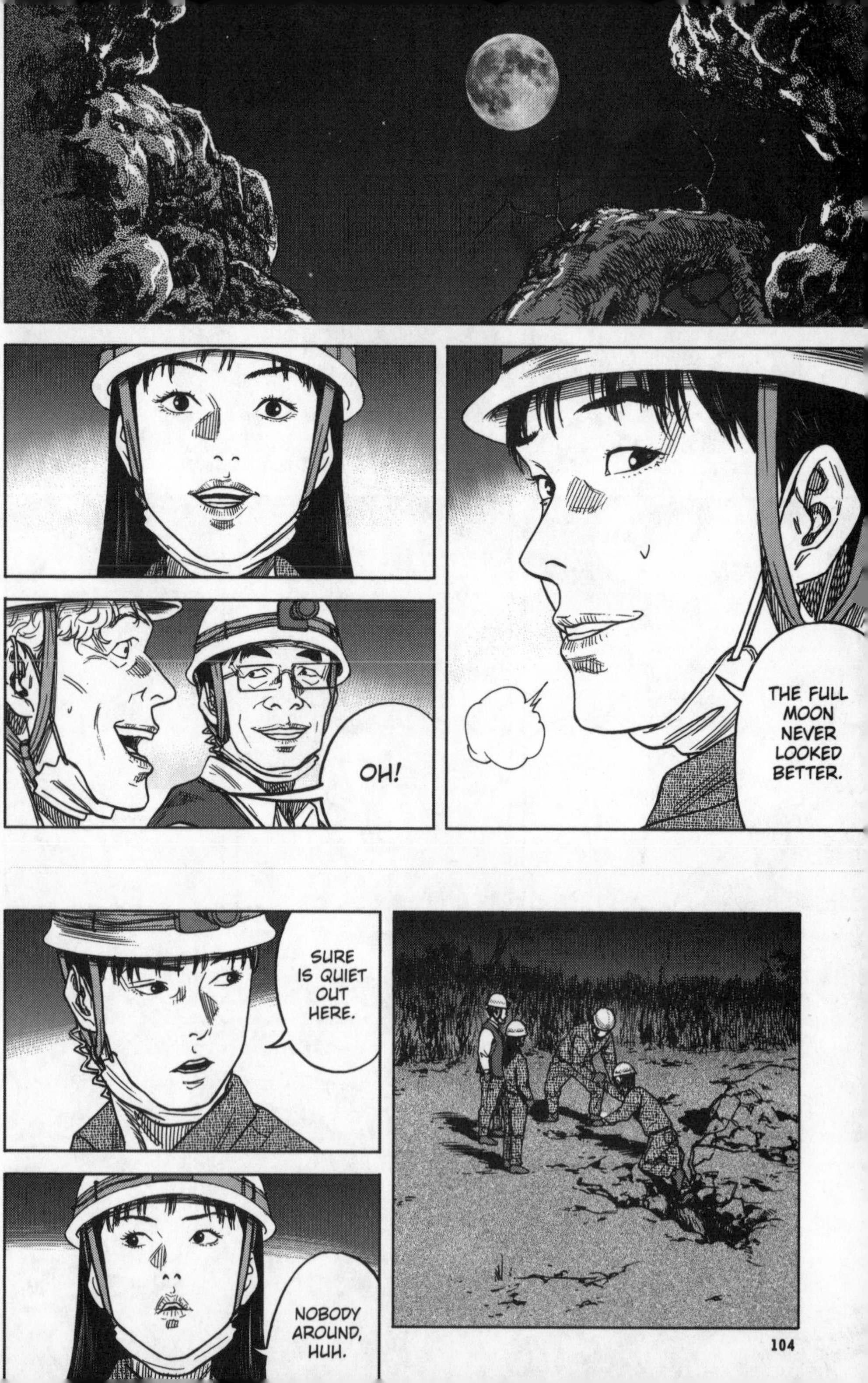
THE FULL MOON NEVER LOOKED BETTER.
OH!
SURE IS QUIET OUT HERE.
NOBODY AROUND, HUH.

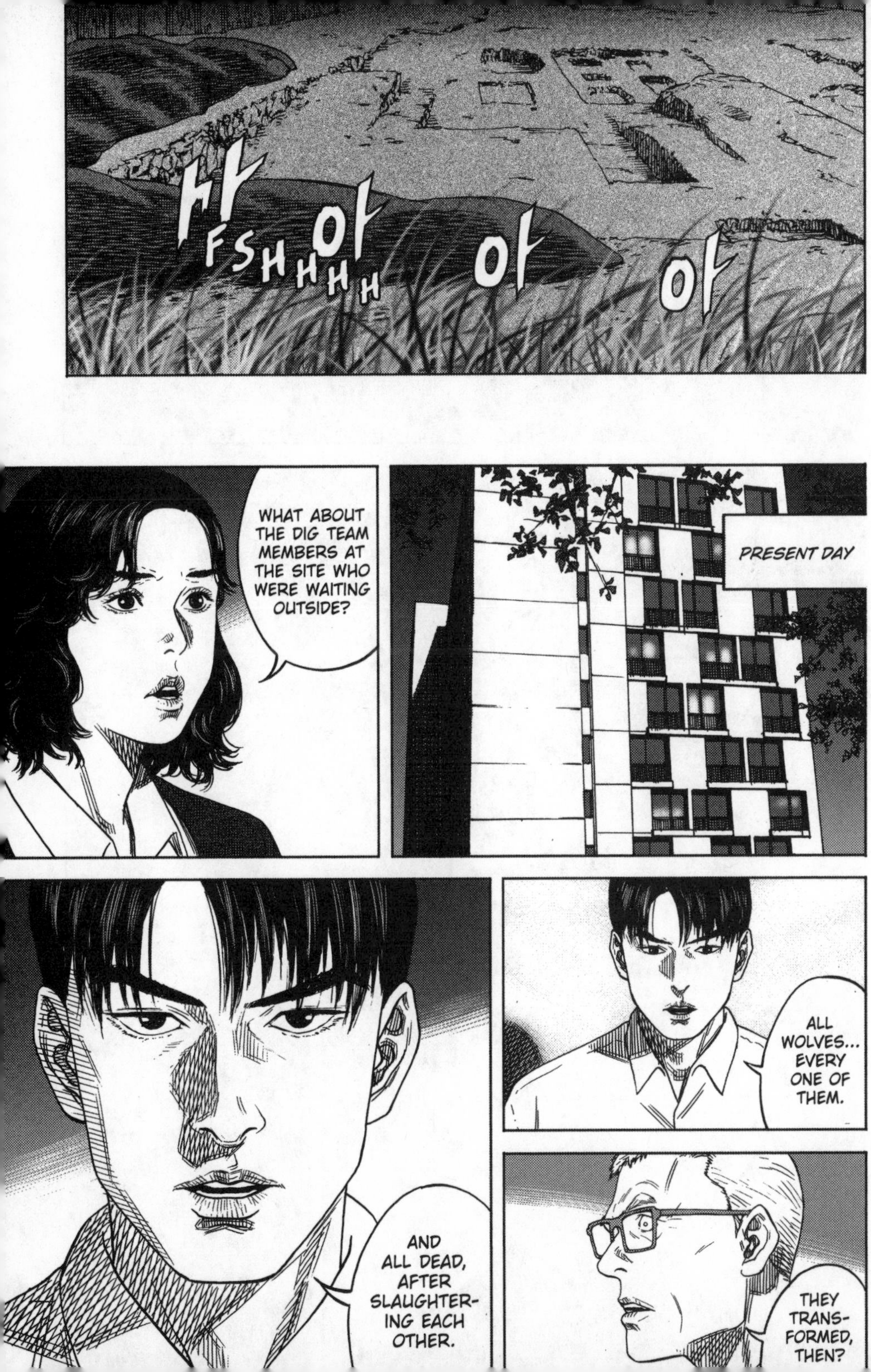
FSHHHH
PRESENT DAY
WHAT ABOUT THE DIG TEAM MEMBERS AT THE SITE WHO WERE WAITING OUTSIDE?
ALL WOLVES... EVERY ONE OF THEM.
THEY TRANS-FORMED, THEN?
AND ALL DEAD, AFTER SLAUGHTER-ING EACH OTHER.

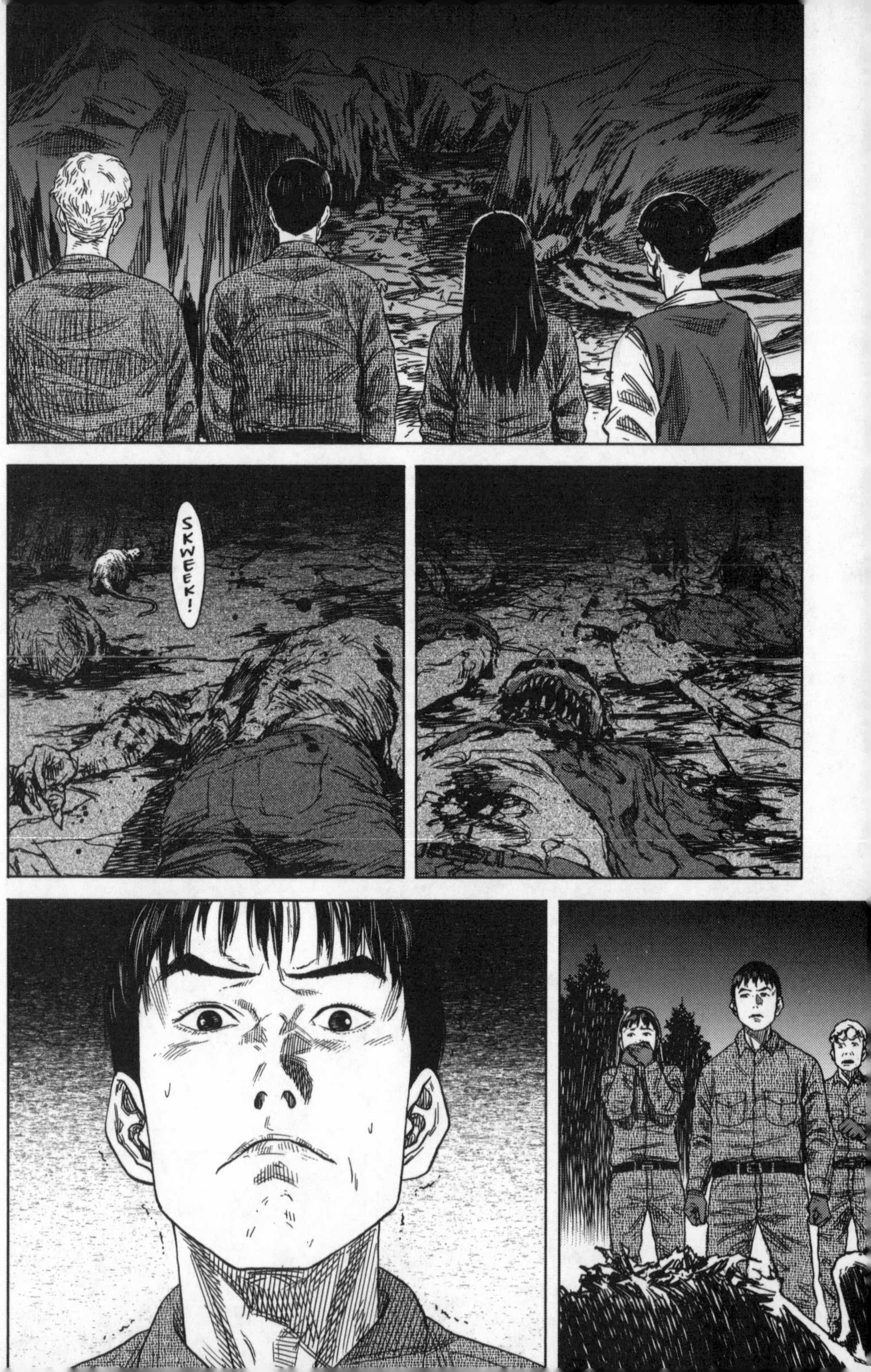
SKWEEK!

KING OF EDEN

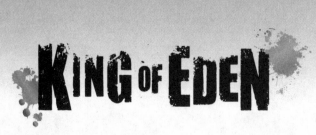

KING OF EDEN

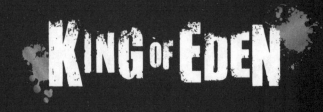

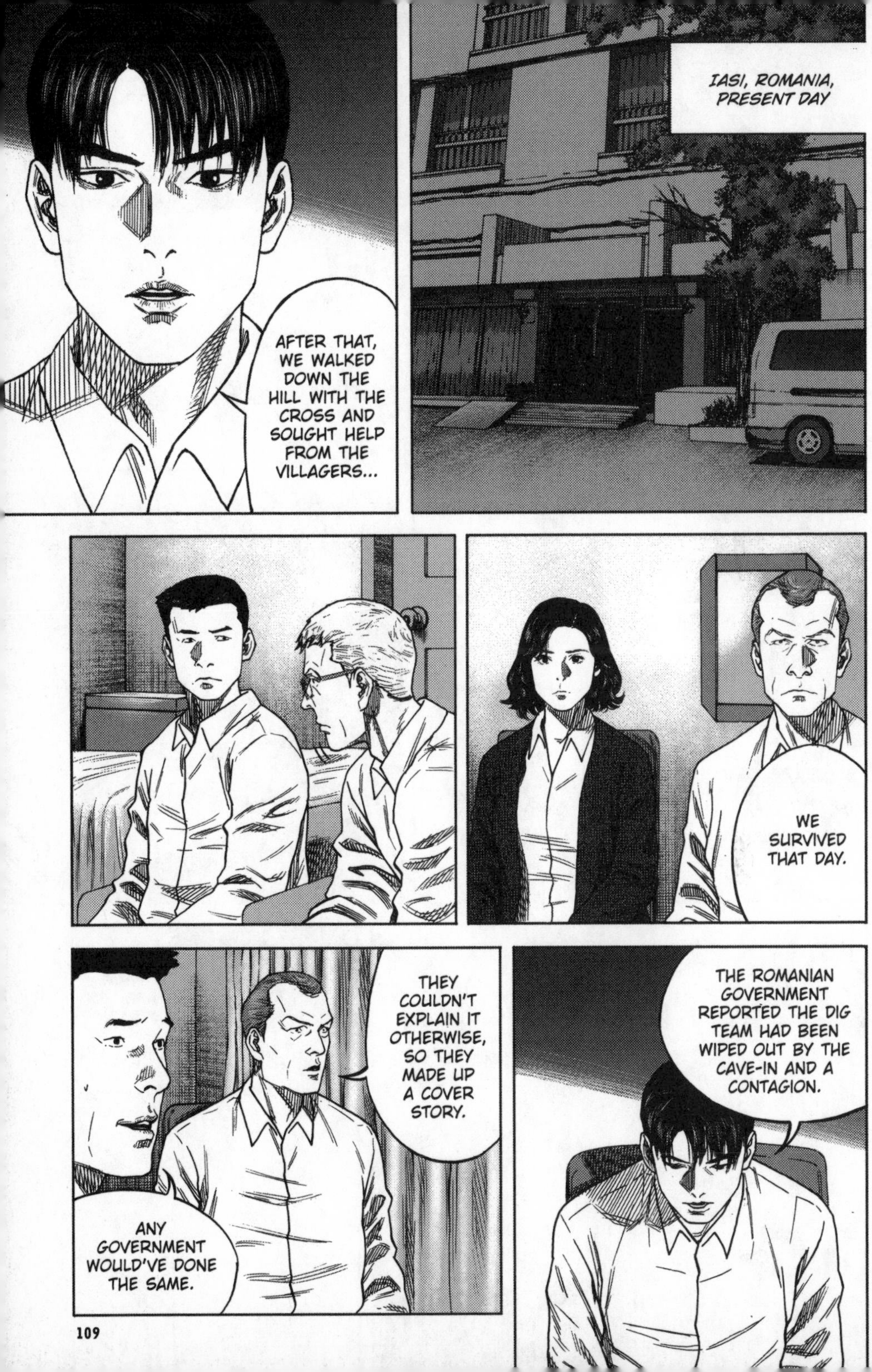
IASI, ROMANIA, PRESENT DAY
AFTER THAT, WE WALKED DOWN THE HILL WITH THE CROSS AND SOUGHT HELP FROM THE VILLAGERS...
WE SURVIVED THAT DAY.
THE ROMANIAN GOVERNMENT REPORTED THE DIG TEAM HAD BEEN WIPED OUT BY THE CAVE-IN AND A CONTAGION.
THEY COULDN'T EXPLAIN IT OTHERWISE, SO THEY MADE UP A COVER STORY.
ANY GOVERNMENT WOULD'VE DONE THE SAME.

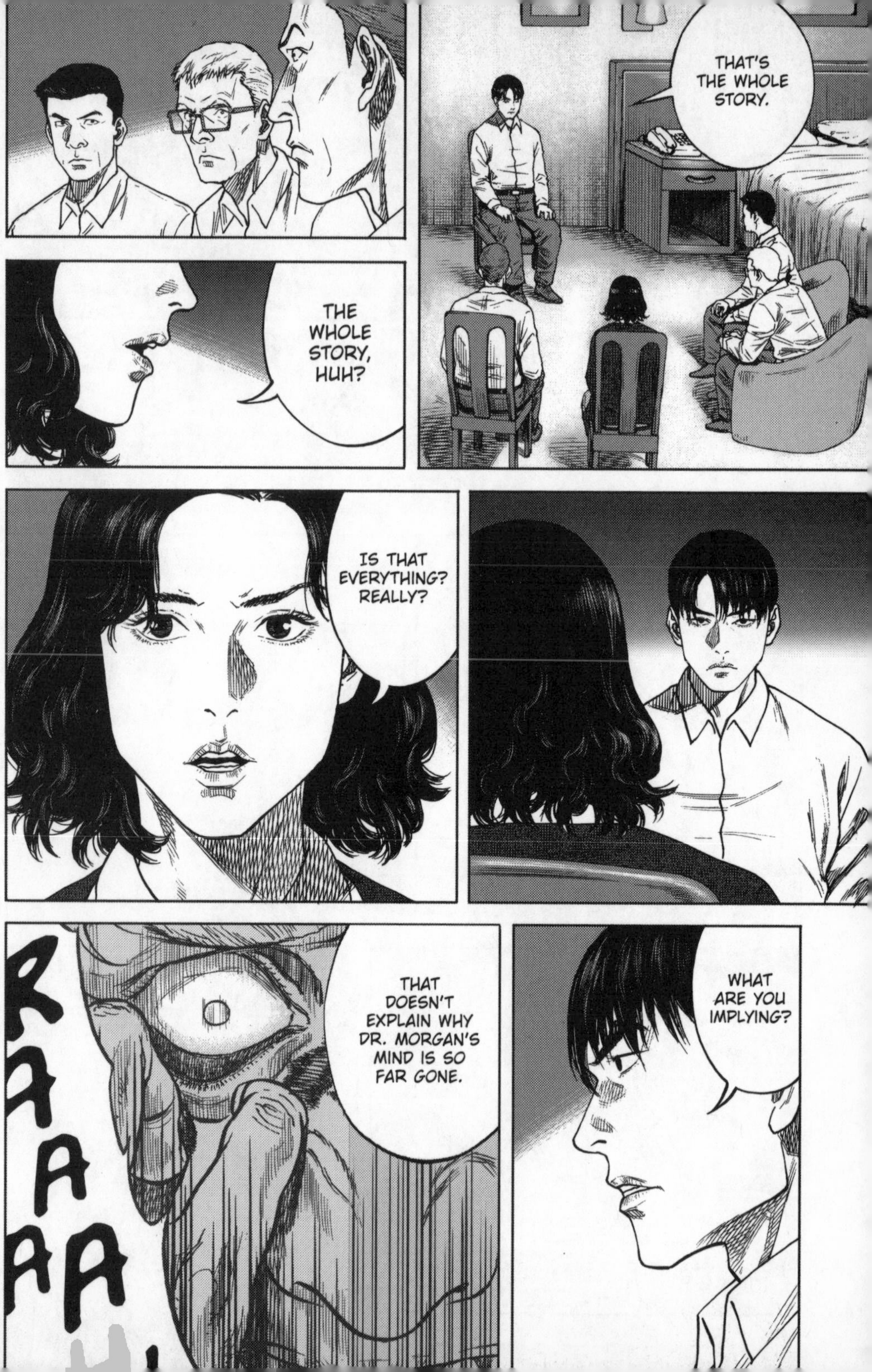
THAT'S THE WHOLE STORY.
THE WHOLE STORY, HUH?
IS THAT EVERYTHING? REALLY?
WHAT ARE YOU IMPLYING?
THAT DOESN'T EXPLAIN WHY DR. MORGAN'S MIND IS SO FAR GONE.
RAAAA

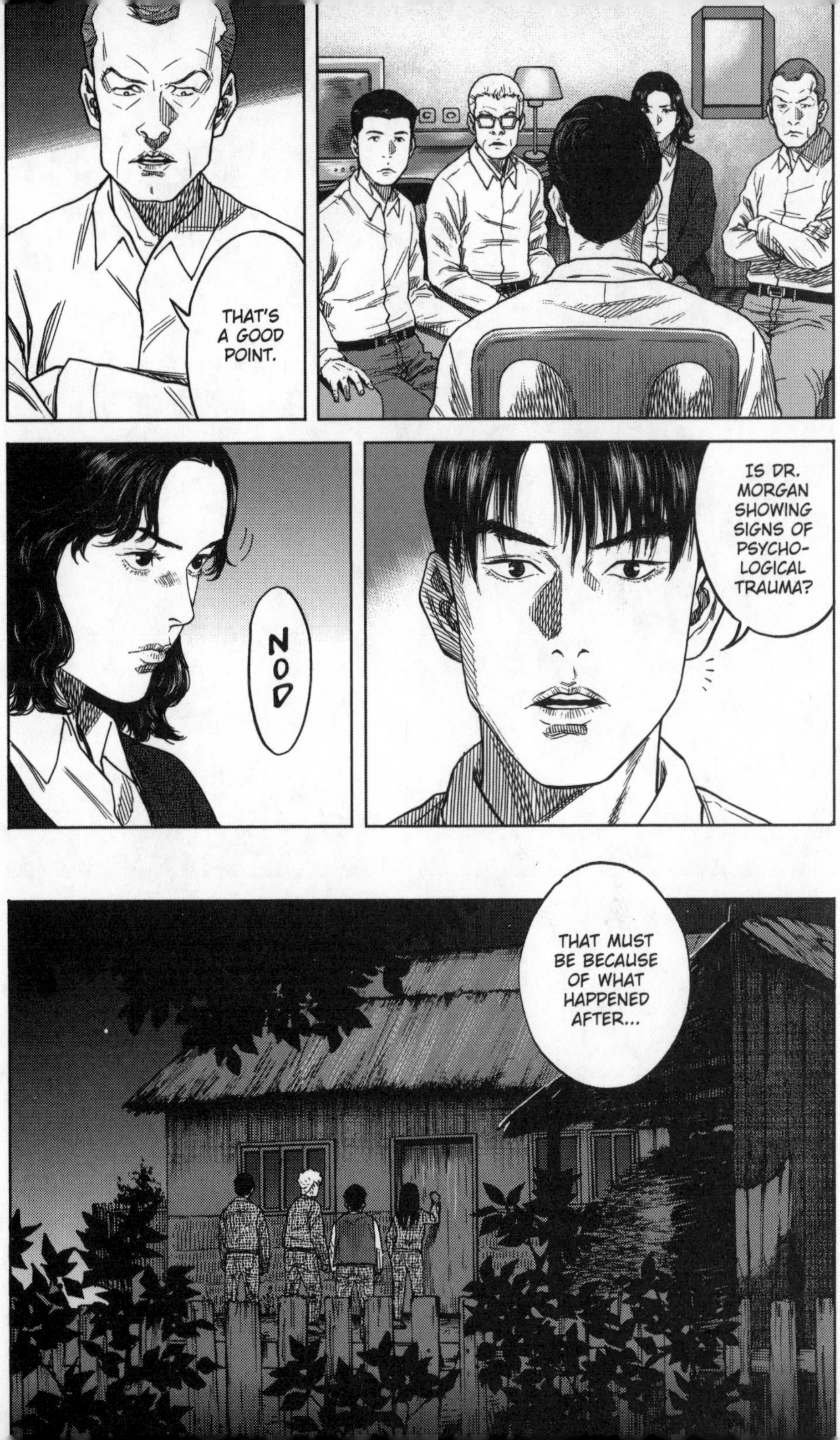
THAT'S A GOOD POINT.
IS DR. MORGAN SHOWING SIGNS OF PSYCHOLOGICAL TRAUMA?
NOD
THAT MUST BE BECAUSE OF WHAT HAPPENED AFTER...

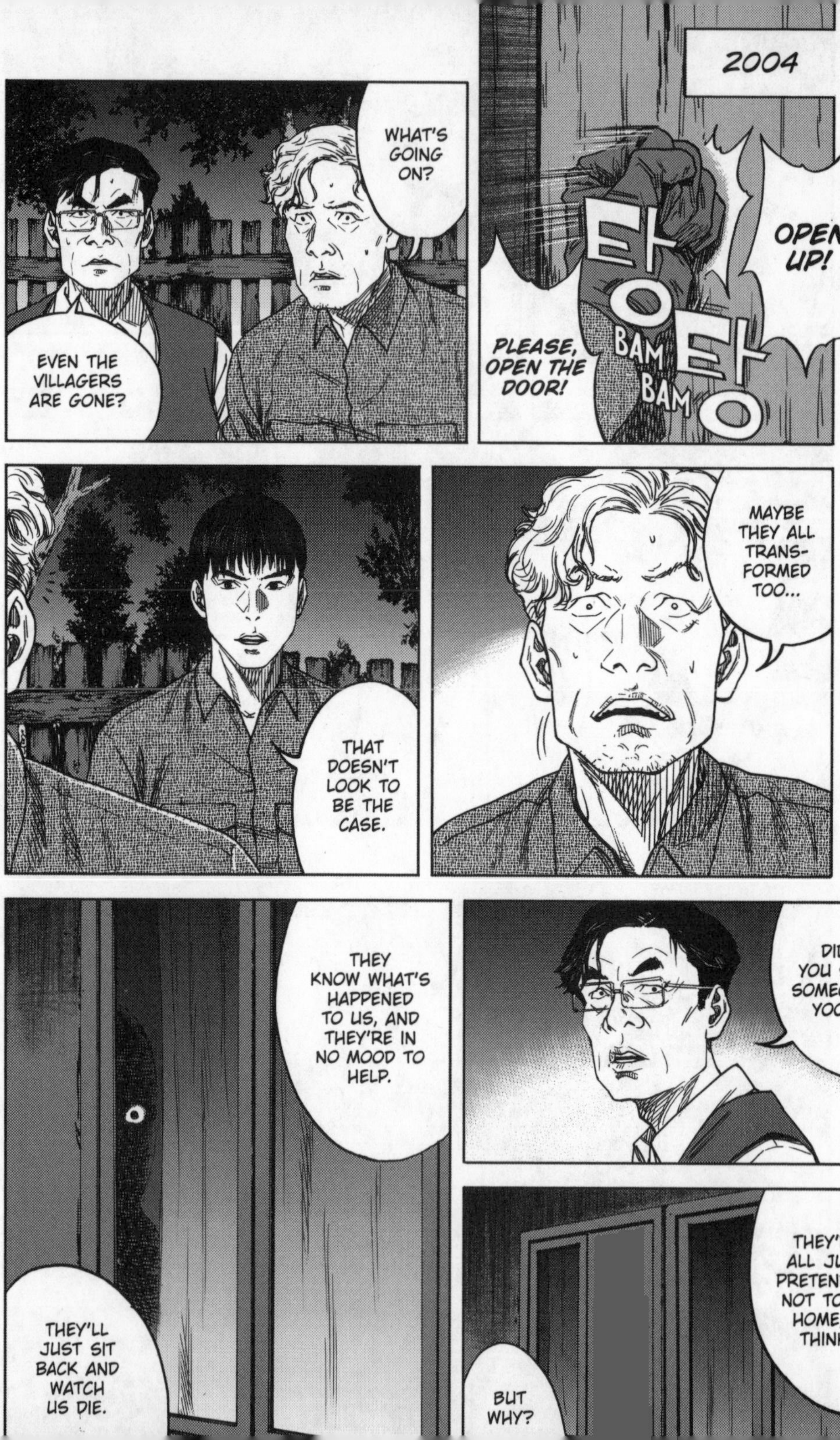
2004
OPEN UP!
탕
BAM
탕
BAM
PLEASE, OPEN THE DOOR!
WHAT'S GOING ON?
EVEN THE VILLAGERS ARE GONE?
MAYBE THEY ALL TRANS-FORMED TOO...
THAT DOESN'T LOOK TO BE THE CASE.
DID YOU SEE SOMEONE, YOO?
THEY'RE ALL JUST PRETENDING NOT TO BE HOME, I THINK.
BUT WHY?
THEY KNOW WHAT'S HAPPENED TO US, AND THEY'RE IN NO MOOD TO HELP.
THEY'LL JUST SIT BACK AND WATCH US DIE.

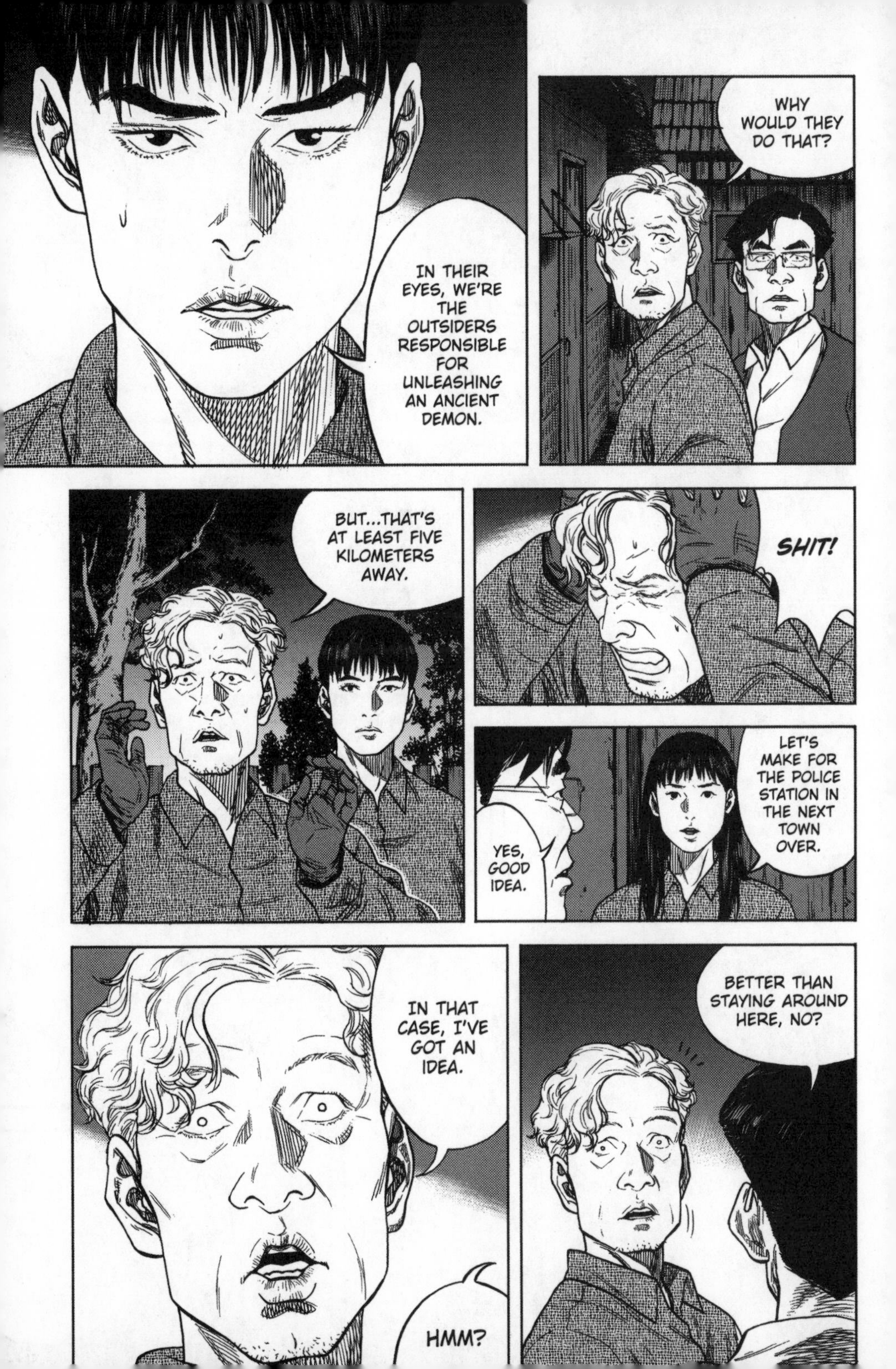
WHY WOULD THEY DO THAT?
IN THEIR EYES, WE'RE THE OUTSIDERS RESPONSIBLE FOR UNLEASHING AN ANCIENT DEMON.
SHIT!
LET'S MAKE FOR THE POLICE STATION IN THE NEXT TOWN OVER.
YES, GOOD IDEA.
BUT...THAT'S AT LEAST FIVE KILOMETERS AWAY.
BETTER THAN STAYING AROUND HERE, NO?
IN THAT CASE, I'VE GOT AN IDEA.
HMM?

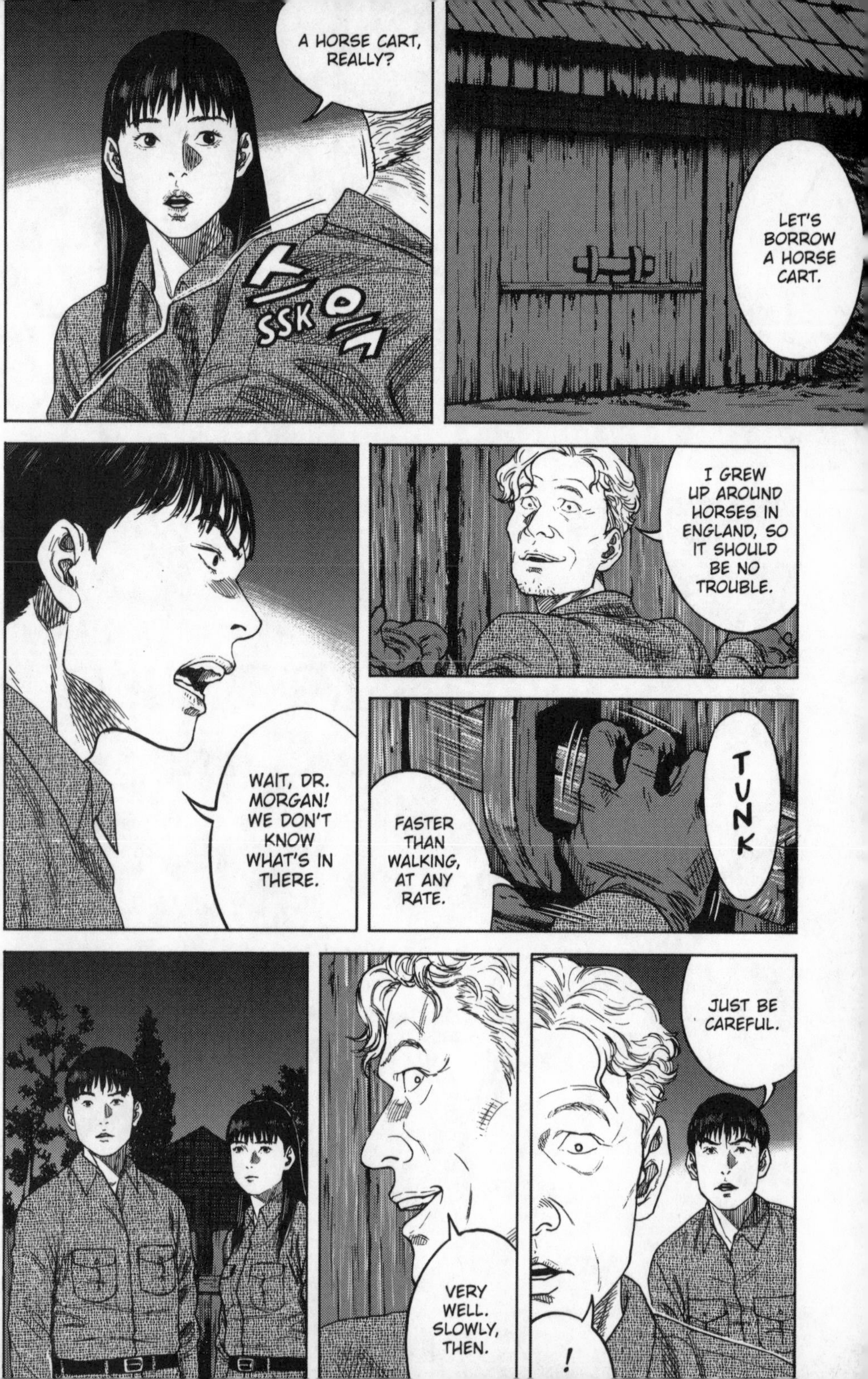
LET'S BORROW A HORSE CART.
A HORSE CART, REALLY?
SSK
I GREW UP AROUND HORSES IN ENGLAND, SO IT SHOULD BE NO TROUBLE.
TUNK
FASTER THAN WALKING, AT ANY RATE.
WAIT, DR. MORGAN! WE DON'T KNOW WHAT'S IN THERE.
JUST BE CAREFUL.
!
VERY WELL. SLOWLY, THEN.

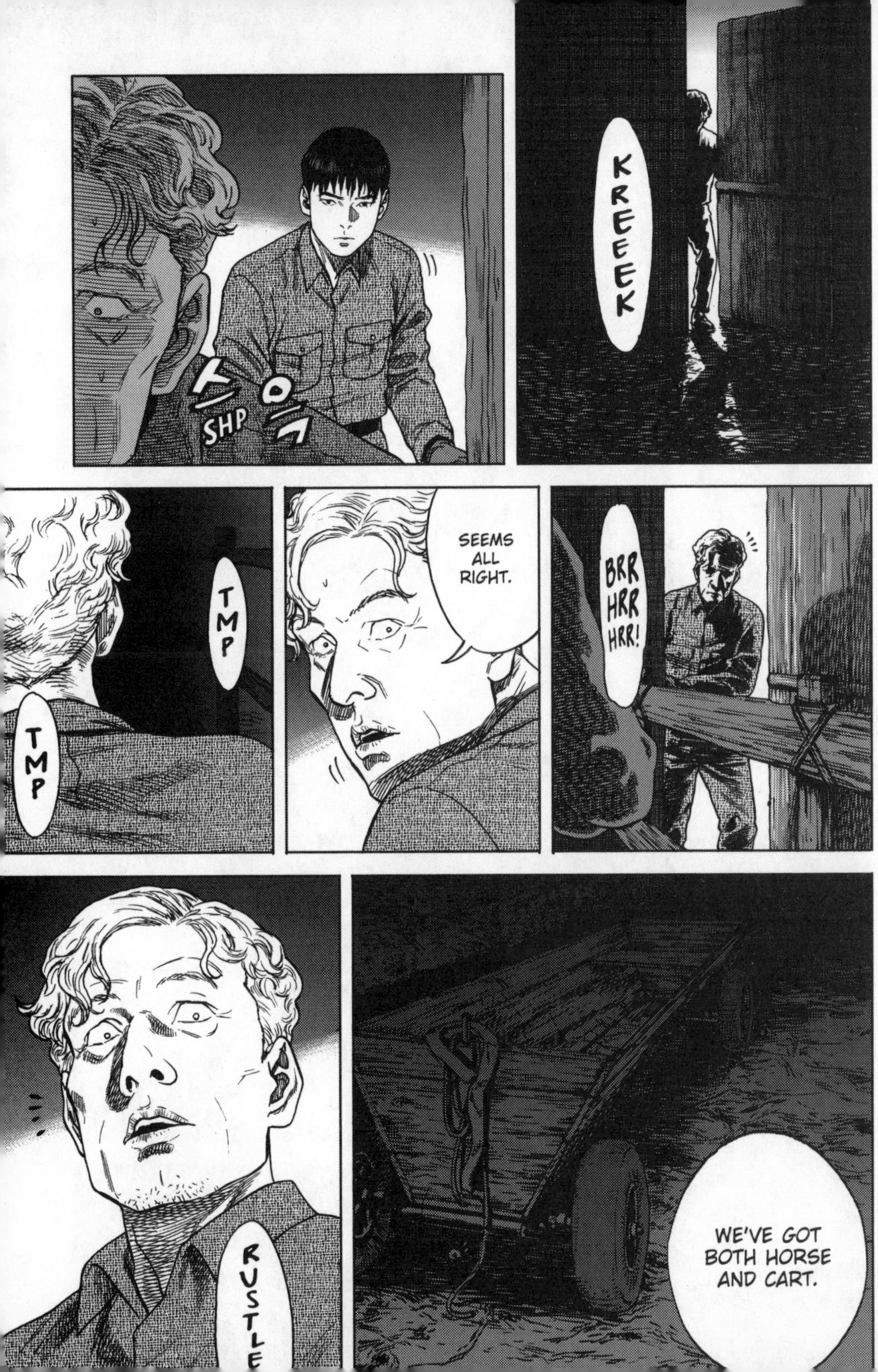
KREEEK
SHP
BRR HRR HRR!
SEEMS ALL RIGHT.
TMP
TMP
WE'VE GOT BOTH HORSE AND CART.
RUSTLE

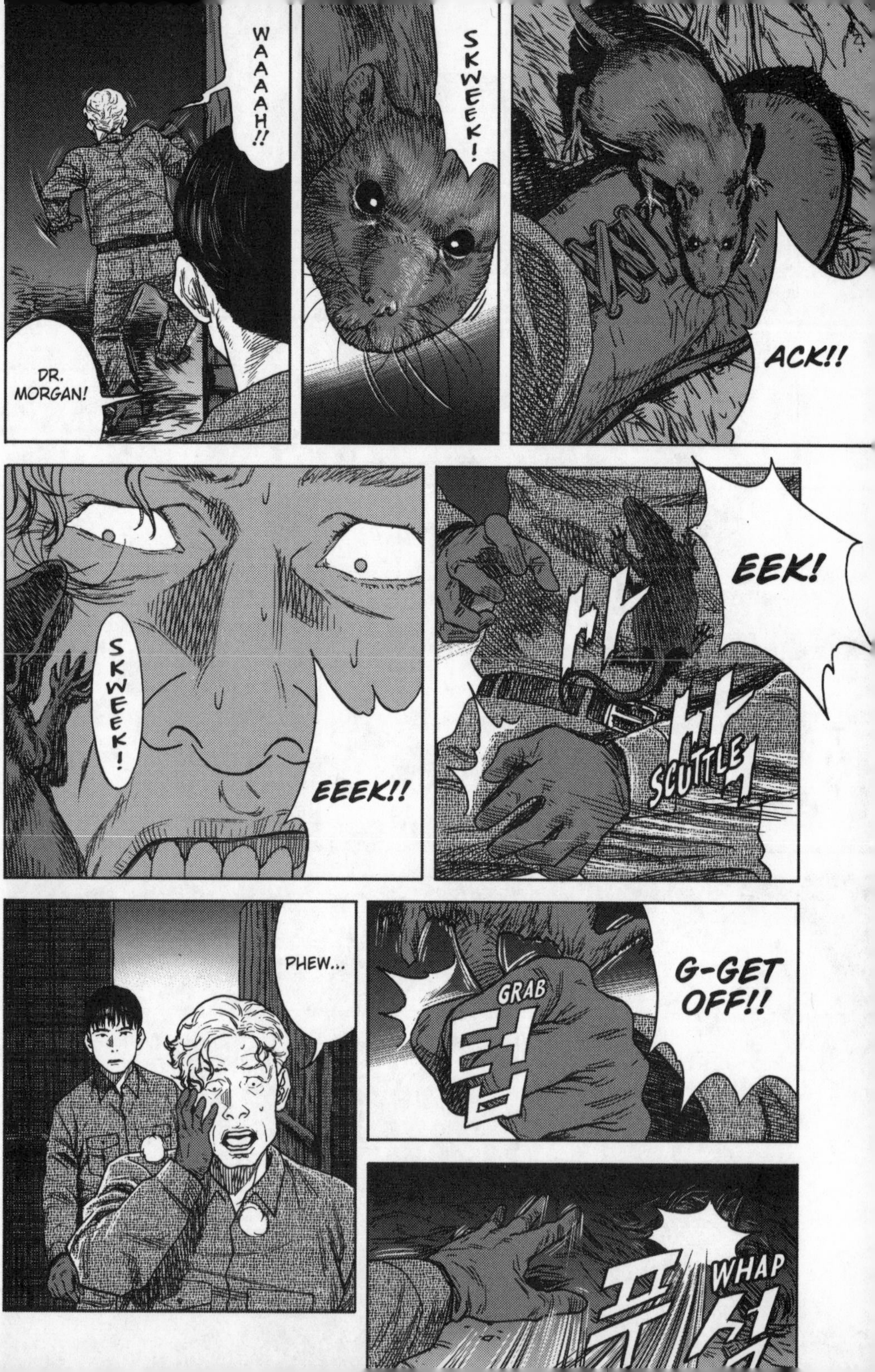
ACK!!
SKWEEK!
WAAAAAH!!
DR. MORGAN!
EEK!
SCUTTLE
SKWEEK!
EEEK!!
G-GET OFF!!
GRAB
텁
WHAP
PHEW...

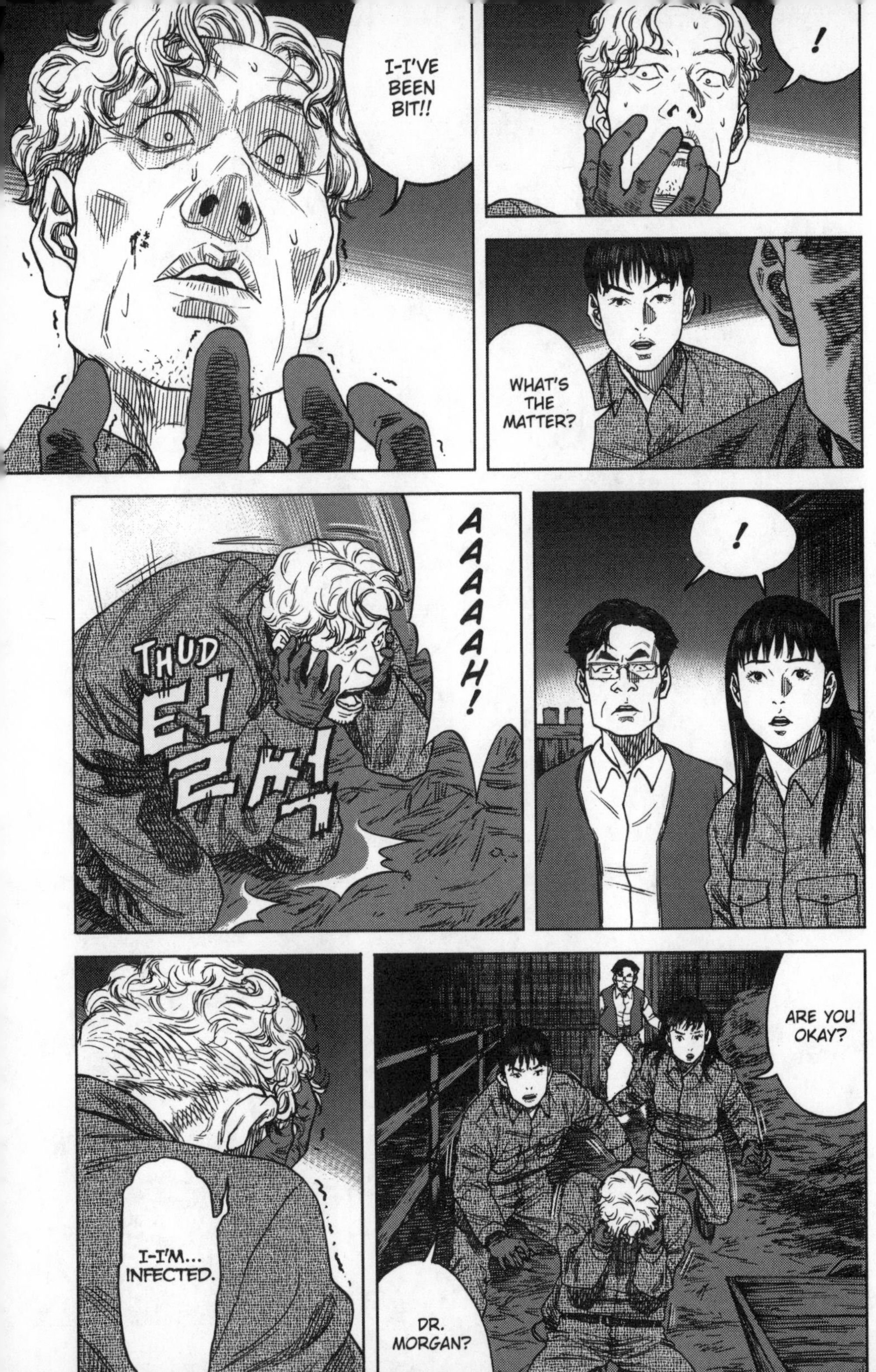
!
WHAT'S THE MATTER?
I-I'VE BEEN BIT!!
!
AAAAAAH!
THUD
털썩
ARE YOU OKAY?
DR. MORGAN?
I-I'M... INFECTED.

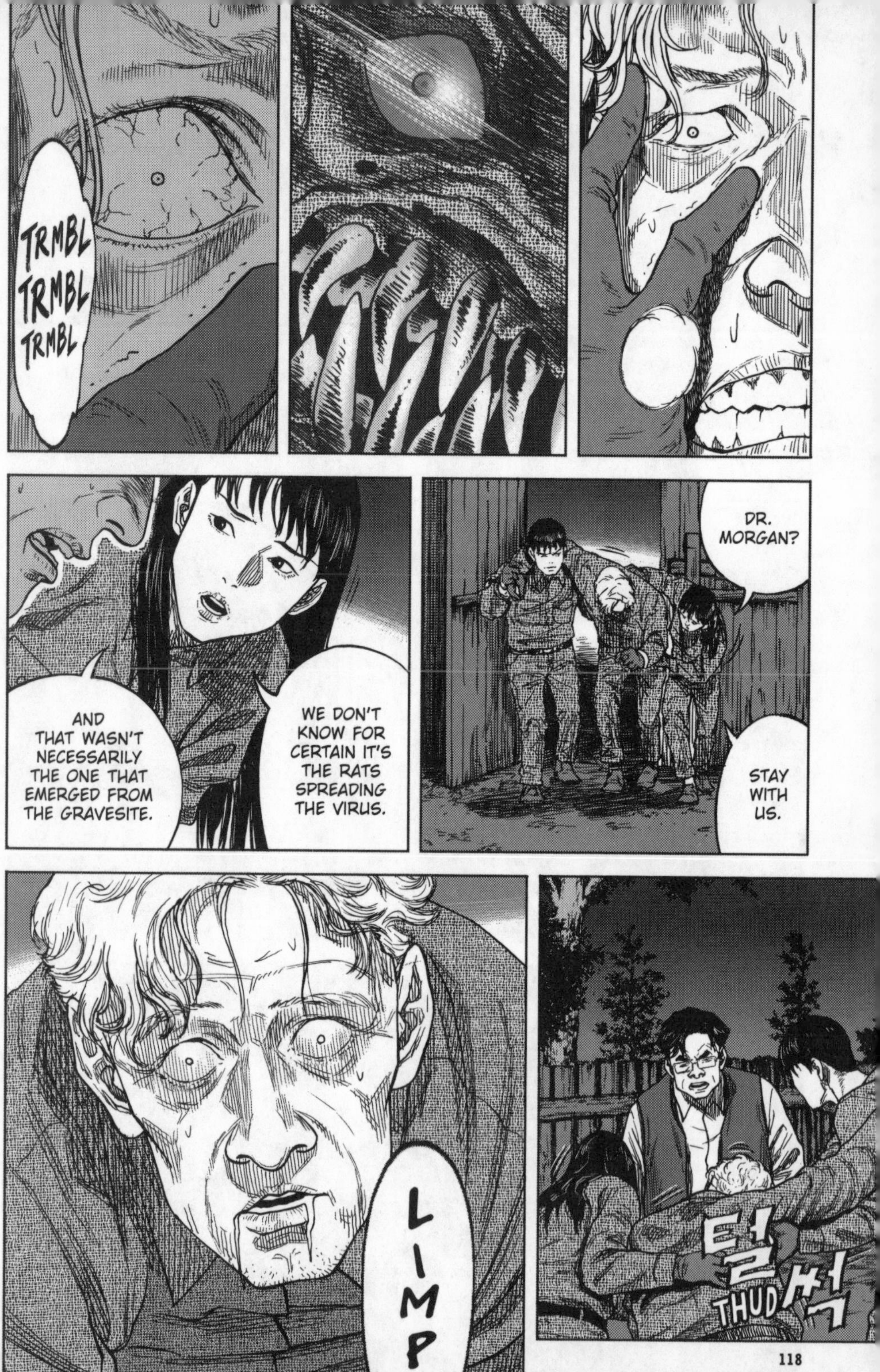
TRMBL TRMBL TRMBL
DR. MORGAN?
STAY WITH US.
WE DON'T KNOW FOR CERTAIN IT'S THE RATS SPREADING THE VIRUS.
AND THAT WASN'T NECESSARILY THE ONE THAT EMERGED FROM THE GRAVESITE.
털썩
THUD
LIMP

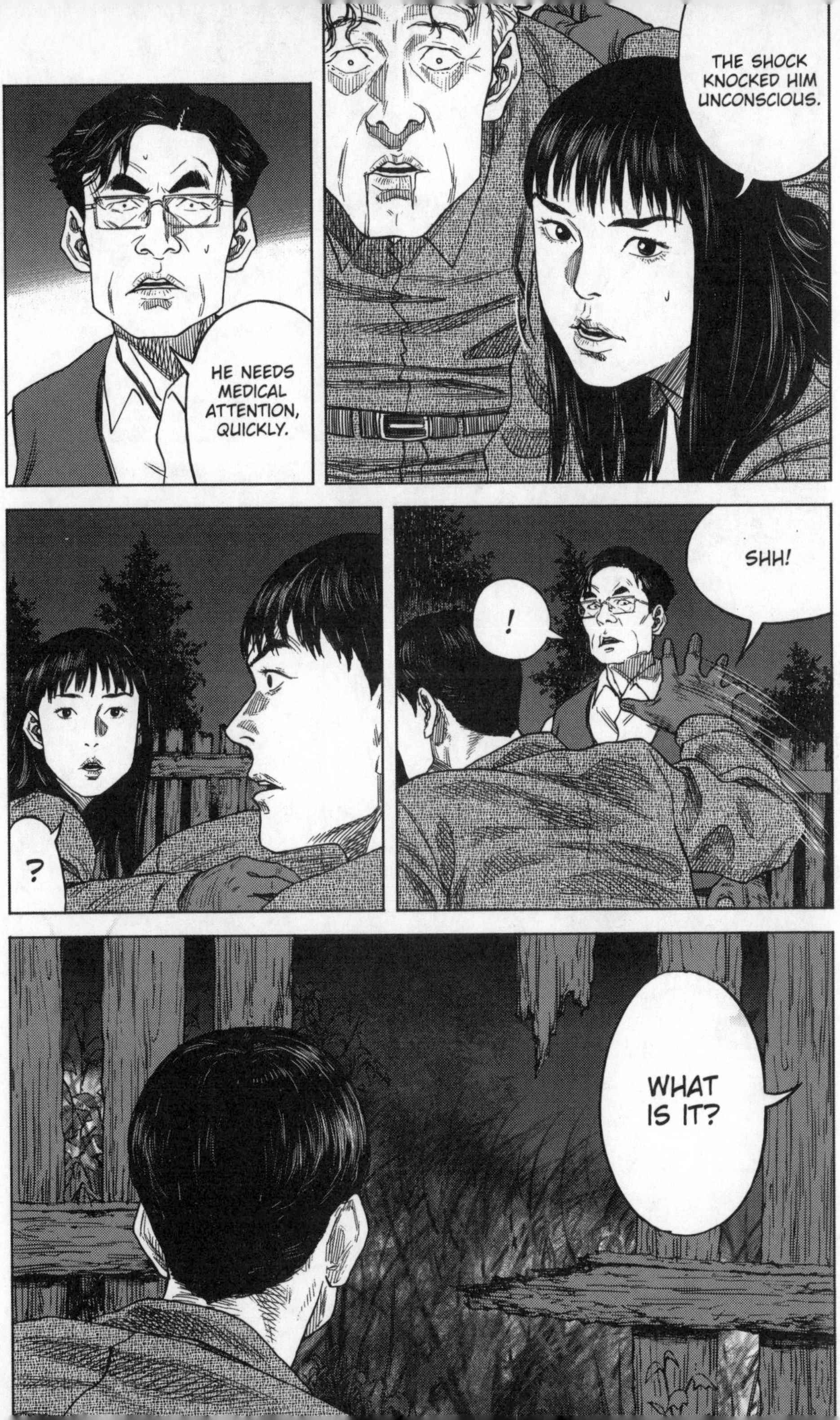
THE SHOCK KNOCKED HIM UNCONSCIOUS.
HE NEEDS MEDICAL ATTENTION, QUICKLY.
SHH!
!
?
WHAT IS IT?

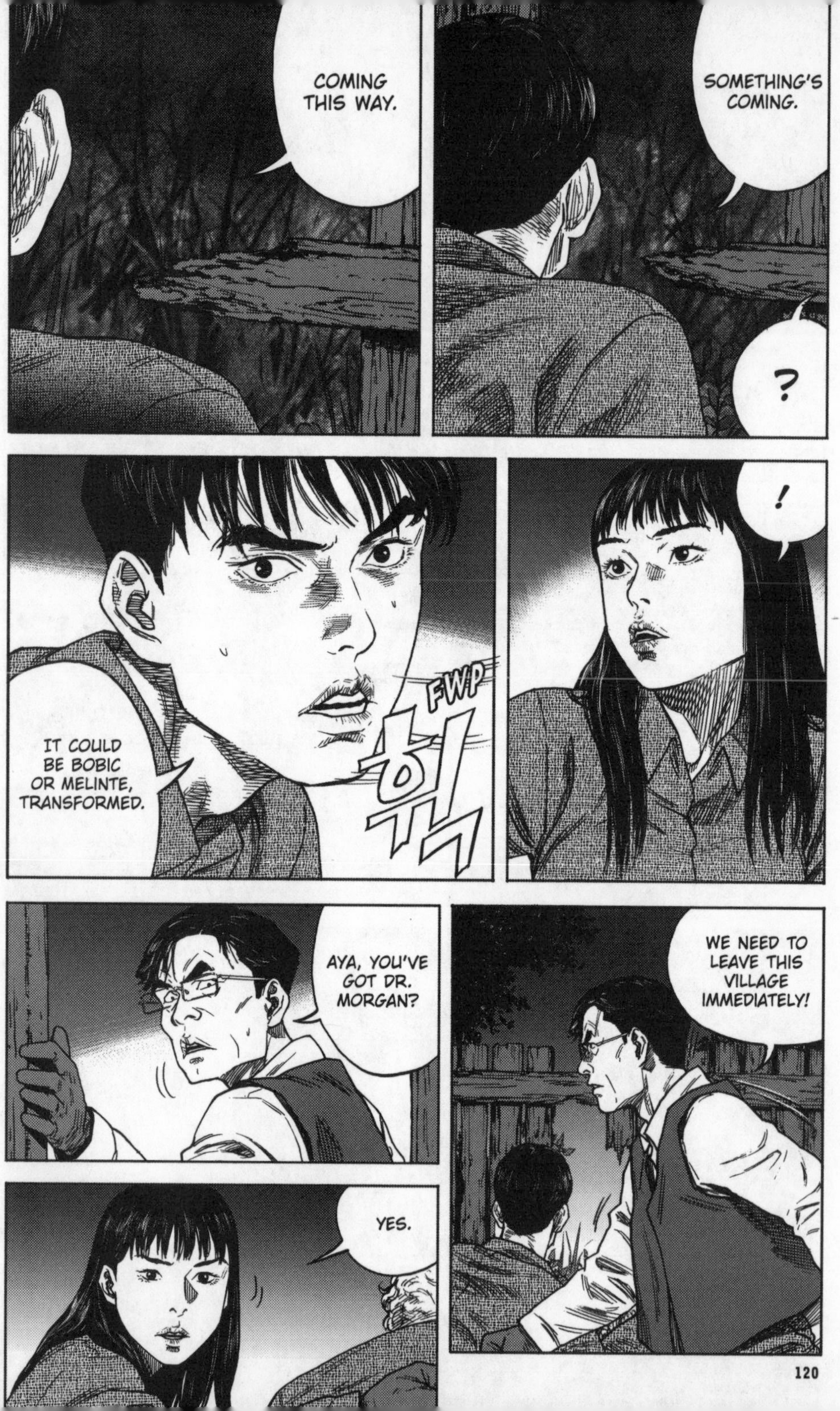
SOMETHING'S COMING.
?
COMING THIS WAY.
!
FWP
휙
IT COULD BE BOBIC OR MELINTE, TRANSFORMED.
WE NEED TO LEAVE THIS VILLAGE IMMEDIATELY!
AYA, YOU'VE GOT DR. MORGAN?
YES.

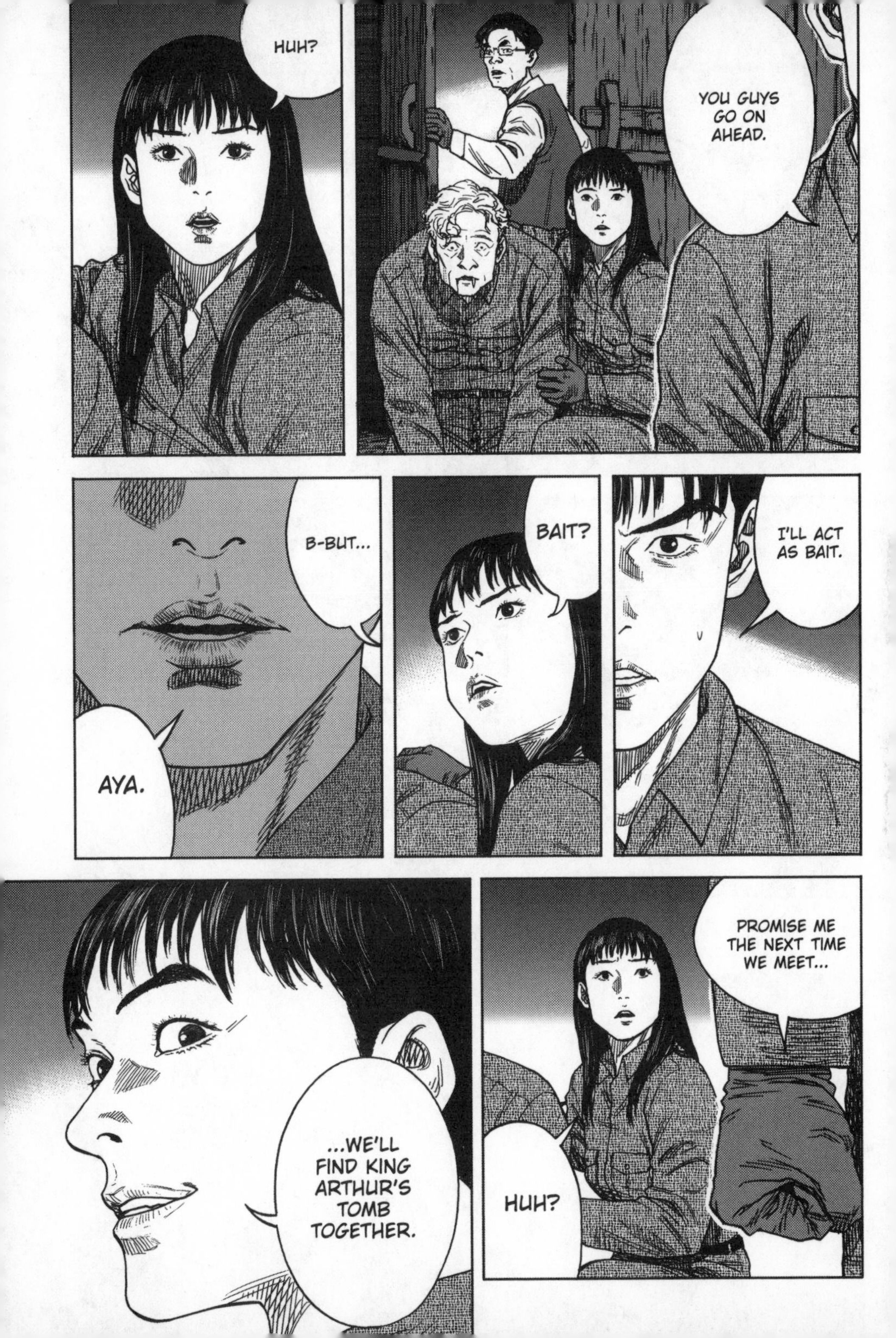
YOU GUYS GO ON AHEAD.
HUH?
I'LL ACT AS BAIT.
BAIT?
B-BUT...
AYA.
PROMISE ME THE NEXT TIME WE MEET...
HUH?
...WE'LL FIND KING ARTHUR'S TOMB TOGETHER.

I PROMISE.

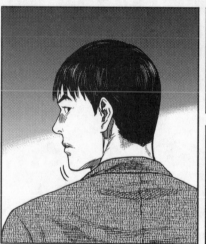

SHF

YOO.

WE WILL MEET AGAIN.

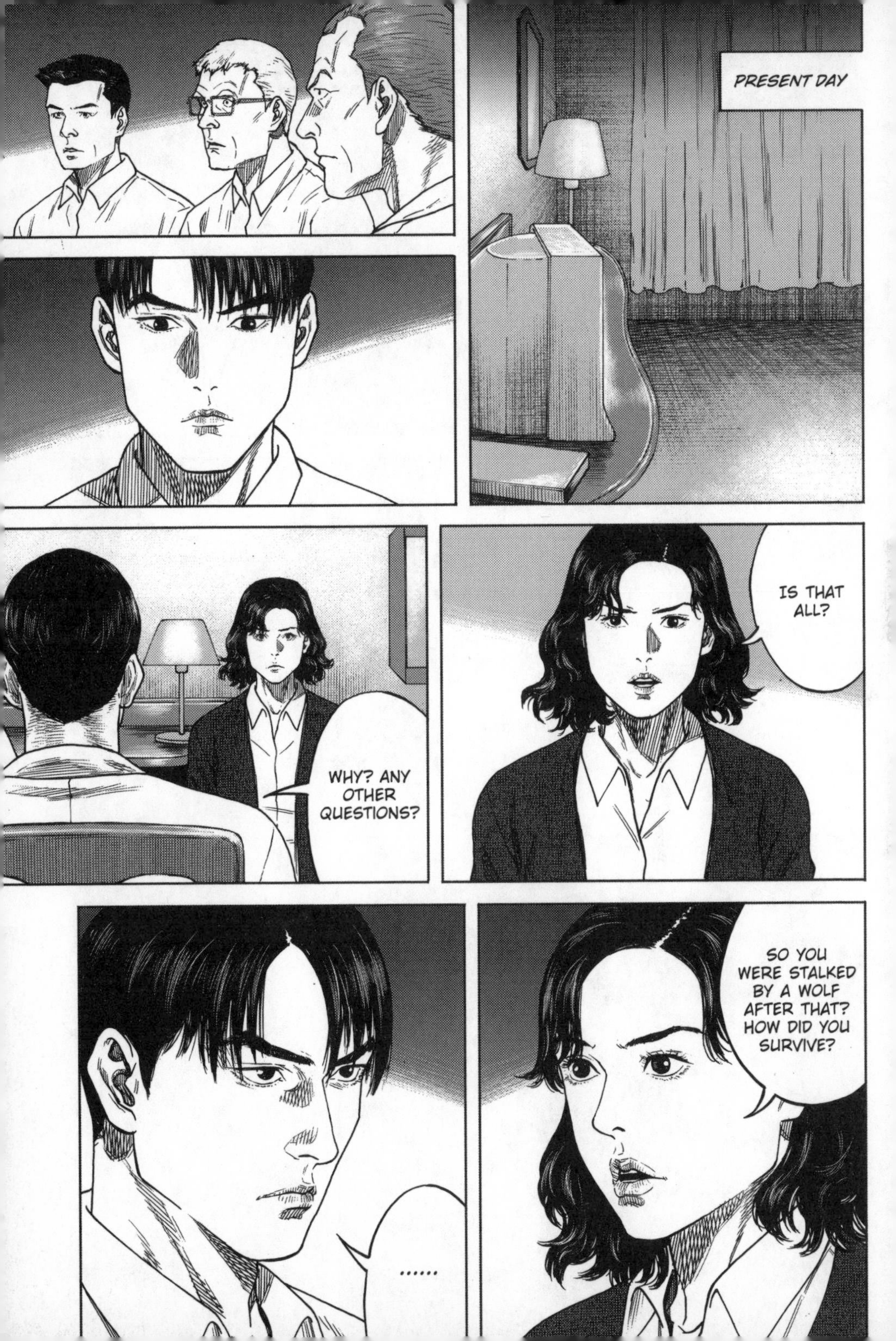
PRESENT DAY
IS THAT ALL?
WHY? ANY OTHER QUESTIONS?
SO YOU WERE STALKED BY A WOLF AFTER THAT? HOW DID YOU SURVIVE?
......

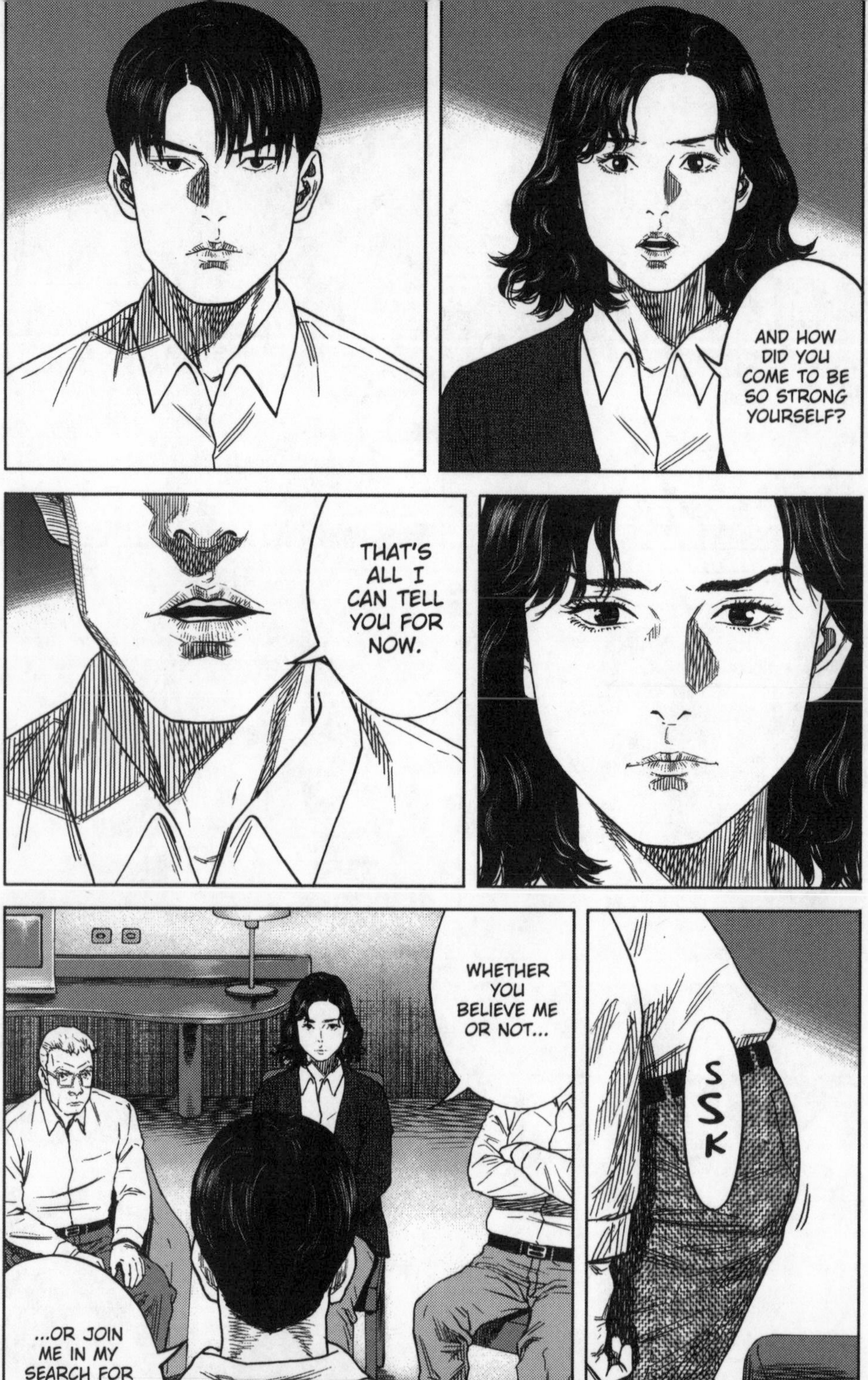
AND HOW DID YOU COME TO BE SO STRONG YOURSELF?
THAT'S ALL I CAN TELL YOU FOR NOW.
SSK
WHETHER YOU BELIEVE ME OR NOT...
...OR JOIN ME IN MY SEARCH FOR THE WOLF KING......

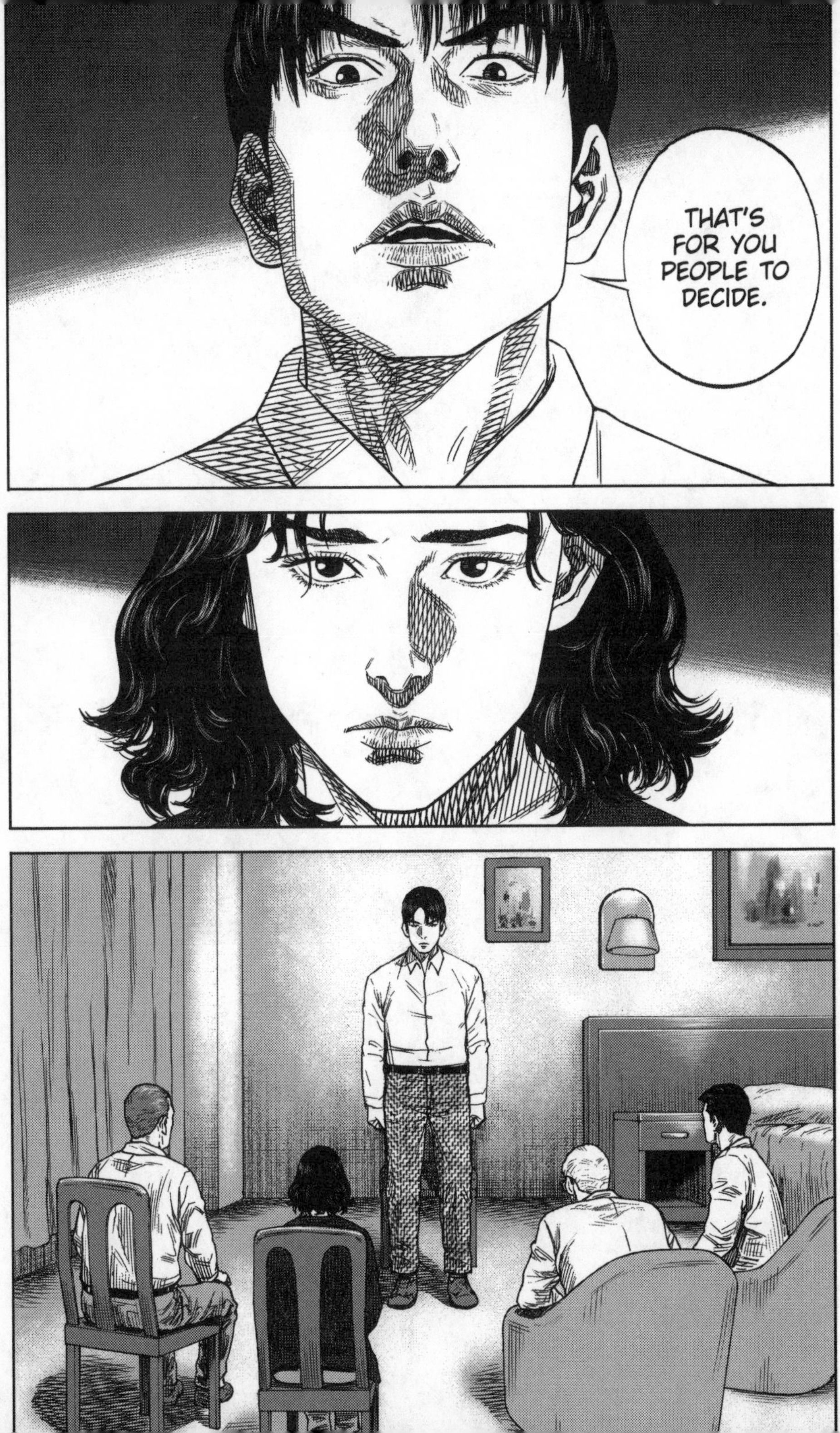
THAT'S FOR YOU PEOPLE TO DECIDE.

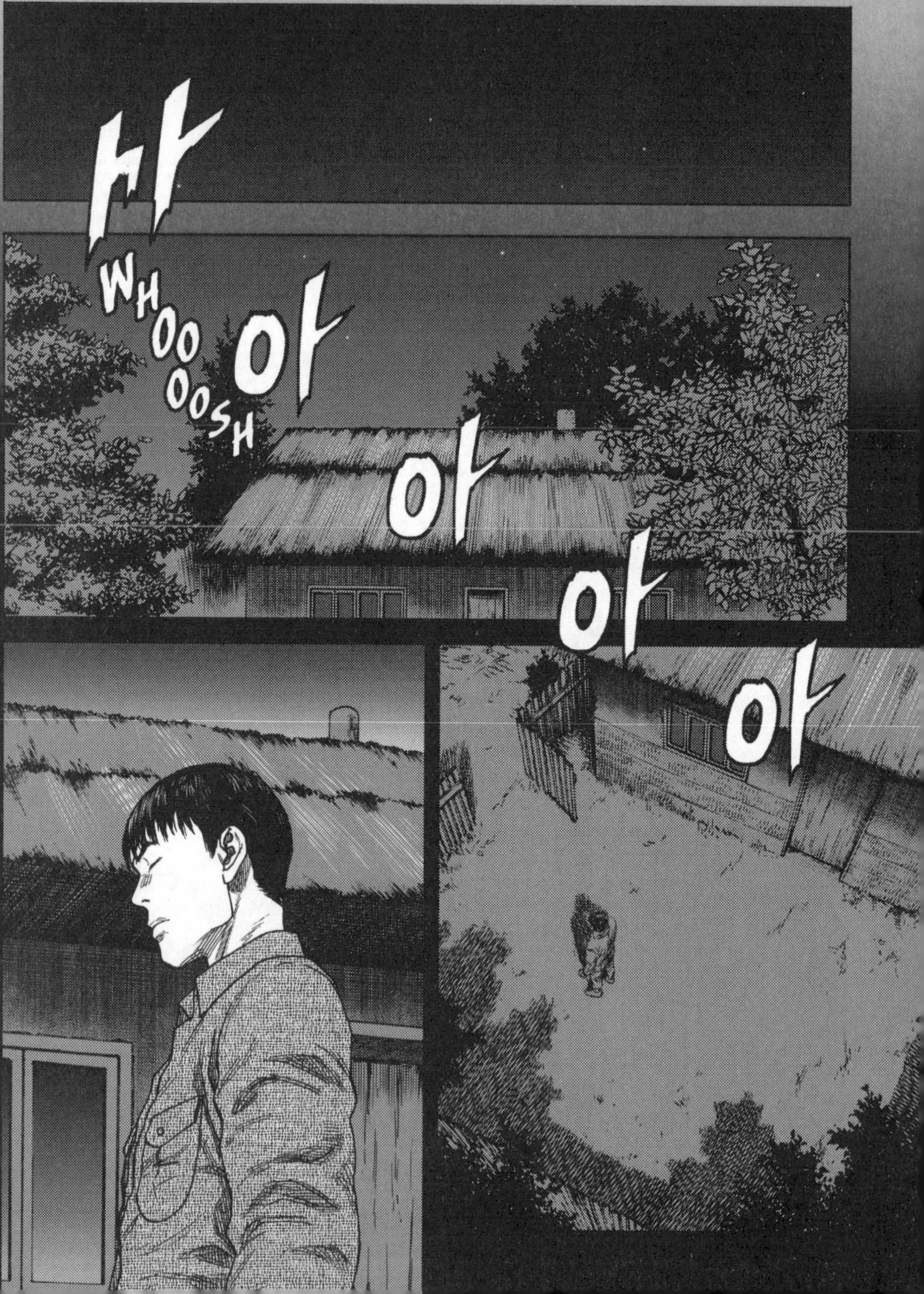
WHOOOOSH
아아아아

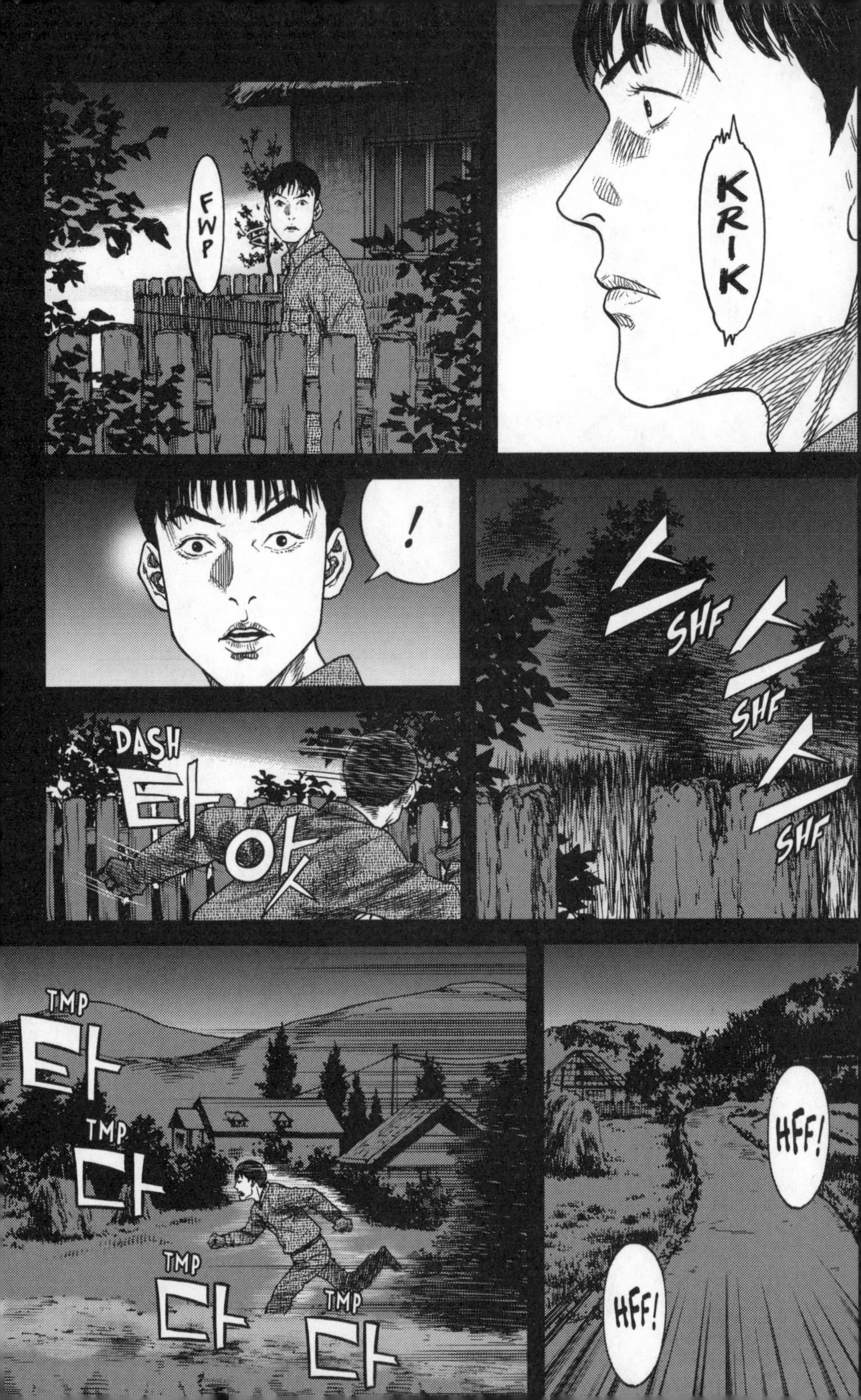
KRIK
FWP
SHF
SHF
SHF
!
DASH
타앗
HFF!
HFF!
TMP
타
TMP
다
TMP
다
TMP
다

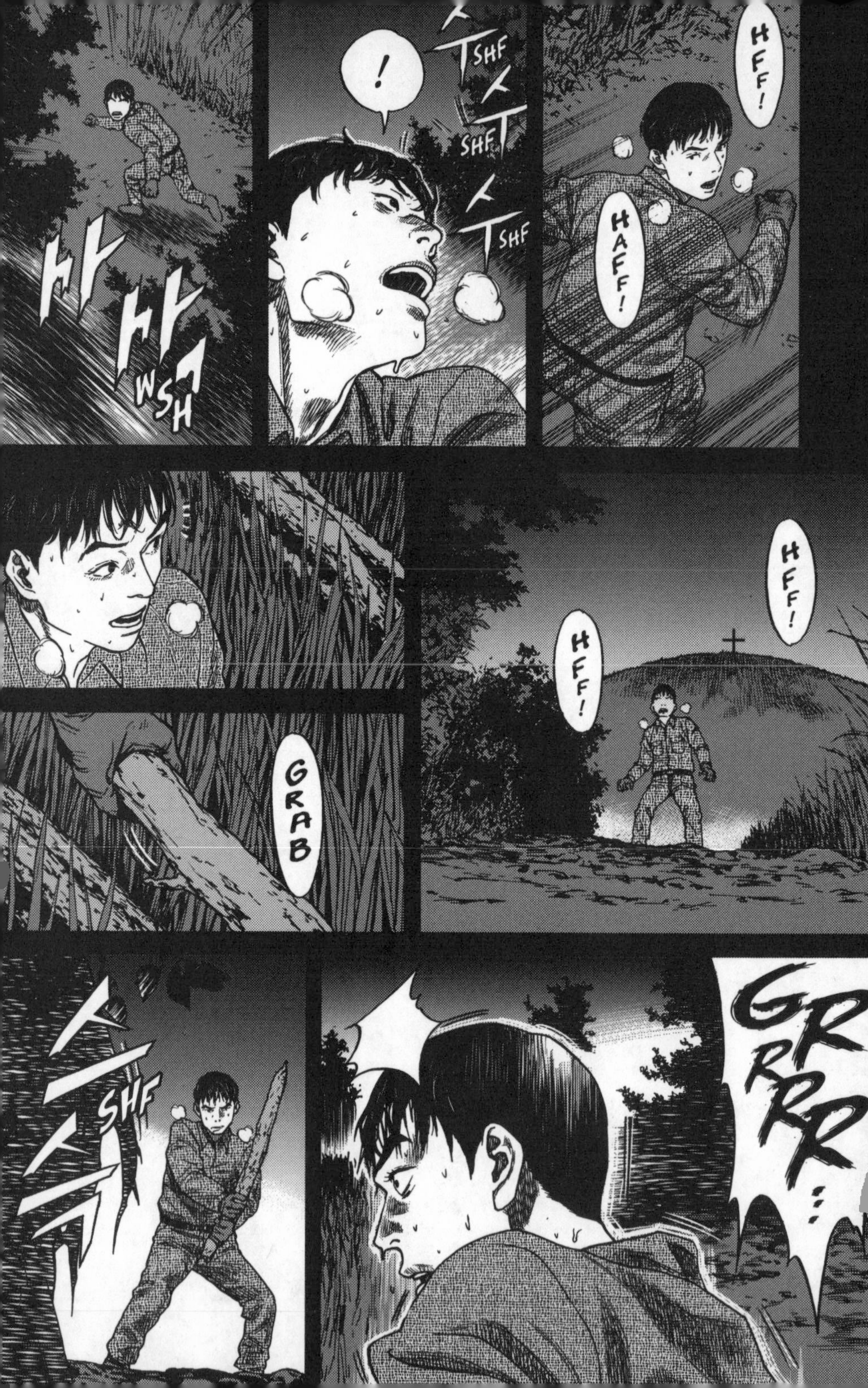
HFF!
HAFF!
!
SHF
SHF
SHF
WSH
HFF!
HFF!
GRAB
GRRRR...
SHF

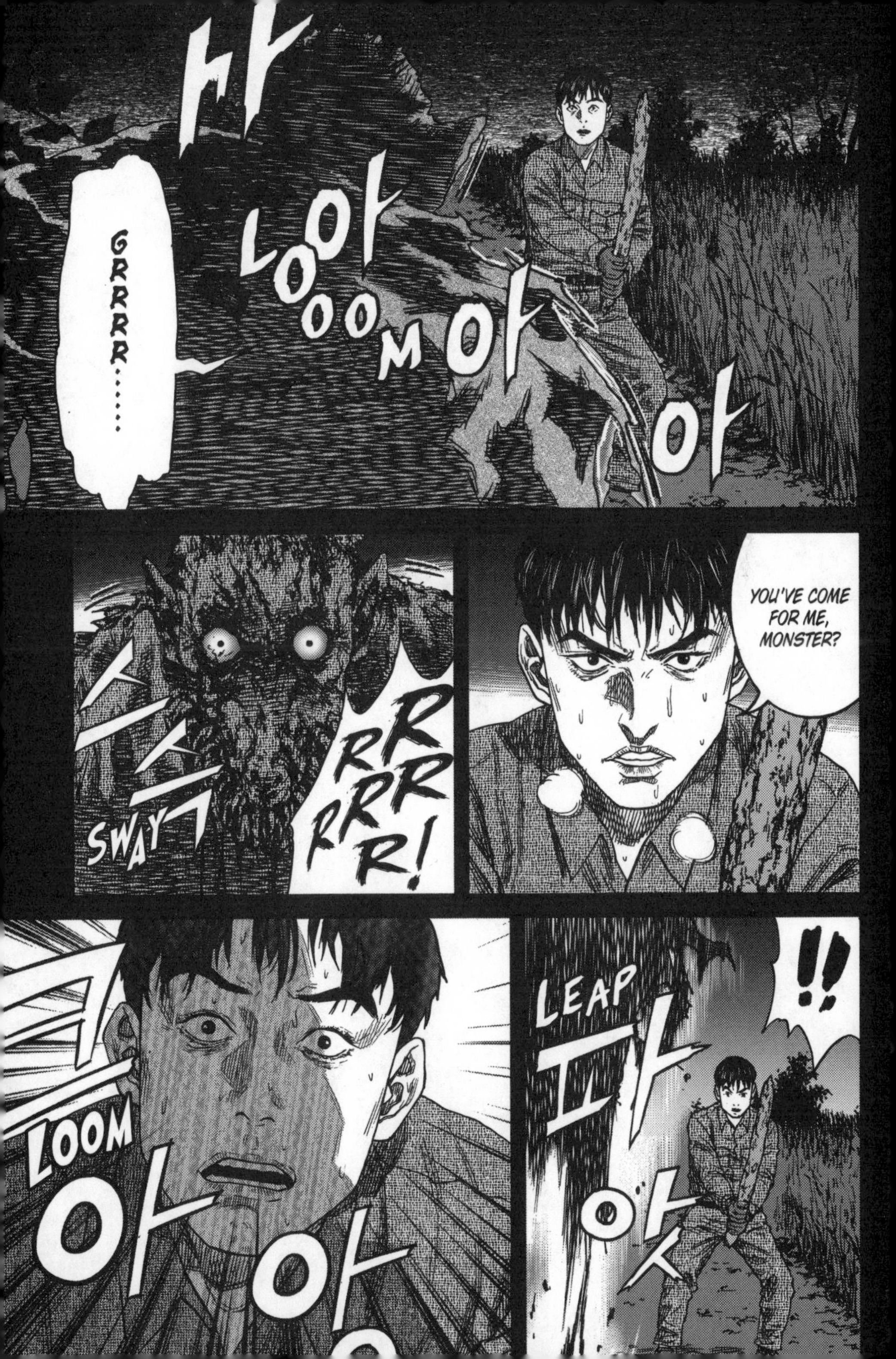
LOOOOOM
GRRRRR......
YOU'VE COME FOR ME, MONSTER?
RRRRRRR!
SWAY
!!
LEAP
LOOM

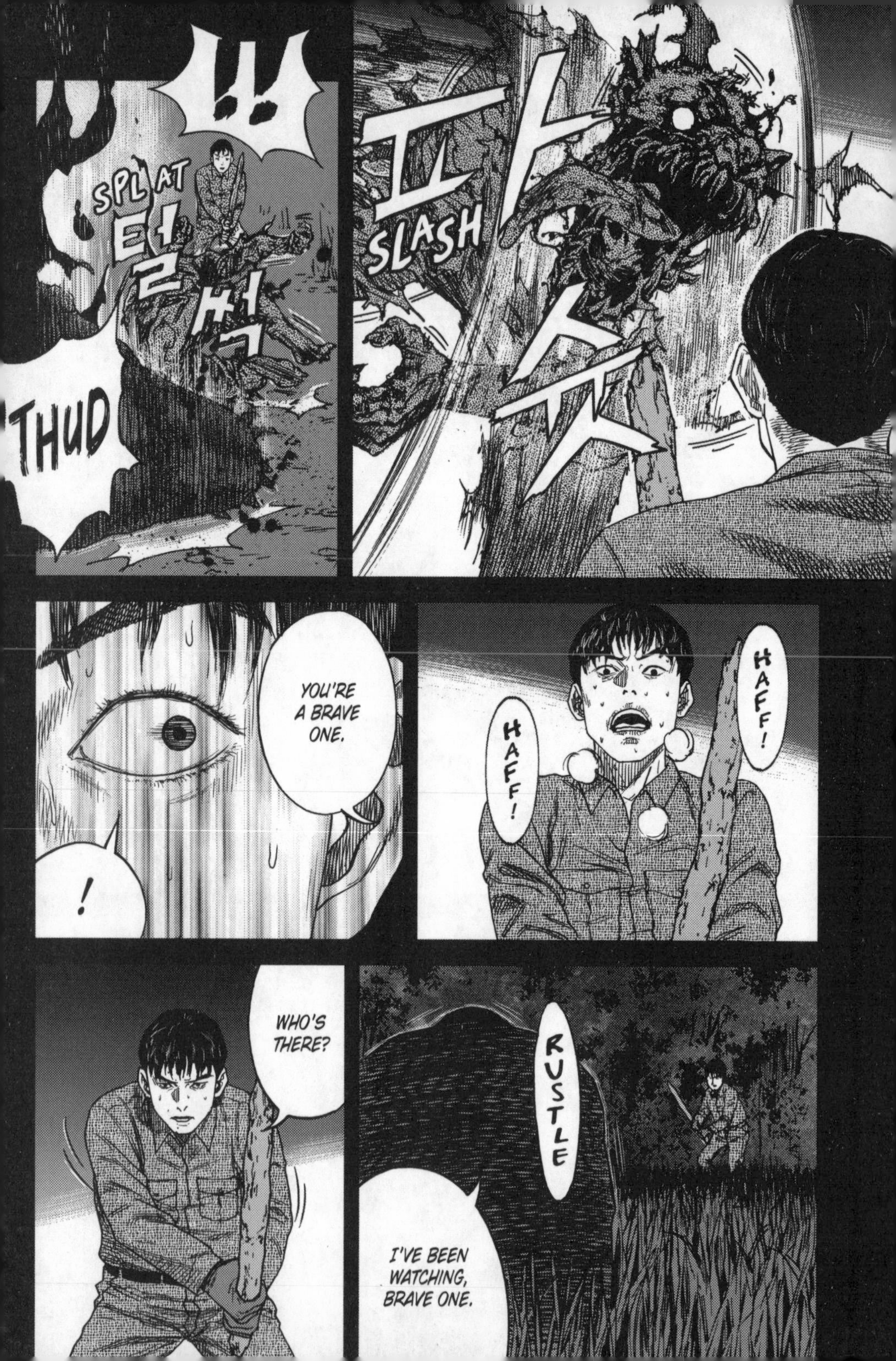
SLASH
!!
SPLAT
털썩
THUD
HAFF!
HAFF!
YOU'RE A BRAVE ONE.
!
RUSTLE
I'VE BEEN WATCHING, BRAVE ONE.
WHO'S THERE?

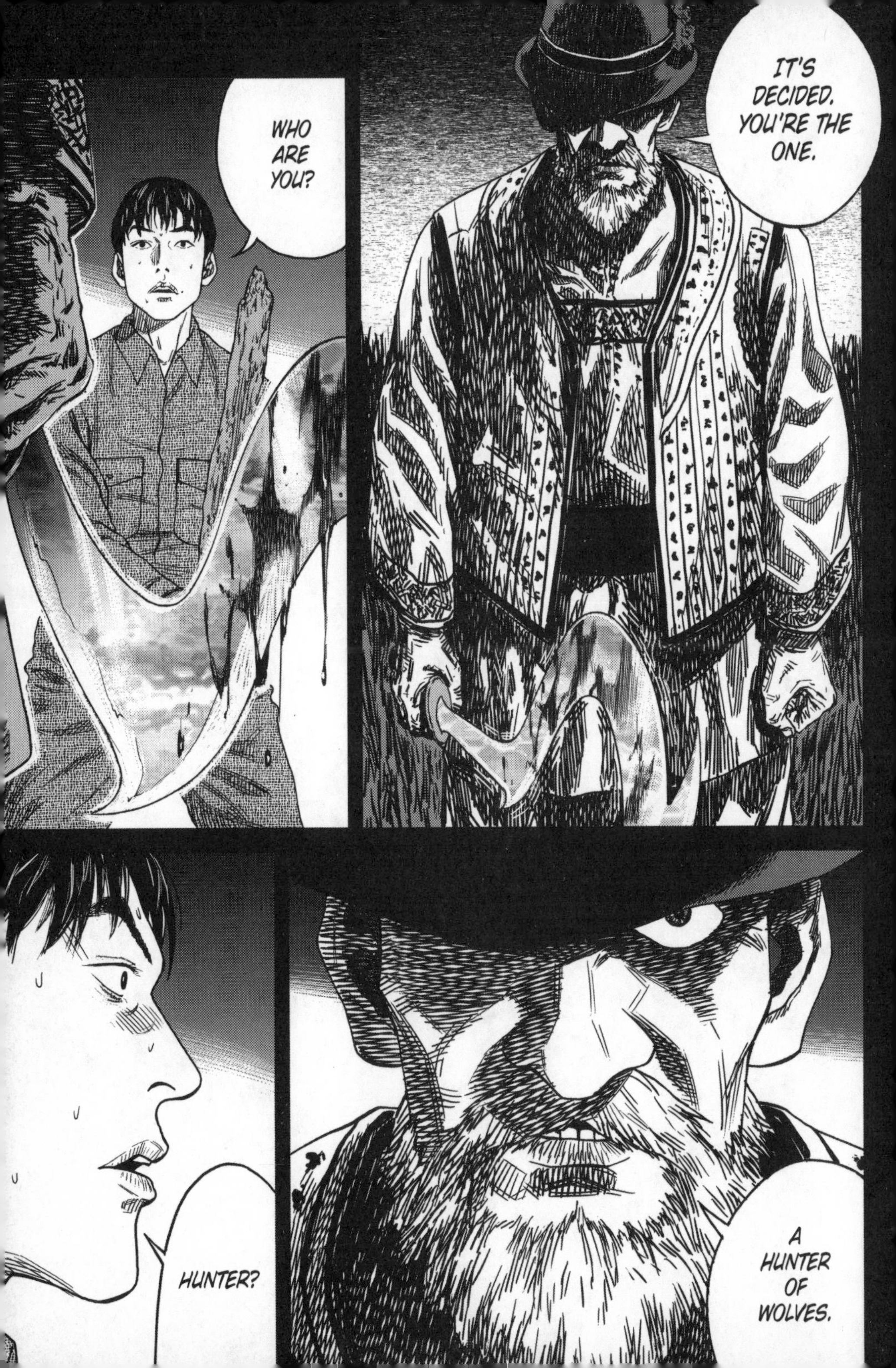
IT'S DECIDED. YOU'RE THE ONE.
WHO ARE YOU?
A HUNTER OF WOLVES.
HUNTER?

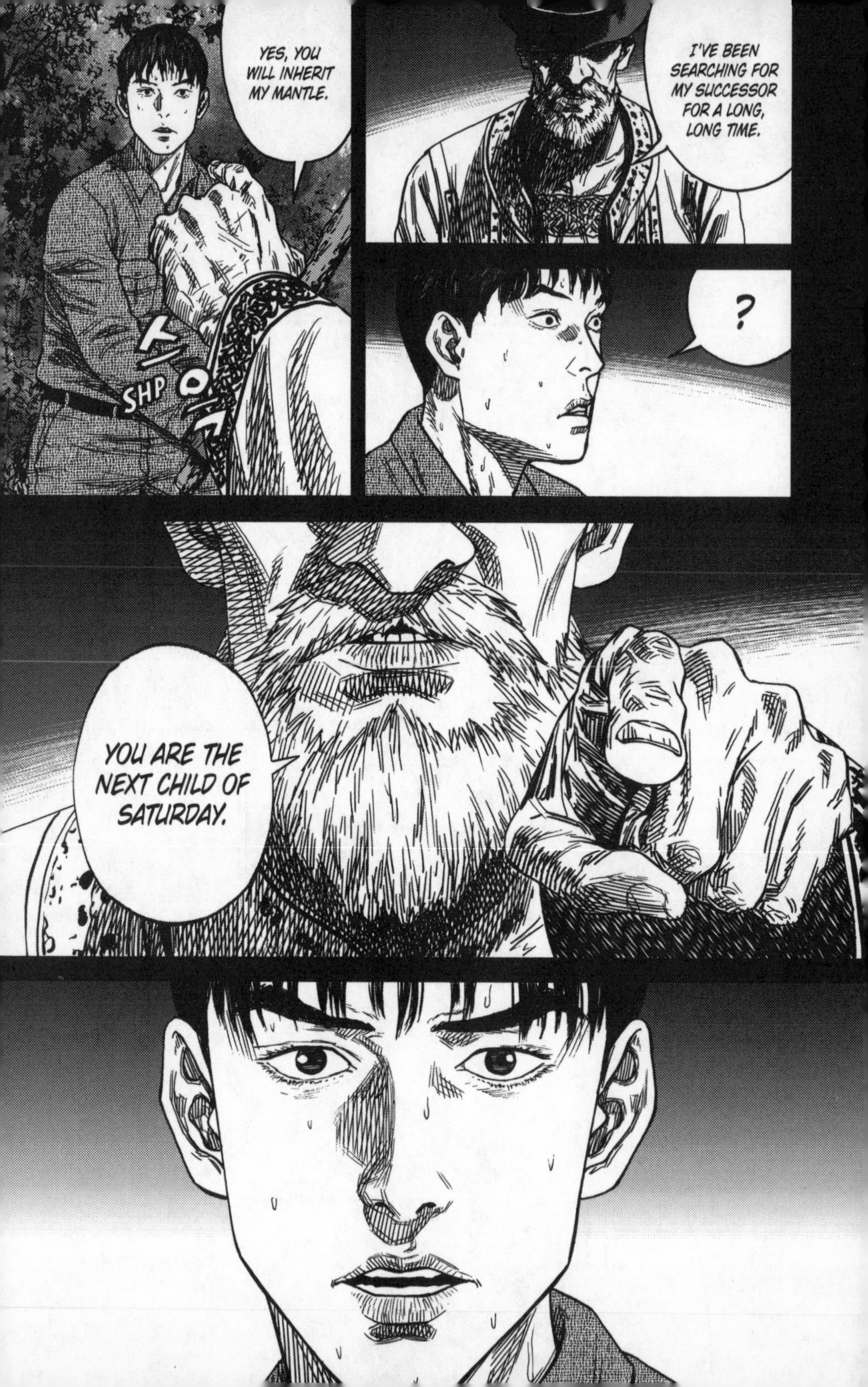
I'VE BEEN SEARCHING FOR MY SUCCESSOR FOR A LONG, LONG TIME.
?
YES, YOU WILL INHERIT MY MANTLE.
SHP
YOU ARE THE NEXT CHILD OF SATURDAY.

KING OF EDEN

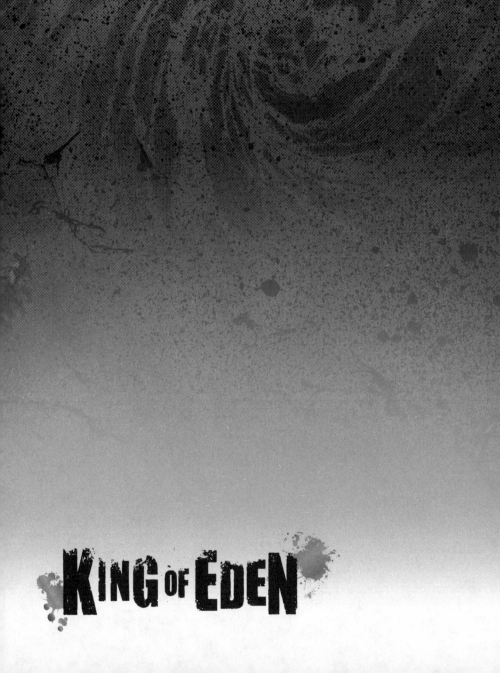

KING OF EDEN

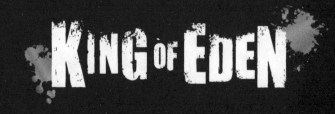

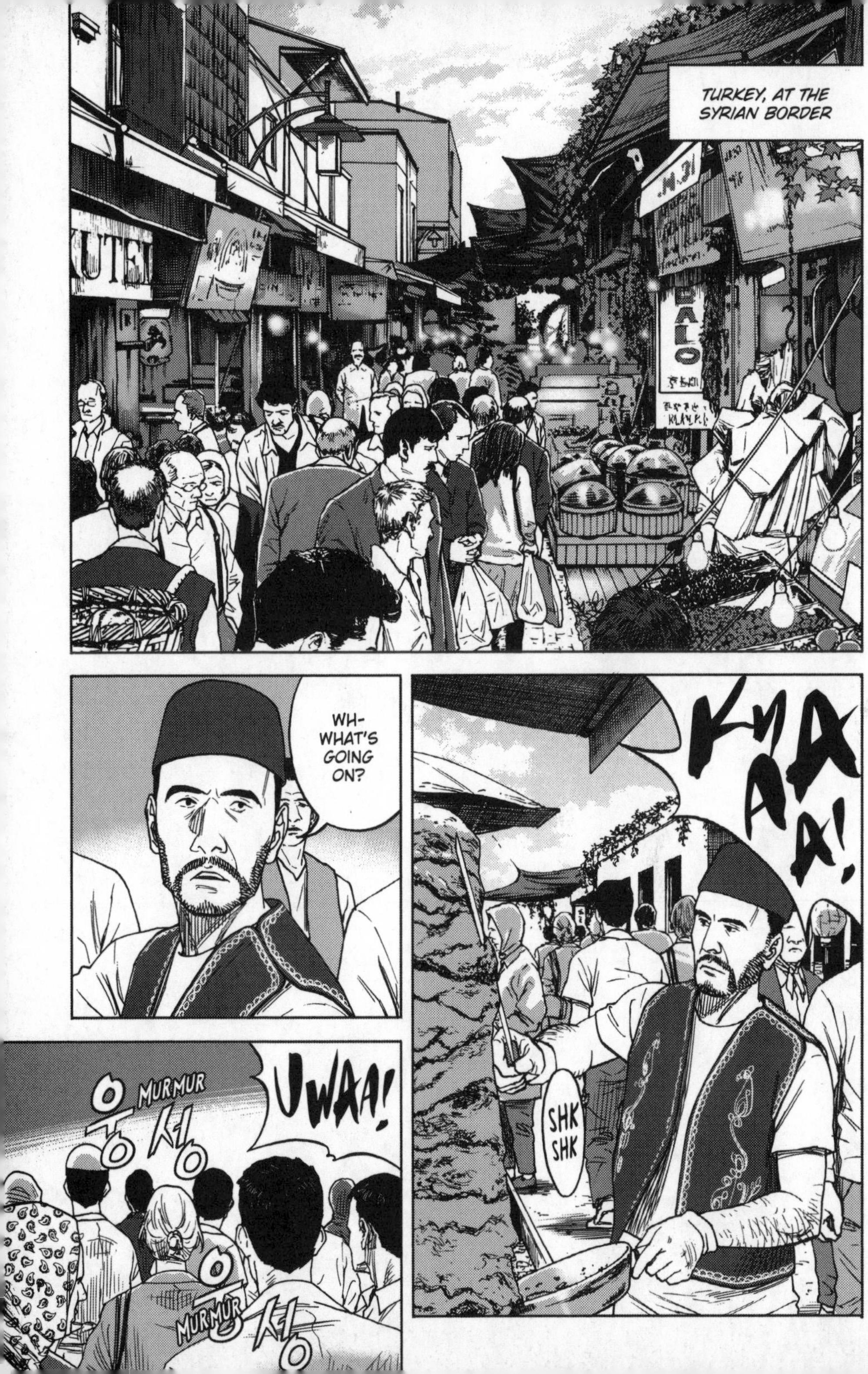
TURKEY, AT THE SYRIAN BORDER
KYAAAAA!
SHK SHK
WH- WHAT'S GOING ON?
UWAA!
MURMUR
MURMUR

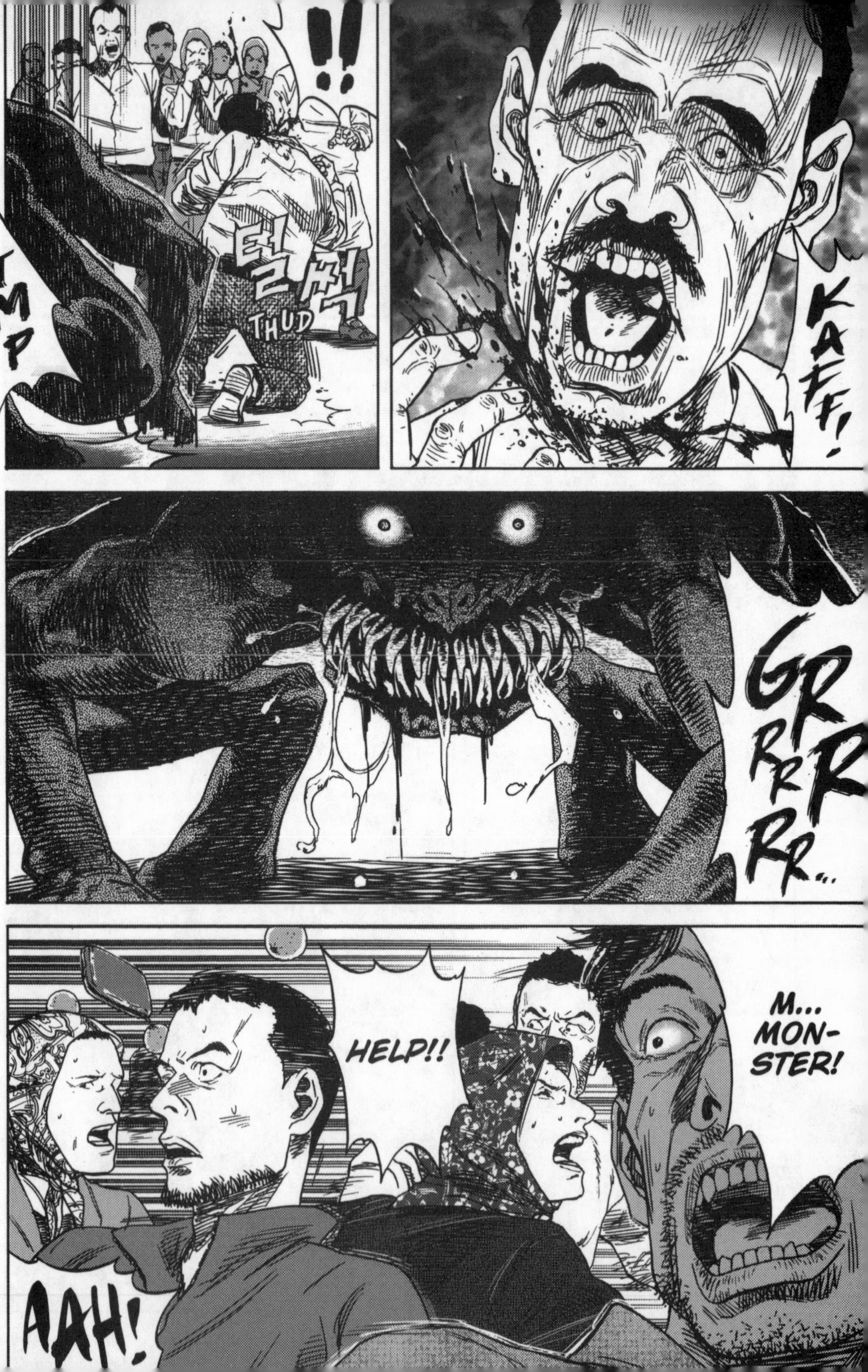
KAFF!
!!
TMP
털썩 THUD
GRRRRRR...
M... MON-STER!
HELP!!
AAH!

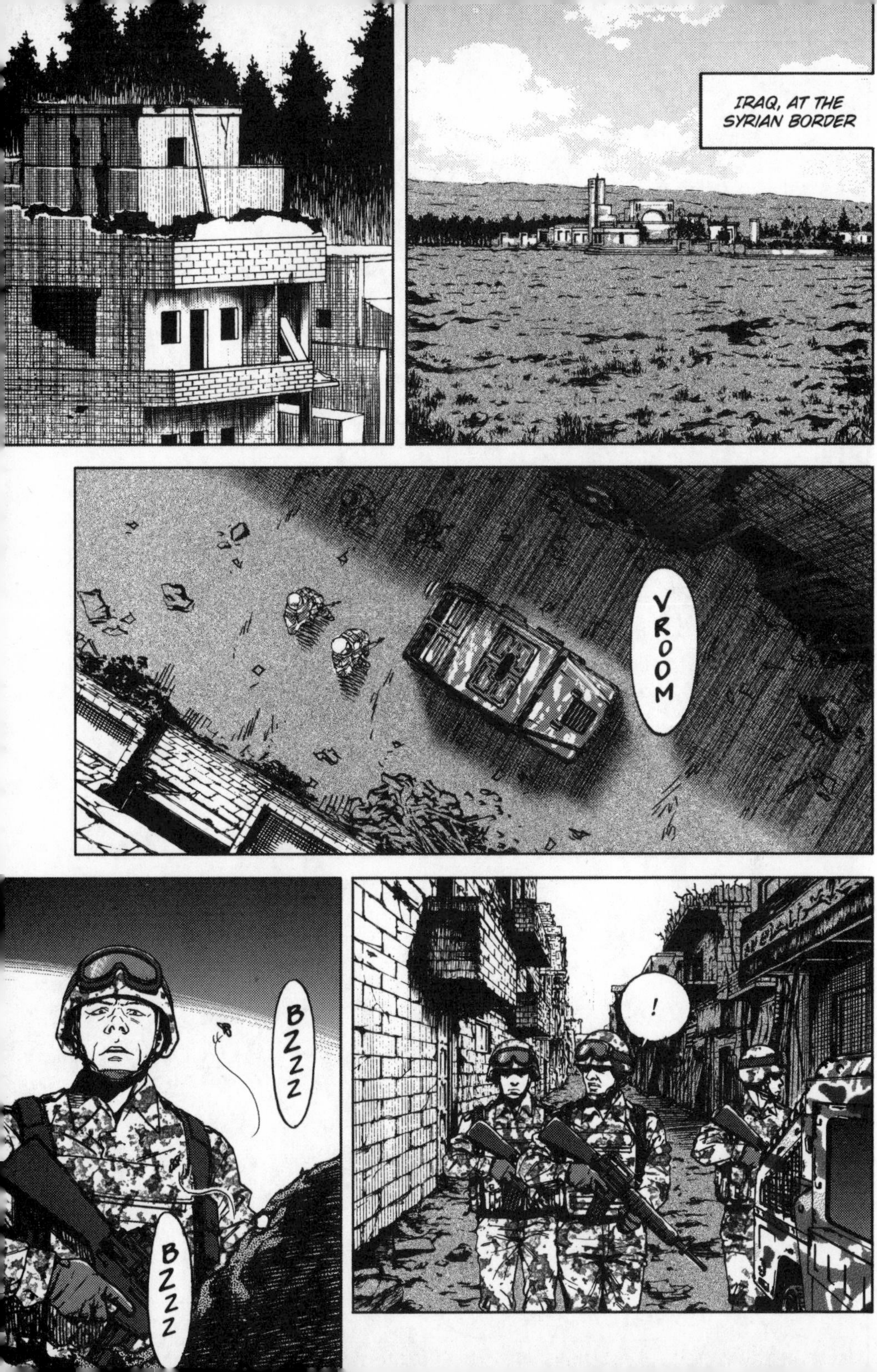
IRAQ, AT THE SYRIAN BORDER
VROOM
!
BZZZ
BZZZ

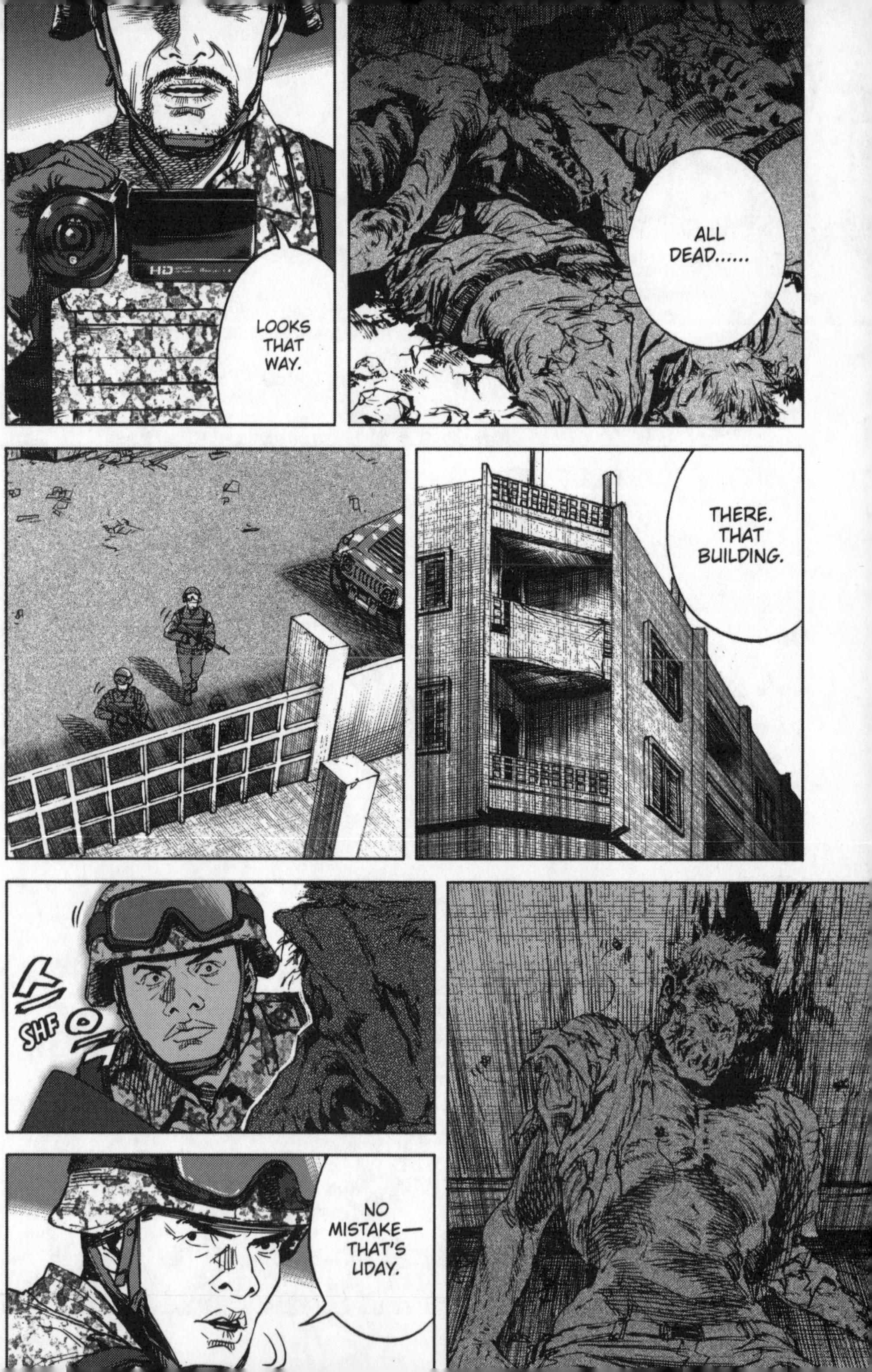
ALL DEAD......
LOOKS THAT WAY.
THERE. THAT BUILDING.
SHF
NO MISTAKE— THAT'S UDAY.

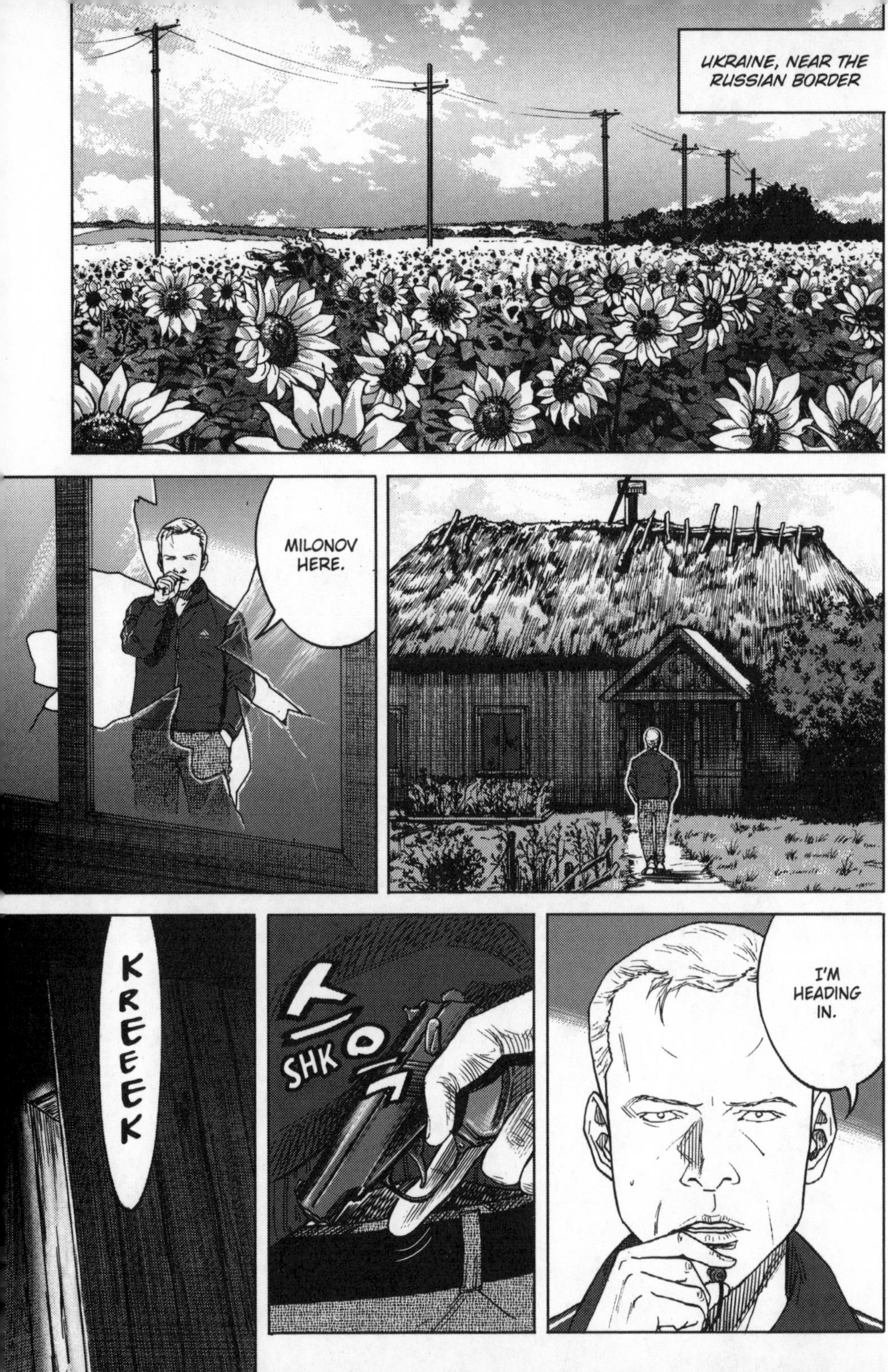
UKRAINE, NEAR THE RUSSIAN BORDER
MILONOV HERE.
I'M HEADING IN.
SHK
KREEEK

UGH!

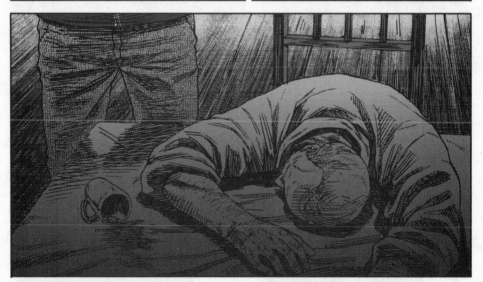

!

SHF

SHF

SHF

TAP

HEY.
LUKASHOV.

140

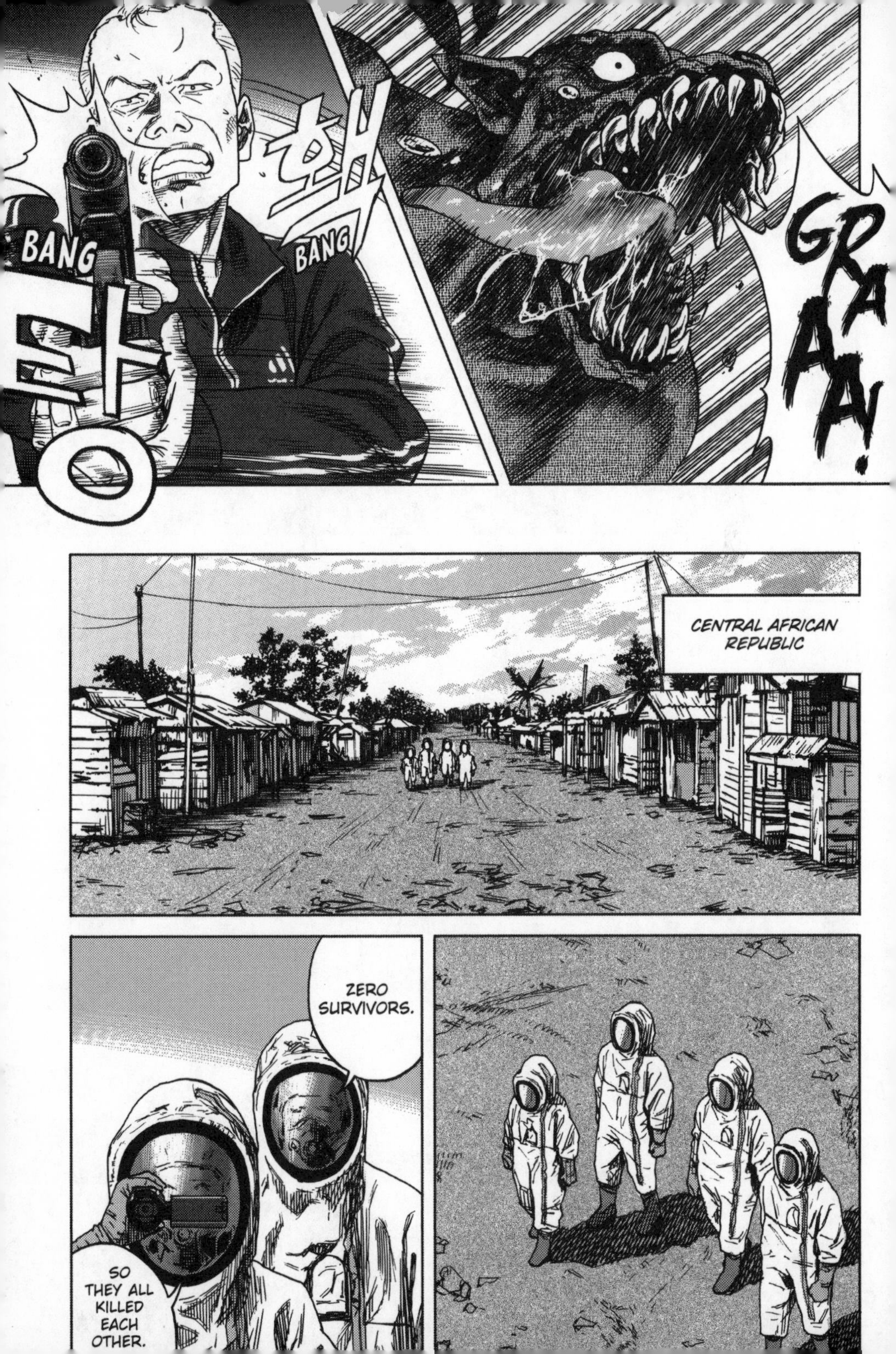
GRAAA!
BANG
BANG
CENTRAL AFRICAN REPUBLIC
ZERO SURVIVORS.
SO THEY ALL KILLED EACH OTHER.

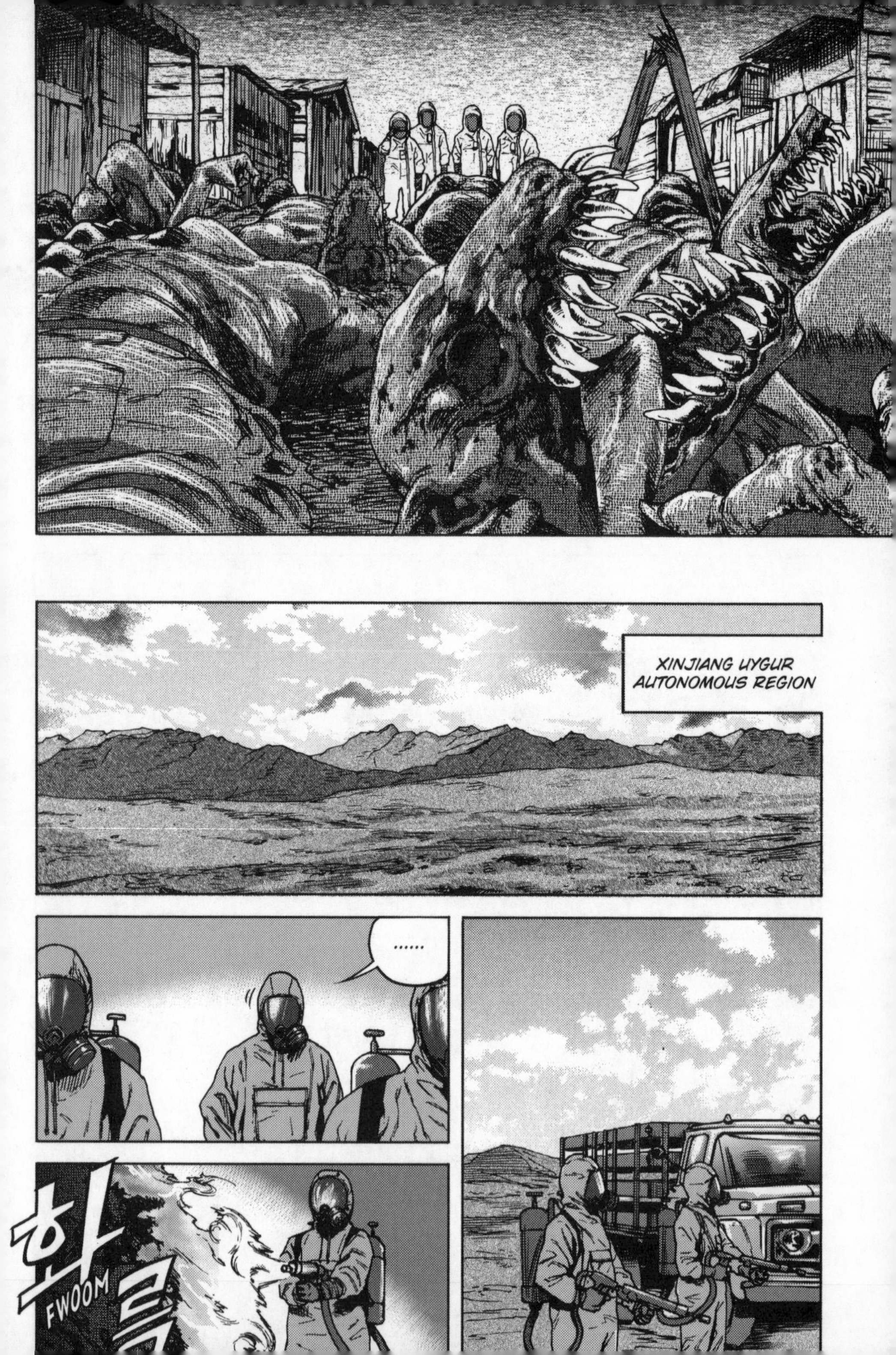
XINJIANG UYGUR AUTONOMOUS REGION
......
FWOOM

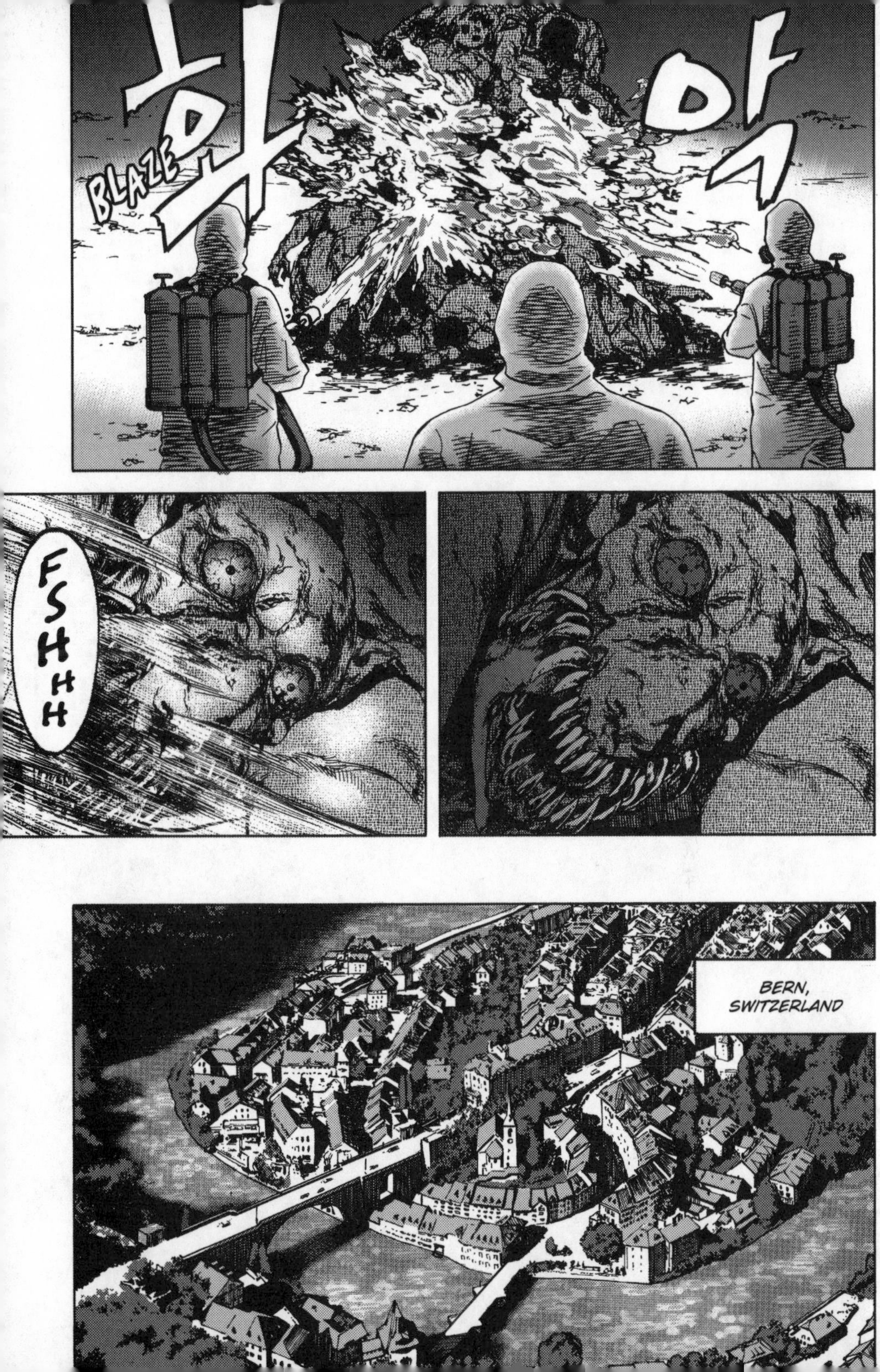
BLAZE
FSHHHH
BERN, SWITZERLAND

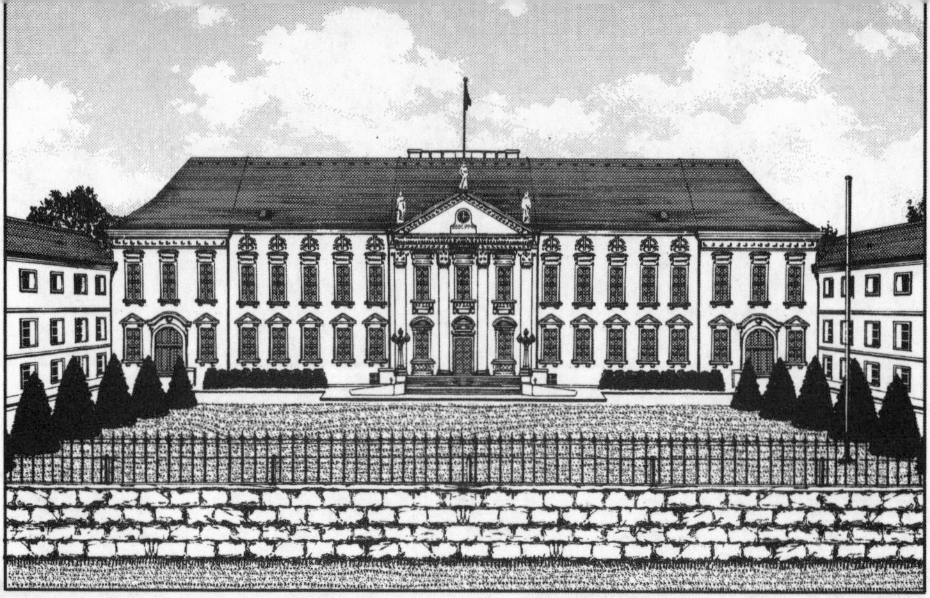

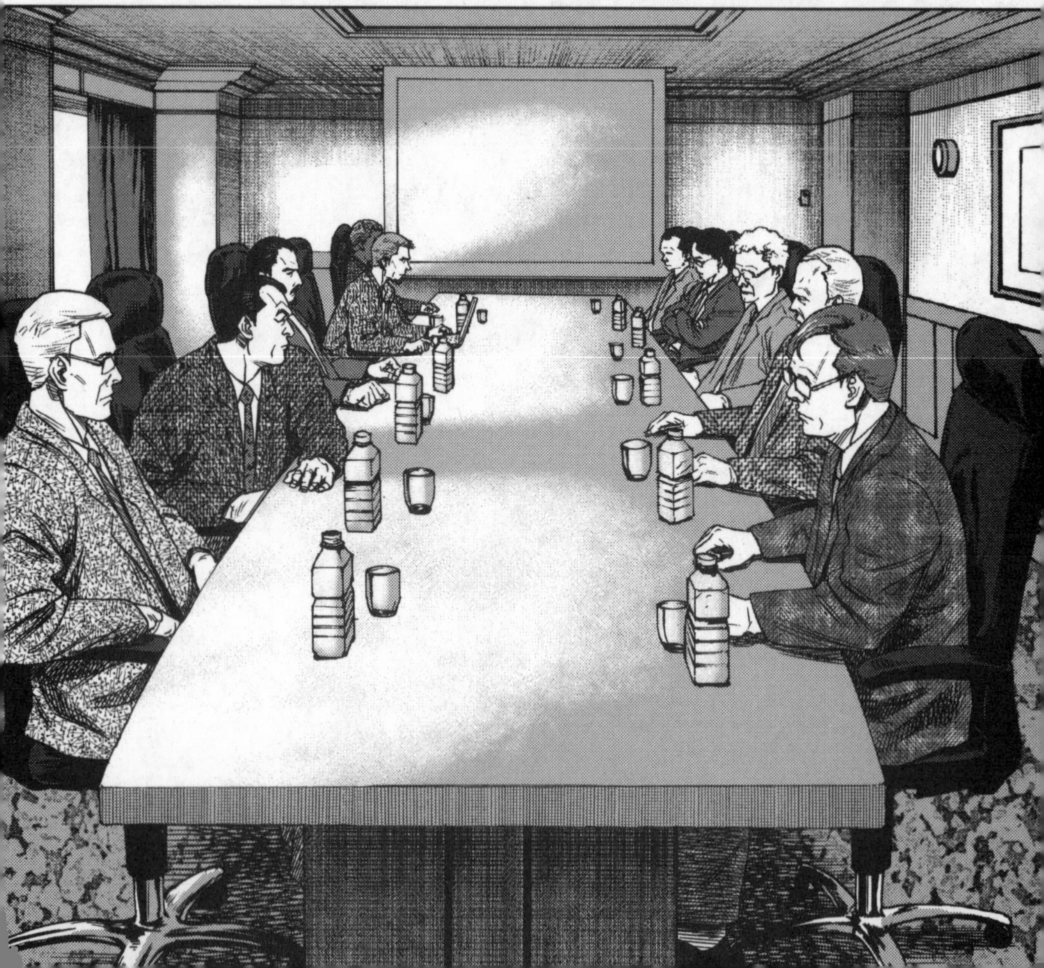

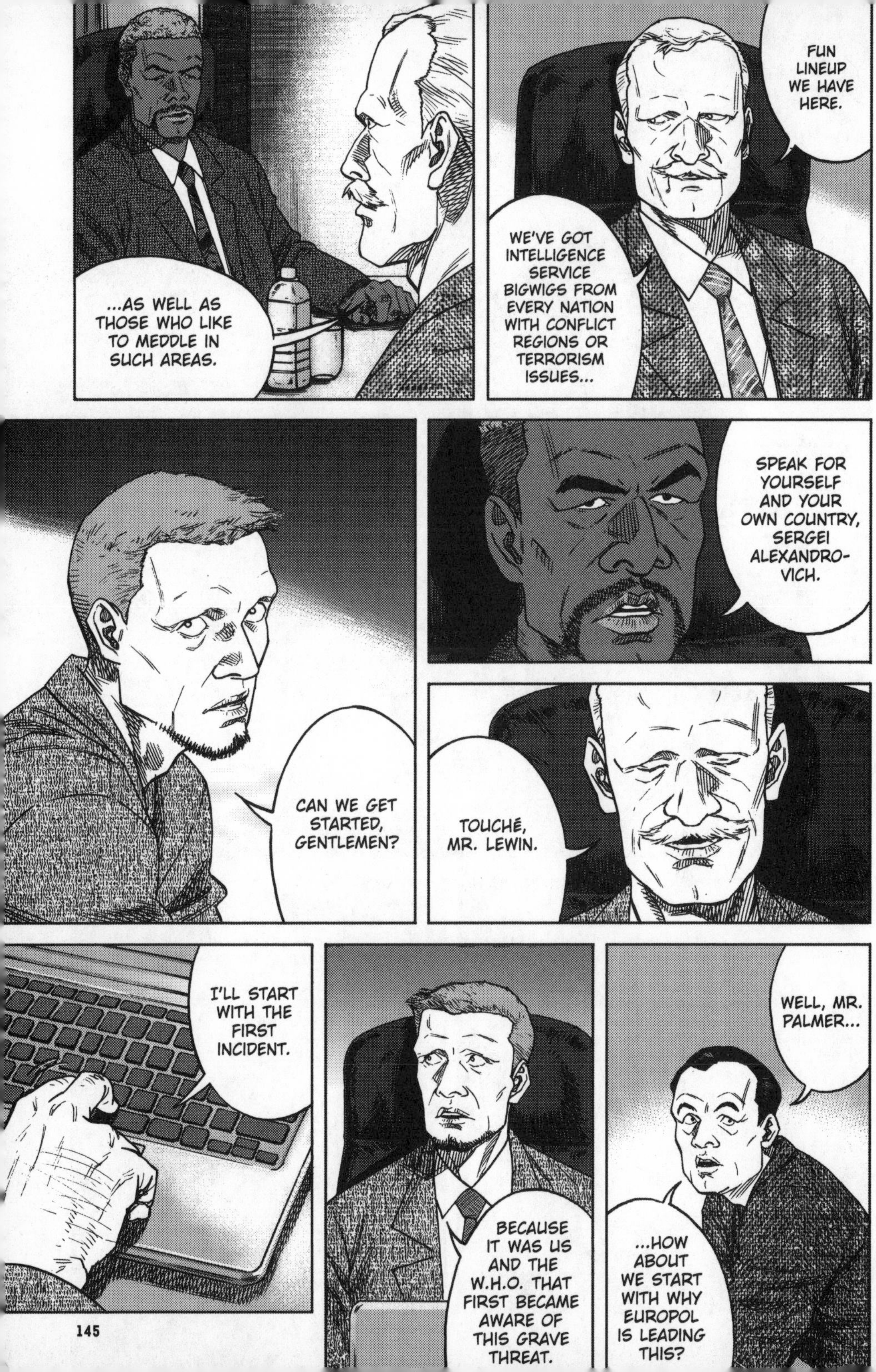

FUN LINEUP WE HAVE HERE.
WE'VE GOT INTELLIGENCE SERVICE BIGWIGS FROM EVERY NATION WITH CONFLICT REGIONS OR TERRORISM ISSUES...
...AS WELL AS THOSE WHO LIKE TO MEDDLE IN SUCH AREAS.
SPEAK FOR YOURSELF AND YOUR OWN COUNTRY, SERGEI ALEXANDRO-VICH.
TOUCHÉ, MR. LEWIN.
CAN WE GET STARTED, GENTLEMEN?
WELL, MR. PALMER...
...HOW ABOUT WE START WITH WHY EUROPOL IS LEADING THIS?
BECAUSE IT WAS US AND THE W.H.O. THAT FIRST BECAME AWARE OF THIS GRAVE THREAT.
I'LL START WITH THE FIRST INCIDENT.

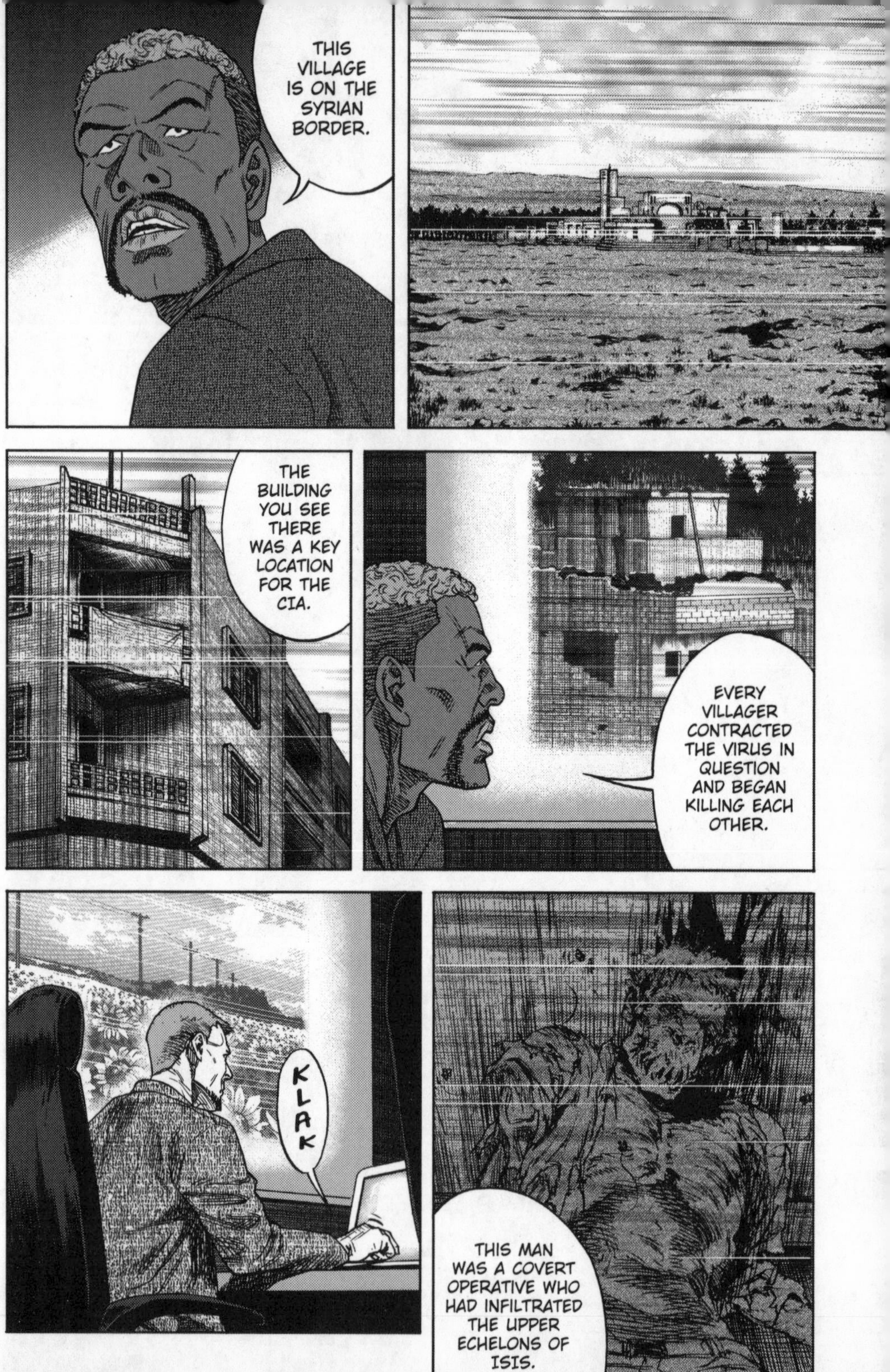
THIS VILLAGE IS ON THE SYRIAN BORDER.
EVERY VILLAGER CONTRACTED THE VIRUS IN QUESTION AND BEGAN KILLING EACH OTHER.
THE BUILDING YOU SEE THERE WAS A KEY LOCATION FOR THE CIA.
THIS MAN WAS A COVERT OPERATIVE WHO HAD INFILTRATED THE UPPER ECHELONS OF ISIS.
KLAK

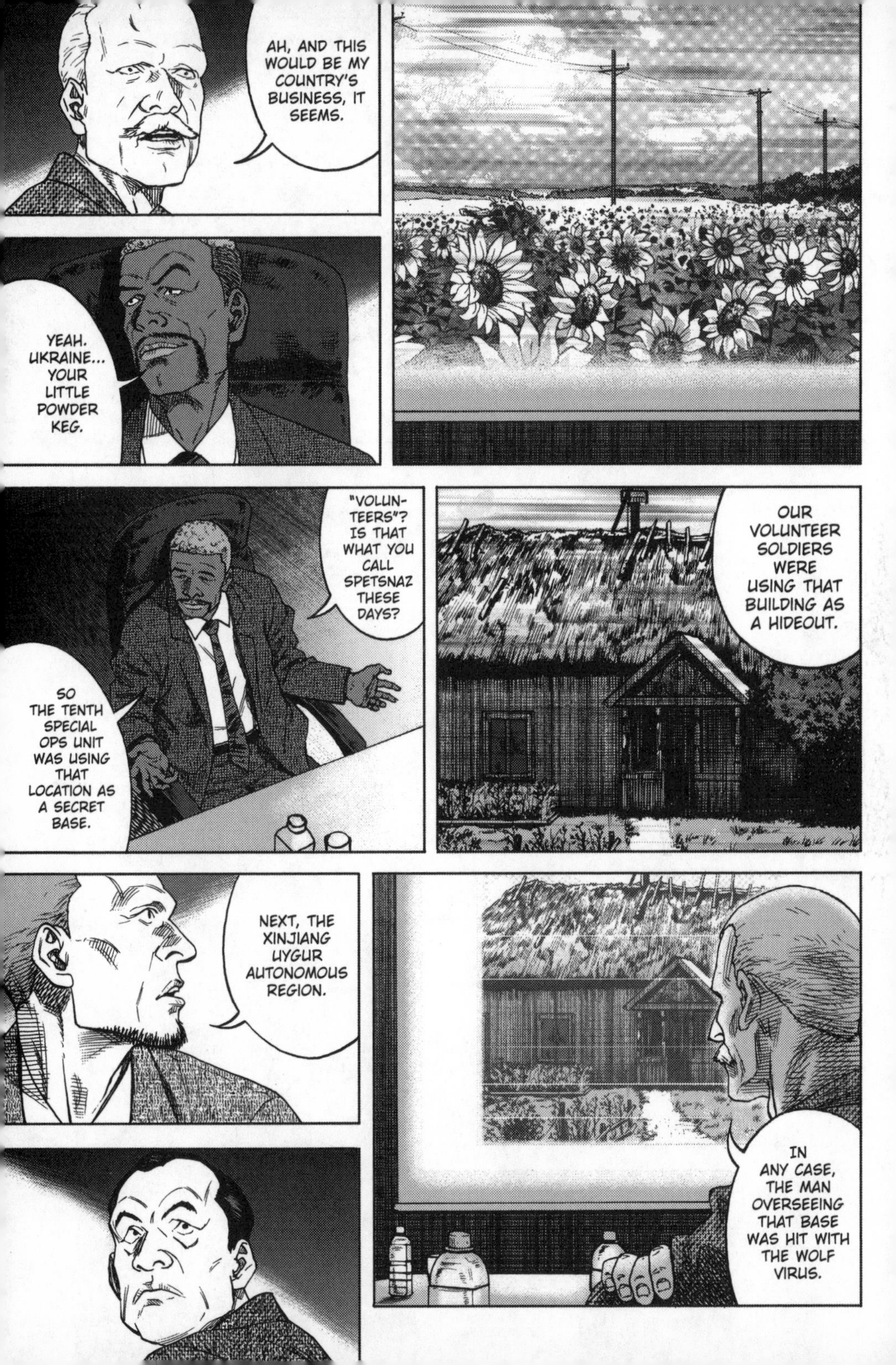
AH, AND THIS WOULD BE MY COUNTRY'S BUSINESS, IT SEEMS.
YEAH. UKRAINE... YOUR LITTLE POWDER KEG.
OUR VOLUNTEER SOLDIERS WERE USING THAT BUILDING AS A HIDEOUT.
"VOLUN-TEERS"? IS THAT WHAT YOU CALL SPETSNAZ THESE DAYS?
SO THE TENTH SPECIAL OPS UNIT WAS USING THAT LOCATION AS A SECRET BASE.
IN ANY CASE, THE MAN OVERSEEING THAT BASE WAS HIT WITH THE WOLF VIRUS.
NEXT, THE XINJIANG UYGUR AUTONOMOUS REGION.

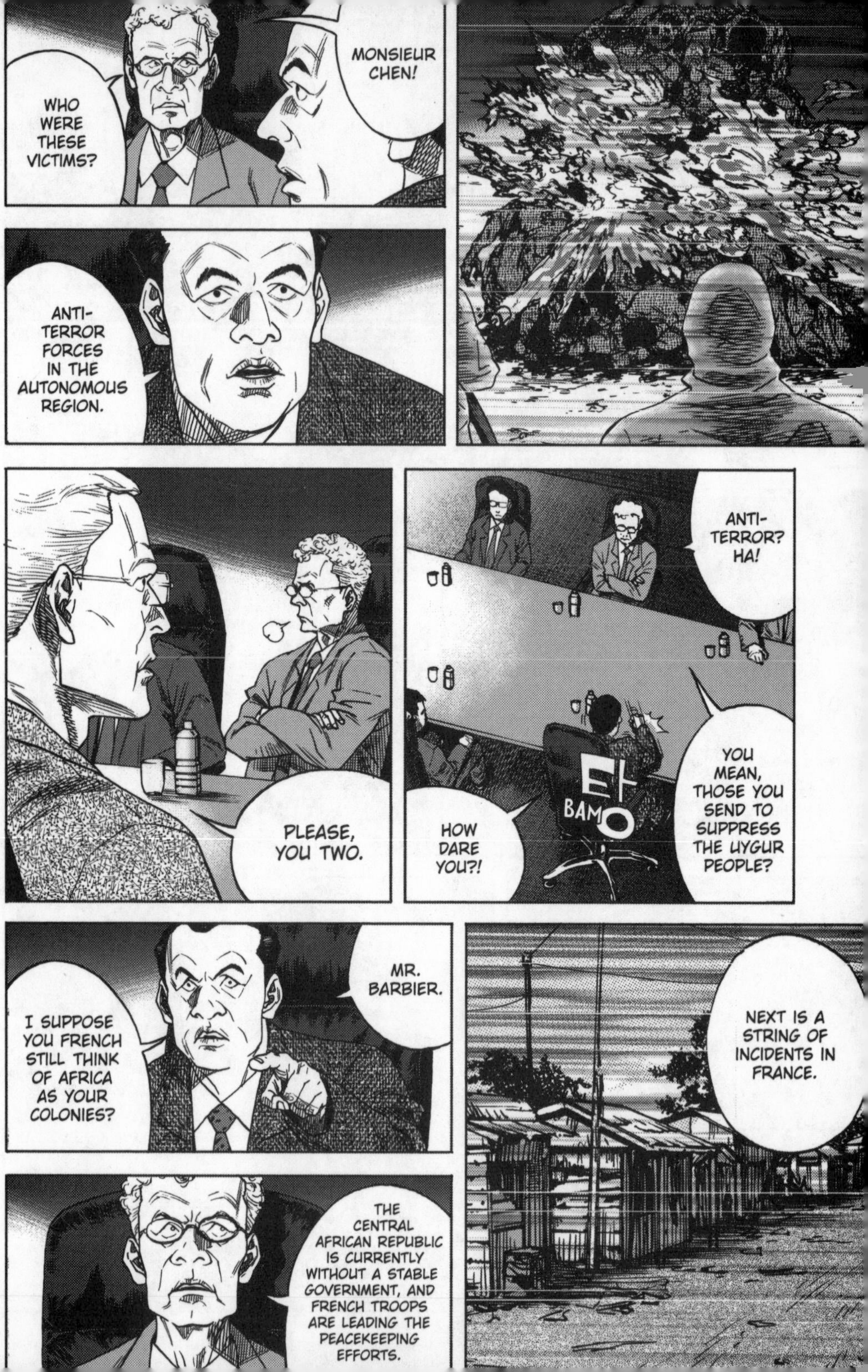
MONSIEUR CHEN!
WHO WERE THESE VICTIMS?
ANTI-TERROR FORCES IN THE AUTONOMOUS REGION.
ANTI-TERROR? HA!
YOU MEAN, THOSE YOU SEND TO SUPPRESS THE UYGUR PEOPLE?
HOW DARE YOU?!
PLEASE, YOU TWO.
NEXT IS A STRING OF INCIDENTS IN FRANCE.
MR. BARBIER.
I SUPPOSE YOU FRENCH STILL THINK OF AFRICA AS YOUR COLONIES?
THE CENTRAL AFRICAN REPUBLIC IS CURRENTLY WITHOUT A STABLE GOVERNMENT, AND FRENCH TROOPS ARE LEADING THE PEACEKEEPING EFFORTS.

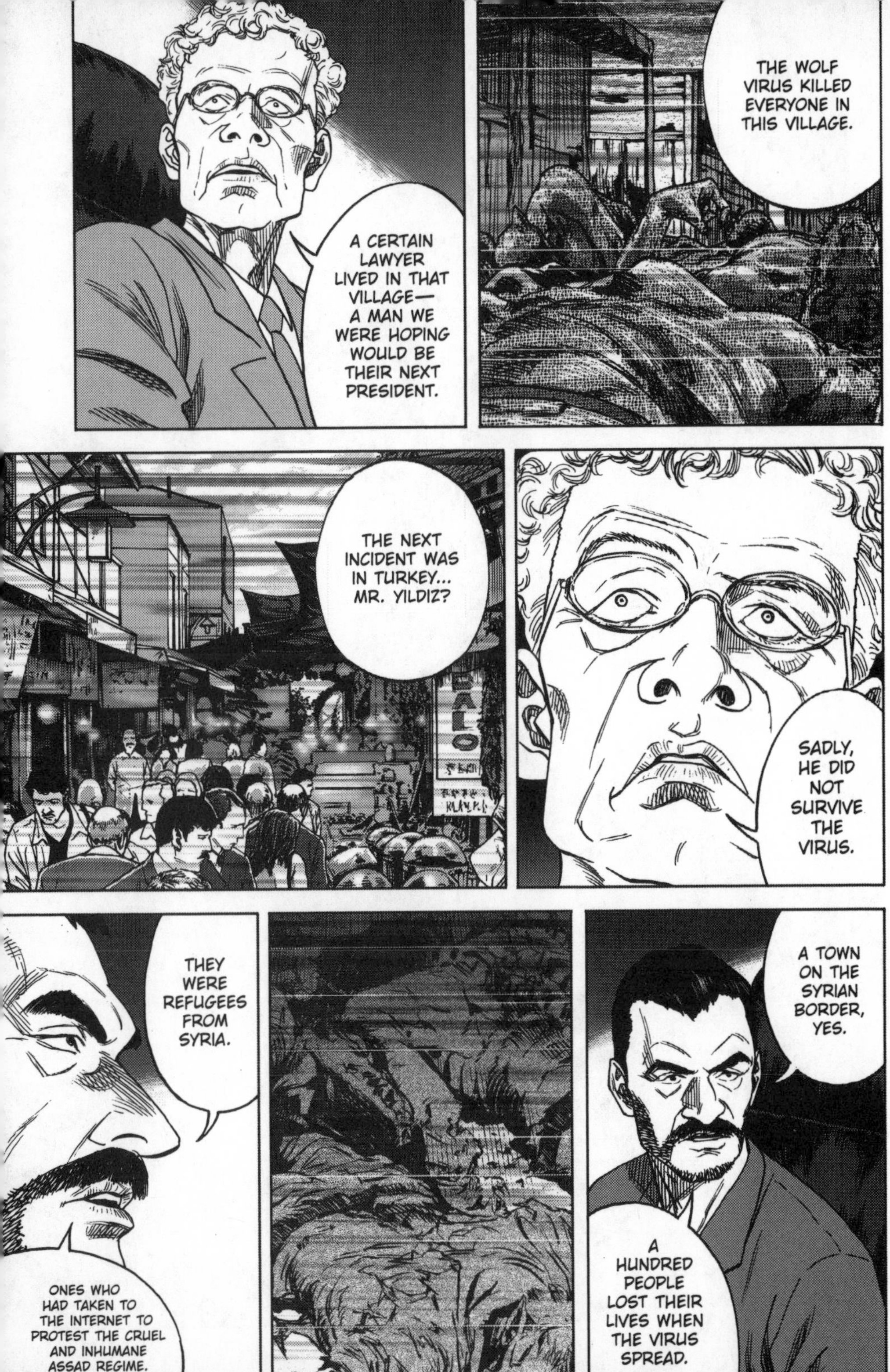
THE WOLF VIRUS KILLED EVERYONE IN THIS VILLAGE.
A CERTAIN LAWYER LIVED IN THAT VILLAGE— A MAN WE WERE HOPING WOULD BE THEIR NEXT PRESIDENT.
SADLY, HE DID NOT SURVIVE THE VIRUS.
THE NEXT INCIDENT WAS IN TURKEY... MR. YILDIZ?
A TOWN ON THE SYRIAN BORDER, YES.
A HUNDRED PEOPLE LOST THEIR LIVES WHEN THE VIRUS SPREAD.
THEY WERE REFUGEES FROM SYRIA.
ONES WHO HAD TAKEN TO THE INTERNET TO PROTEST THE CRUEL AND INHUMANE ASSAD REGIME.

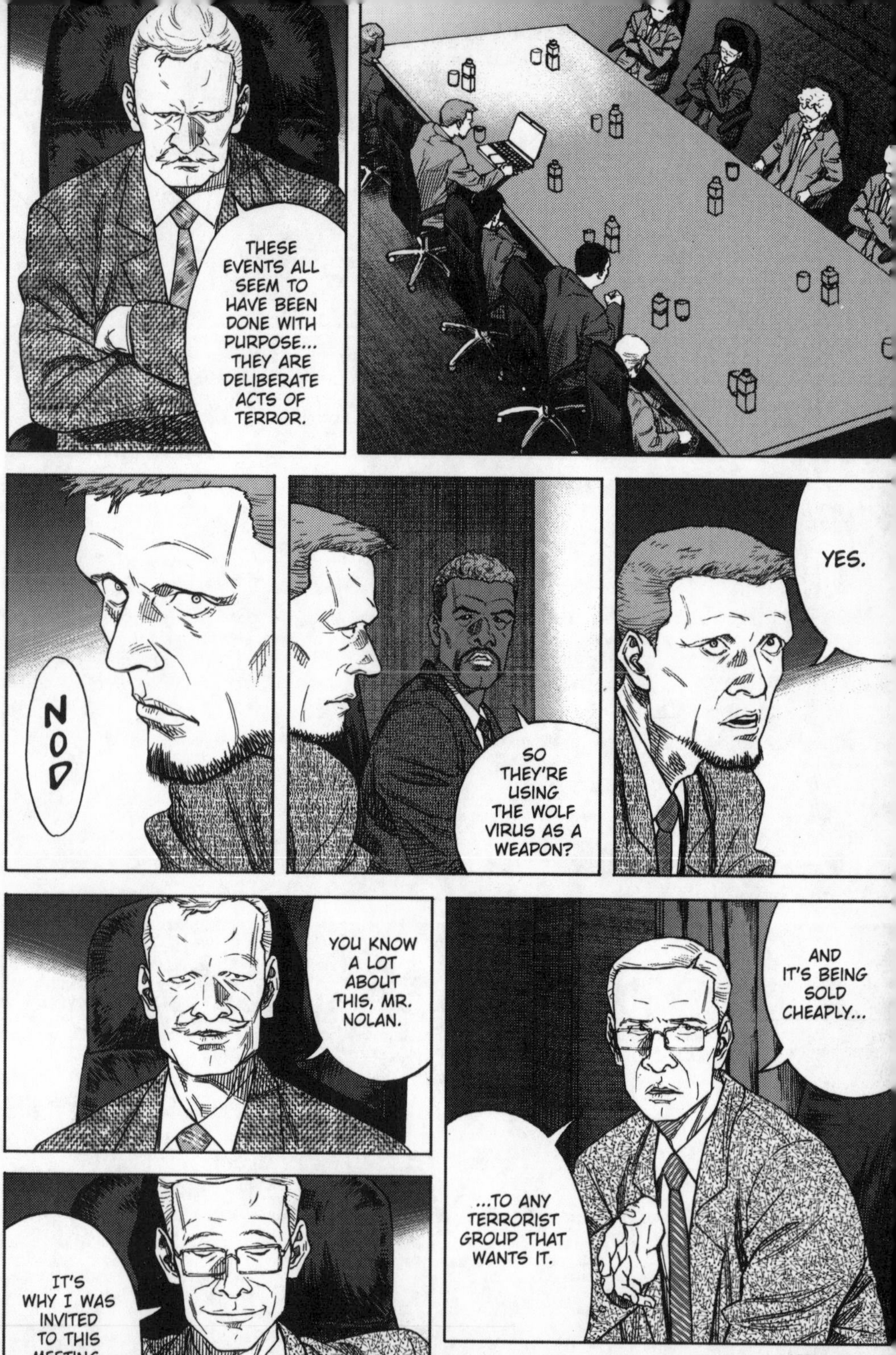
THESE EVENTS ALL SEEM TO HAVE BEEN DONE WITH PURPOSE... THEY ARE DELIBERATE ACTS OF TERROR.
YES.
SO THEY'RE USING THE WOLF VIRUS AS A WEAPON?
NOD
AND IT'S BEING SOLD CHEAPLY...
...TO ANY TERRORIST GROUP THAT WANTS IT.
YOU KNOW A LOT ABOUT THIS, MR. NOLAN.
IT'S WHY I WAS INVITED TO THIS MEETING.

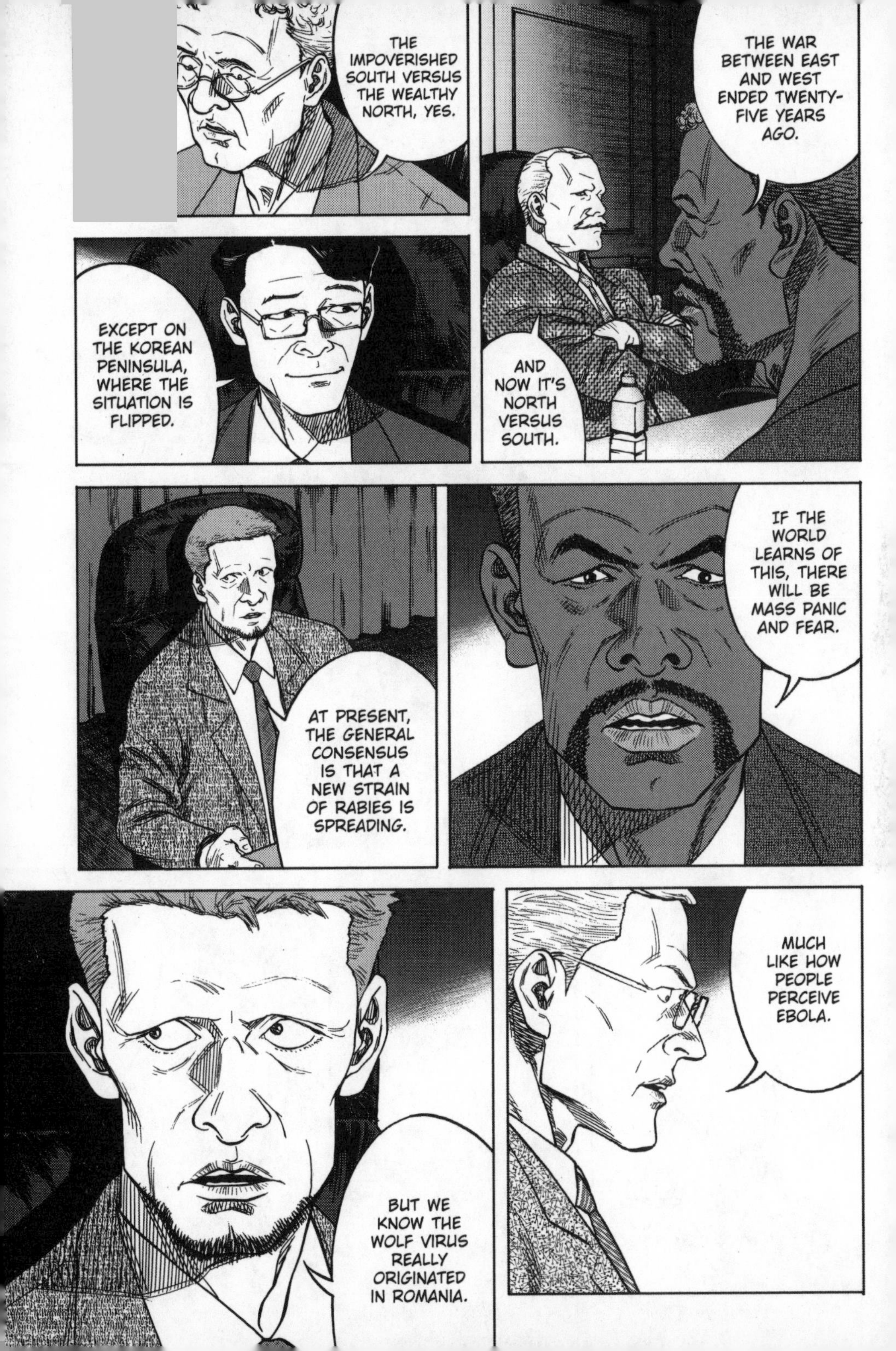
THE WAR BETWEEN EAST AND WEST ENDED TWENTY-FIVE YEARS AGO.
AND NOW IT'S NORTH VERSUS SOUTH.
THE IMPOVERISHED SOUTH VERSUS THE WEALTHY NORTH, YES.
EXCEPT ON THE KOREAN PENINSULA, WHERE THE SITUATION IS FLIPPED.
IF THE WORLD LEARNS OF THIS, THERE WILL BE MASS PANIC AND FEAR.
AT PRESENT, THE GENERAL CONSENSUS IS THAT A NEW STRAIN OF RABIES IS SPREADING.
MUCH LIKE HOW PEOPLE PERCEIVE EBOLA.
BUT WE KNOW THE WOLF VIRUS REALLY ORIGINATED IN ROMANIA.

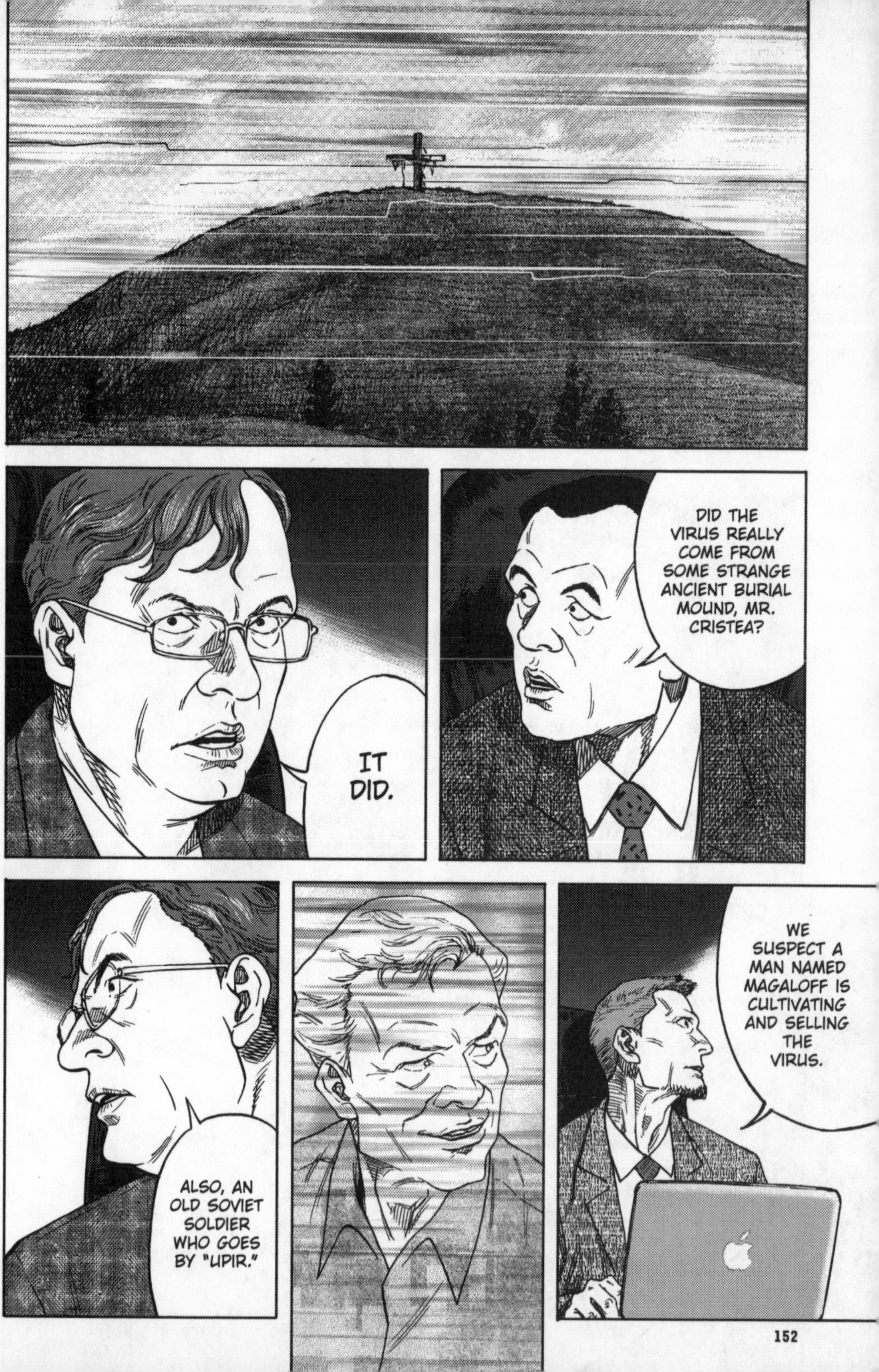
DID THE VIRUS REALLY COME FROM SOME STRANGE ANCIENT BURIAL MOUND, MR. CRISTEA?
IT DID.
WE SUSPECT A MAN NAMED MAGALOFF IS CULTIVATING AND SELLING THE VIRUS.
ALSO, AN OLD SOVIET SOLDIER WHO GOES BY "UPIR."

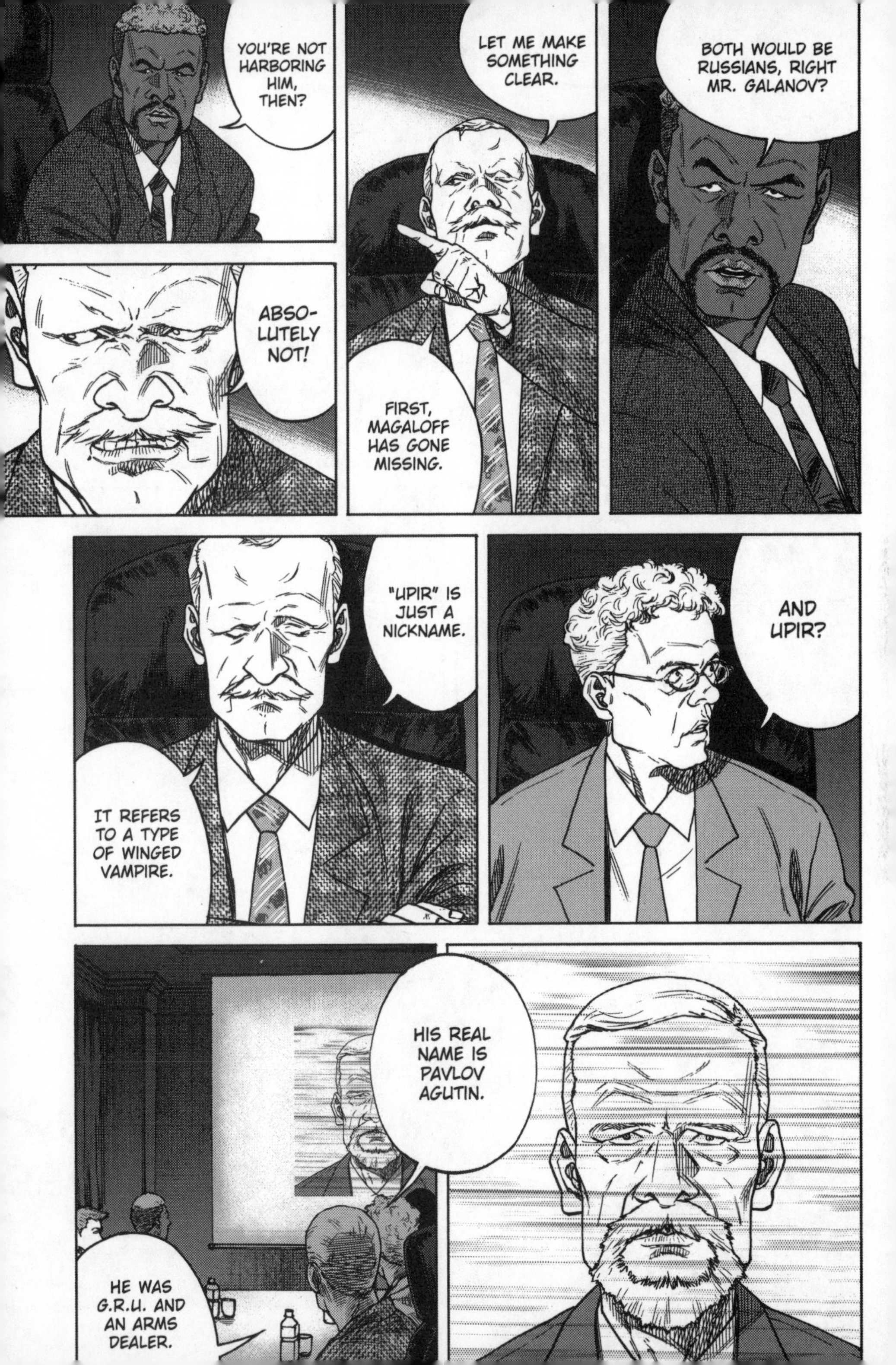
BOTH WOULD BE RUSSIANS, RIGHT MR. GALANOV?
LET ME MAKE SOMETHING CLEAR.
FIRST, MAGALOFF HAS GONE MISSING.
YOU'RE NOT HARBORING HIM, THEN?
ABSO-LUTELY NOT!
AND UPIR?
"UPIR" IS JUST A NICKNAME.
IT REFERS TO A TYPE OF WINGED VAMPIRE.
HIS REAL NAME IS PAVLOV AGUTIN.
HE WAS G.R.U. AND AN ARMS DEALER.

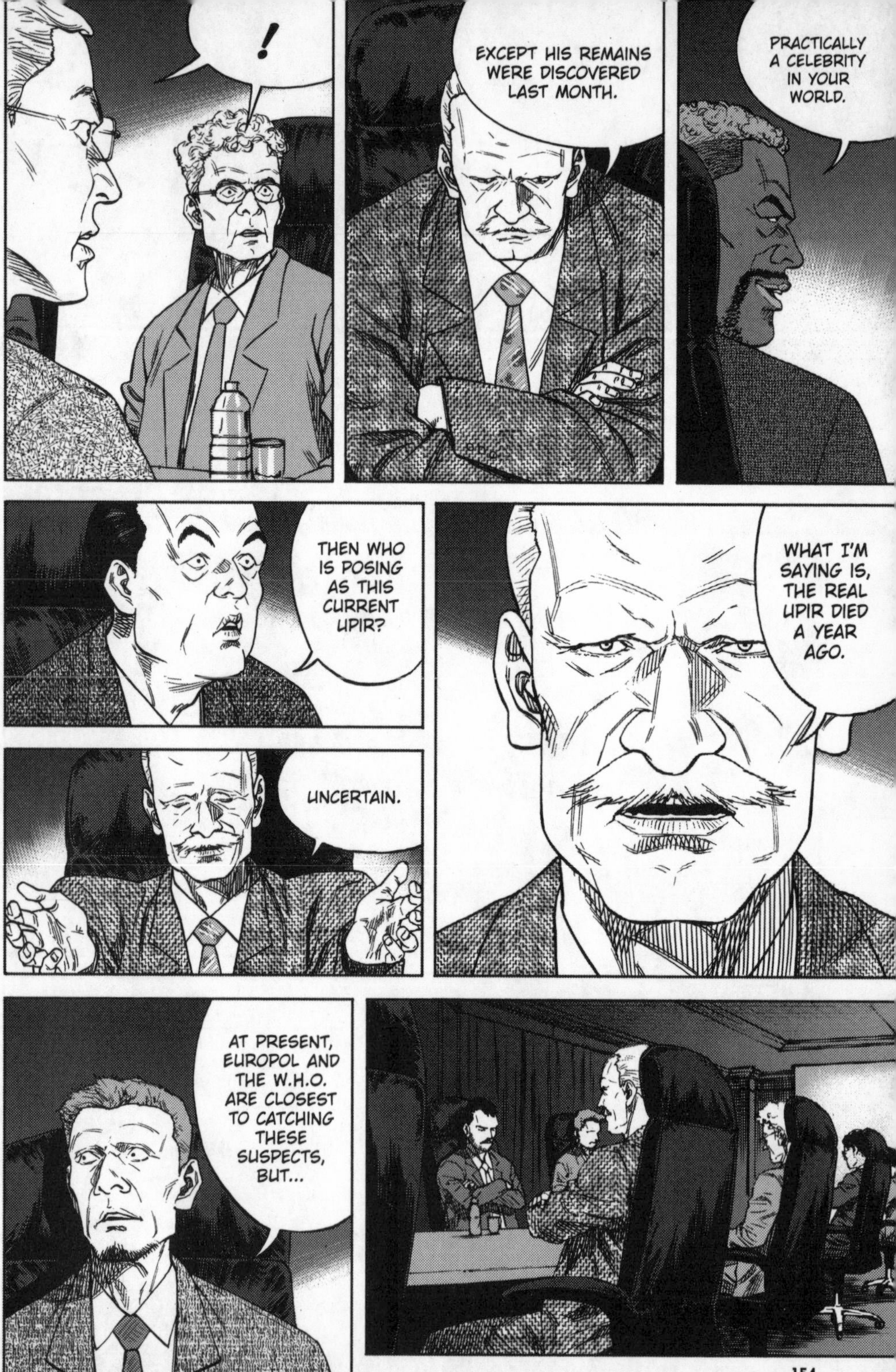
PRACTICALLY A CELEBRITY IN YOUR WORLD.
EXCEPT HIS REMAINS WERE DISCOVERED LAST MONTH.
!
WHAT I'M SAYING IS, THE REAL UPIR DIED A YEAR AGO.
THEN WHO IS POSING AS THIS CURRENT UPIR?
UNCERTAIN.
AT PRESENT, EUROPOL AND THE W.H.O. ARE CLOSEST TO CATCHING THESE SUSPECTS, BUT...

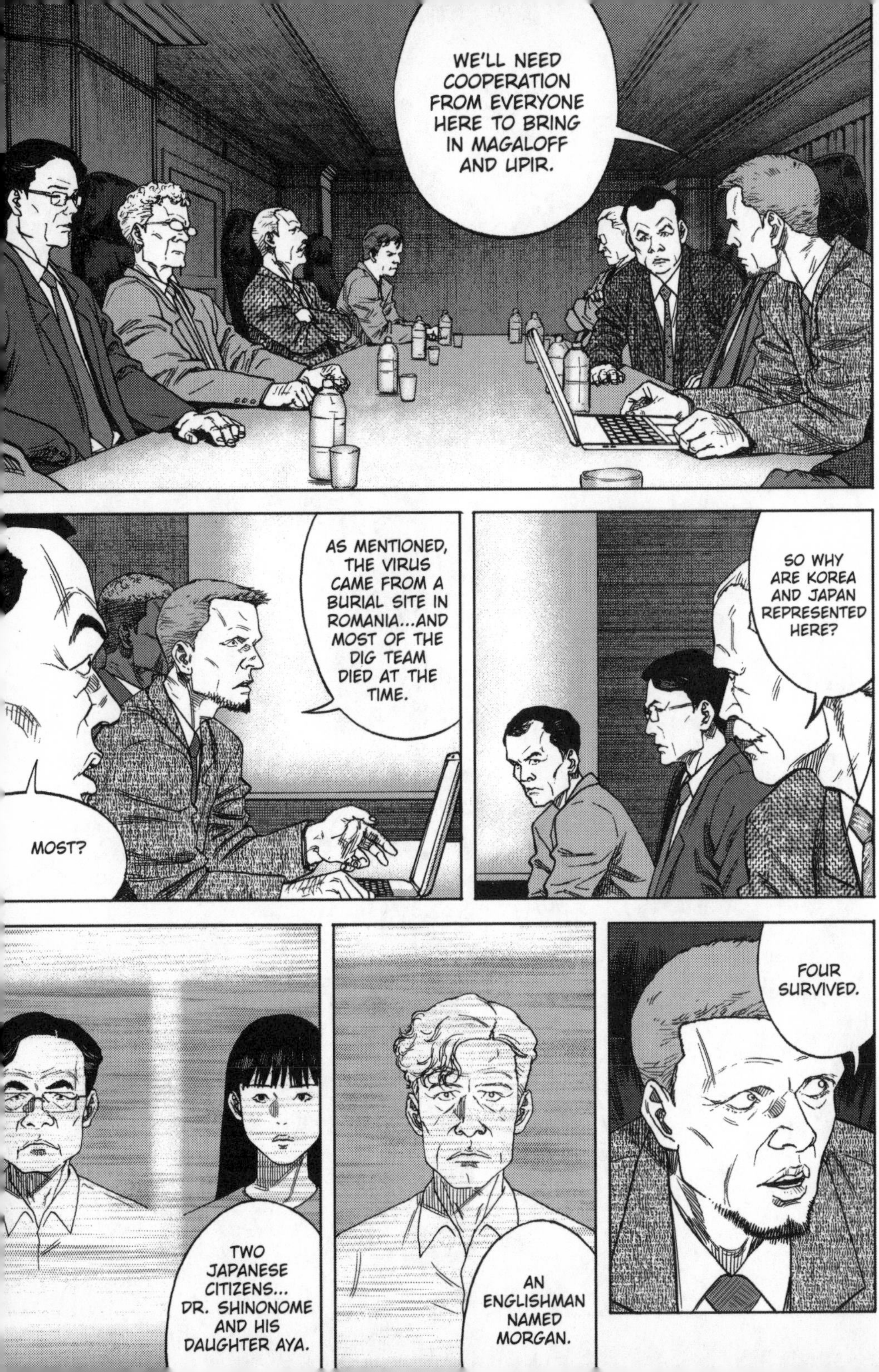
WE'LL NEED COOPERATION FROM EVERYONE HERE TO BRING IN MAGALOFF AND UPIR.
SO WHY ARE KOREA AND JAPAN REPRESENTED HERE?
AS MENTIONED, THE VIRUS CAME FROM A BURIAL SITE IN ROMANIA...AND MOST OF THE DIG TEAM DIED AT THE TIME.
MOST?
FOUR SURVIVED.
AN ENGLISHMAN NAMED MORGAN.
TWO JAPANESE CITIZENS... DR. SHINONOME AND HIS DAUGHTER AYA.

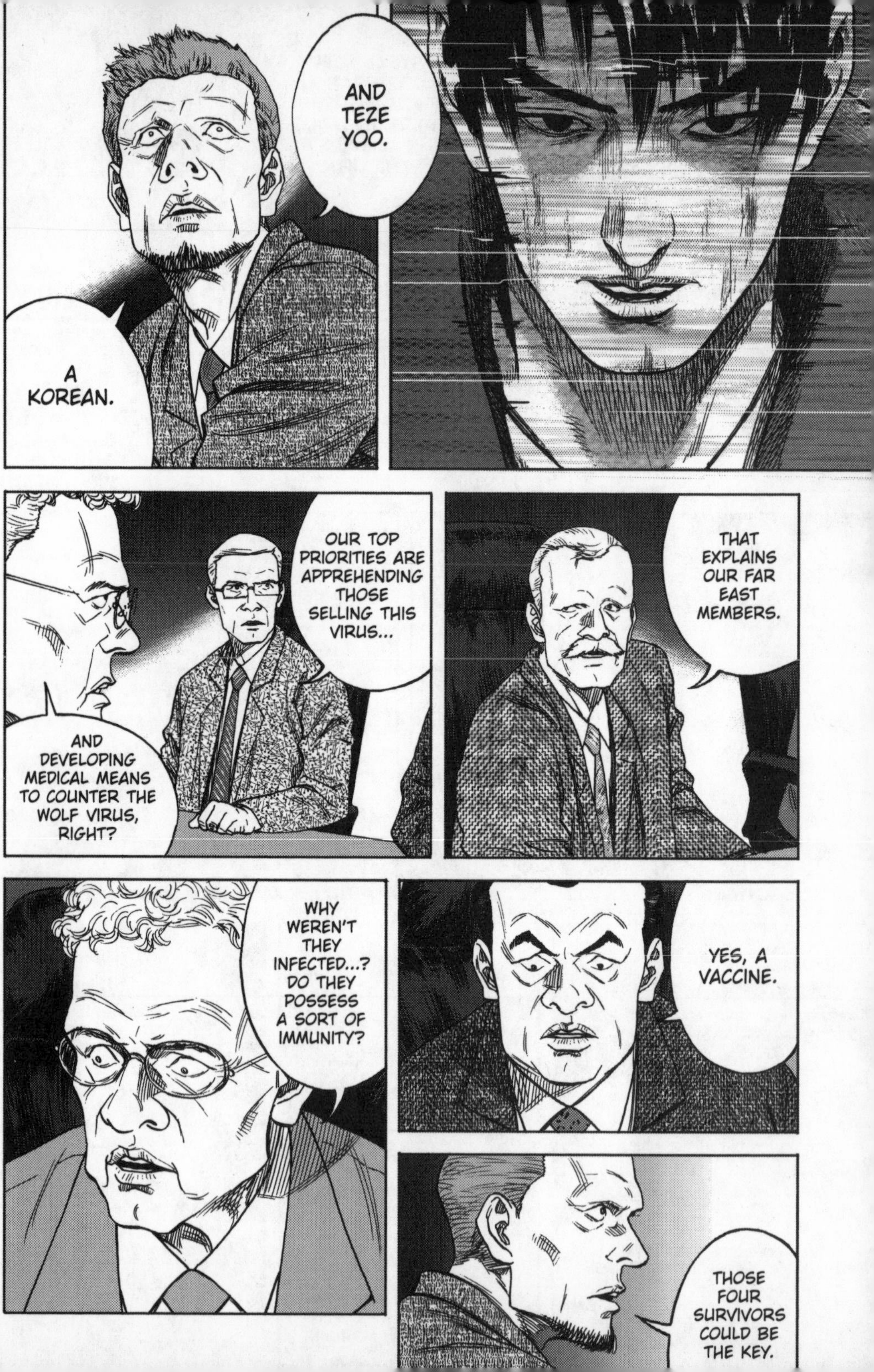
AND TEZE YOO.
A KOREAN.
THAT EXPLAINS OUR FAR EAST MEMBERS.
OUR TOP PRIORITIES ARE APPREHENDING THOSE SELLING THIS VIRUS...
AND DEVELOPING MEDICAL MEANS TO COUNTER THE WOLF VIRUS, RIGHT?
YES, A VACCINE.
THOSE FOUR SURVIVORS COULD BE THE KEY.
WHY WEREN'T THEY INFECTED...? DO THEY POSSESS A SORT OF IMMUNITY?

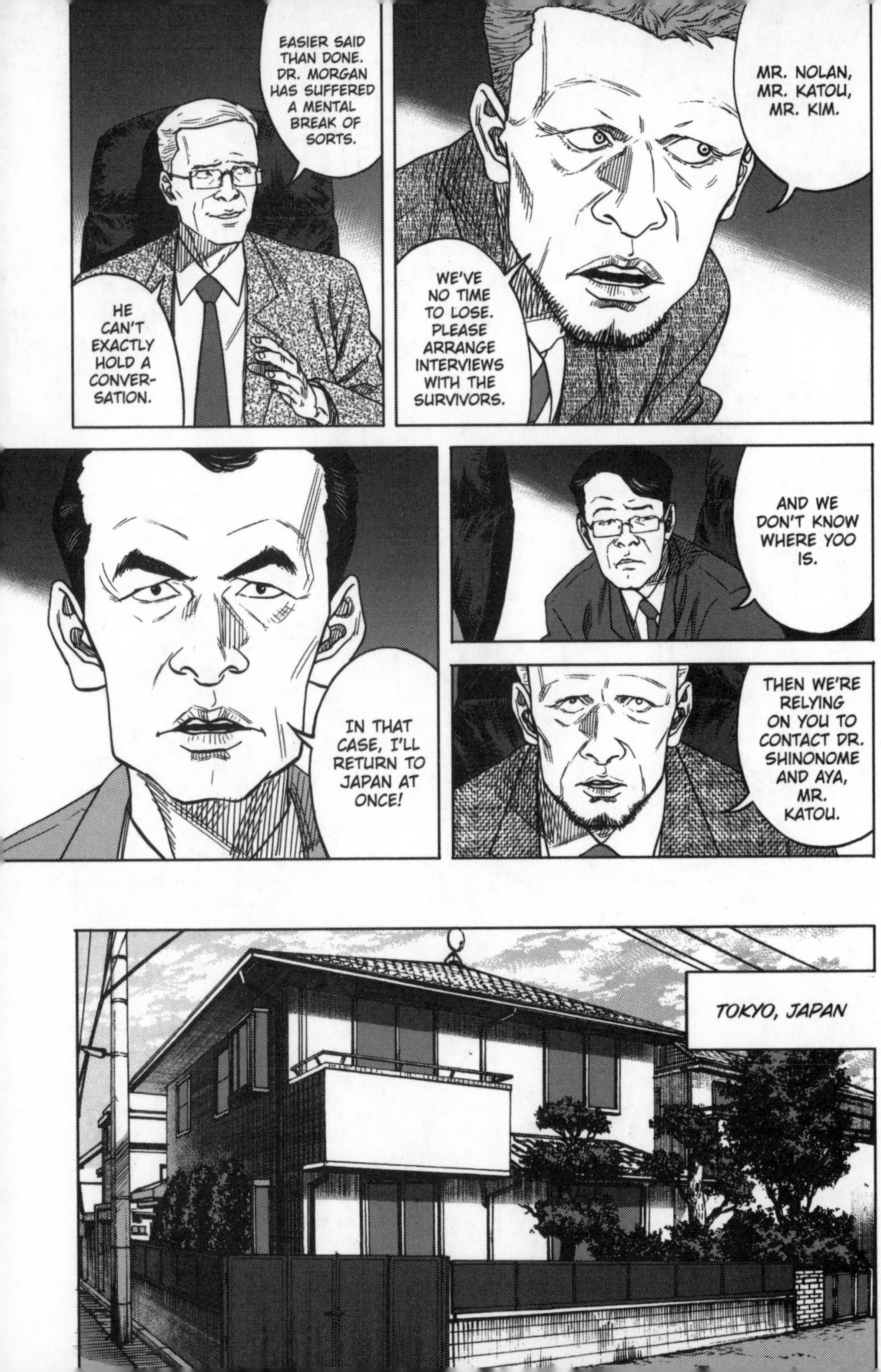
MR. NOLAN, MR. KATOU, MR. KIM.
WE'VE NO TIME TO LOSE. PLEASE ARRANGE INTERVIEWS WITH THE SURVIVORS.
EASIER SAID THAN DONE. DR. MORGAN HAS SUFFERED A MENTAL BREAK OF SORTS.
HE CAN'T EXACTLY HOLD A CONVER-SATION.
AND WE DON'T KNOW WHERE YOO IS.
THEN WE'RE RELYING ON YOU TO CONTACT DR. SHINONOME AND AYA, MR. KATOU.
IN THAT CASE, I'LL RETURN TO JAPAN AT ONCE!
TOKYO, JAPAN

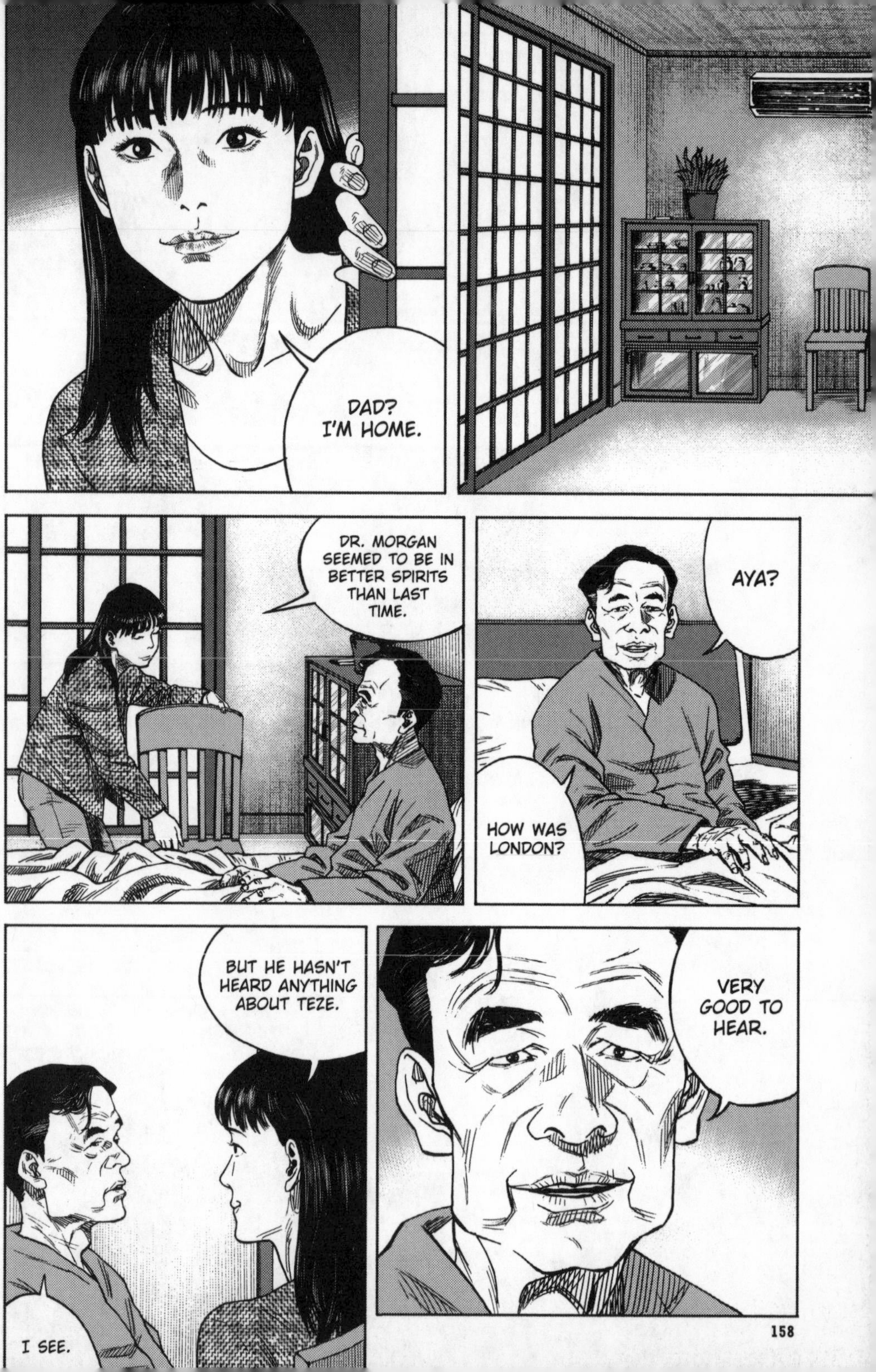
DAD? I'M HOME.
AYA?
HOW WAS LONDON?
DR. MORGAN SEEMED TO BE IN BETTER SPIRITS THAN LAST TIME.
VERY GOOD TO HEAR.
BUT HE HASN'T HEARD ANYTHING ABOUT TEZE.
I SEE.

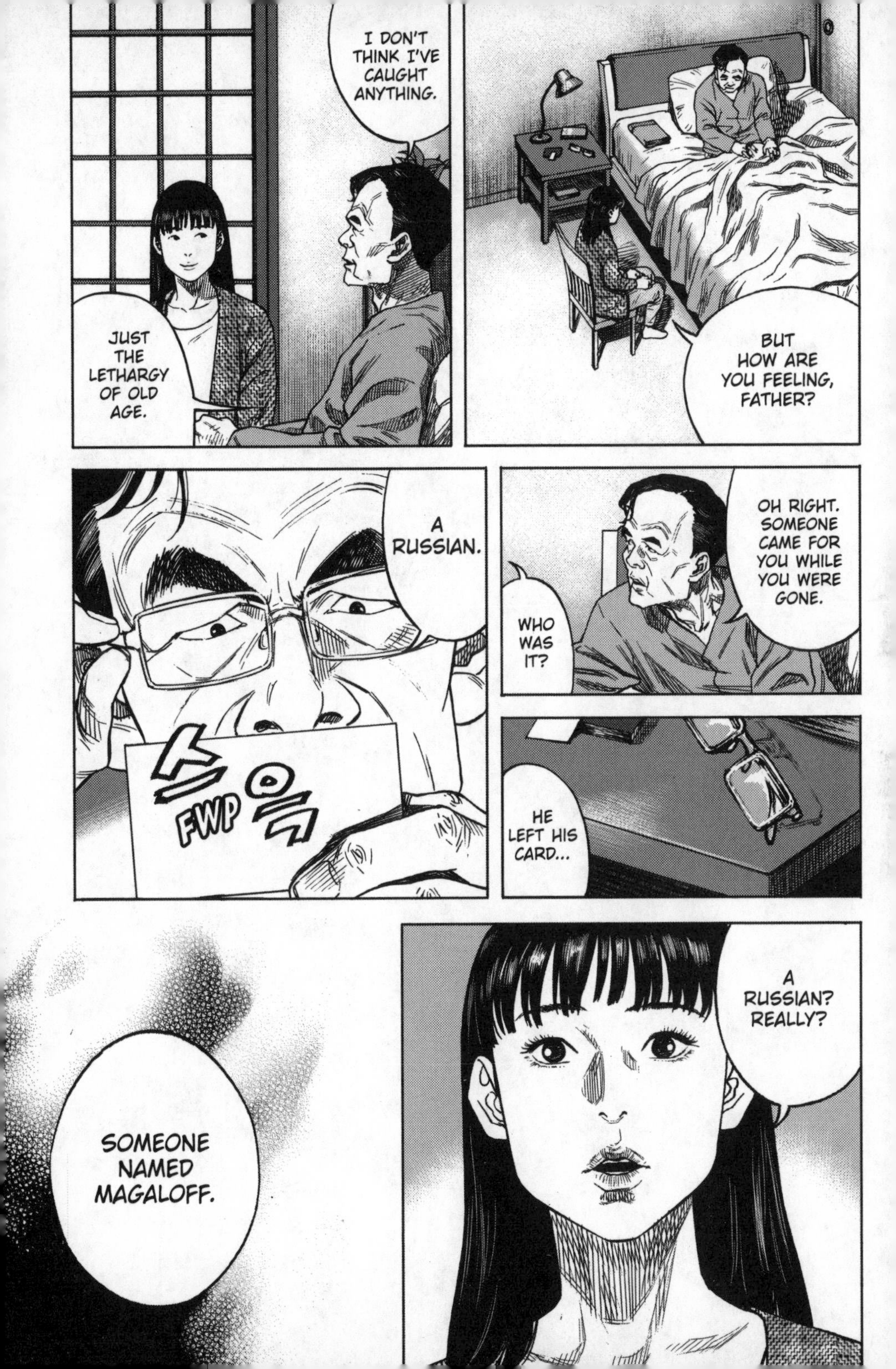
BUT HOW ARE YOU FEELING, FATHER?
I DON'T THINK I'VE CAUGHT ANYTHING.
JUST THE LETHARGY OF OLD AGE.
OH RIGHT. SOMEONE CAME FOR YOU WHILE YOU WERE GONE.
WHO WAS IT?
HE LEFT HIS CARD...
A RUSSIAN.
FWP
A RUSSIAN? REALLY?
SOMEONE NAMED MAGALOFF.

KING OF EDEN

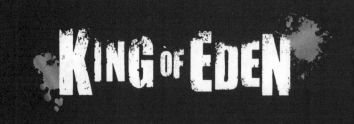

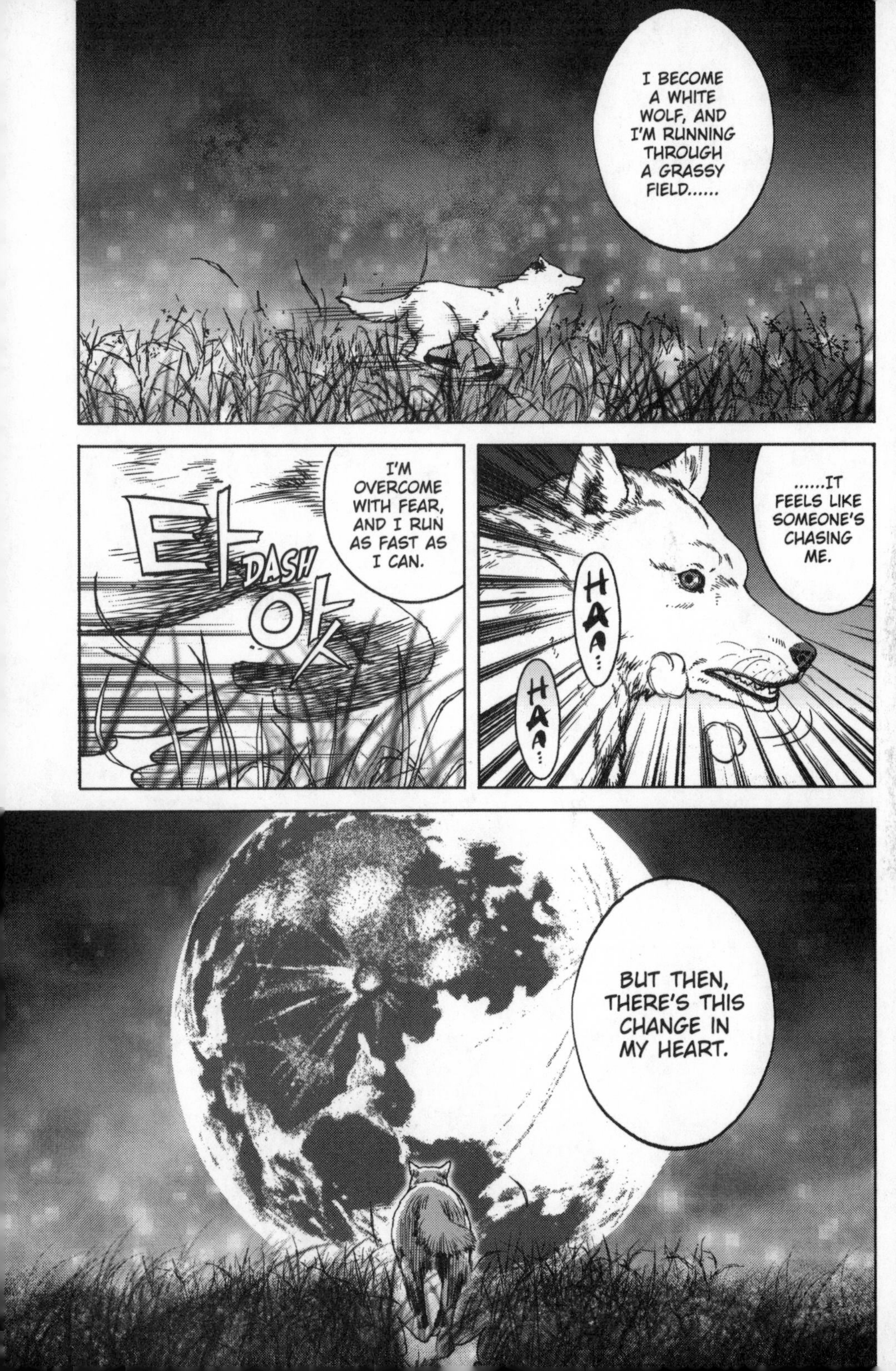
I BECOME A WHITE WOLF, AND I'M RUNNING THROUGH A GRASSY FIELD......
......IT FEELS LIKE SOMEONE'S CHASING ME.
HAA...
HAA...
I'M OVERCOME WITH FEAR, AND I RUN AS FAST AS I CAN.
타악
DASH
BUT THEN, THERE'S THIS CHANGE IN MY HEART.

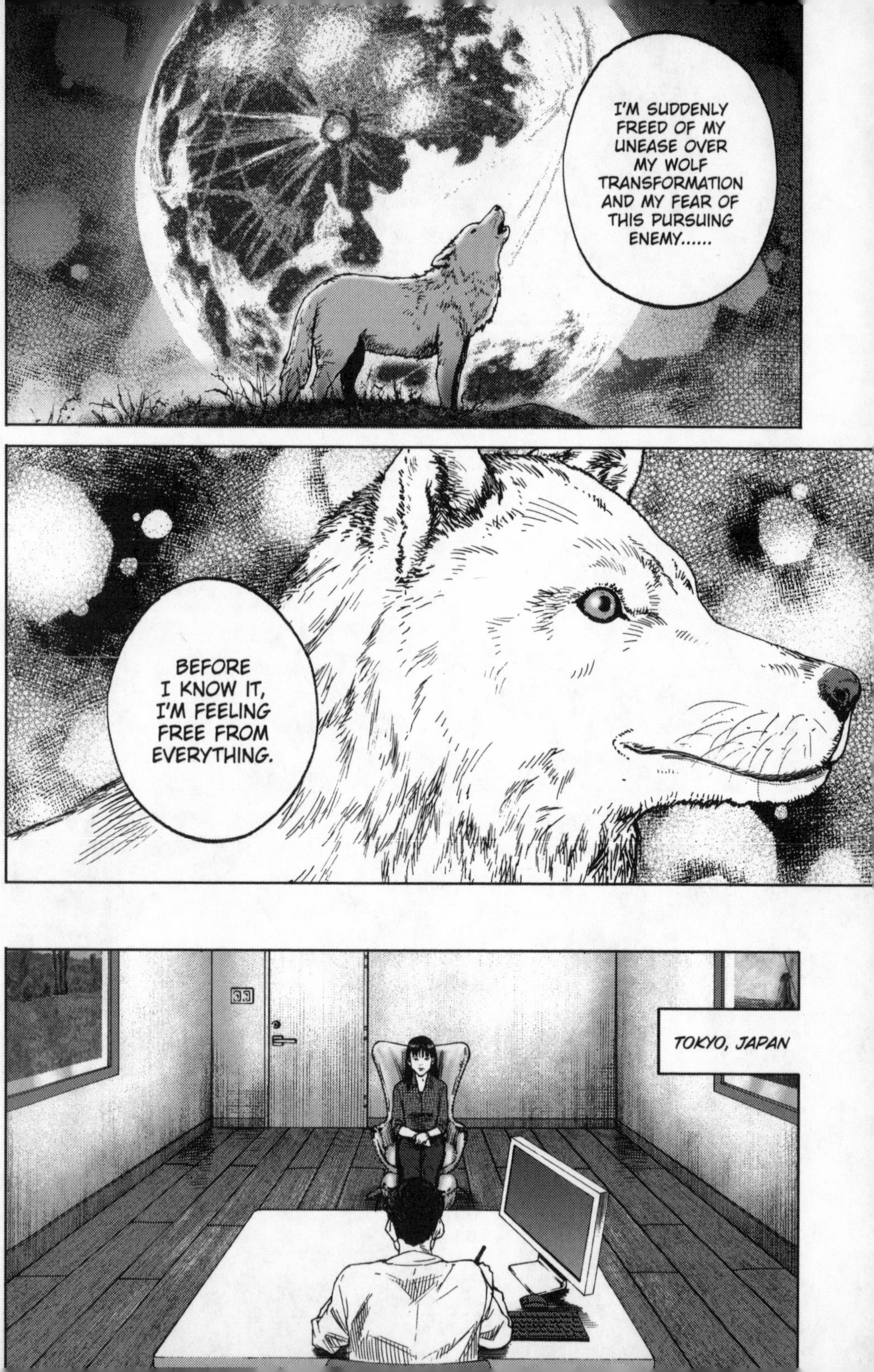
I'M SUDDENLY FREED OF MY UNEASE OVER MY WOLF TRANSFORMATION AND MY FEAR OF THIS PURSUING ENEMY......
BEFORE I KNOW IT, I'M FEELING FREE FROM EVERYTHING.
TOKYO, JAPAN

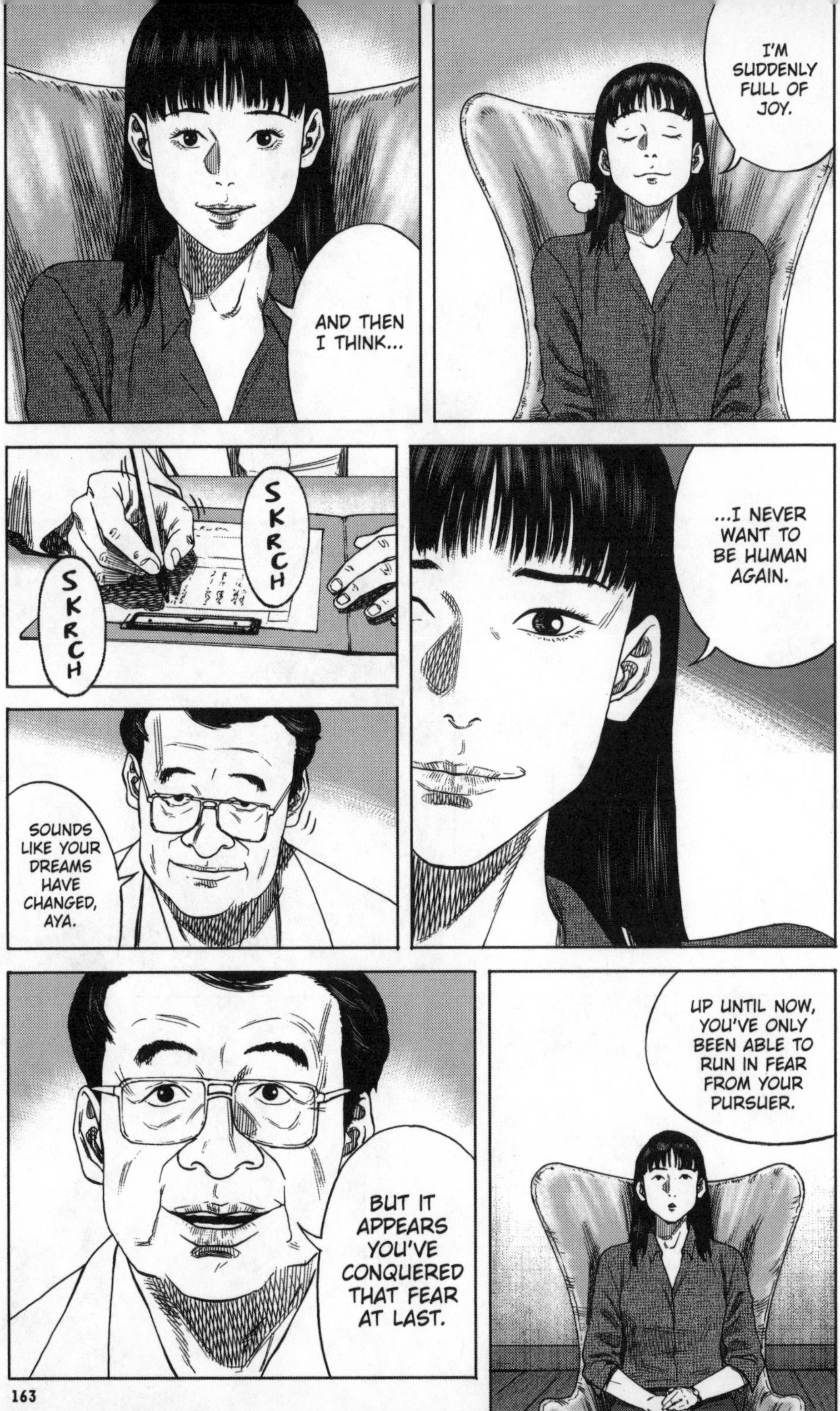
I'M SUDDENLY FULL OF JOY.
AND THEN I THINK...
...I NEVER WANT TO BE HUMAN AGAIN.
SKRCH
SKRCH
SOUNDS LIKE YOUR DREAMS HAVE CHANGED, AYA.
UP UNTIL NOW, YOU'VE ONLY BEEN ABLE TO RUN IN FEAR FROM YOUR PURSUER.
BUT IT APPEARS YOU'VE CONQUERED THAT FEAR AT LAST.

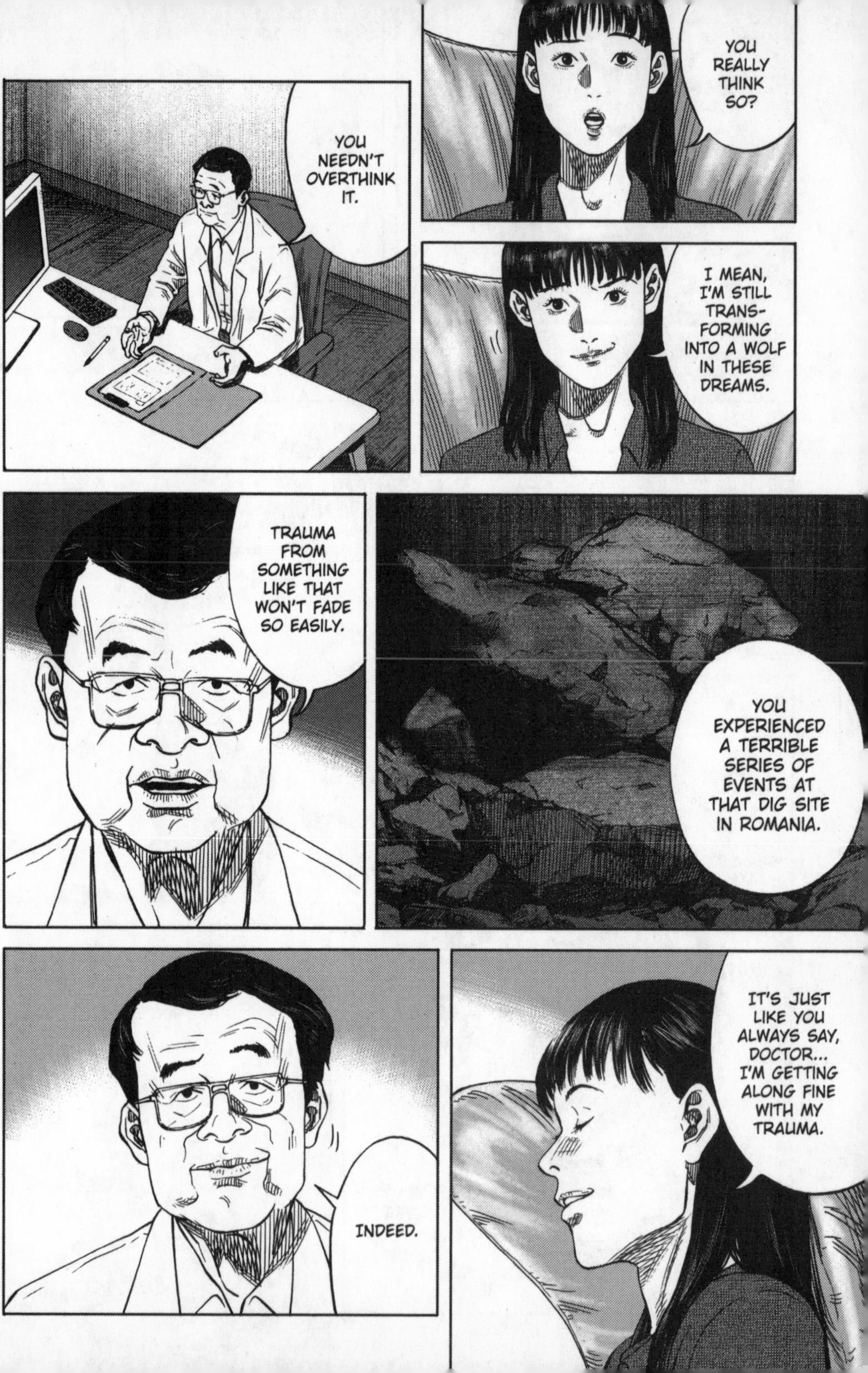
YOU REALLY THINK SO?
I MEAN, I'M STILL TRANS-FORMING INTO A WOLF IN THESE DREAMS.
YOU NEEDN'T OVERTHINK IT.
YOU EXPERIENCED A TERRIBLE SERIES OF EVENTS AT THAT DIG SITE IN ROMANIA.
TRAUMA FROM SOMETHING LIKE THAT WON'T FADE SO EASILY.
IT'S JUST LIKE YOU ALWAYS SAY, DOCTOR... I'M GETTING ALONG FINE WITH MY TRAUMA.
INDEED.

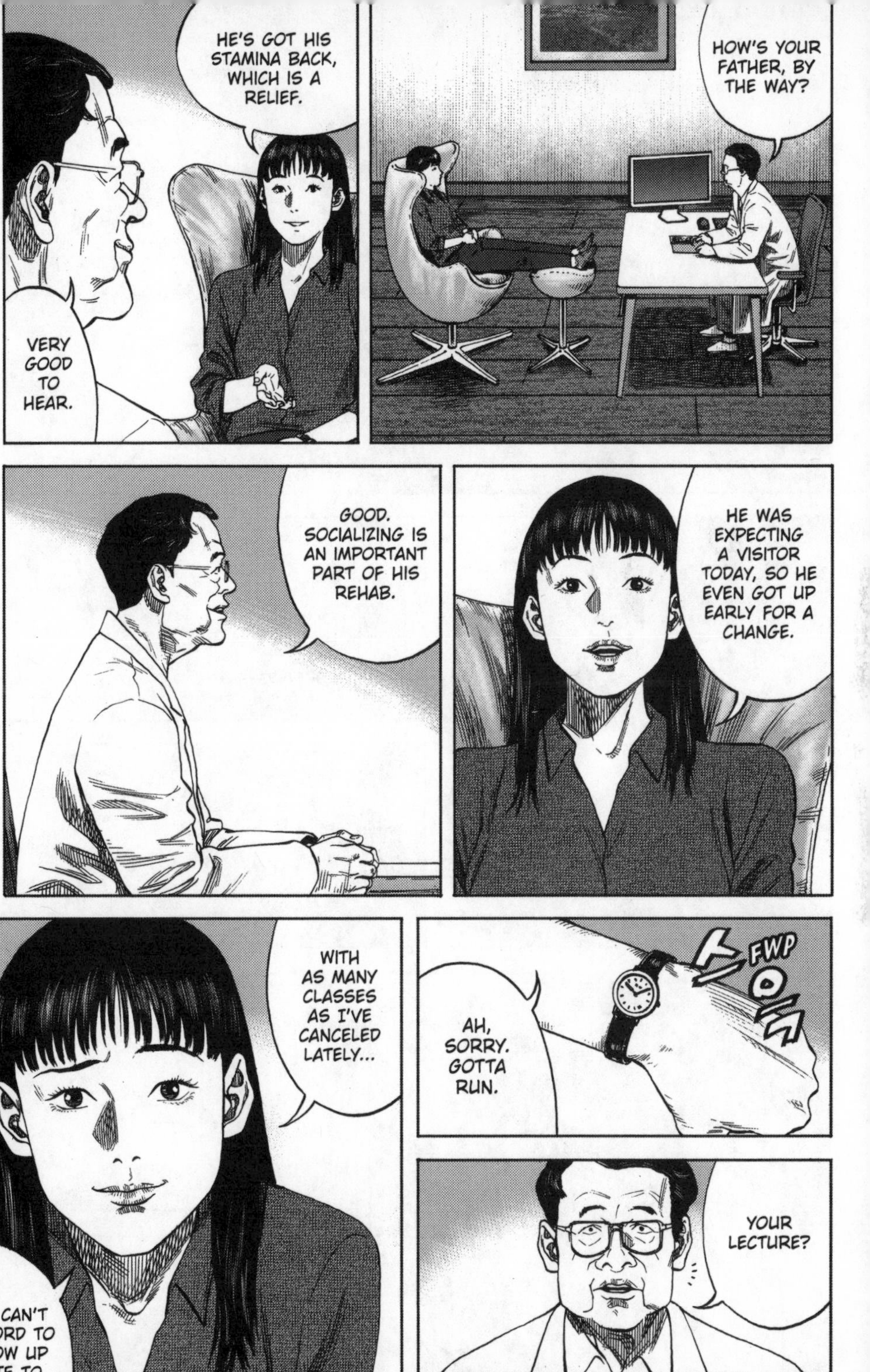
HOW'S YOUR FATHER, BY THE WAY?
HE'S GOT HIS STAMINA BACK, WHICH IS A RELIEF.
VERY GOOD TO HEAR.
HE WAS EXPECTING A VISITOR TODAY, SO HE EVEN GOT UP EARLY FOR A CHANGE.
GOOD. SOCIALIZING IS AN IMPORTANT PART OF HIS REHAB.
FWP
AH, SORRY. GOTTA RUN.
YOUR LECTURE?
WITH AS MANY CLASSES AS I'VE CANCELED LATELY...
...I CAN'T AFFORD TO SHOW UP LATE TO THIS ONE.

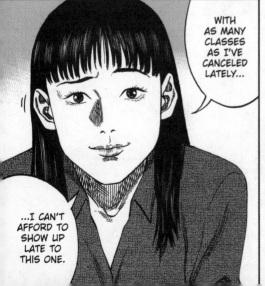

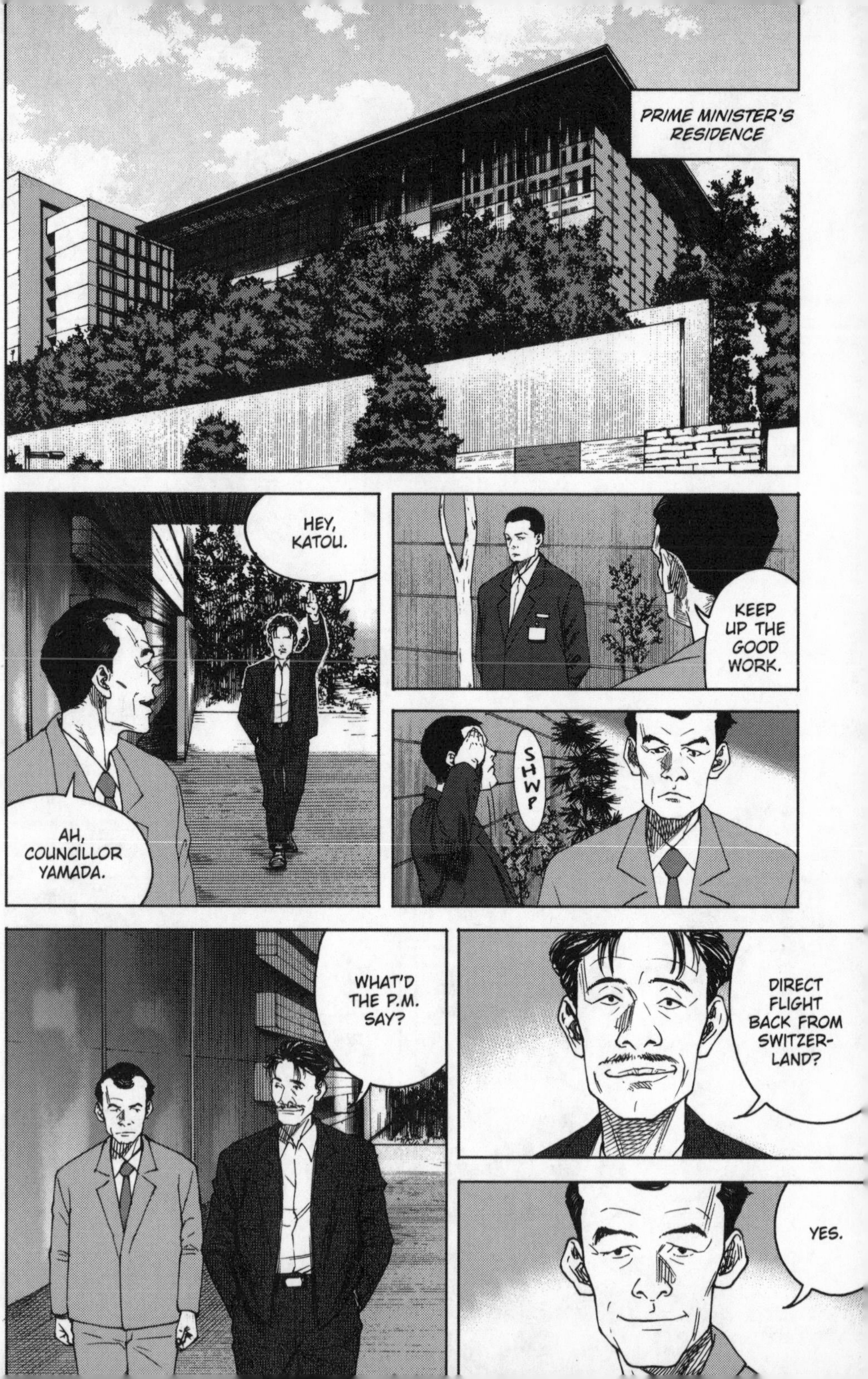
PRIME MINISTER'S RESIDENCE
KEEP UP THE GOOD WORK.
SHWP
HEY, KATOU.
AH, COUNCILLOR YAMADA.
DIRECT FLIGHT BACK FROM SWITZER-LAND?
YES.
WHAT'D THE P.M. SAY?

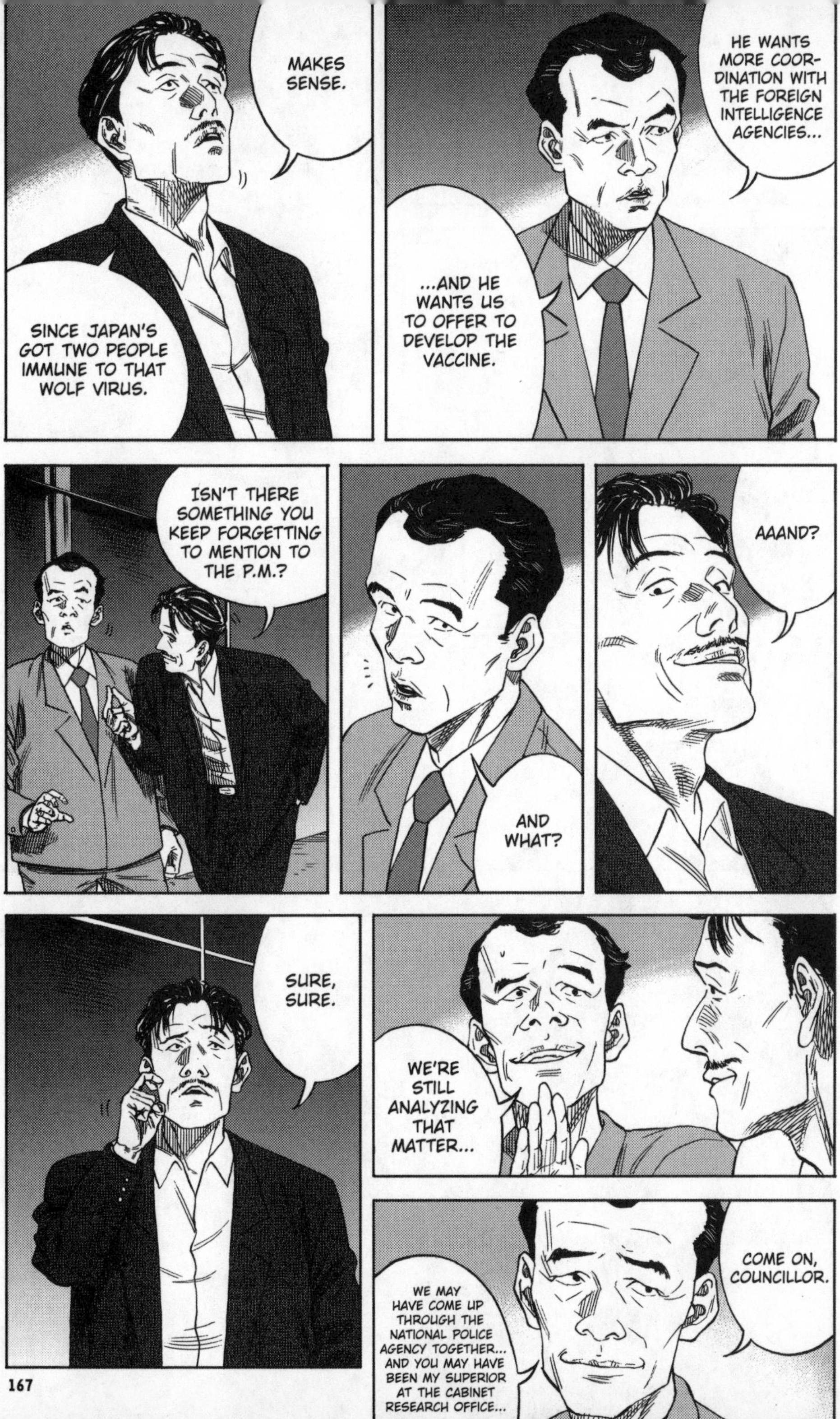
HE WANTS MORE COORDINATION WITH THE FOREIGN INTELLIGENCE AGENCIES...
...AND HE WANTS US TO OFFER TO DEVELOP THE VACCINE.
MAKES SENSE.
SINCE JAPAN'S GOT TWO PEOPLE IMMUNE TO THAT WOLF VIRUS.
AAAND?
AND WHAT?
ISN'T THERE SOMETHING YOU KEEP FORGETTING TO MENTION TO THE P.M.?
WE'RE STILL ANALYZING THAT MATTER...
COME ON, COUNCILLOR.
WE MAY HAVE COME UP THROUGH THE NATIONAL POLICE AGENCY TOGETHER... AND YOU MAY HAVE BEEN MY SUPERIOR AT THE CABINET RESEARCH OFFICE...
SURE, SURE.

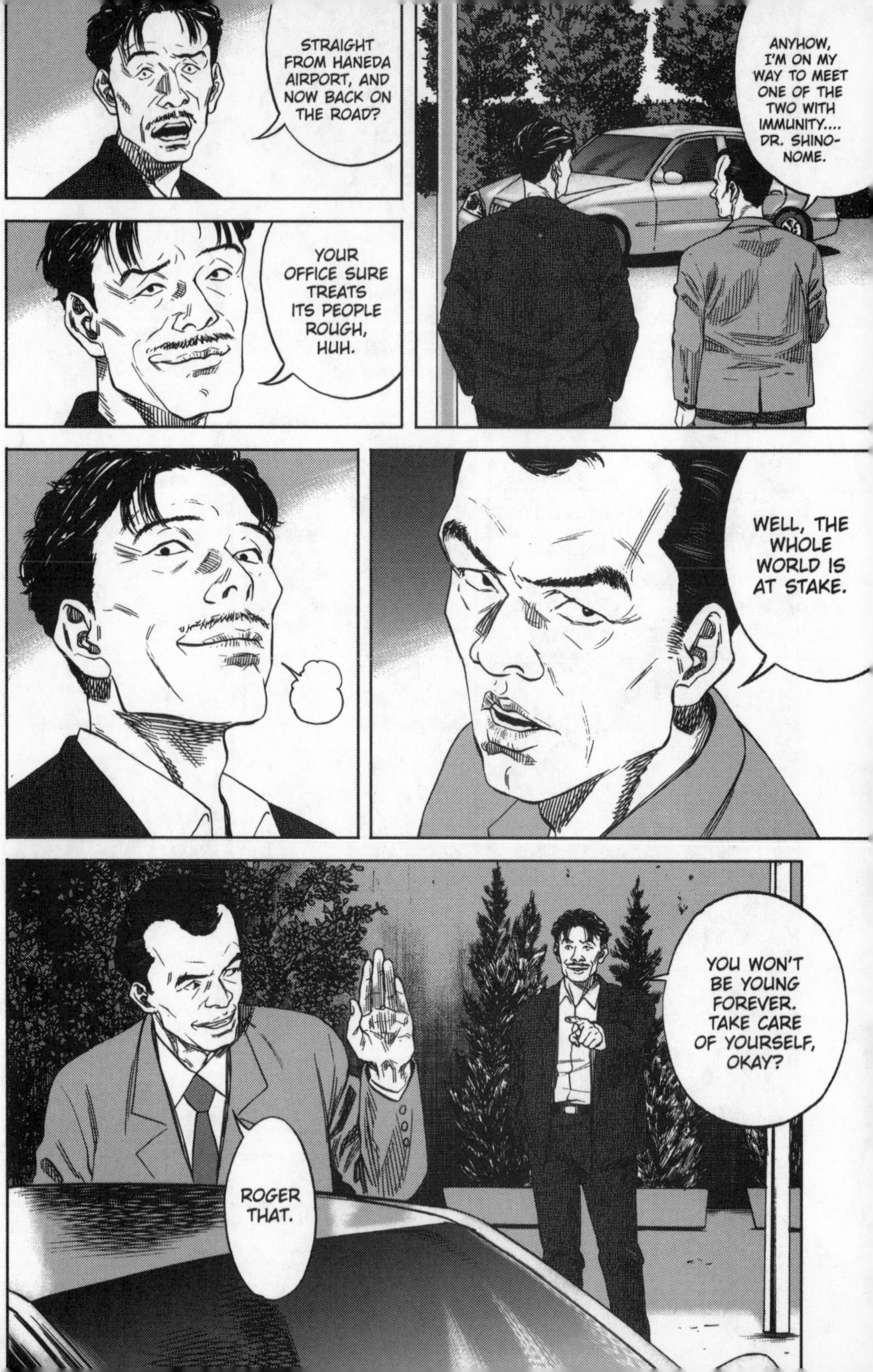
ANYHOW, I'M ON MY WAY TO MEET ONE OF THE TWO WITH IMMUNITY.... DR. SHINO-NOME.
STRAIGHT FROM HANEDA AIRPORT, AND NOW BACK ON THE ROAD?
YOUR OFFICE SURE TREATS ITS PEOPLE ROUGH, HUH.
WELL, THE WHOLE WORLD IS AT STAKE.
YOU WON'T BE YOUNG FOREVER. TAKE CARE OF YOURSELF, OKAY?
ROGER THAT.

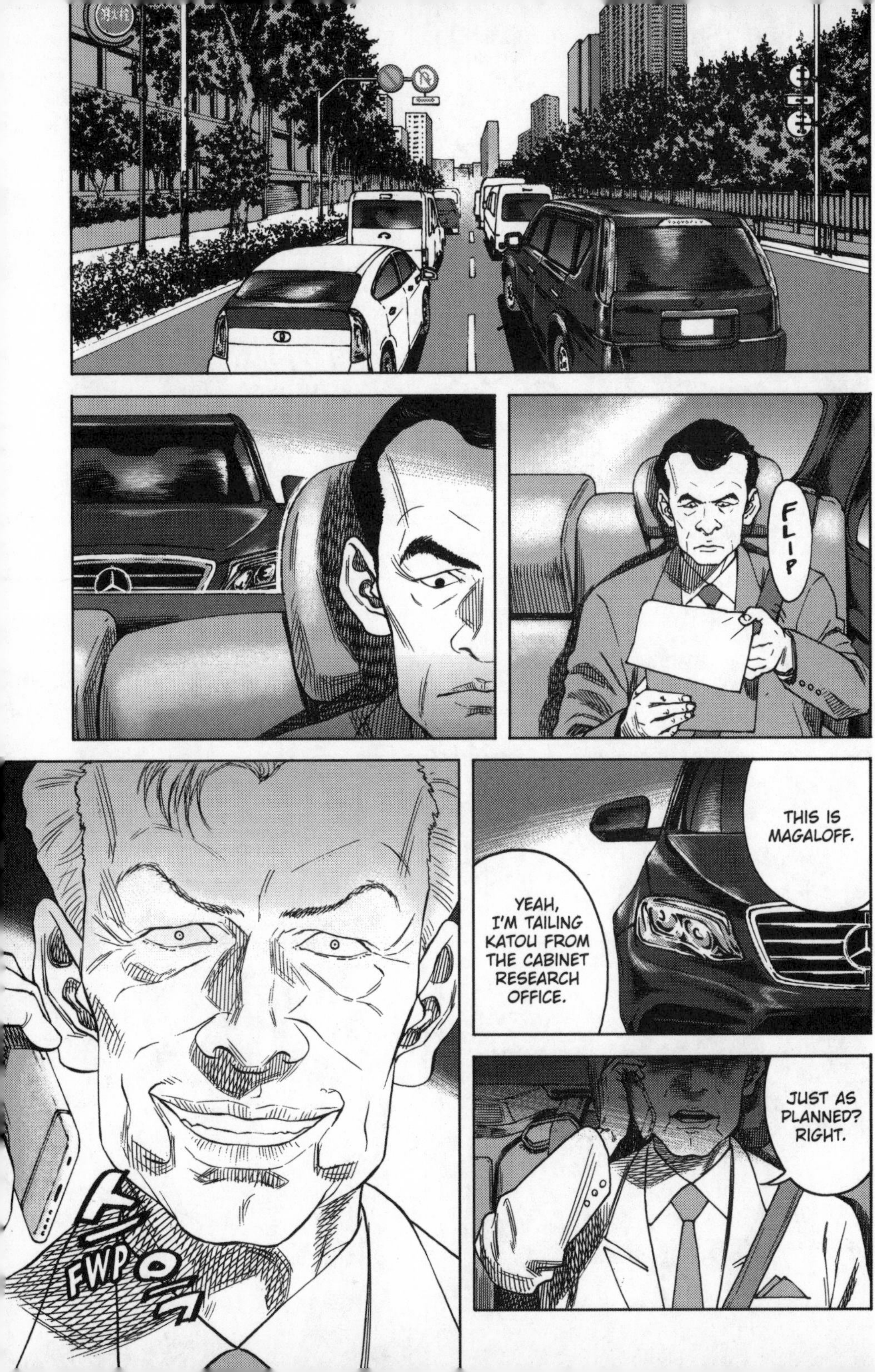
FLIP
THIS IS MAGALOFF.
YEAH, I'M TAILING KATOU FROM THE CABINET RESEARCH OFFICE.
JUST AS PLANNED? RIGHT.
FWP

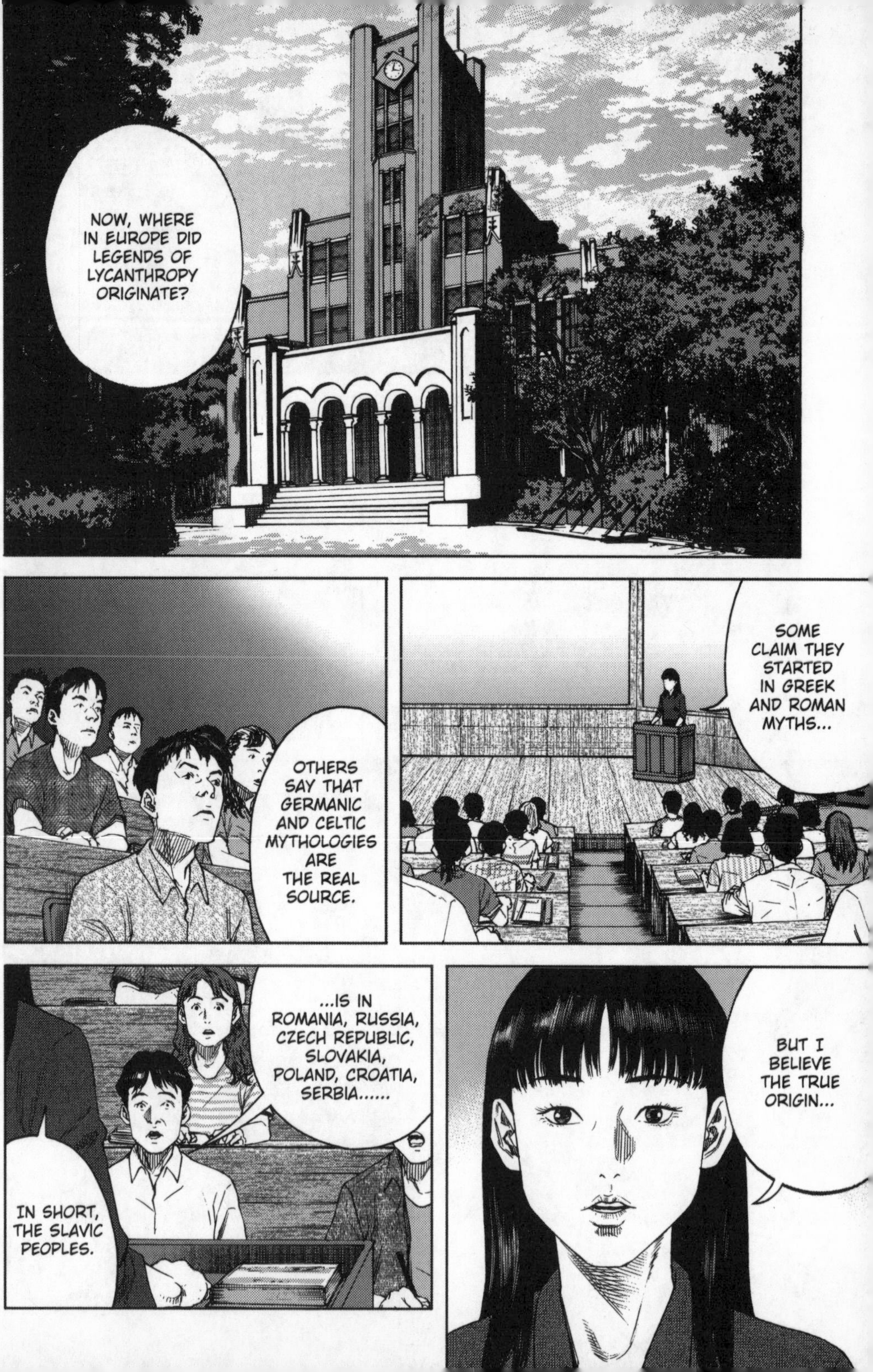
NOW, WHERE IN EUROPE DID LEGENDS OF LYCANTHROPY ORIGINATE?
SOME CLAIM THEY STARTED IN GREEK AND ROMAN MYTHS...
OTHERS SAY THAT GERMANIC AND CELTIC MYTHOLOGIES ARE THE REAL SOURCE.
BUT I BELIEVE THE TRUE ORIGIN...
...IS IN ROMANIA, RUSSIA, CZECH REPUBLIC, SLOVAKIA, POLAND, CROATIA, SERBIA......
IN SHORT, THE SLAVIC PEOPLES.

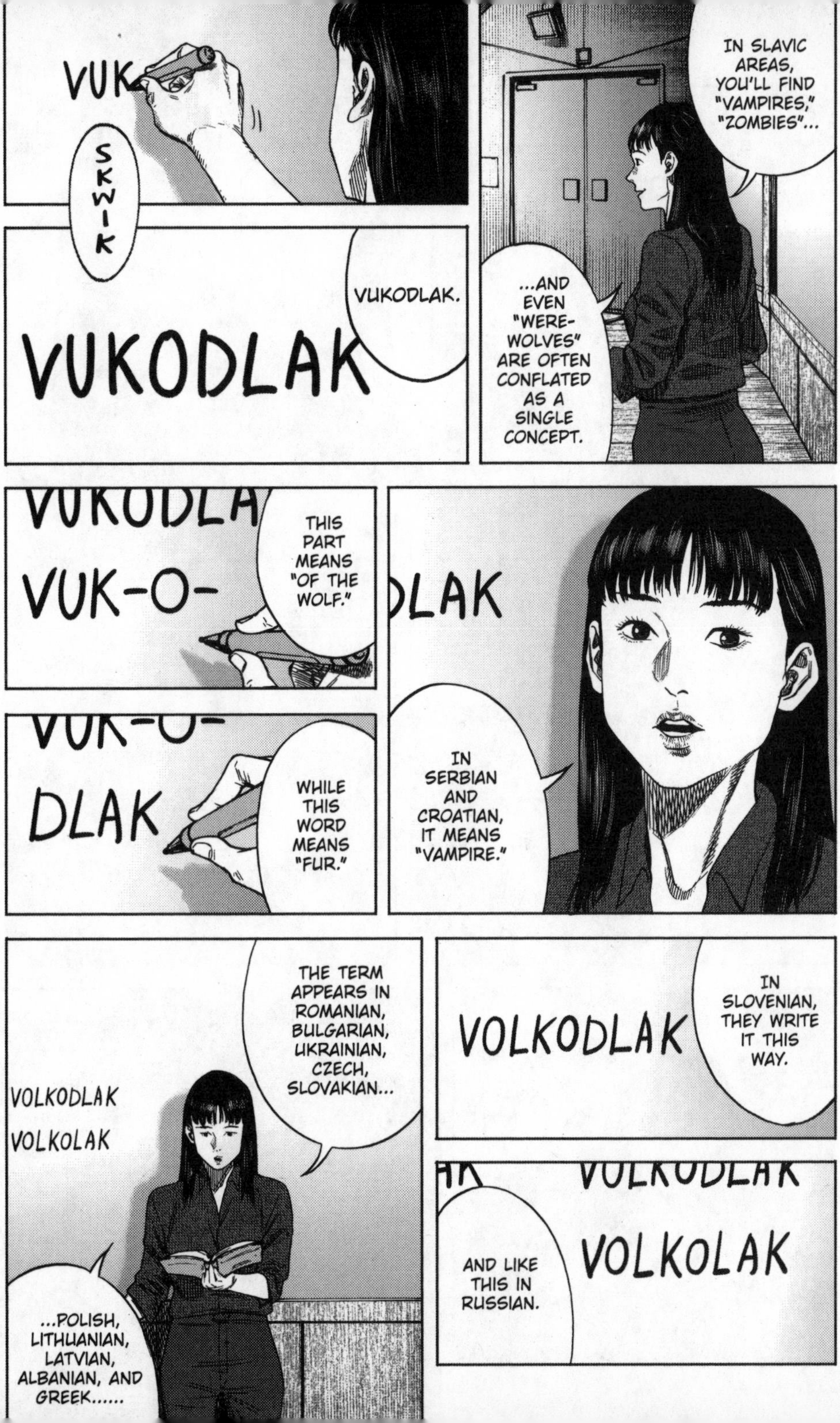
IN SLAVIC AREAS, YOU'LL FIND "VAMPIRES," "ZOMBIES"...
...AND EVEN "WERE-WOLVES" ARE OFTEN CONFLATED AS A SINGLE CONCEPT.
VUK
SKWIK
VUKODLAK.
VUKODLAK
IN SERBIAN AND CROATIAN, IT MEANS "VAMPIRE."
THIS PART MEANS "OF THE WOLF."
VUK-O-
DLAK
WHILE THIS WORD MEANS "FUR."
DLAK
IN SLOVENIAN, THEY WRITE IT THIS WAY.
VOLKODLAK
VOLKOLAK
AND LIKE THIS IN RUSSIAN.
THE TERM APPEARS IN ROMANIAN, BULGARIAN, UKRAINIAN, CZECH, SLOVAKIAN...
VOLKODLAK
VOLKOLAK
...POLISH, LITHUANIAN, LATVIAN, ALBANIAN, AND GREEK......

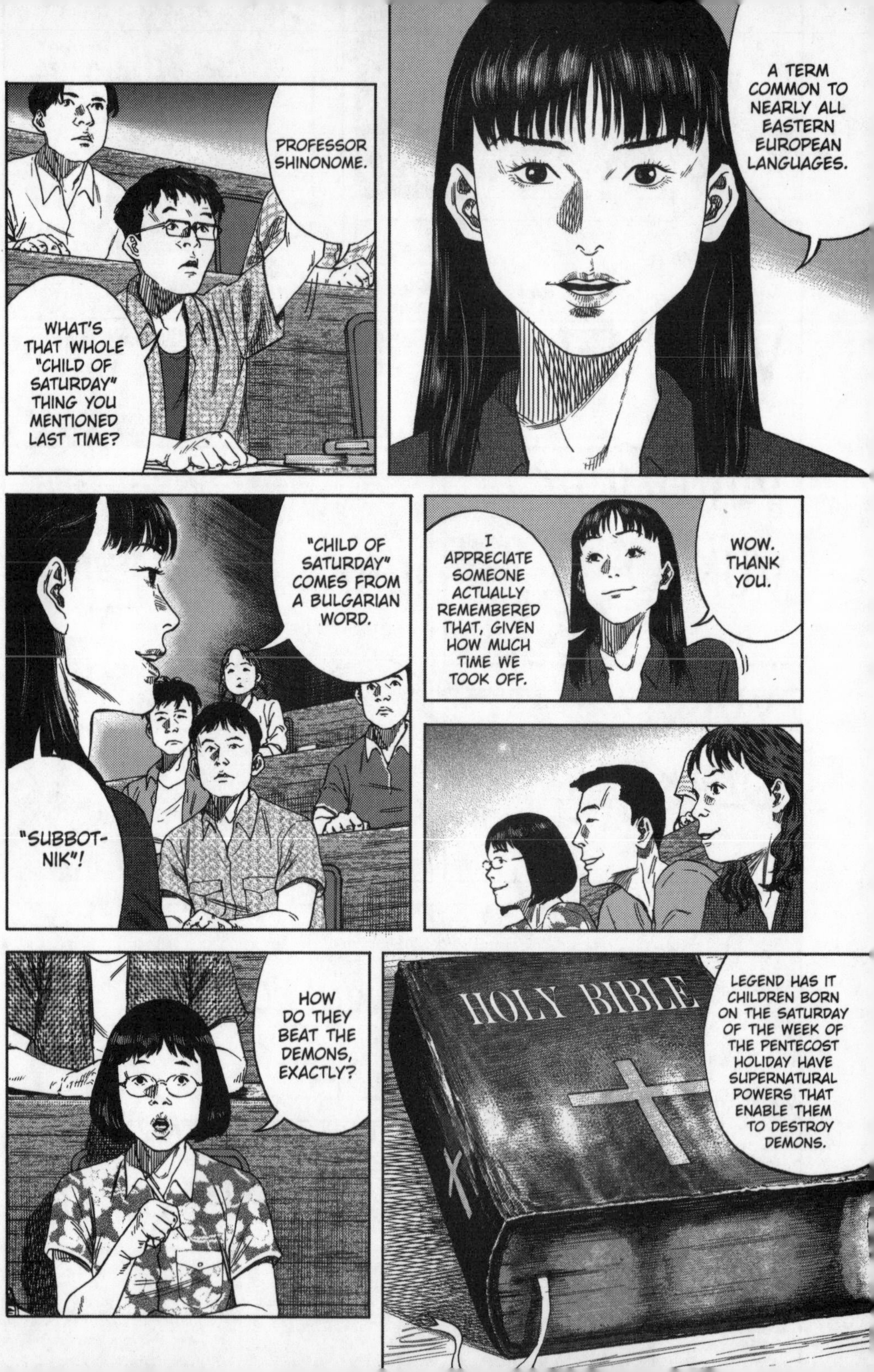
A TERM COMMON TO NEARLY ALL EASTERN EUROPEAN LANGUAGES.
PROFESSOR SHINONOME.
WHAT'S THAT WHOLE "CHILD OF SATURDAY" THING YOU MENTIONED LAST TIME?
WOW. THANK YOU.
I APPRECIATE SOMEONE ACTUALLY REMEMBERED THAT, GIVEN HOW MUCH TIME WE TOOK OFF.
"CHILD OF SATURDAY" COMES FROM A BULGARIAN WORD.
"SUBBOT-NIK"!
HOLY BIBLE
LEGEND HAS IT CHILDREN BORN ON THE SATURDAY OF THE WEEK OF THE PENTECOST HOLIDAY HAVE SUPERNATURAL POWERS THAT ENABLE THEM TO DESTROY DEMONS.
HOW DO THEY BEAT THE DEMONS, EXACTLY?

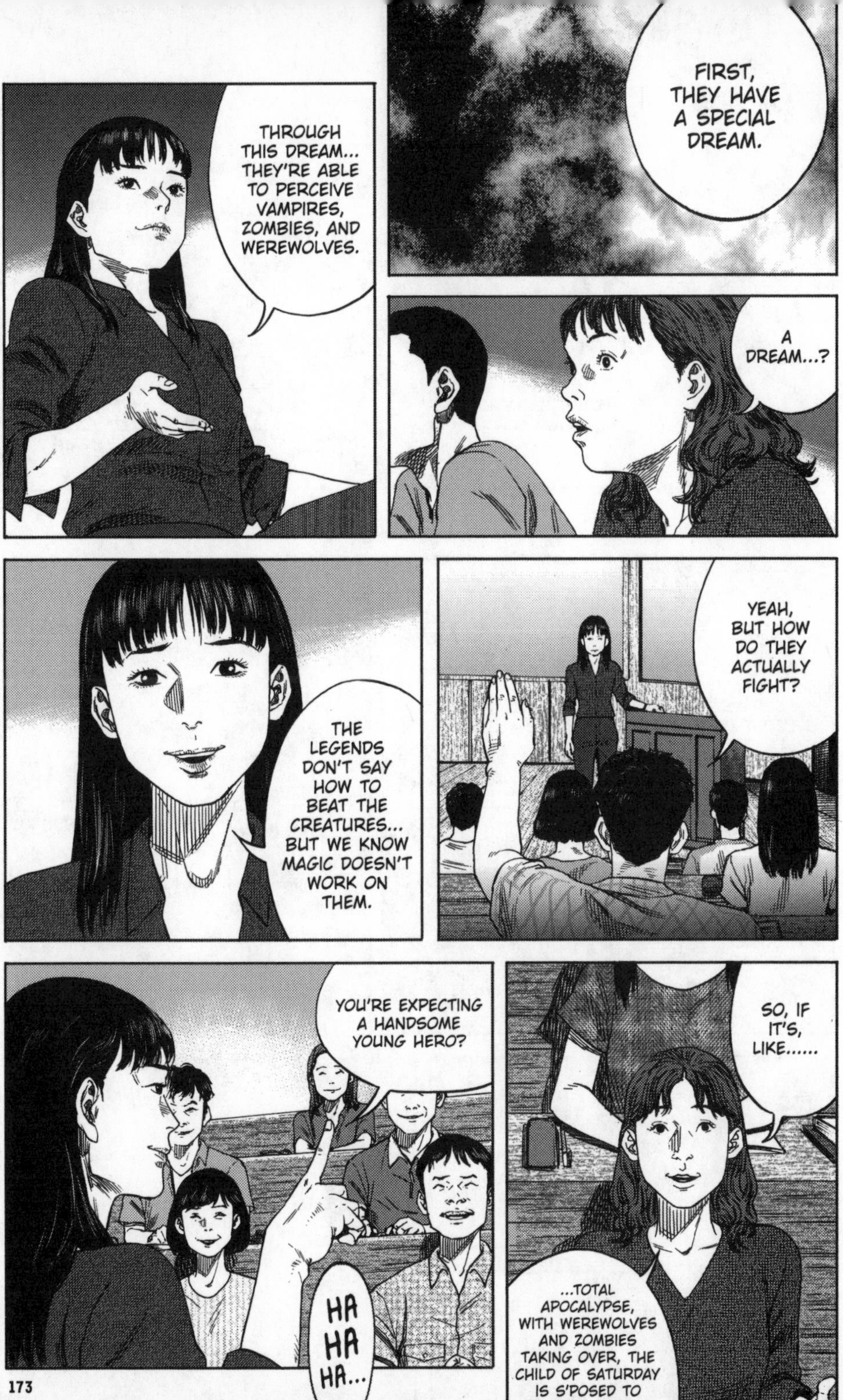
FIRST, THEY HAVE A SPECIAL DREAM.
A DREAM...?
THROUGH THIS DREAM... THEY'RE ABLE TO PERCEIVE VAMPIRES, ZOMBIES, AND WEREWOLVES.
YEAH, BUT HOW DO THEY ACTUALLY FIGHT?
THE LEGENDS DON'T SAY HOW TO BEAT THE CREATURES... BUT WE KNOW MAGIC DOESN'T WORK ON THEM.
SO, IF IT'S, LIKE......
...TOTAL APOCALYPSE, WITH WEREWOLVES AND ZOMBIES TAKING OVER, THE CHILD OF SATURDAY IS S'POSED TO PROTECT US ALL?
YOU'RE EXPECTING A HANDSOME YOUNG HERO?
HA HA HA...

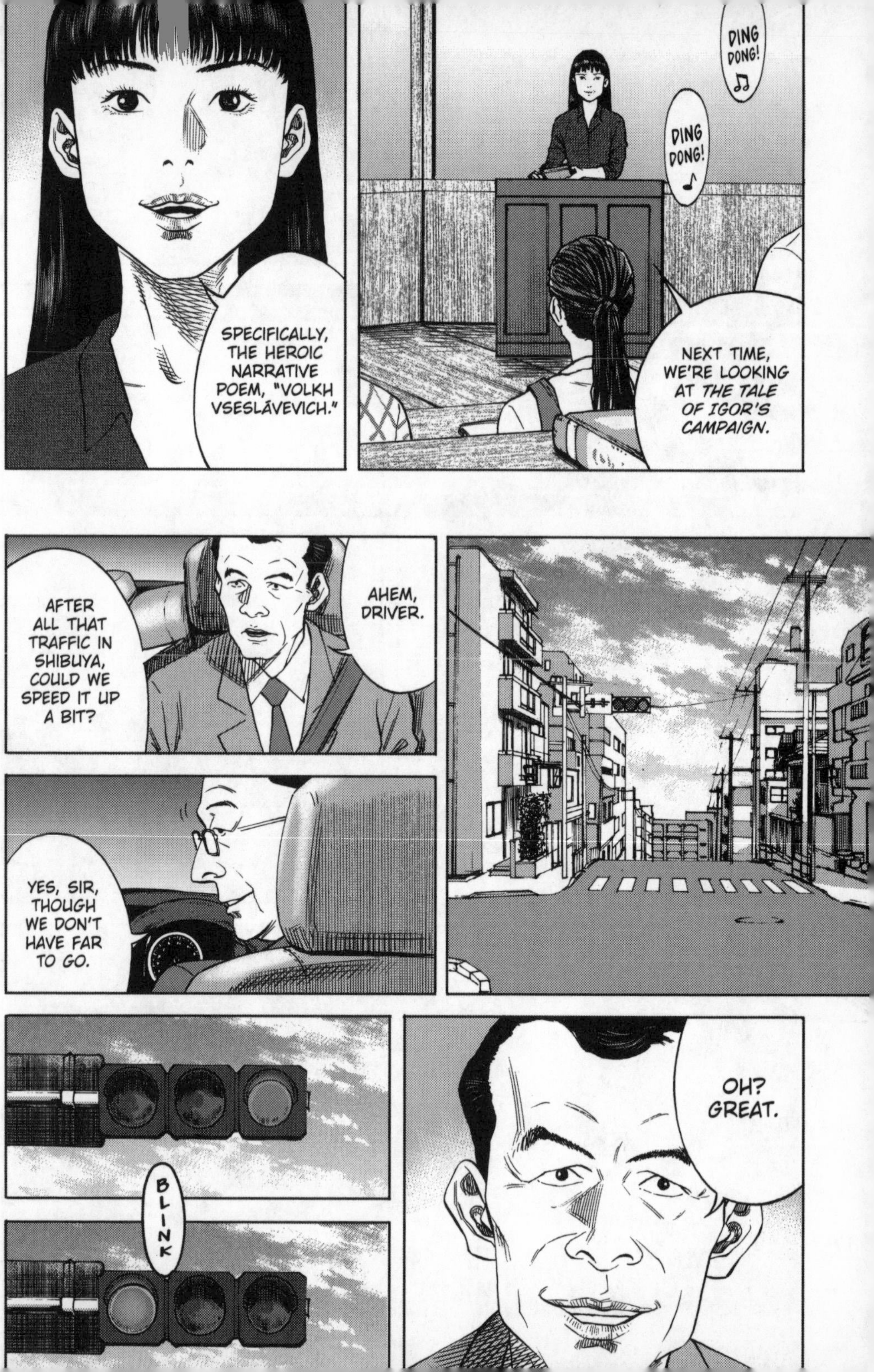
DING DONG! ♫
DING DONG! ♪
NEXT TIME, WE'RE LOOKING AT *THE TALE OF IGOR'S CAMPAIGN*.
SPECIFICALLY, THE HEROIC NARRATIVE POEM, "VOLKH VSESLÁVEVICH."
AHEM, DRIVER.
AFTER ALL THAT TRAFFIC IN SHIBUYA, COULD WE SPEED IT UP A BIT?
YES, SIR, THOUGH WE DON'T HAVE FAR TO GO.
OH? GREAT.
BLINK

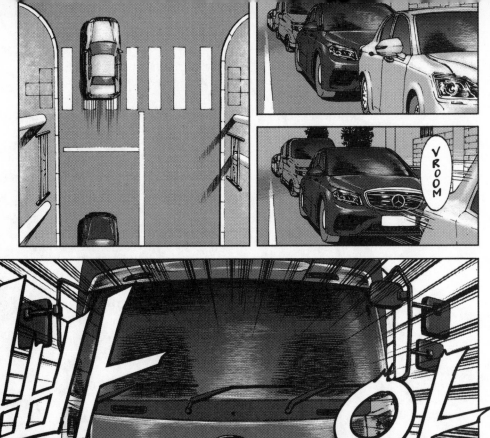

VROOM

BAM

야

아

!!

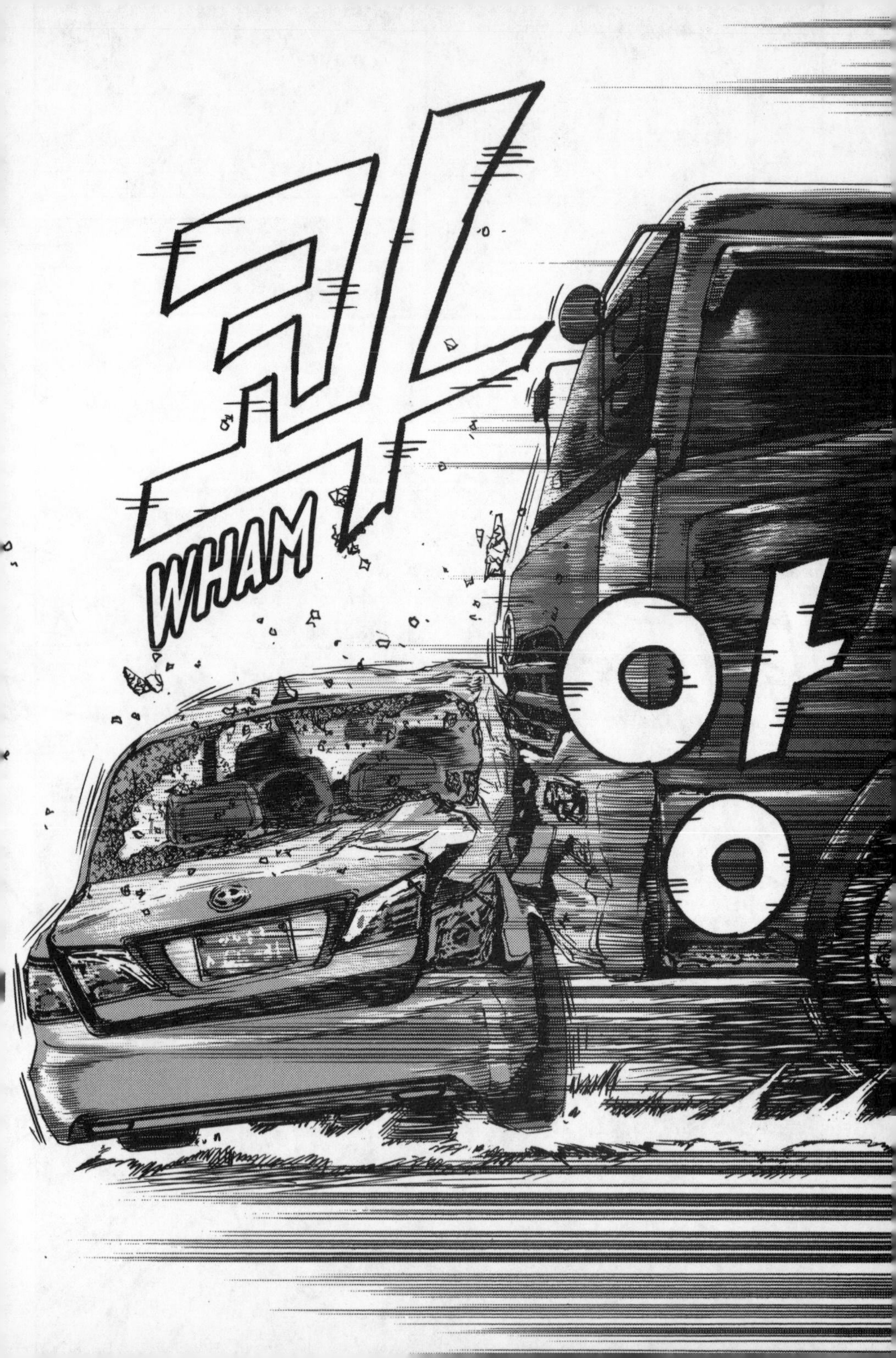
WHAM

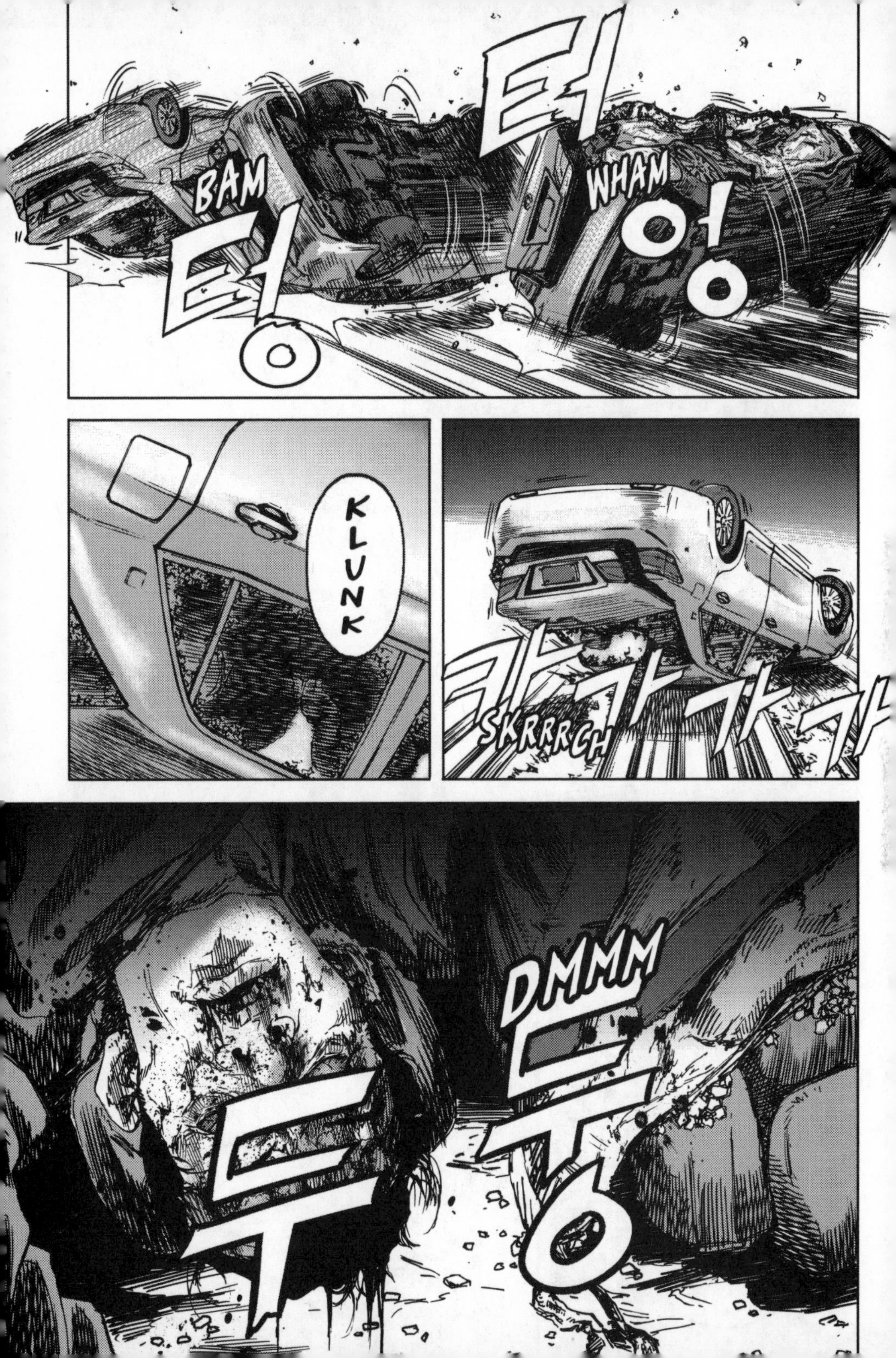
WHAM
BAM
SKRRRCH
KLUNK
DMMM

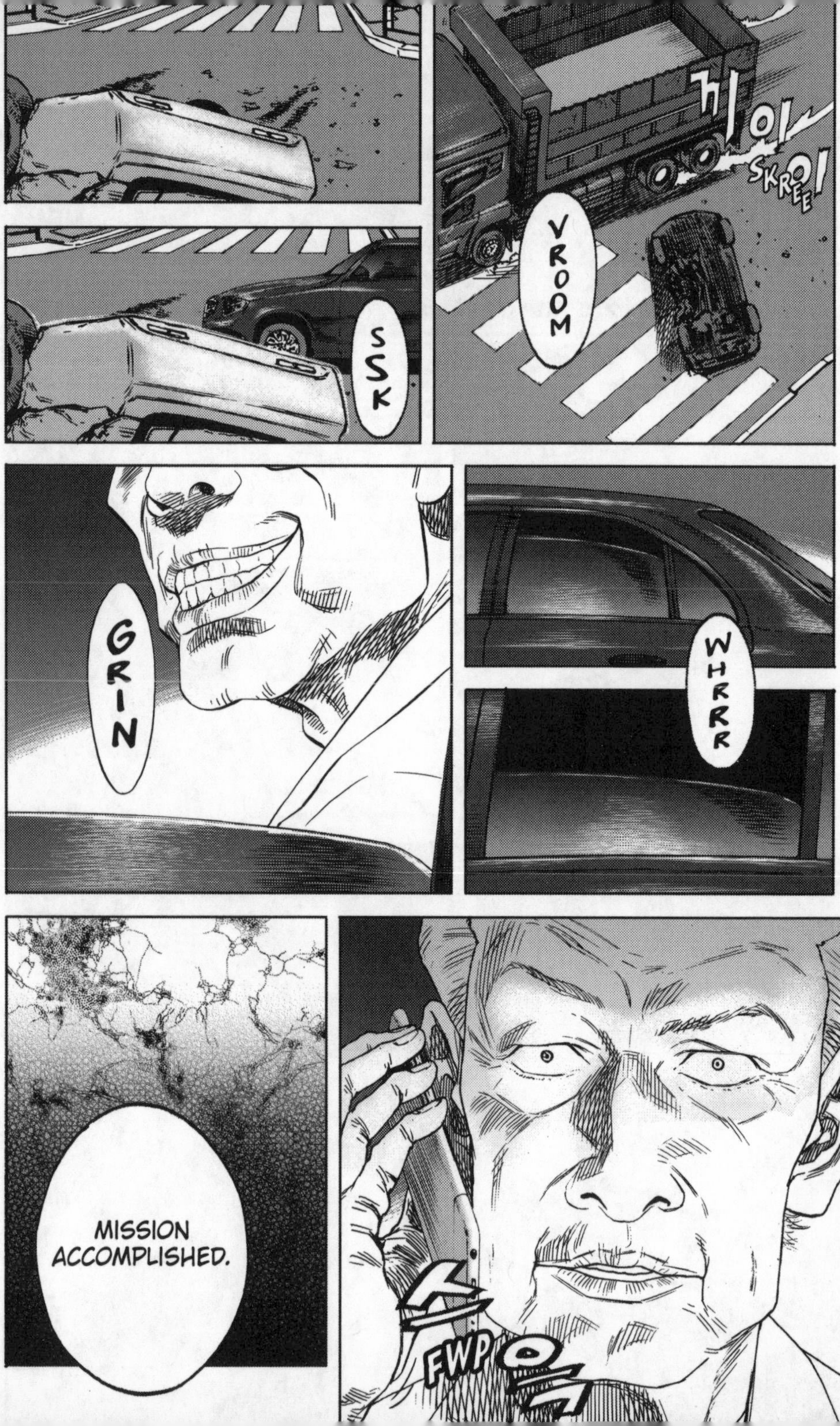
SKREE
VROOM
SSK
WHRRR
GRIN
FWP
MISSION ACCOMPLISHED.

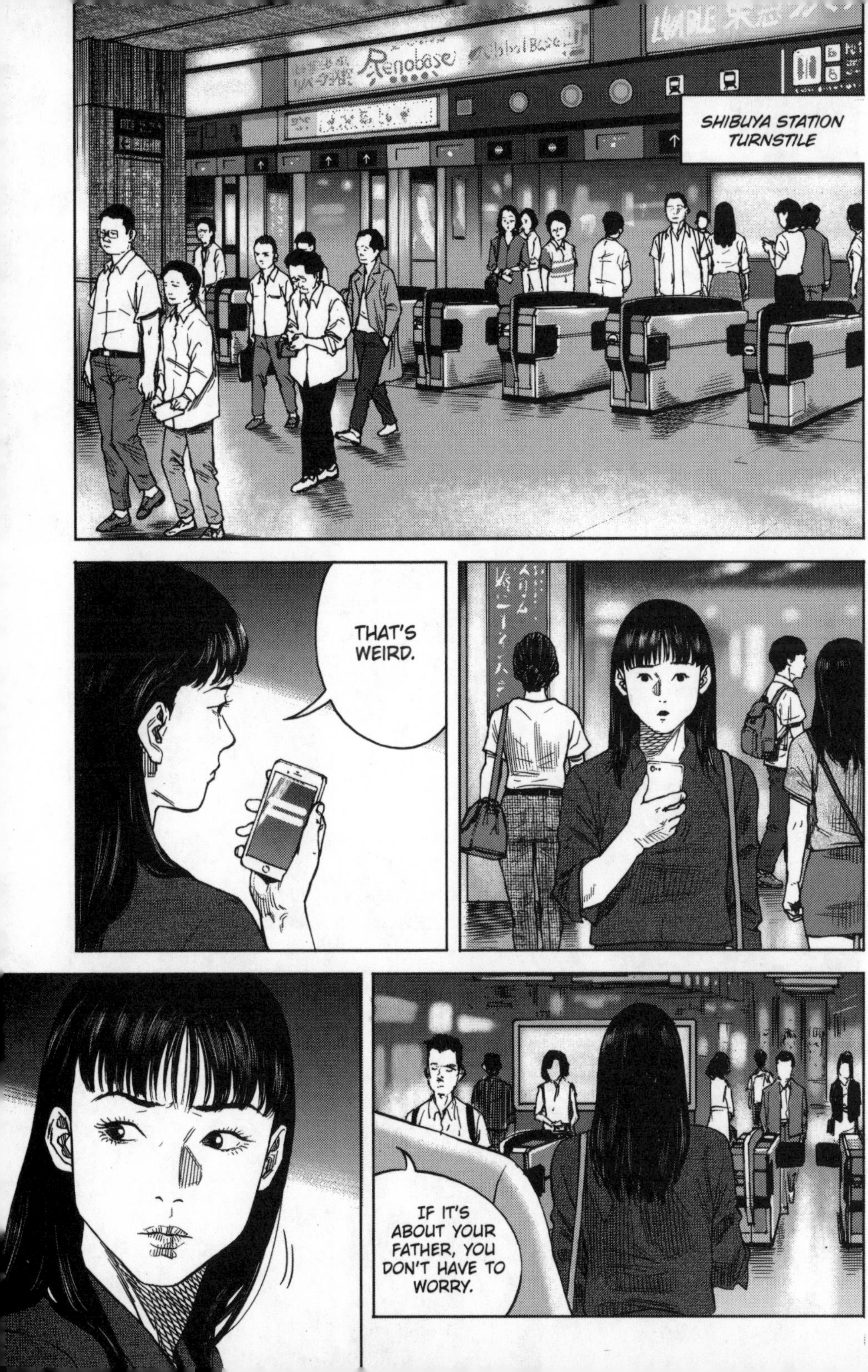
SHIBUYA STATION TURNSTILE
THAT'S WEIRD.
IF IT'S ABOUT YOUR FATHER, YOU DON'T HAVE TO WORRY.

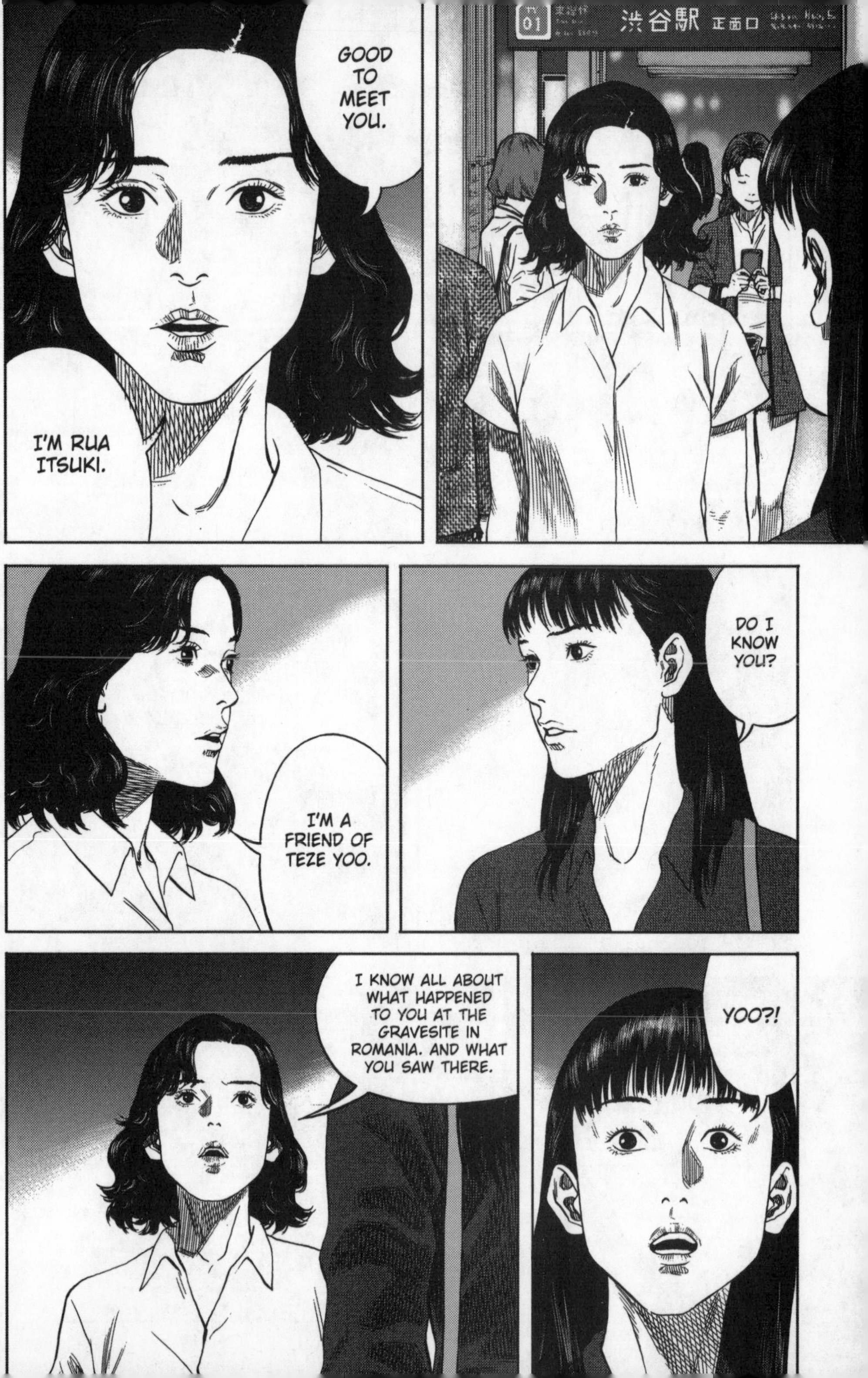
渋谷駅 正面口
GOOD TO MEET YOU.
I'M RUA ITSUKI.
DO I KNOW YOU?
I'M A FRIEND OF TEZE YOO.
YOO?!
I KNOW ALL ABOUT WHAT HAPPENED TO YOU AT THE GRAVESITE IN ROMANIA. AND WHAT YOU SAW THERE.

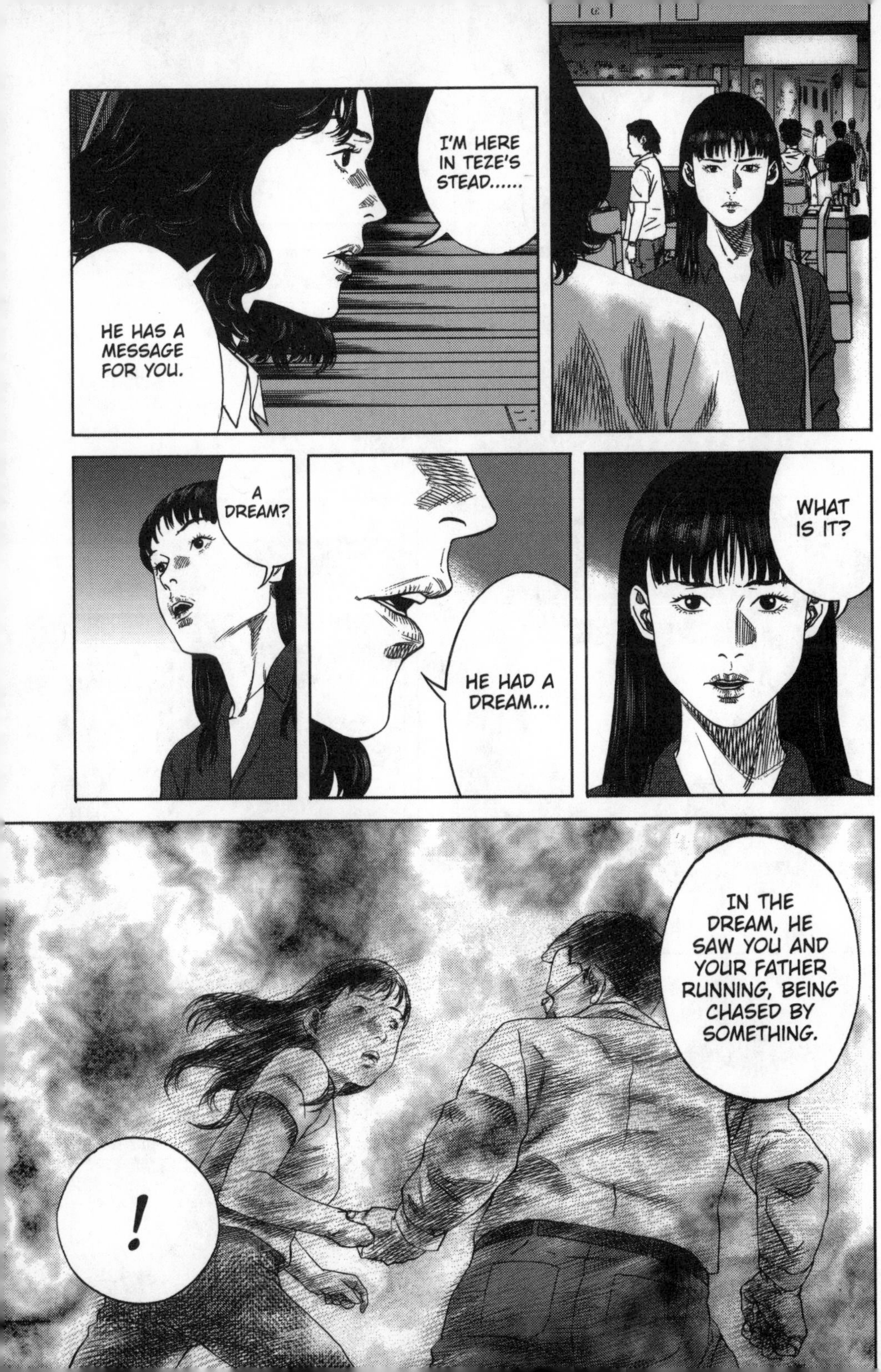
I'M HERE IN TEZE'S STEAD......
HE HAS A MESSAGE FOR YOU.
WHAT IS IT?
HE HAD A DREAM...
A DREAM?
IN THE DREAM, HE SAW YOU AND YOUR FATHER RUNNING, BEING CHASED BY SOMETHING.
!

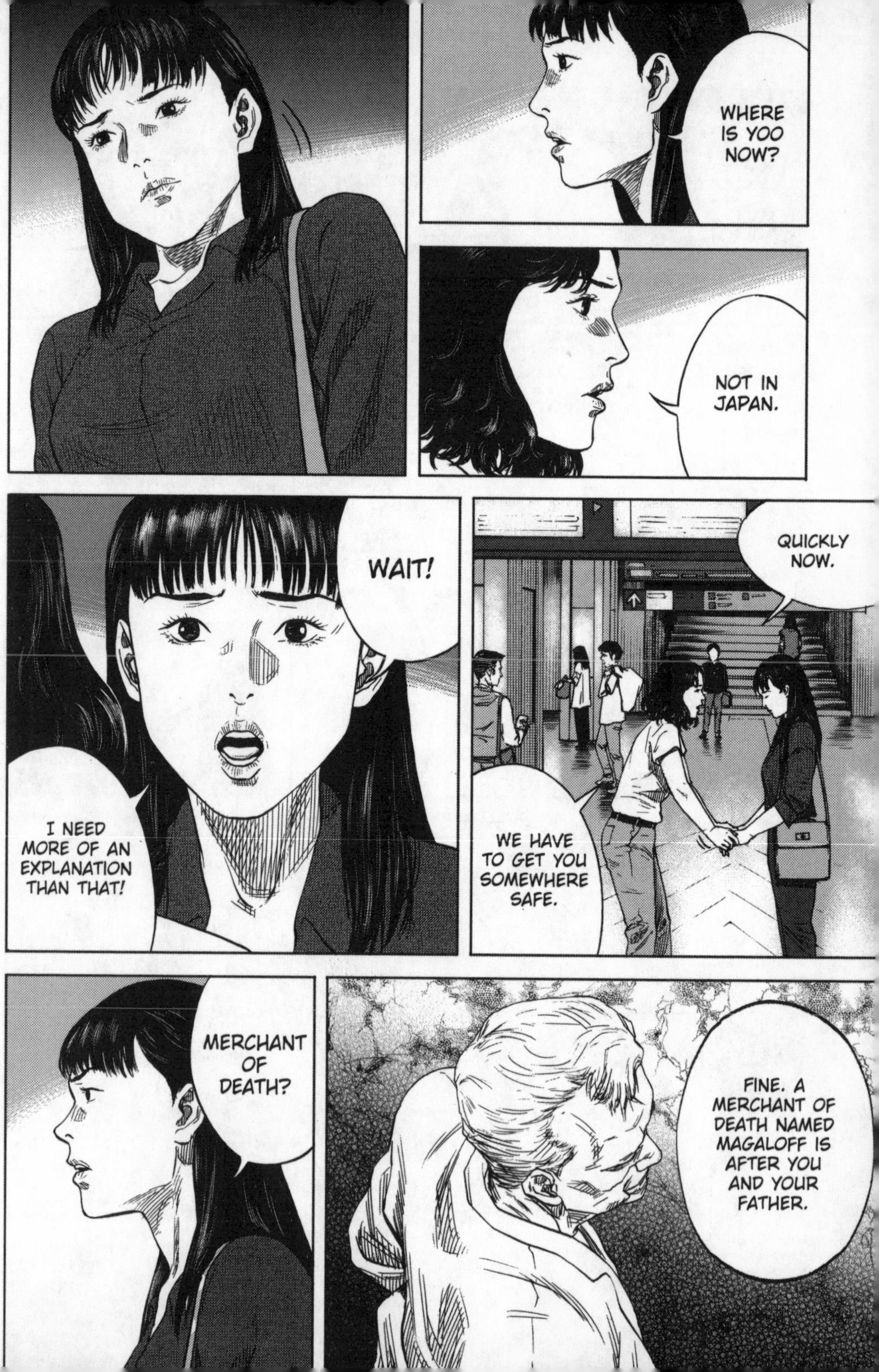
WHERE IS YOO NOW?
NOT IN JAPAN.
QUICKLY NOW.
WE HAVE TO GET YOU SOMEWHERE SAFE.
WAIT!
I NEED MORE OF AN EXPLANATION THAN THAT!
FINE. A MERCHANT OF DEATH NAMED MAGALOFF IS AFTER YOU AND YOUR FATHER.
MERCHANT OF DEATH?

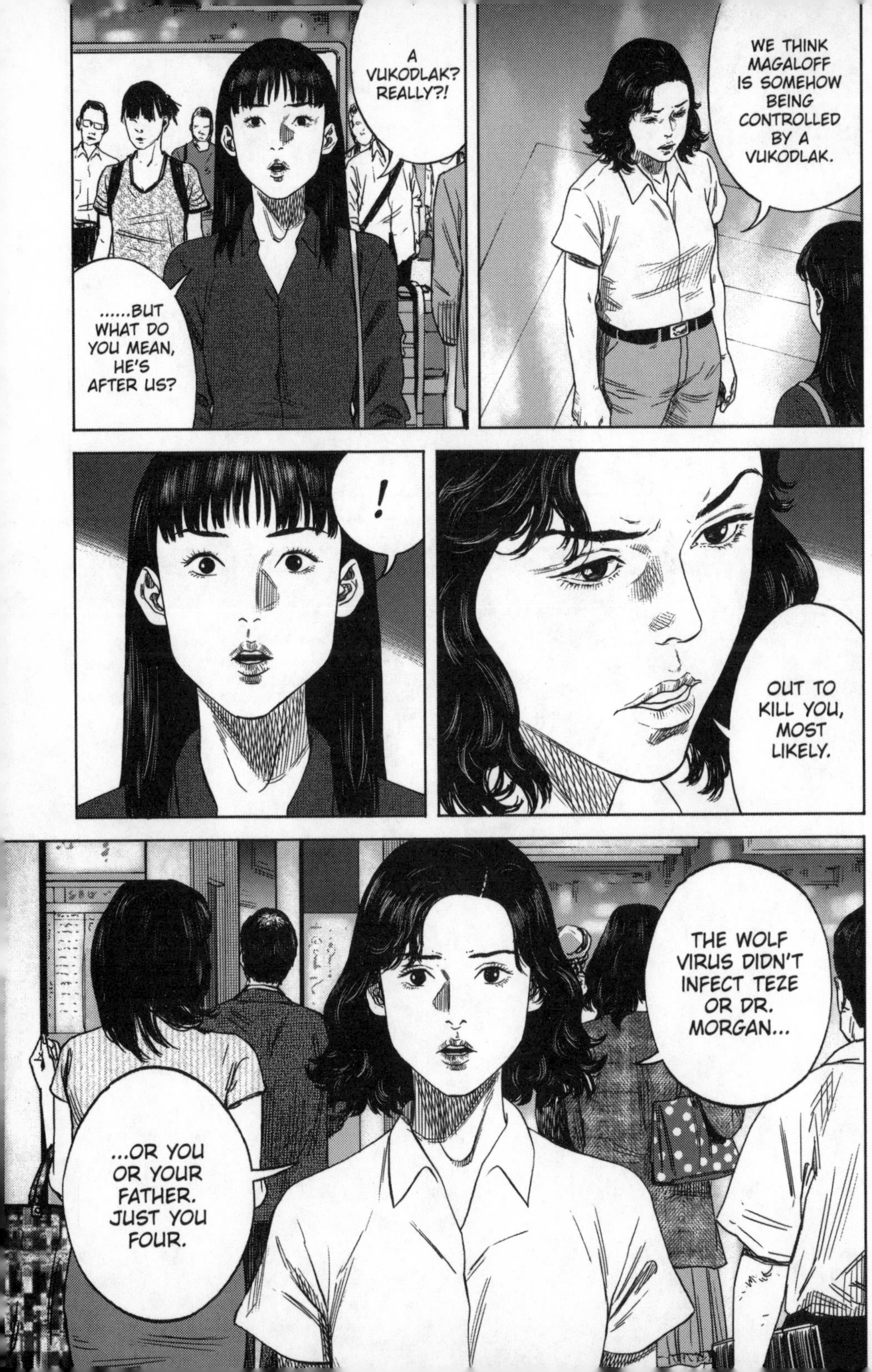
WE THINK MAGALOFF IS SOMEHOW BEING CONTROLLED BY A VUKODLAK.
A VUKODLAK? REALLY?!
......BUT WHAT DO YOU MEAN, HE'S AFTER US?
OUT TO KILL YOU, MOST LIKELY.
!
THE WOLF VIRUS DIDN'T INFECT TEZE OR DR. MORGAN...
...OR YOU OR YOUR FATHER. JUST YOU FOUR.

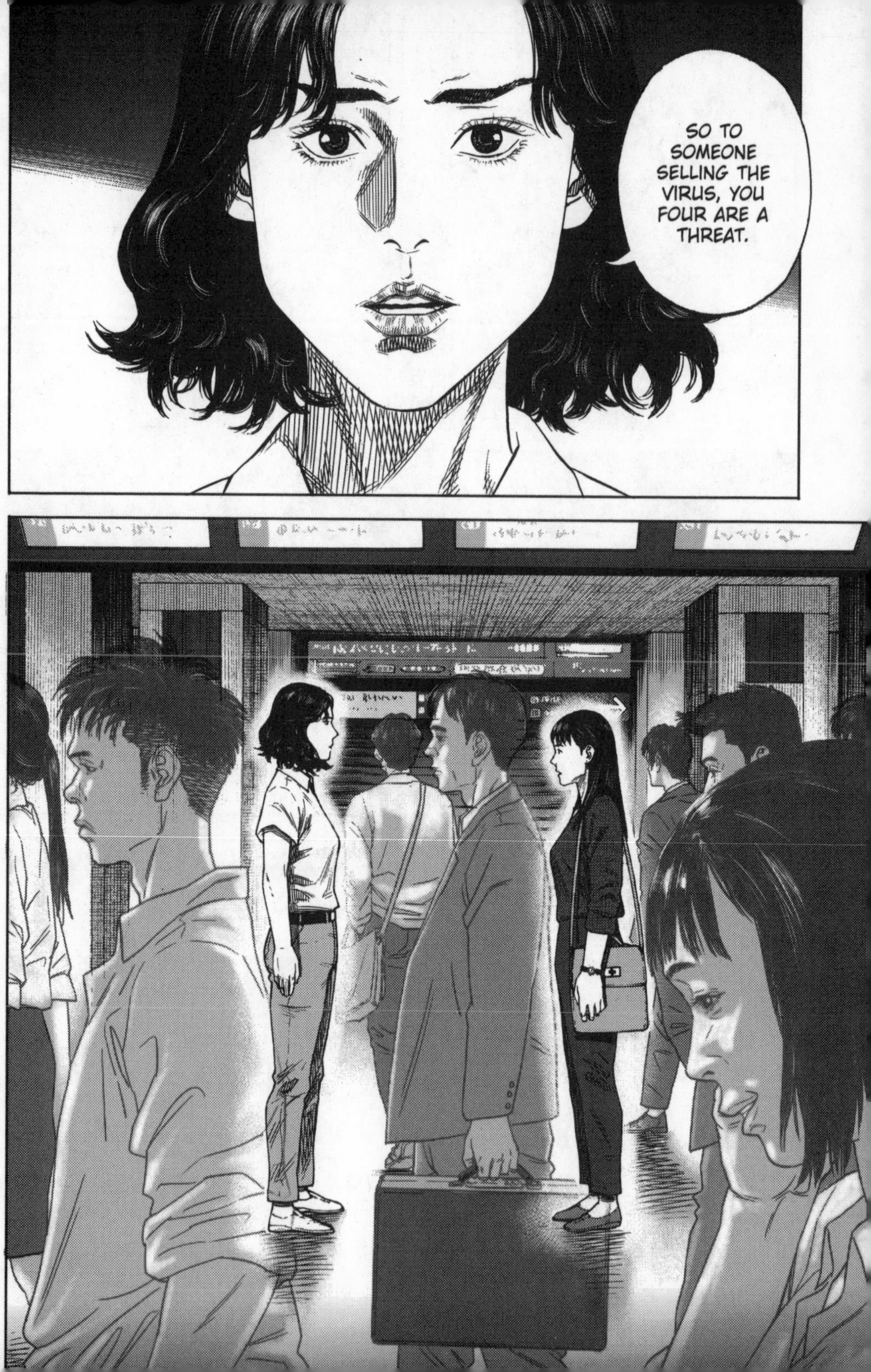
SO TO SOMEONE SELLING THE VIRUS, YOU FOUR ARE A THREAT.

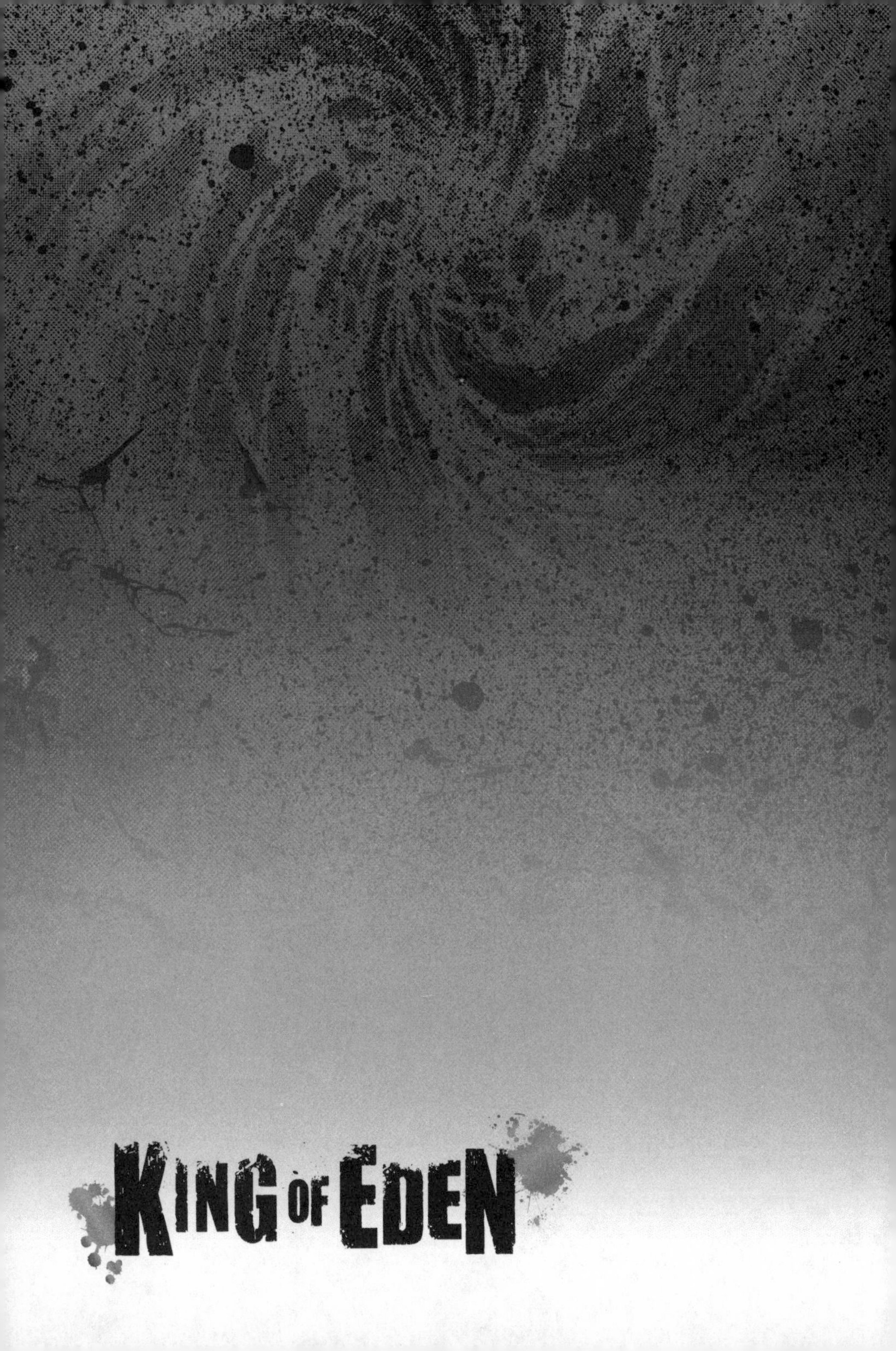
KING OF EDEN

KING OF EDEN

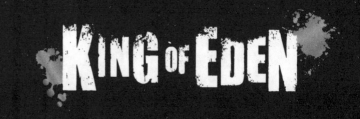

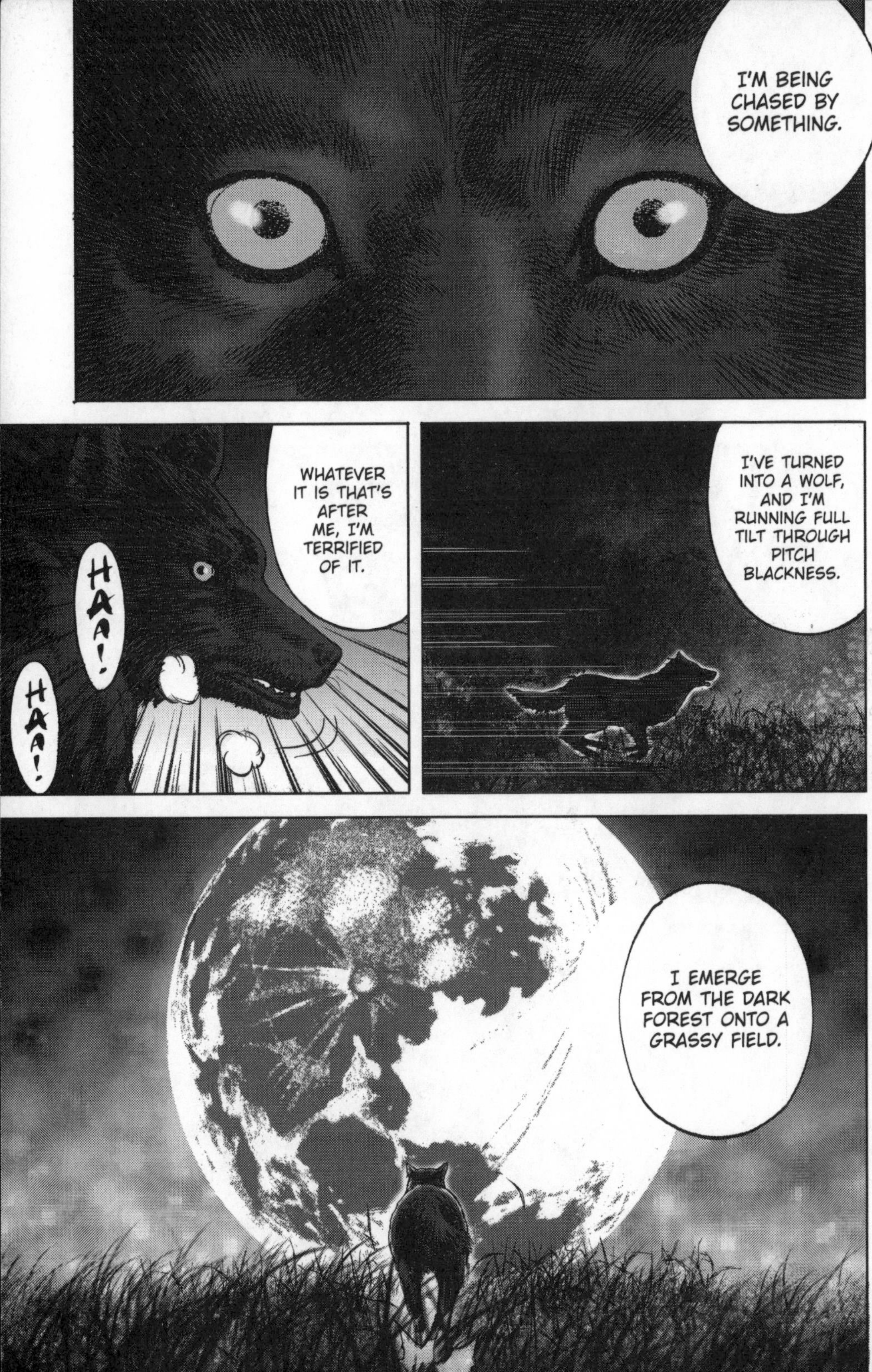
I'M BEING CHASED BY SOMETHING.
I'VE TURNED INTO A WOLF, AND I'M RUNNING FULL TILT THROUGH PITCH BLACKNESS.
WHATEVER IT IS THAT'S AFTER ME, I'M TERRIFIED OF IT.
HAA!
HAA!
I EMERGE FROM THE DARK FOREST ONTO A GRASSY FIELD.

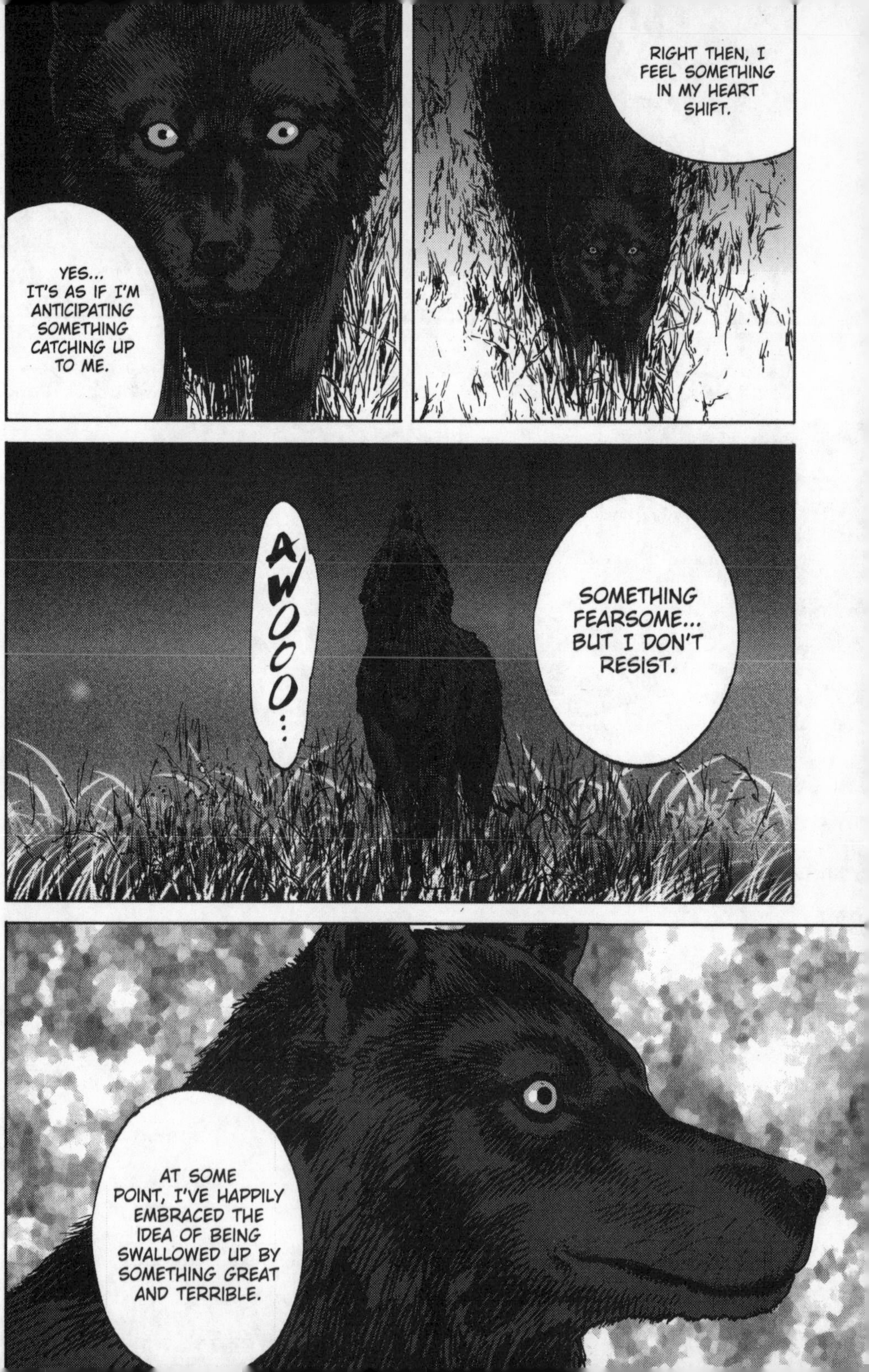
RIGHT THEN, I FEEL SOMETHING IN MY HEART SHIFT.
YES... IT'S AS IF I'M ANTICIPATING SOMETHING CATCHING UP TO ME.
SOMETHING FEARSOME... BUT I DON'T RESIST.
AWOOO...
AT SOME POINT, I'VE HAPPILY EMBRACED THE IDEA OF BEING SWALLOWED UP BY SOMETHING GREAT AND TERRIBLE.

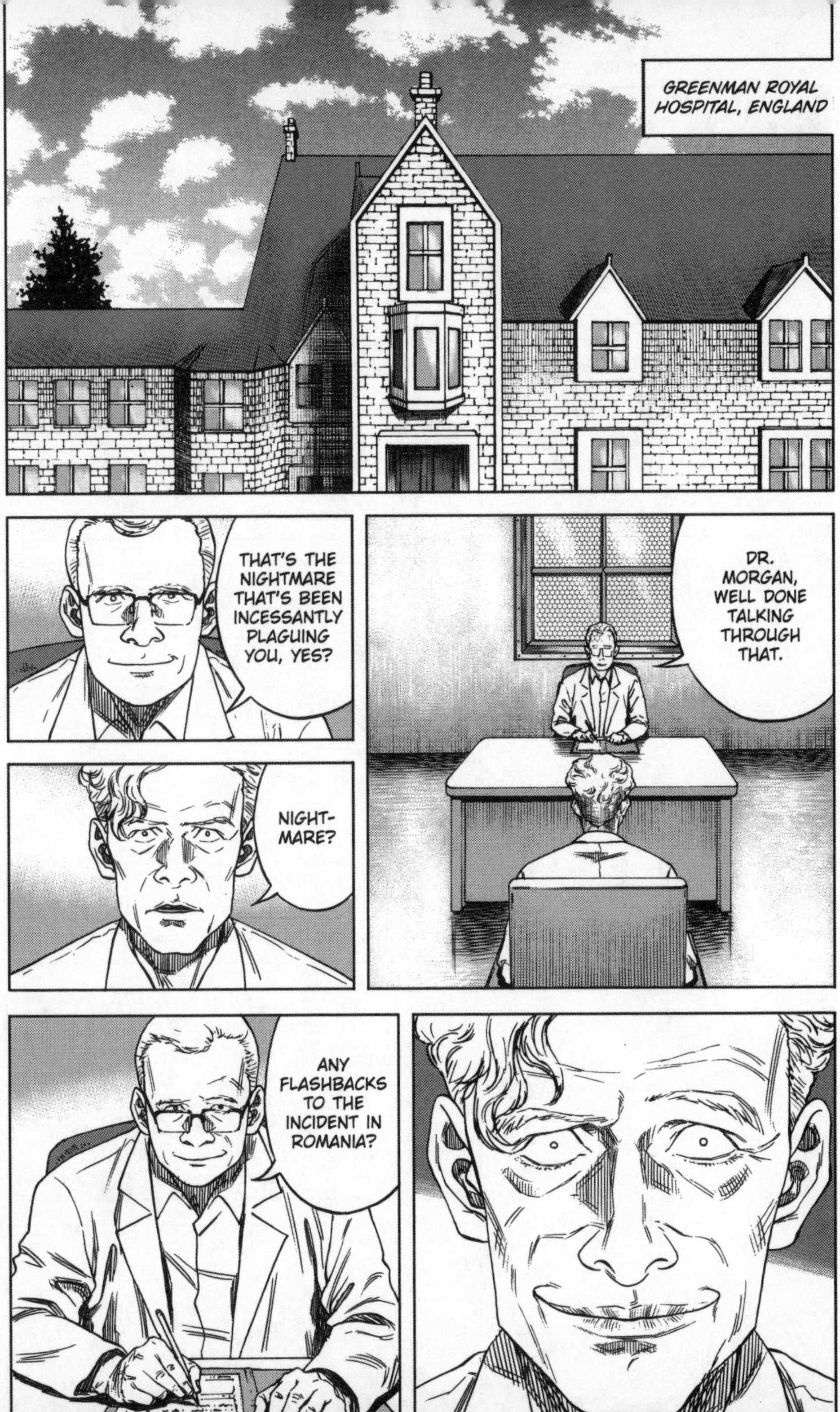
GREENMAN ROYAL HOSPITAL, ENGLAND
DR. MORGAN, WELL DONE TALKING THROUGH THAT.
THAT'S THE NIGHTMARE THAT'S BEEN INCESSANTLY PLAGUING YOU, YES?
NIGHT-MARE?
ANY FLASHBACKS TO THE INCIDENT IN ROMANIA?

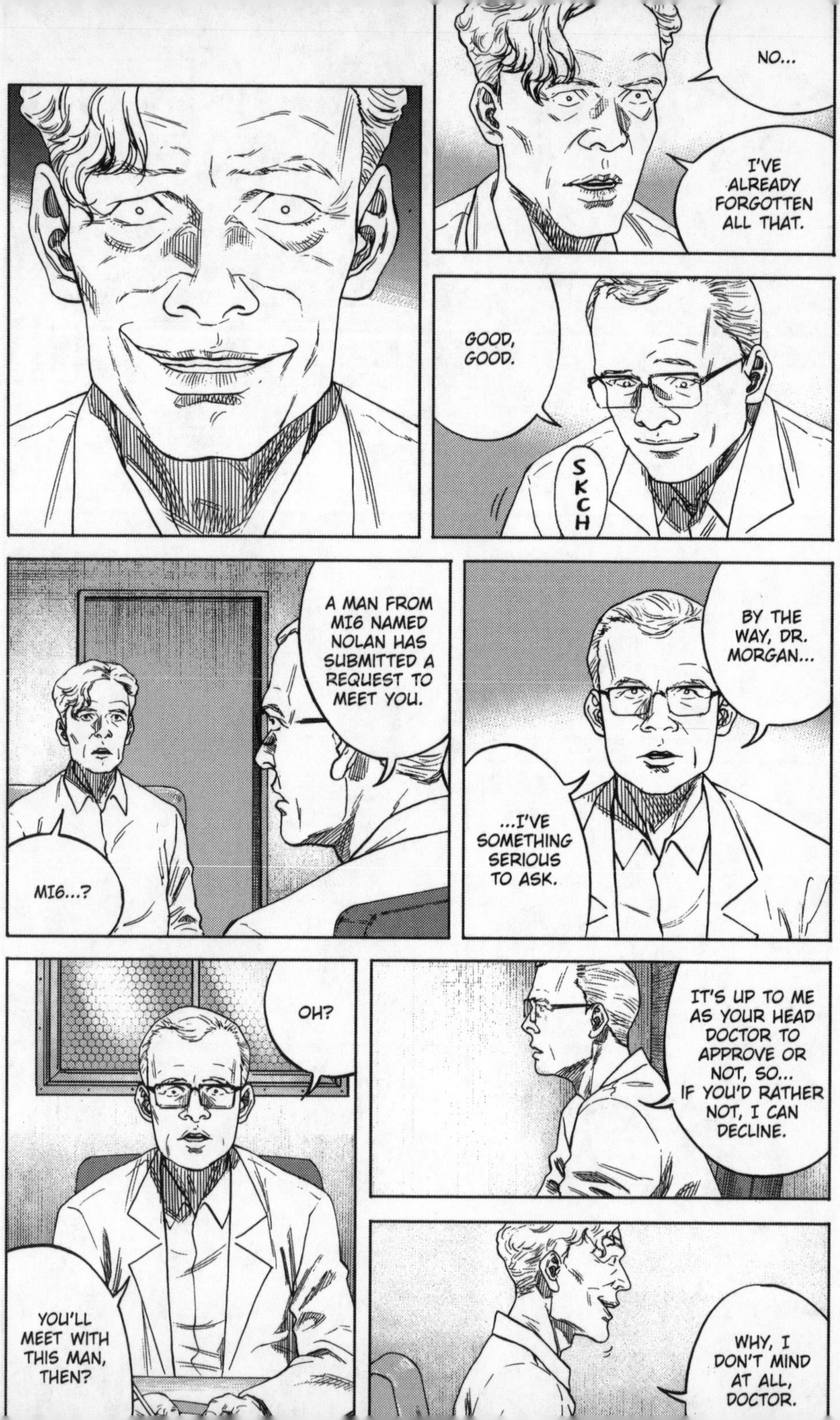
NO...
I'VE ALREADY FORGOTTEN ALL THAT.
GOOD, GOOD.
SKCH
BY THE WAY, DR. MORGAN...
...I'VE SOMETHING SERIOUS TO ASK.
A MAN FROM MI6 NAMED NOLAN HAS SUBMITTED A REQUEST TO MEET YOU.
MI6...?
IT'S UP TO ME AS YOUR HEAD DOCTOR TO APPROVE OR NOT, SO... IF YOU'D RATHER NOT, I CAN DECLINE.
WHY, I DON'T MIND AT ALL, DOCTOR.
OH?
YOU'LL MEET WITH THIS MAN, THEN?

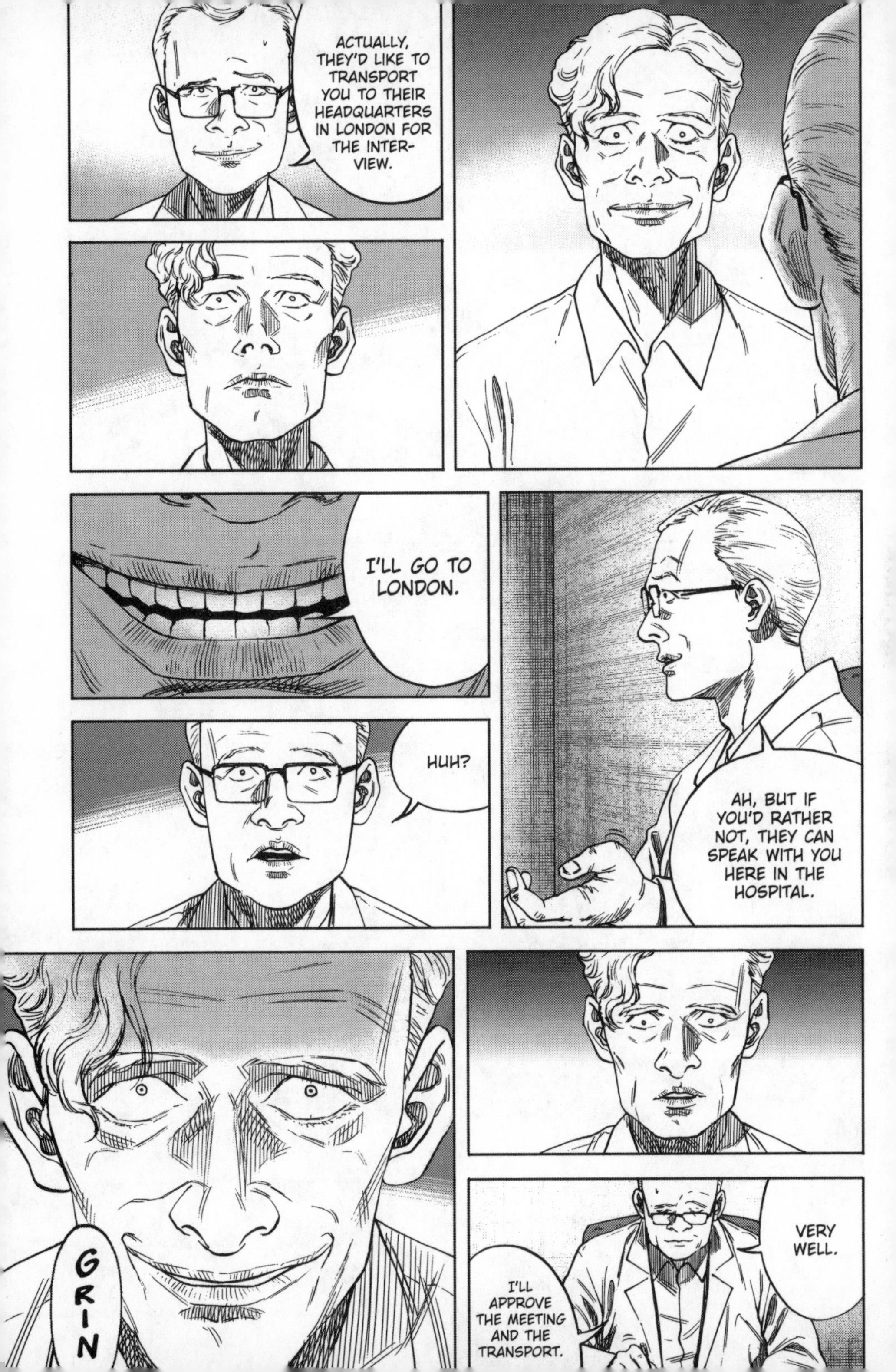
ACTUALLY, THEY'D LIKE TO TRANSPORT YOU TO THEIR HEADQUARTERS IN LONDON FOR THE INTER-VIEW.
AH, BUT IF YOU'D RATHER NOT, THEY CAN SPEAK WITH YOU HERE IN THE HOSPITAL.
I'LL GO TO LONDON.
HUH?
VERY WELL.
I'LL APPROVE THE MEETING AND THE TRANSPORT.
GRIN

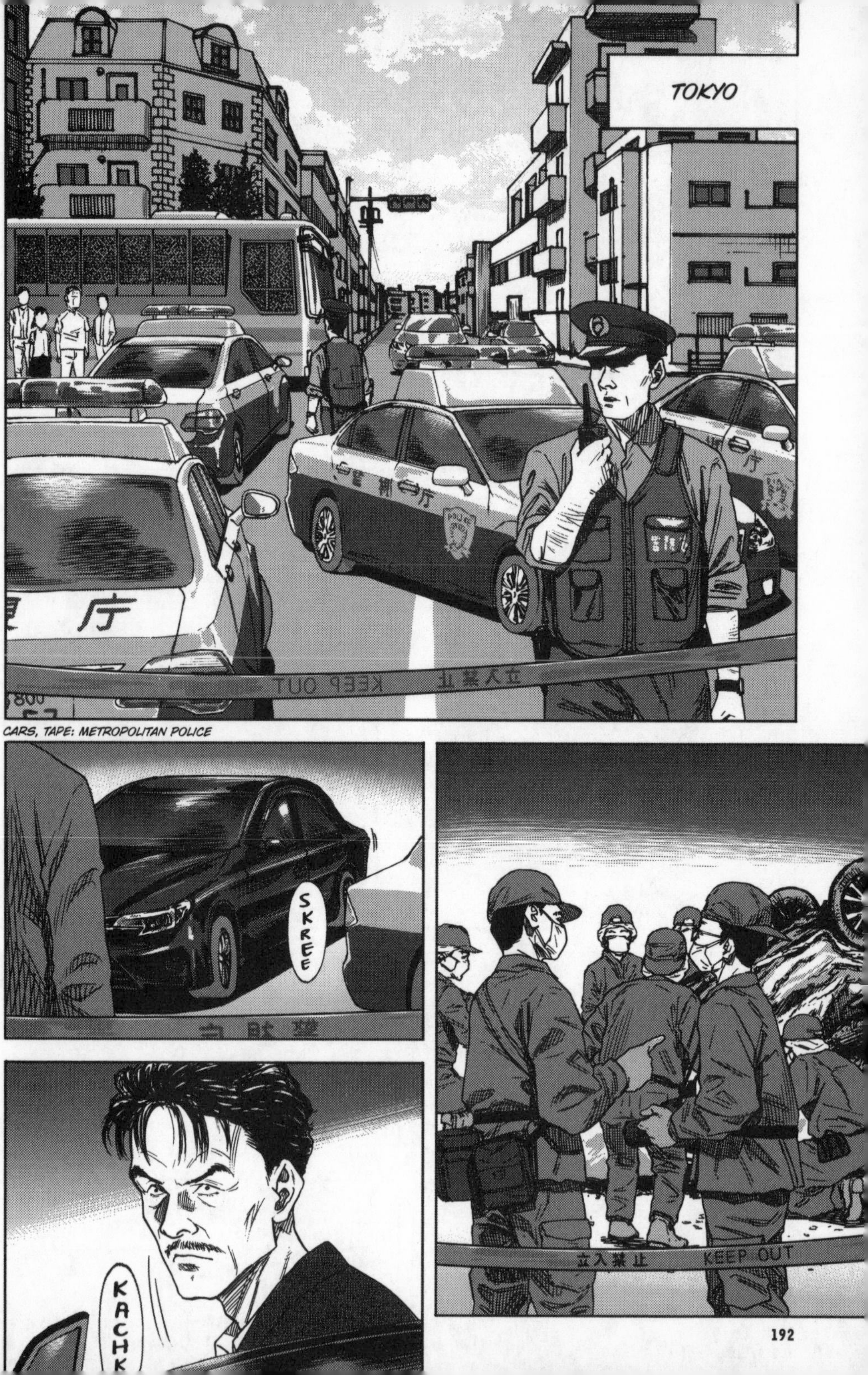
TOKYO
CARS, TAPE: METROPOLITAN POLICE
立入禁止
KEEP OUT
SKREE
KACHK

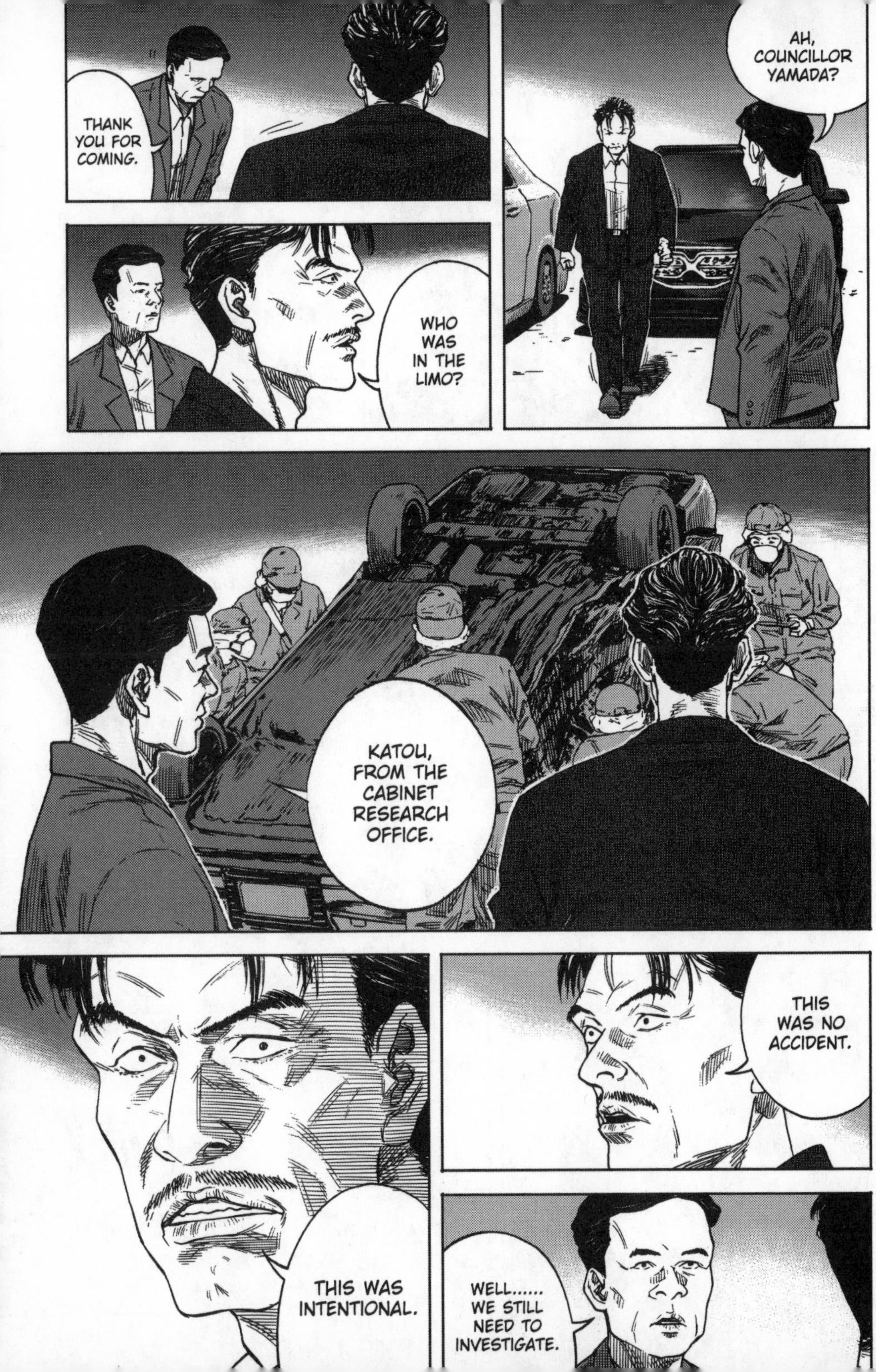
AH, COUNCILLOR YAMADA?
THANK YOU FOR COMING.
WHO WAS IN THE LIMO?
KATOU, FROM THE CABINET RESEARCH OFFICE.
THIS WAS NO ACCIDENT.
WELL...... WE STILL NEED TO INVESTIGATE.
THIS WAS INTENTIONAL.

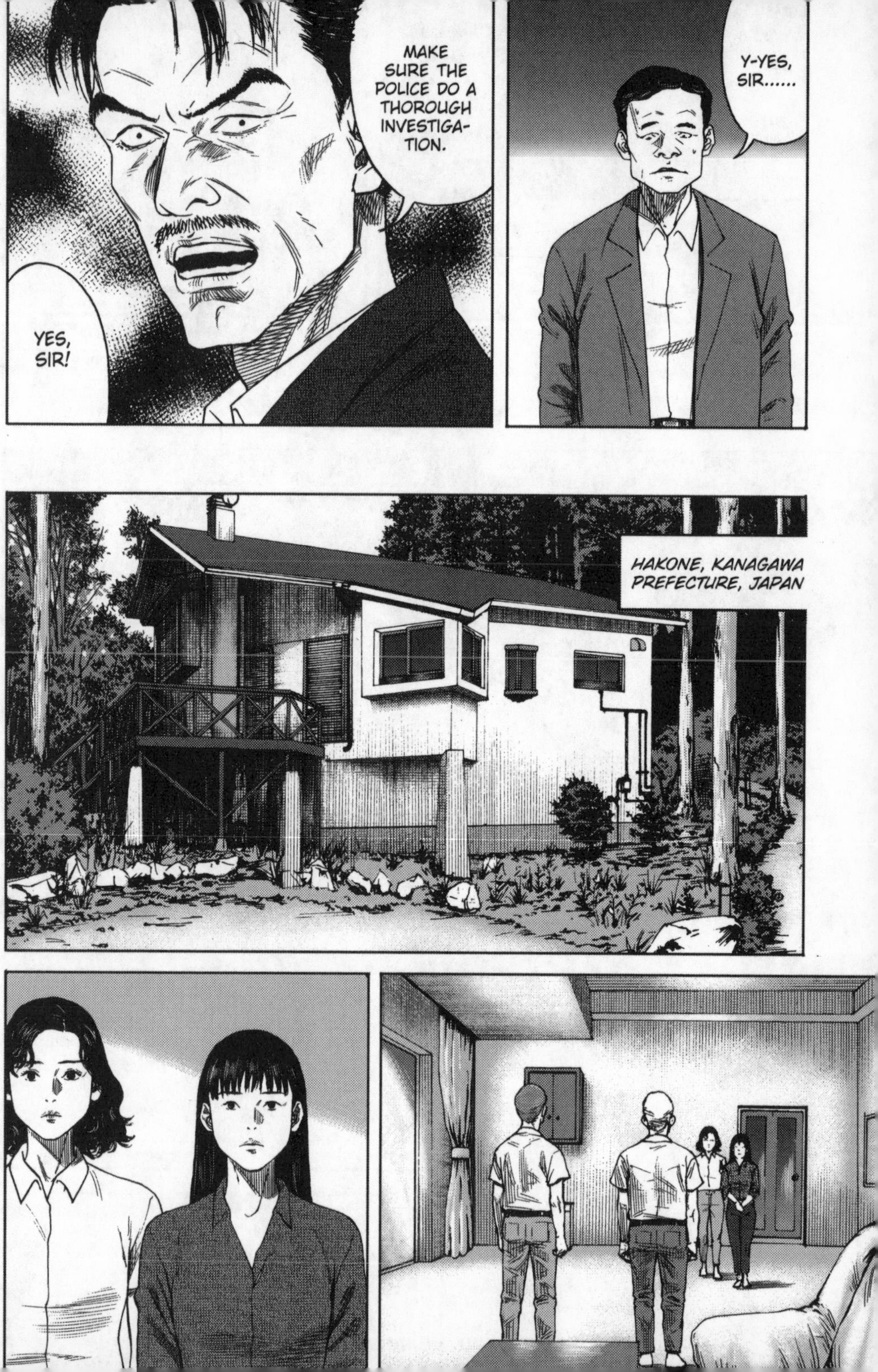
Y-YES, SIR......
MAKE SURE THE POLICE DO A THOROUGH INVESTIGATION.
YES, SIR!
HAKONE, KANAGAWA PREFECTURE, JAPAN

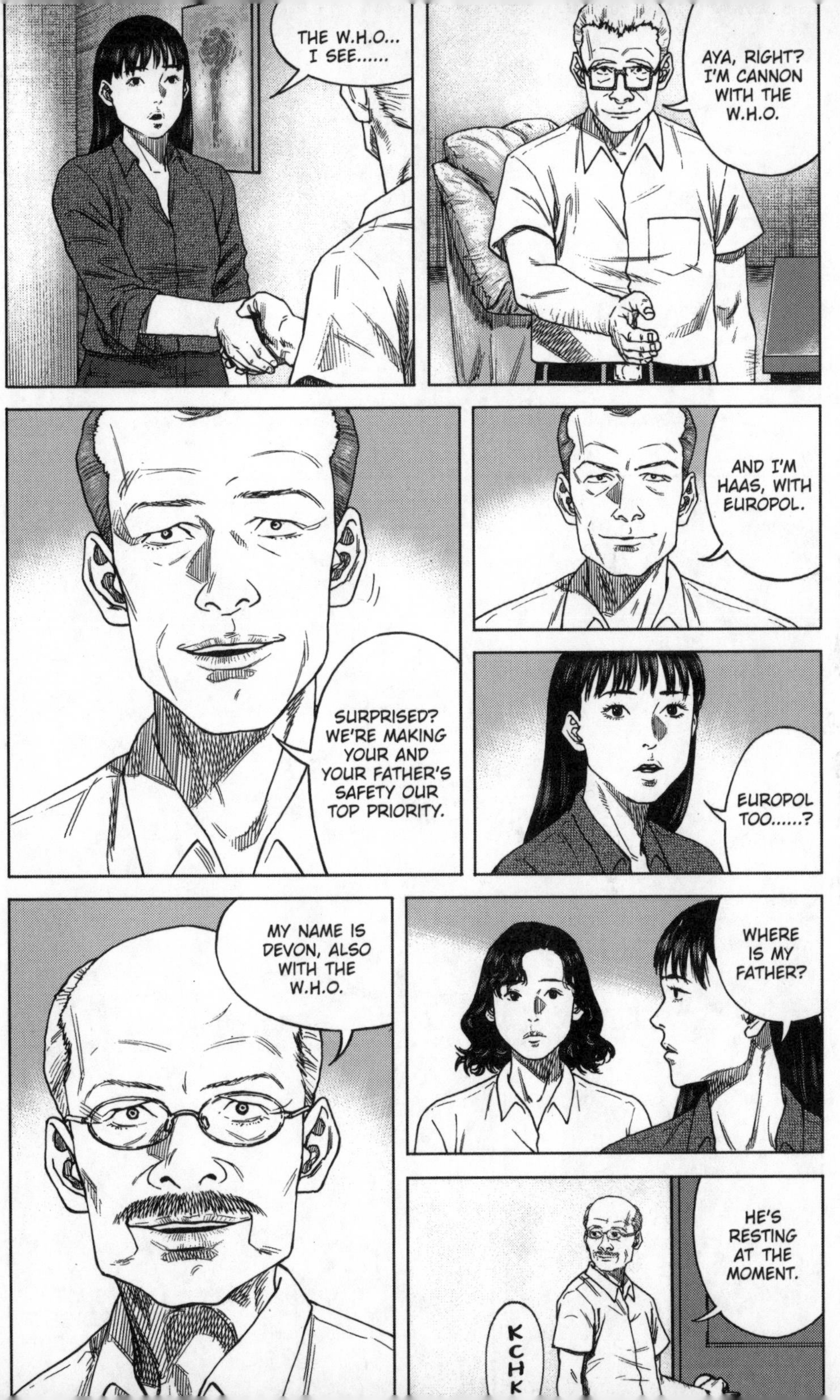
AYA, RIGHT? I'M CANNON WITH THE W.H.O.
THE W.H.O... I SEE......
AND I'M HAAS, WITH EUROPOL.
EUROPOL TOO......?
SURPRISED? WE'RE MAKING YOUR AND YOUR FATHER'S SAFETY OUR TOP PRIORITY.
WHERE IS MY FATHER?
HE'S RESTING AT THE MOMENT.
KCHK
MY NAME IS DEVON, ALSO WITH THE W.H.O.

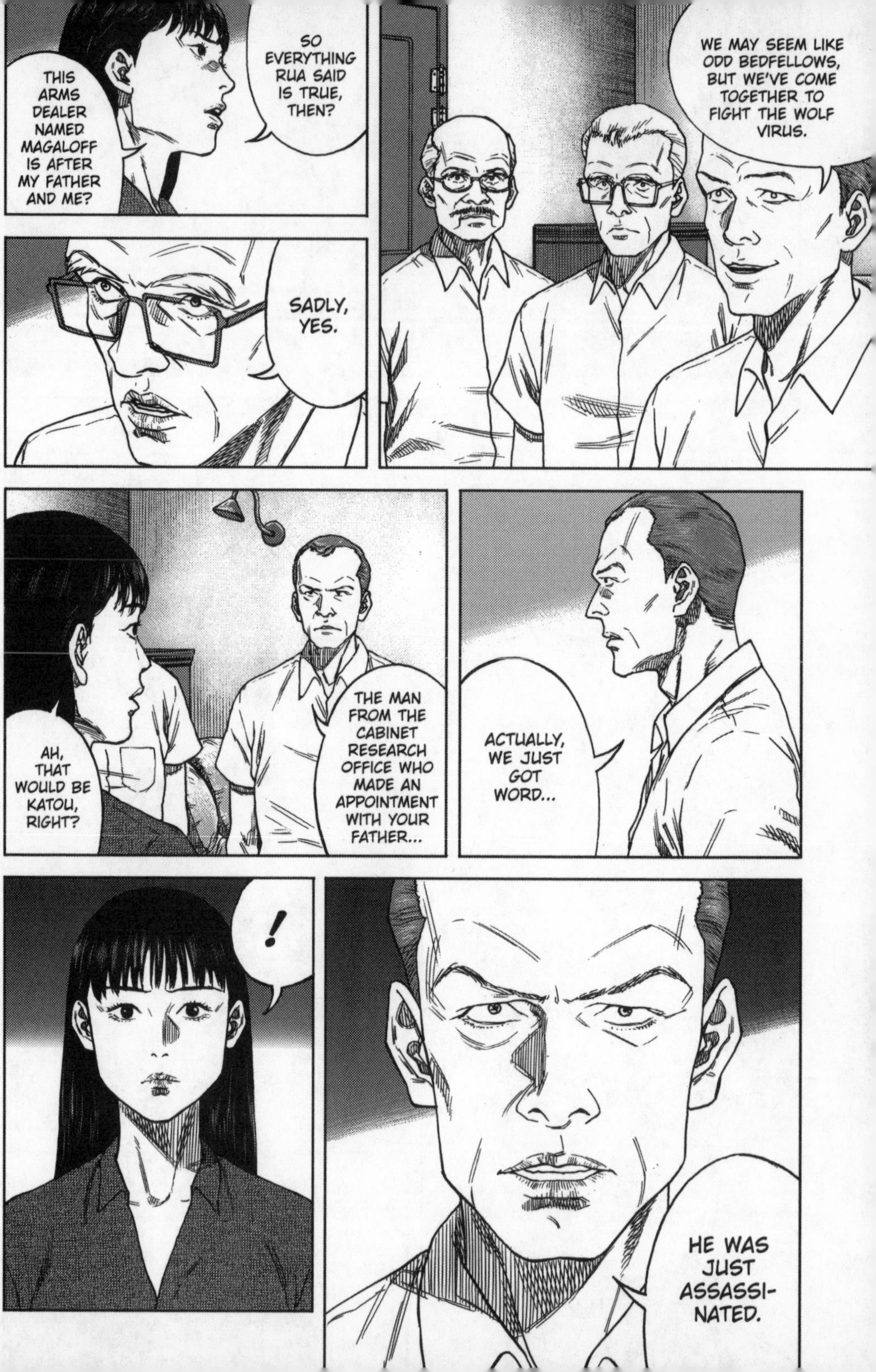
WE MAY SEEM LIKE ODD BEDFELLOWS, BUT WE'VE COME TOGETHER TO FIGHT THE WOLF VIRUS.
SO EVERYTHING RUA SAID IS TRUE, THEN?
THIS ARMS DEALER NAMED MAGALOFF IS AFTER MY FATHER AND ME?
SADLY, YES.
ACTUALLY, WE JUST GOT WORD...
THE MAN FROM THE CABINET RESEARCH OFFICE WHO MADE AN APPOINTMENT WITH YOUR FATHER...
AH, THAT WOULD BE KATOU, RIGHT?
HE WAS JUST ASSASSINATED.
!

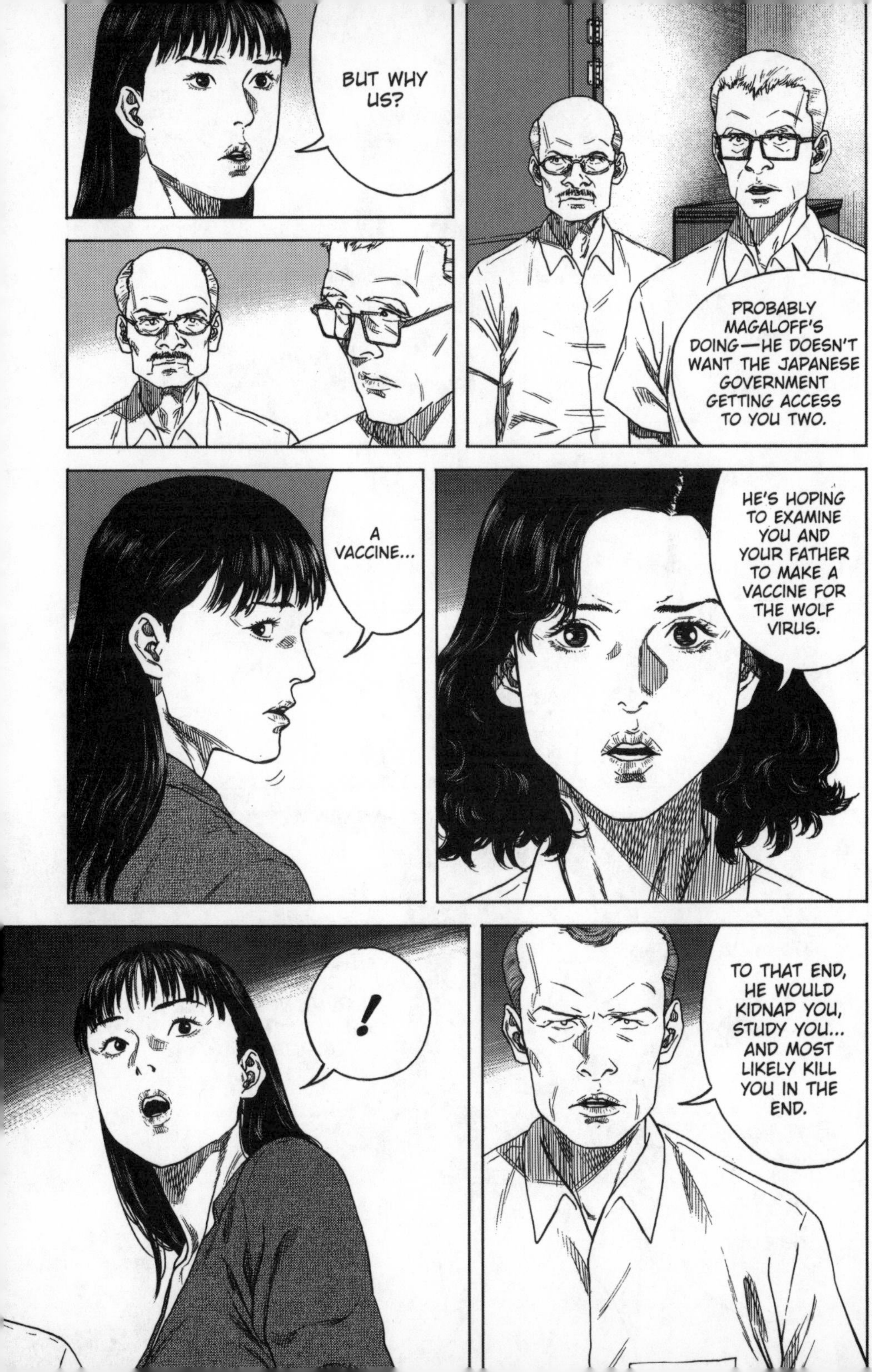

PROBABLY MAGALOFF'S DOING—HE DOESN'T WANT THE JAPANESE GOVERNMENT GETTING ACCESS TO YOU TWO.
BUT WHY US?
HE'S HOPING TO EXAMINE YOU AND YOUR FATHER TO MAKE A VACCINE FOR THE WOLF VIRUS.
A VACCINE...
TO THAT END, HE WOULD KIDNAP YOU, STUDY YOU... AND MOST LIKELY KILL YOU IN THE END.
!

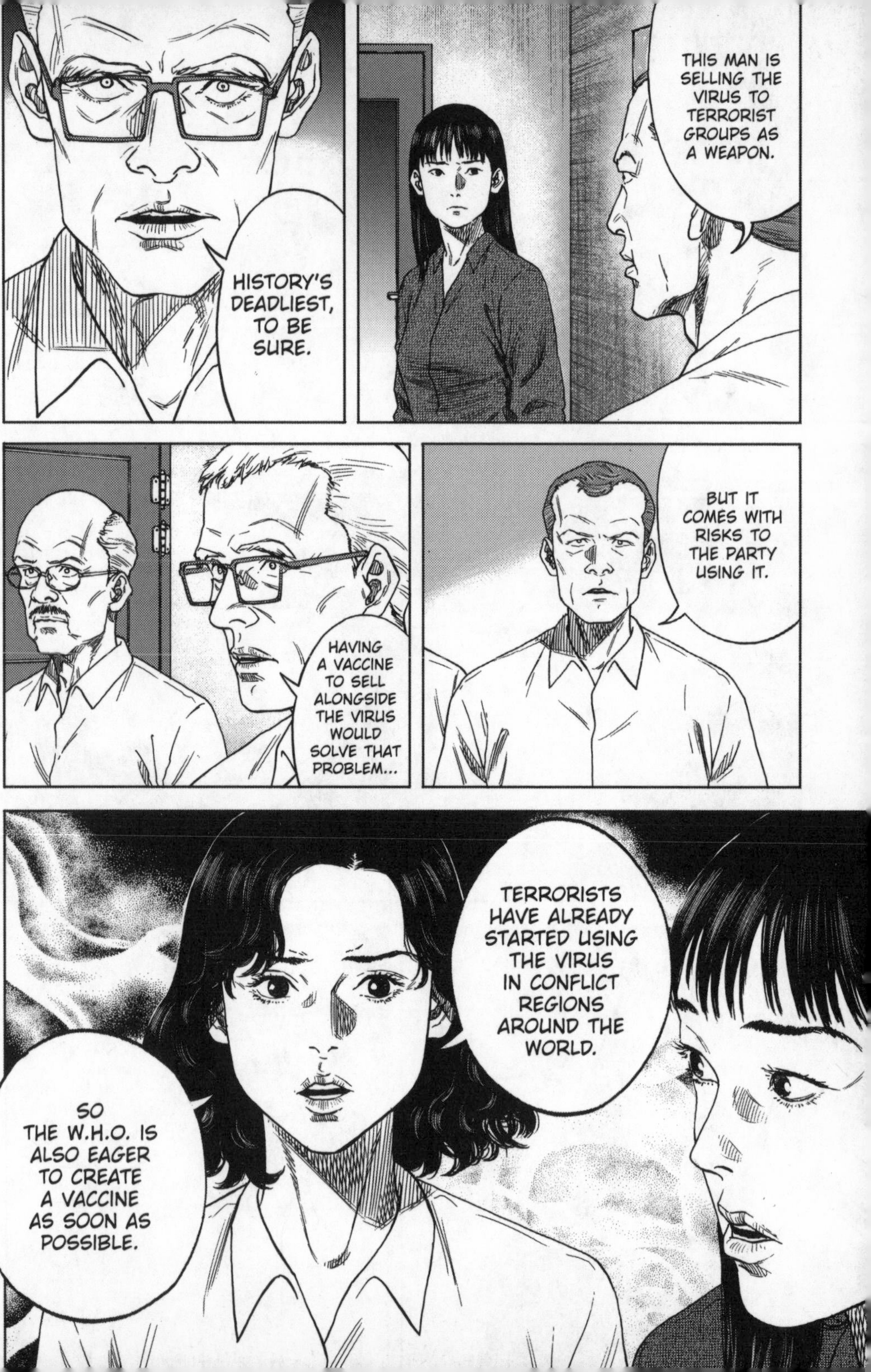
THIS MAN IS SELLING THE VIRUS TO TERRORIST GROUPS AS A WEAPON.
HISTORY'S DEADLIEST, TO BE SURE.
BUT IT COMES WITH RISKS TO THE PARTY USING IT.
HAVING A VACCINE TO SELL ALONGSIDE THE VIRUS WOULD SOLVE THAT PROBLEM...
TERRORISTS HAVE ALREADY STARTED USING THE VIRUS IN CONFLICT REGIONS AROUND THE WORLD.
SO THE W.H.O. IS ALSO EAGER TO CREATE A VACCINE AS SOON AS POSSIBLE.

PRECISELY.

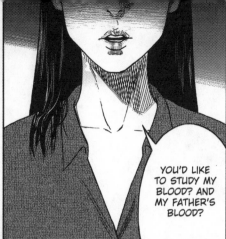

YOU'D LIKE TO STUDY MY BLOOD? AND MY FATHER'S BLOOD?

IF THE FUTURE OF HUMANITY HANGS IN THE BALANCE...

...TAKE AS MUCH FROM ME AS YOU NEED!

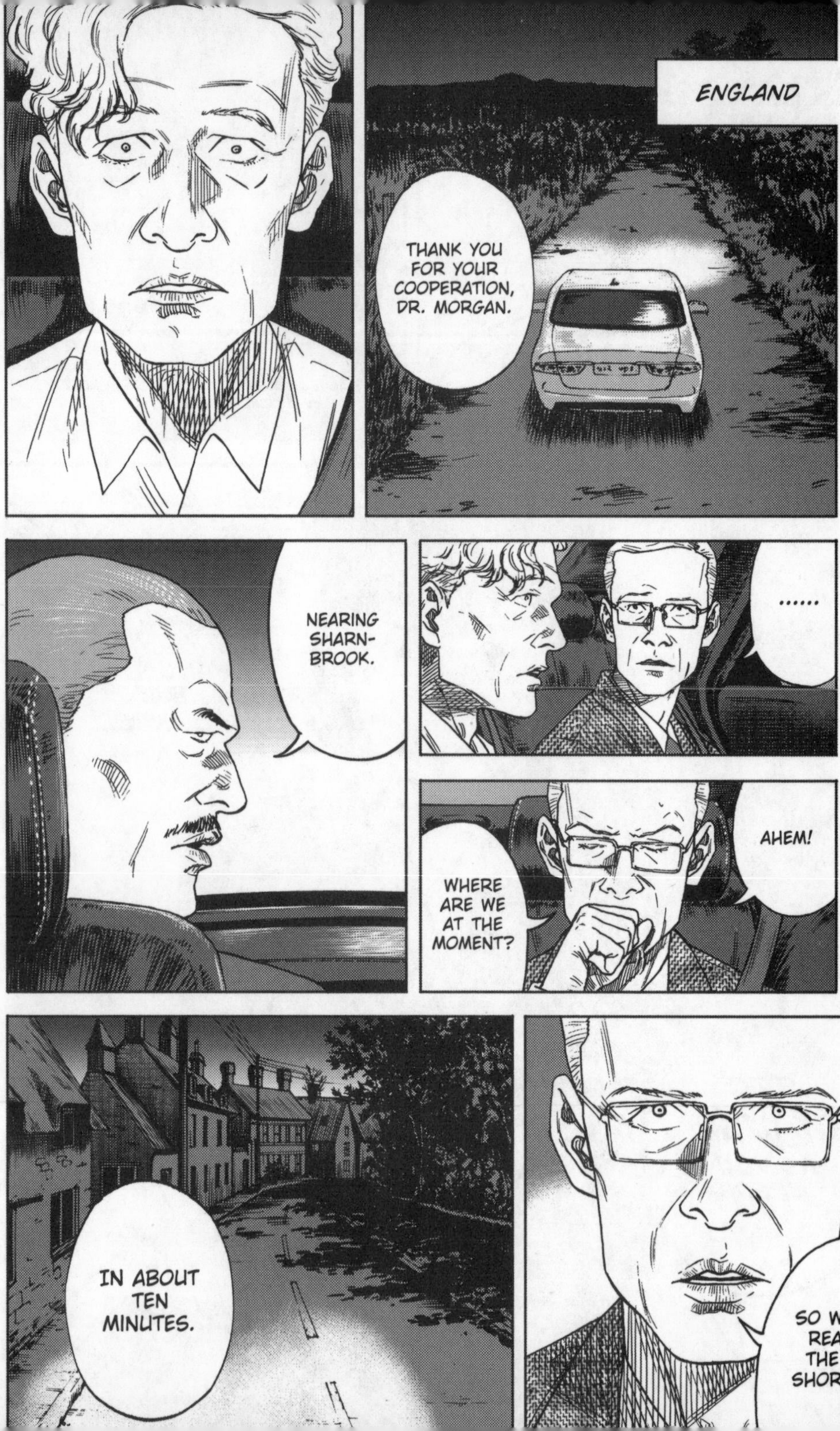
ENGLAND
THANK YOU FOR YOUR COOPERATION, DR. MORGAN.
......
AHEM!
WHERE ARE WE AT THE MOMENT?
NEARING SHARN-BROOK.
SO WE'LL REACH THE A6 SHORTLY?
IN ABOUT TEN MINUTES.

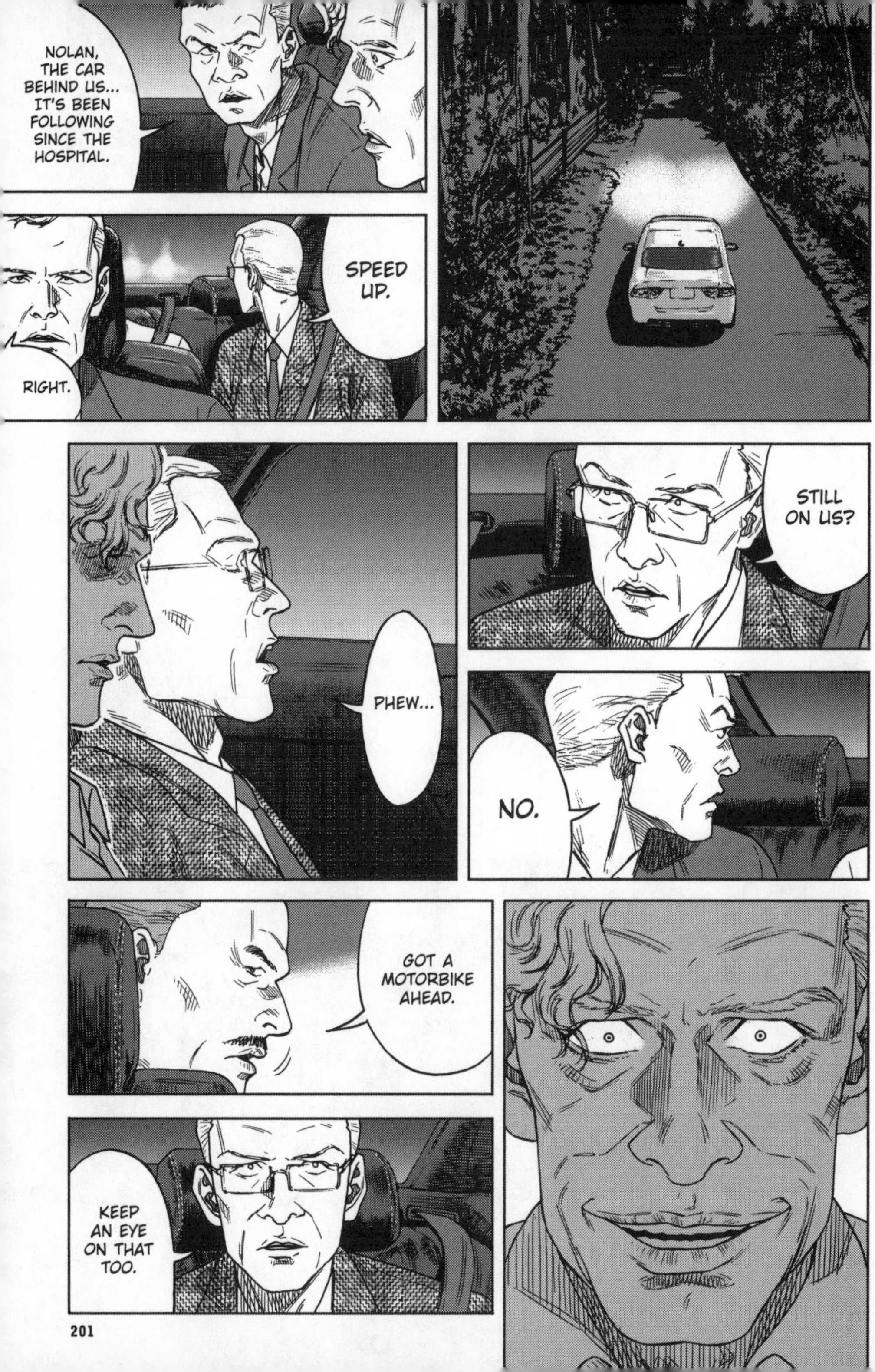
NOLAN, THE CAR BEHIND US... IT'S BEEN FOLLOWING SINCE THE HOSPITAL.
SPEED UP.
RIGHT.
STILL ON US?
NO.
PHEW...
GOT A MOTORBIKE AHEAD.
KEEP AN EYE ON THAT TOO.

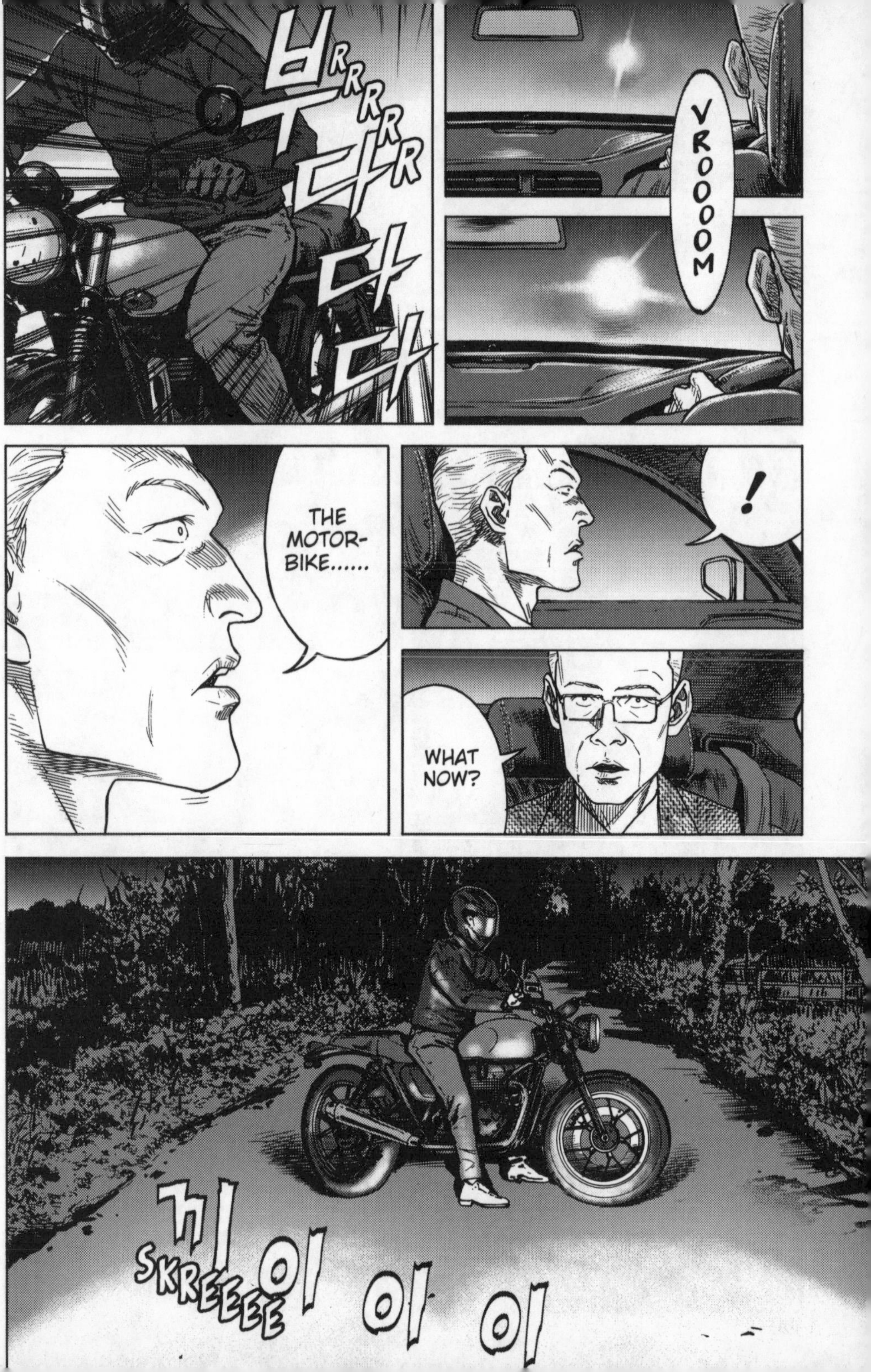

VROOOOM
부다다다
RRRRR
!
WHAT NOW?
THE MOTOR-BIKE......
끼이이이
SKREEEEE

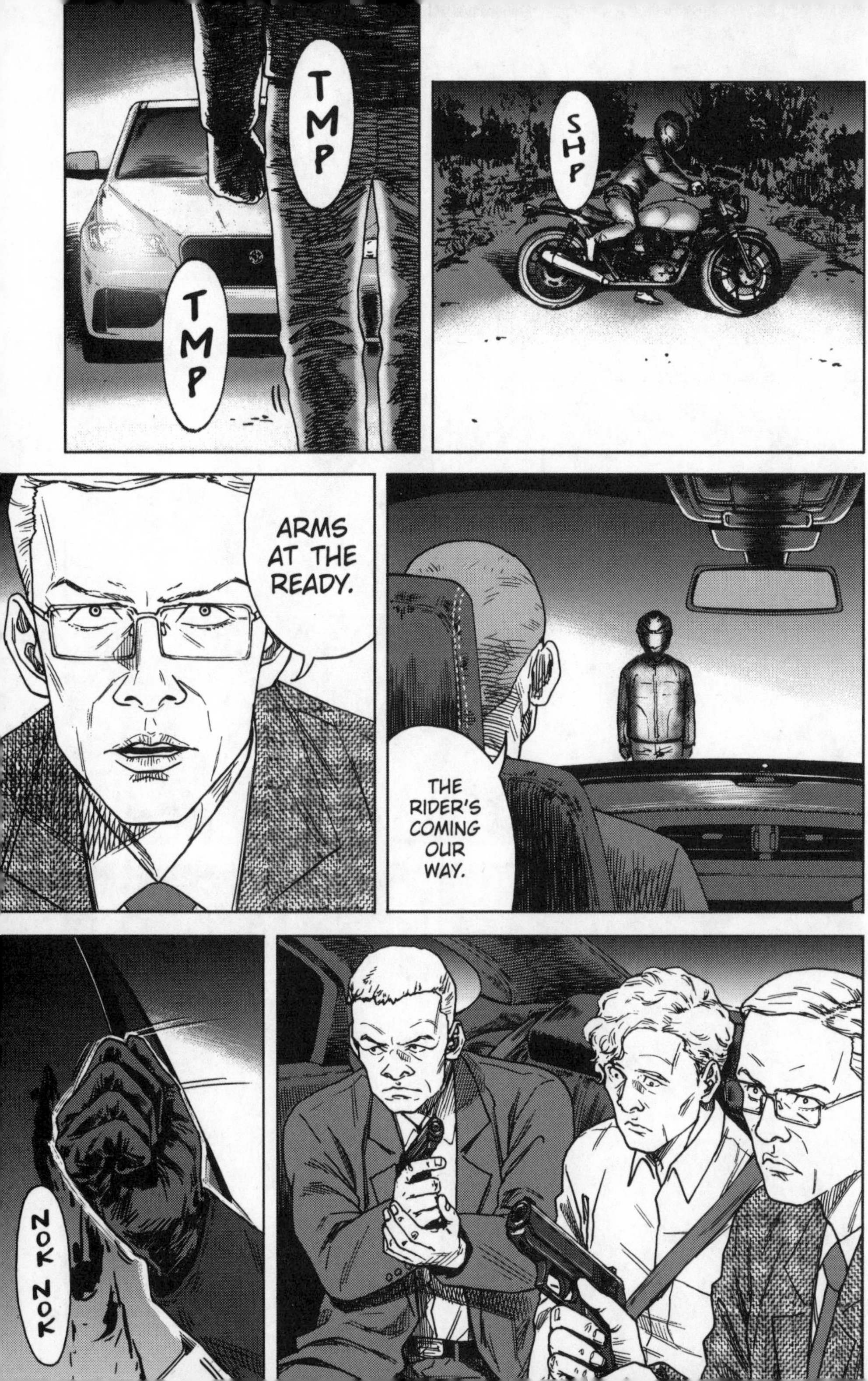
SHP
TMP
TMP
THE RIDER'S COMING OUR WAY.
ARMS AT THE READY.
NOK NOK

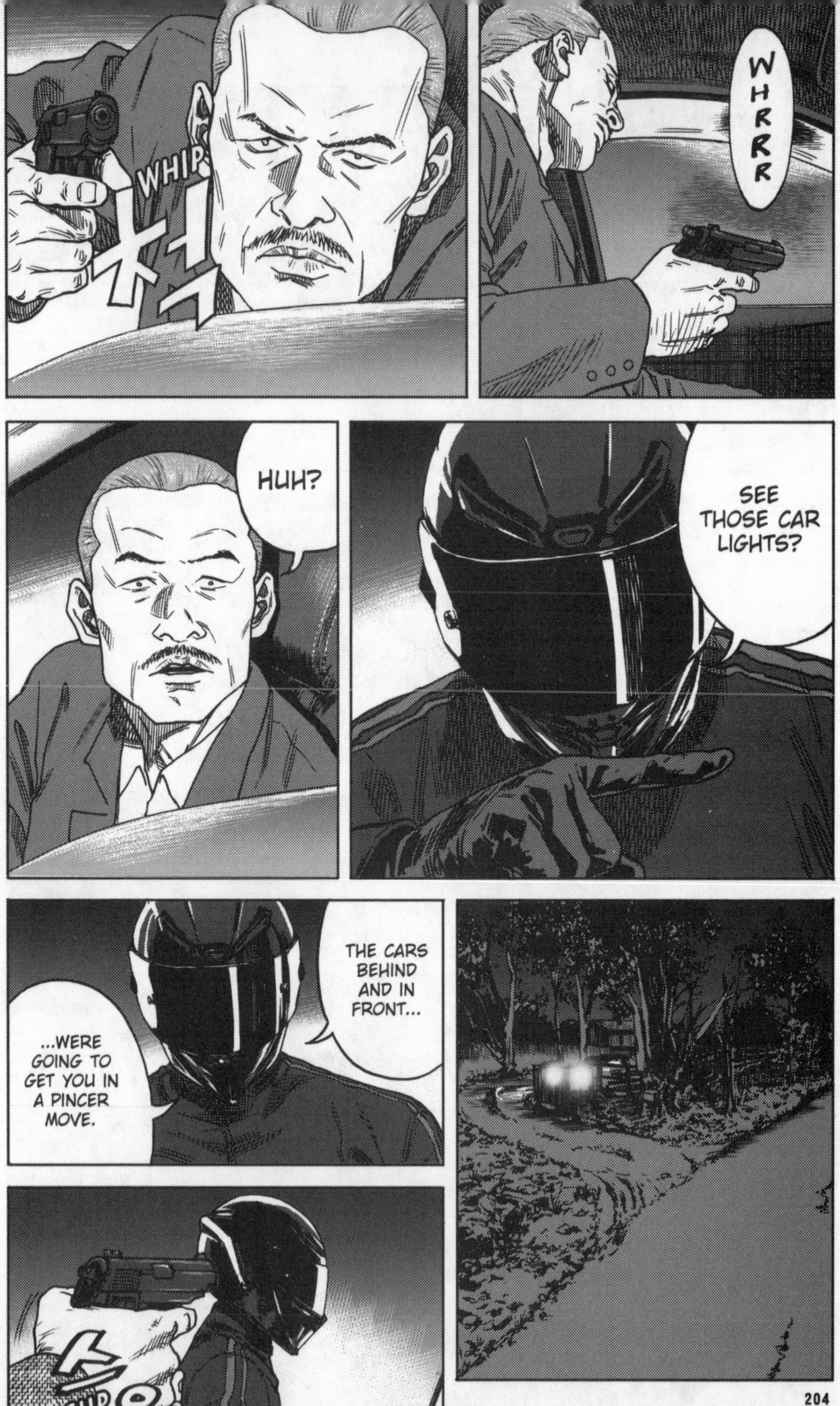
WHRRR
WHIP
SEE THOSE CAR LIGHTS?
HUH?
THE CARS BEHIND AND IN FRONT...
...WERE GOING TO GET YOU IN A PINCER MOVE.
SHP

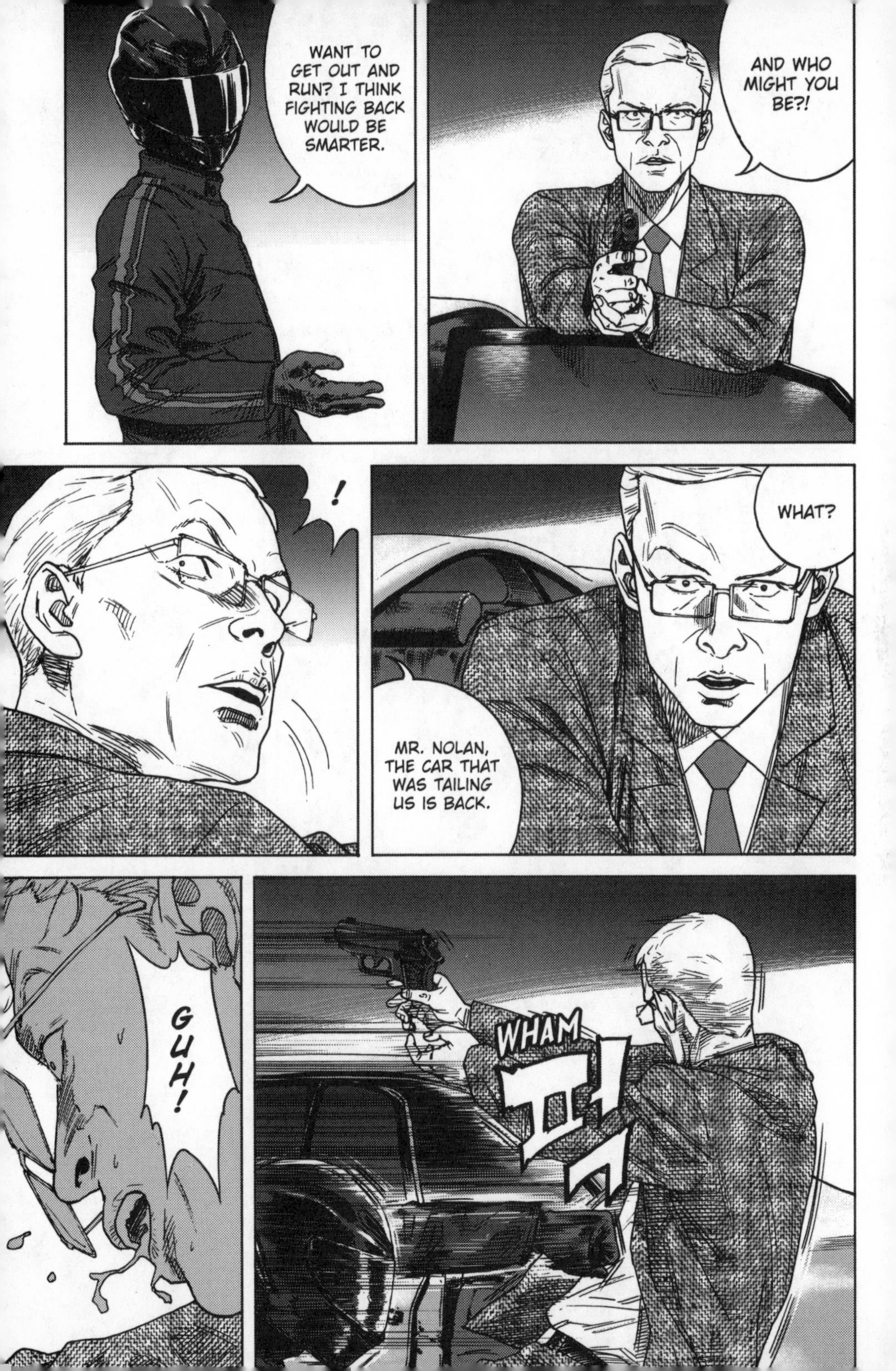
AND WHO MIGHT YOU BE?!
WANT TO GET OUT AND RUN? I THINK FIGHTING BACK WOULD BE SMARTER.
WHAT?
MR. NOLAN, THE CAR THAT WAS TAILING US IS BACK.
!
WHAM
GUH!

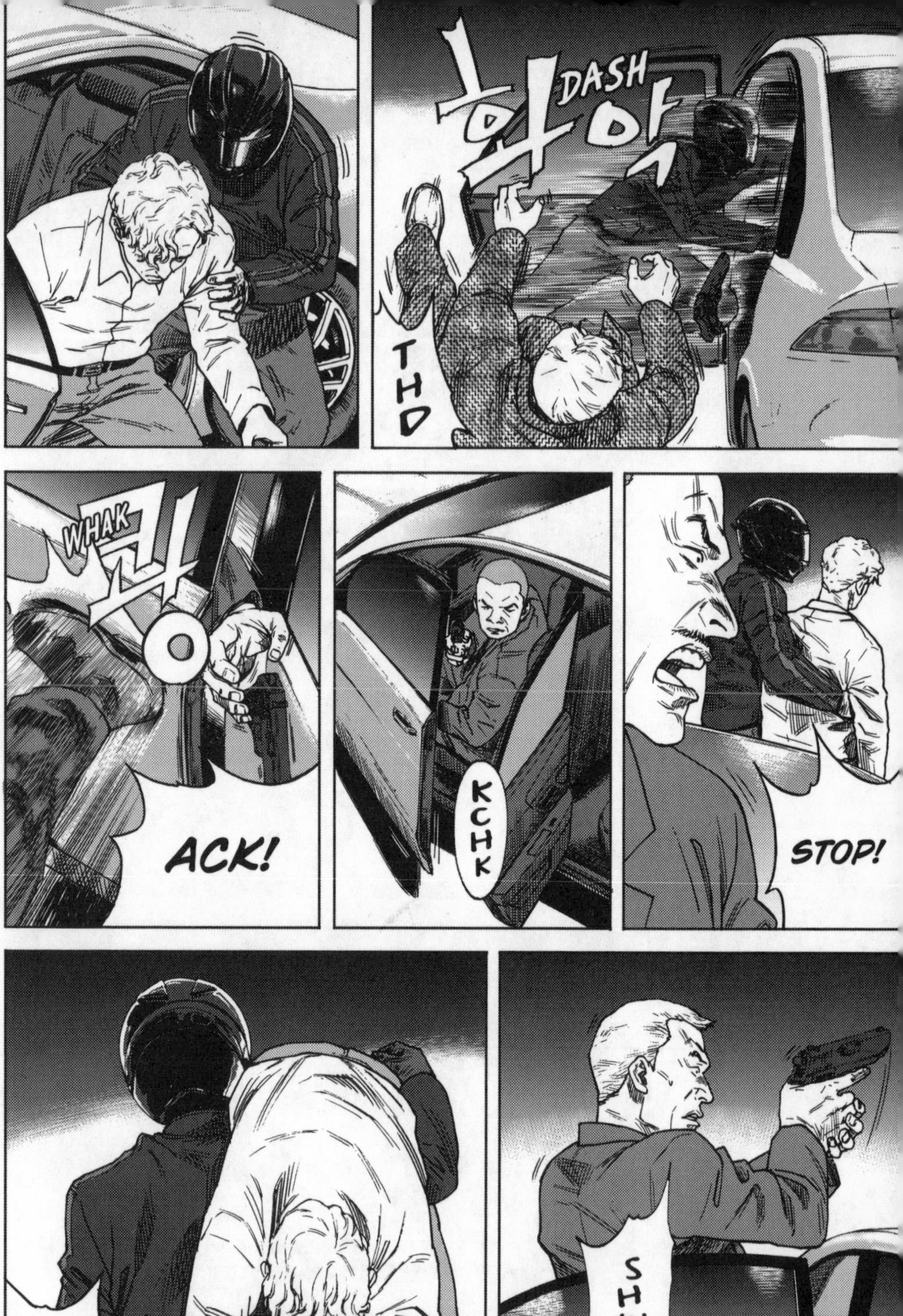
DASH
THD
STOP!
KCHK
WHAK
ACK!
SHWP
HUH?

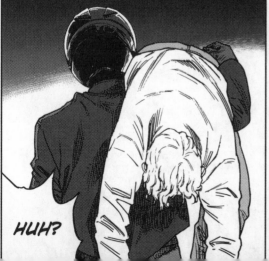

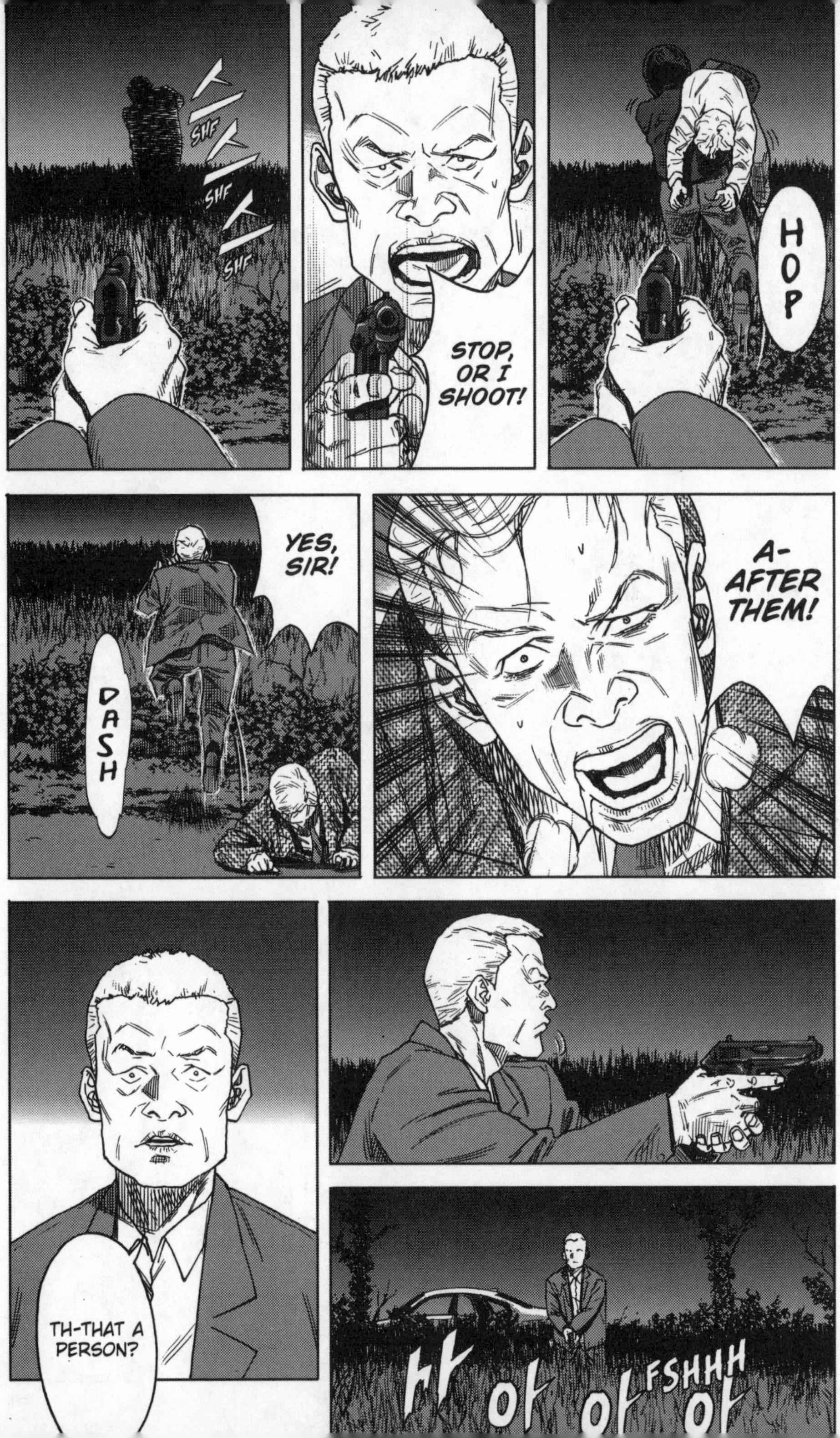
HOP
STOP, OR I SHOOT!
SHF
SHF
SHF
A- AFTER THEM!
YES, SIR!
DASH
FSHHH
TH-THAT A PERSON?

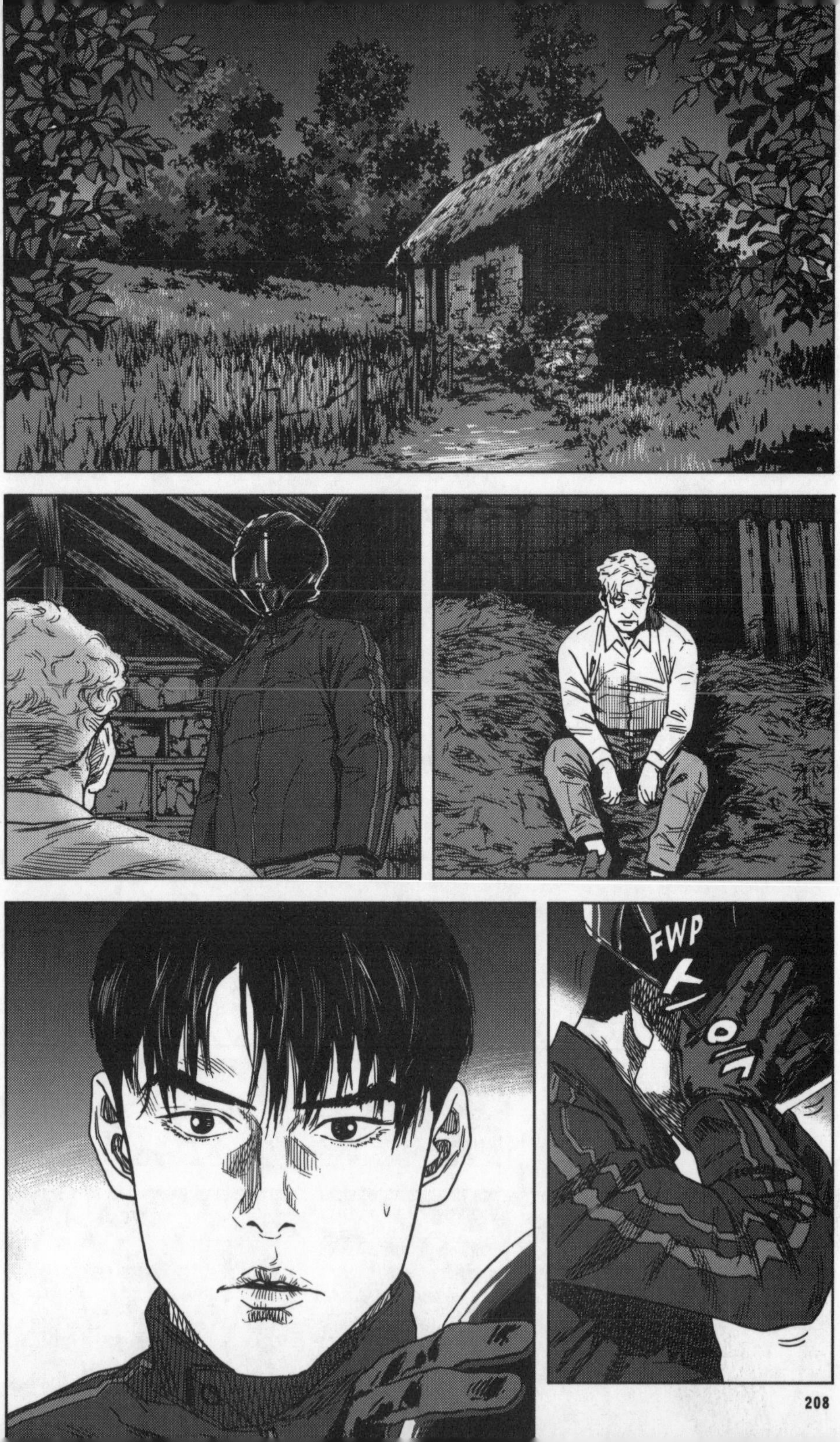
FWP

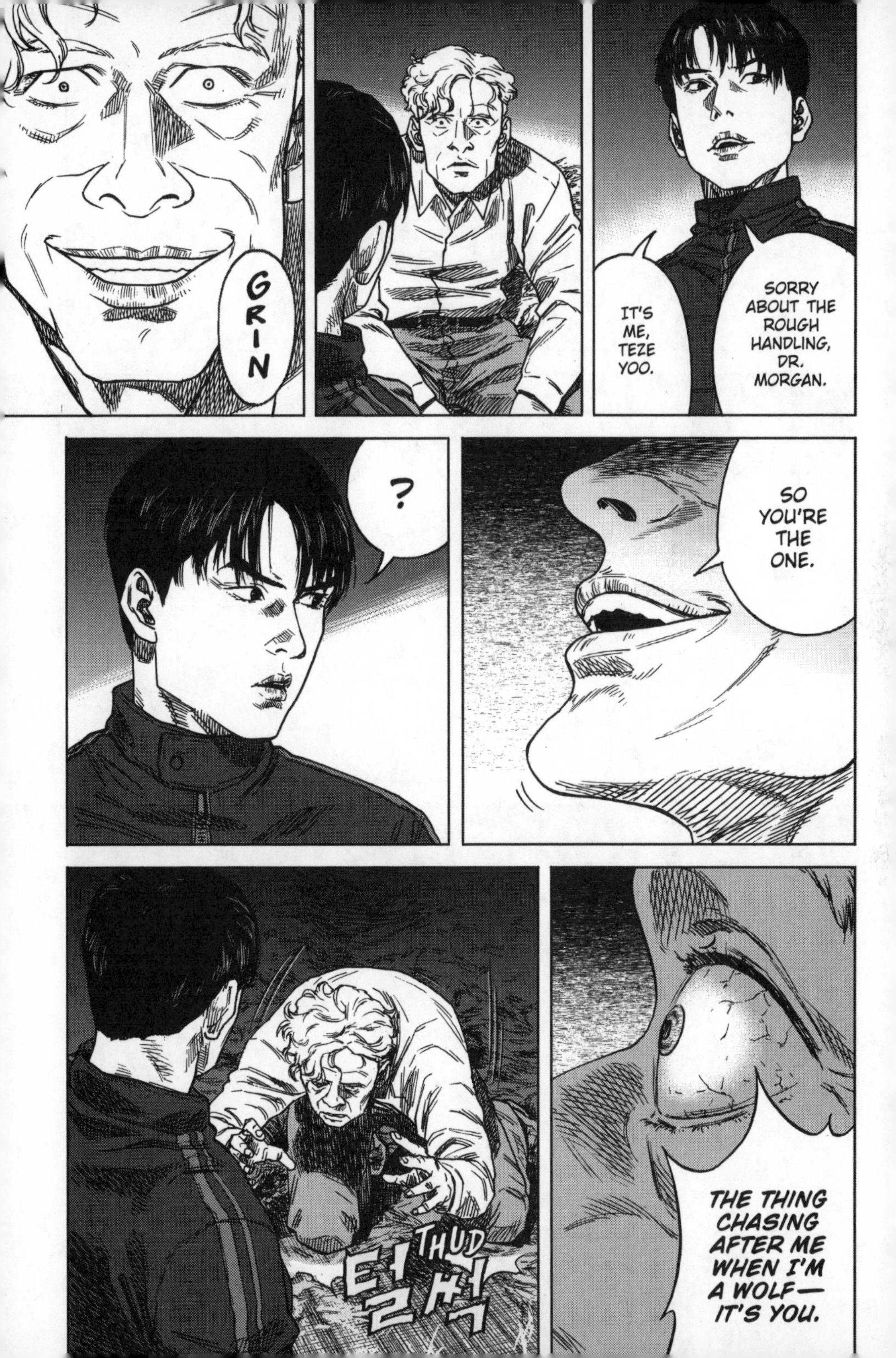
SORRY ABOUT THE ROUGH HANDLING, DR. MORGAN.
IT'S ME, TEZE YOO.
GRIN
SO YOU'RE THE ONE.
?
THE THING CHASING AFTER ME WHEN I'M A WOLF— IT'S YOU.
THUD
털썩

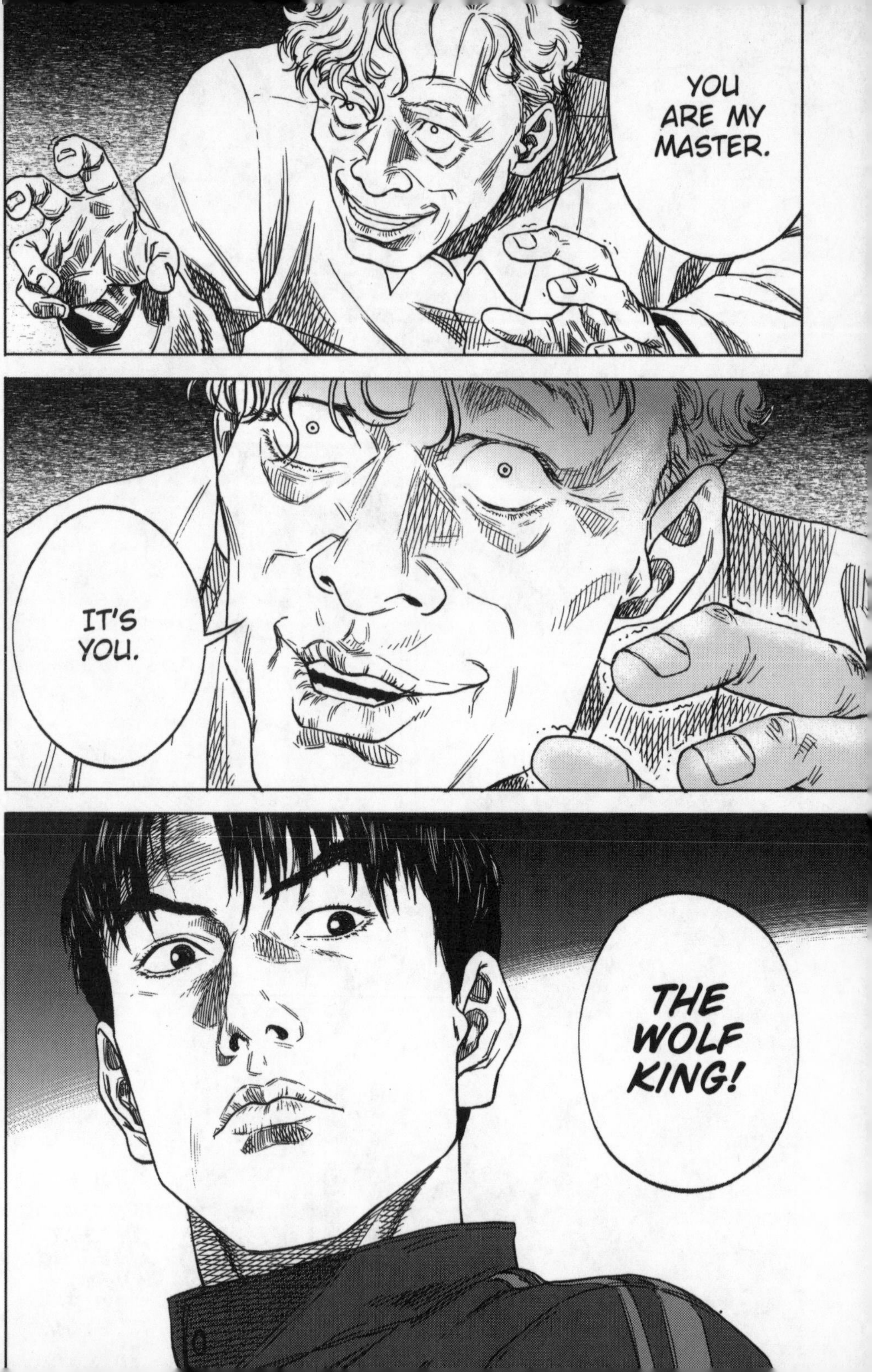
YOU ARE MY MASTER.
IT'S YOU.
THE WOLF KING!

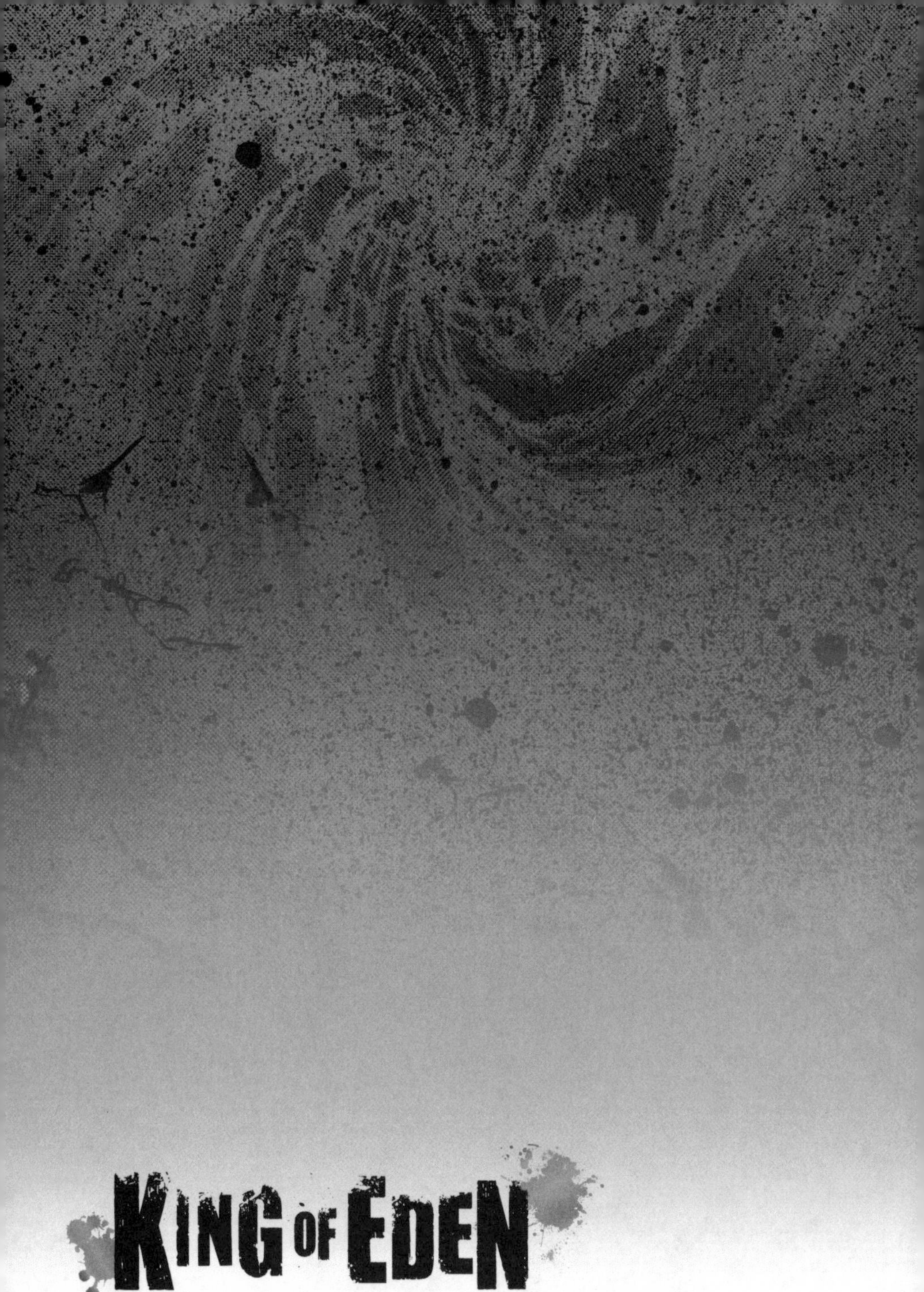

KING OF EDEN

KING OF EDEN

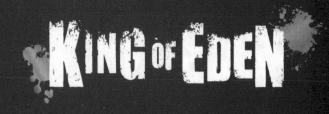

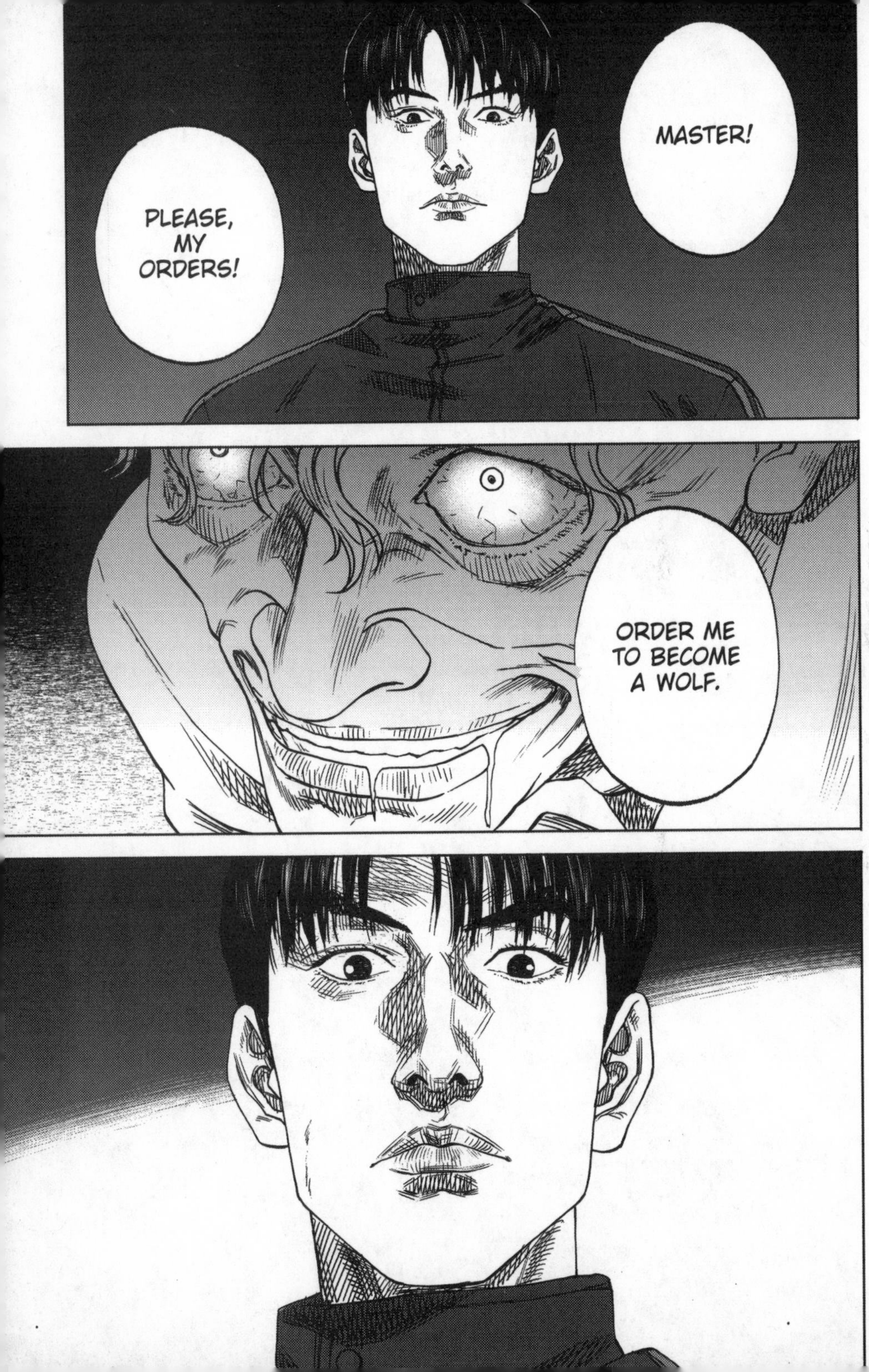
MASTER!
PLEASE, MY ORDERS!
ORDER ME TO BECOME A WOLF.

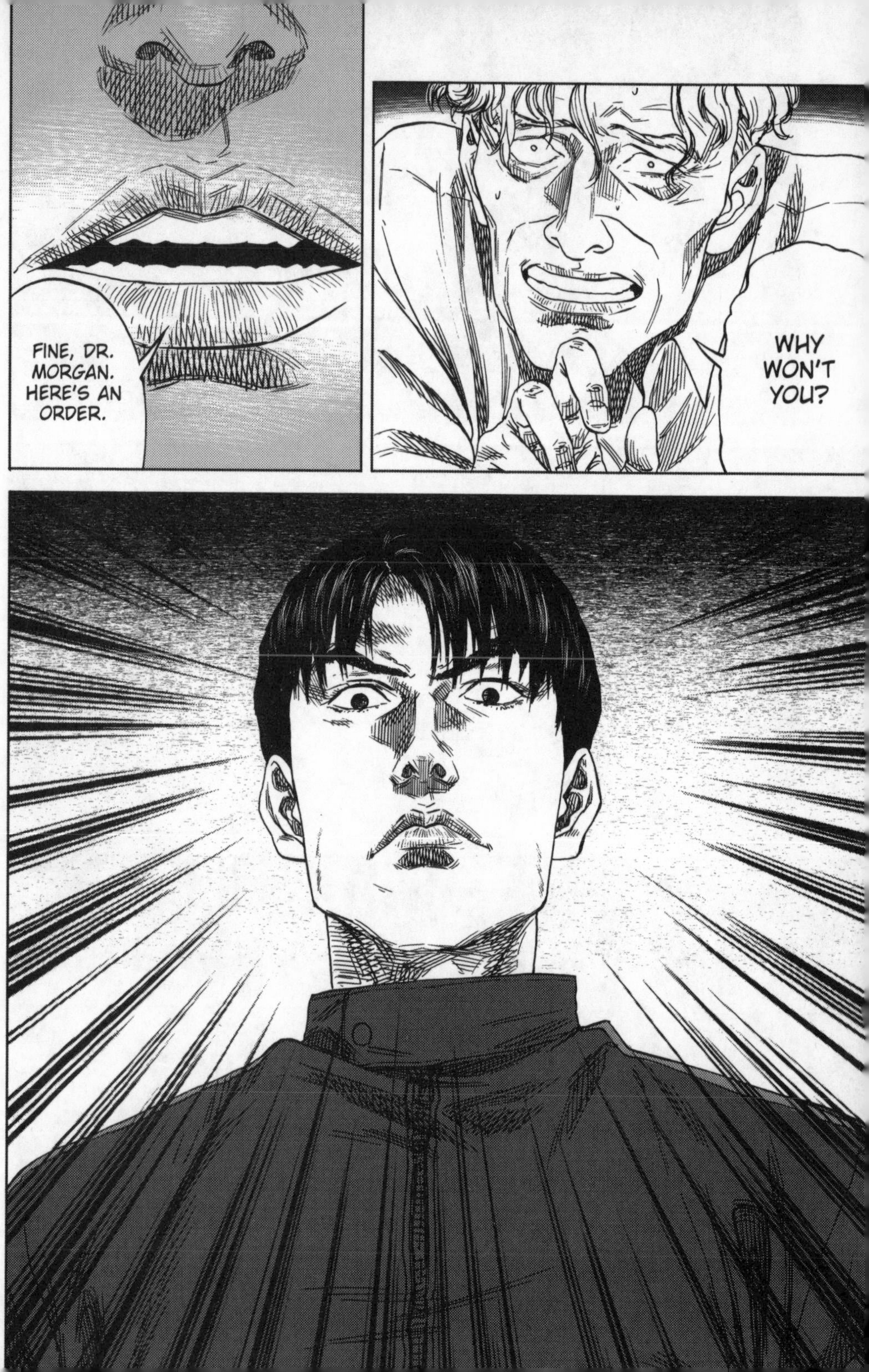
WHY WON'T YOU?
FINE, DR. MORGAN. HERE'S AN ORDER.

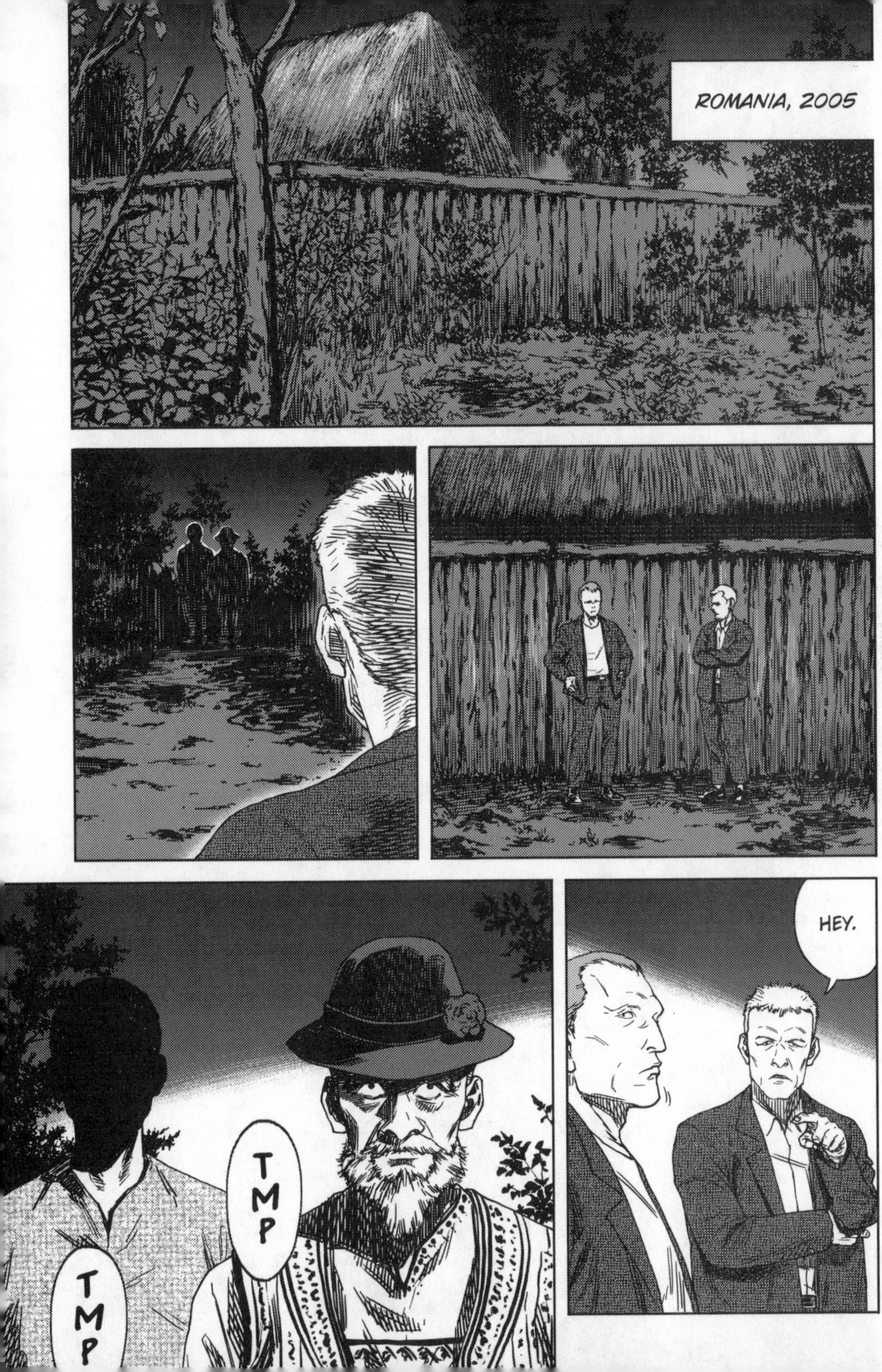
ROMANIA, 2005
HEY.
TMP
TMP

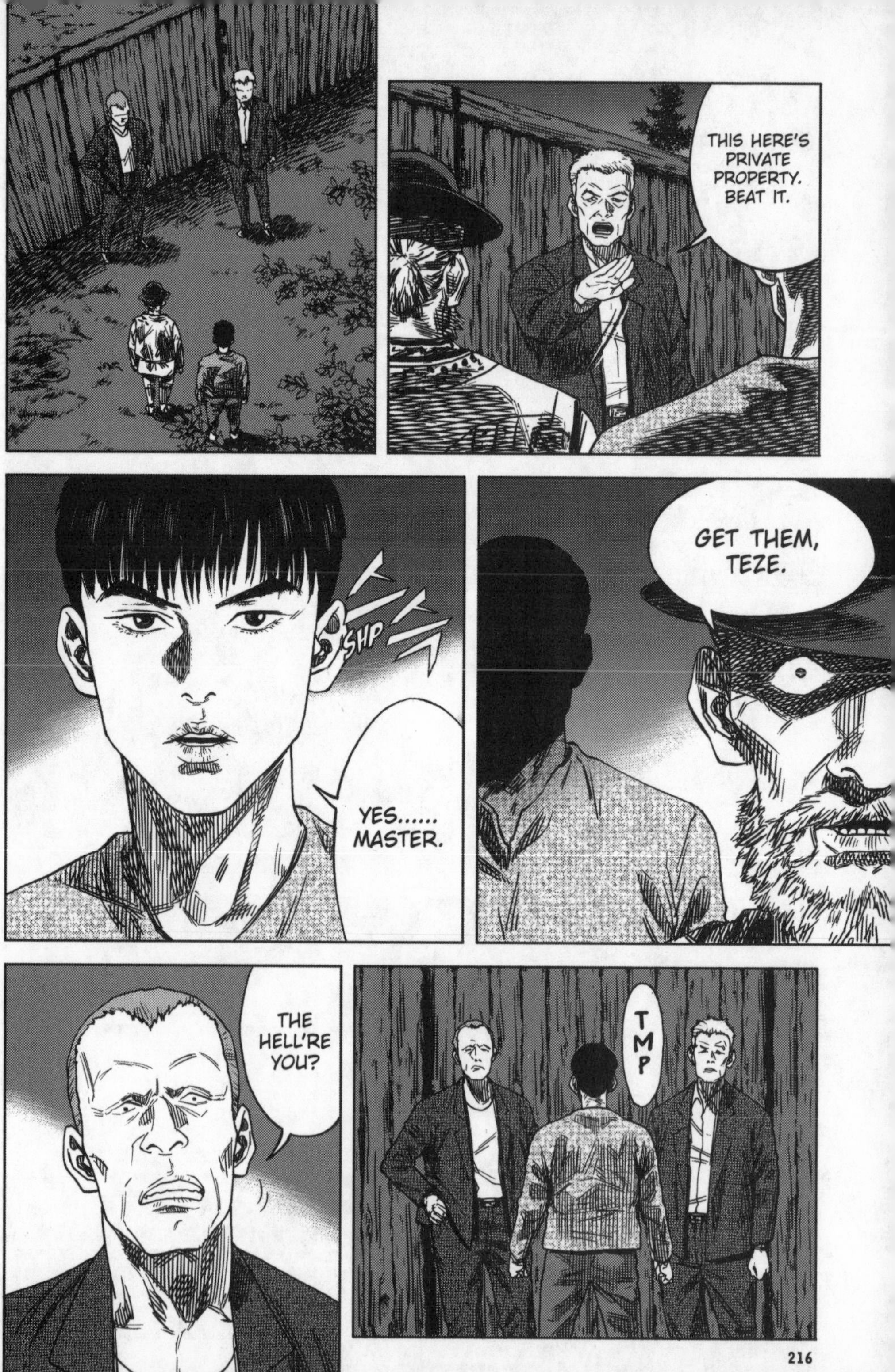
THIS HERE'S PRIVATE PROPERTY. BEAT IT.
GET THEM, TEZE.
SHP
YES...... MASTER.
TMP
THE HELL'RE YOU?

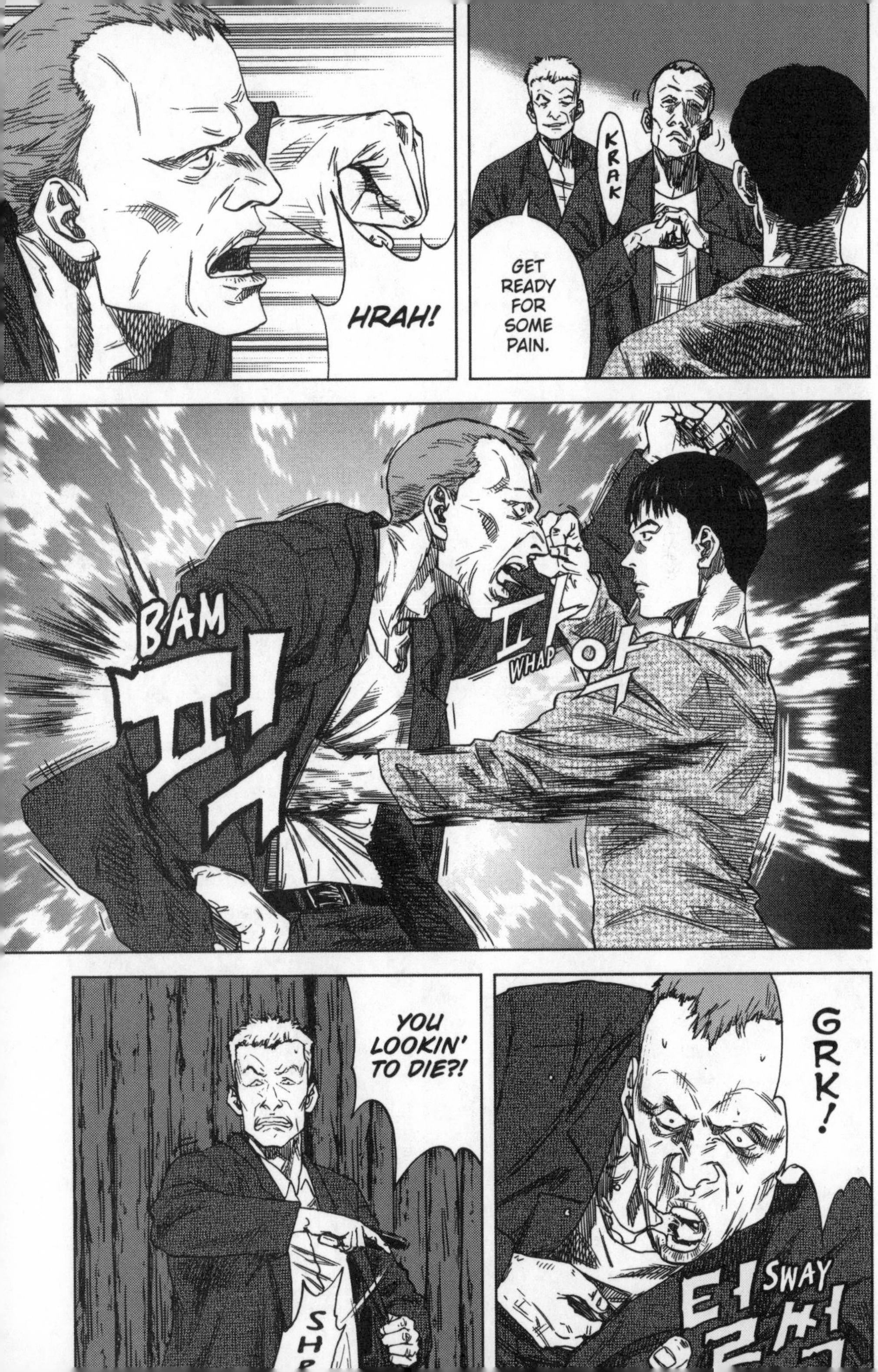
KRAK
GET READY FOR SOME PAIN.
HRAH!
BAM
WHAP
GRK!
SWAY
YOU LOOKIN' TO DIE?!

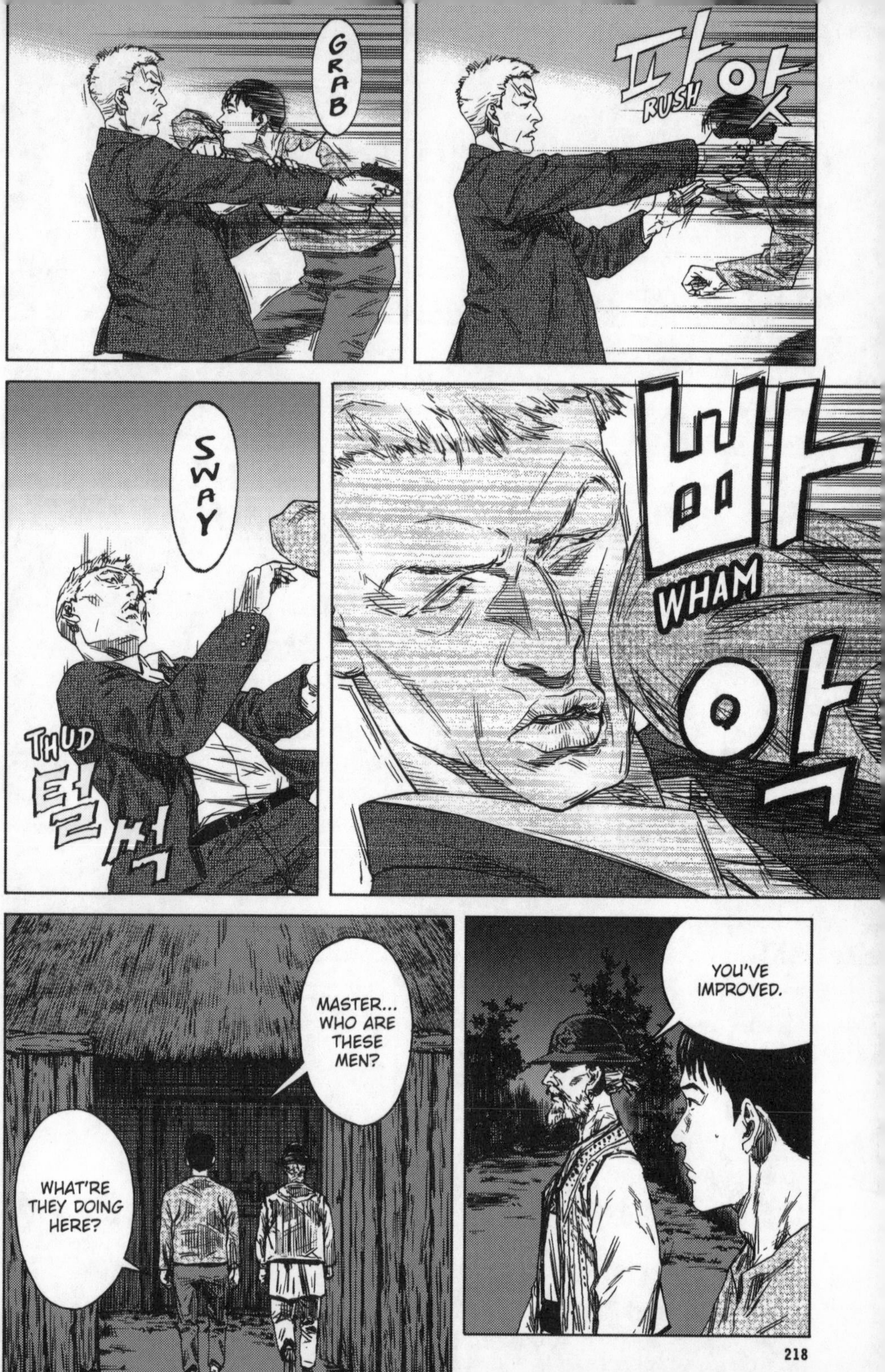
파앗
RUSH
GRAB
빠악
WHAM
SWAY
THUD
털썩
YOU'VE IMPROVED.
MASTER... WHO ARE THESE MEN?
WHAT'RE THEY DOING HERE?

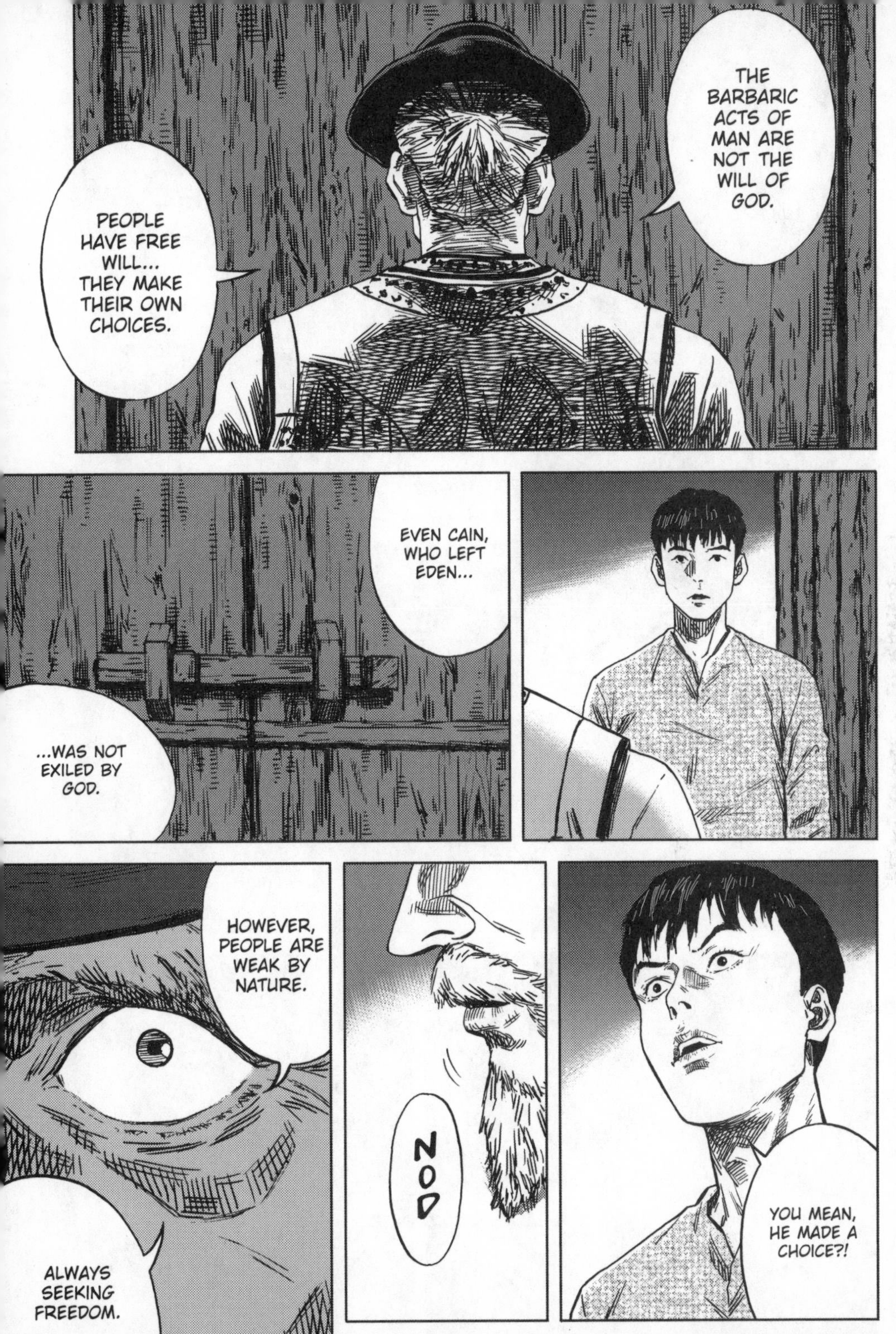
THE BARBARIC ACTS OF MAN ARE NOT THE WILL OF GOD.
PEOPLE HAVE FREE WILL... THEY MAKE THEIR OWN CHOICES.
EVEN CAIN, WHO LEFT EDEN...
...WAS NOT EXILED BY GOD.
YOU MEAN, HE MADE A CHOICE?!
NOD
HOWEVER, PEOPLE ARE WEAK BY NATURE.
ALWAYS SEEKING FREEDOM.

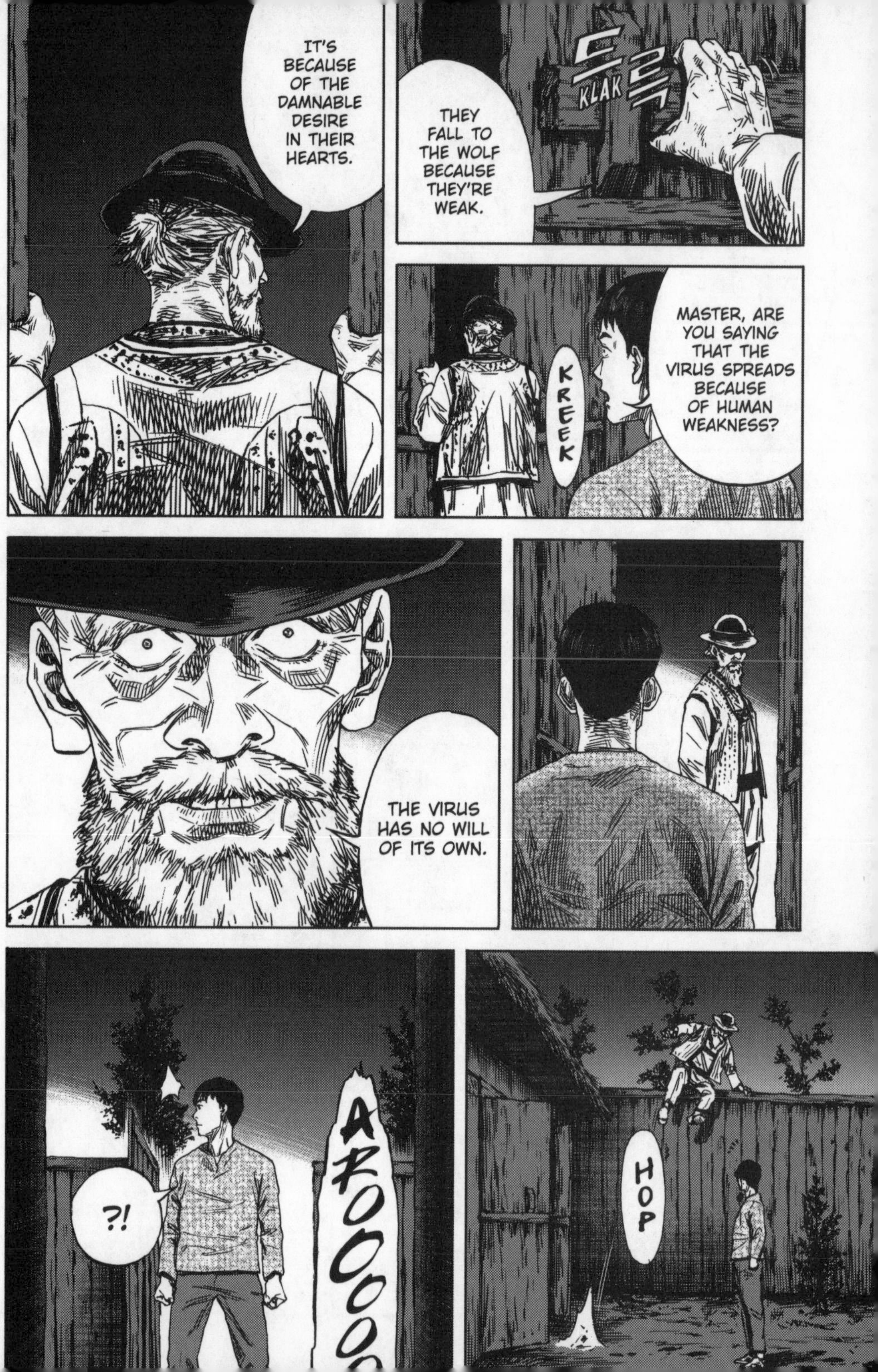

KLAK
THEY FALL TO THE WOLF BECAUSE THEY'RE WEAK.
MASTER, ARE YOU SAYING THAT THE VIRUS SPREADS BECAUSE OF HUMAN WEAKNESS?
KREEK
IT'S BECAUSE OF THE DAMNABLE DESIRE IN THEIR HEARTS.
THE VIRUS HAS NO WILL OF ITS OWN.
HOP
AROOOOO
?!

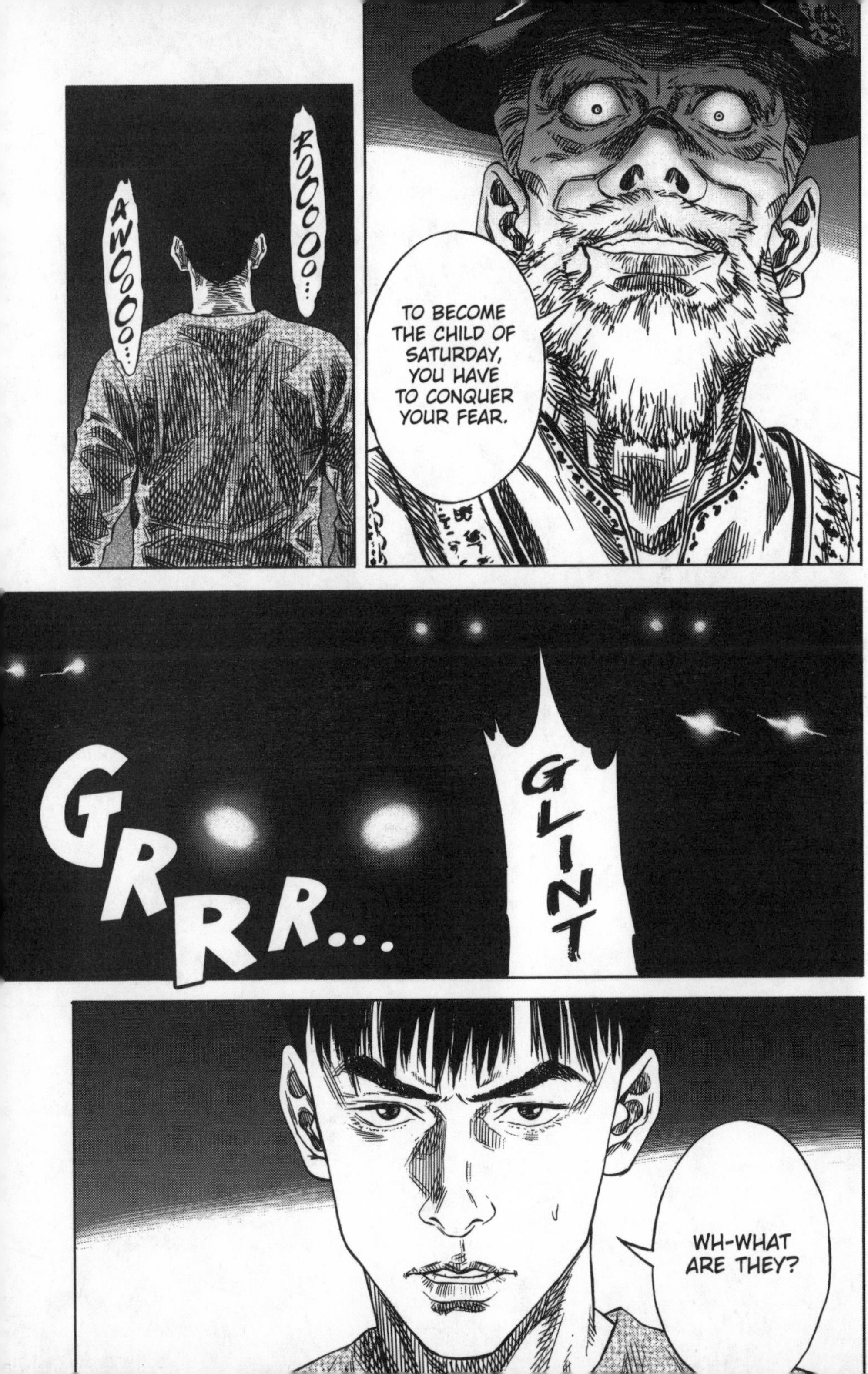
TO BECOME THE CHILD OF SATURDAY, YOU HAVE TO CONQUER YOUR FEAR.
ROOOOOO...
AWOOOOO...
GLINT
GRRR...
WH-WHAT ARE THEY?

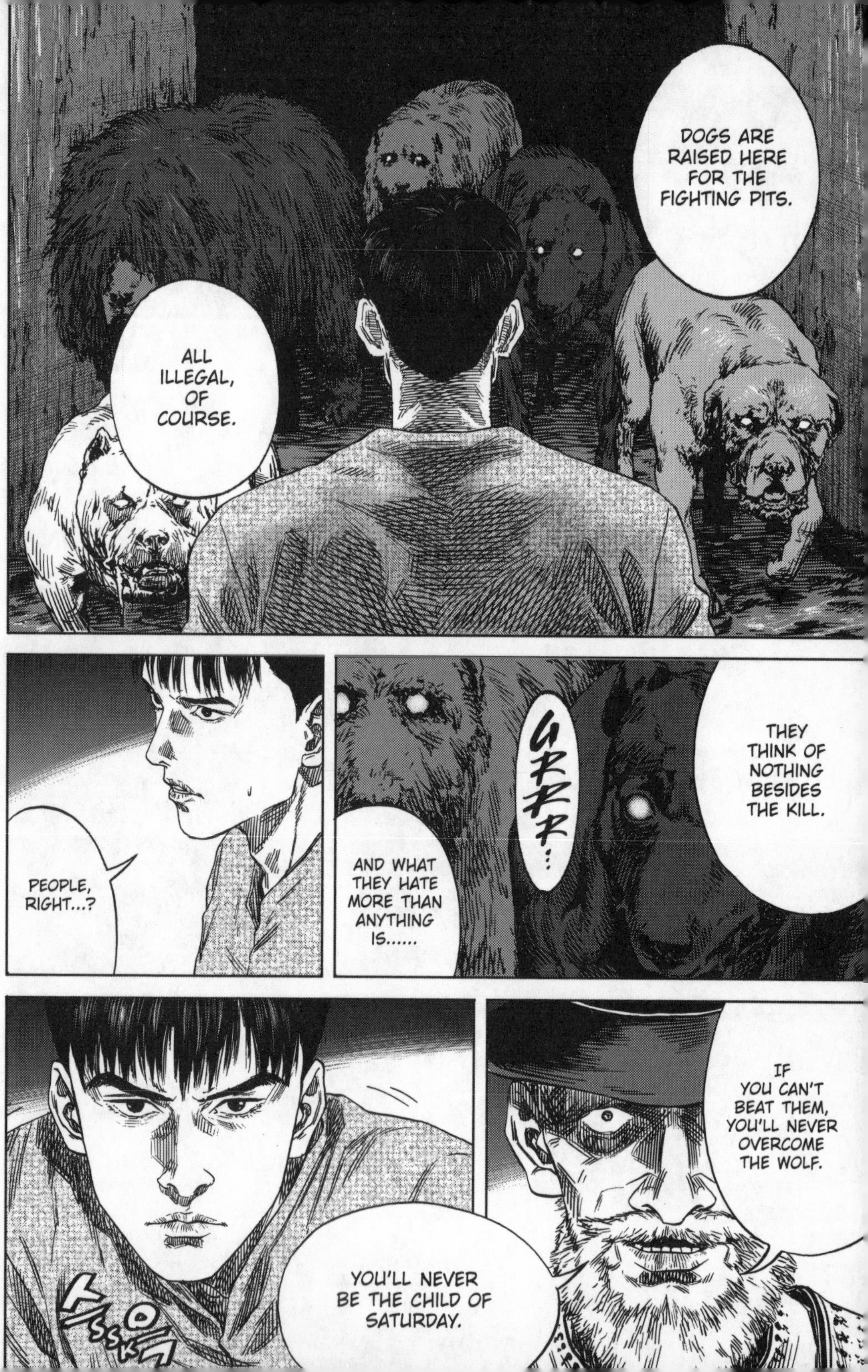
DOGS ARE RAISED HERE FOR THE FIGHTING PITS.
ALL ILLEGAL, OF COURSE.
THEY THINK OF NOTHING BESIDES THE KILL.
GRRRR...
AND WHAT THEY HATE MORE THAN ANYTHING IS......
PEOPLE, RIGHT...?
IF YOU CAN'T BEAT THEM, YOU'LL NEVER OVERCOME THE WOLF.
YOU'LL NEVER BE THE CHILD OF SATURDAY.
SSK

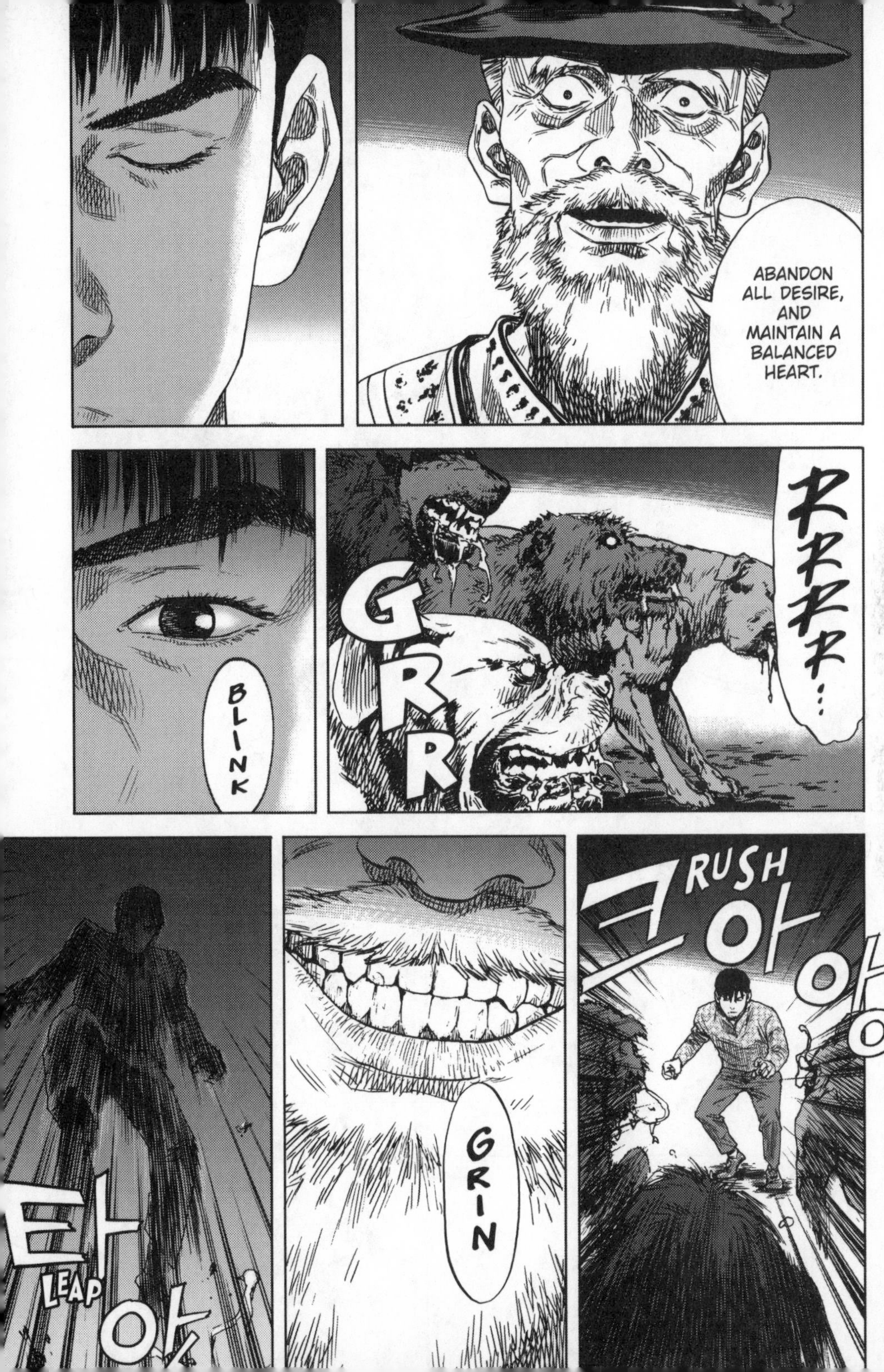
ABANDON ALL DESIRE, AND MAINTAIN A BALANCED HEART.
RRRRR...
GRR
BLINK
크아아아
RUSH
GRIN
타아
LEAP

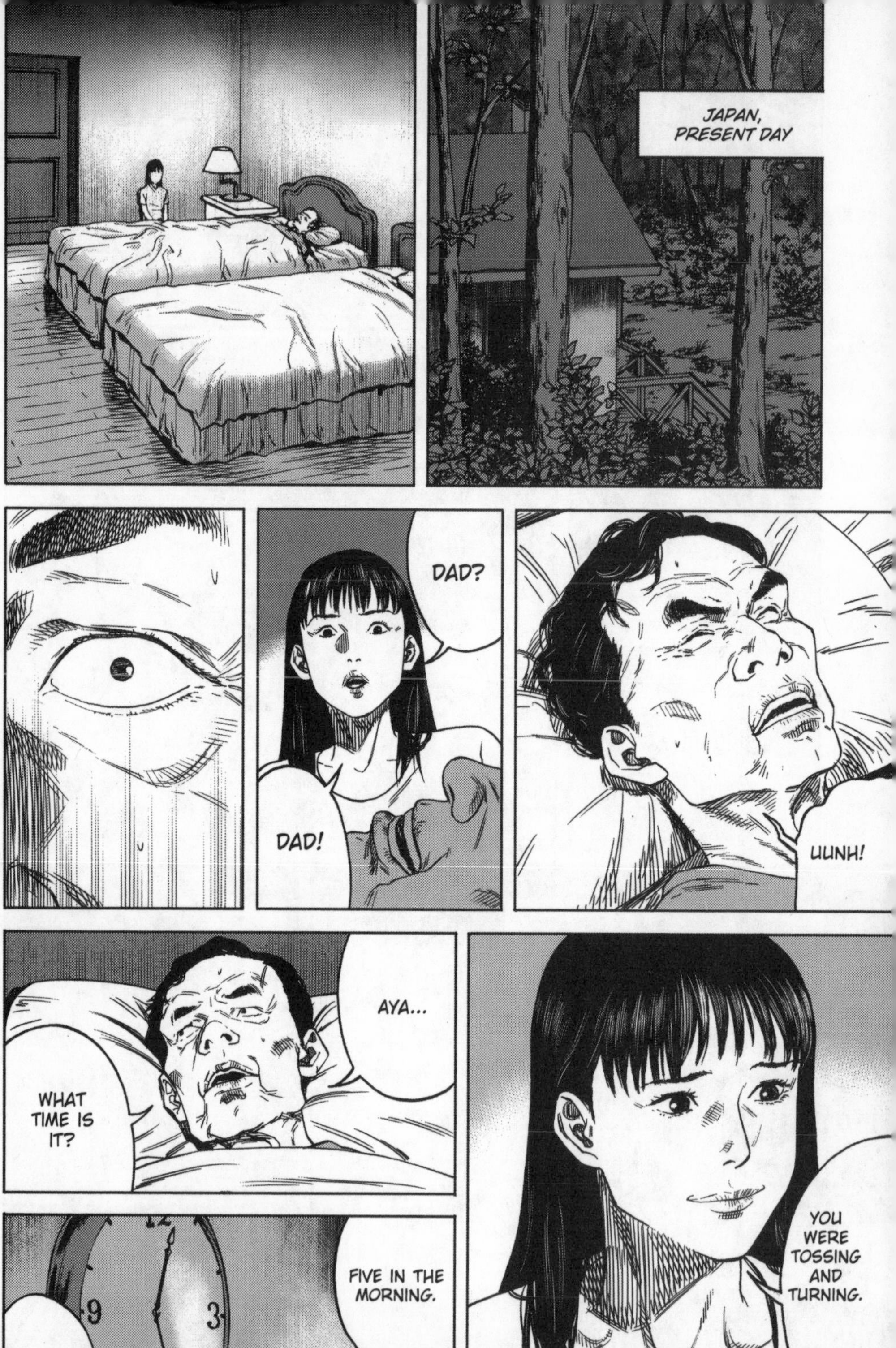
JAPAN, PRESENT DAY
UUNH!
DAD?
DAD!
YOU WERE TOSSING AND TURNING.
AYA...
WHAT TIME IS IT?
FIVE IN THE MORNING.
I SEE.

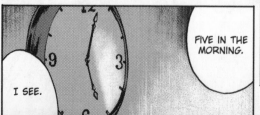

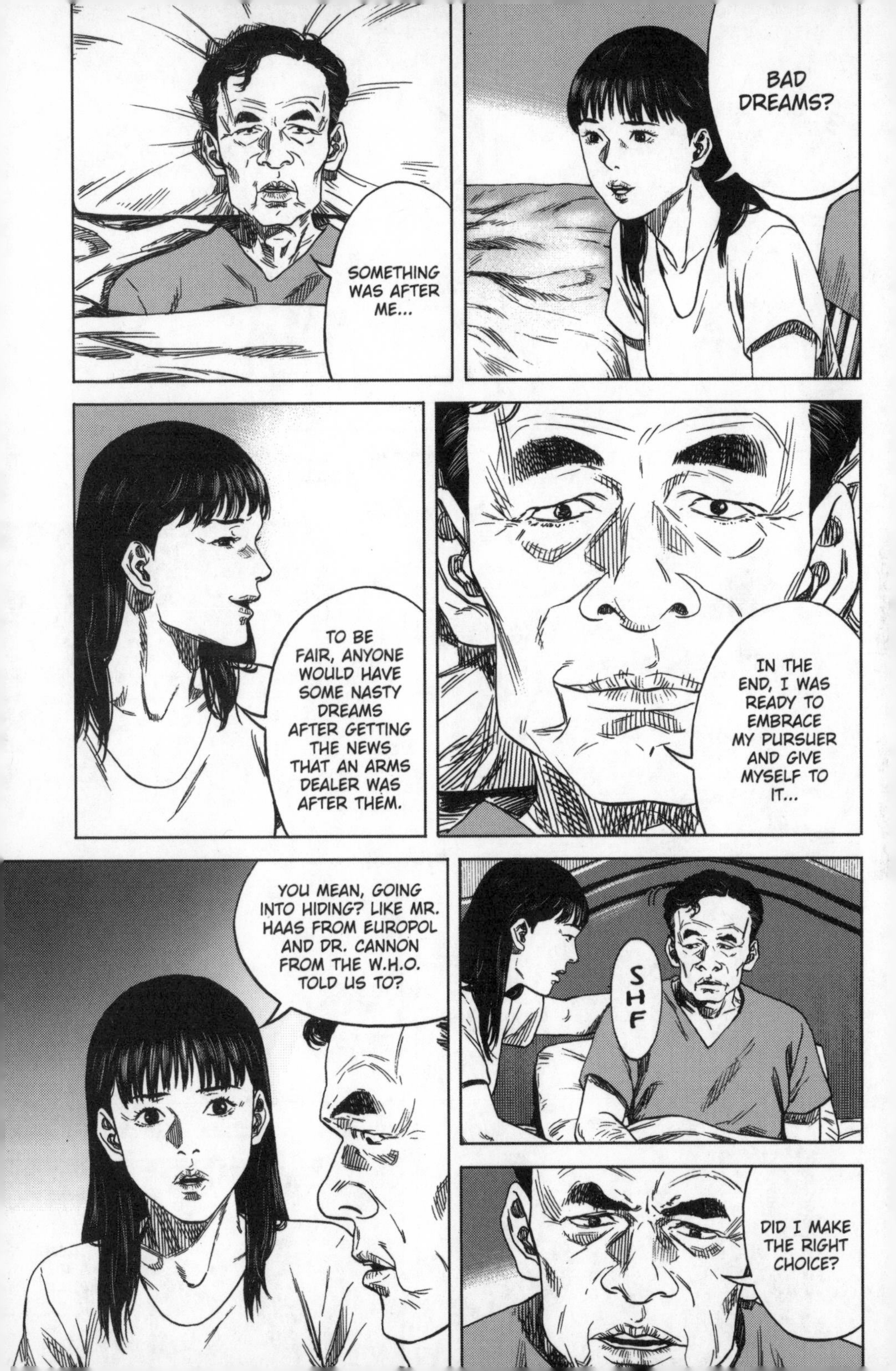
BAD DREAMS?
SOMETHING WAS AFTER ME...
IN THE END, I WAS READY TO EMBRACE MY PURSUER AND GIVE MYSELF TO IT...
TO BE FAIR, ANYONE WOULD HAVE SOME NASTY DREAMS AFTER GETTING THE NEWS THAT AN ARMS DEALER WAS AFTER THEM.
SHF
DID I MAKE THE RIGHT CHOICE?
YOU MEAN, GOING INTO HIDING? LIKE MR. HAAS FROM EUROPOL AND DR. CANNON FROM THE W.H.O. TOLD US TO?

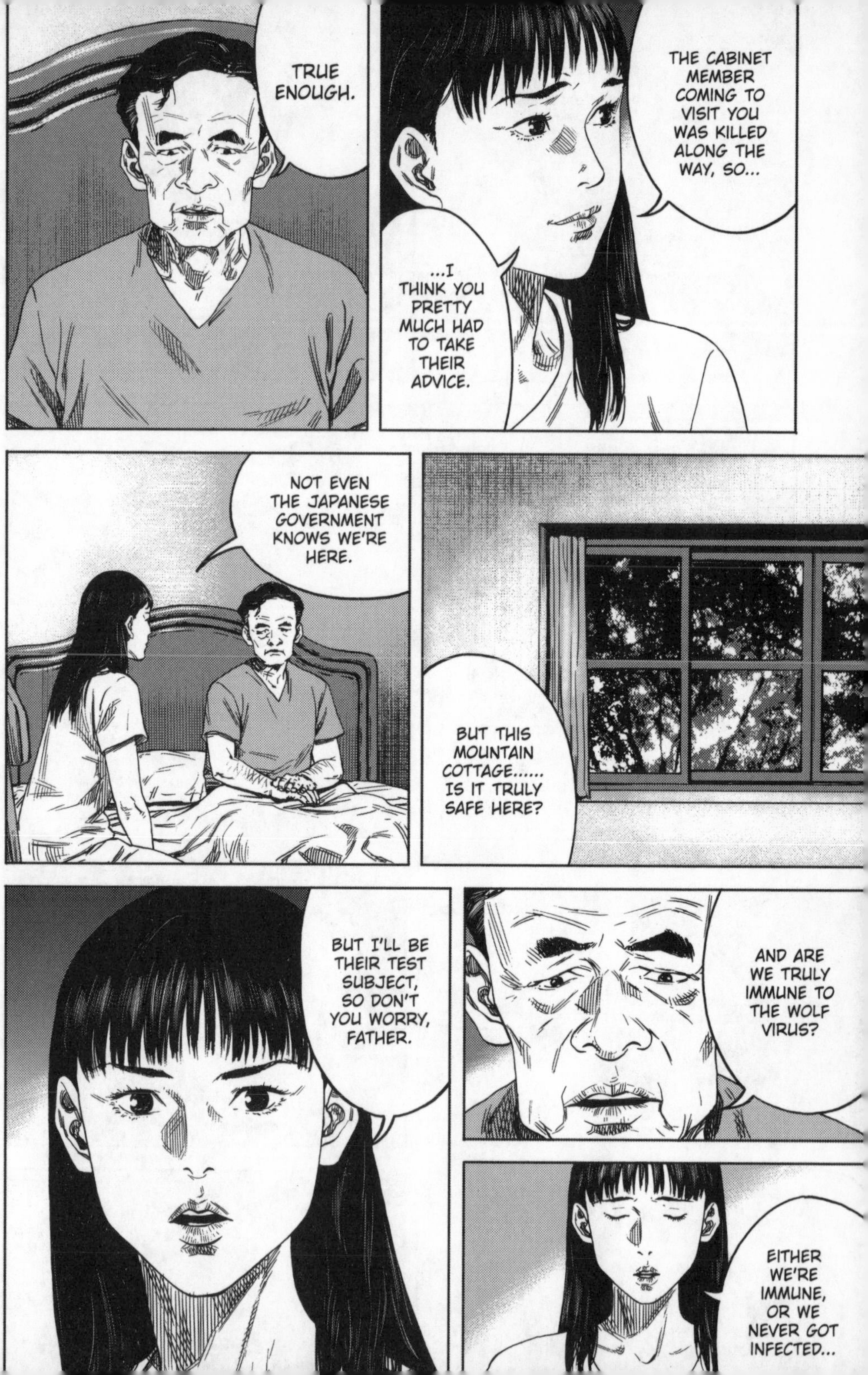
THE CABINET MEMBER COMING TO VISIT YOU WAS KILLED ALONG THE WAY, SO...
...I THINK YOU PRETTY MUCH HAD TO TAKE THEIR ADVICE.
TRUE ENOUGH.
BUT THIS MOUNTAIN COTTAGE...... IS IT TRULY SAFE HERE?
NOT EVEN THE JAPANESE GOVERNMENT KNOWS WE'RE HERE.
AND ARE WE TRULY IMMUNE TO THE WOLF VIRUS?
EITHER WE'RE IMMUNE, OR WE NEVER GOT INFECTED...
BUT I'LL BE THEIR TEST SUBJECT, SO DON'T YOU WORRY, FATHER.

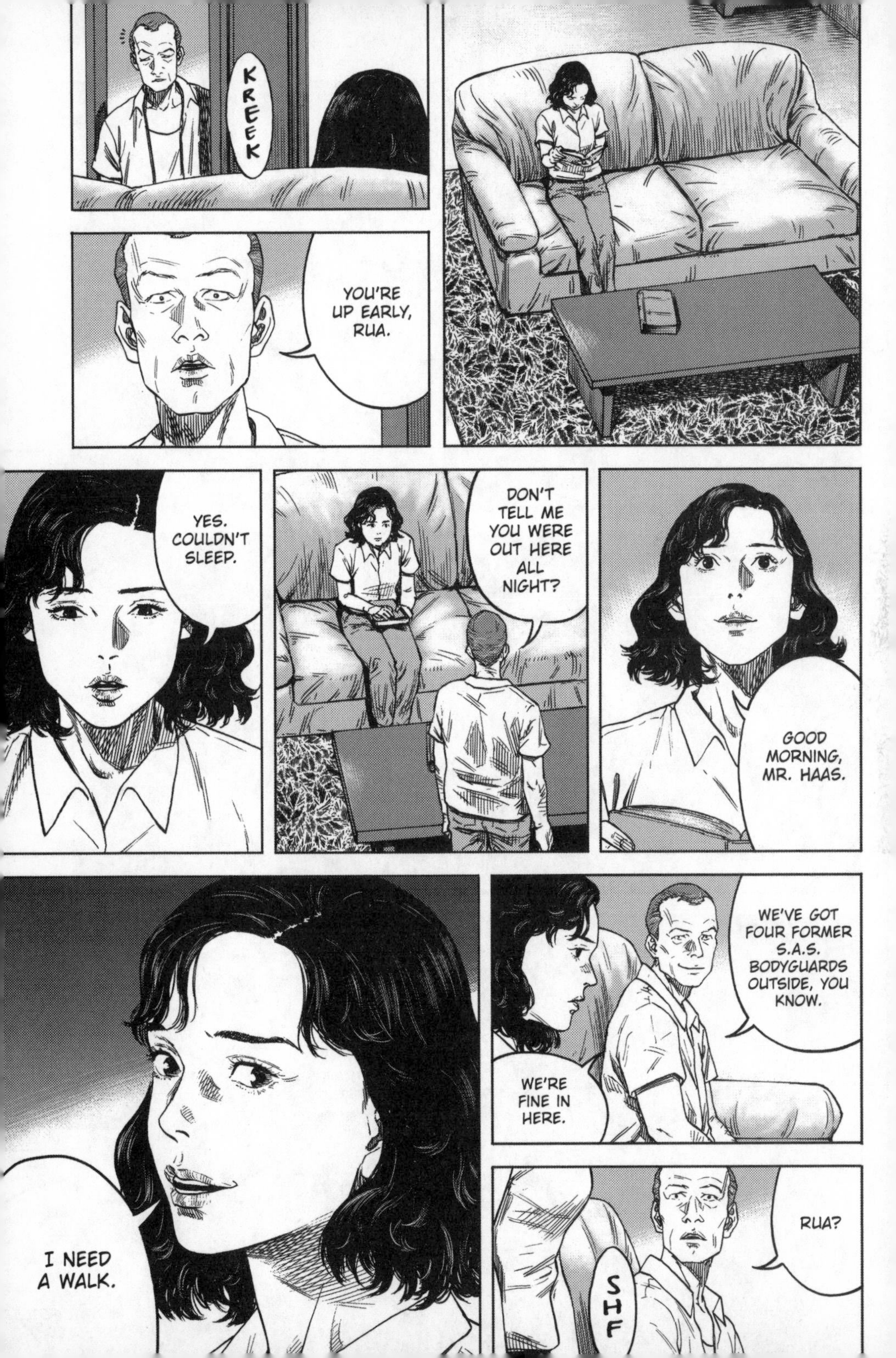
KREEK
YOU'RE UP EARLY, RUA.
GOOD MORNING, MR. HAAS.
DON'T TELL ME YOU WERE OUT HERE ALL NIGHT?
YES. COULDN'T SLEEP.
WE'VE GOT FOUR FORMER S.A.S. BODYGUARDS OUTSIDE, YOU KNOW.
WE'RE FINE IN HERE.
RUA?
SHF
I NEED A WALK.

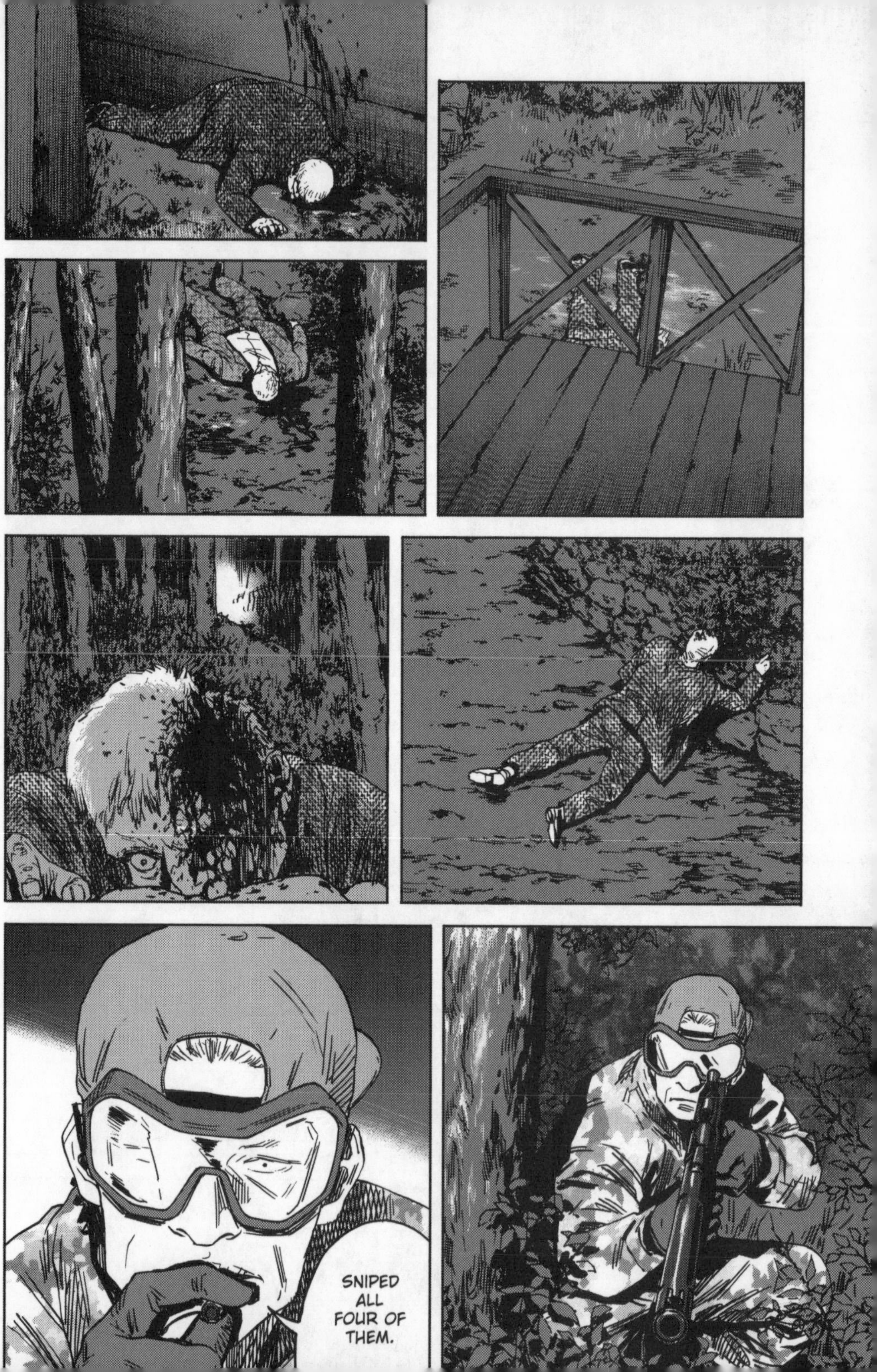
SNIPED ALL FOUR OF THEM.

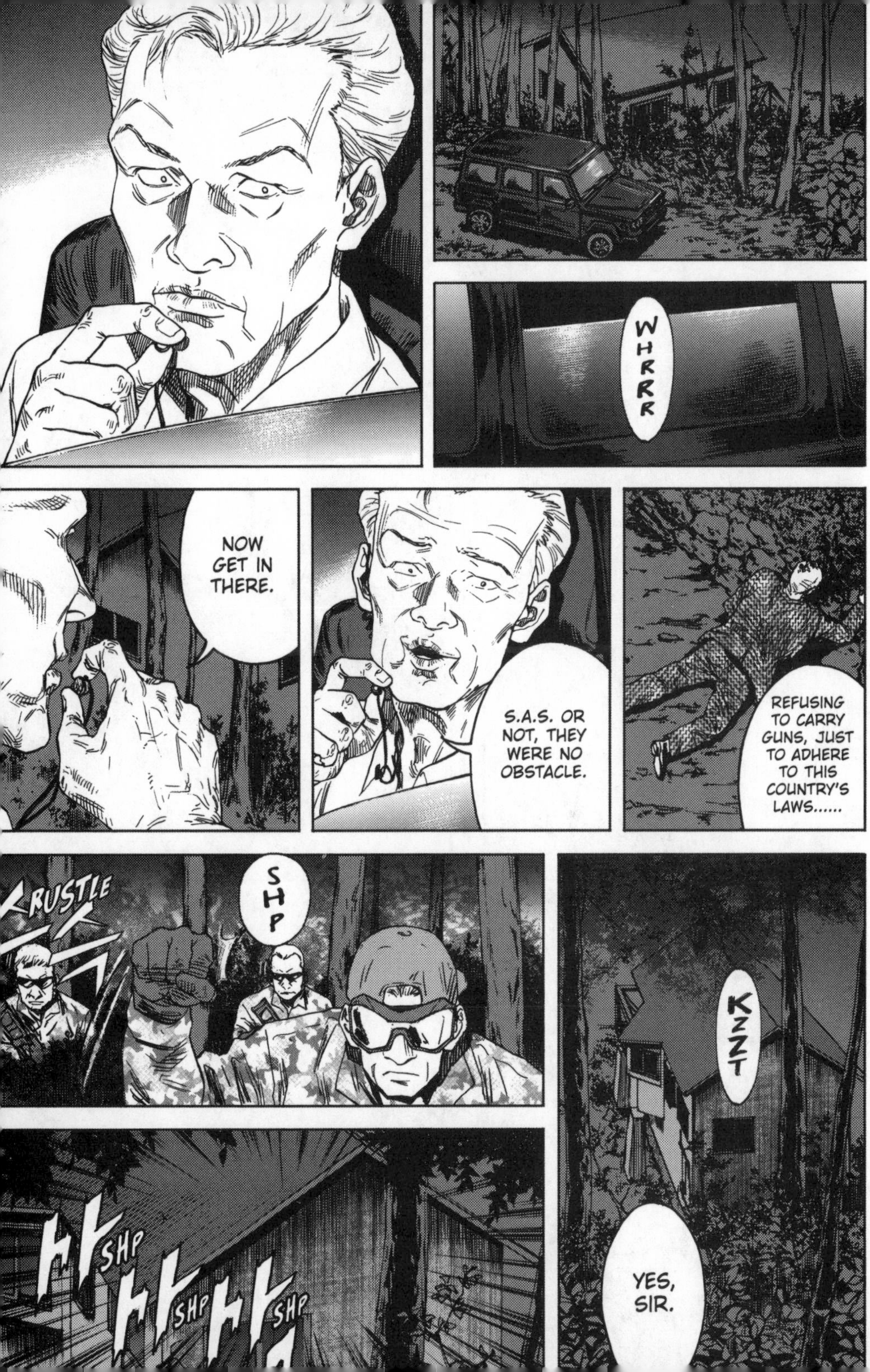
WHRRR
REFUSING TO CARRY GUNS, JUST TO ADHERE TO THIS COUNTRY'S LAWS......
S.A.S. OR NOT, THEY WERE NO OBSTACLE.
NOW GET IN THERE.
KZZT
YES, SIR.
SHP
RUSTLE
SHP
SHP
SHP

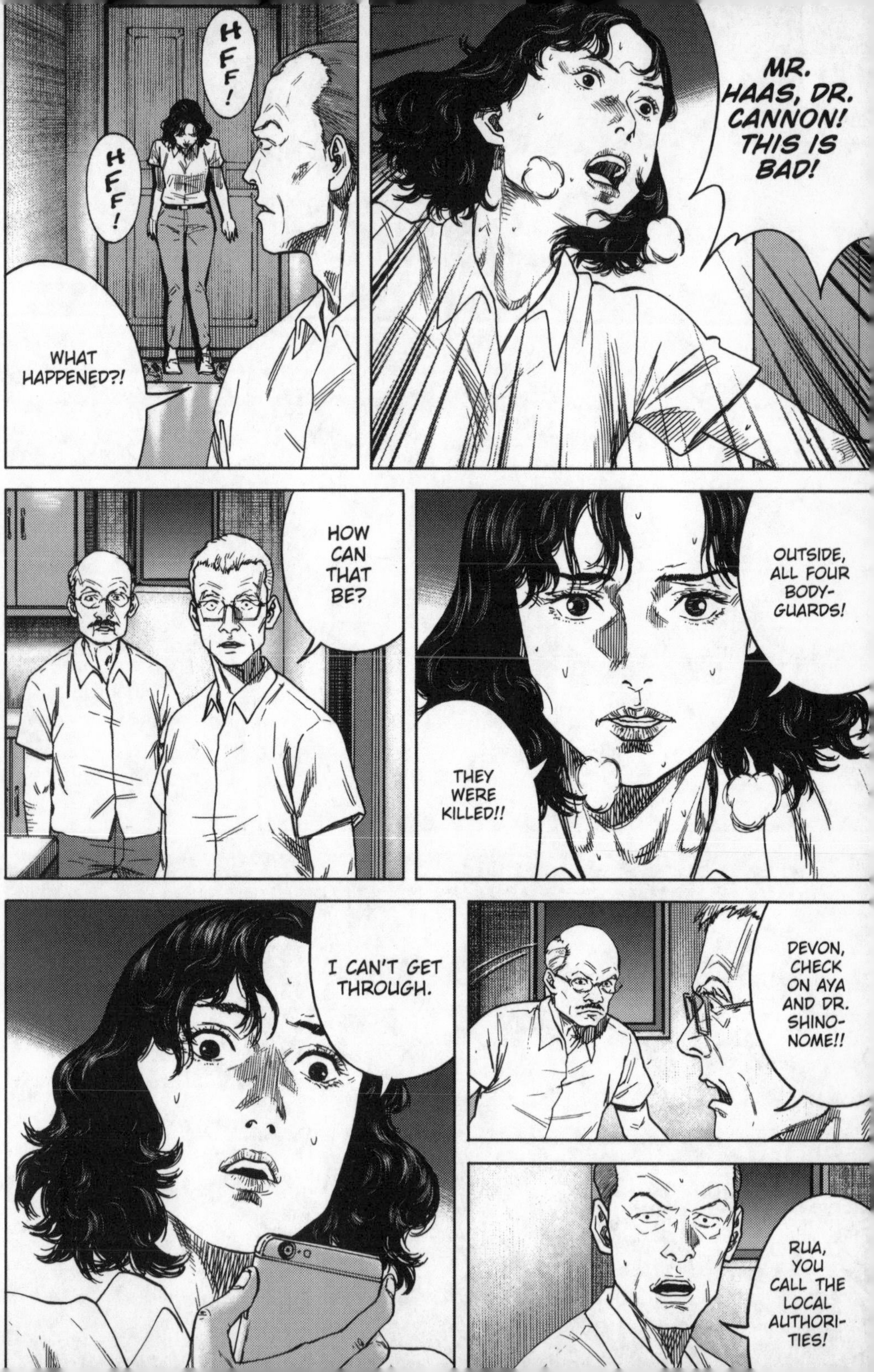
MR. HAAS, DR. CANNON! THIS IS BAD!
HFF!
HFF!
WHAT HAPPENED?!
OUTSIDE, ALL FOUR BODYGUARDS!
THEY WERE KILLED!!
HOW CAN THAT BE?
DEVON, CHECK ON AYA AND DR. SHINONOME!!
RUA, YOU CALL THE LOCAL AUTHORITIES!
I CAN'T GET THROUGH.

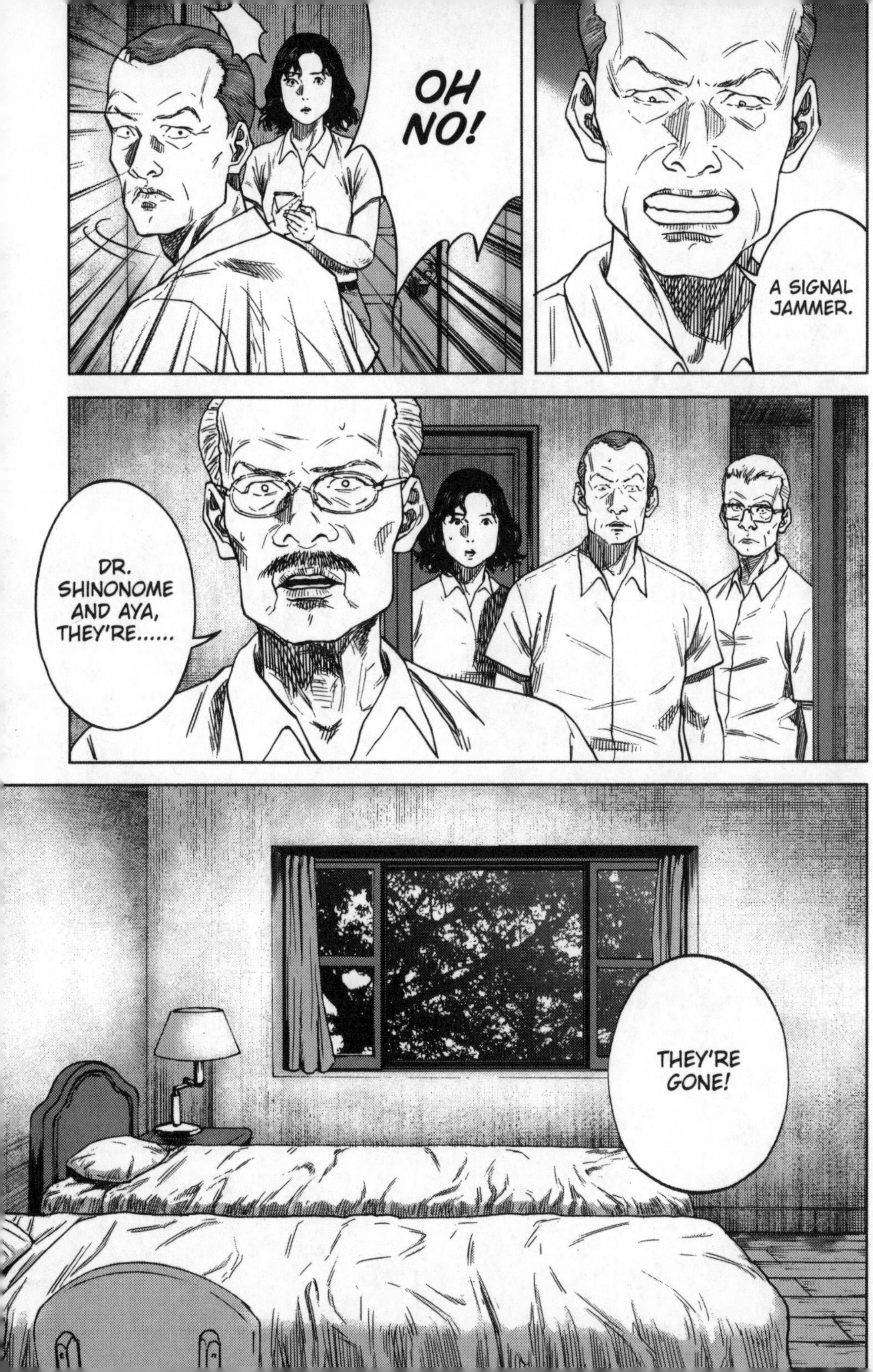
A SIGNAL JAMMER.
OH NO!
DR. SHINONOME AND AYA, THEY'RE......
THEY'RE GONE!

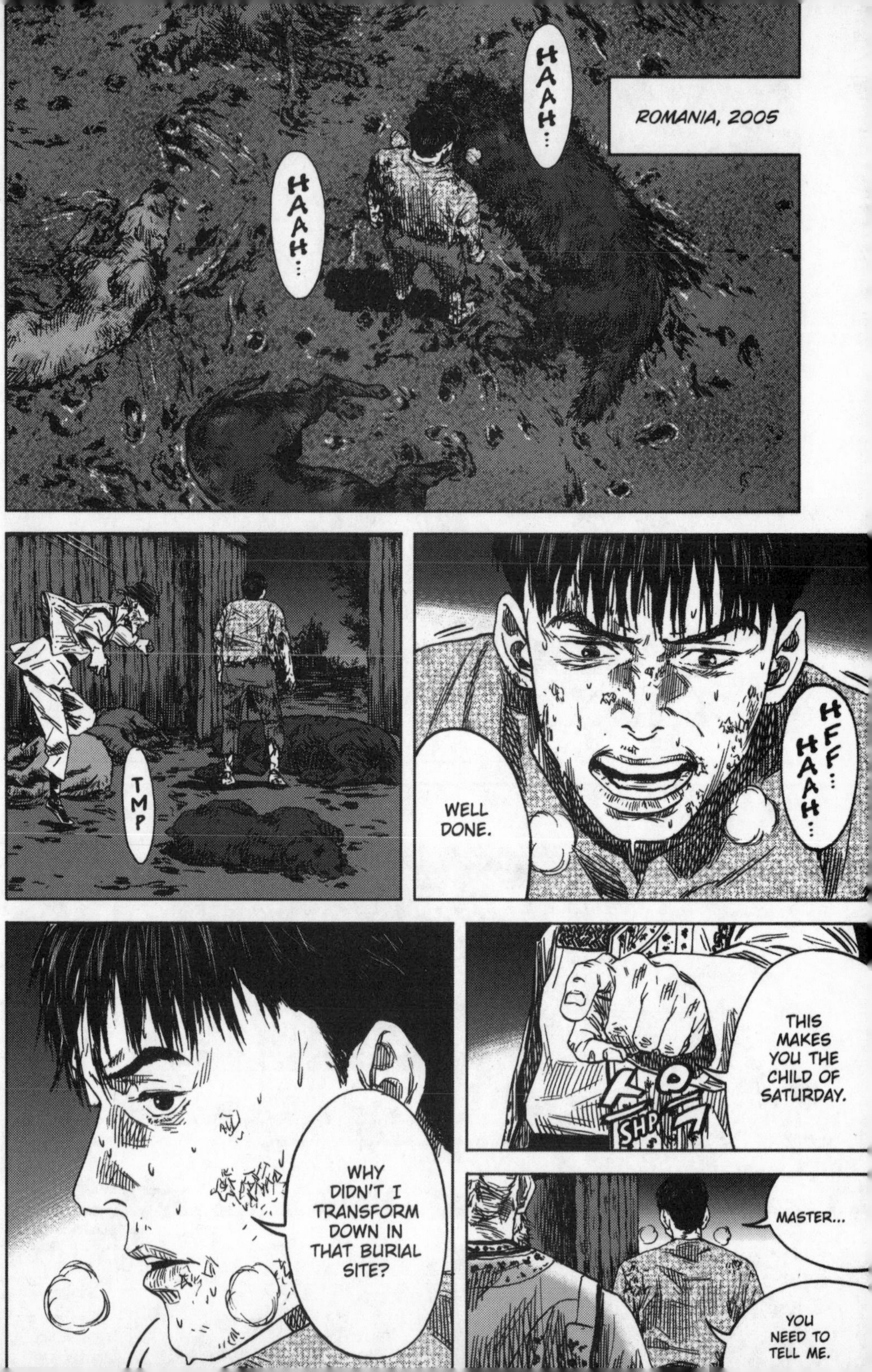

ROMANIA, 2005
HAAH...
HAAH...
HFF... HAAH...
WELL DONE.
TMP
THIS MAKES YOU THE CHILD OF SATURDAY.
SHP
MASTER...
YOU NEED TO TELL ME.
WHY DIDN'T I TRANSFORM DOWN IN THAT BURIAL SITE?

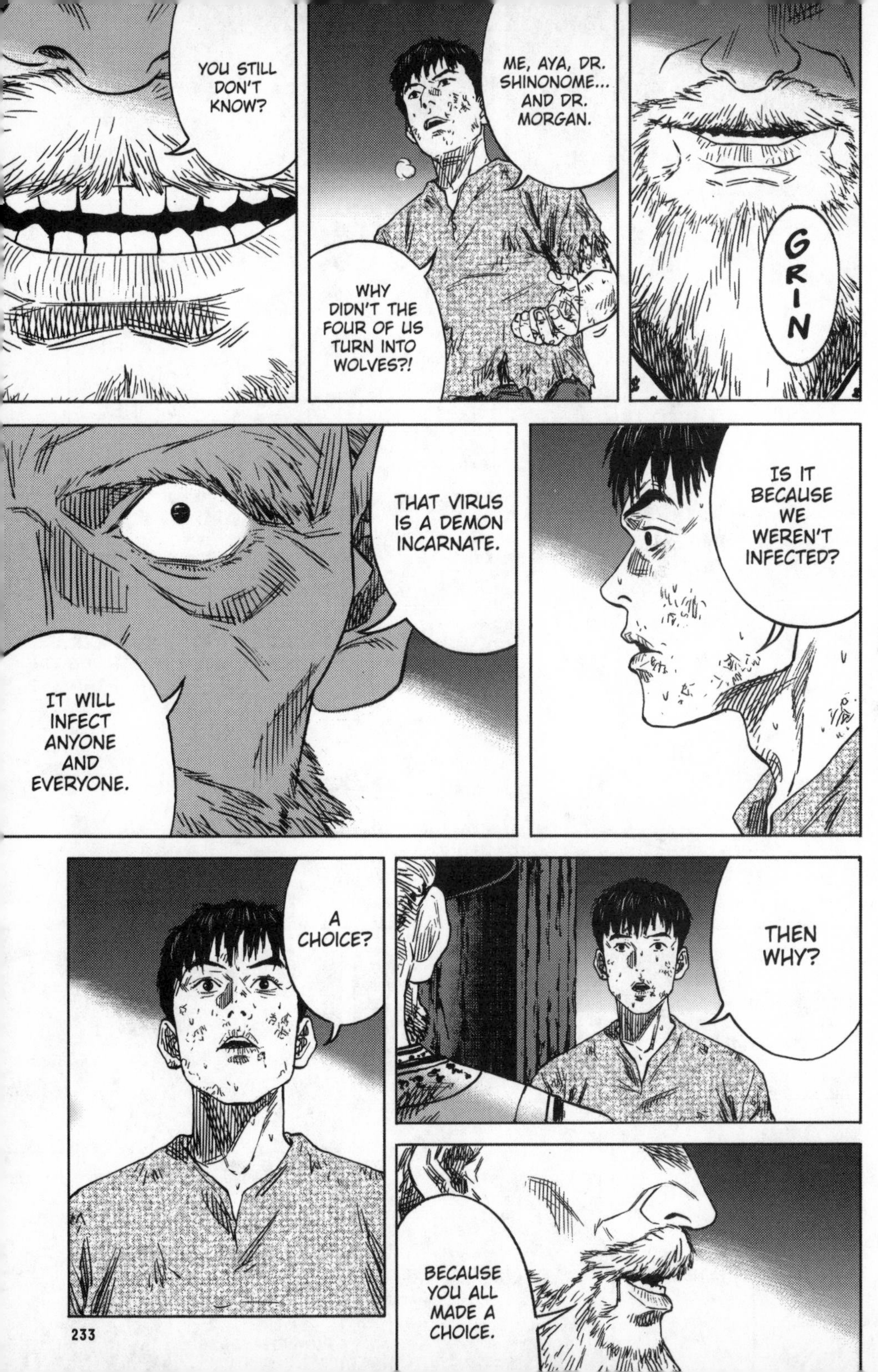
GRIN
ME, AYA, DR. SHINONOME... AND DR. MORGAN.
WHY DIDN'T THE FOUR OF US TURN INTO WOLVES?!
YOU STILL DON'T KNOW?
IS IT BECAUSE WE WEREN'T INFECTED?
THAT VIRUS IS A DEMON INCARNATE.
IT WILL INFECT ANYONE AND EVERYONE.
THEN WHY?
BECAUSE YOU ALL MADE A CHOICE.
A CHOICE?

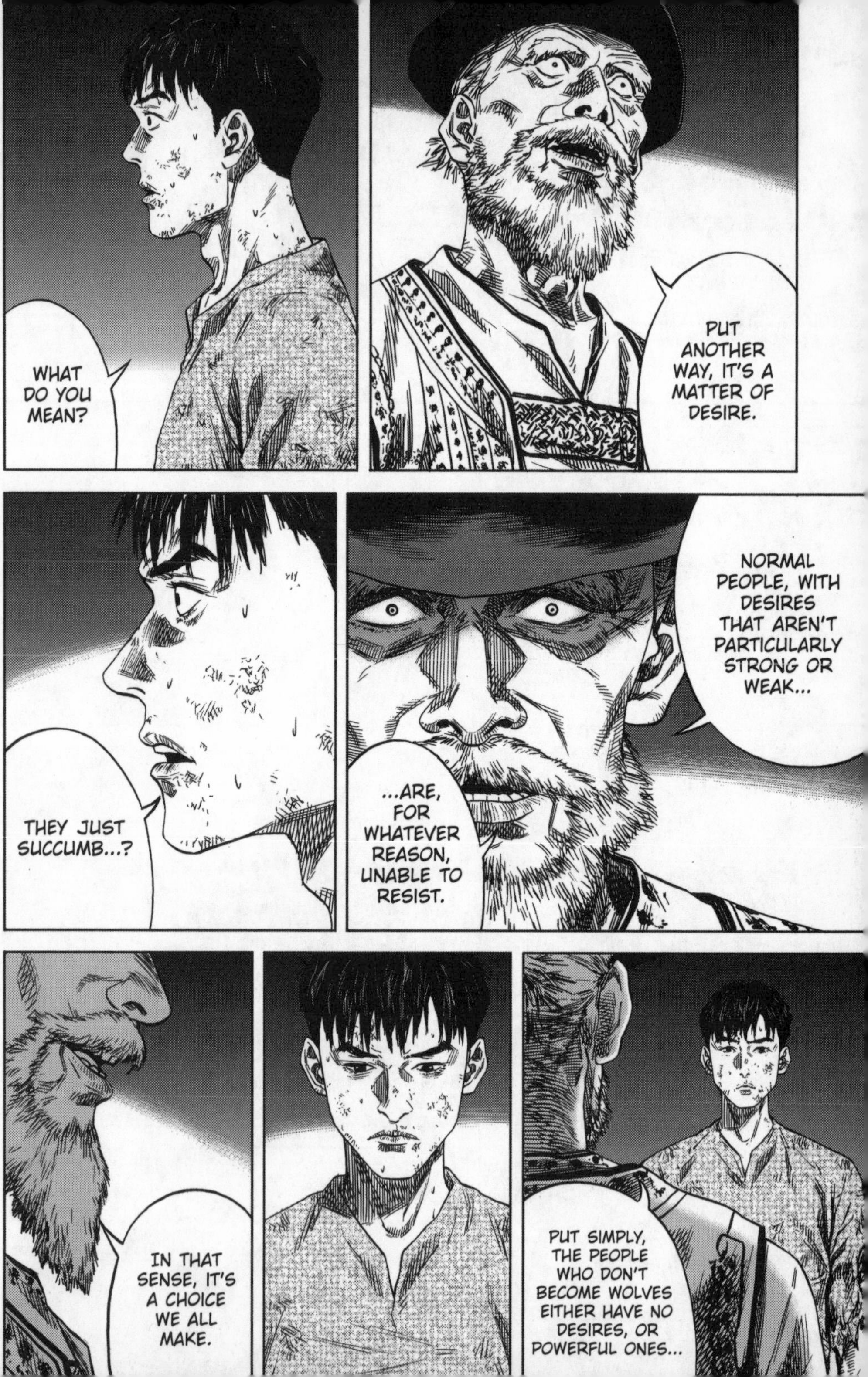
PUT ANOTHER WAY, IT'S A MATTER OF DESIRE.
WHAT DO YOU MEAN?
NORMAL PEOPLE, WITH DESIRES THAT AREN'T PARTICULARLY STRONG OR WEAK...
...ARE, FOR WHATEVER REASON, UNABLE TO RESIST.
THEY JUST SUCCUMB...?
PUT SIMPLY, THE PEOPLE WHO DON'T BECOME WOLVES EITHER HAVE NO DESIRES, OR POWERFUL ONES...
IN THAT SENSE, IT'S A CHOICE WE ALL MAKE.

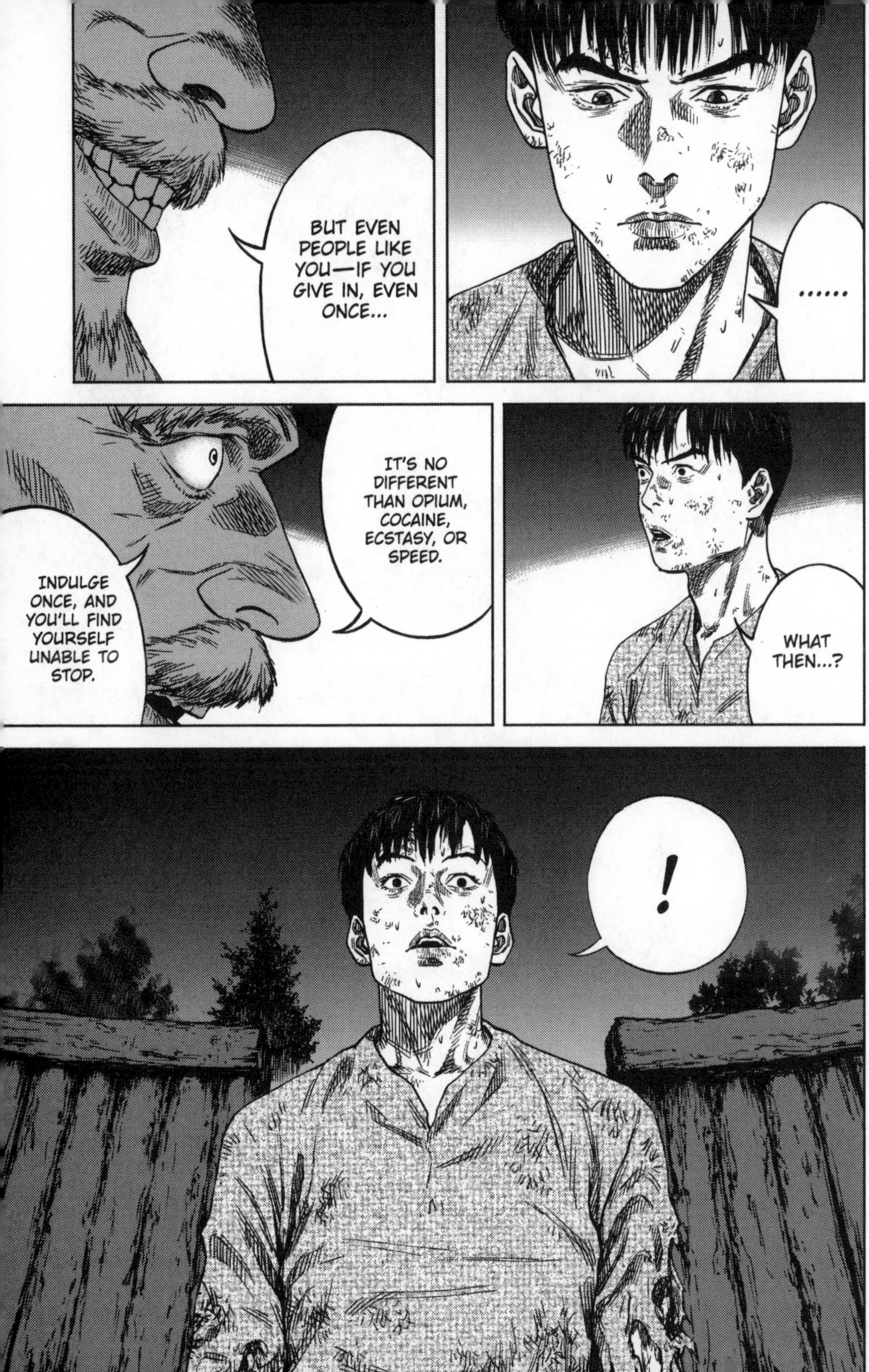
......
BUT EVEN PEOPLE LIKE YOU—IF YOU GIVE IN, EVEN ONCE...
WHAT THEN...?
IT'S NO DIFFERENT THAN OPIUM, COCAINE, ECSTASY, OR SPEED.
INDULGE ONCE, AND YOU'LL FIND YOURSELF UNABLE TO STOP.
!

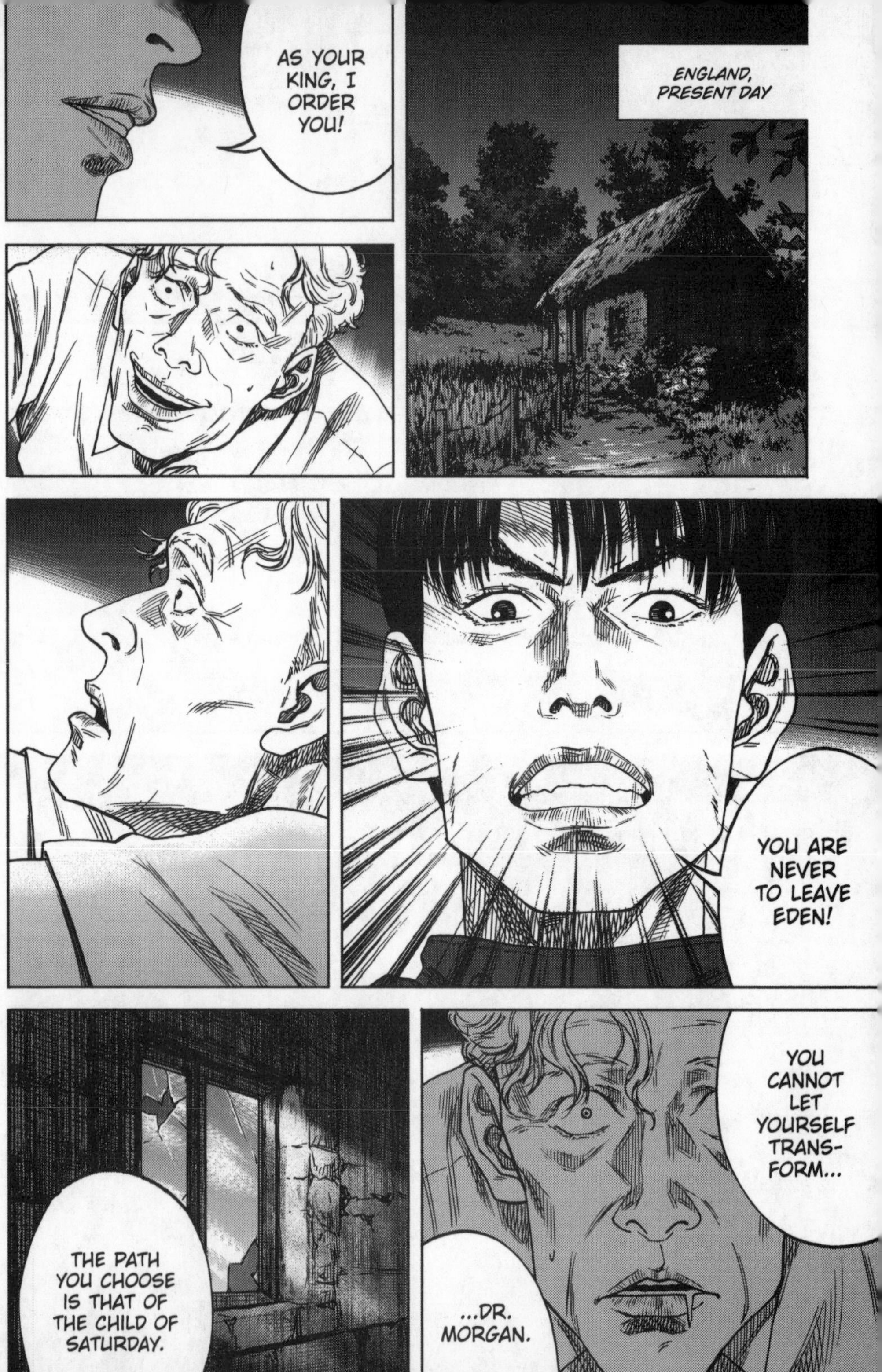
ENGLAND, PRESENT DAY
AS YOUR KING, I ORDER YOU!
YOU ARE NEVER TO LEAVE EDEN!
YOU CANNOT LET YOURSELF TRANS-FORM...
...DR. MORGAN.
THE PATH YOU CHOOSE IS THAT OF THE CHILD OF SATURDAY.

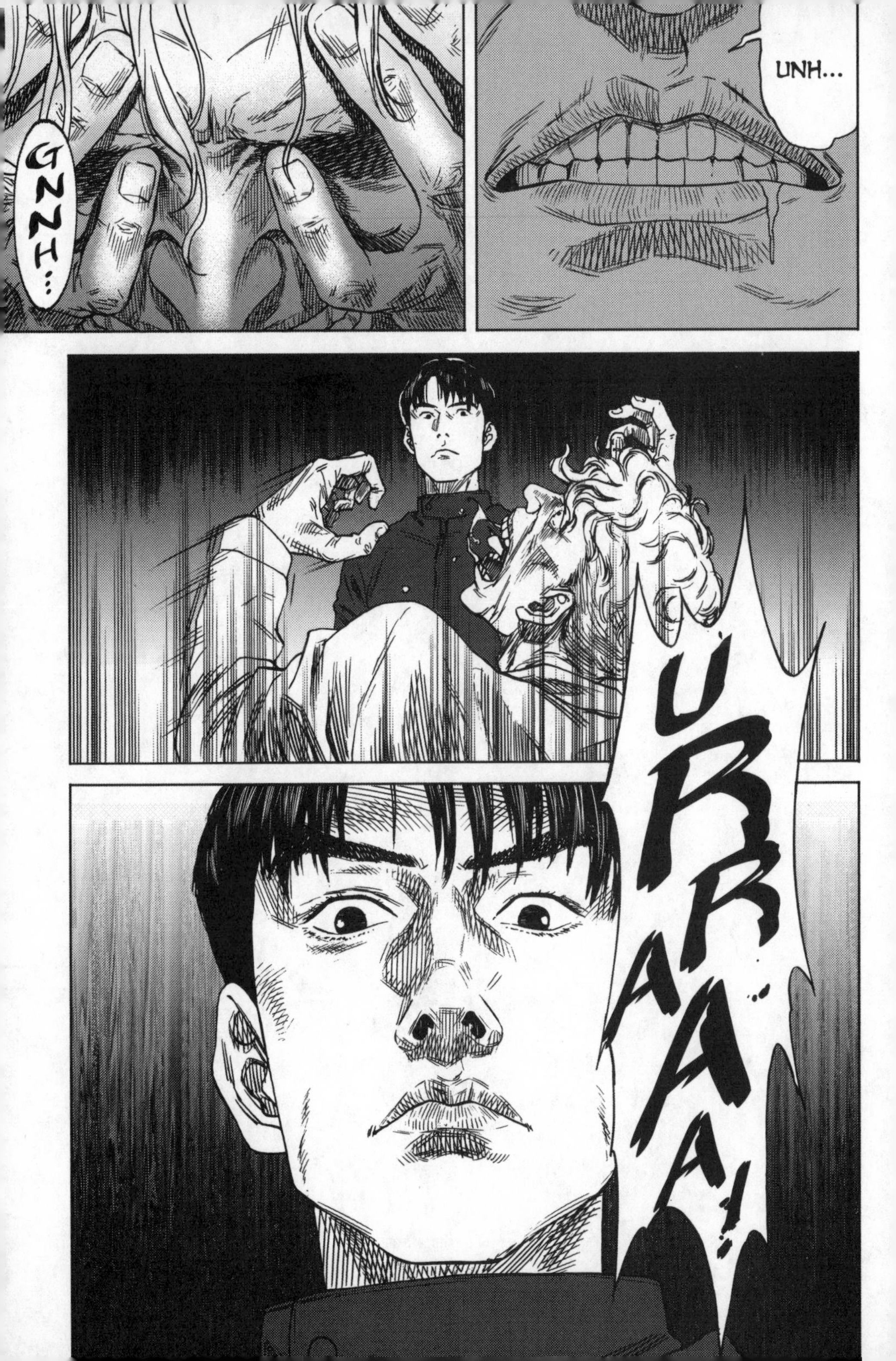
UNH...
GNNH...
URRAAA!!

KING OF EDEN

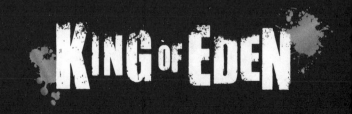

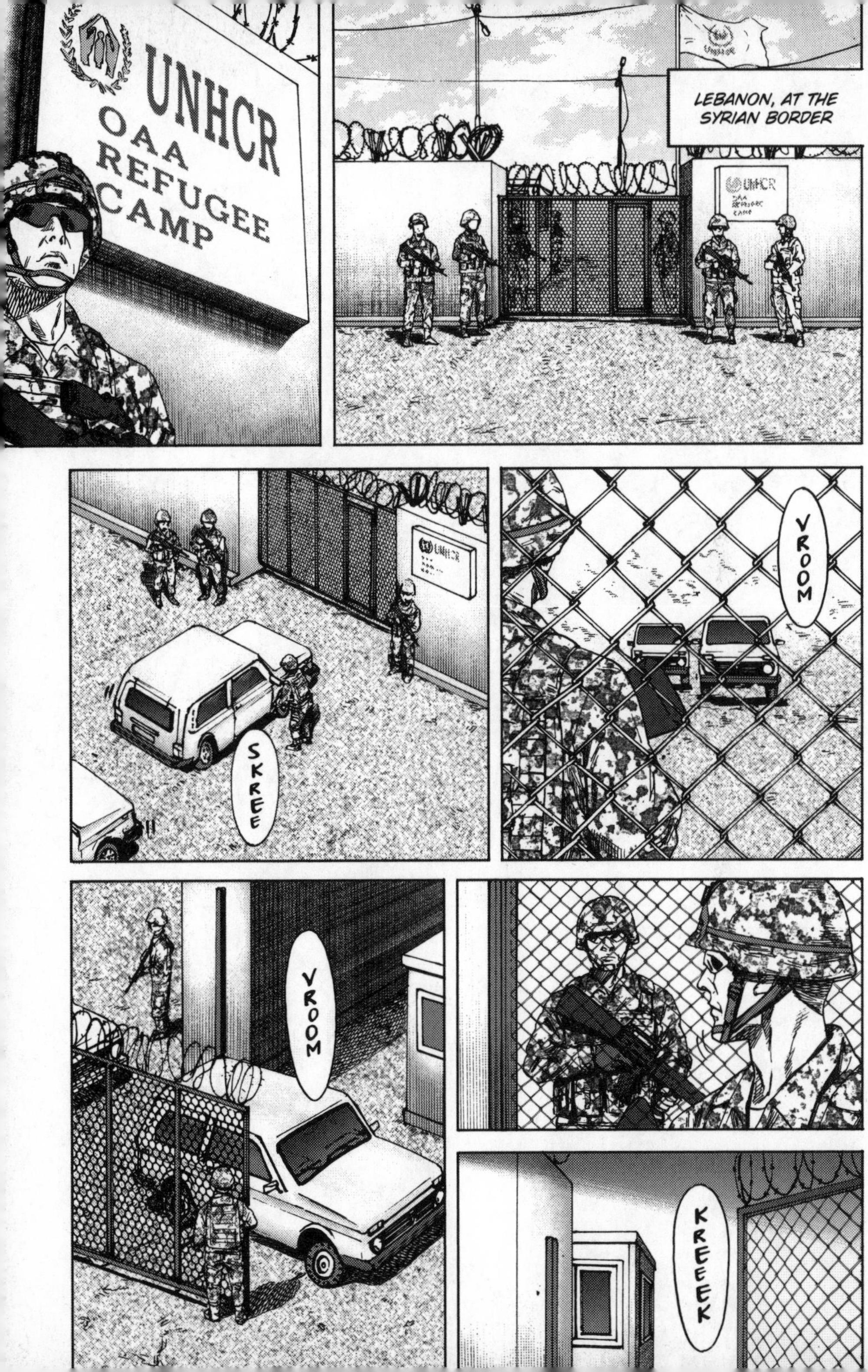
LEBANON, AT THE SYRIAN BORDER
UNHCR
UNHCR
OAA
REFUGEE
CAMP
VROOM
UNHCR
SKREE
KREEEK
VROOM

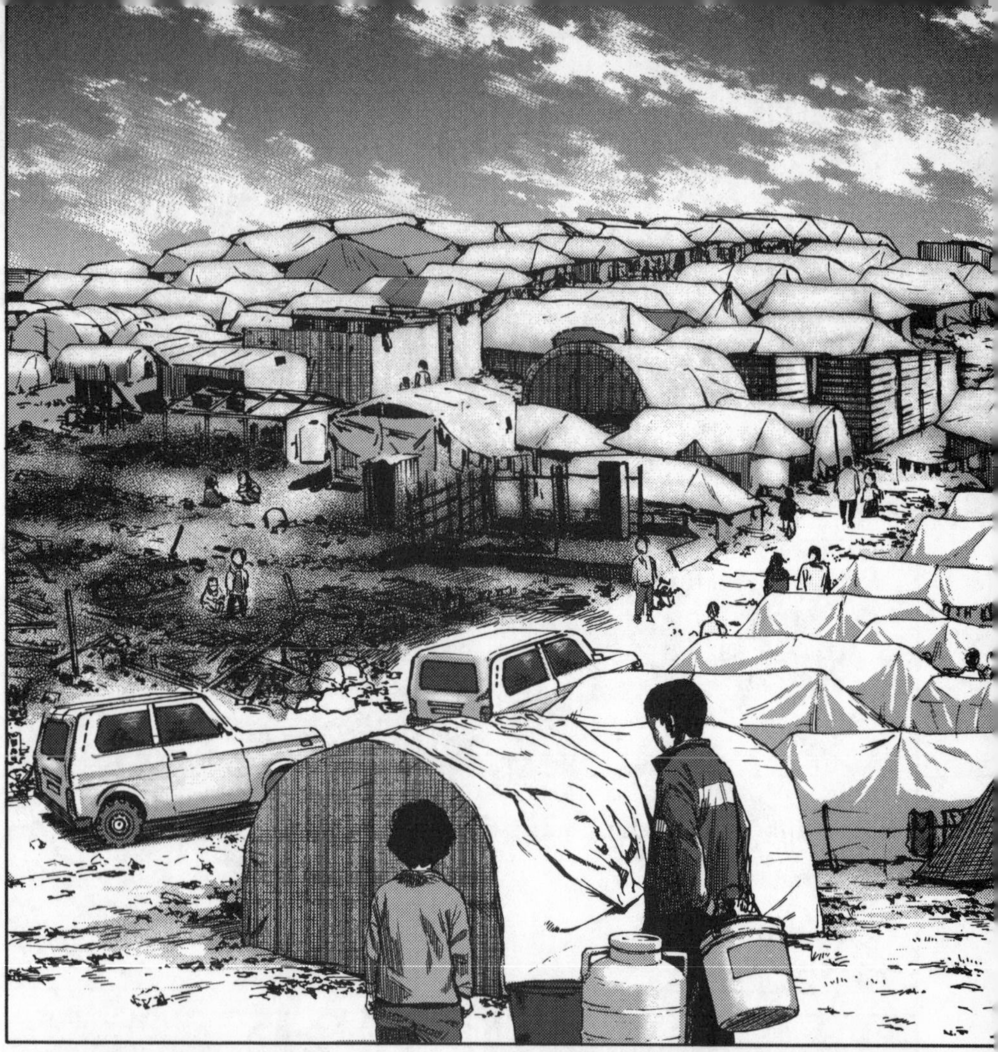
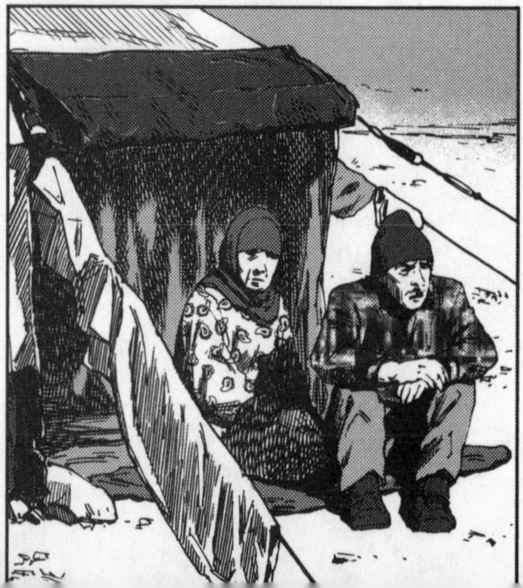
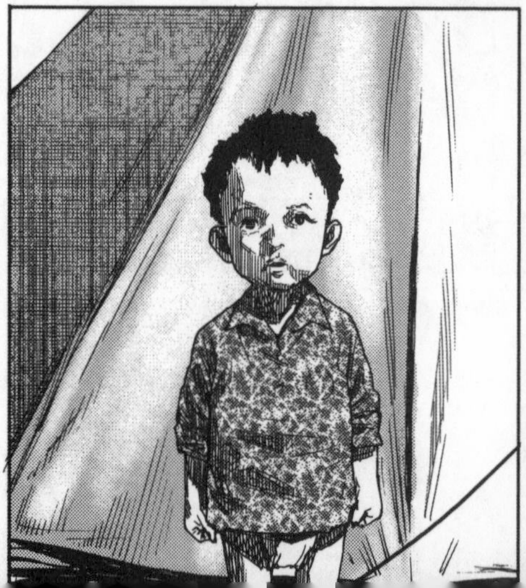

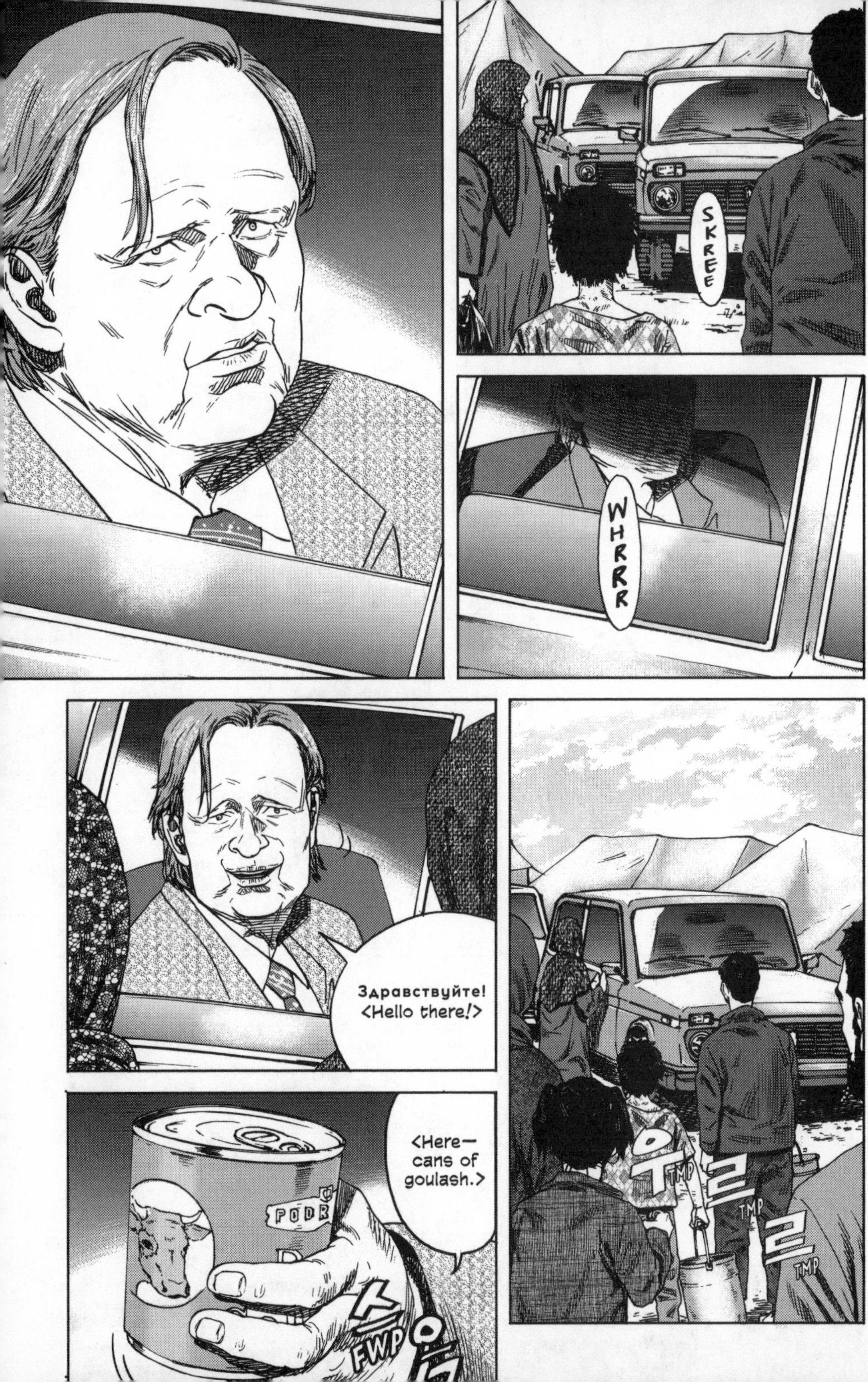
SKREE
WHRRR
TMP
TMP
TMP
Здравствуйте!
<Hello there!>
<Here—
cans of
goulash.>
PODR
FWP

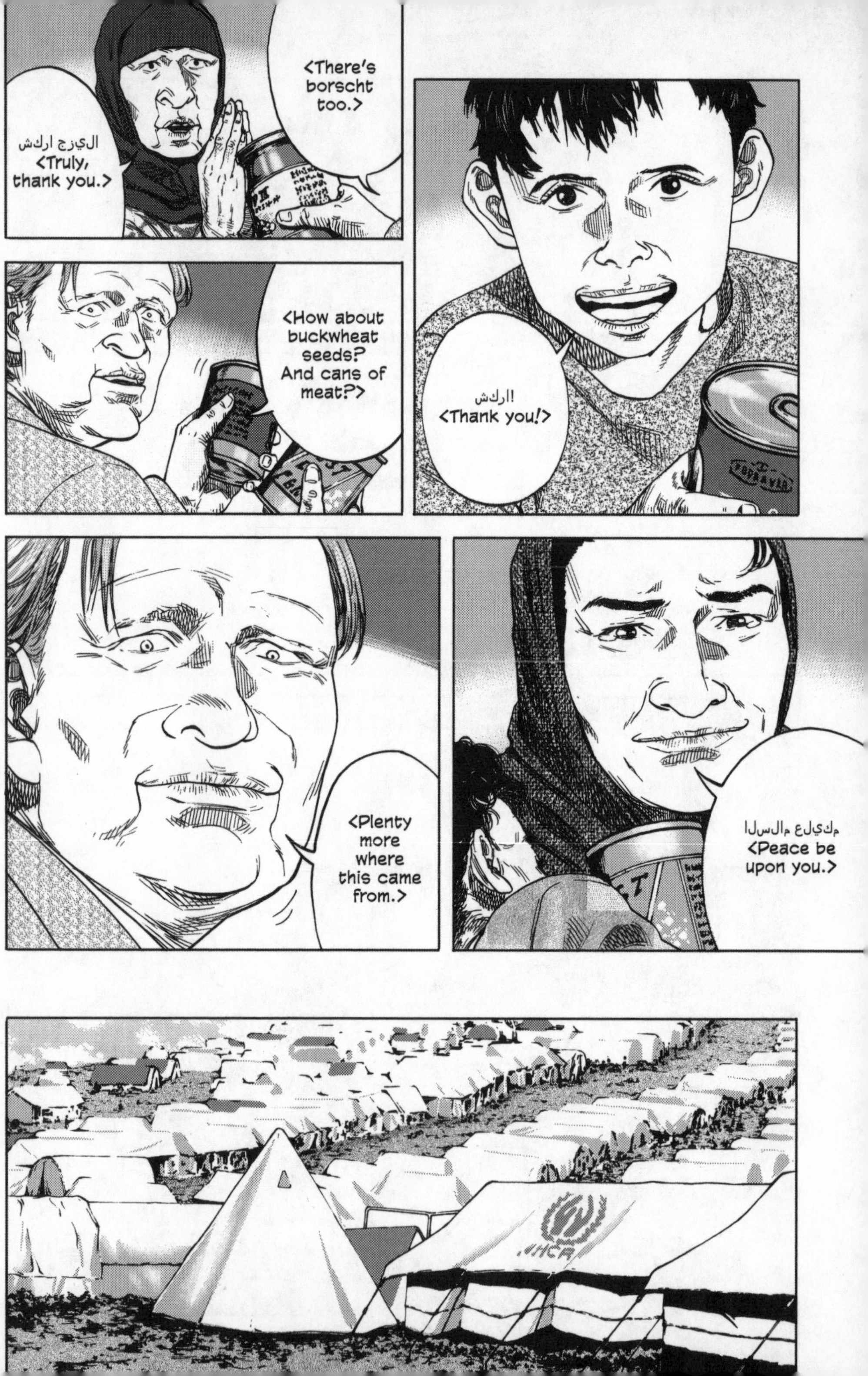
اركش!
<Thank you!>
<There's borscht too.>
اليزج اركش
<Truly, thank you.>
<How about buckwheat seeds? And cans of meat?>
السلام عليكم
<Peace be upon you.>
<Plenty more where this came from.>

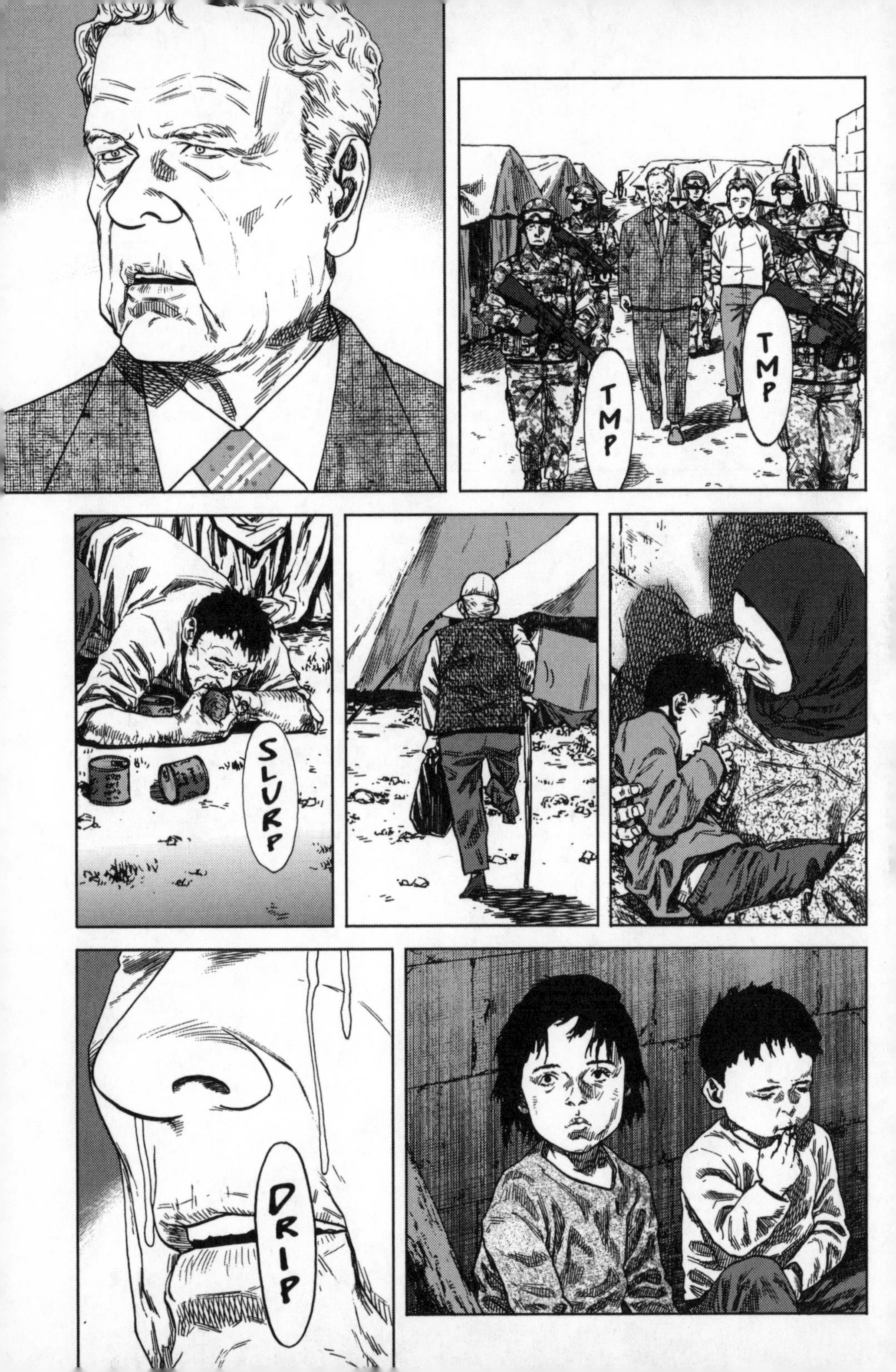
TMP
TMP
SLURP
DRIP

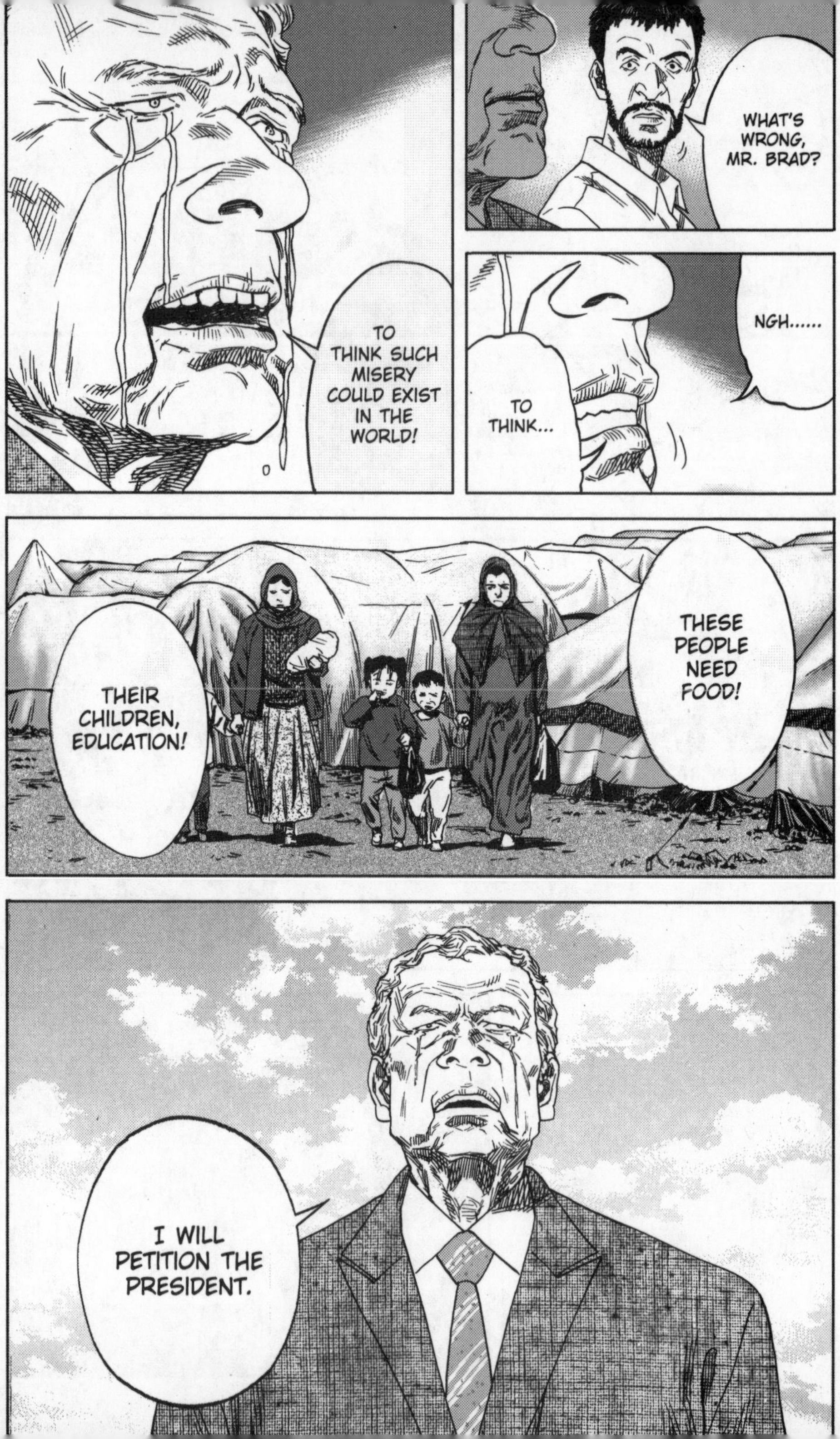
WHAT'S WRONG, MR. BRAD?
NGH......
TO THINK...
TO THINK SUCH MISERY COULD EXIST IN THE WORLD!
THESE PEOPLE NEED FOOD!
THEIR CHILDREN, EDUCATION!
I WILL PETITION THE PRESIDENT.

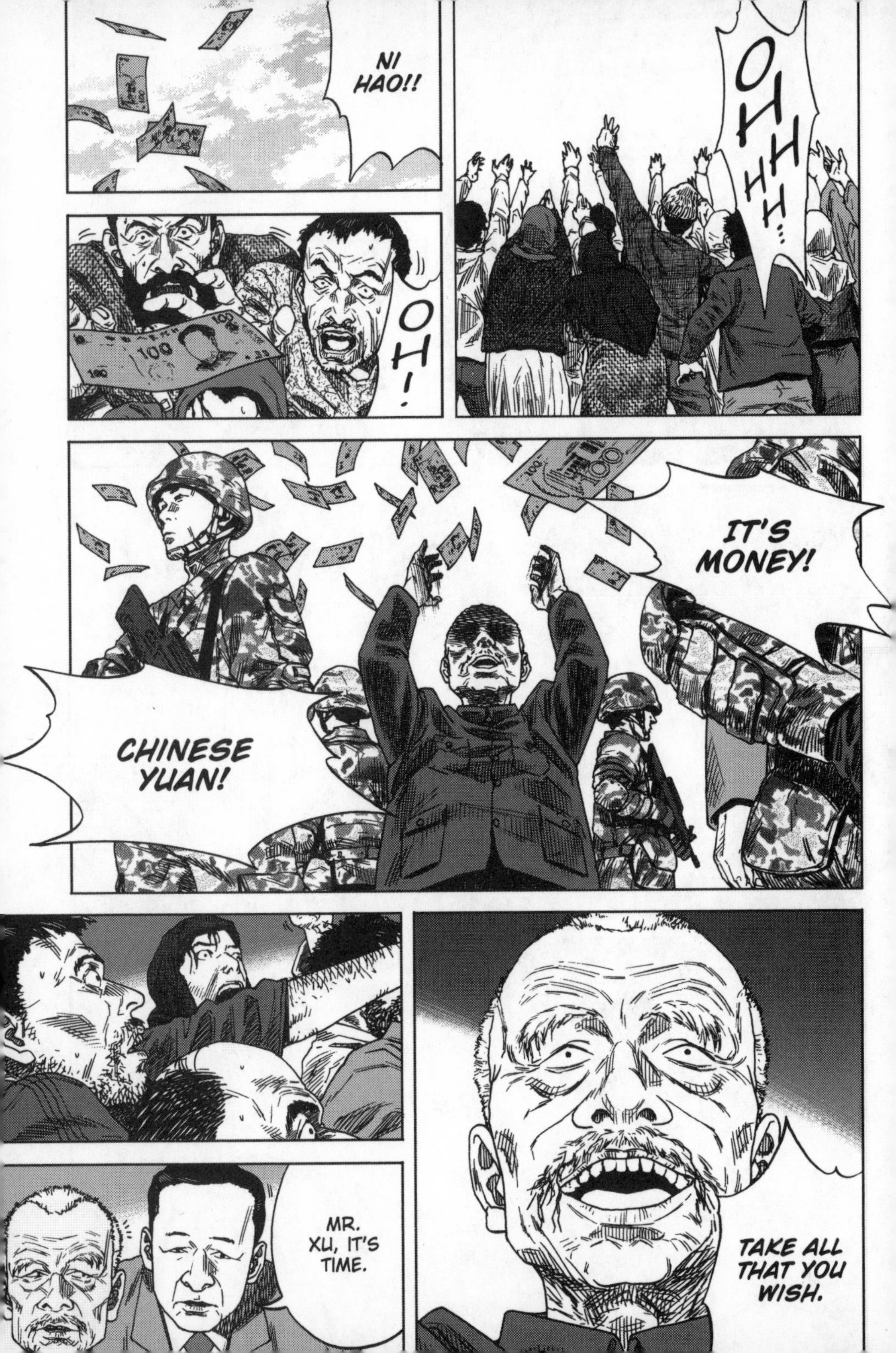
OHHHH...
NI HAO!!
OH!
IT'S MONEY!
CHINESE YUAN!
TAKE ALL THAT YOU WISH.
MR. XU, IT'S TIME.

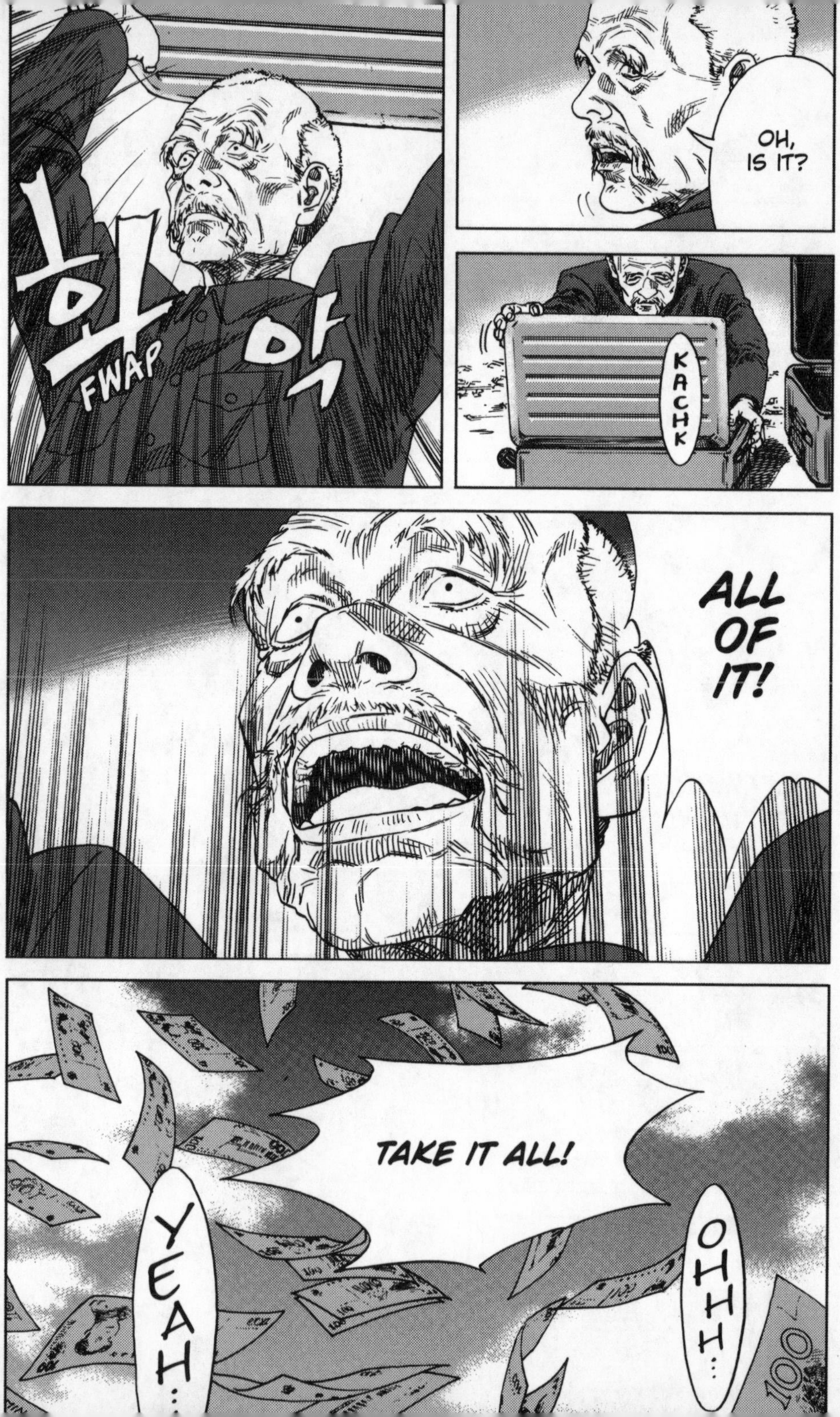
OH, IS IT?
KACHK
FWAP
ALL OF IT!
TAKE IT ALL!
OHHH...
YEAH...

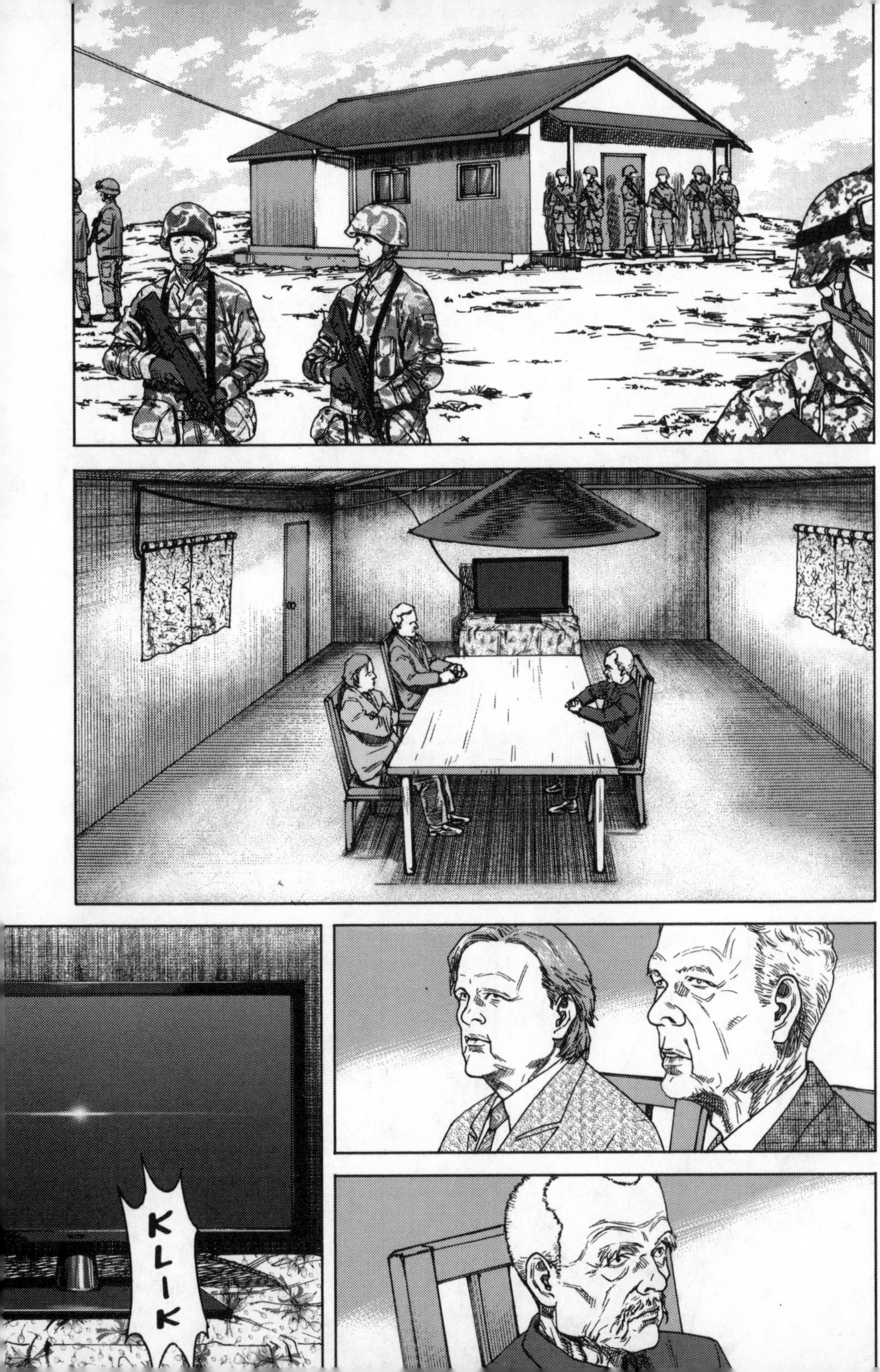
KLIK

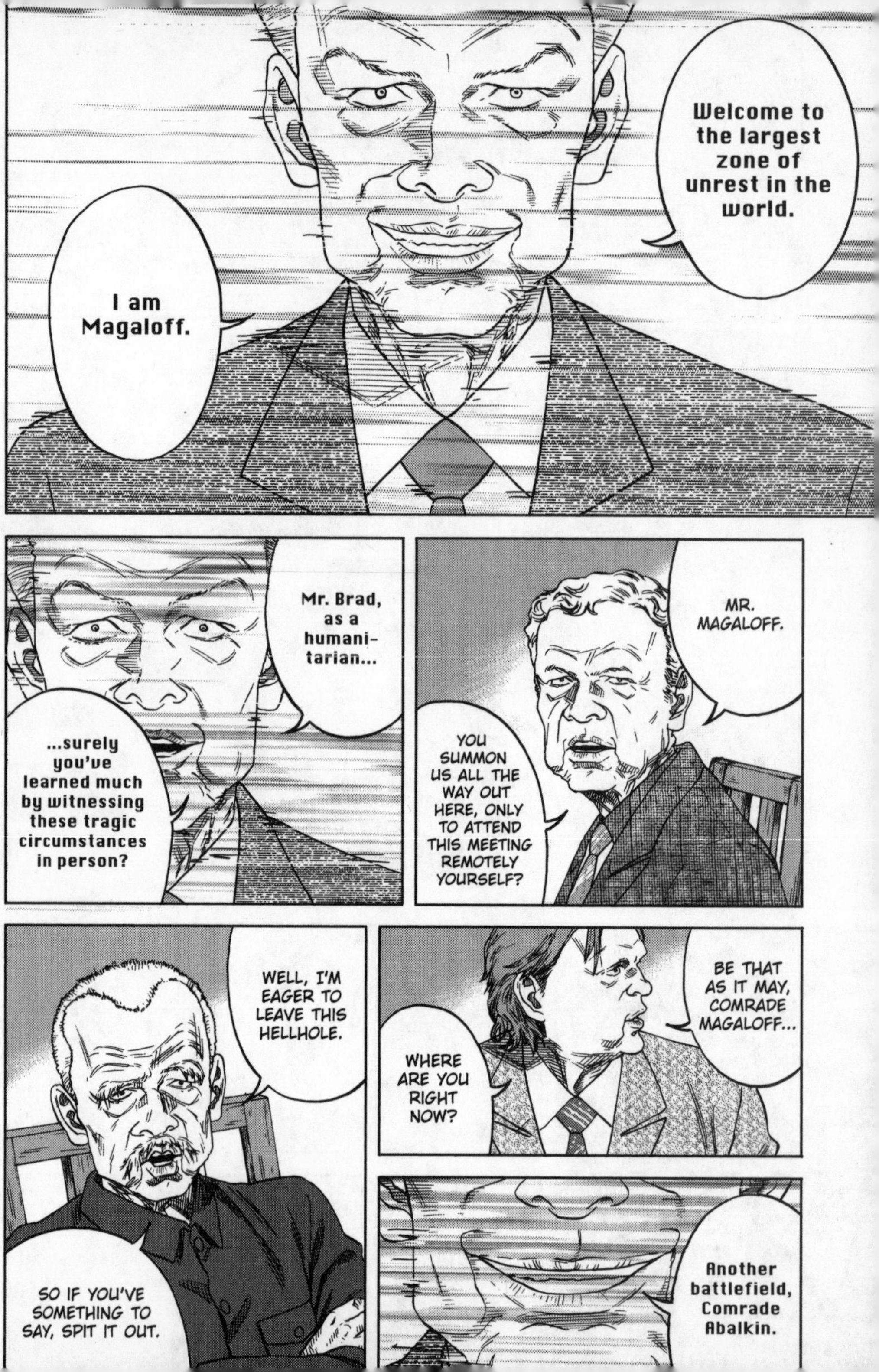
Welcome to the largest zone of unrest in the world.
I am Magaloff.
MR. MAGALOFF.
YOU SUMMON US ALL THE WAY OUT HERE, ONLY TO ATTEND THIS MEETING REMOTELY YOURSELF?
Mr. Brad, as a humani-tarian...
...surely you've learned much by witnessing these tragic circumstances in person?
BE THAT AS IT MAY, COMRADE MAGALOFF...
WHERE ARE YOU RIGHT NOW?
Another battlefield, Comrade Abalkin.
WELL, I'M EAGER TO LEAVE THIS HELLHOLE.
SO IF YOU'VE SOMETHING TO SAY, SPIT IT OUT.

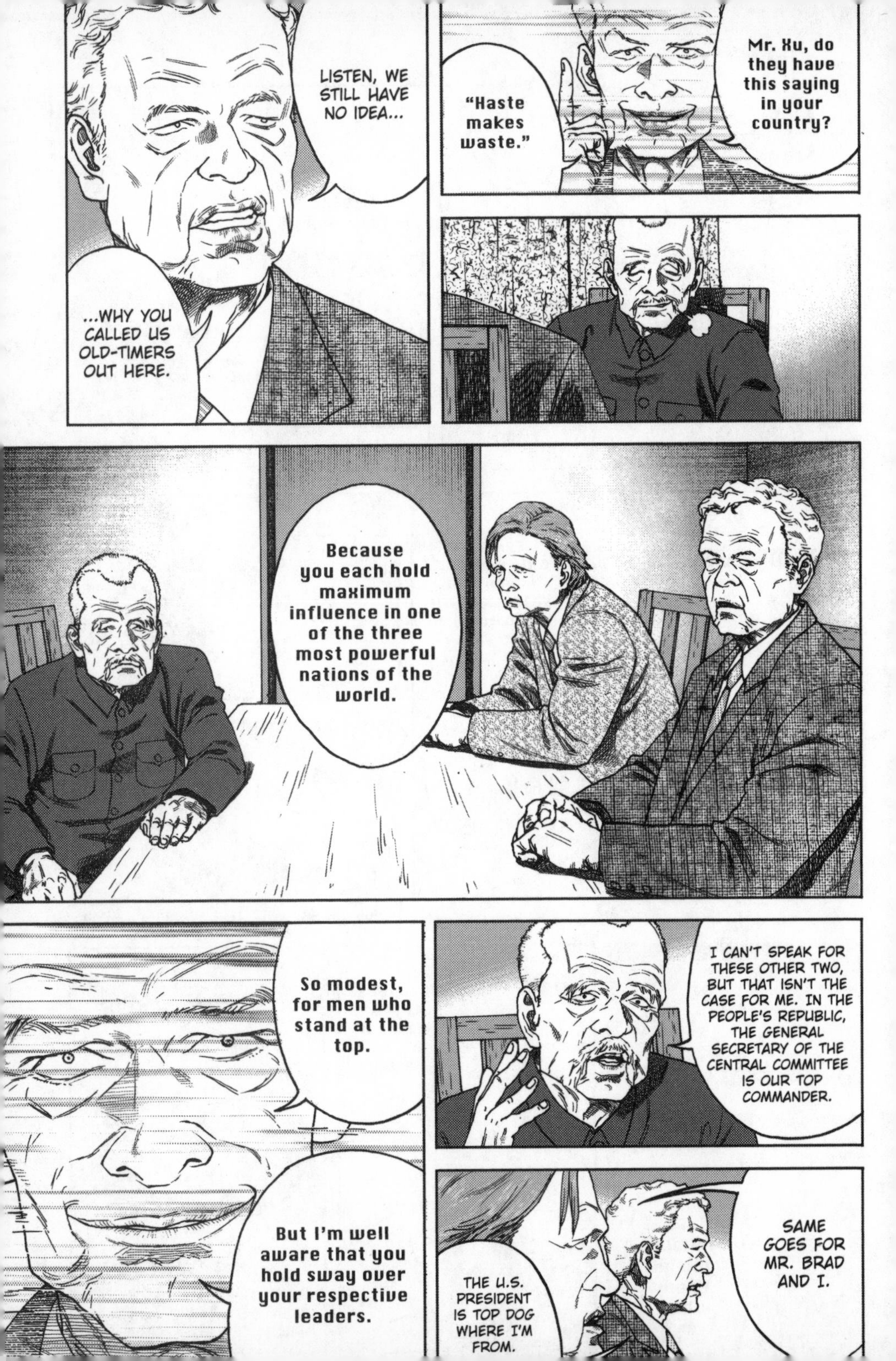
Mr. Xu, do they have this saying in your country?
"Haste makes waste."
LISTEN, WE STILL HAVE NO IDEA...
...WHY YOU CALLED US OLD-TIMERS OUT HERE.
Because you each hold maximum influence in one of the three most powerful nations of the world.
I CAN'T SPEAK FOR THESE OTHER TWO, BUT THAT ISN'T THE CASE FOR ME. IN THE PEOPLE'S REPUBLIC, THE GENERAL SECRETARY OF THE CENTRAL COMMITTEE IS OUR TOP COMMANDER.
SAME GOES FOR MR. BRAD AND I.
THE U.S. PRESIDENT IS TOP DOG WHERE I'M FROM.
So modest, for men who stand at the top.
But I'm well aware that you hold sway over your respective leaders.

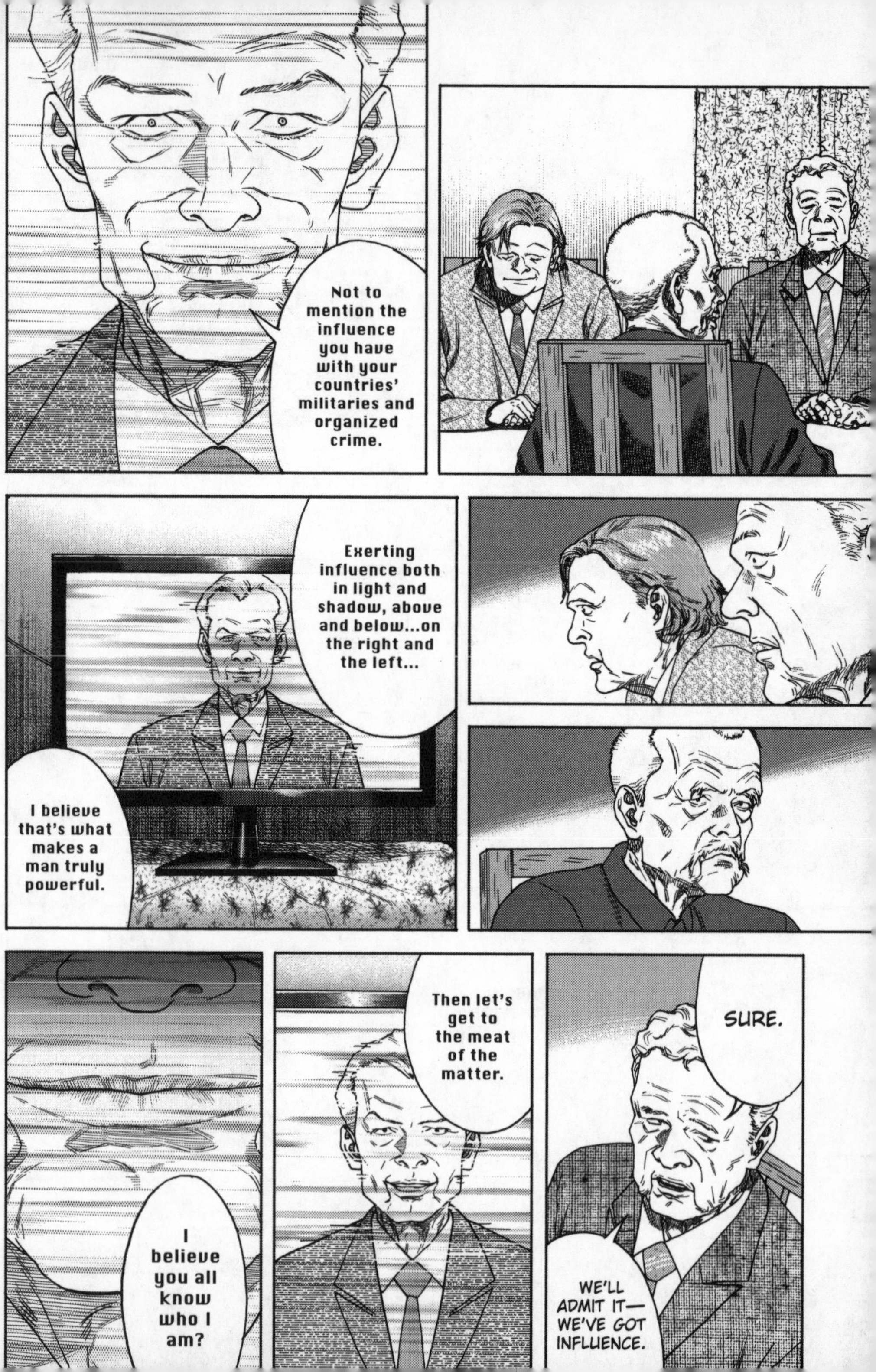
Not to mention the influence you have with your countries' militaries and organized crime.
Exerting influence both in light and shadow, above and below...on the right and the left...
I believe that's what makes a man truly powerful.
SURE.
WE'LL ADMIT IT— WE'VE GOT INFLUENCE.
Then let's get to the meat of the matter.
I believe you all know who I am?

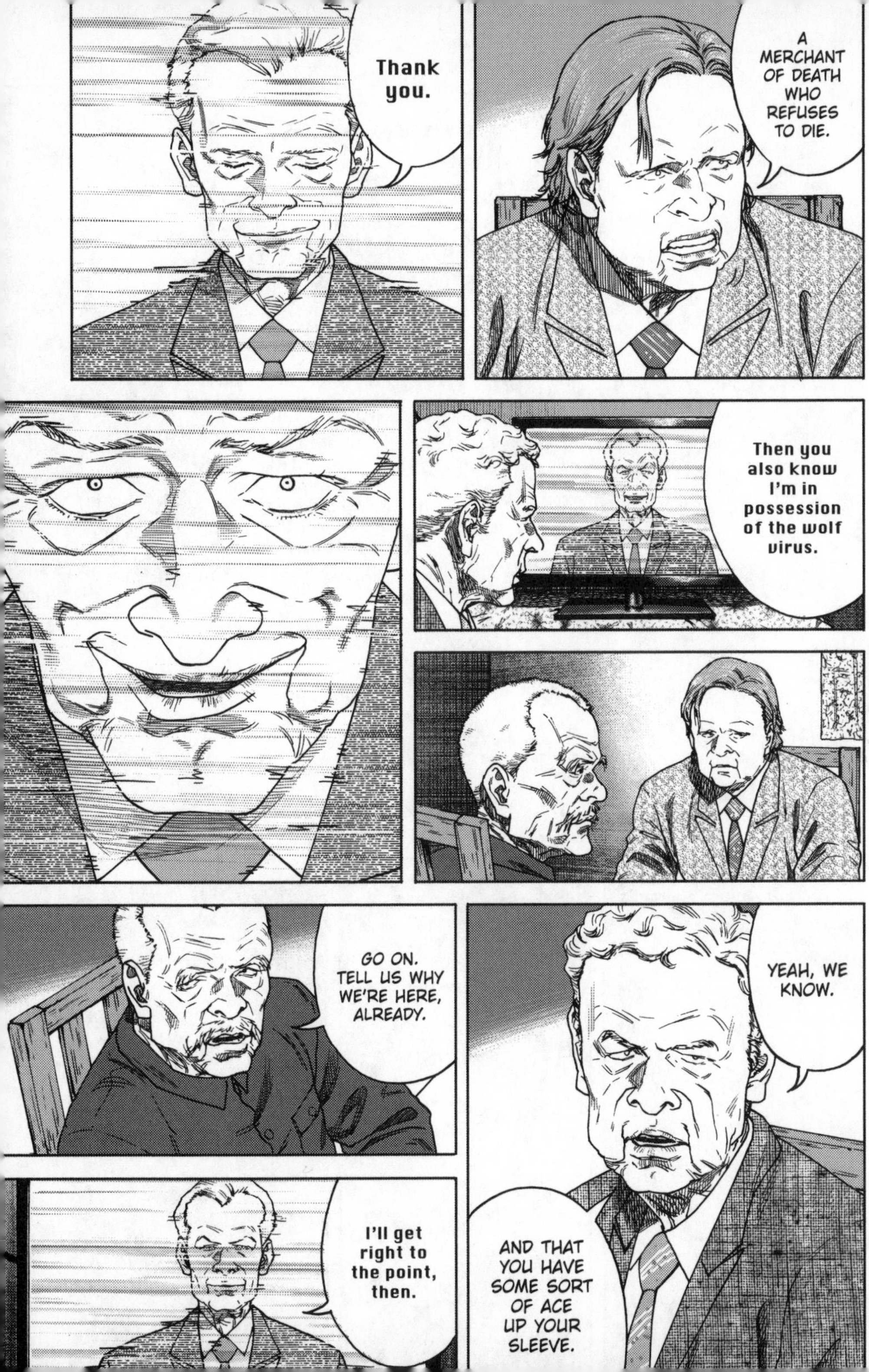
A MERCHANT OF DEATH WHO REFUSES TO DIE.
Thank you.
Then you also know I'm in possession of the wolf virus.
YEAH, WE KNOW.
AND THAT YOU HAVE SOME SORT OF ACE UP YOUR SLEEVE.
GO ON. TELL US WHY WE'RE HERE, ALREADY.
I'll get right to the point, then.

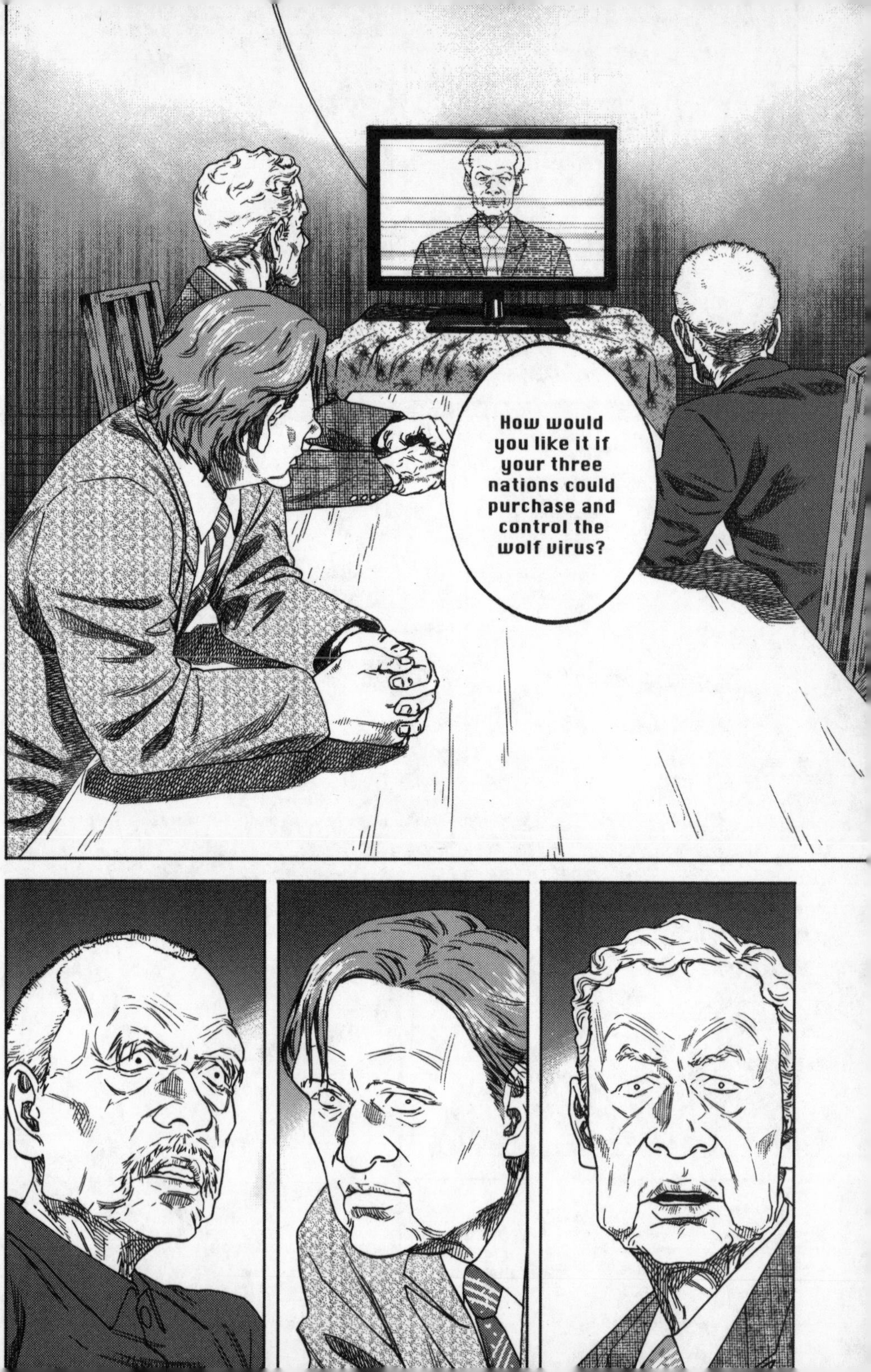
How would you like it if your three nations could purchase and control the wolf virus?

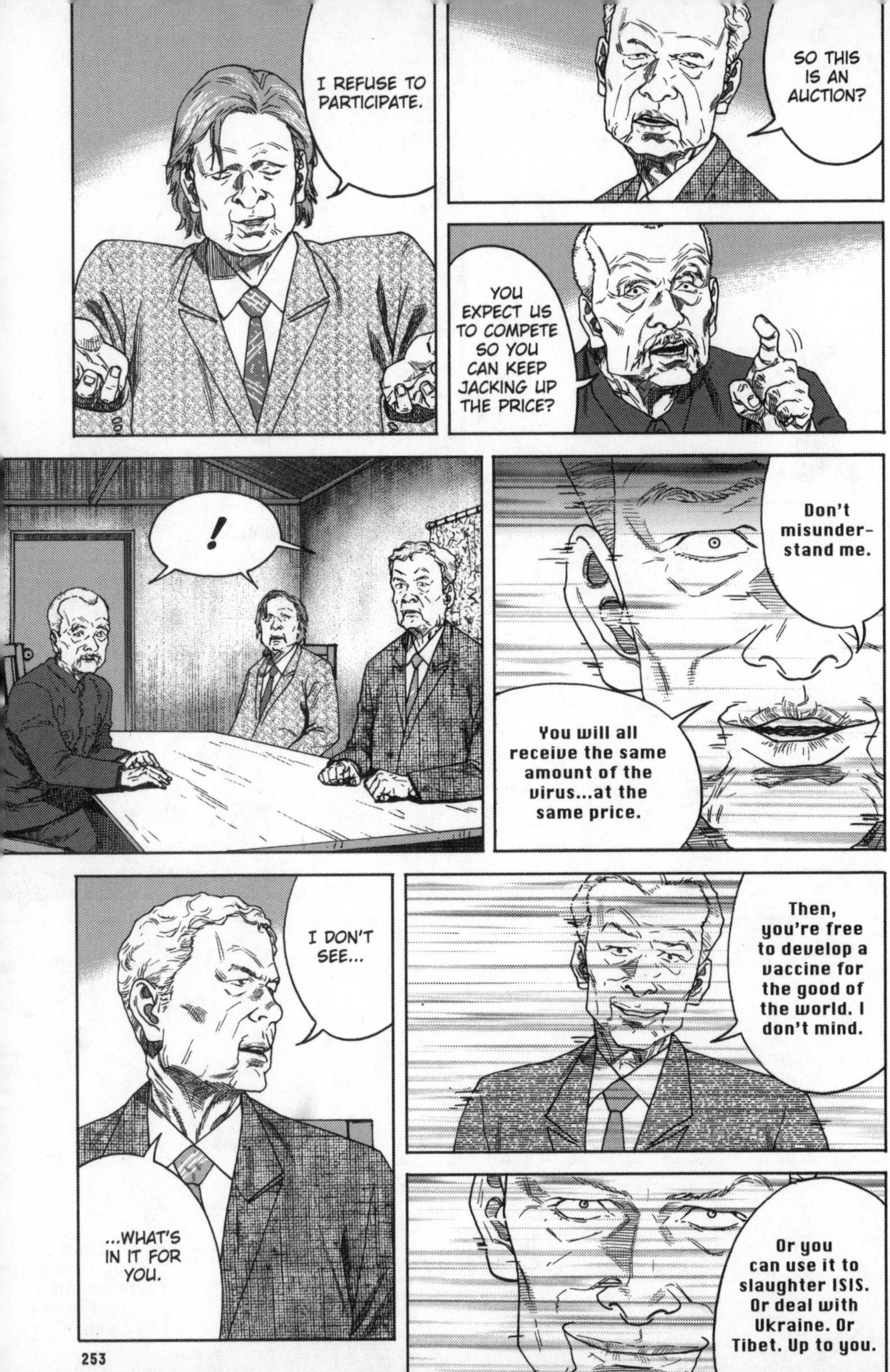
SO THIS IS AN AUCTION?
YOU EXPECT US TO COMPETE SO YOU CAN KEEP JACKING UP THE PRICE?
I REFUSE TO PARTICIPATE.
Don't misunder-stand me.
You will all receive the same amount of the virus...at the same price.
!
Then, you're free to develop a vaccine for the good of the world. I don't mind.
Or you can use it to slaughter ISIS. Or deal with Ukraine. Or Tibet. Up to you.
I DON'T SEE...
...WHAT'S IN IT FOR YOU.

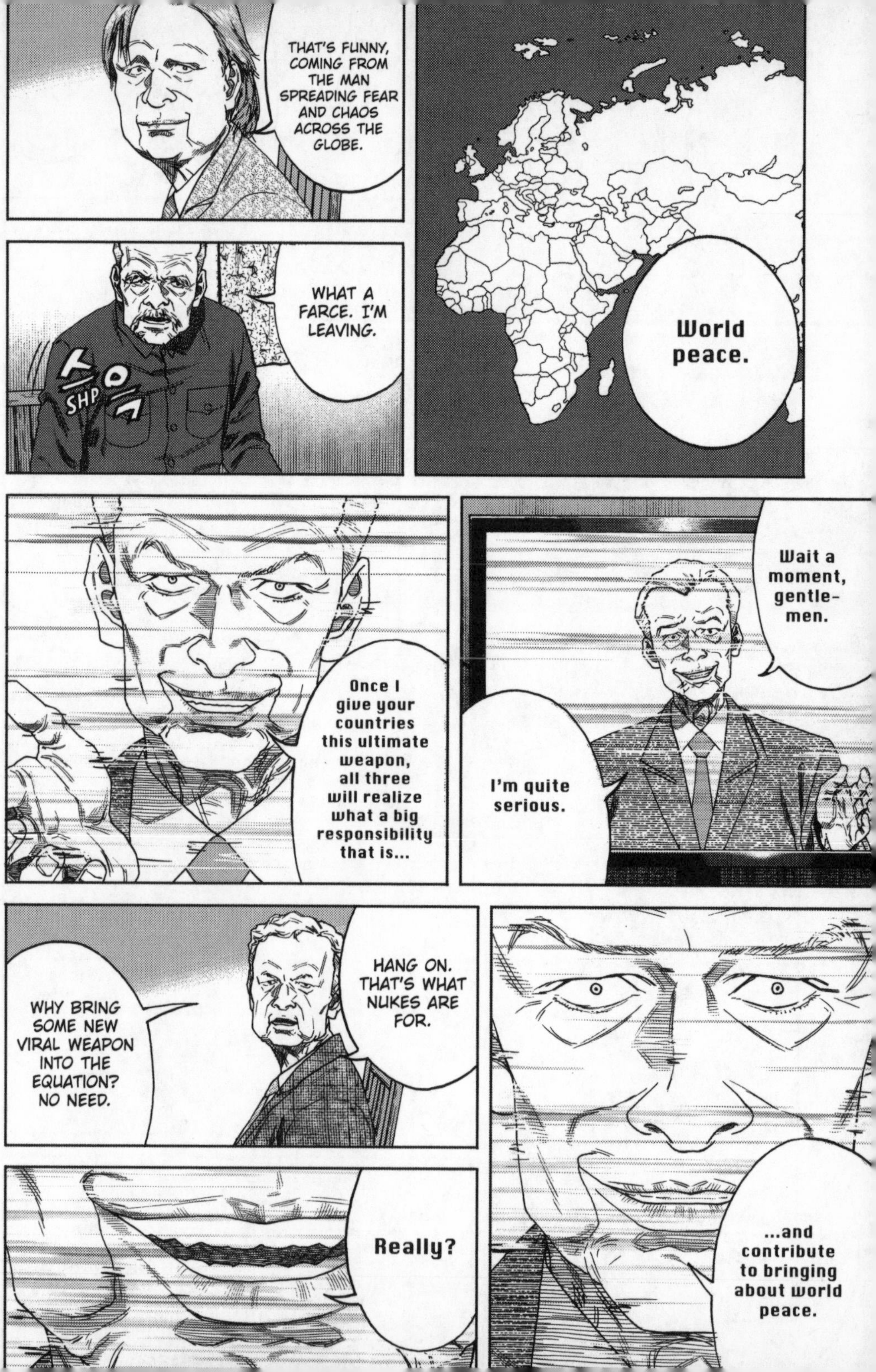
World peace.
THAT'S FUNNY, COMING FROM THE MAN SPREADING FEAR AND CHAOS ACROSS THE GLOBE.
WHAT A FARCE. I'M LEAVING.
SHP
Wait a moment, gentlemen.
I'm quite serious.
Once I give your countries this ultimate weapon, all three will realize what a big responsibility that is...
...and contribute to bringing about world peace.
HANG ON. THAT'S WHAT NUKES ARE FOR.
WHY BRING SOME NEW VIRAL WEAPON INTO THE EQUATION? NO NEED.
Really?

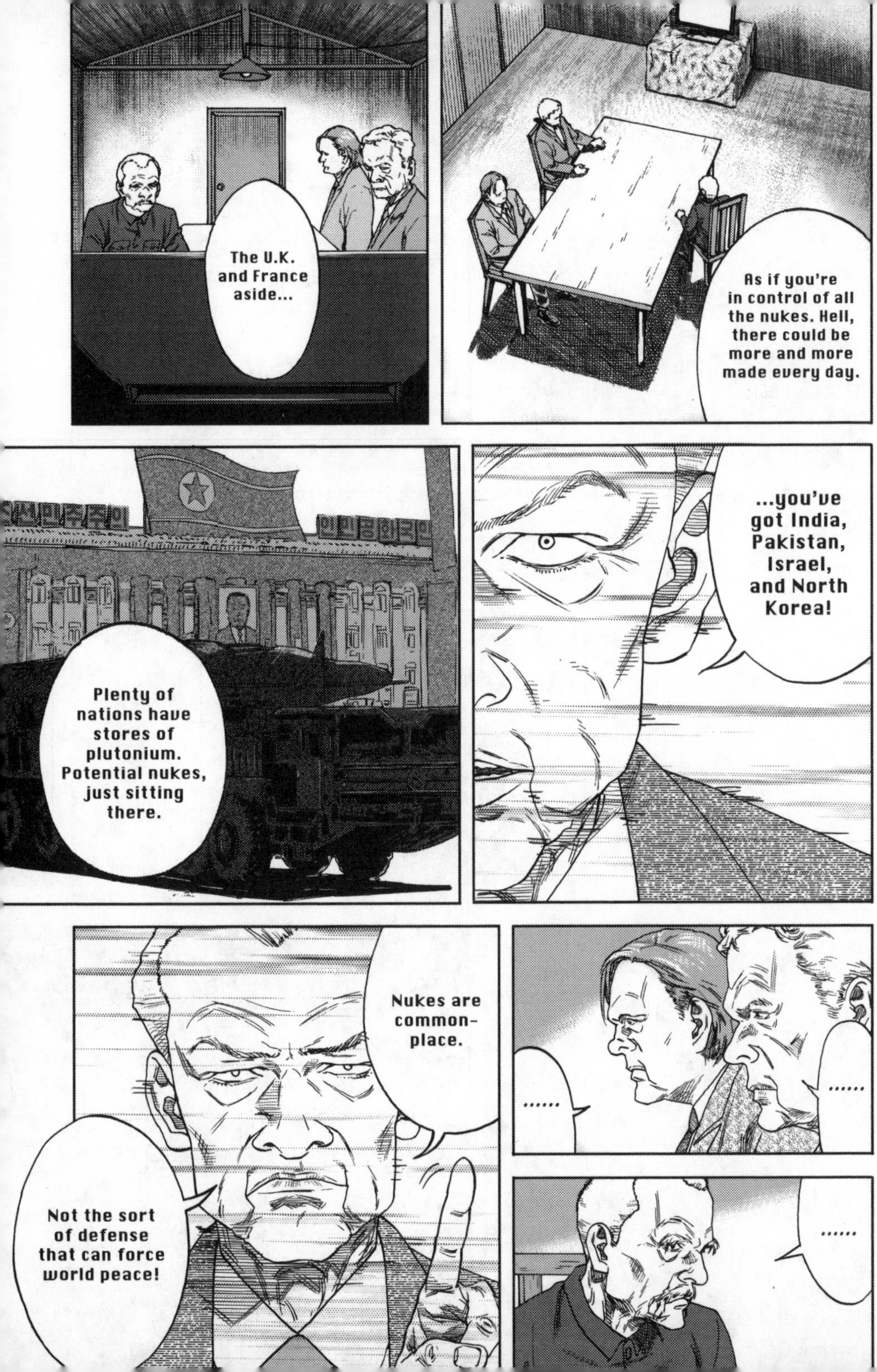
As if you're in control of all the nukes. Hell, there could be more and more made every day.
The U.K. and France aside...
...you've got India, Pakistan, Israel, and North Korea!
Plenty of nations have stores of plutonium. Potential nukes, just sitting there.
......
......
......
Nukes are commonplace.
Not the sort of defense that can force world peace!

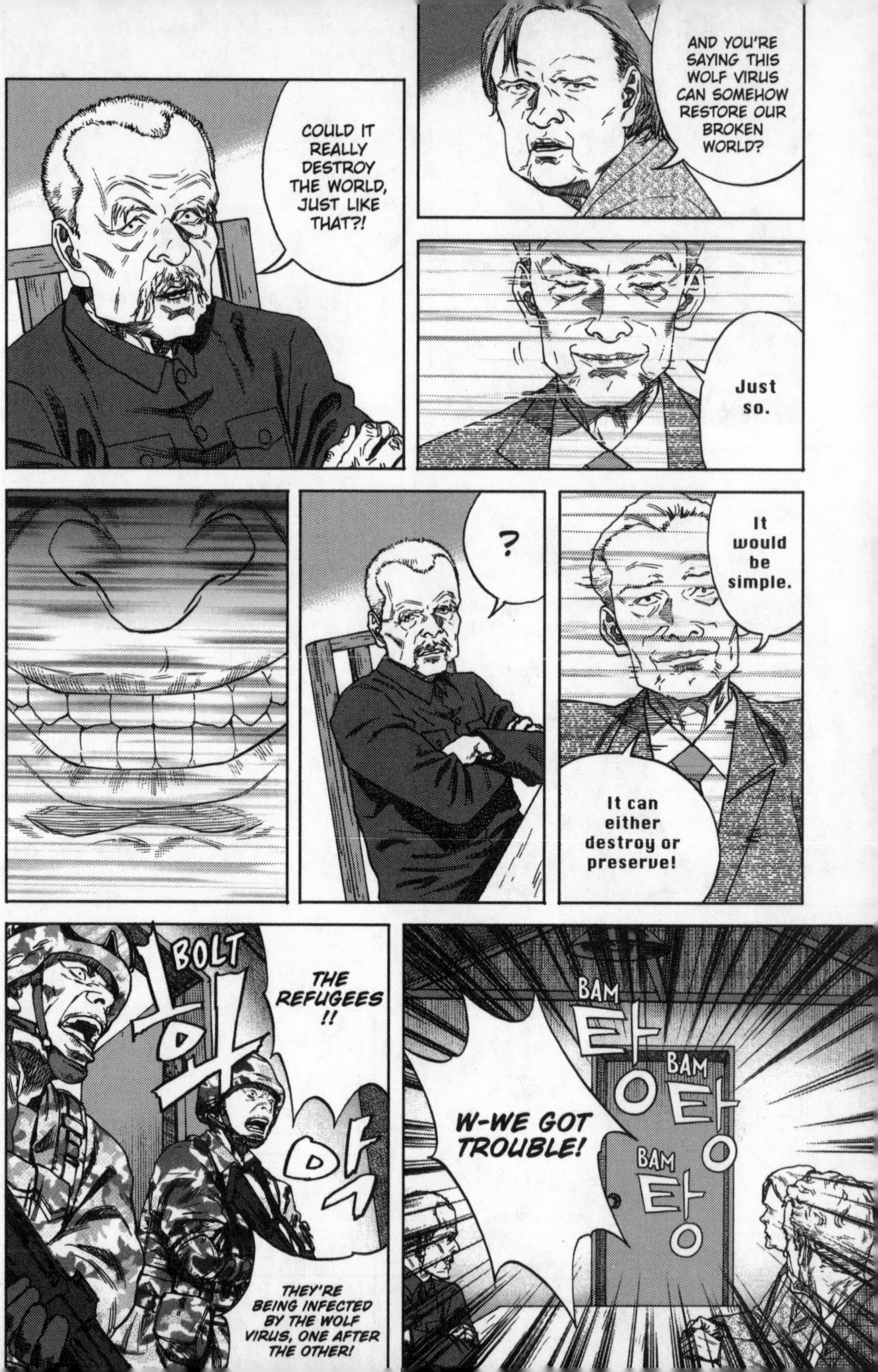
AND YOU'RE SAYING THIS WOLF VIRUS CAN SOMEHOW RESTORE OUR BROKEN WORLD?
Just so.
COULD IT REALLY DESTROY THE WORLD, JUST LIKE THAT?!
It would be simple.
It can either destroy or preserve!
?
BAM
BAM
BAM
W-WE GOT TROUBLE!
BOLT
THE REFUGEES !!
THEY'RE BEING INFECTED BY THE WOLF VIRUS, ONE AFTER THE OTHER!

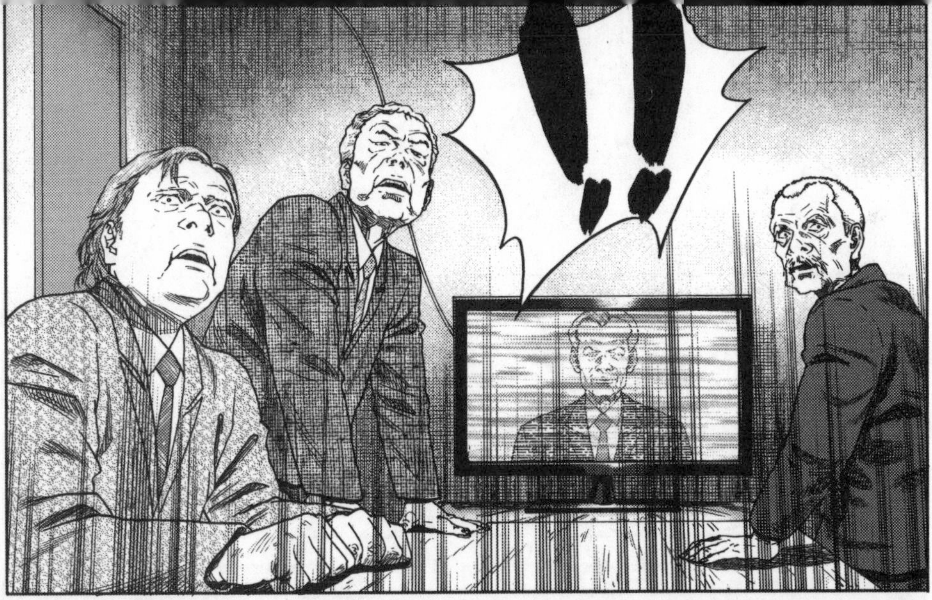
!!
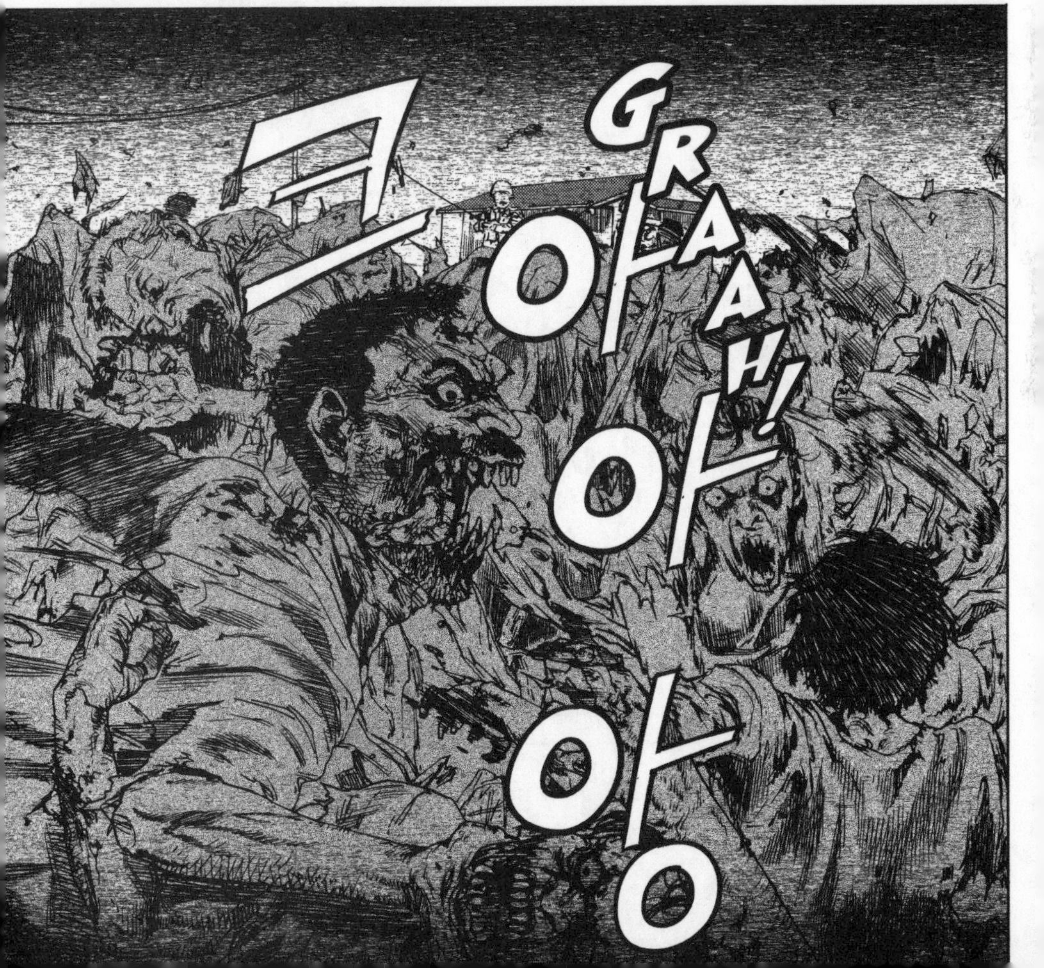
GRAAH!

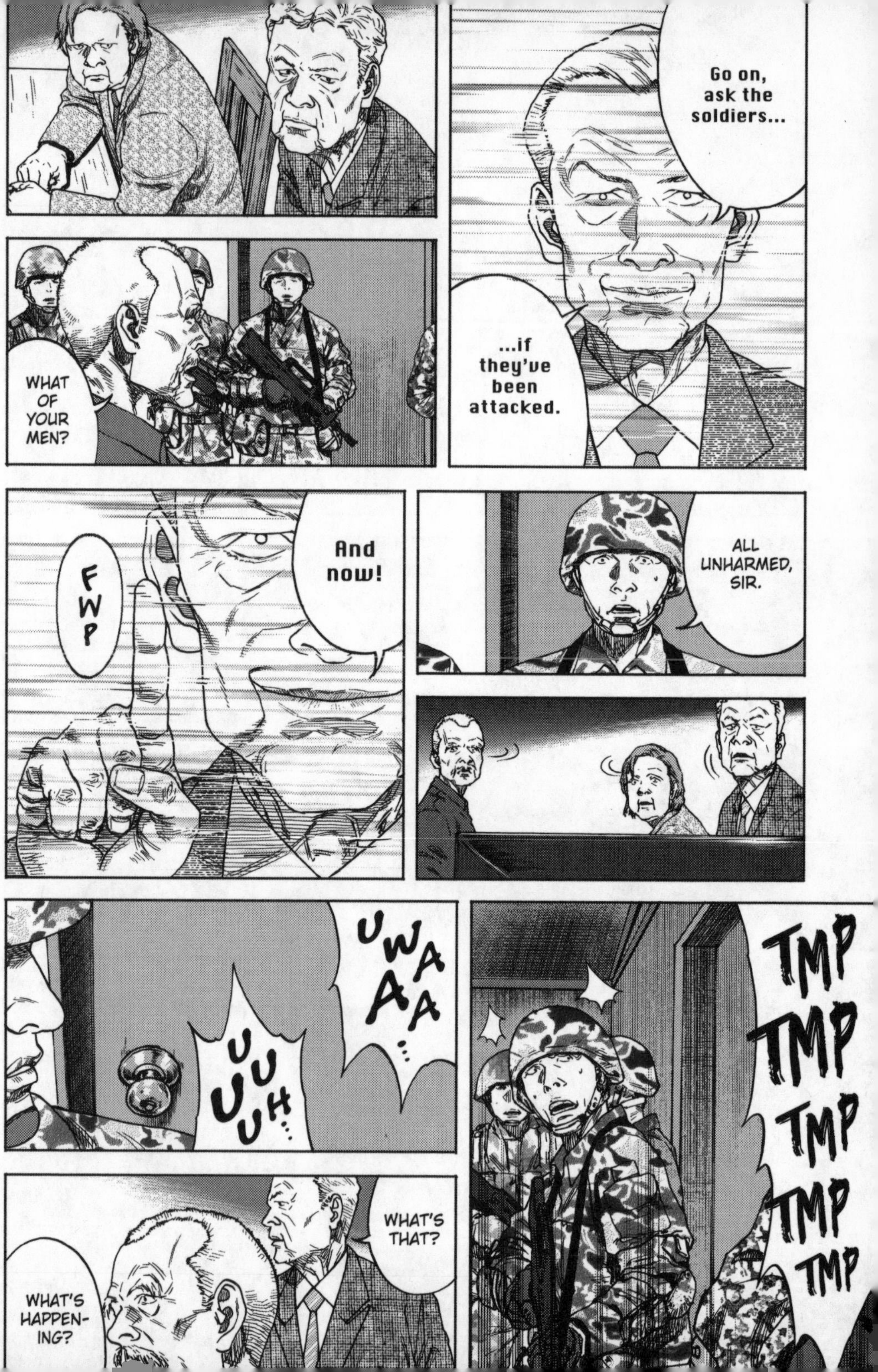
Go on, ask the soldiers...
...if they've been attacked.
WHAT OF YOUR MEN?
ALL UNHARMED, SIR.
And now!
FWP
TMP TMP TMP TMP TMP
UWAAA...
UUUUH...
WHAT'S THAT?
WHAT'S HAPPEN-ING?

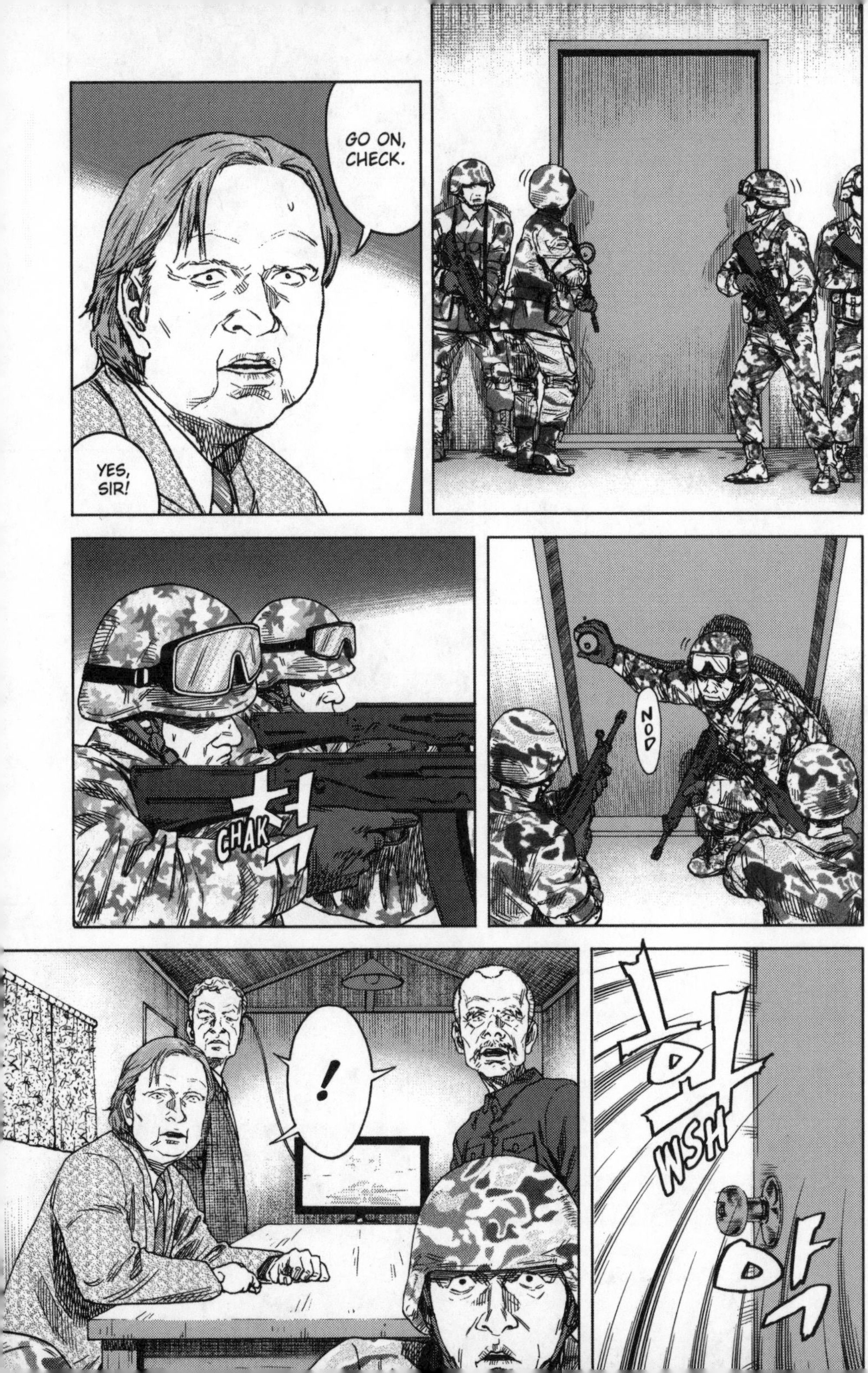
GO ON, CHECK.
YES, SIR!
NOD
CHAK
WSH
!

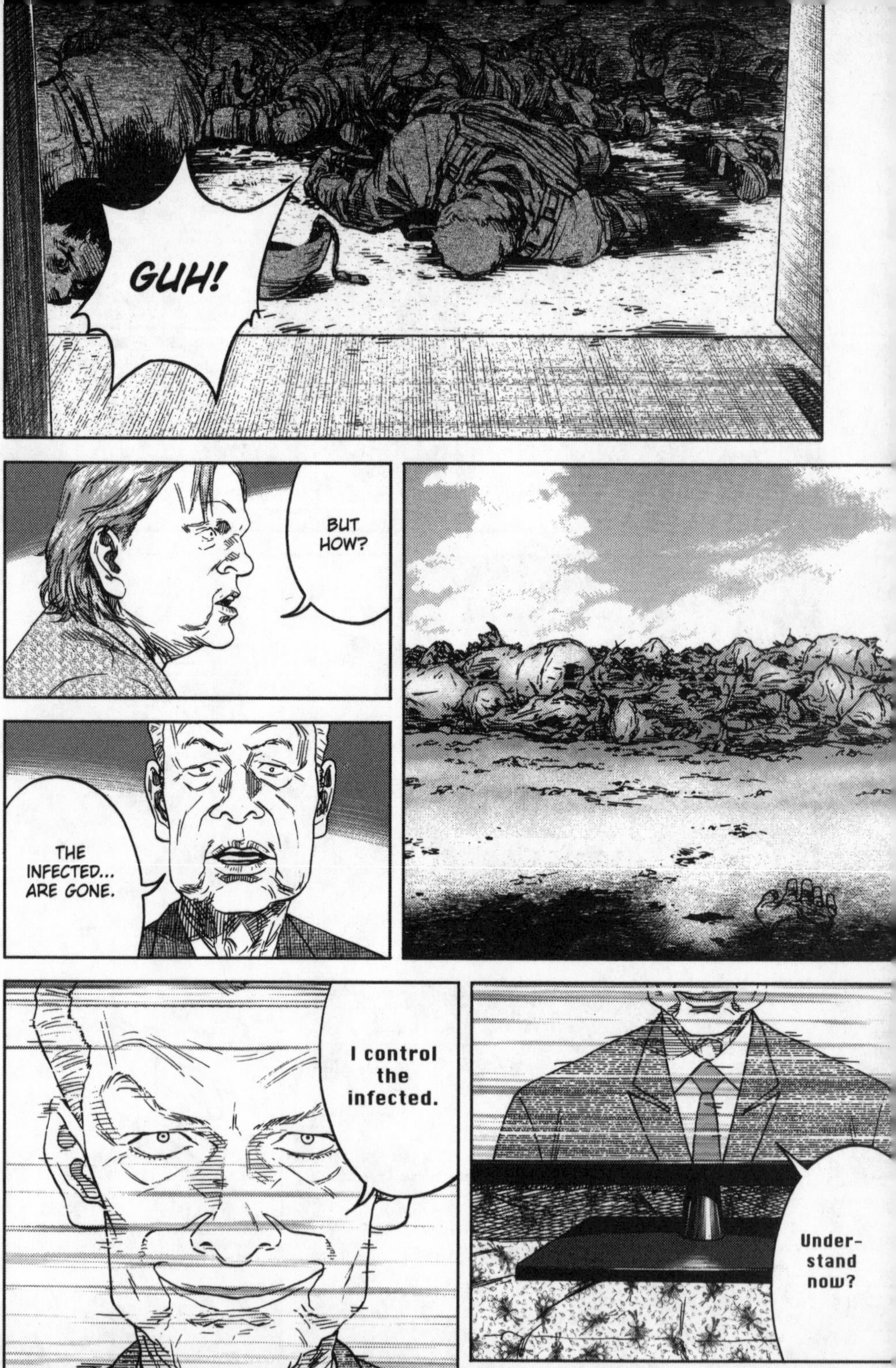
GUH!
BUT HOW?
THE INFECTED... ARE GONE.
Under-stand now?
I control the infected.

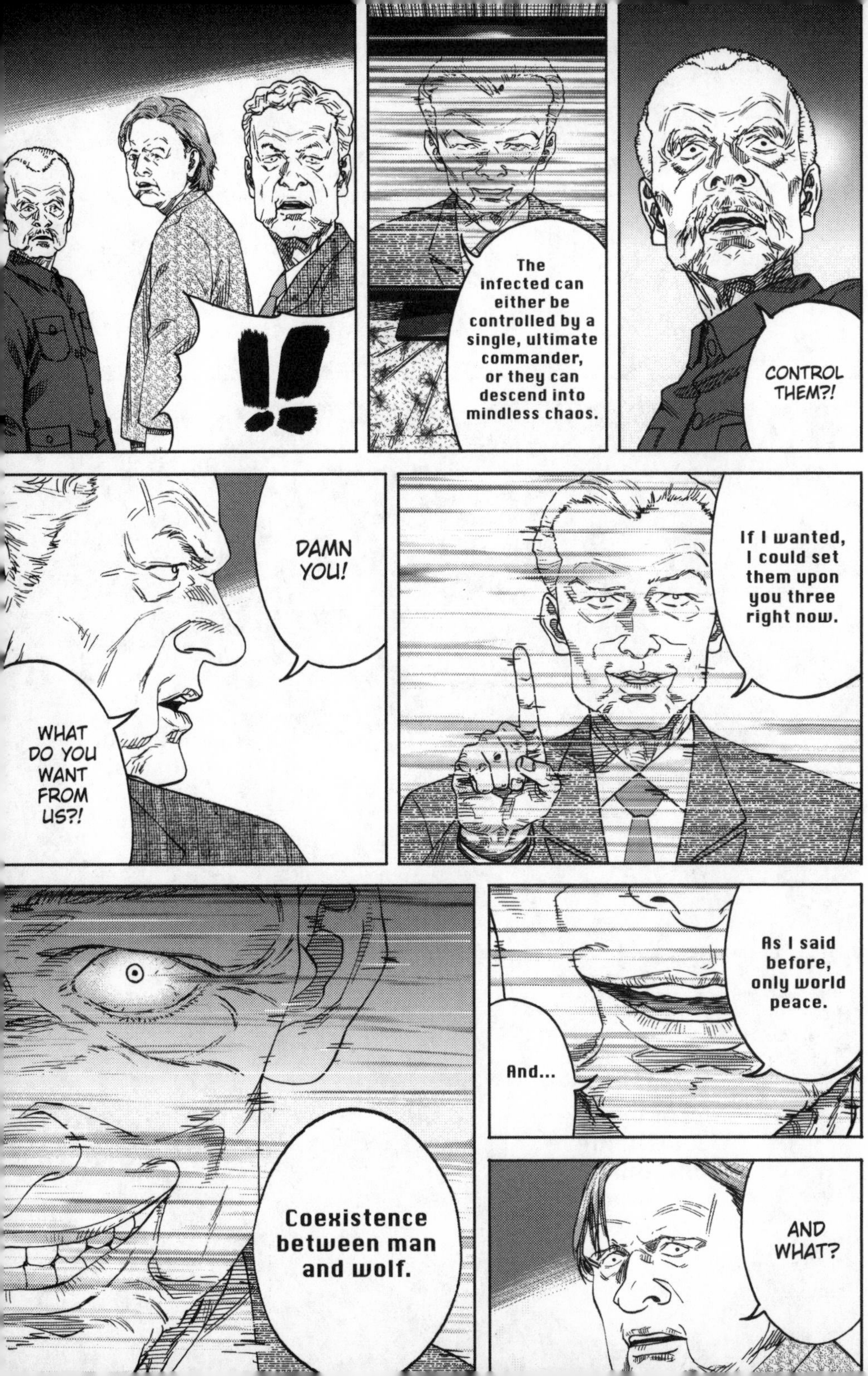
CONTROL THEM?!
The infected can either be controlled by a single, ultimate commander, or they can descend into mindless chaos.
!!
If I wanted, I could set them upon you three right now.
DAMN YOU!
WHAT DO YOU WANT FROM US?!
As I said before, only world peace.
And...
AND WHAT?
Coexistence between man and wolf.

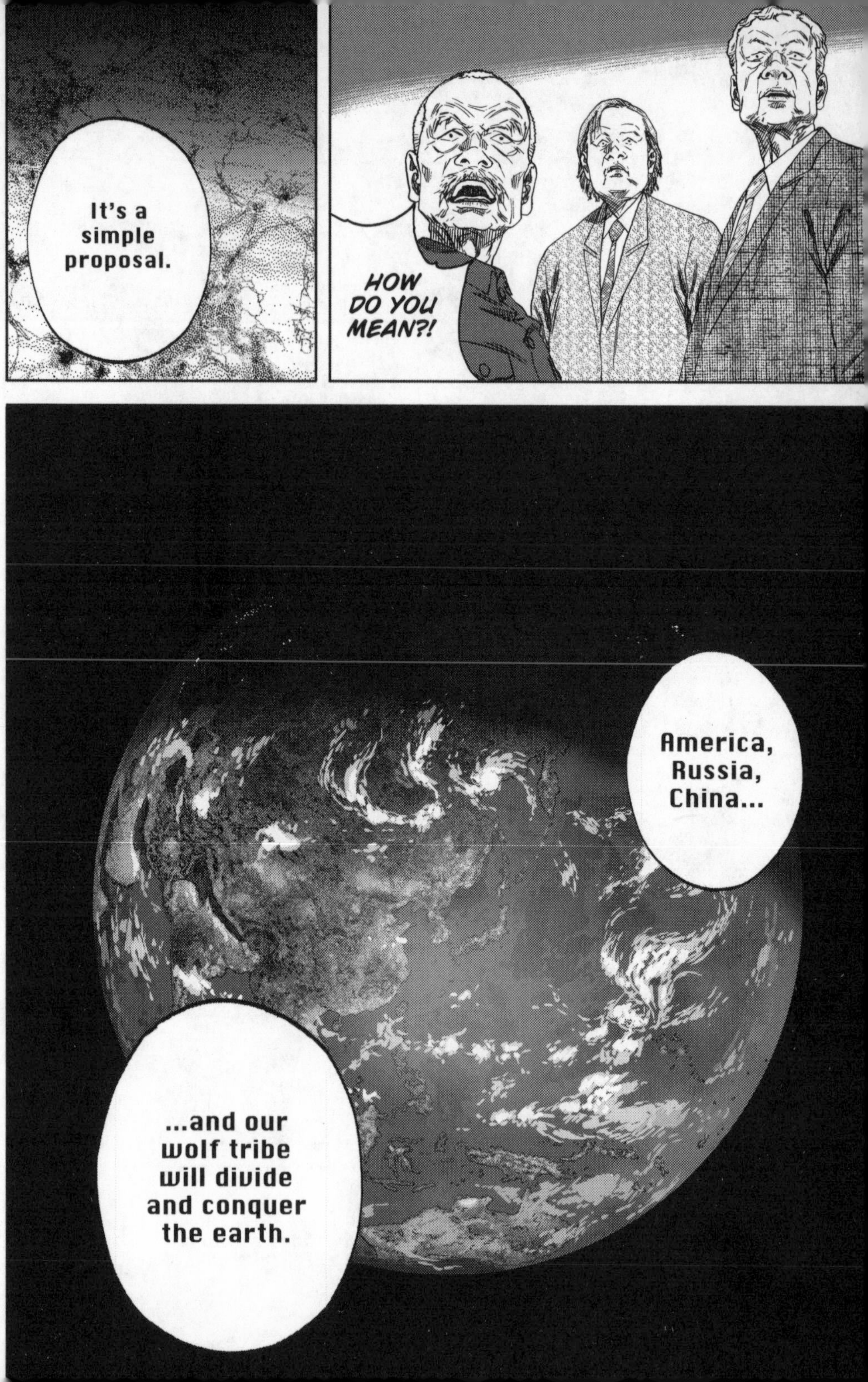
HOW DO YOU MEAN?!
It's a simple proposal.
America, Russia, China...
...and our wolf tribe will divide and conquer the earth.

KING OF EDEN

KING OF EDEN

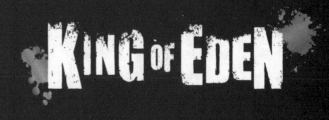

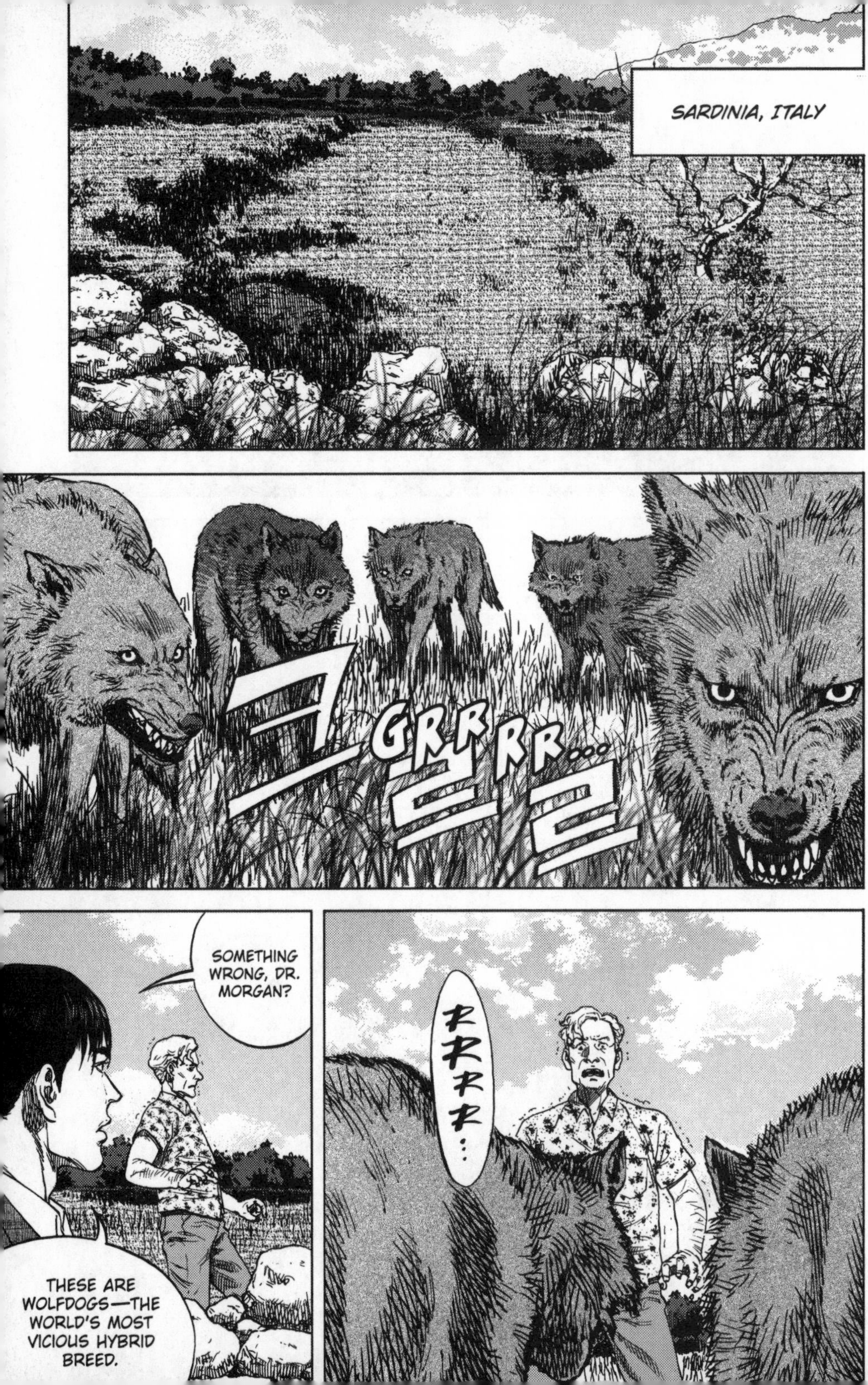
SARDINIA, ITALY
GRRRRR...
RRRRR...
SOMETHING WRONG, DR. MORGAN?
THESE ARE WOLFDOGS—THE WORLD'S MOST VICIOUS HYBRID BREED.

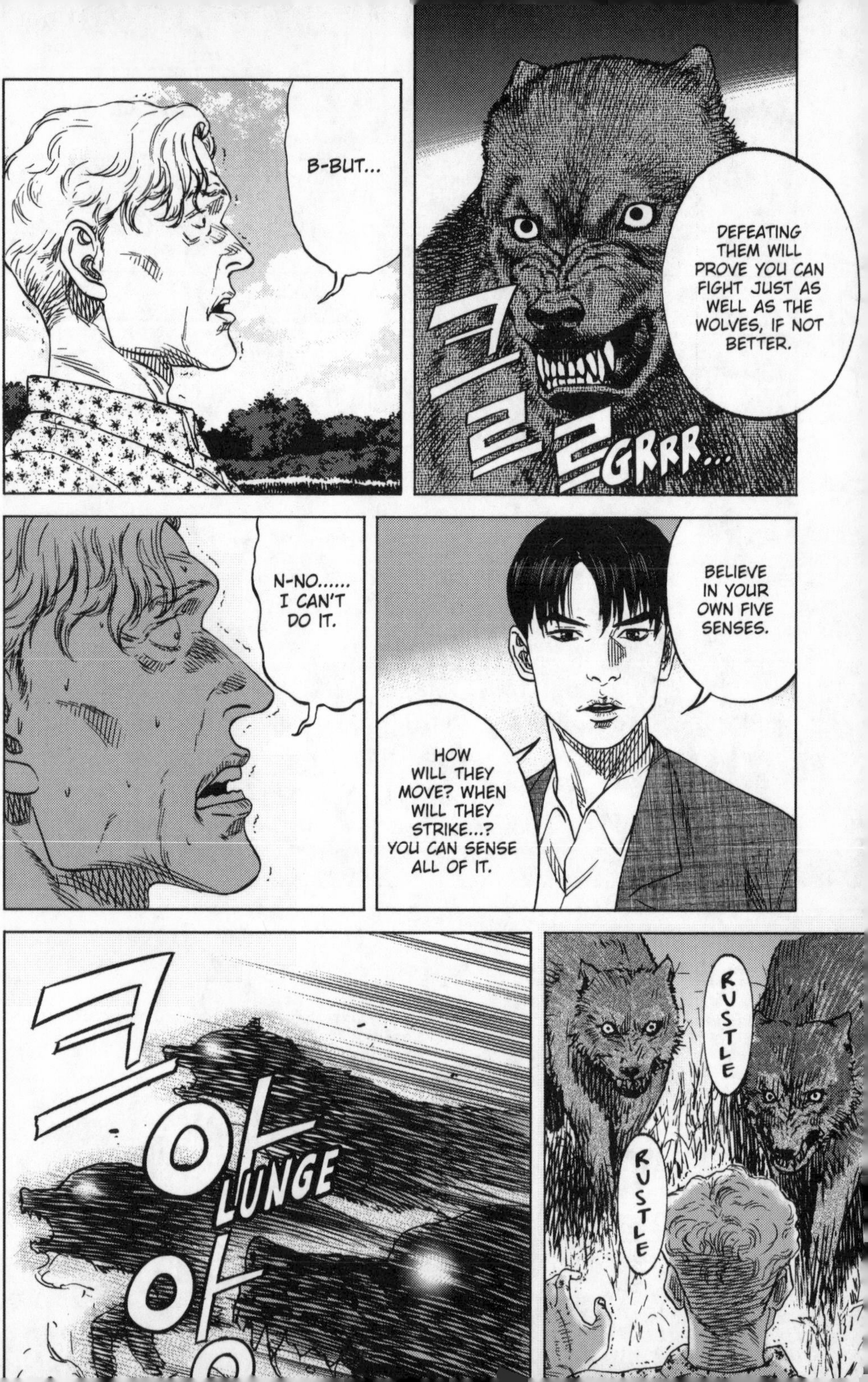
DEFEATING THEM WILL PROVE YOU CAN FIGHT JUST AS WELL AS THE WOLVES, IF NOT BETTER.
크르르
GRRR...
B-BUT...
BELIEVE IN YOUR OWN FIVE SENSES.
HOW WILL THEY MOVE? WHEN WILL THEY STRIKE...? YOU CAN SENSE ALL OF IT.
N-NO...... I CAN'T DO IT.
RUSTLE
RUSTLE
LUNGE

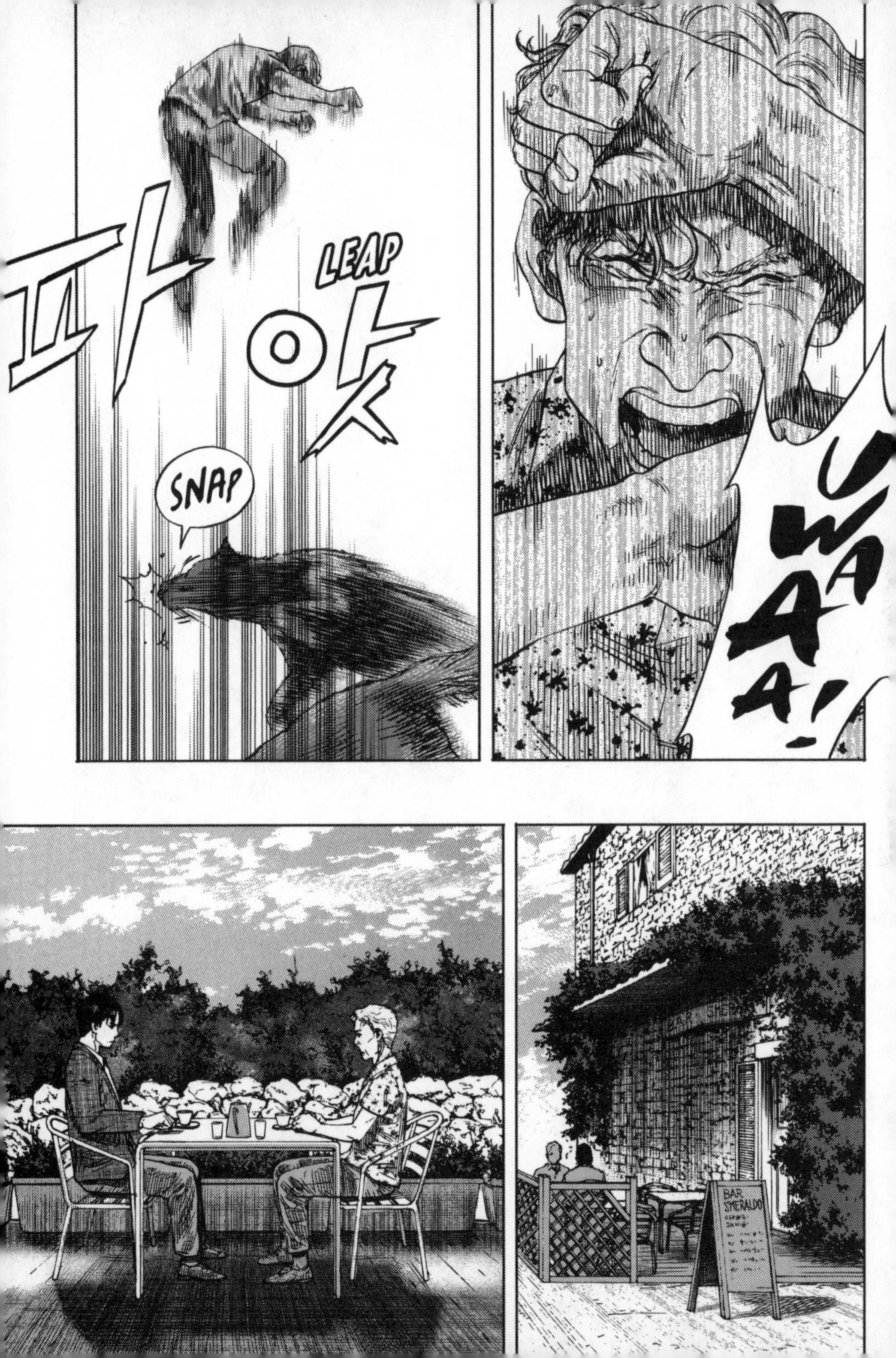
UWAAAA!!
파앗
LEAP
SNAP
BAR SMERALDO

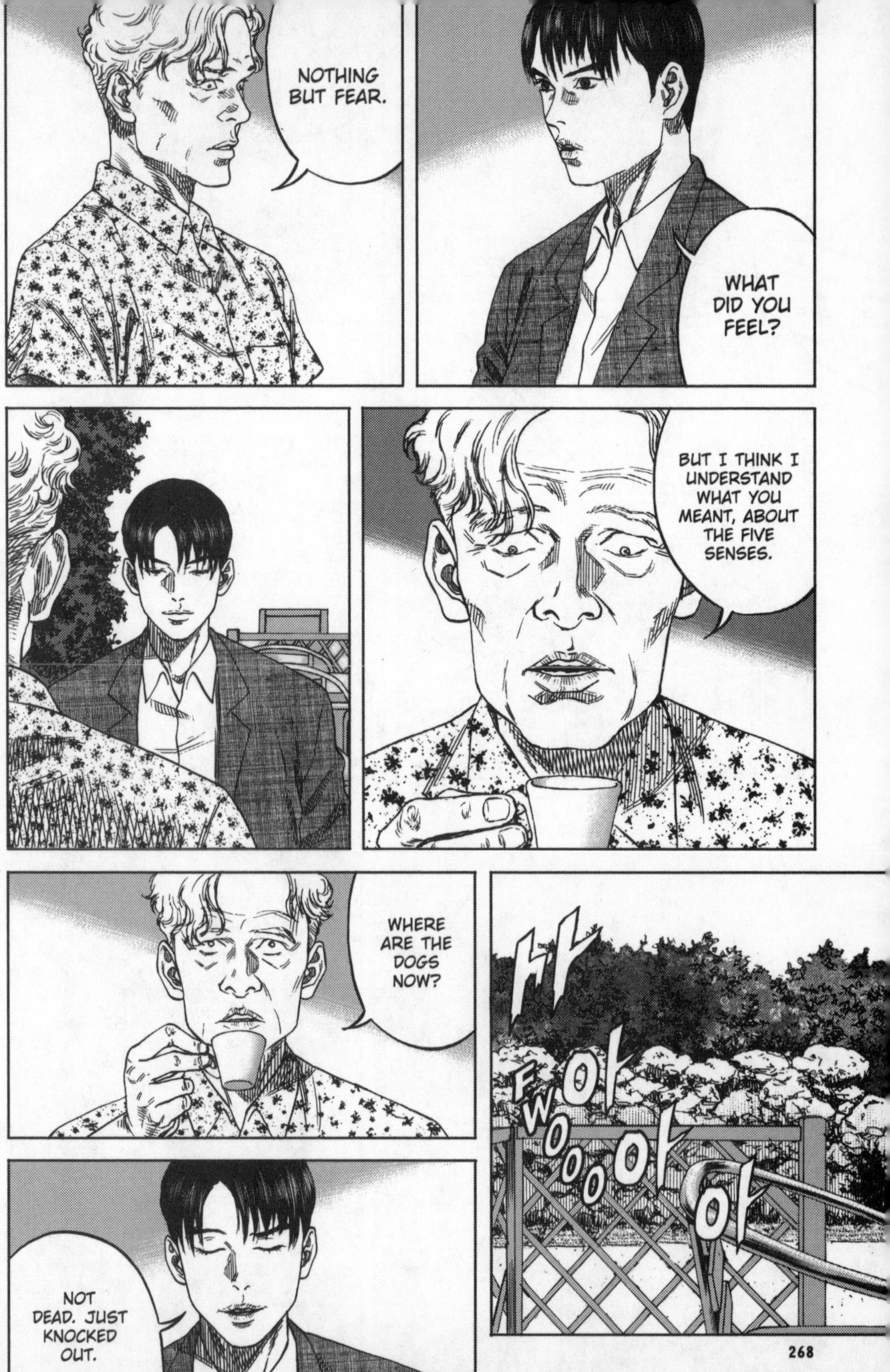
WHAT DID YOU FEEL?
NOTHING BUT FEAR.
BUT I THINK I UNDERSTAND WHAT YOU MEANT, ABOUT THE FIVE SENSES.
FWOOOO
WHERE ARE THE DOGS NOW?
NOT DEAD. JUST KNOCKED OUT.

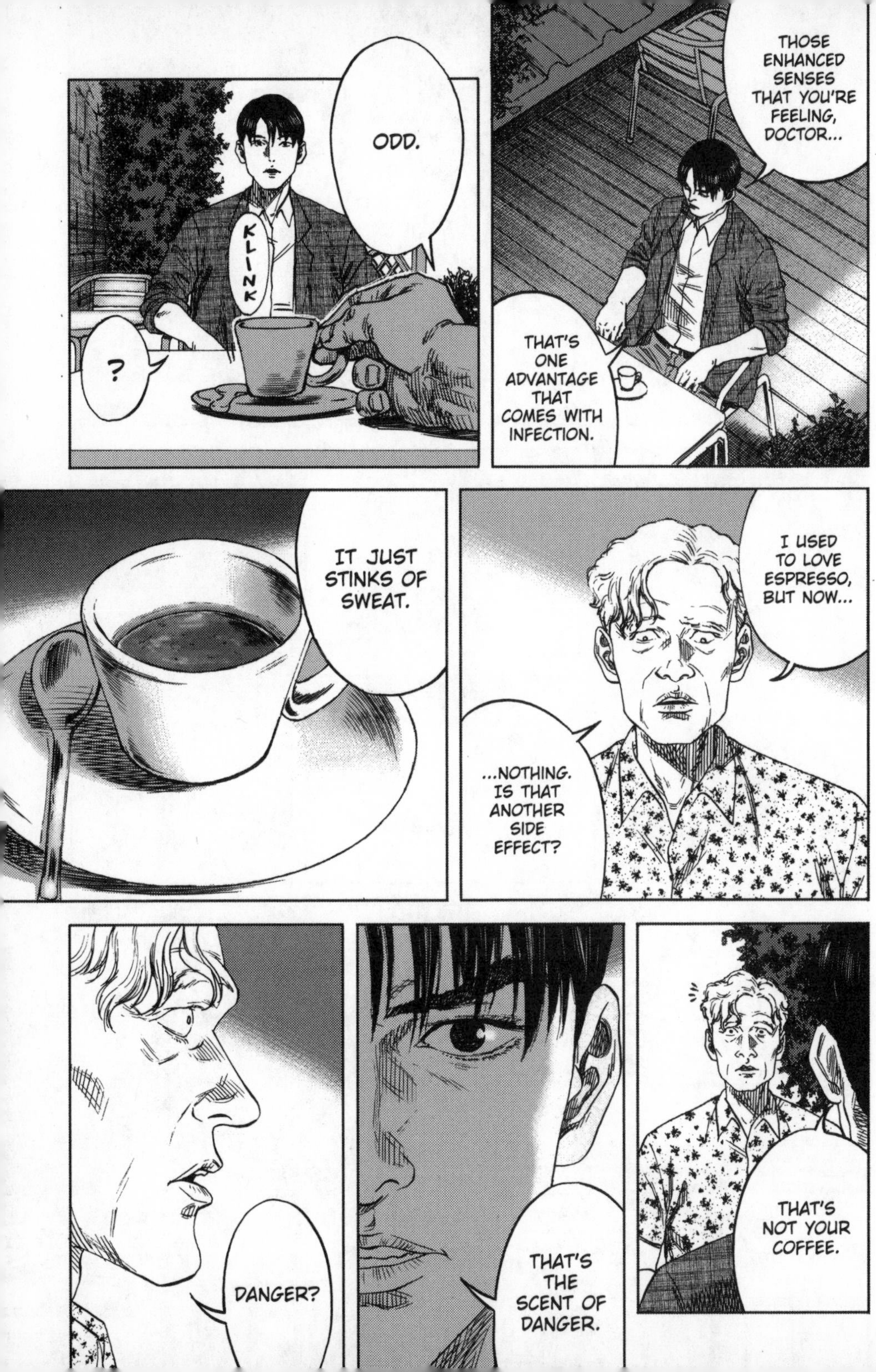
THOSE ENHANCED SENSES THAT YOU'RE FEELING, DOCTOR...
THAT'S ONE ADVANTAGE THAT COMES WITH INFECTION.
ODD.
KLINK
?
I USED TO LOVE ESPRESSO, BUT NOW...
...NOTHING. IS THAT ANOTHER SIDE EFFECT?
IT JUST STINKS OF SWEAT.
THAT'S NOT YOUR COFFEE.
THAT'S THE SCENT OF DANGER.
DANGER?

NOD

I'M GOING TO COUNT TO FIVE. THEN WE JUMP.

FOUR...

TWO...

THREE...

KLINK

ONE...

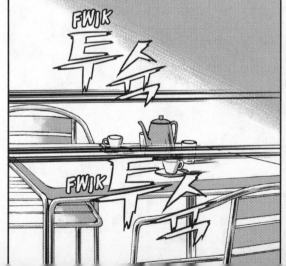

FWIK

FWIK

LEAP

FIVE!!

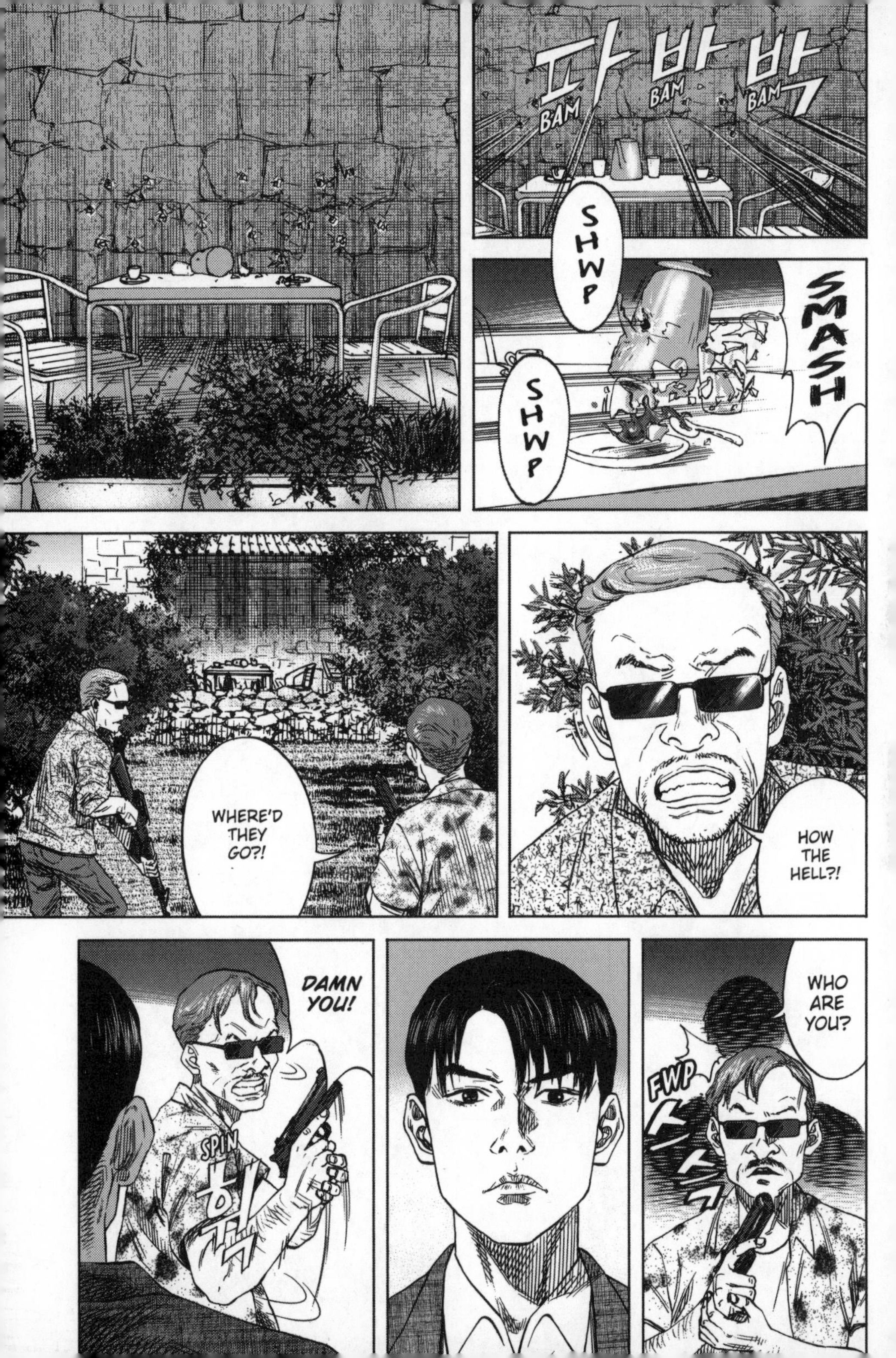
파바박
BAM BAM BAM
SHWP
SHWP
SMASH
HOW THE HELL?!
WHERE'D THEY GO?!
WHO ARE YOU?
FWP
DAMN YOU!
SPIN

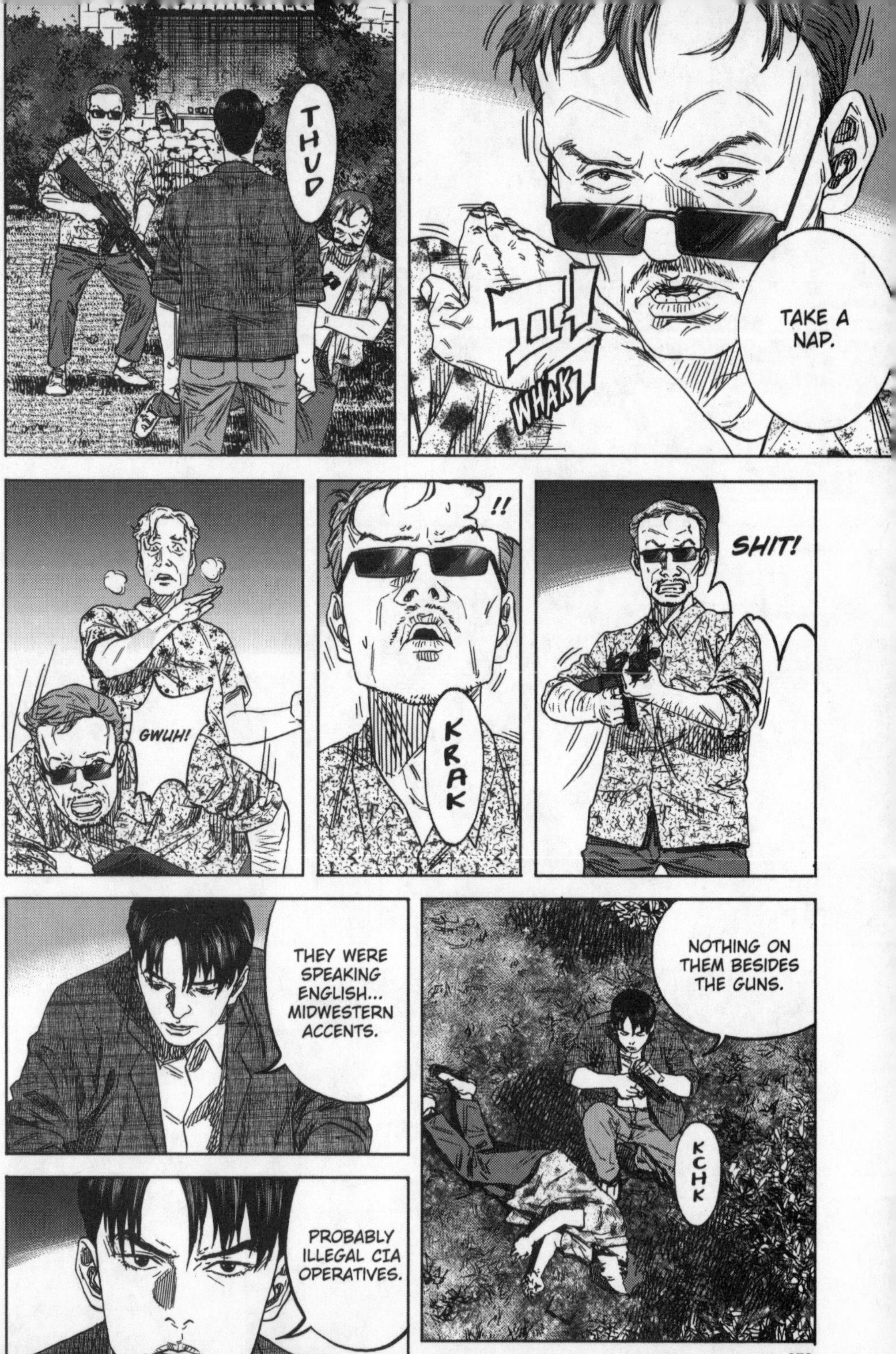
TAKE A NAP.
WHAK
THUD
SHIT!
!!
KRAK
GWUH!
NOTHING ON THEM BESIDES THE GUNS.
KCHK
THEY WERE SPEAKING ENGLISH... MIDWESTERN ACCENTS.
PROBABLY ILLEGAL CIA OPERATIVES.

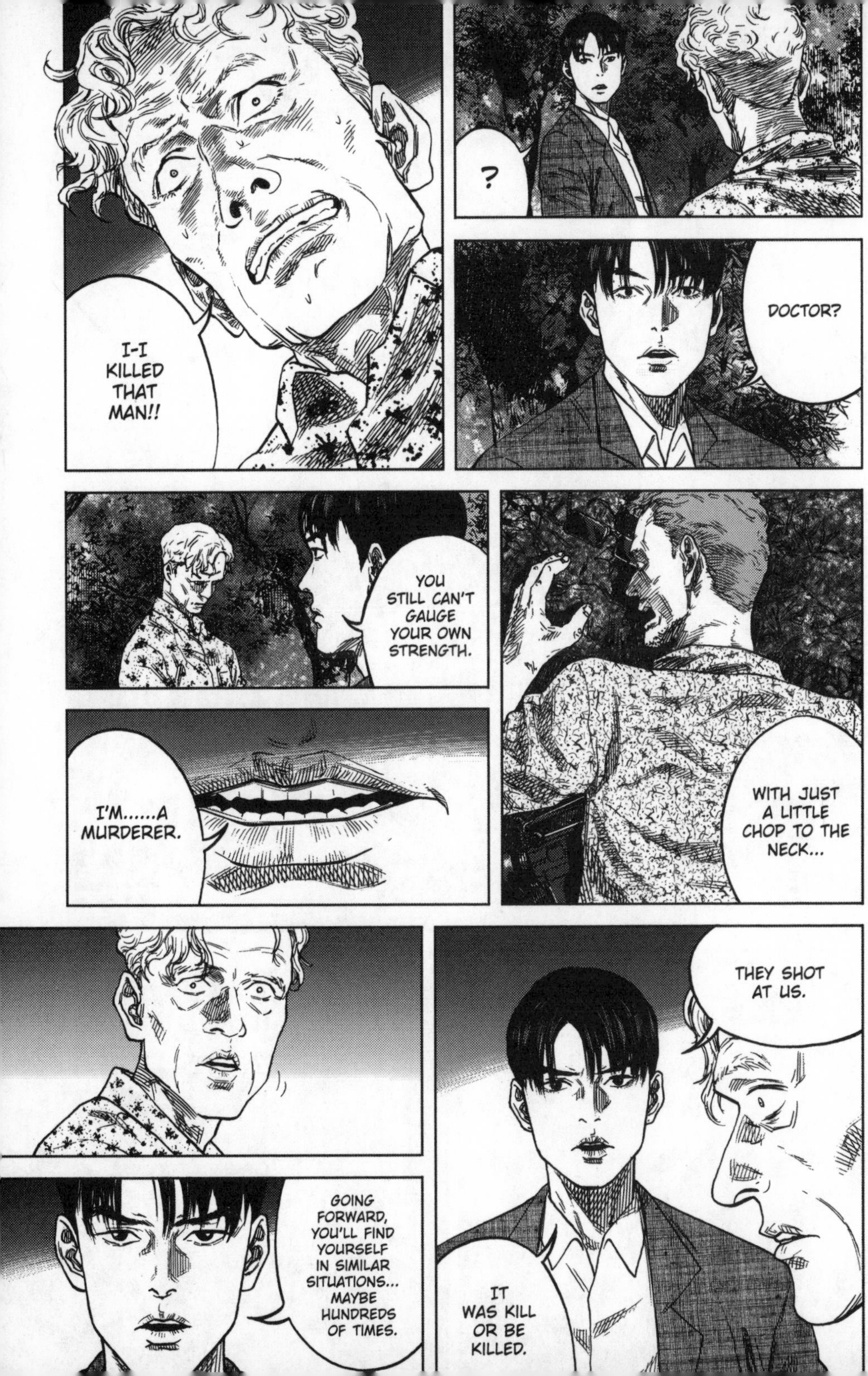
?
DOCTOR?
I-I KILLED THAT MAN!!
WITH JUST A LITTLE CHOP TO THE NECK...
YOU STILL CAN'T GAUGE YOUR OWN STRENGTH.
I'M......A MURDERER.
THEY SHOT AT US.
IT WAS KILL OR BE KILLED.
GOING FORWARD, YOU'LL FIND YOURSELF IN SIMILAR SITUATIONS... MAYBE HUNDREDS OF TIMES.

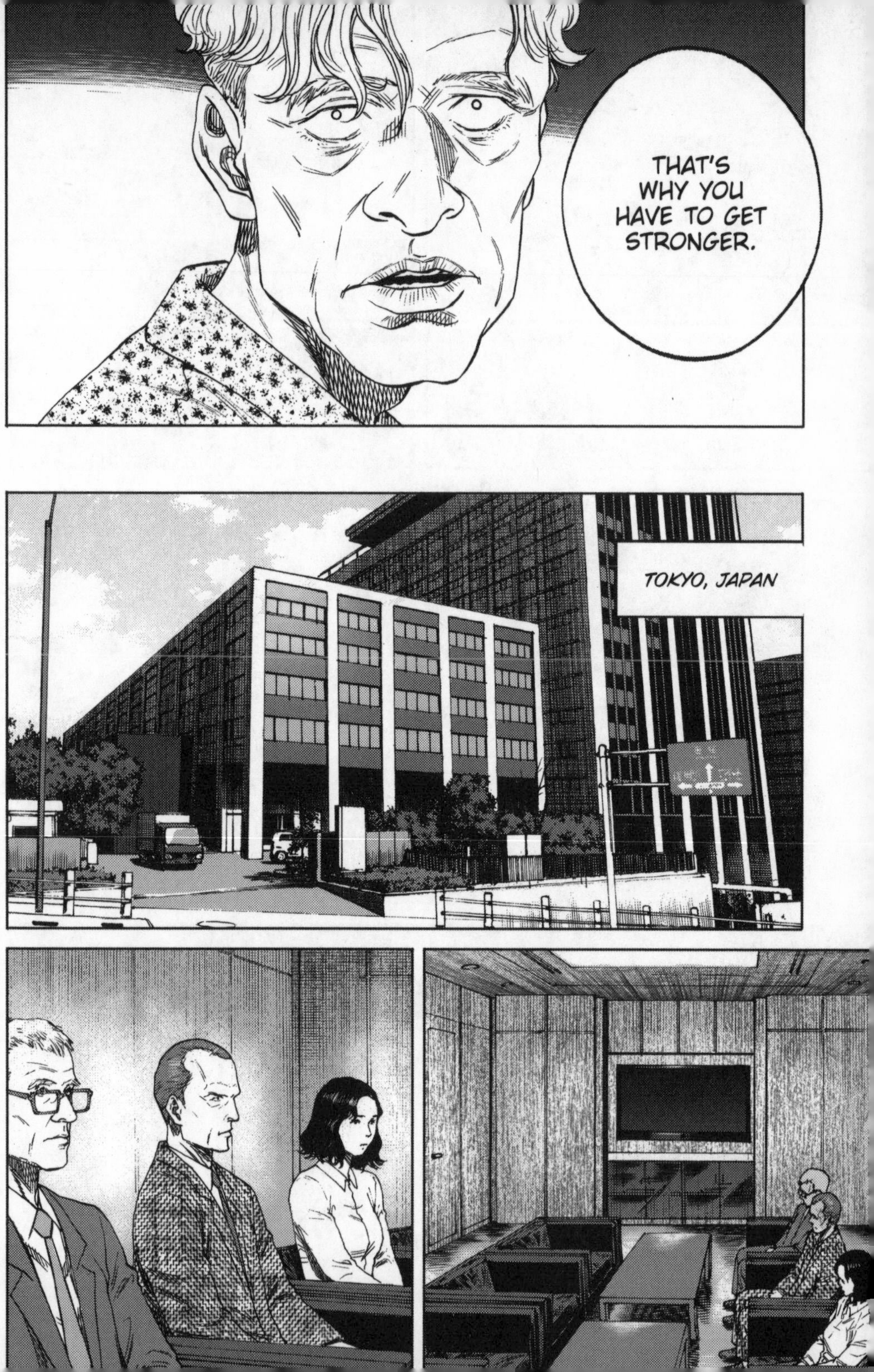
THAT'S WHY YOU HAVE TO GET STRONGER.
TOKYO, JAPAN

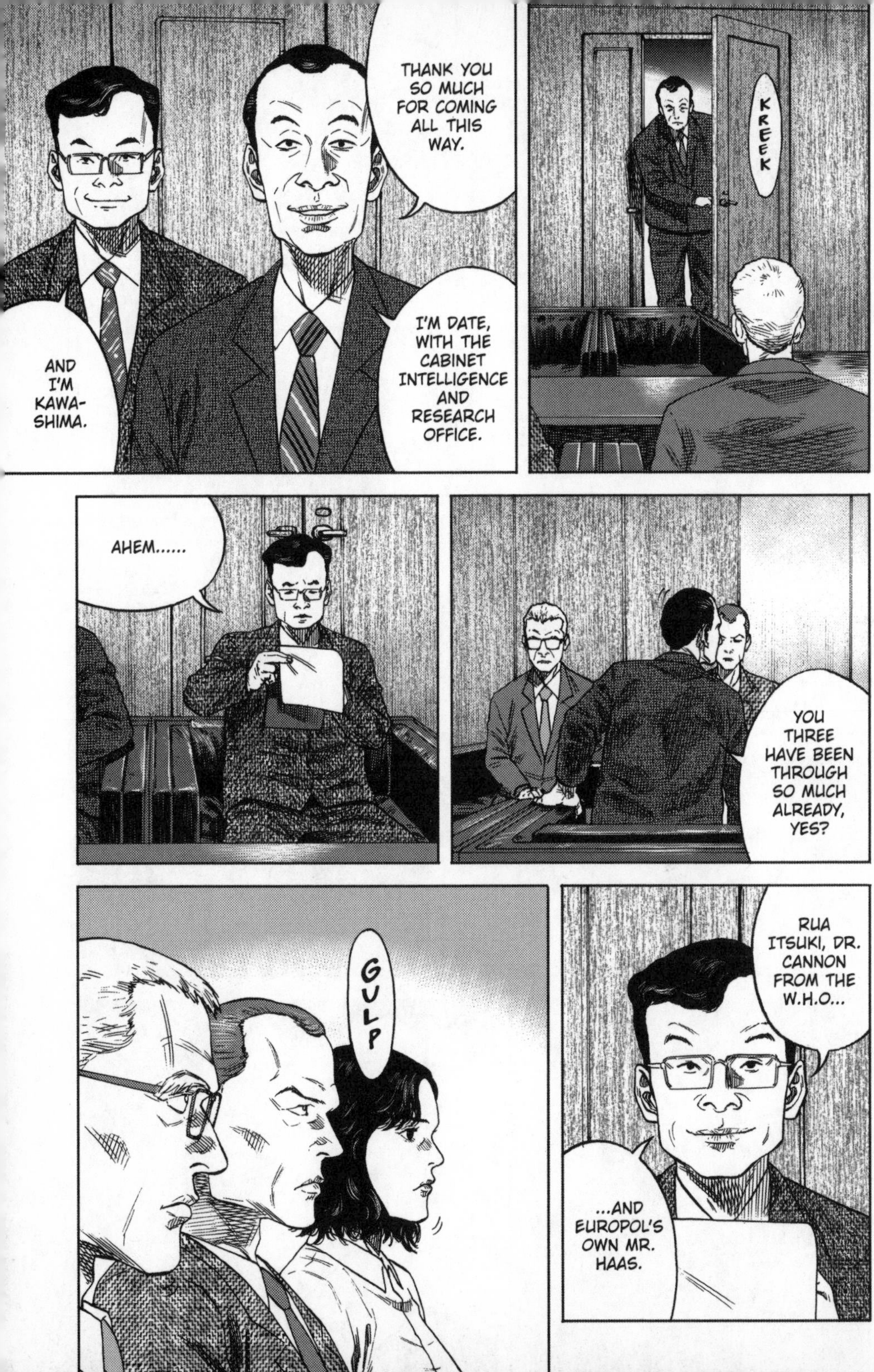
KREEK
THANK YOU SO MUCH FOR COMING ALL THIS WAY.
I'M DATE, WITH THE CABINET INTELLIGENCE AND RESEARCH OFFICE.
AND I'M KAWA-SHIMA.
YOU THREE HAVE BEEN THROUGH SO MUCH ALREADY, YES?
AHEM......
RUA ITSUKI, DR. CANNON FROM THE W.H.O...
...AND EUROPOL'S OWN MR. HAAS.
GULP

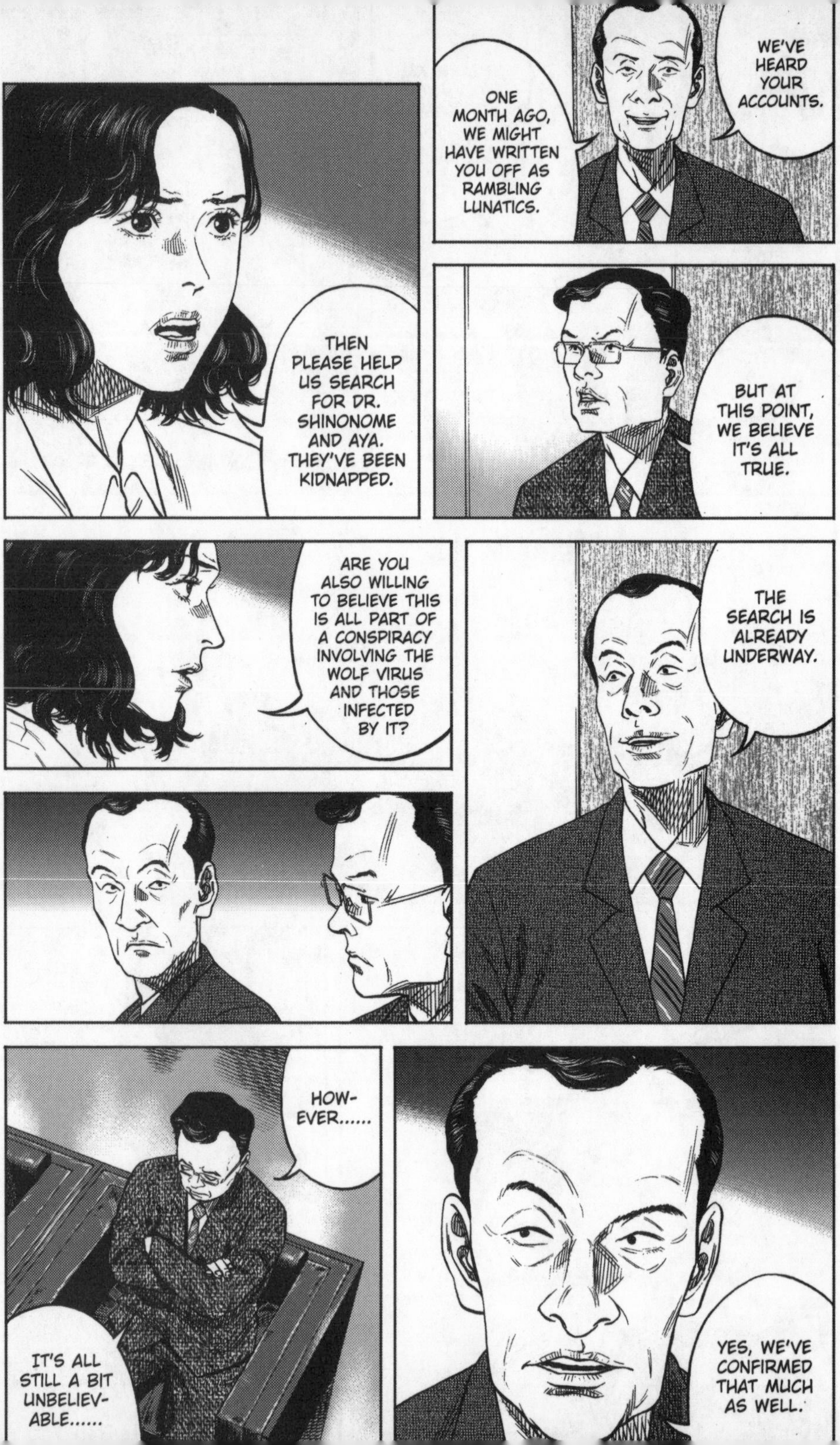

WE'VE HEARD YOUR ACCOUNTS.
ONE MONTH AGO, WE MIGHT HAVE WRITTEN YOU OFF AS RAMBLING LUNATICS.
BUT AT THIS POINT, WE BELIEVE IT'S ALL TRUE.
THEN PLEASE HELP US SEARCH FOR DR. SHINONOME AND AYA. THEY'VE BEEN KIDNAPPED.
THE SEARCH IS ALREADY UNDERWAY.
ARE YOU ALSO WILLING TO BELIEVE THIS IS ALL PART OF A CONSPIRACY INVOLVING THE WOLF VIRUS AND THOSE INFECTED BY IT?
YES, WE'VE CONFIRMED THAT MUCH AS WELL.
HOW-EVER......
IT'S ALL STILL A BIT UNBELIEV-ABLE......

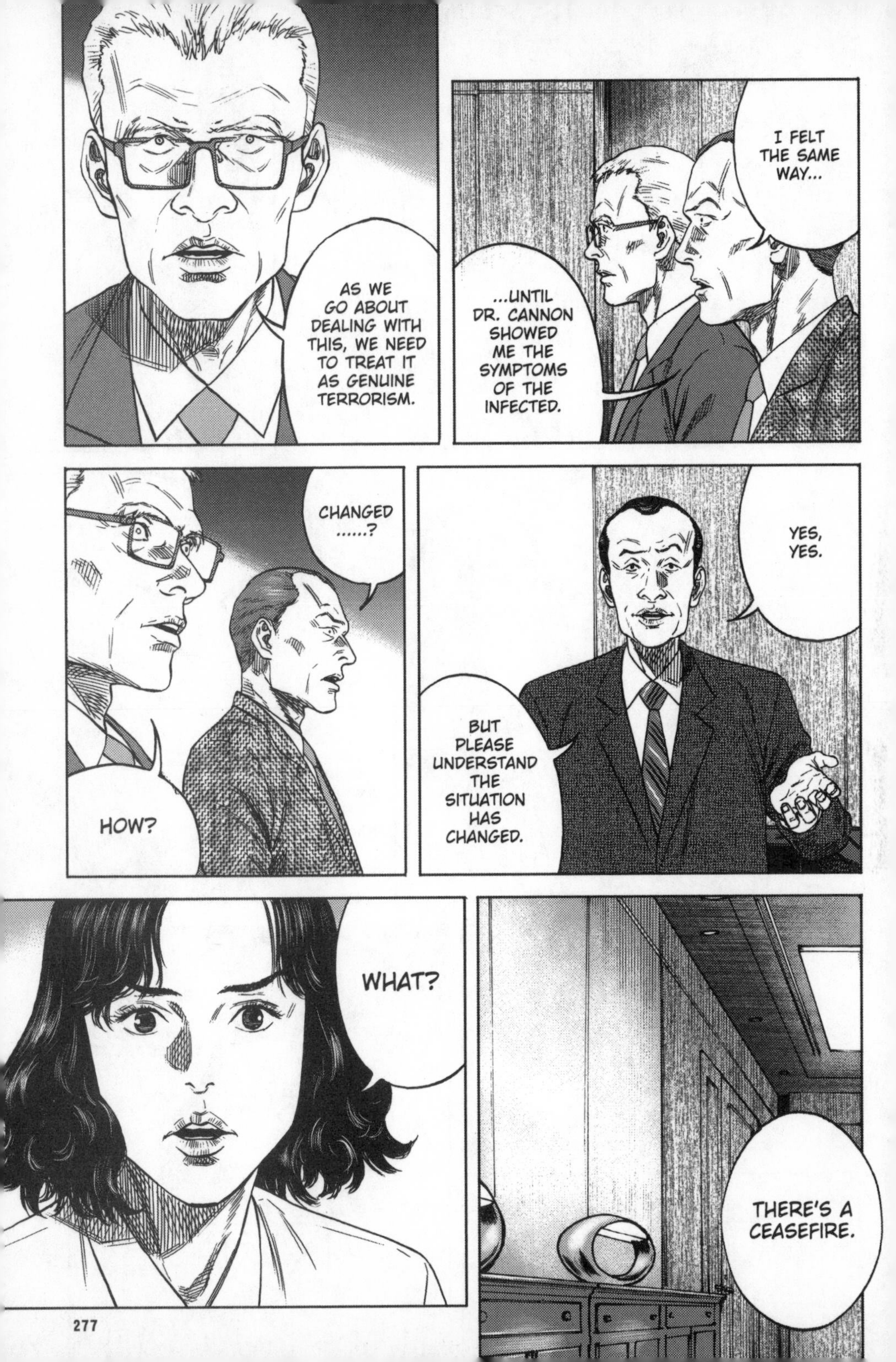
I FELT THE SAME WAY...
...UNTIL DR. CANNON SHOWED ME THE SYMPTOMS OF THE INFECTED.
AS WE GO ABOUT DEALING WITH THIS, WE NEED TO TREAT IT AS GENUINE TERRORISM.
YES, YES.
BUT PLEASE UNDERSTAND THE SITUATION HAS CHANGED.
CHANGED ......?
HOW?
THERE'S A CEASEFIRE.
WHAT?

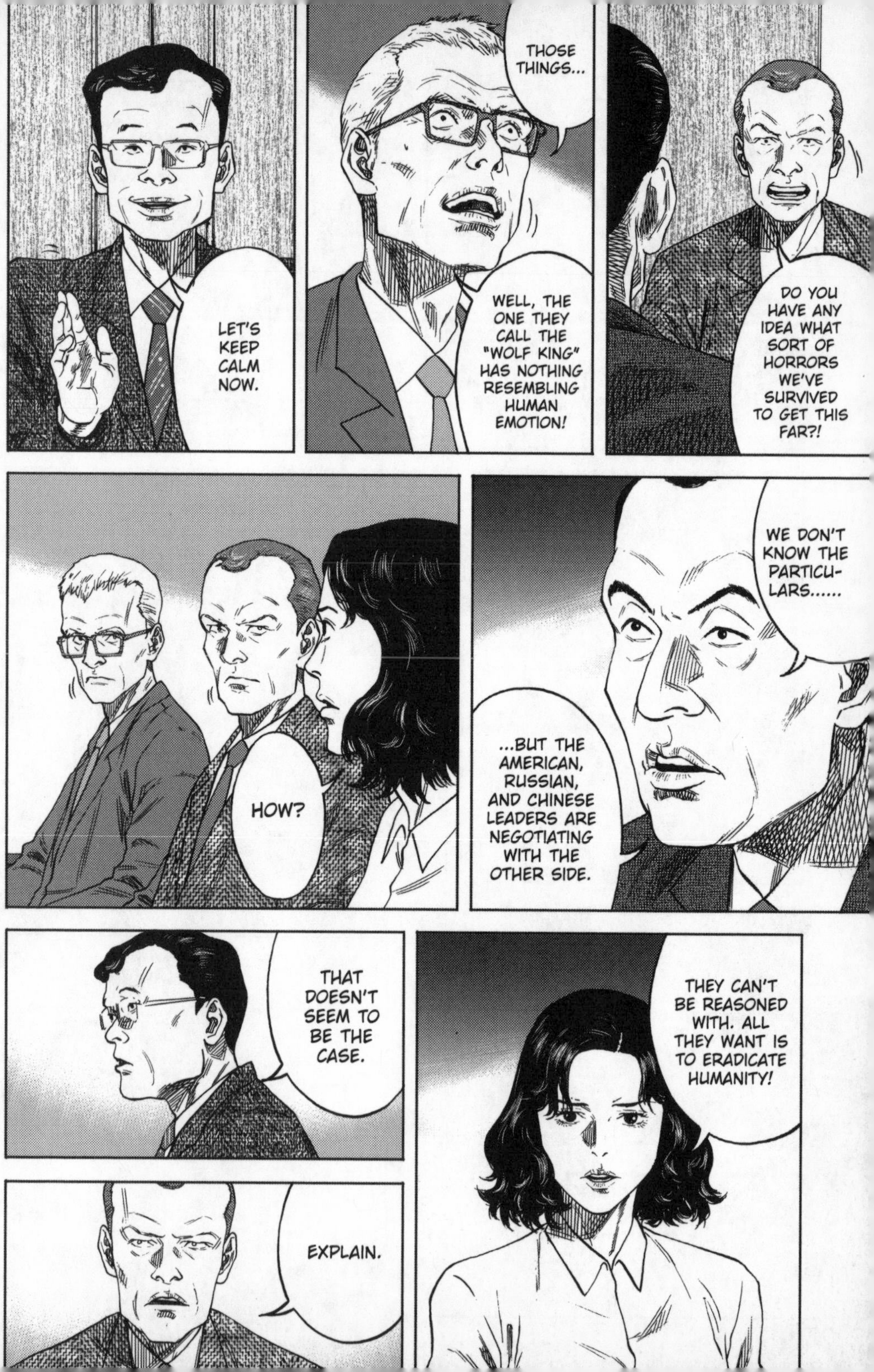
DO YOU HAVE ANY IDEA WHAT SORT OF HORRORS WE'VE SURVIVED TO GET THIS FAR?!
THOSE THINGS...
WELL, THE ONE THEY CALL THE "WOLF KING" HAS NOTHING RESEMBLING HUMAN EMOTION!
LET'S KEEP CALM NOW.
WE DON'T KNOW THE PARTICU-LARS......
...BUT THE AMERICAN, RUSSIAN, AND CHINESE LEADERS ARE NEGOTIATING WITH THE OTHER SIDE.
HOW?
THEY CAN'T BE REASONED WITH. ALL THEY WANT IS TO ERADICATE HUMANITY!
THAT DOESN'T SEEM TO BE THE CASE.
EXPLAIN.

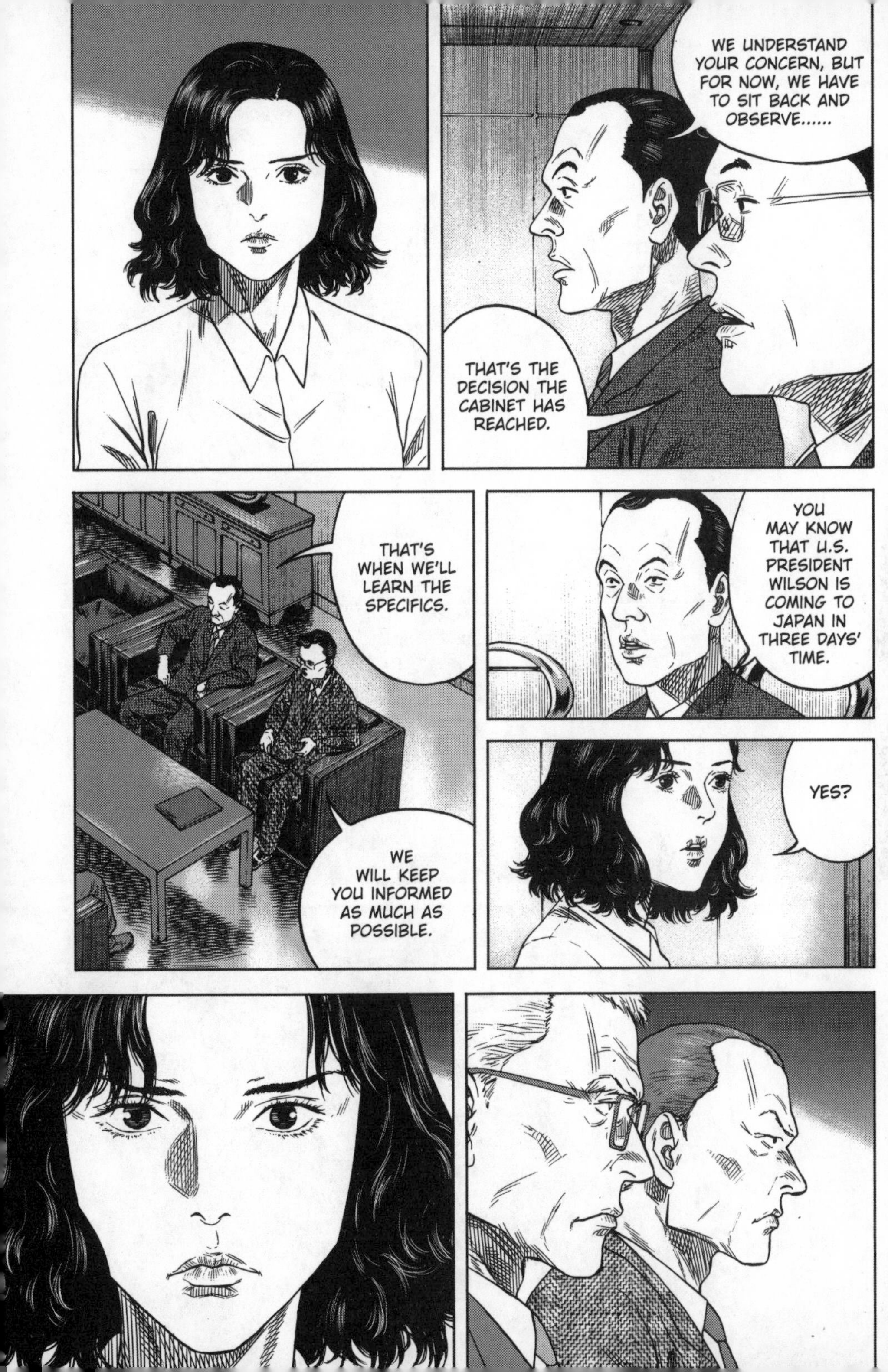
WE UNDERSTAND YOUR CONCERN, BUT FOR NOW, WE HAVE TO SIT BACK AND OBSERVE......
THAT'S THE DECISION THE CABINET HAS REACHED.
YOU MAY KNOW THAT U.S. PRESIDENT WILSON IS COMING TO JAPAN IN THREE DAYS' TIME.
YES?
THAT'S WHEN WE'LL LEARN THE SPECIFICS.
WE WILL KEEP YOU INFORMED AS MUCH AS POSSIBLE.

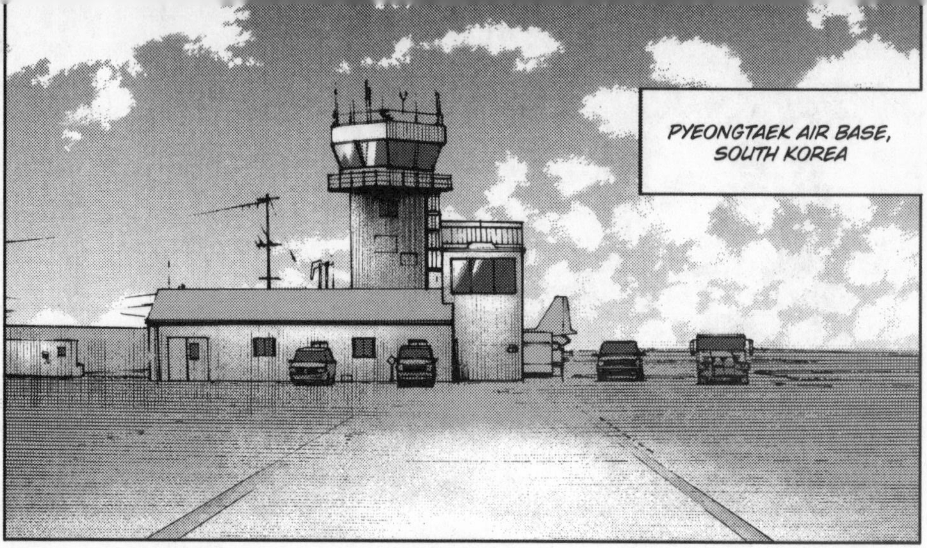
PYEONGTAEK AIR BASE,
SOUTH KOREA

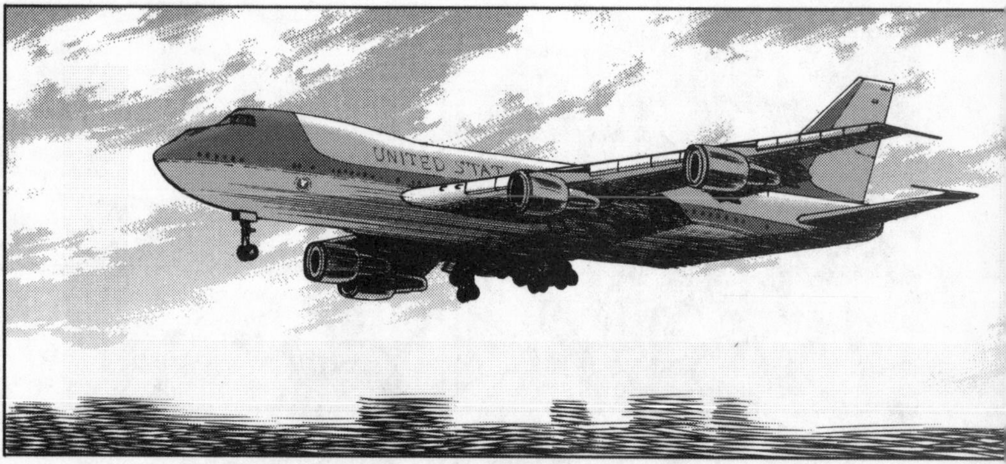
UNITED STAT

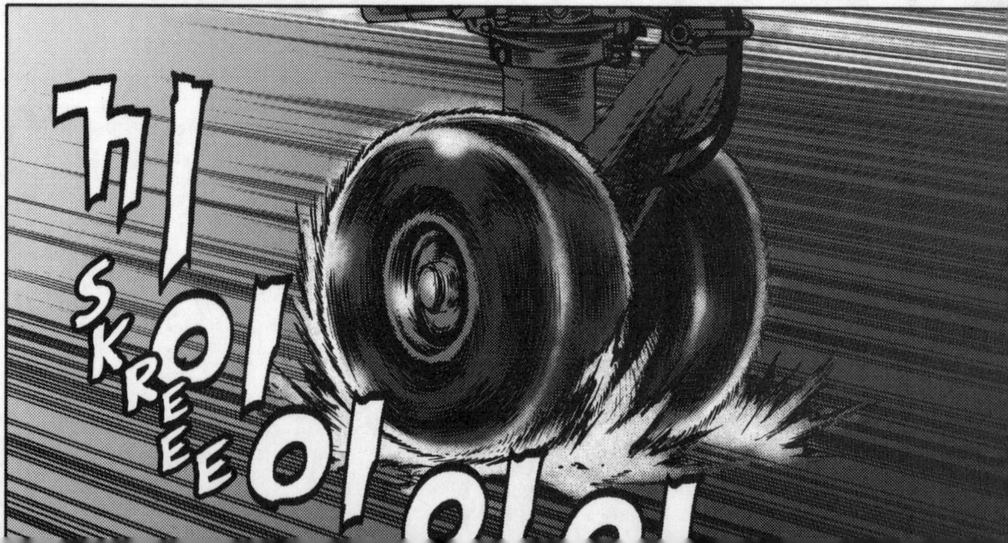
끼이
SKREEE

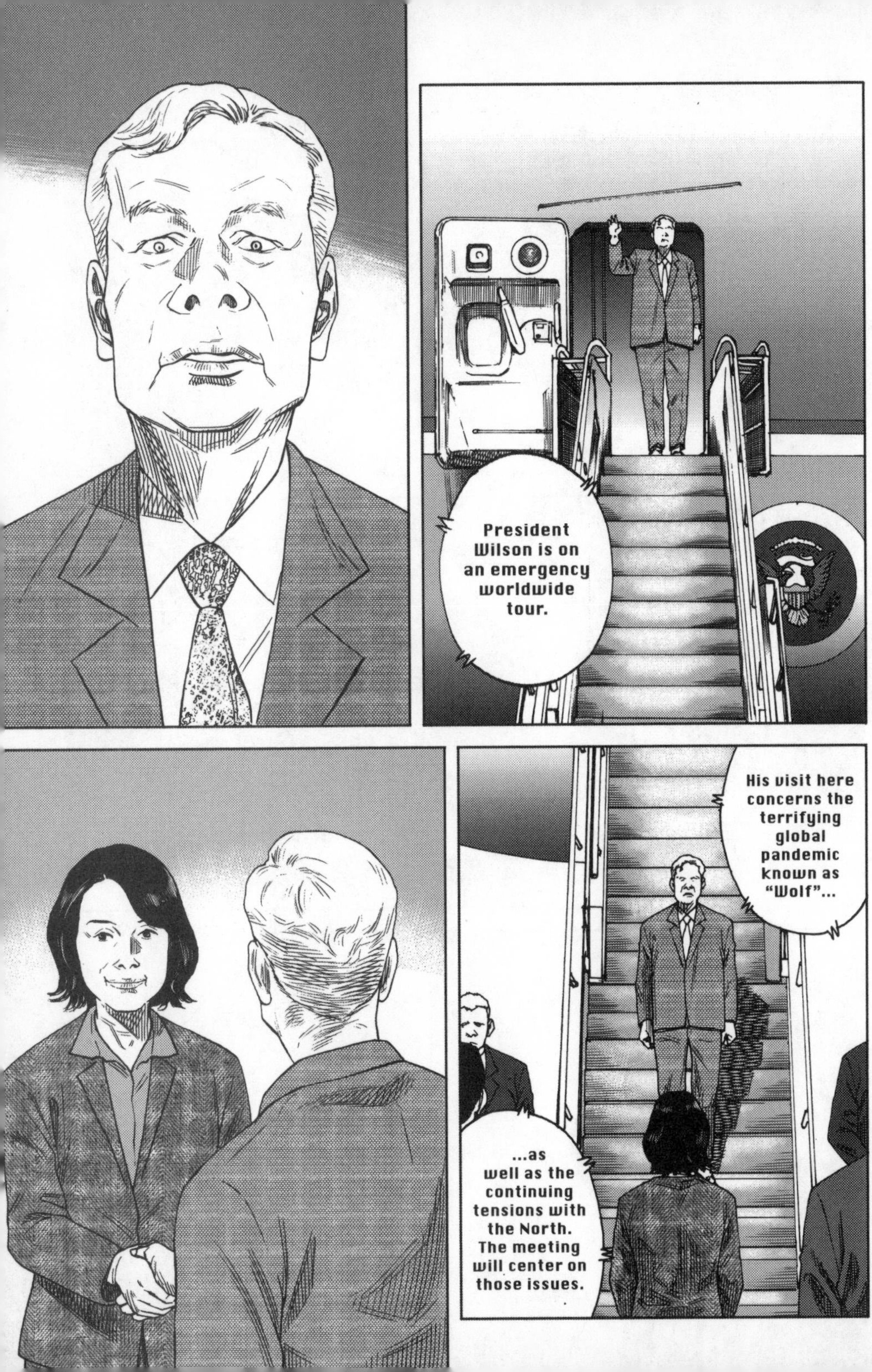
President Wilson is on an emergency worldwide tour.
His visit here concerns the terrifying global pandemic known as "Wolf"...
...as well as the continuing tensions with the North. The meeting will center on those issues.

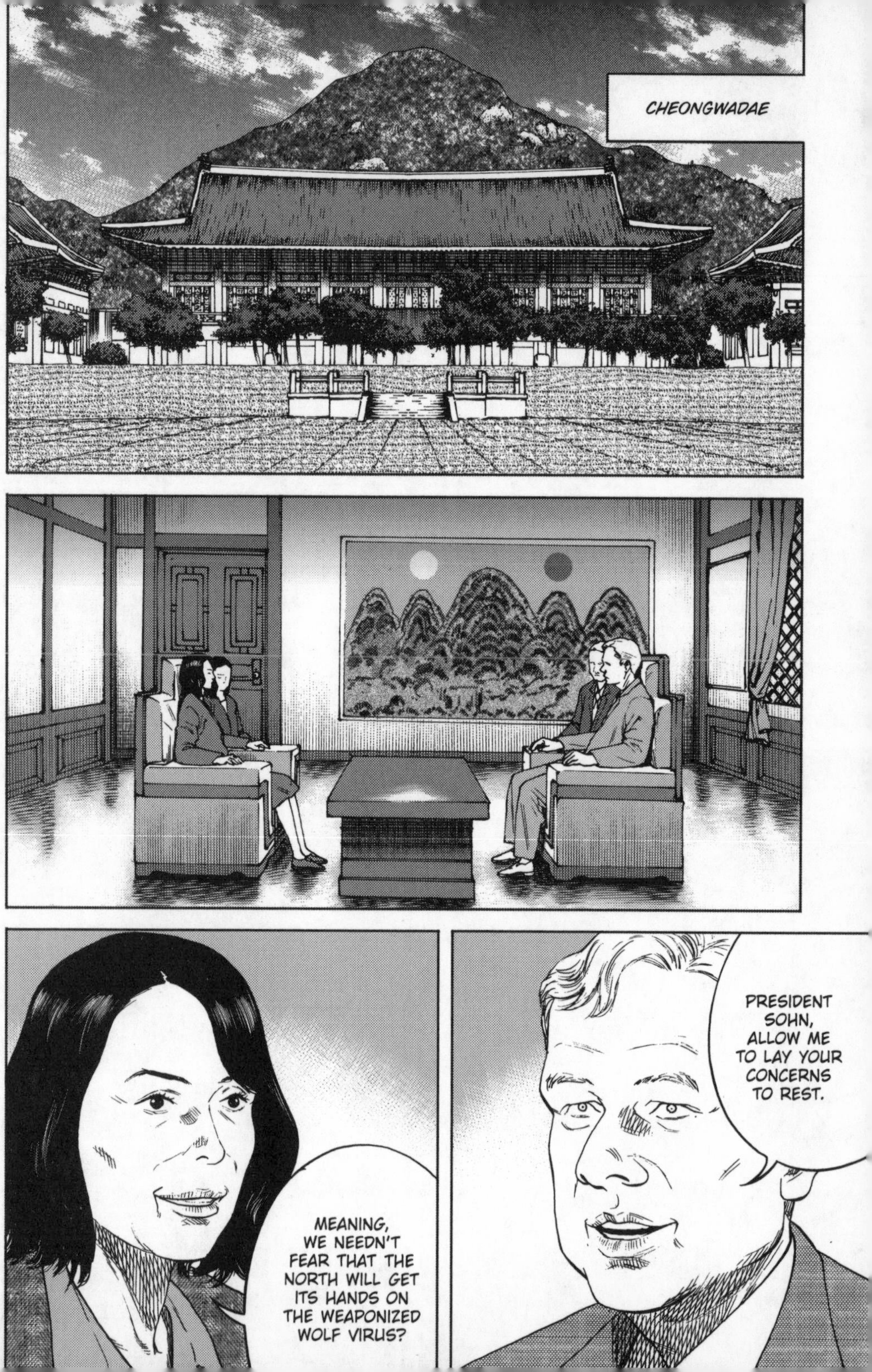
CHEONGWADAE
PRESIDENT SOHN, ALLOW ME TO LAY YOUR CONCERNS TO REST.
MEANING, WE NEEDN'T FEAR THAT THE NORTH WILL GET ITS HANDS ON THE WEAPONIZED WOLF VIRUS?

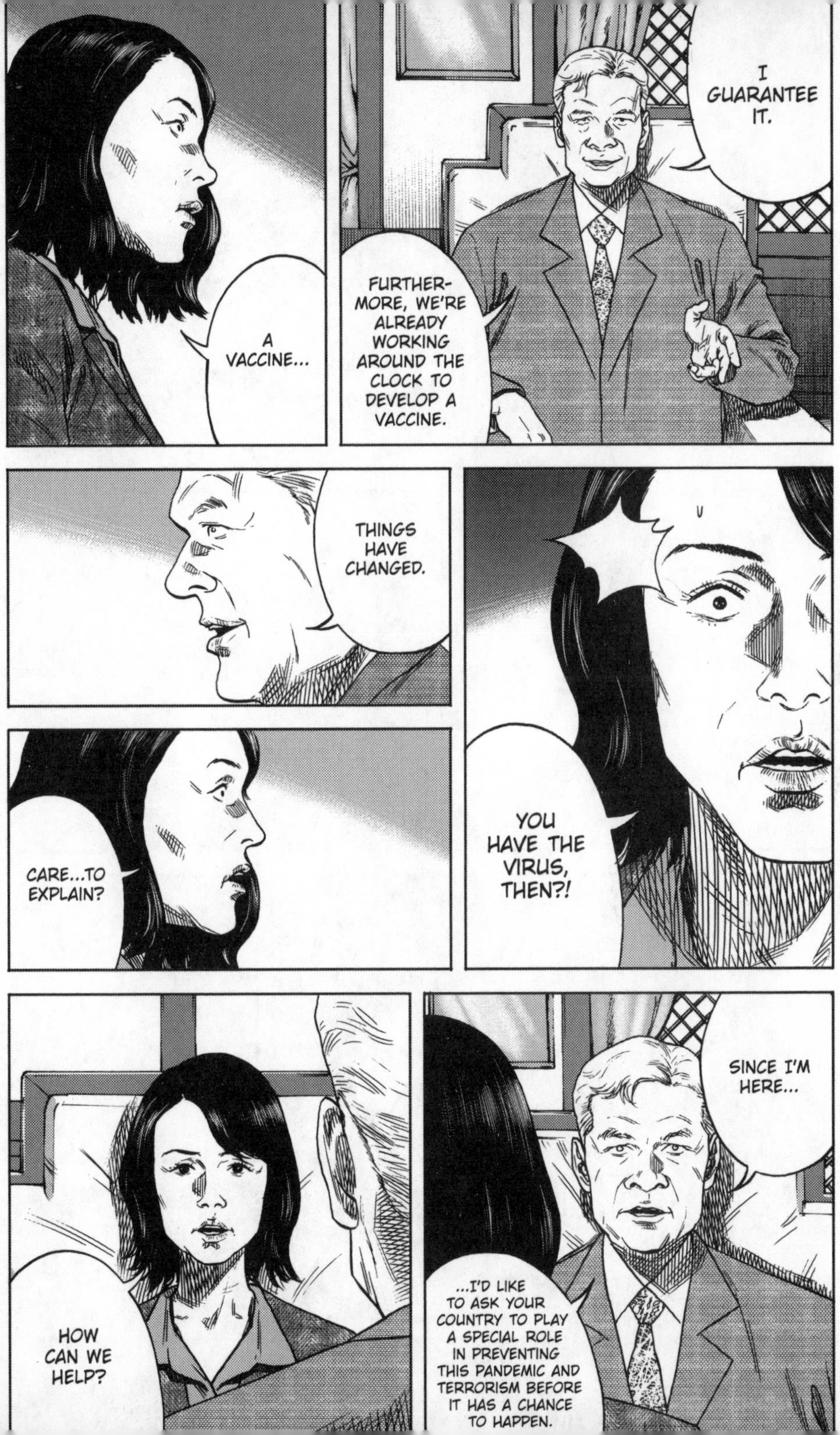
I GUARANTEE IT.
FURTHERMORE, WE'RE ALREADY WORKING AROUND THE CLOCK TO DEVELOP A VACCINE.
A VACCINE...
YOU HAVE THE VIRUS, THEN?!
THINGS HAVE CHANGED.
CARE...TO EXPLAIN?
SINCE I'M HERE...
...I'D LIKE TO ASK YOUR COUNTRY TO PLAY A SPECIAL ROLE IN PREVENTING THIS PANDEMIC AND TERRORISM BEFORE IT HAS A CHANCE TO HAPPEN.
HOW CAN WE HELP?

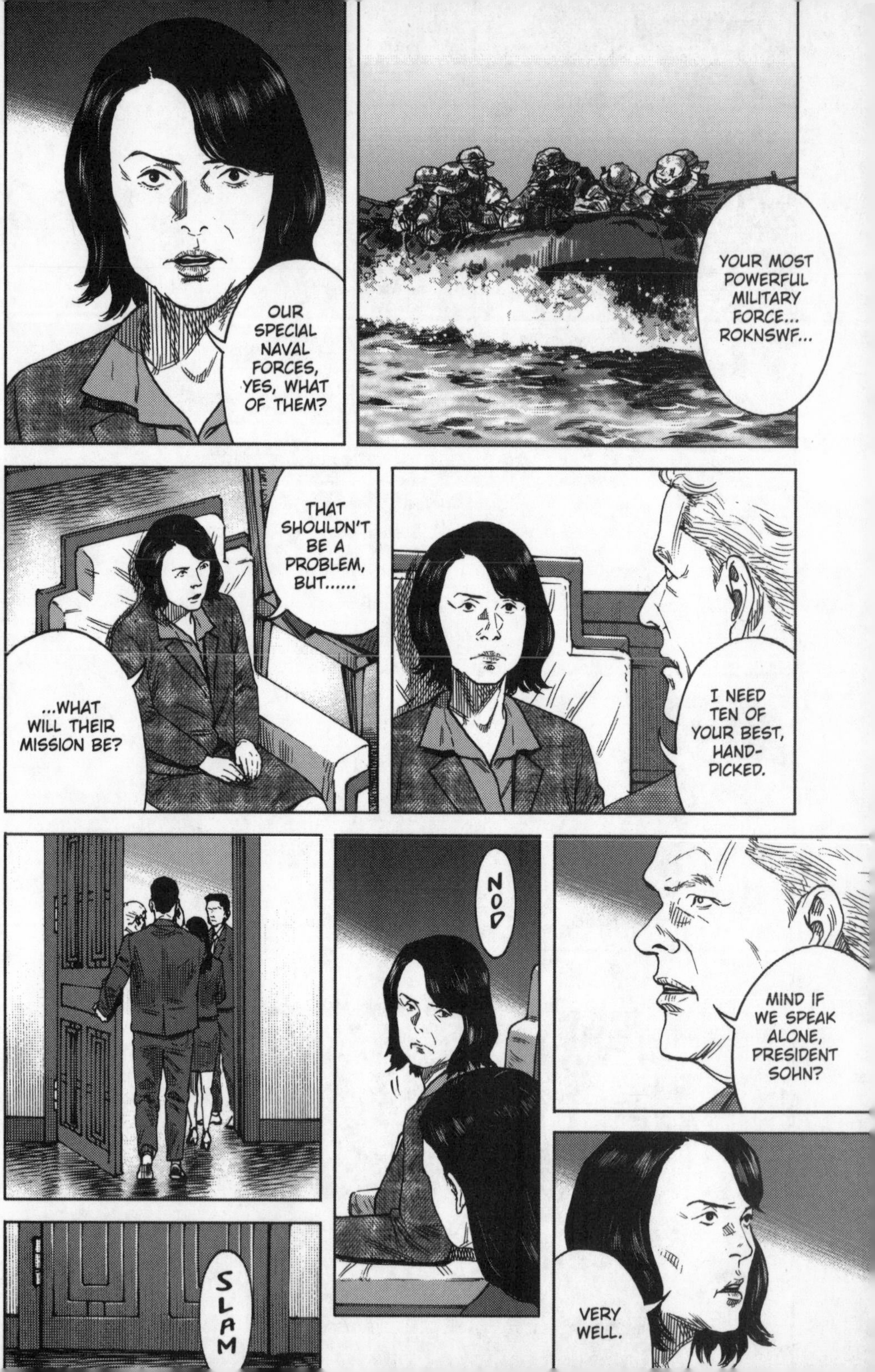
YOUR MOST POWERFUL MILITARY FORCE... ROKNSWF...
OUR SPECIAL NAVAL FORCES, YES, WHAT OF THEM?
I NEED TEN OF YOUR BEST, HAND-PICKED.
THAT SHOULDN'T BE A PROBLEM, BUT......
...WHAT WILL THEIR MISSION BE?
MIND IF WE SPEAK ALONE, PRESIDENT SOHN?
VERY WELL.
NOD
SLAM

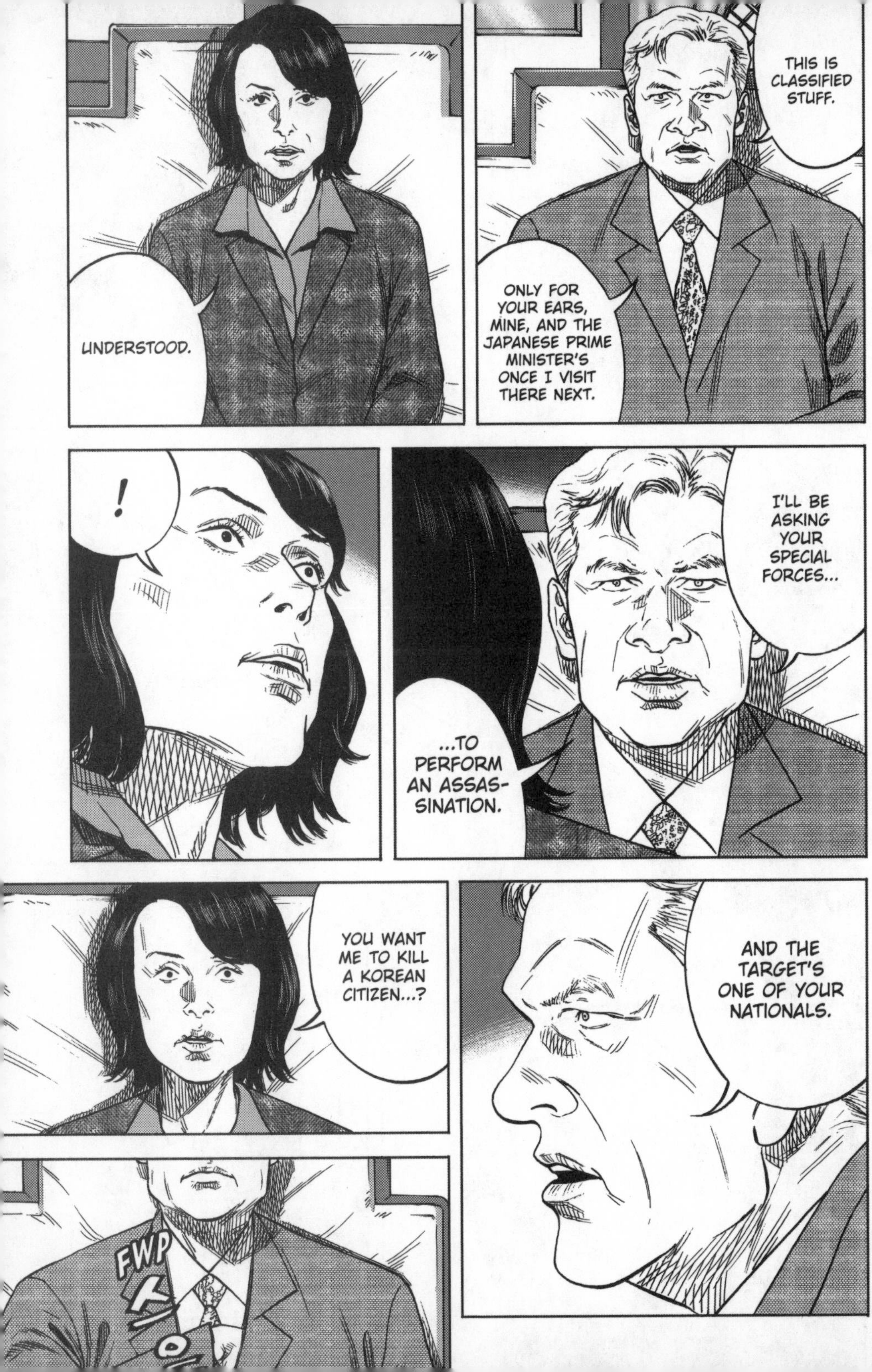
THIS IS CLASSIFIED STUFF.
ONLY FOR YOUR EARS, MINE, AND THE JAPANESE PRIME MINISTER'S ONCE I VISIT THERE NEXT.
UNDERSTOOD.
I'LL BE ASKING YOUR SPECIAL FORCES...
...TO PERFORM AN ASSAS-SINATION.
!
AND THE TARGET'S ONE OF YOUR NATIONALS.
YOU WANT ME TO KILL A KOREAN CITIZEN...?
FWP

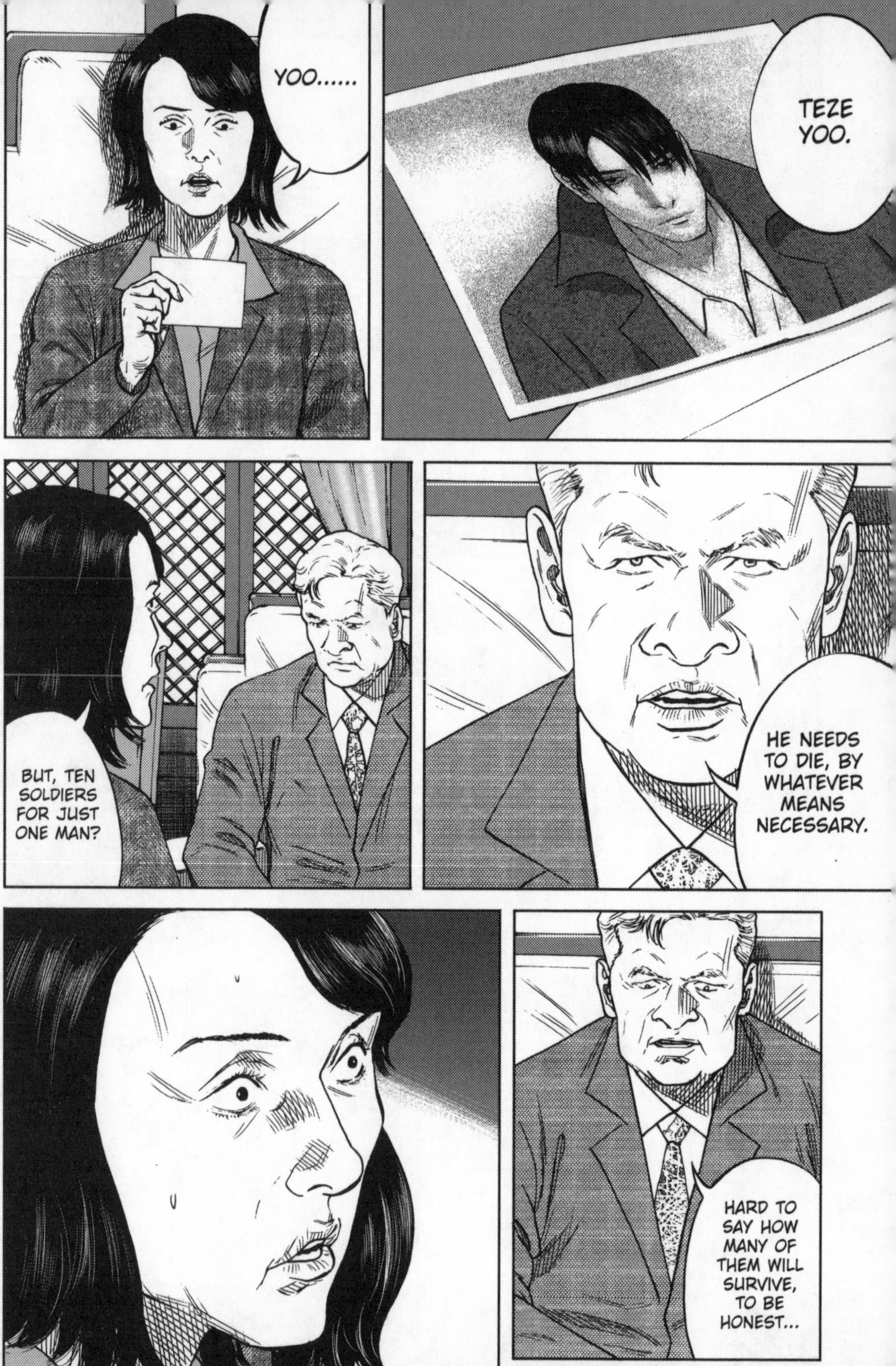
TEZE YOO.
YOO......
HE NEEDS TO DIE, BY WHATEVER MEANS NECESSARY.
BUT, TEN SOLDIERS FOR JUST ONE MAN?
HARD TO SAY HOW MANY OF THEM WILL SURVIVE, TO BE HONEST...

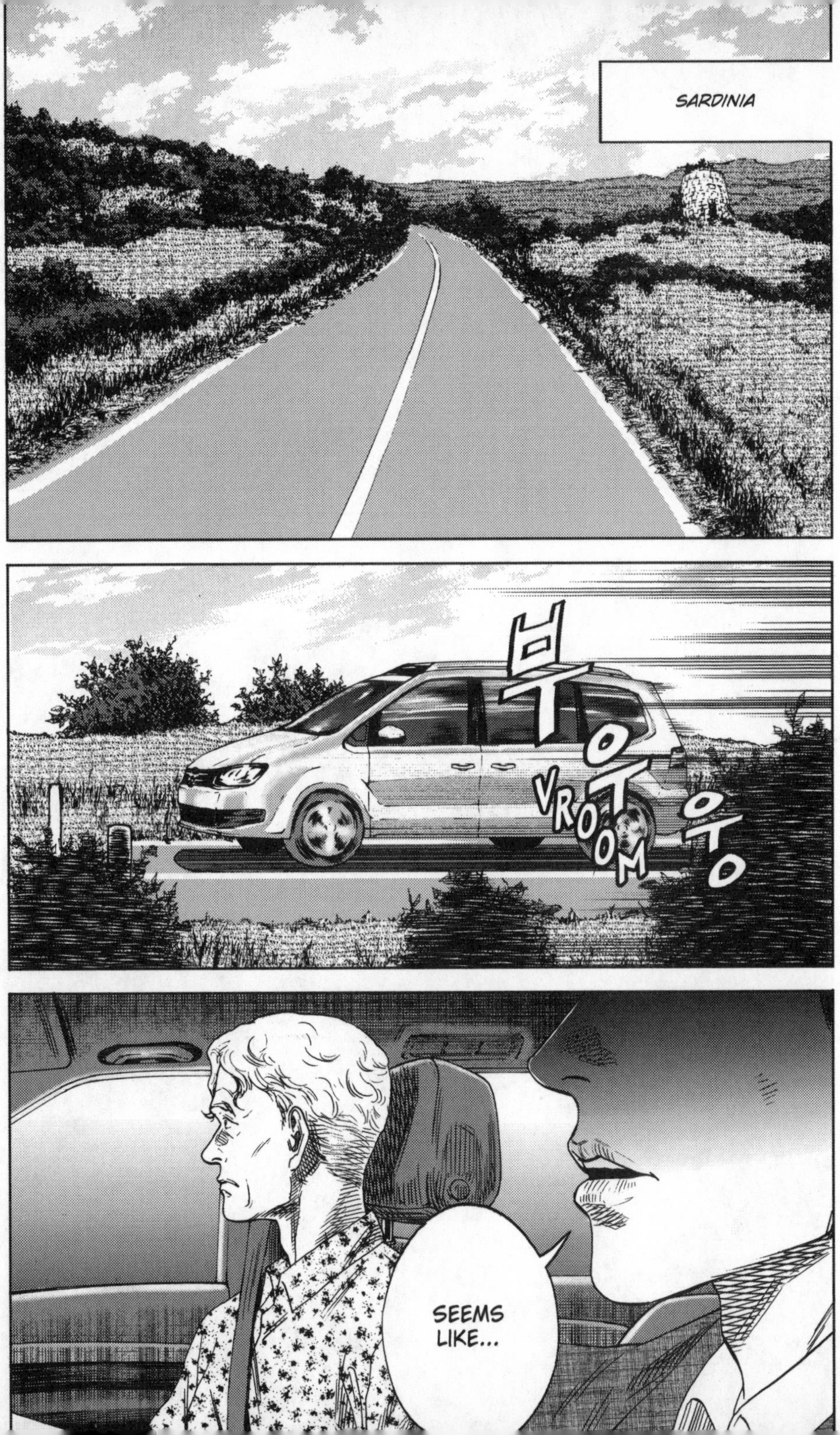
SARDINIA
VROOM
SEEMS LIKE...

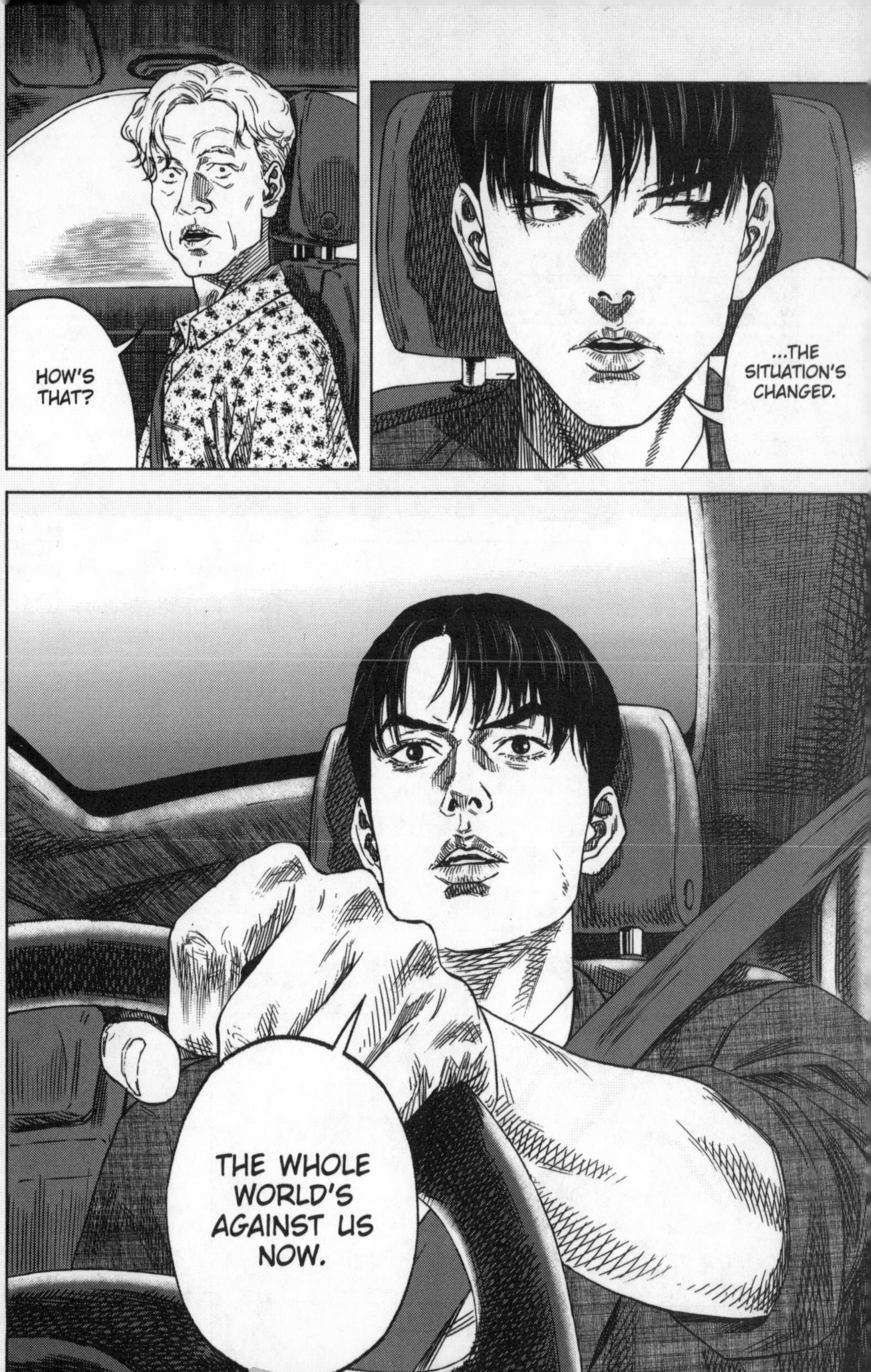
...THE SITUATION'S CHANGED.
HOW'S THAT?
THE WHOLE WORLD'S AGAINST US NOW.

KING OF EDEN

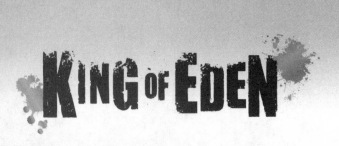

KING OF EDEN

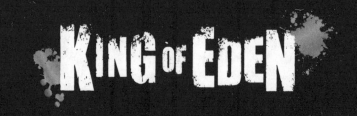

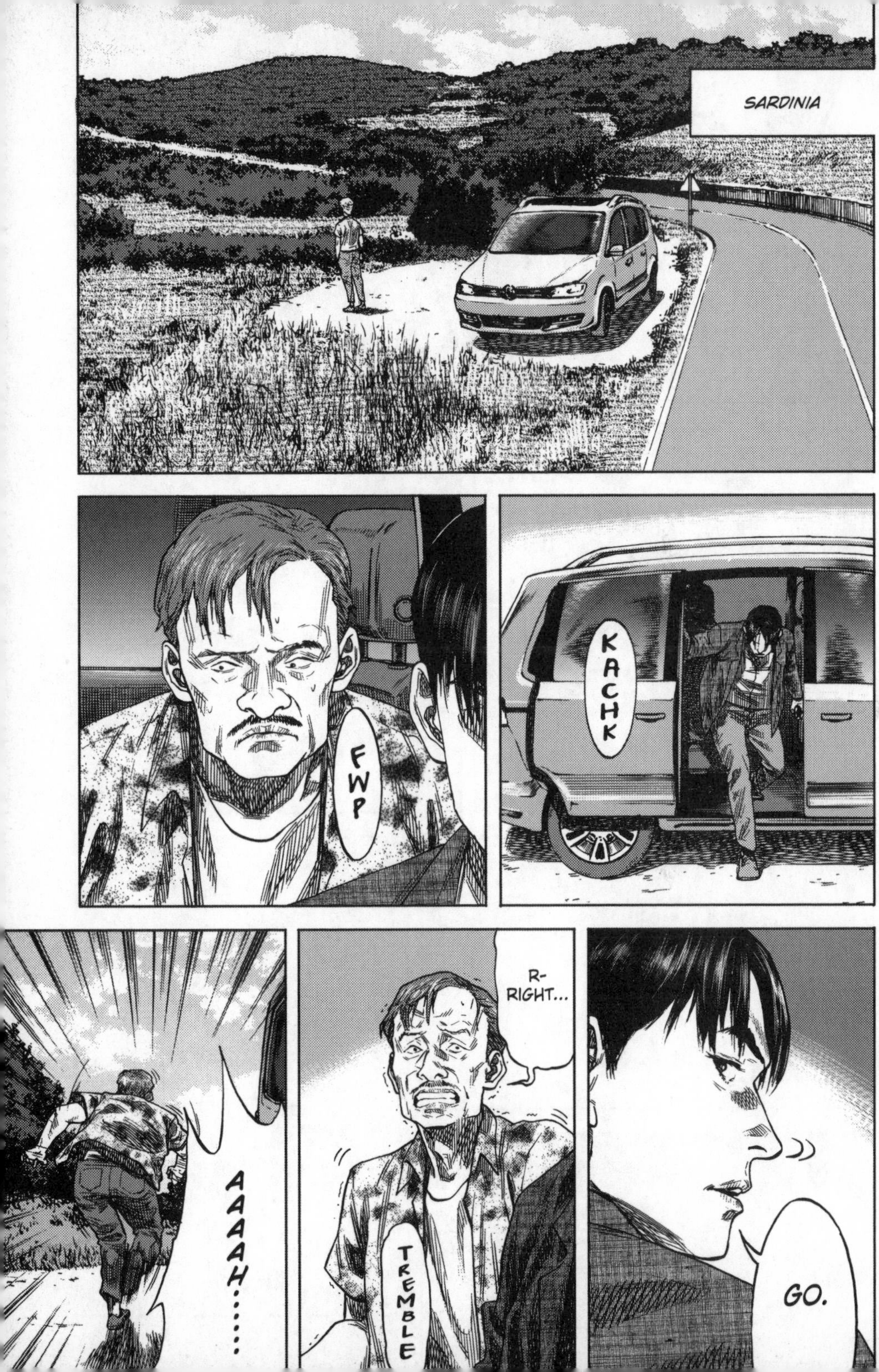
SARDINIA
KACHK
FWP
GO.
R-RIGHT...
TREMBLE
AAAAH......

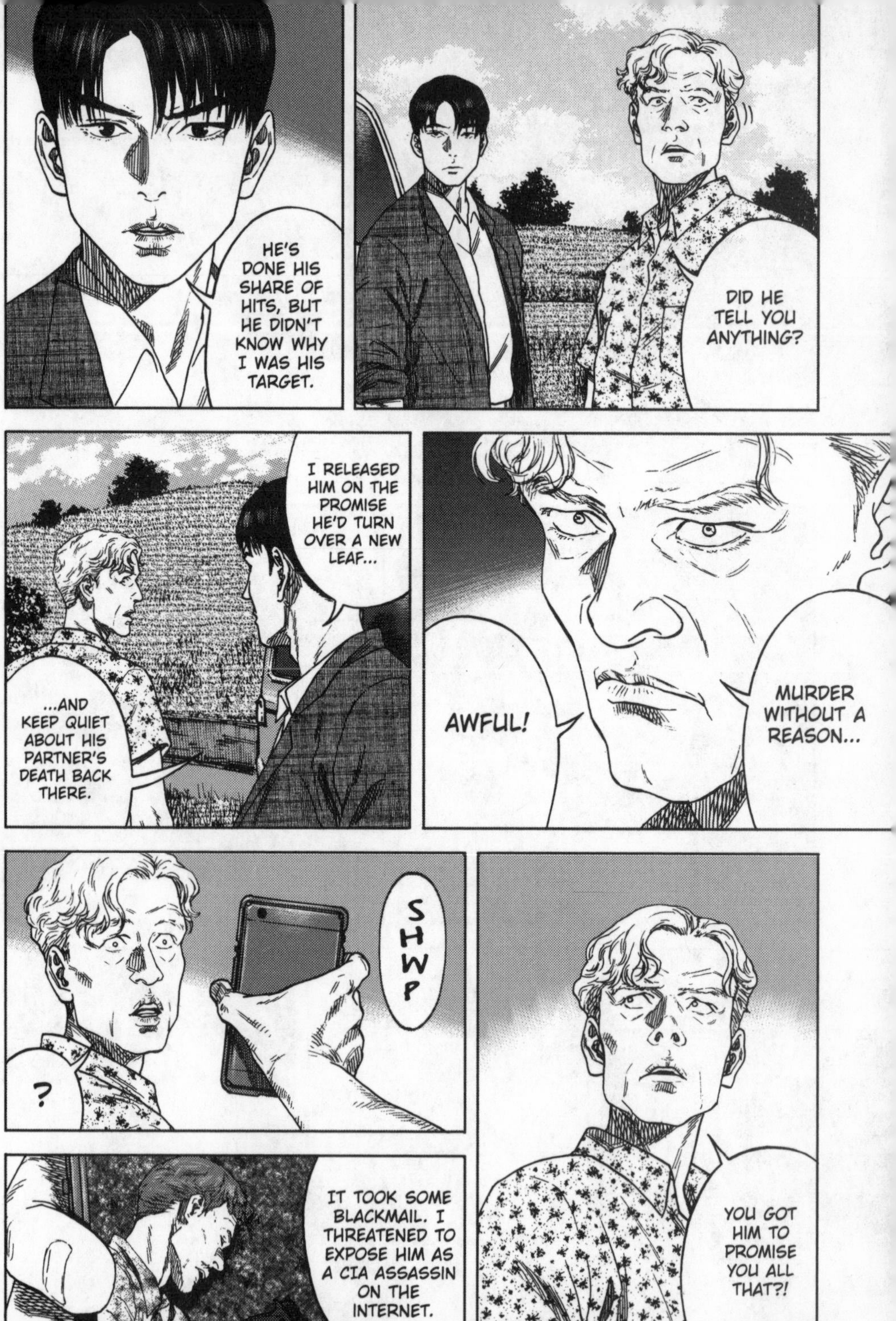
DID HE TELL YOU ANYTHING?
HE'S DONE HIS SHARE OF HITS, BUT HE DIDN'T KNOW WHY I WAS HIS TARGET.
MURDER WITHOUT A REASON...
AWFUL!
I RELEASED HIM ON THE PROMISE HE'D TURN OVER A NEW LEAF...
...AND KEEP QUIET ABOUT HIS PARTNER'S DEATH BACK THERE.
YOU GOT HIM TO PROMISE YOU ALL THAT?!
SHWP
?
IT TOOK SOME BLACKMAIL. I THREATENED TO EXPOSE HIM AS A CIA ASSASSIN ON THE INTERNET.

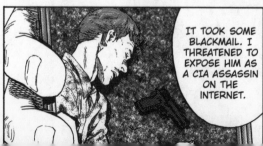

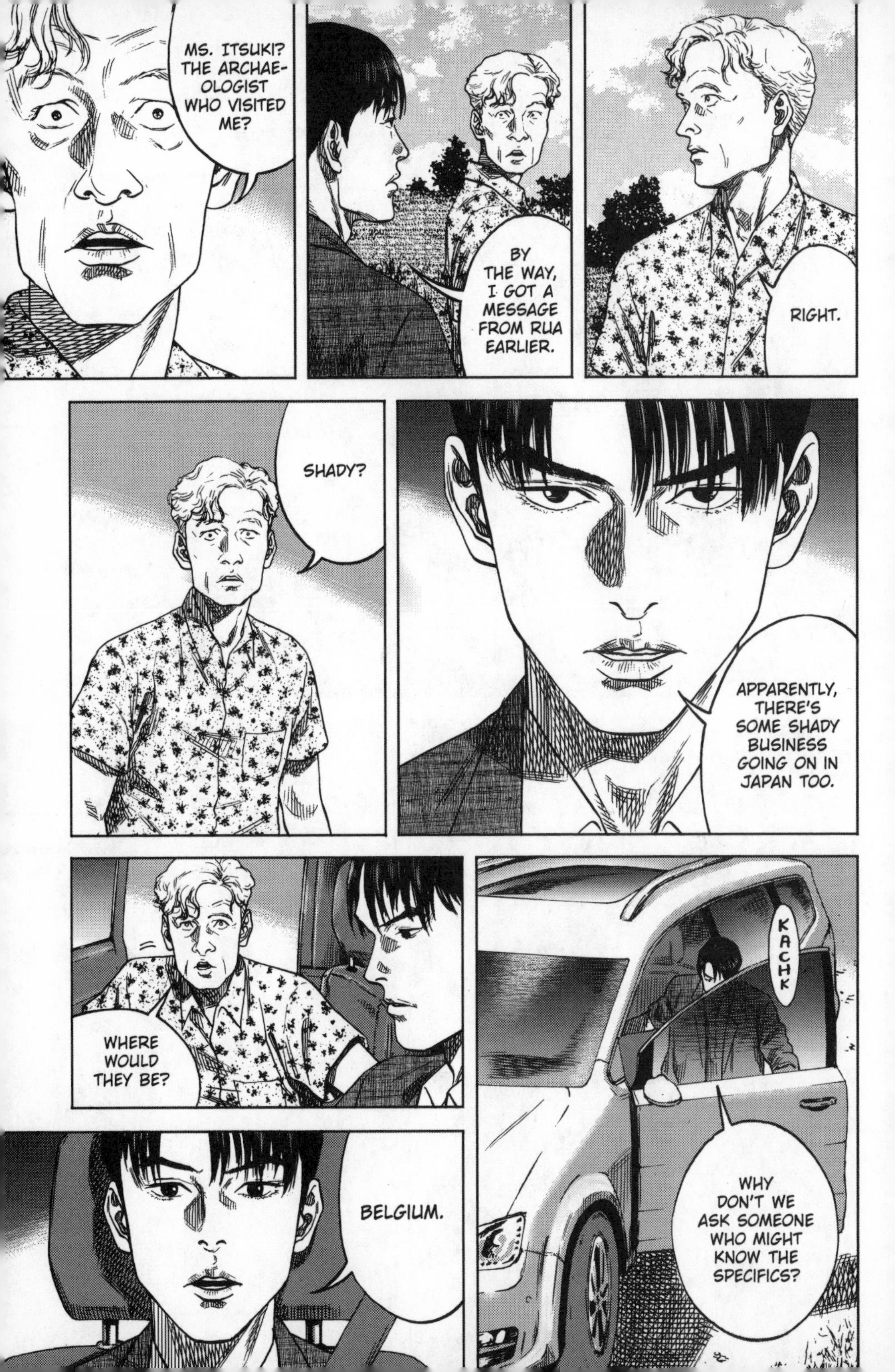
RIGHT.
BY THE WAY, I GOT A MESSAGE FROM RUA EARLIER.
MS. ITSUKI? THE ARCHAEOLOGIST WHO VISITED ME?
APPARENTLY, THERE'S SOME SHADY BUSINESS GOING ON IN JAPAN TOO.
SHADY?
KACHK
WHY DON'T WE ASK SOMEONE WHO MIGHT KNOW THE SPECIFICS?
WHERE WOULD THEY BE?
BELGIUM.

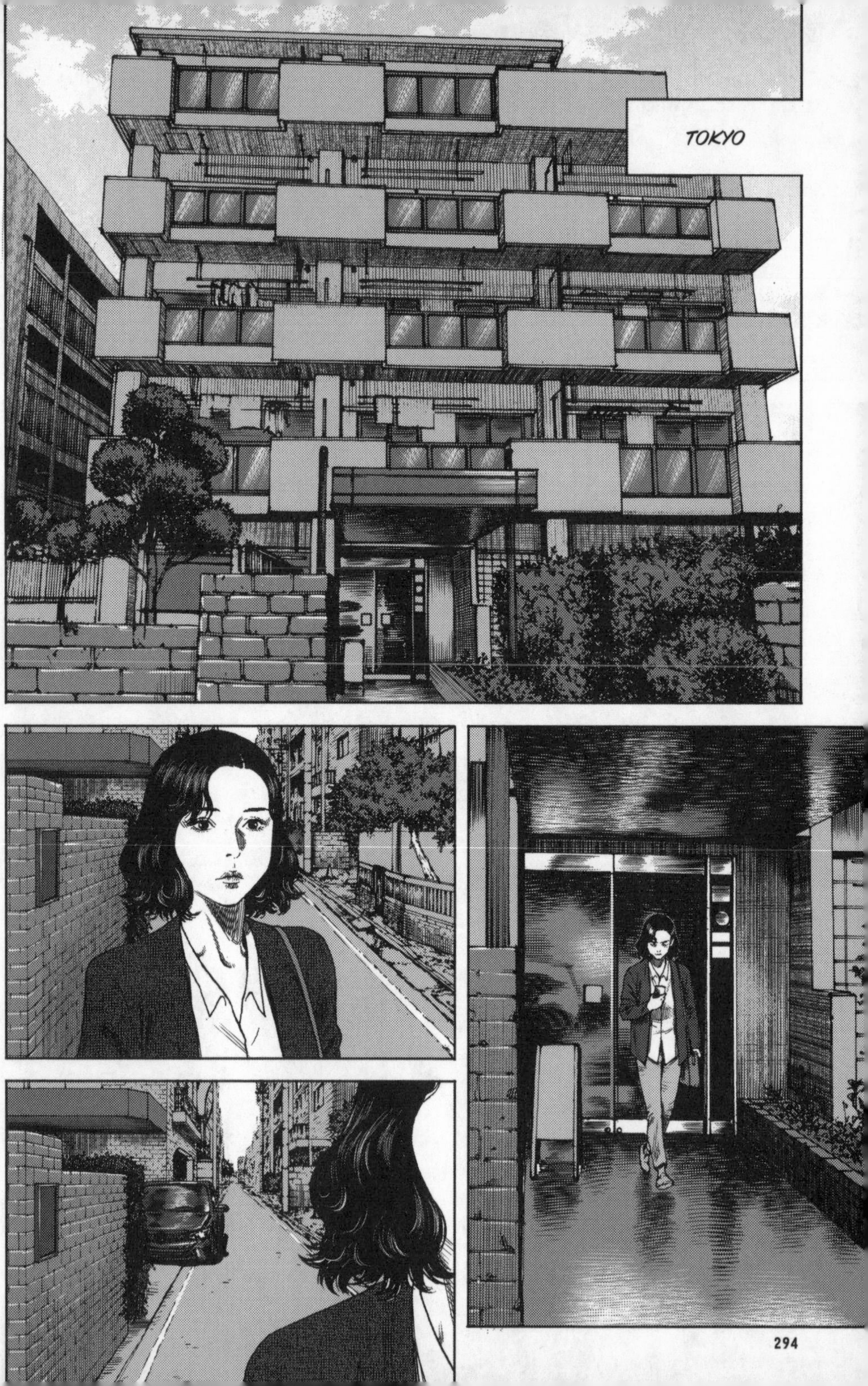
TOKYO

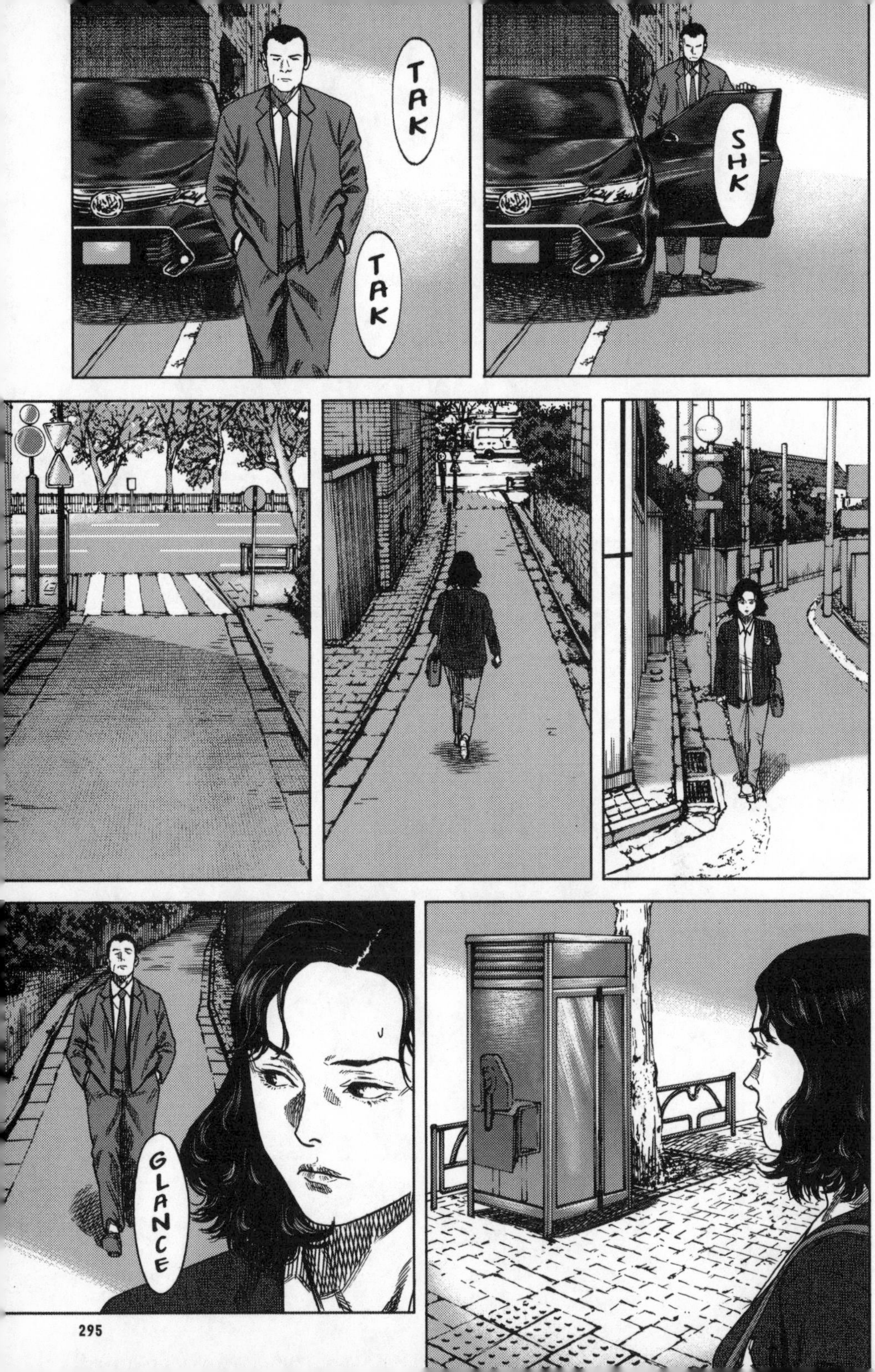
SHK
TAK
TAK
GLANCE

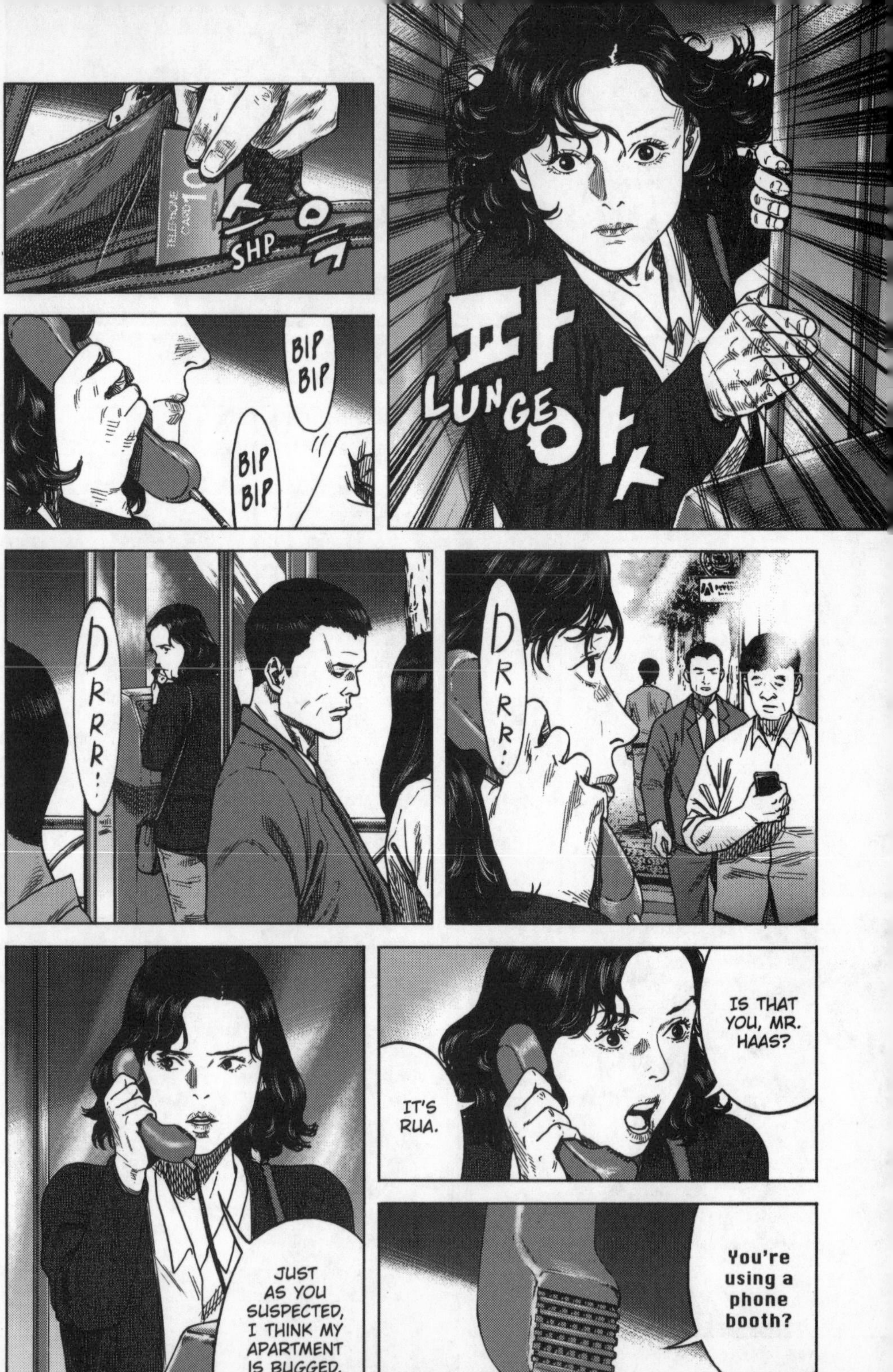

파아
LUNGE
스윽
SHP
BIP BIP
BIP BIP
Drrr..
Drrr..
IS THAT YOU, MR. HAAS?
IT'S RUA.
You're using a phone booth?
JUST AS YOU SUSPECTED, I THINK MY APARTMENT IS BUGGED.

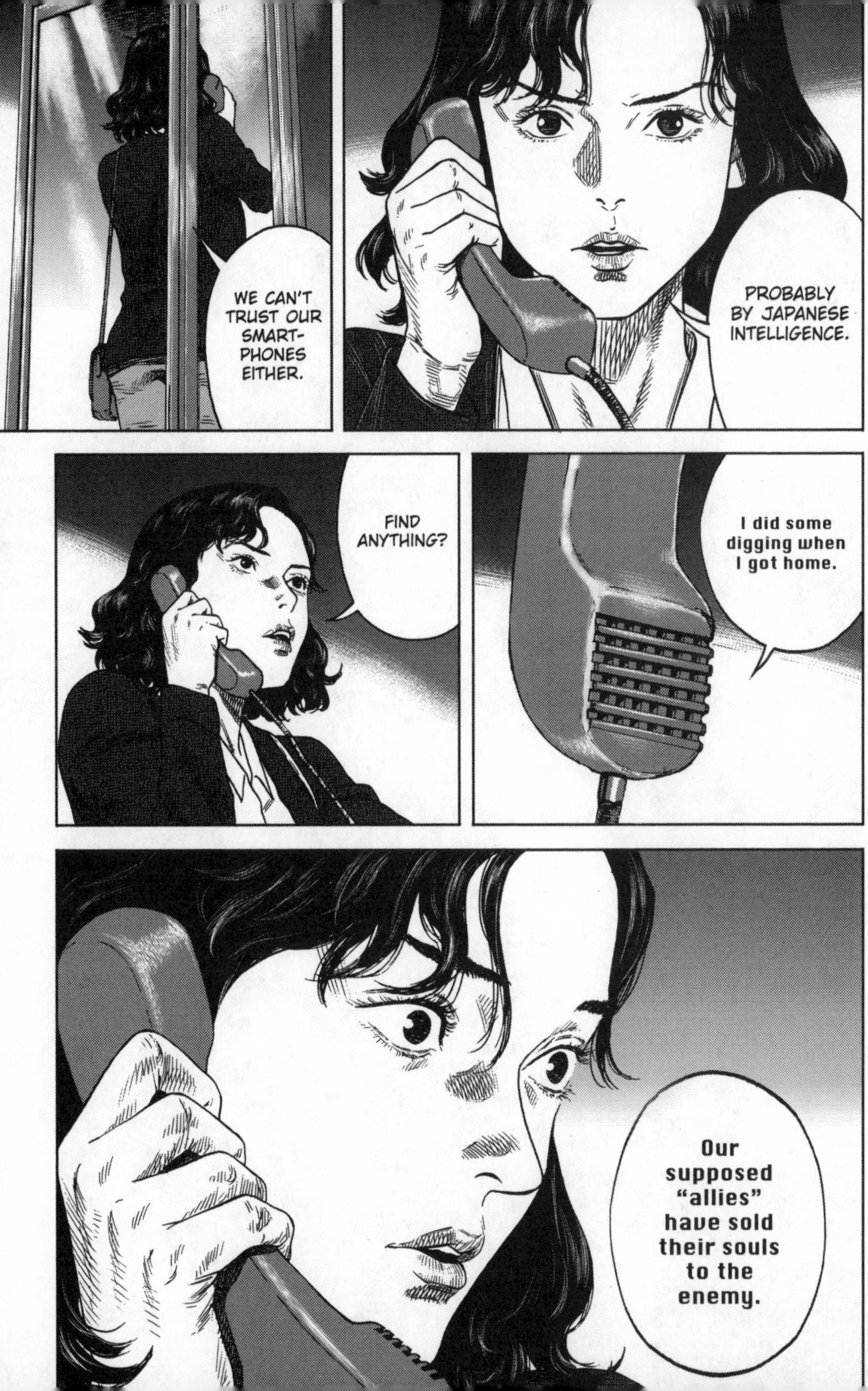
PROBABLY BY JAPANESE INTELLIGENCE.
WE CAN'T TRUST OUR SMART-PHONES EITHER.
I did some digging when I got home.
FIND ANYTHING?
Our supposed "allies" have sold their souls to the enemy.

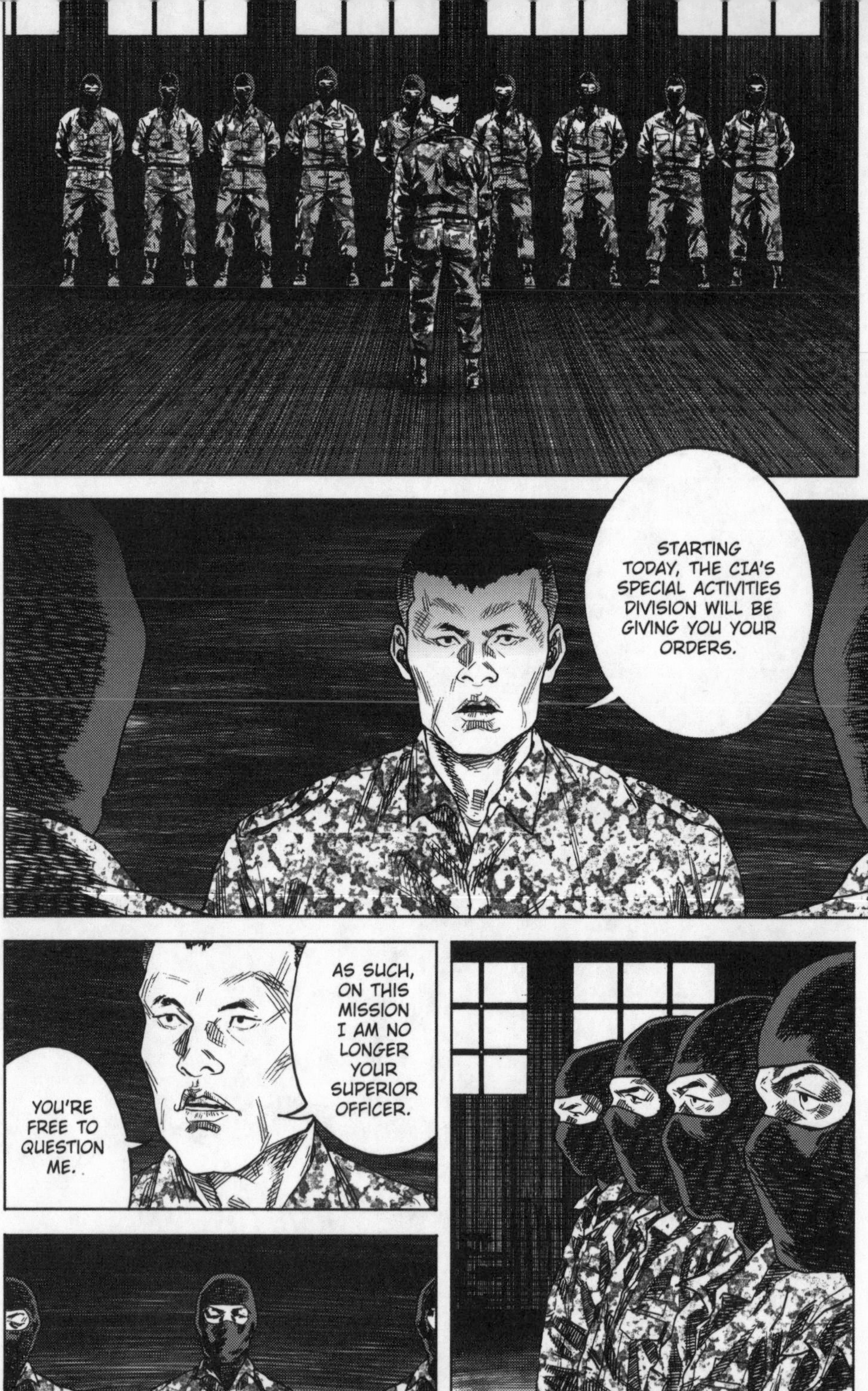
STARTING TODAY, THE CIA'S SPECIAL ACTIVITIES DIVISION WILL BE GIVING YOU YOUR ORDERS.
AS SUCH, ON THIS MISSION I AM NO LONGER YOUR SUPERIOR OFFICER.
YOU'RE FREE TO QUESTION ME.

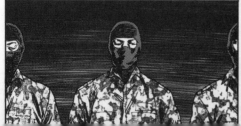

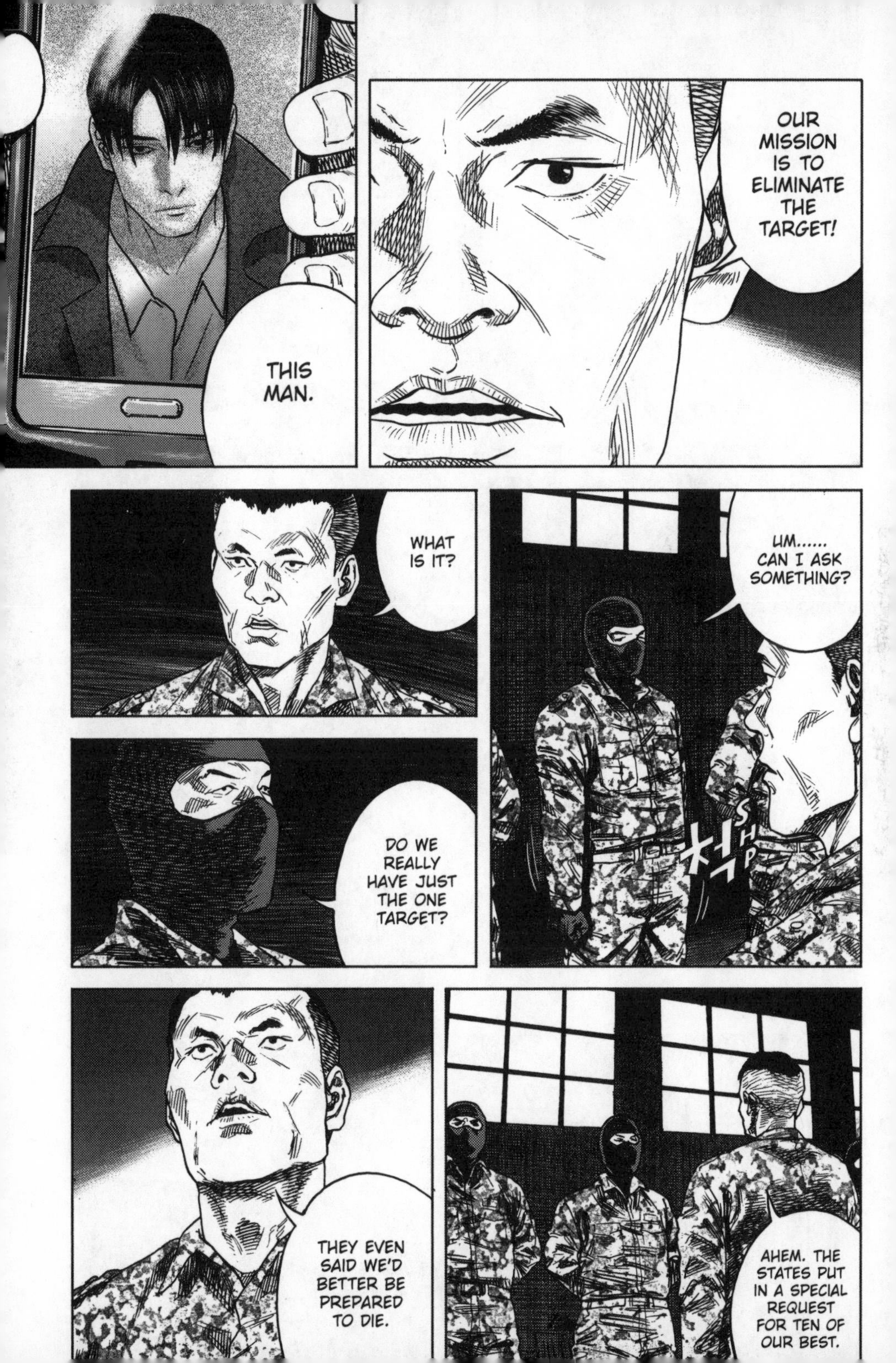
OUR MISSION IS TO ELIMINATE THE TARGET!
THIS MAN.
UM...... CAN I ASK SOMETHING?
척
SHP
WHAT IS IT?
DO WE REALLY HAVE JUST THE ONE TARGET?
AHEM. THE STATES PUT IN A SPECIAL REQUEST FOR TEN OF OUR BEST.
THEY EVEN SAID WE'D BETTER BE PREPARED TO DIE.

AND YEAH—
ALL TO TAKE
OUT JUST
ONE MAN!

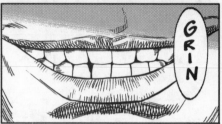

GRIN

CLENCH

NOW LET'S
SHOW THOSE
FUCKING
YANKEES
WHAT KOREA'S
ROKNSWF IS
MADE OF!

BRUSSELS, BELGIUM

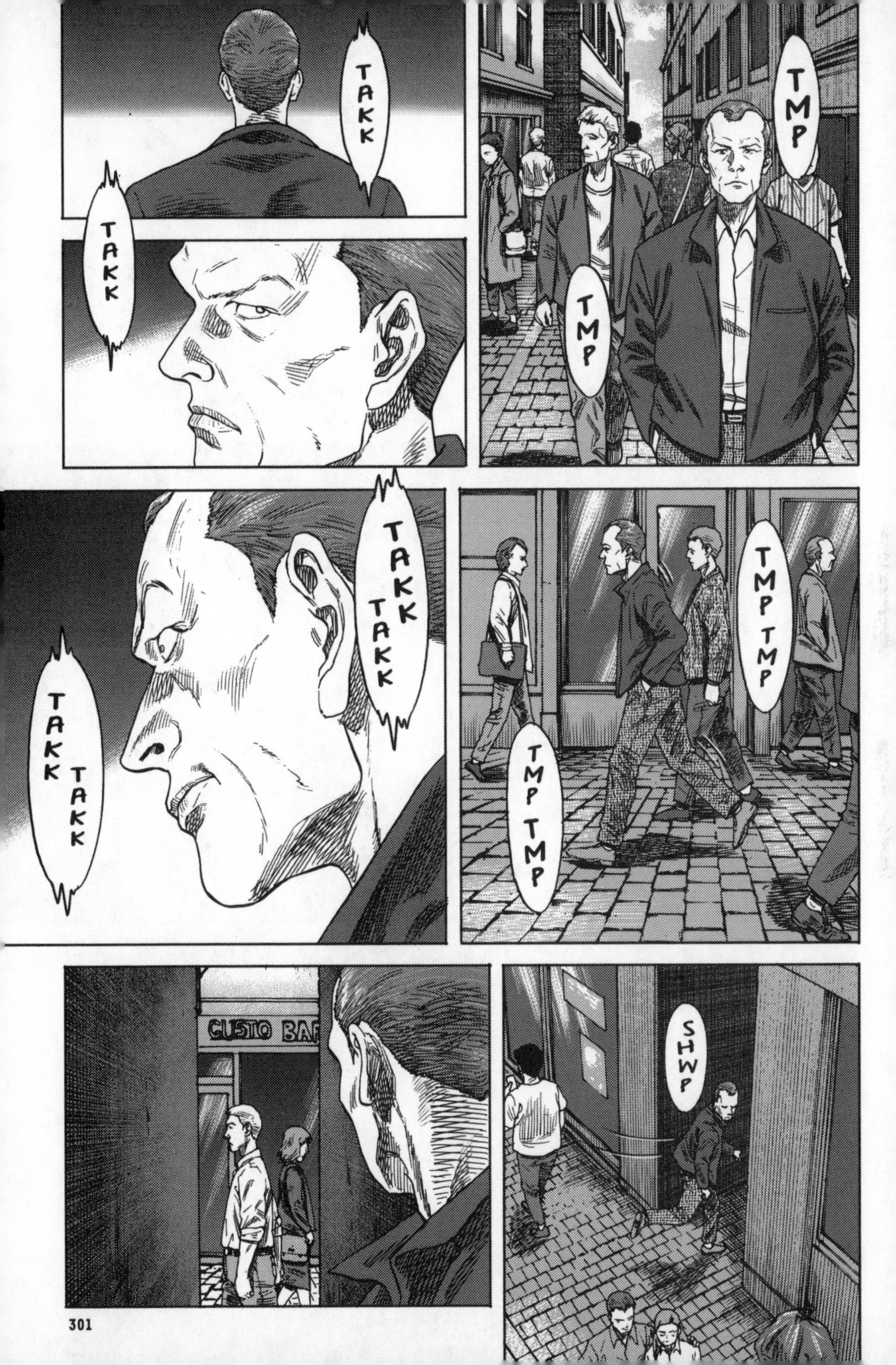
TMP
TMP
TAKK
TAKK
TMP TMP
TMP TMP
TAKK TAKK
TAKK TAKK
SHWP
GUSTO BA

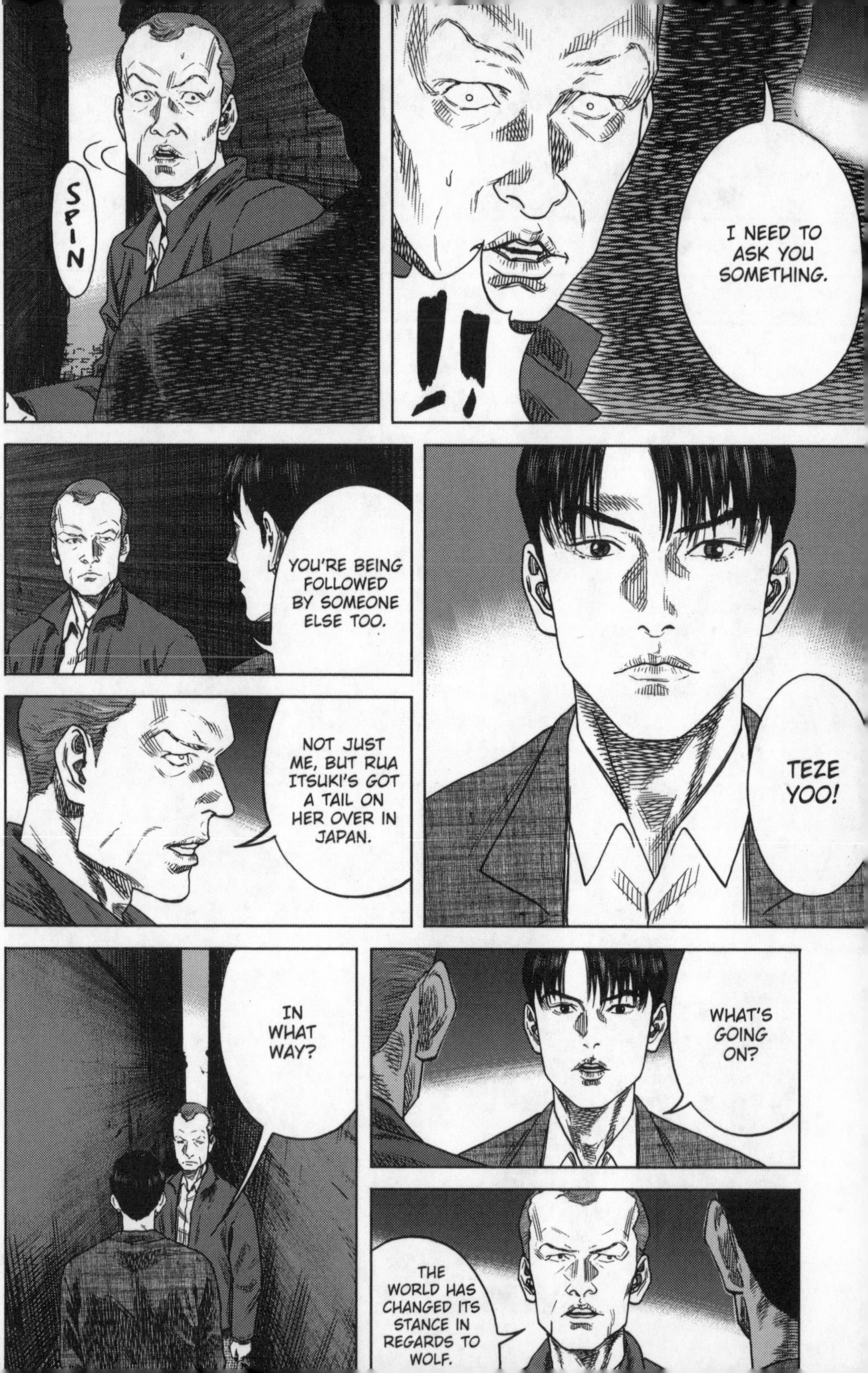
I NEED TO ASK YOU SOMETHING.
!!
SPIN
TEZE YOO!
YOU'RE BEING FOLLOWED BY SOMEONE ELSE TOO.
NOT JUST ME, BUT RUA ITSUKI'S GOT A TAIL ON HER OVER IN JAPAN.
WHAT'S GOING ON?
THE WORLD HAS CHANGED ITS STANCE IN REGARDS TO WOLF.
IN WHAT WAY?

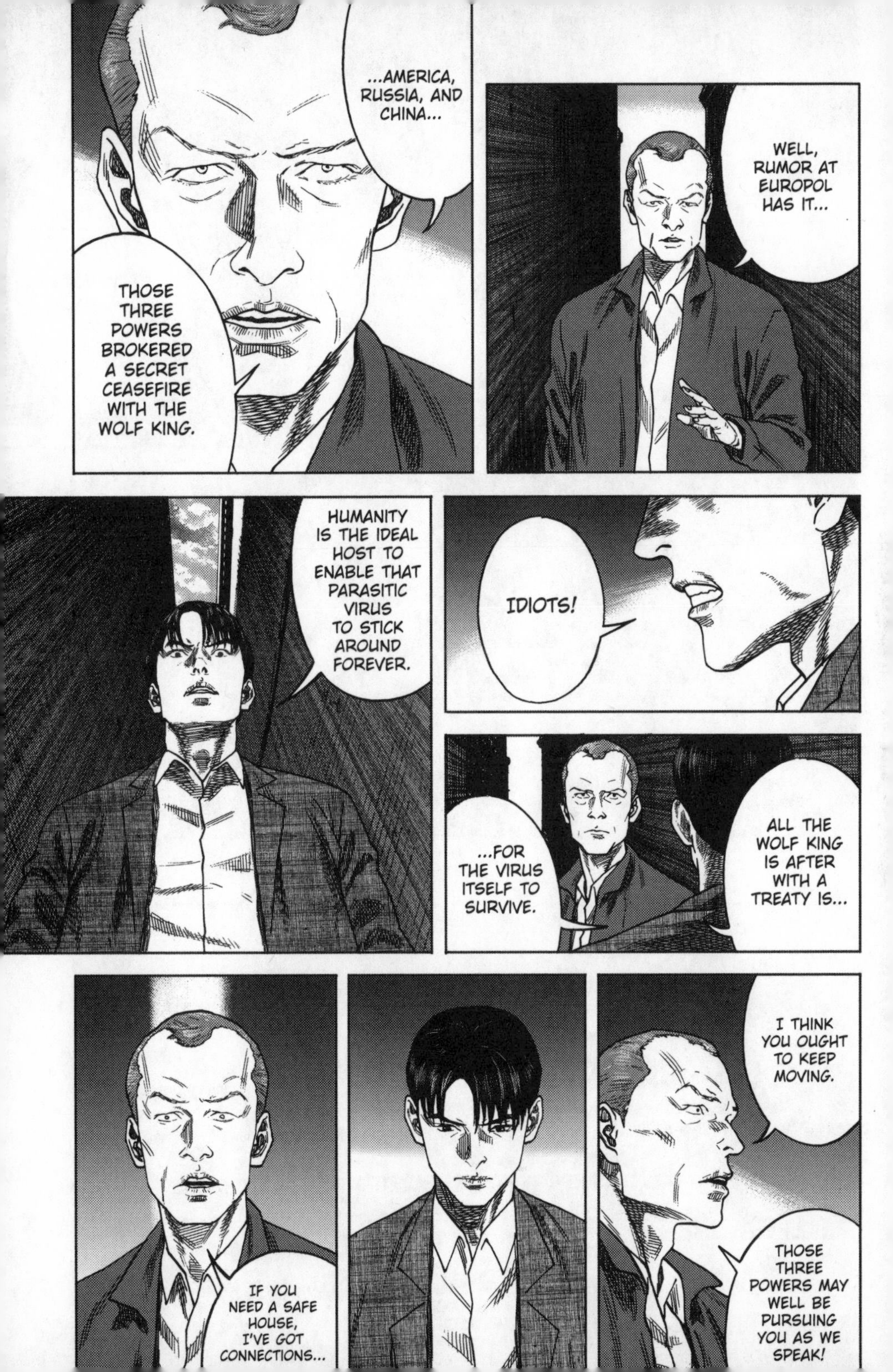
WELL, RUMOR AT EUROPOL HAS IT...
...AMERICA, RUSSIA, AND CHINA...
THOSE THREE POWERS BROKERED A SECRET CEASEFIRE WITH THE WOLF KING.
IDIOTS!
ALL THE WOLF KING IS AFTER WITH A TREATY IS...
...FOR THE VIRUS ITSELF TO SURVIVE.
HUMANITY IS THE IDEAL HOST TO ENABLE THAT PARASITIC VIRUS TO STICK AROUND FOREVER.
I THINK YOU OUGHT TO KEEP MOVING.
THOSE THREE POWERS MAY WELL BE PURSUING YOU AS WE SPEAK!
IF YOU NEED A SAFE HOUSE, I'VE GOT CONNECTIONS...

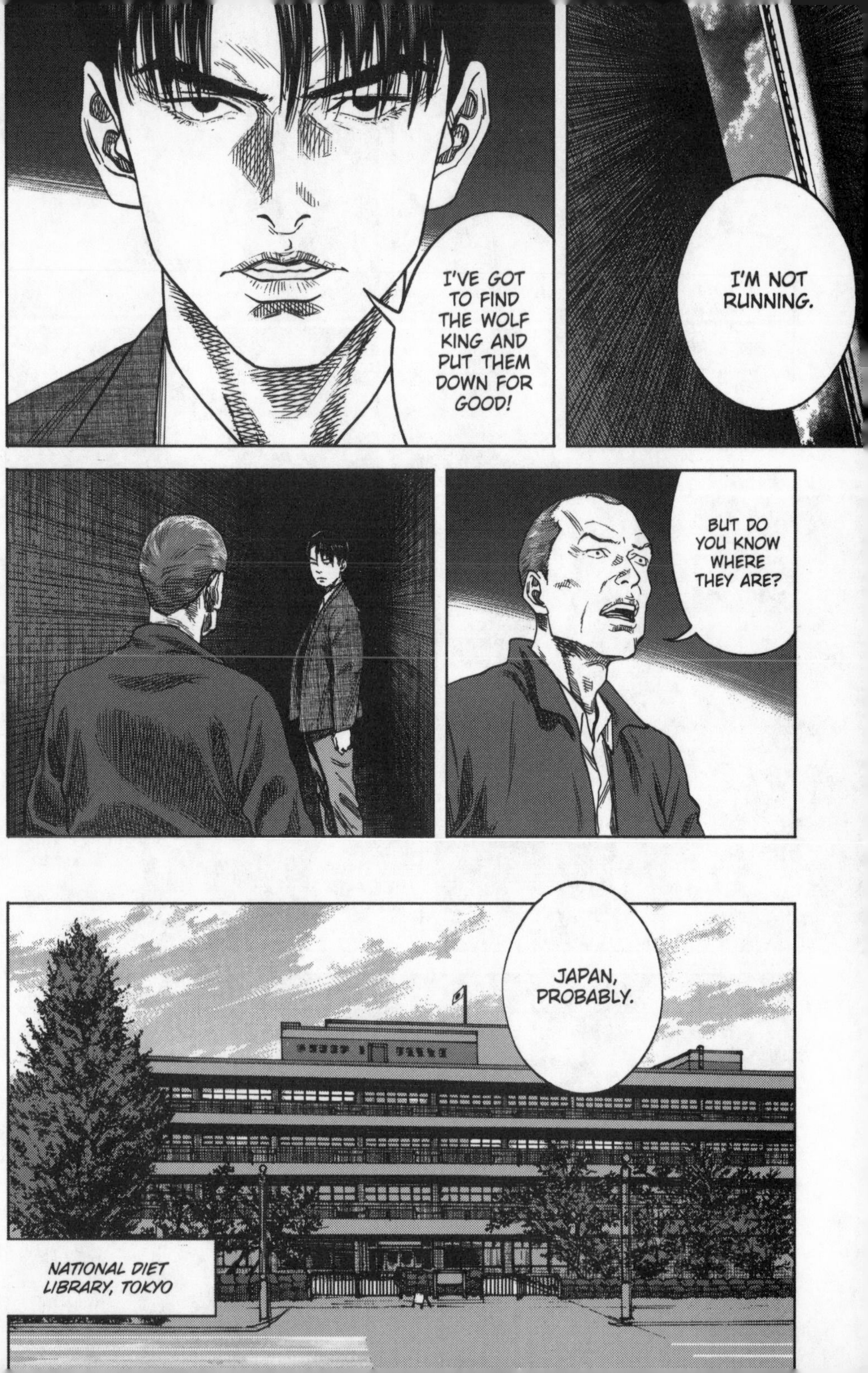
I'M NOT RUNNING.
I'VE GOT TO FIND THE WOLF KING AND PUT THEM DOWN FOR GOOD!
BUT DO YOU KNOW WHERE THEY ARE?
JAPAN, PROBABLY.
NATIONAL DIET LIBRARY, TOKYO

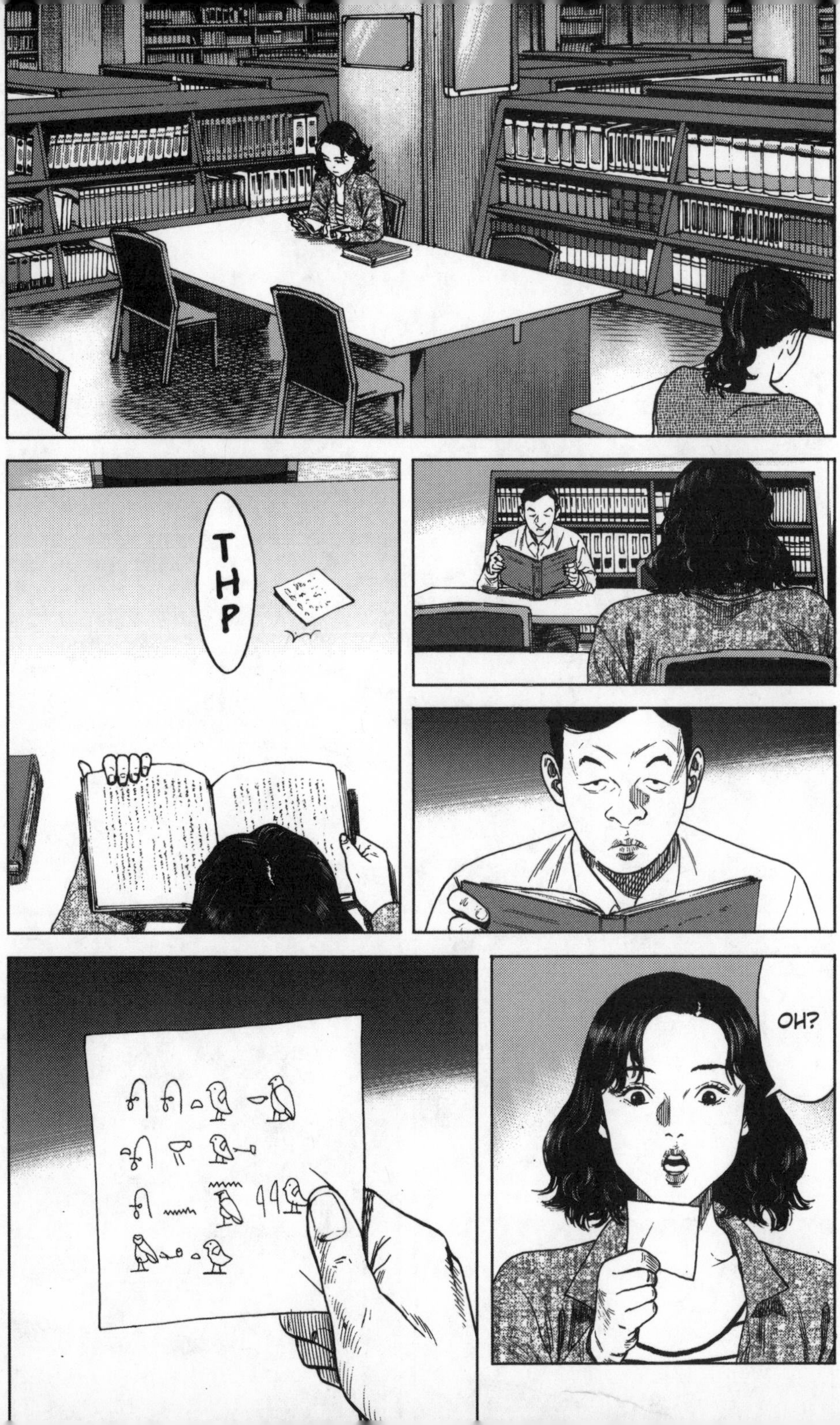
THP
OH?

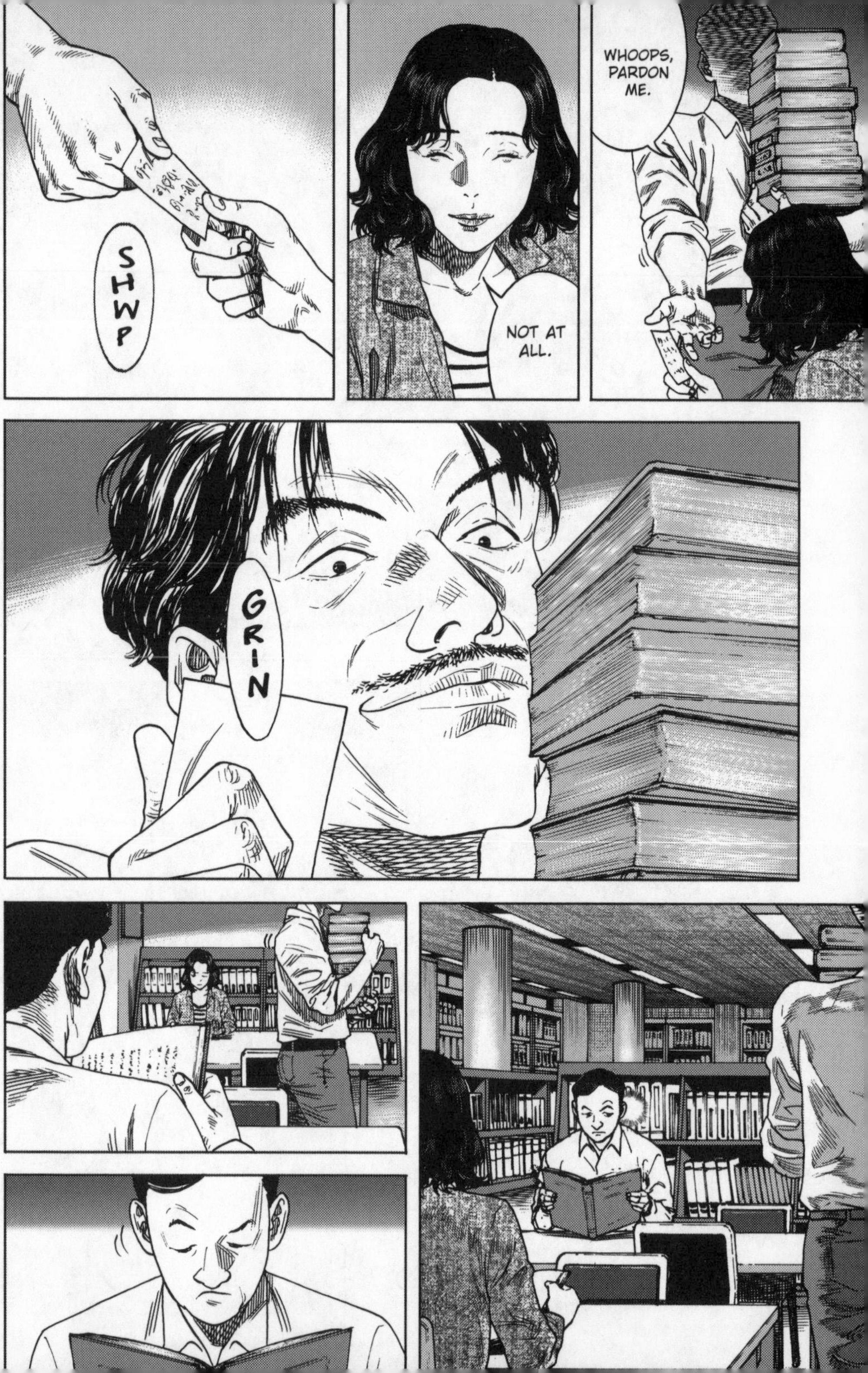
WHOOPS, PARDON ME.
NOT AT ALL.
SHWP
GRIN

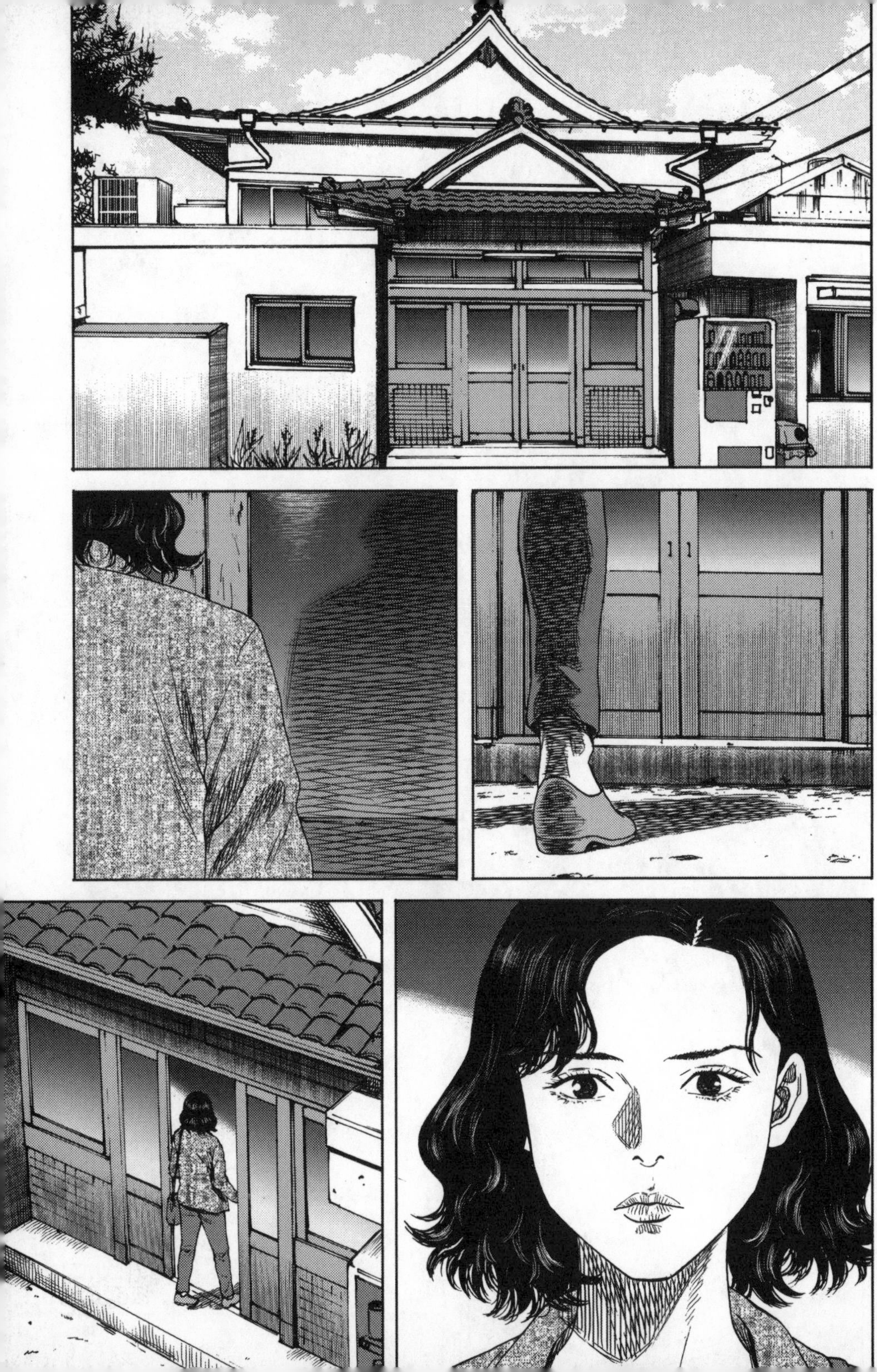

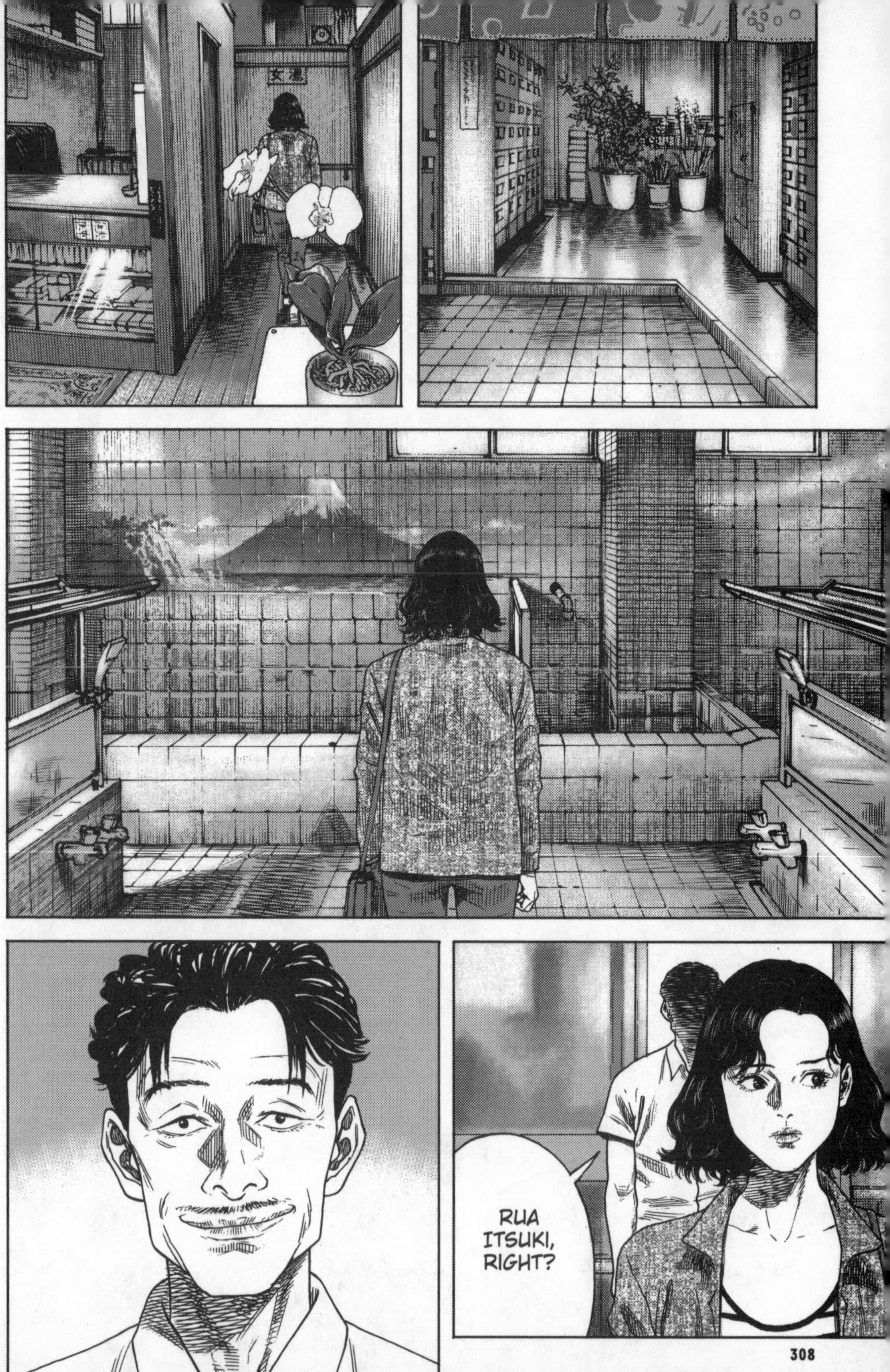
女湯
RUA ITSUKI, RIGHT?

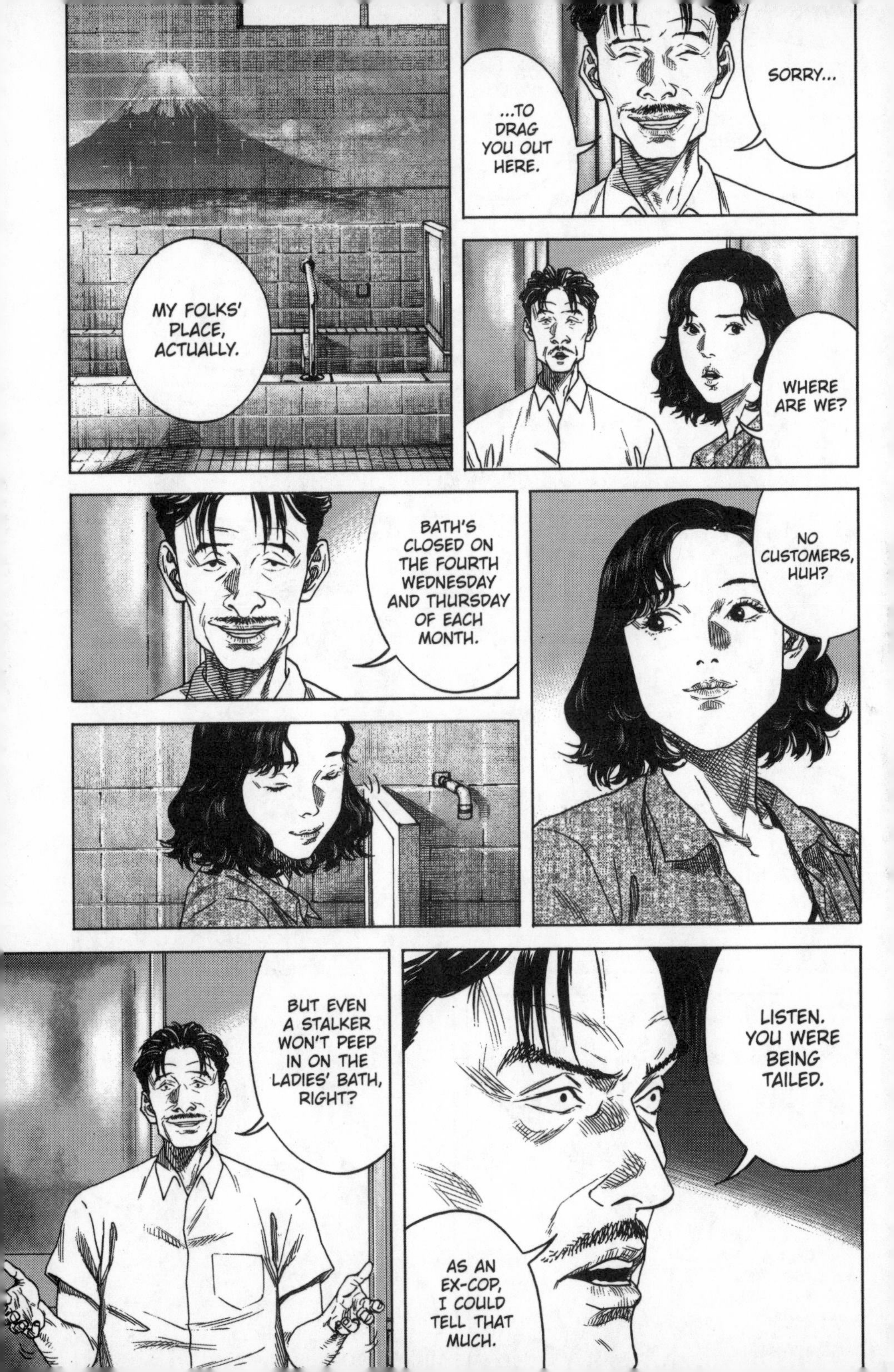
SORRY...
...TO DRAG YOU OUT HERE.
WHERE ARE WE?
MY FOLKS' PLACE, ACTUALLY.
NO CUSTOMERS, HUH?
BATH'S CLOSED ON THE FOURTH WEDNESDAY AND THURSDAY OF EACH MONTH.
LISTEN. YOU WERE BEING TAILED.
AS AN EX-COP, I COULD TELL THAT MUCH.
BUT EVEN A STALKER WON'T PEEP IN ON THE LADIES' BATH, RIGHT?

NOTE: EACH GLYPH CORRESPONDS TO A JAPANESE LETTER. "OOTSUKA" AND "TOKIWA" SPECIFY THE LOCATION, "ONNAYU" MEANS "LADIES' BATH," AND "MATSU" MEANS "WAIT."

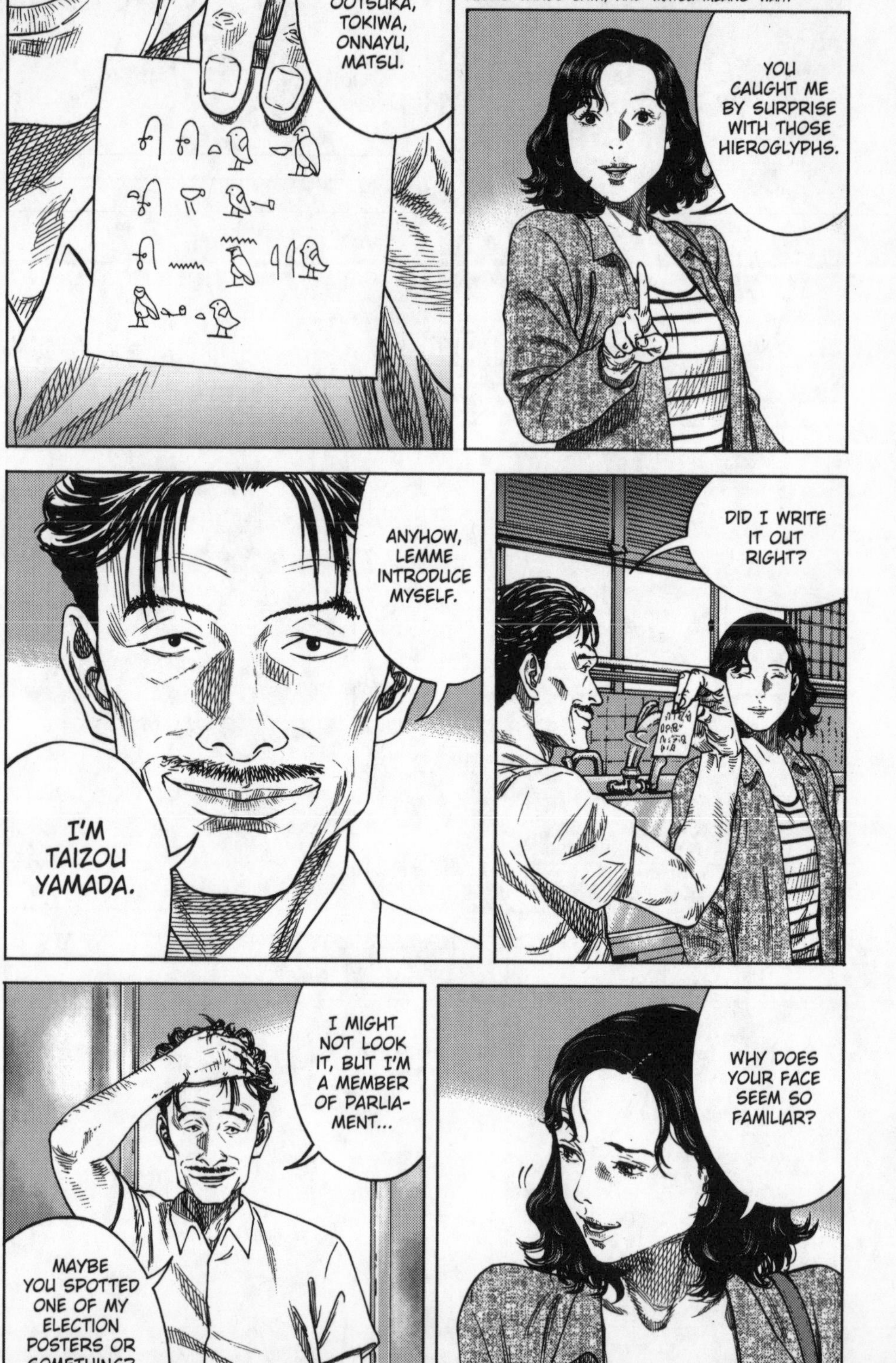
YOU CAUGHT ME BY SURPRISE WITH THOSE HIEROGLYPHS.
OOTSUKA, TOKIWA, ONNAYU, MATSU.
DID I WRITE IT OUT RIGHT?
ANYHOW, LEMME INTRODUCE MYSELF.
I'M TAIZOU YAMADA.
WHY DOES YOUR FACE SEEM SO FAMILIAR?
I MIGHT NOT LOOK IT, BUT I'M A MEMBER OF PARLIA-MENT...
MAYBE YOU SPOTTED ONE OF MY ELECTION POSTERS OR SOMETHING?

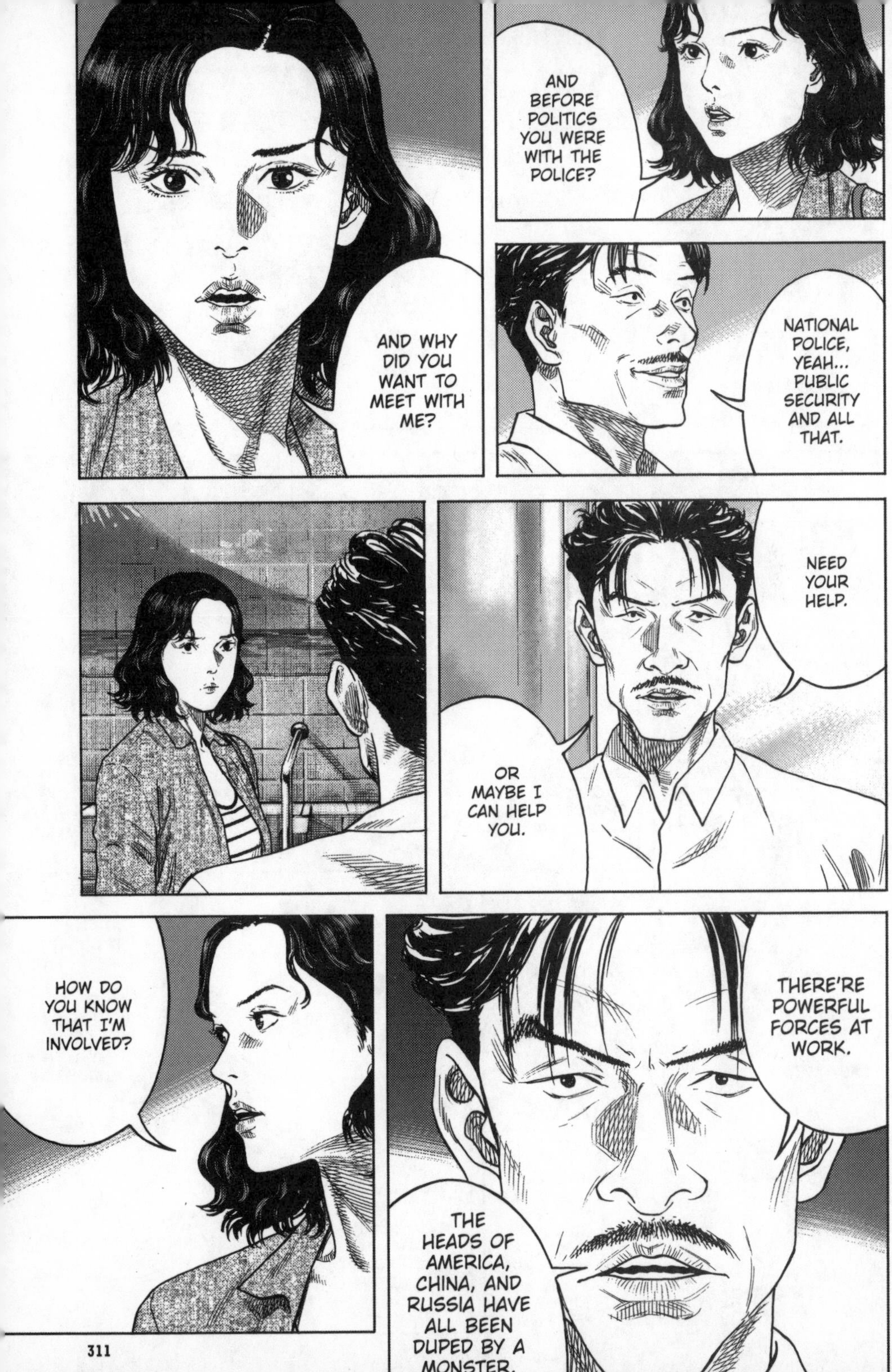
AND BEFORE POLITICS YOU WERE WITH THE POLICE?
NATIONAL POLICE, YEAH... PUBLIC SECURITY AND ALL THAT.
AND WHY DID YOU WANT TO MEET WITH ME?
NEED YOUR HELP.
OR MAYBE I CAN HELP YOU.
THERE'RE POWERFUL FORCES AT WORK.
THE HEADS OF AMERICA, CHINA, AND RUSSIA HAVE ALL BEEN DUPED BY A MONSTER.
HOW DO YOU KNOW THAT I'M INVOLVED?

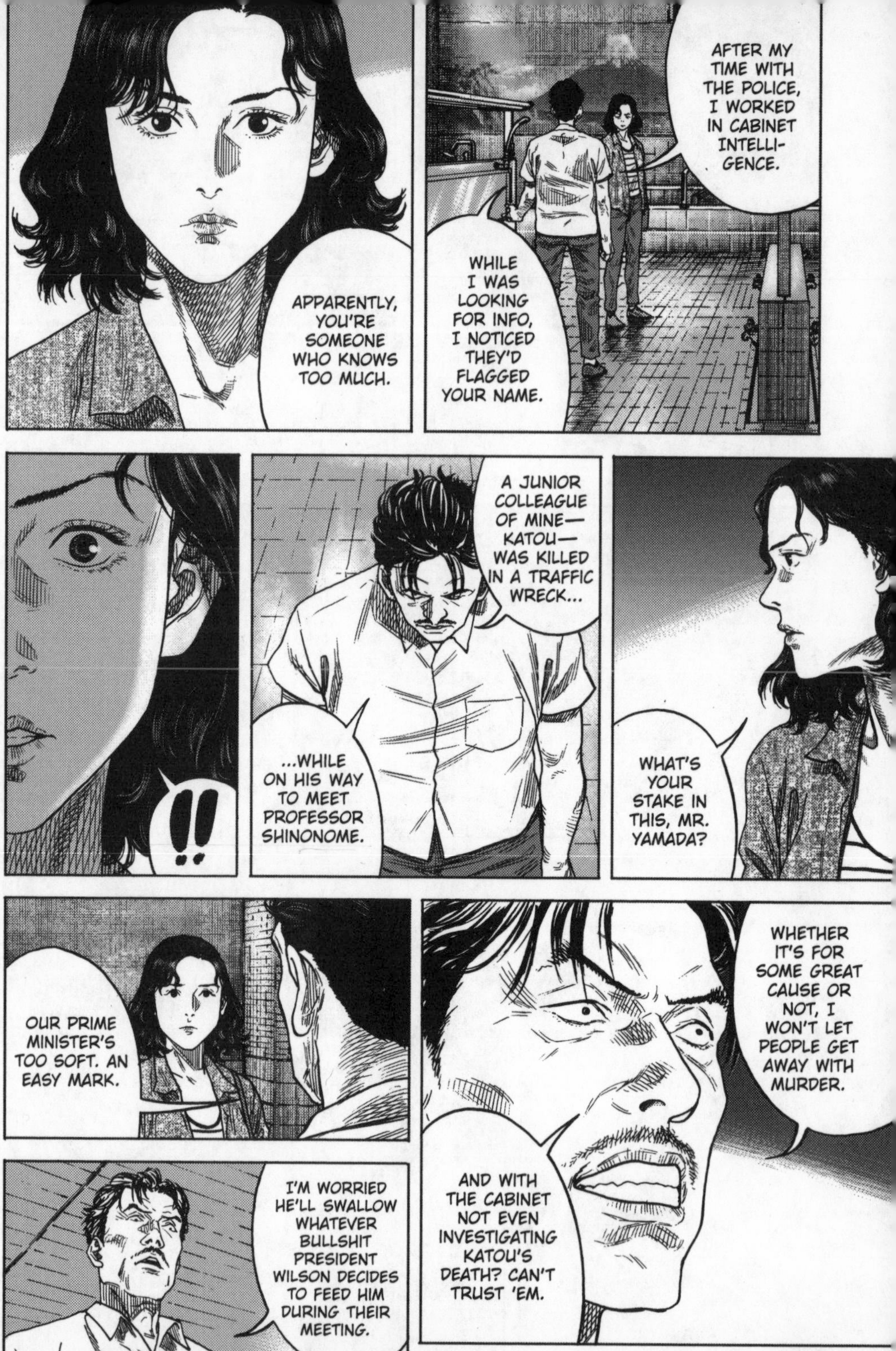
AFTER MY TIME WITH THE POLICE, I WORKED IN CABINET INTELLI-GENCE.
WHILE I WAS LOOKING FOR INFO, I NOTICED THEY'D FLAGGED YOUR NAME.
APPARENTLY, YOU'RE SOMEONE WHO KNOWS TOO MUCH.
WHAT'S YOUR STAKE IN THIS, MR. YAMADA?
A JUNIOR COLLEAGUE OF MINE—KATOU—WAS KILLED IN A TRAFFIC WRECK...
...WHILE ON HIS WAY TO MEET PROFESSOR SHINONOME.
!!
WHETHER IT'S FOR SOME GREAT CAUSE OR NOT, I WON'T LET PEOPLE GET AWAY WITH MURDER.
AND WITH THE CABINET NOT EVEN INVESTIGATING KATOU'S DEATH? CAN'T TRUST 'EM.
OUR PRIME MINISTER'S TOO SOFT. AN EASY MARK.
I'M WORRIED HE'LL SWALLOW WHATEVER BULLSHIT PRESIDENT WILSON DECIDES TO FEED HIM DURING THEIR MEETING.

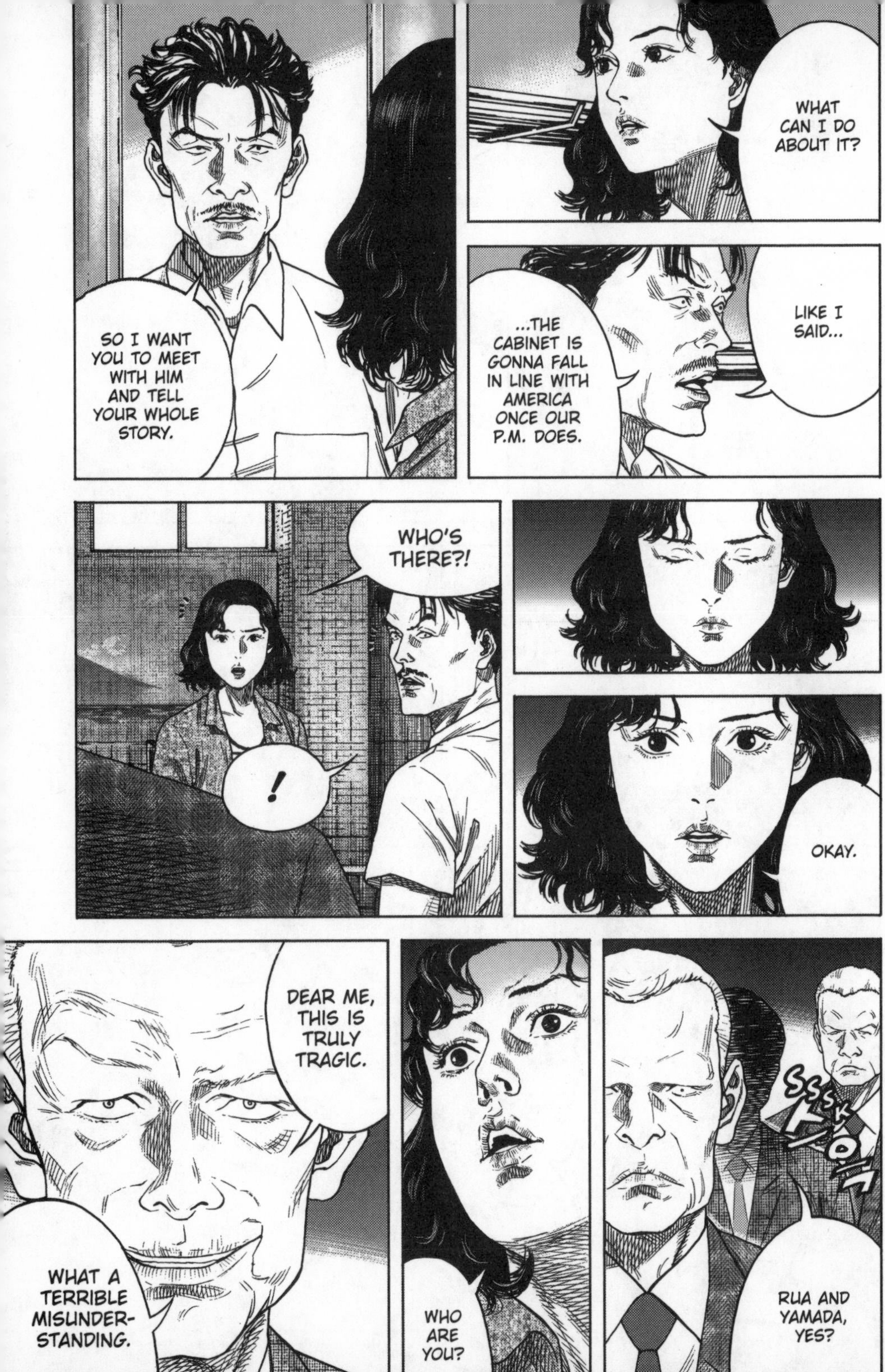
WHAT CAN I DO ABOUT IT?
LIKE I SAID...
...THE CABINET IS GONNA FALL IN LINE WITH AMERICA ONCE OUR P.M. DOES.
SO I WANT YOU TO MEET WITH HIM AND TELL YOUR WHOLE STORY.
OKAY.
WHO'S THERE?!
!
RUA AND YAMADA, YES?
WHO ARE YOU?
DEAR ME, THIS IS TRULY TRAGIC.
WHAT A TERRIBLE MISUNDERSTANDING.

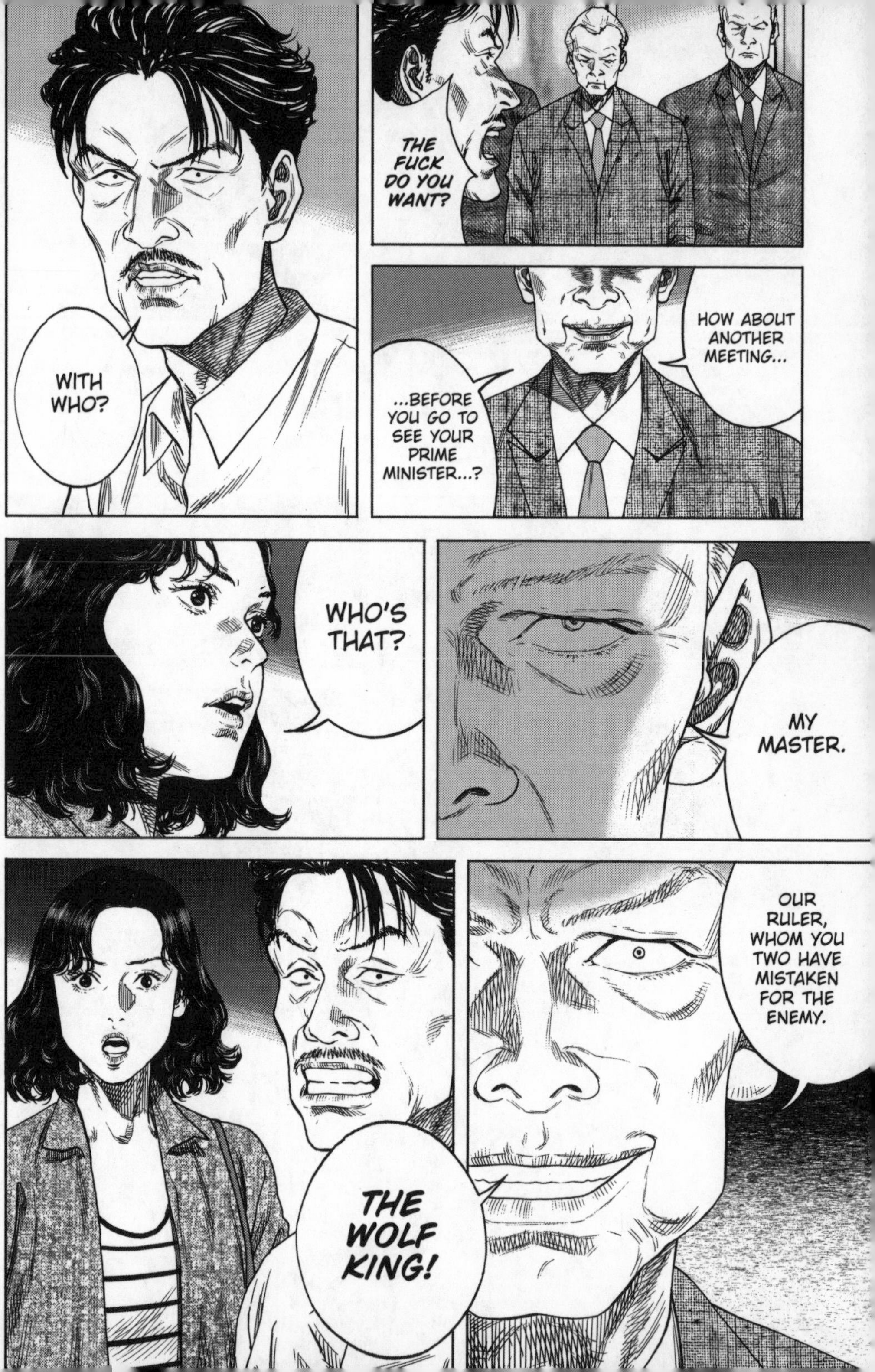
THE FUCK DO YOU WANT?
HOW ABOUT ANOTHER MEETING...
...BEFORE YOU GO TO SEE YOUR PRIME MINISTER...?
WITH WHO?
MY MASTER.
WHO'S THAT?
OUR RULER, WHOM YOU TWO HAVE MISTAKEN FOR THE ENEMY.
THE WOLF KING!

KING OF EDEN

KING OF EDEN

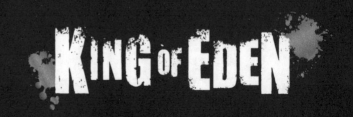

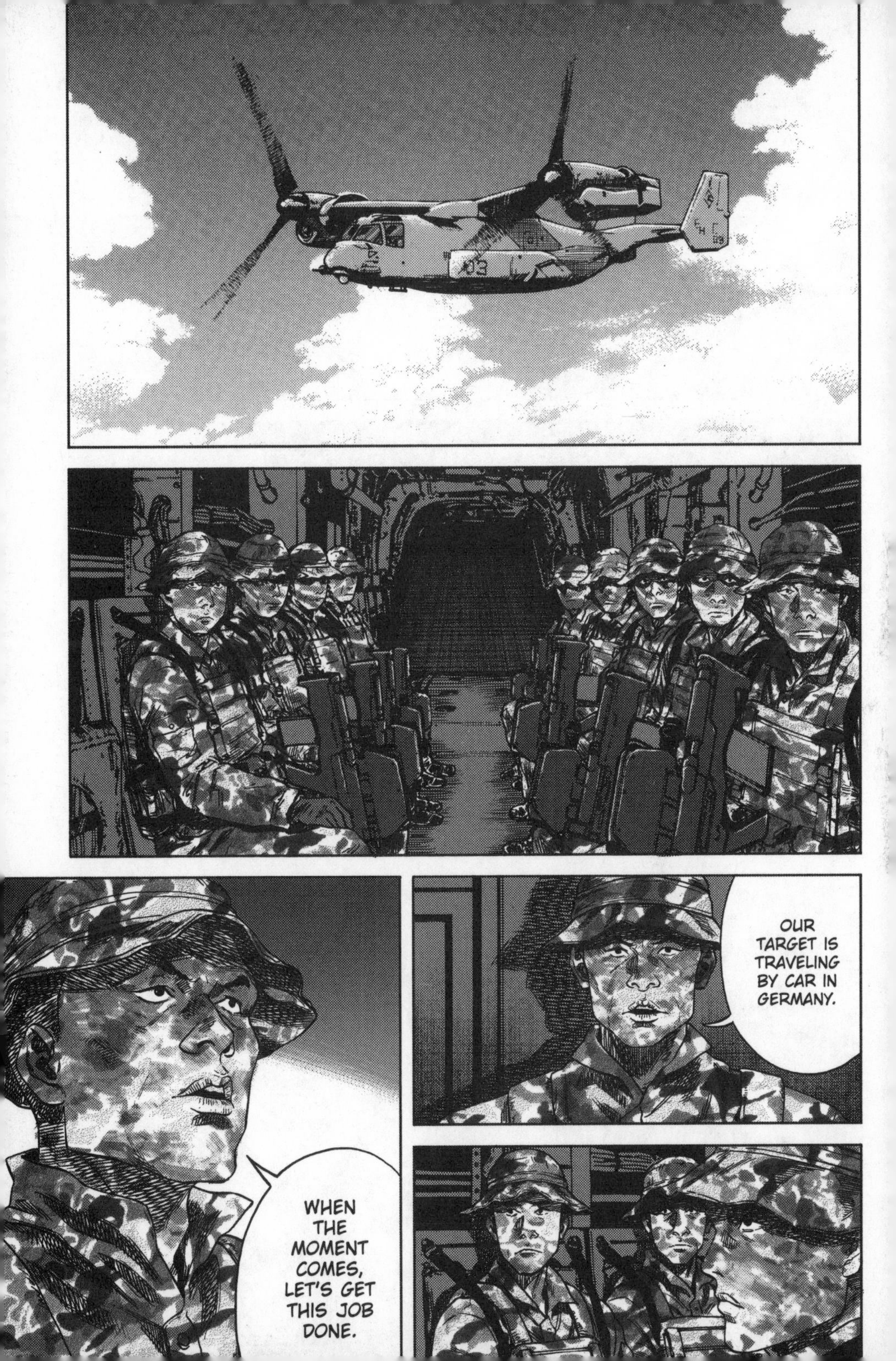
OUR TARGET IS TRAVELING BY CAR IN GERMANY.
WHEN THE MOMENT COMES, LET'S GET THIS JOB DONE.

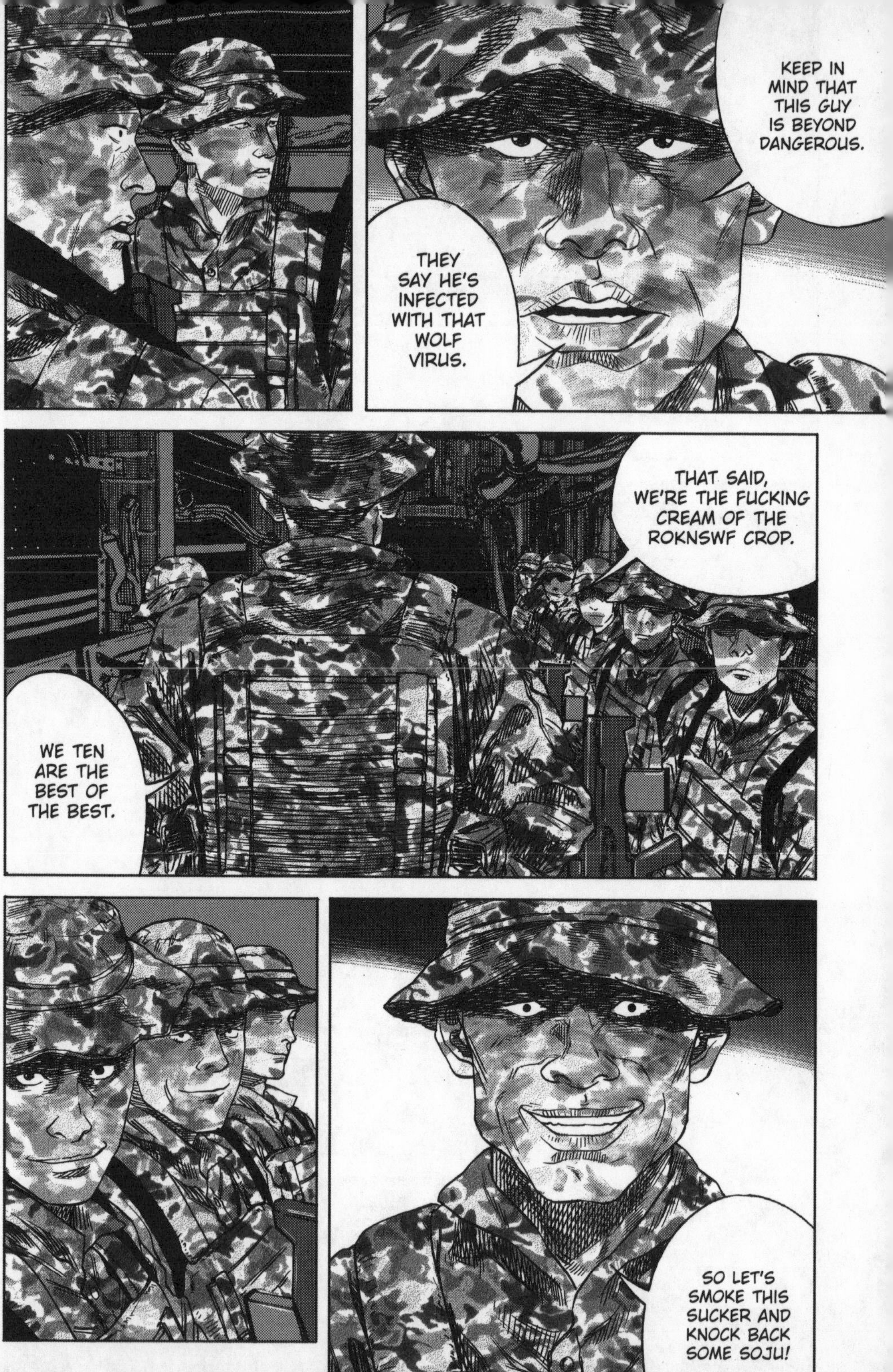
KEEP IN MIND THAT THIS GUY IS BEYOND DANGEROUS.
THEY SAY HE'S INFECTED WITH THAT WOLF VIRUS.
THAT SAID, WE'RE THE FUCKING CREAM OF THE ROKNSWF CROP.
WE TEN ARE THE BEST OF THE BEST.
SO LET'S SMOKE THIS SUCKER AND KNOCK BACK SOME SOJU!

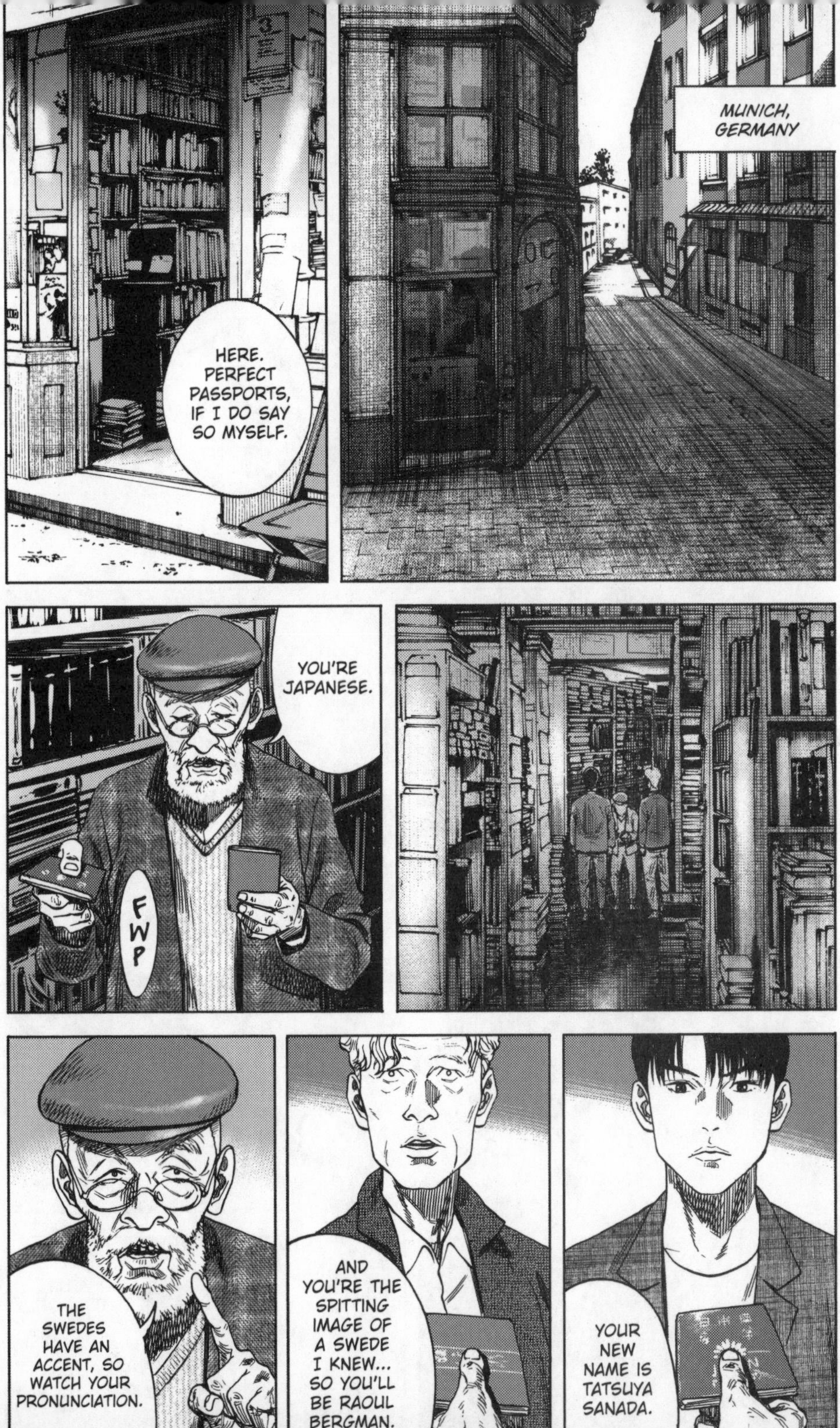
MUNICH, GERMANY
HERE. PERFECT PASSPORTS, IF I DO SAY SO MYSELF.
YOU'RE JAPANESE.
FWP
YOUR NEW NAME IS TATSUYA SANADA.
AND YOU'RE THE SPITTING IMAGE OF A SWEDE I KNEW... SO YOU'LL BE RAOUL BERGMAN.
THE SWEDES HAVE AN ACCENT, SO WATCH YOUR PRONUNCIATION.

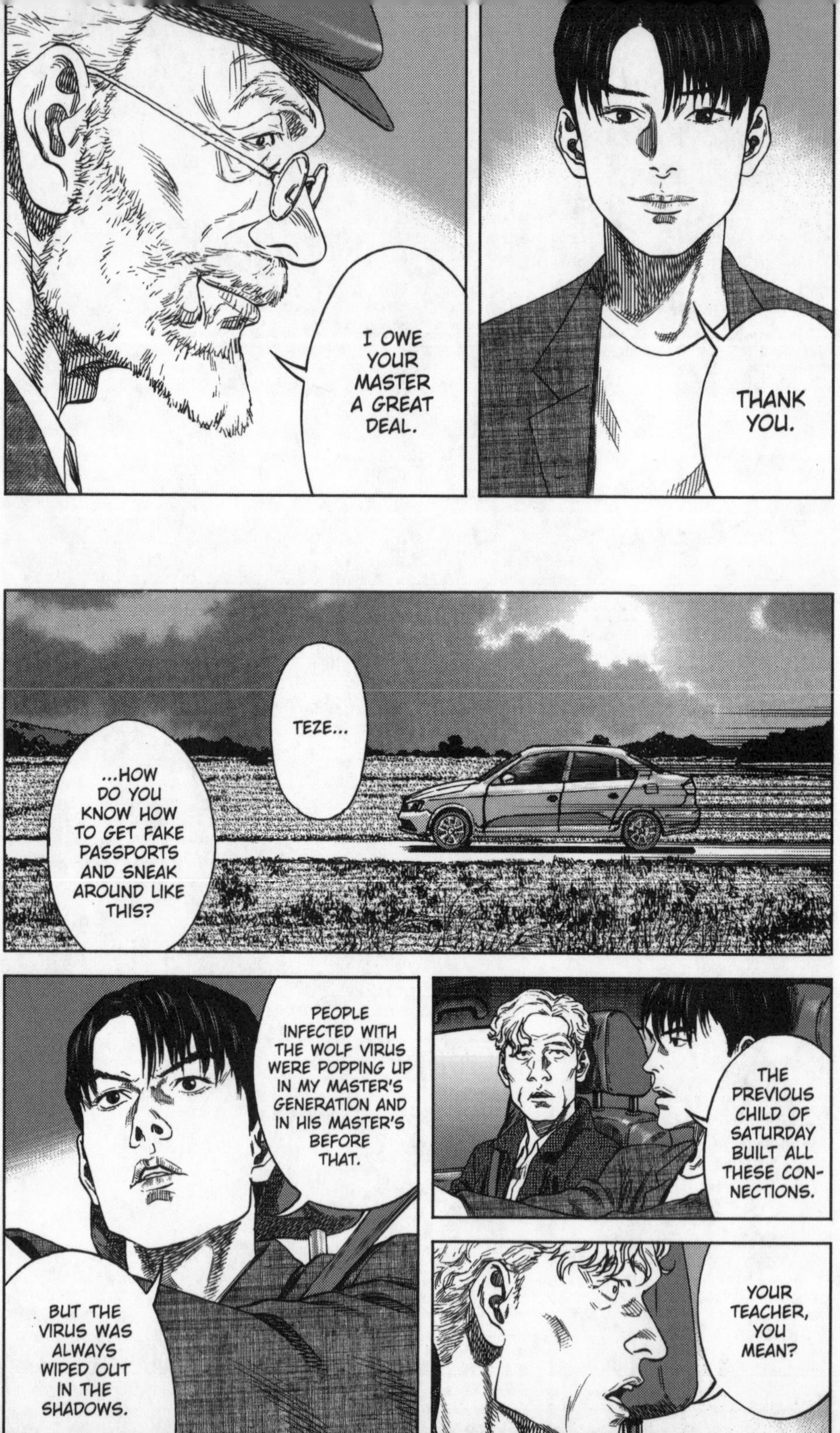
THANK YOU.
I OWE YOUR MASTER A GREAT DEAL.
TEZE...
...HOW DO YOU KNOW HOW TO GET FAKE PASSPORTS AND SNEAK AROUND LIKE THIS?
THE PREVIOUS CHILD OF SATURDAY BUILT ALL THESE CON-NECTIONS.
YOUR TEACHER, YOU MEAN?
PEOPLE INFECTED WITH THE WOLF VIRUS WERE POPPING UP IN MY MASTER'S GENERATION AND IN HIS MASTER'S BEFORE THAT.
BUT THE VIRUS WAS ALWAYS WIPED OUT IN THE SHADOWS.

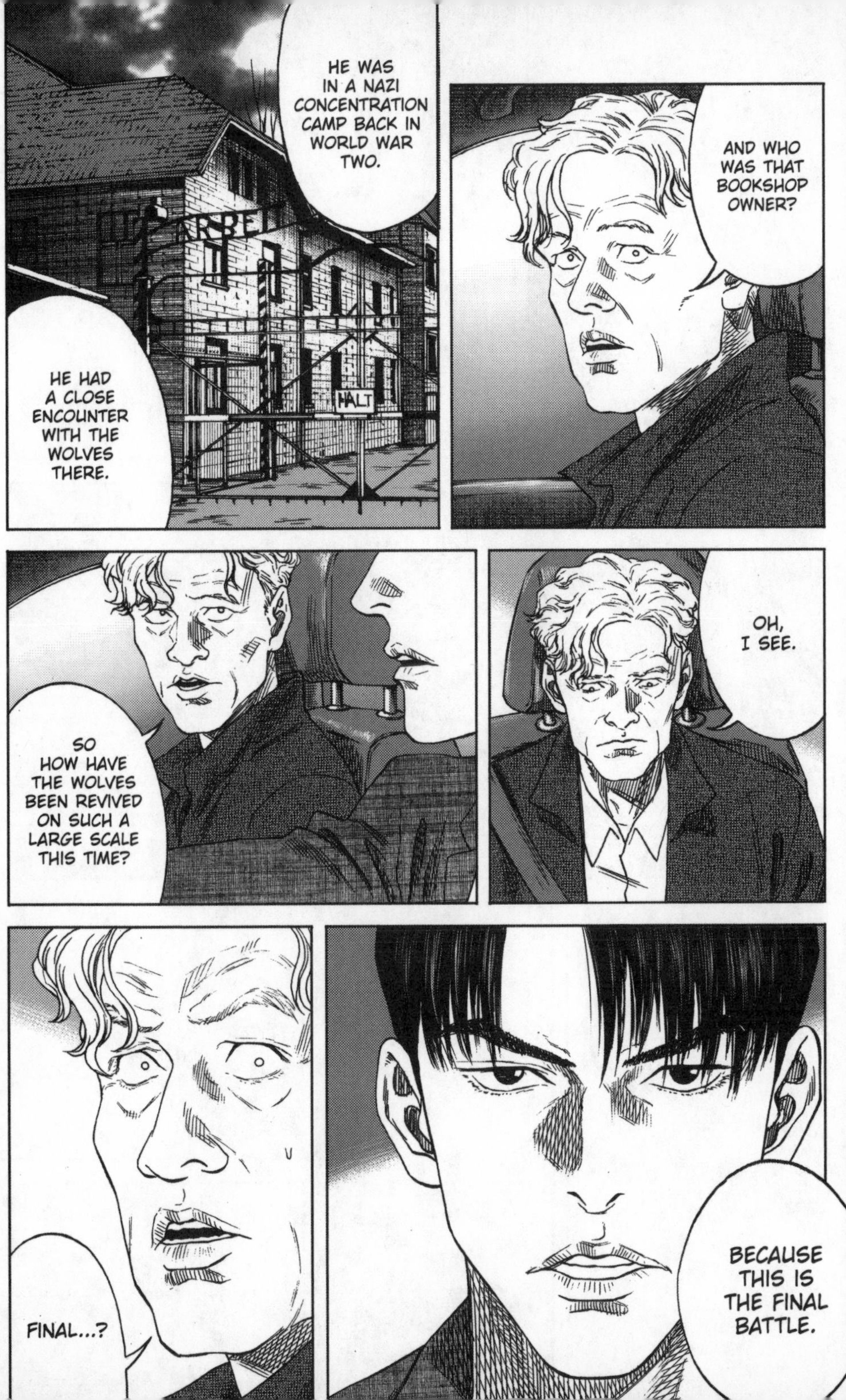
AND WHO WAS THAT BOOKSHOP OWNER?
HE WAS IN A NAZI CONCENTRATION CAMP BACK IN WORLD WAR TWO.
HALT
HE HAD A CLOSE ENCOUNTER WITH THE WOLVES THERE.
OH, I SEE.
SO HOW HAVE THE WOLVES BEEN REVIVED ON SUCH A LARGE SCALE THIS TIME?
BECAUSE THIS IS THE FINAL BATTLE.
FINAL...?

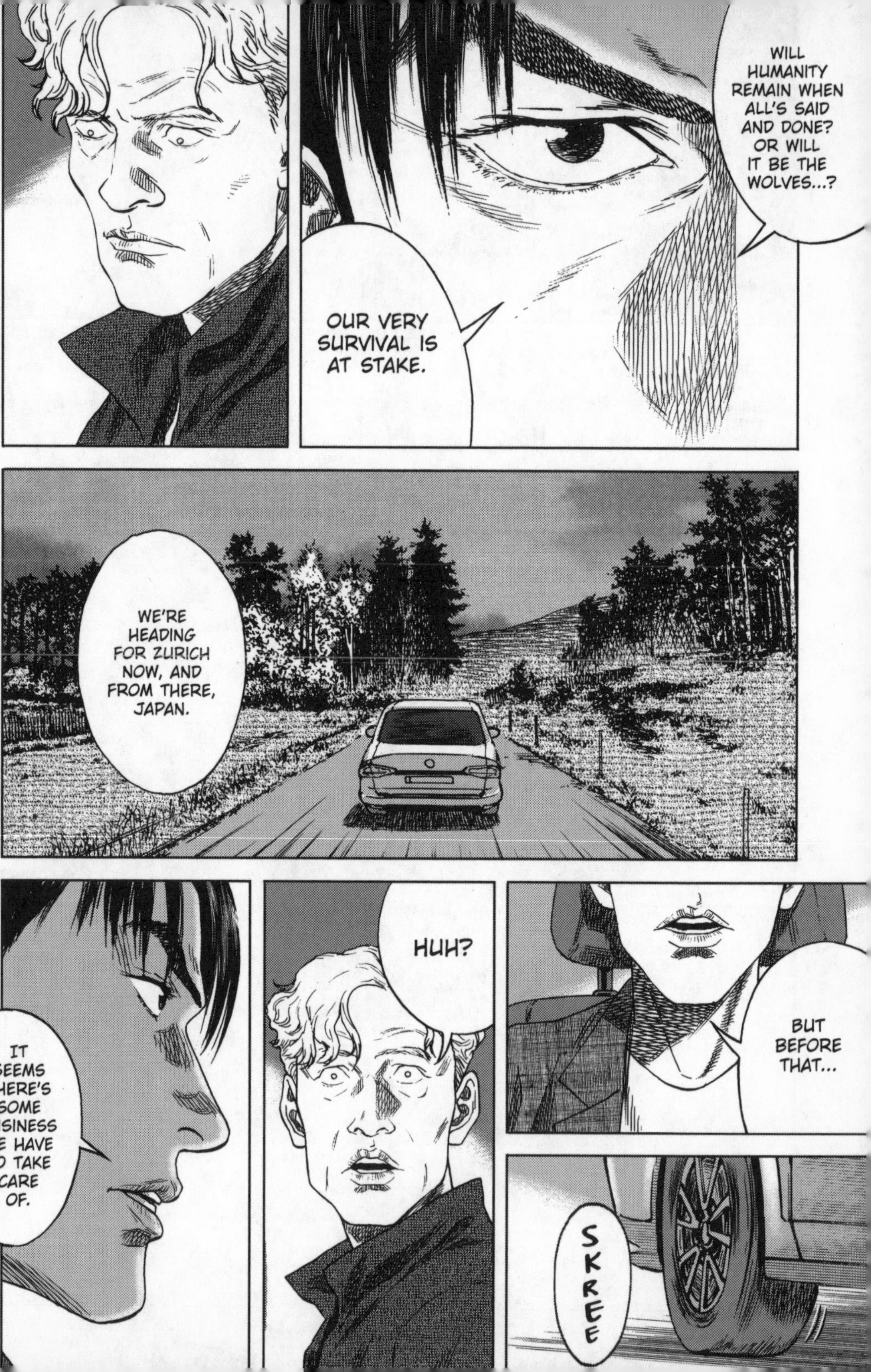
WILL HUMANITY REMAIN WHEN ALL'S SAID AND DONE? OR WILL IT BE THE WOLVES...?
OUR VERY SURVIVAL IS AT STAKE.
WE'RE HEADING FOR ZURICH NOW, AND FROM THERE, JAPAN.
BUT BEFORE THAT...
SKREE
HUH?
IT SEEMS THERE'S SOME BUSINESS WE HAVE TO TAKE CARE OF.

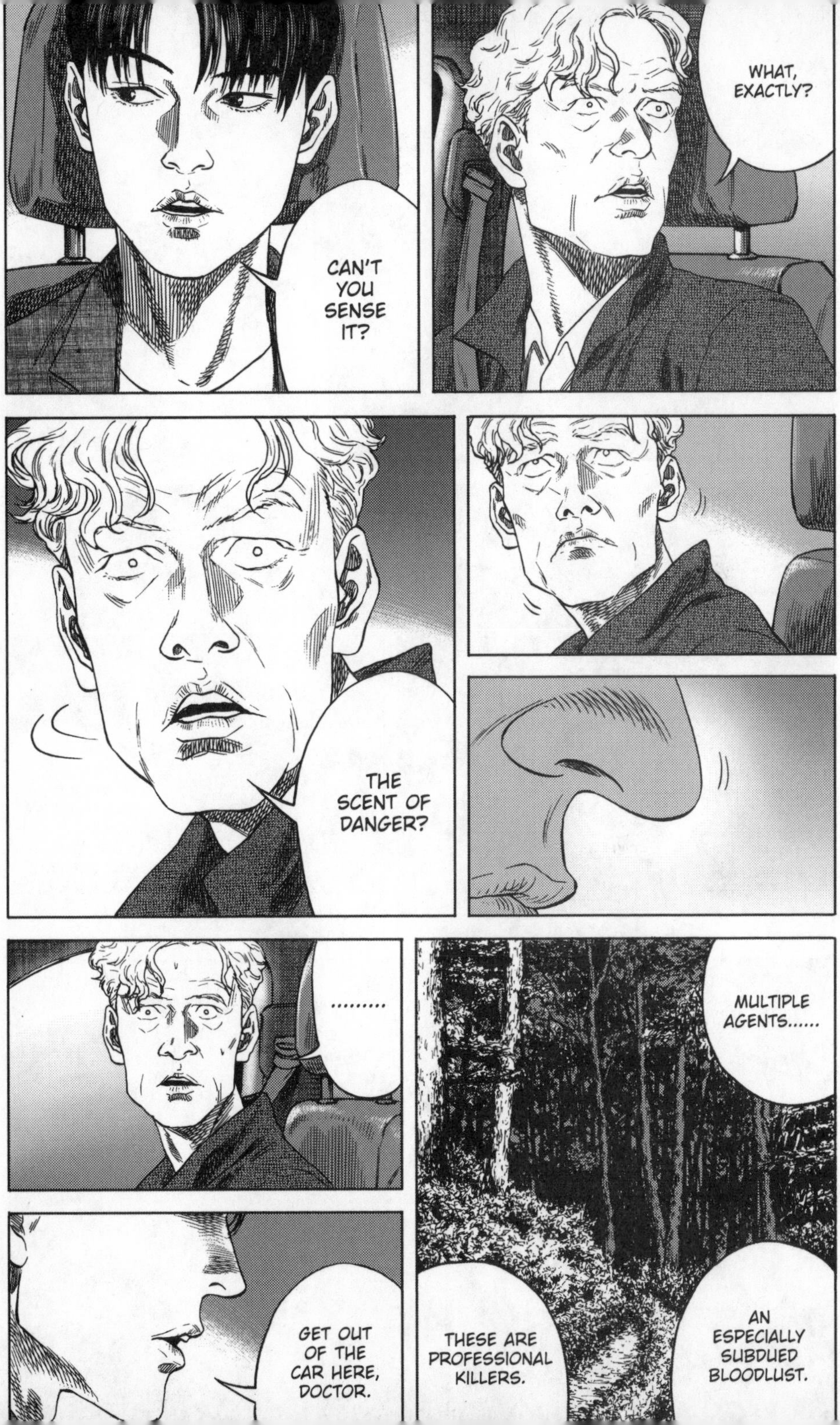

WHAT, EXACTLY?
CAN'T YOU SENSE IT?
THE SCENT OF DANGER?
MULTIPLE AGENTS......
AN ESPECIALLY SUBDUED BLOODLUST.
THESE ARE PROFESSIONAL KILLERS.
....
GET OUT OF THE CAR HERE, DOCTOR.

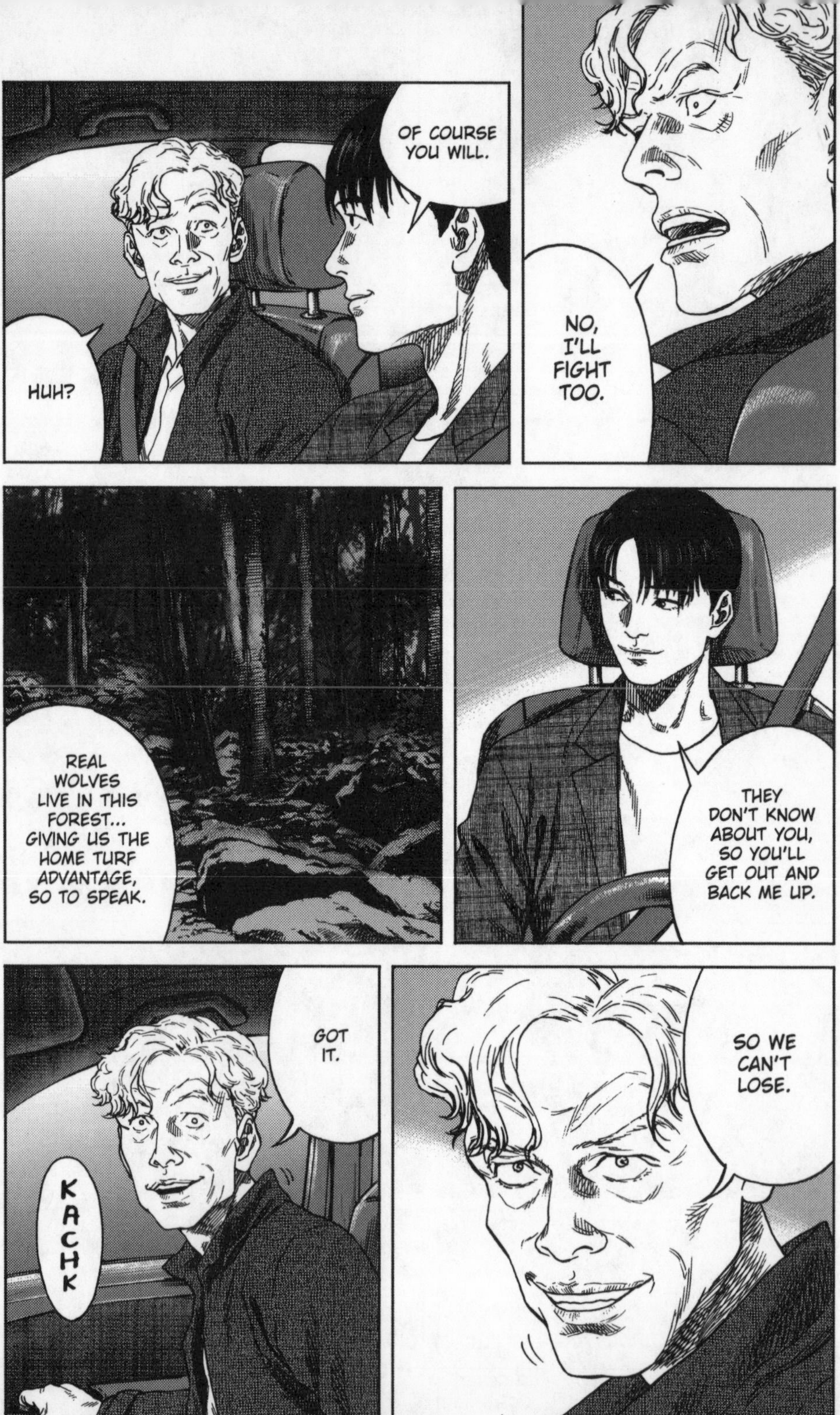
NO, I'LL FIGHT TOO.
OF COURSE YOU WILL.
HUH?
THEY DON'T KNOW ABOUT YOU, SO YOU'LL GET OUT AND BACK ME UP.
REAL WOLVES LIVE IN THIS FOREST... GIVING US THE HOME TURF ADVANTAGE, SO TO SPEAK.
SO WE CAN'T LOSE.
GOT IT.
KACHK

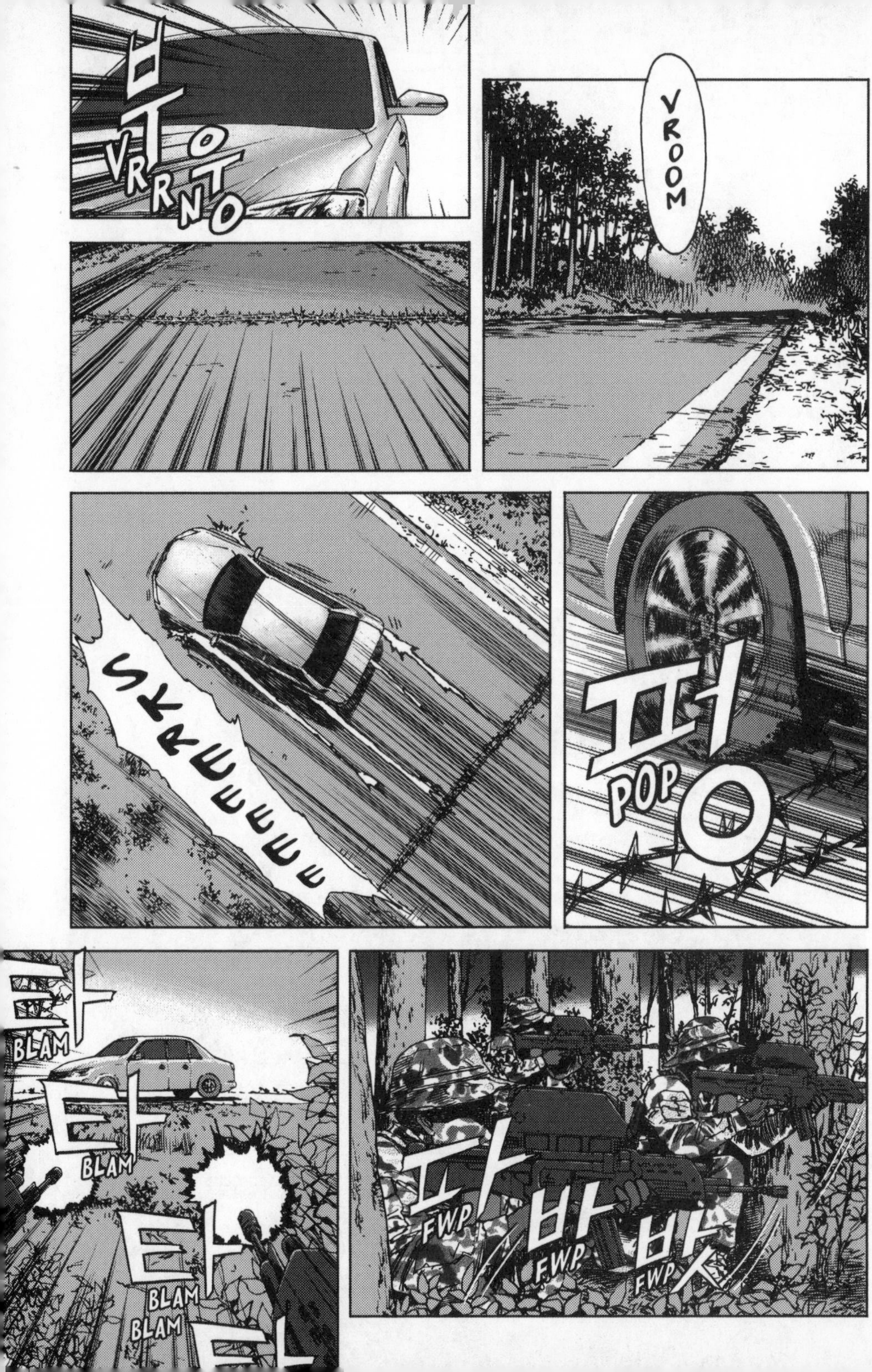

VROOM
VRRN
SKREEEEEE
POP
FWP
FWP
FWP
BLAM
BLAM
BLAM
BLAM

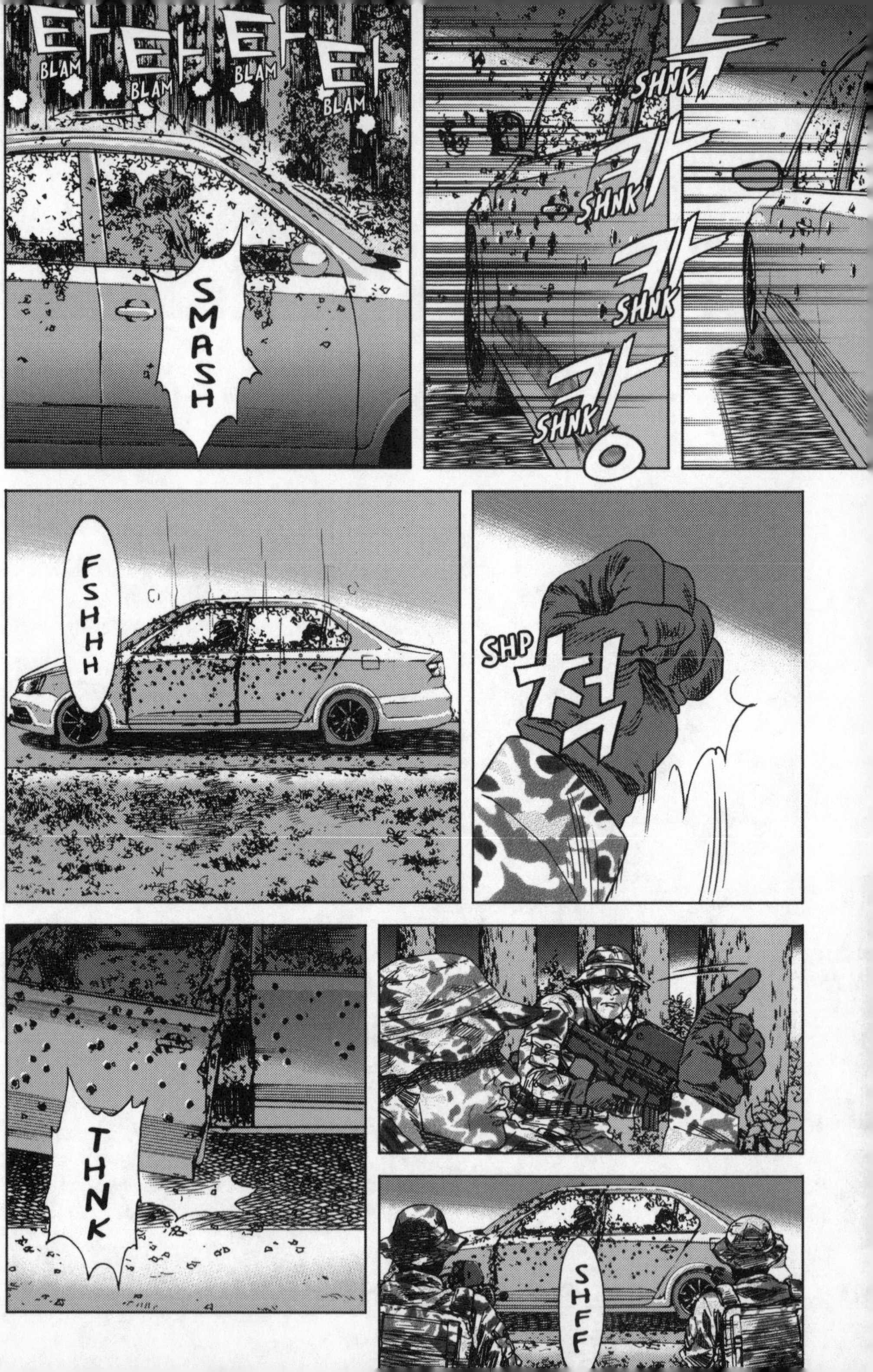
투
SHNK
카
SHNK
카
SHNK
캉
SHNK
타타타타
BLAM
BLAM
BLAM
BLAM
SMASH
SHP
척
FSHHH
SHFF
THNK

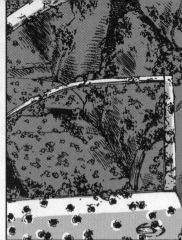

!

HE
SAW US
COMING?

!

FWP

WHERE'S
THE
TARGET?

BLAM

BLAM

BLAM

BLAM

THERE.

SPLIT
UP!

AFTER
HIM!

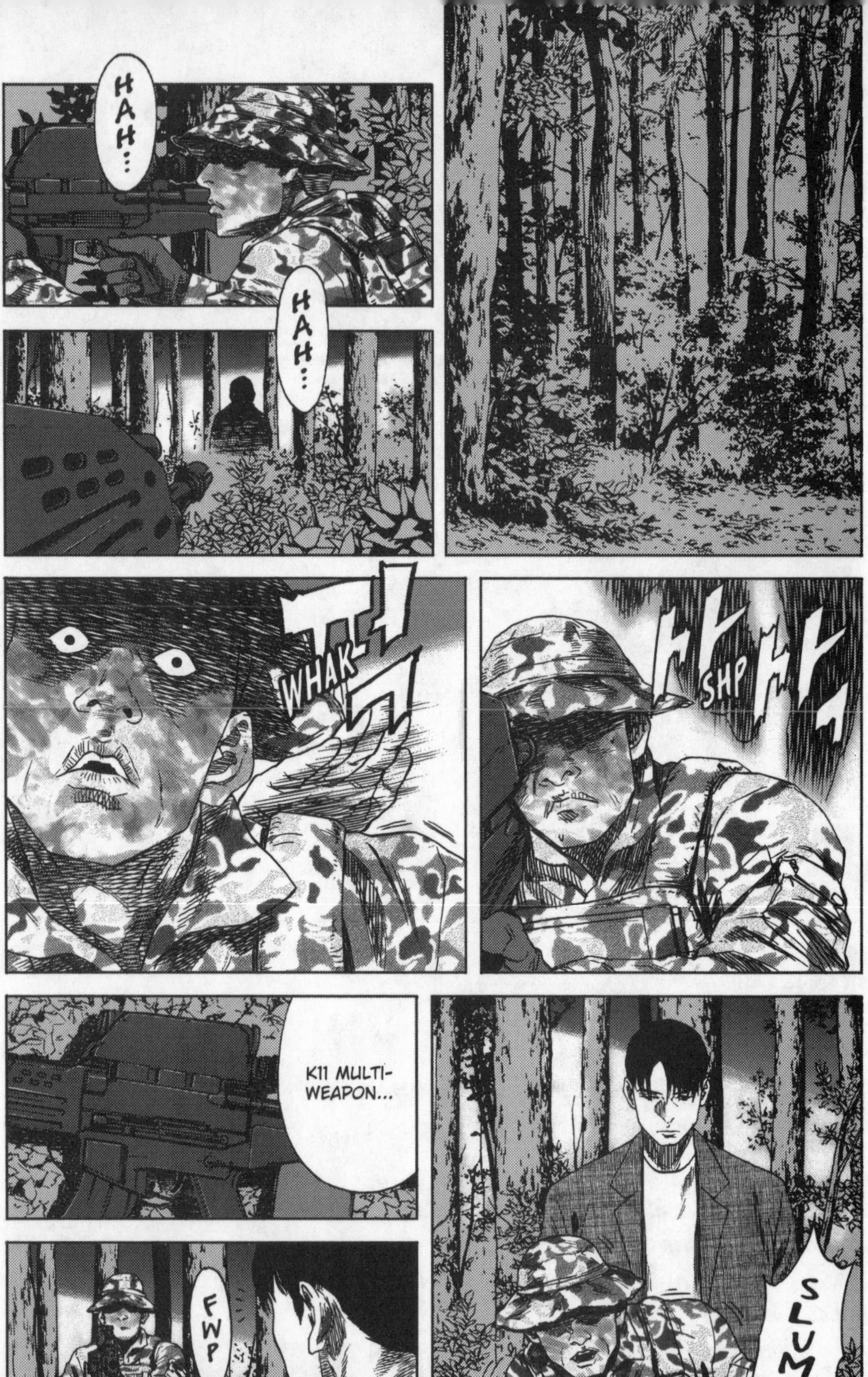
HAH...
HAH...
SHP
WHAK
SLUMP
K11 MULTI-WEAPON...
FWP

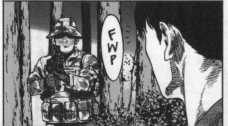

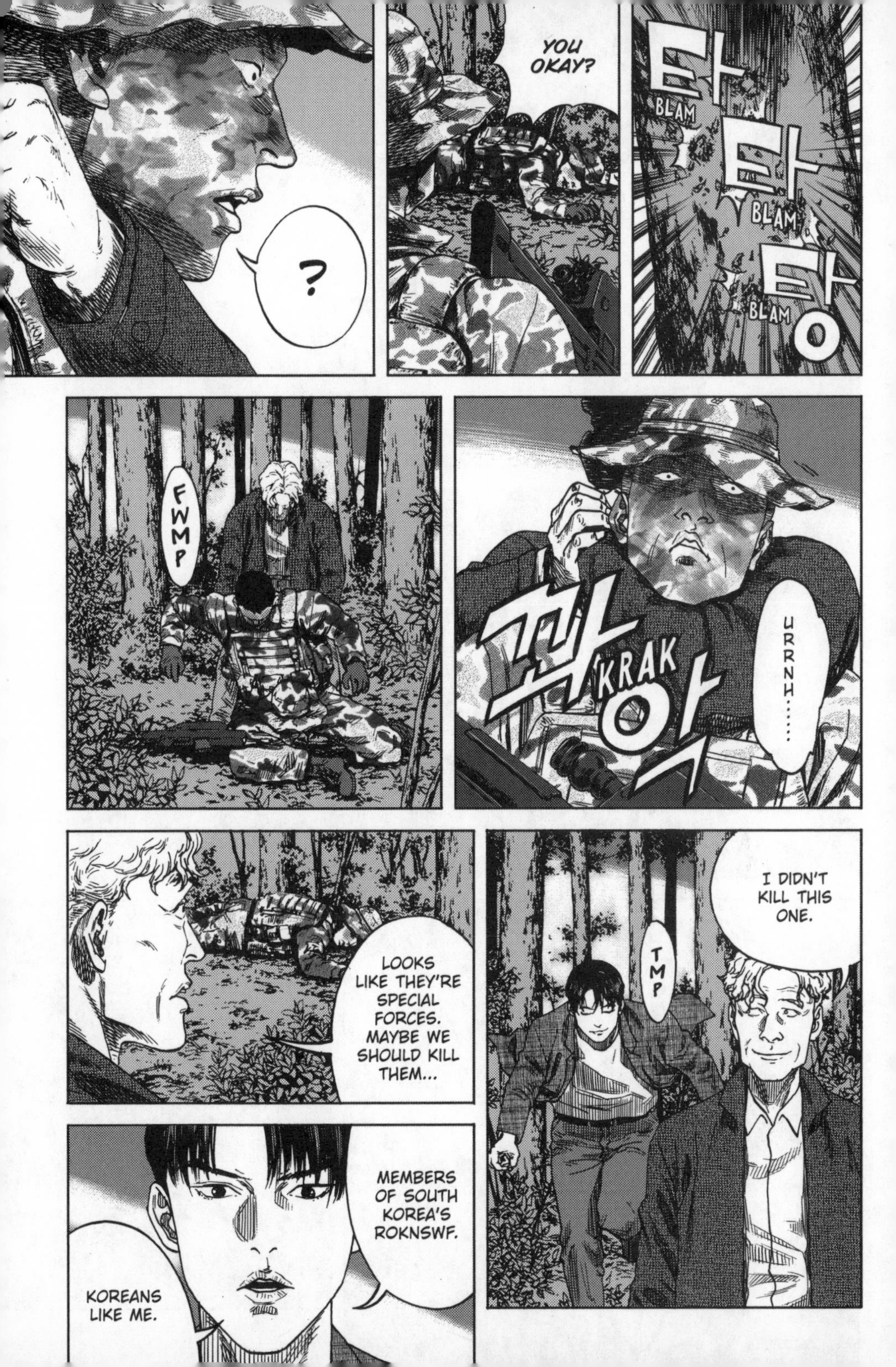

타
BLAM
타
BLAM
타
BLAM
YOU OKAY?
?
팍
KRAK
URRNH......
FWMP
I DIDN'T KILL THIS ONE.
TMP
LOOKS LIKE THEY'RE SPECIAL FORCES. MAYBE WE SHOULD KILL THEM...
MEMBERS OF SOUTH KOREA'S ROKNSWF.
KOREANS LIKE ME.

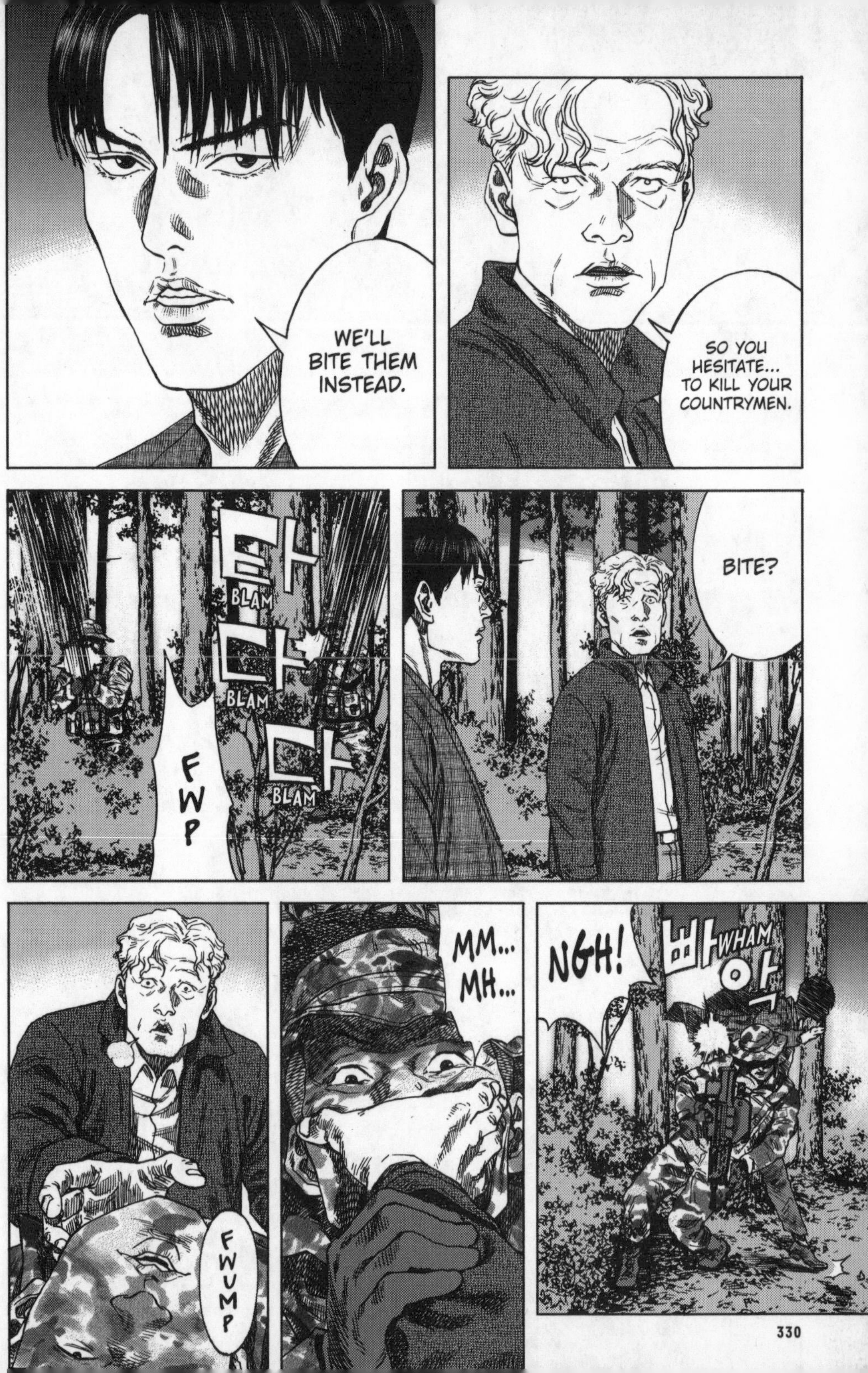
SO YOU HESITATE... TO KILL YOUR COUNTRYMEN.
WE'LL BITE THEM INSTEAD.
BITE?
타 BLAM
다 BLAM
다 BLAM
FWP
NGH!
빠악 WHAM
MM... MH...
FWUMP

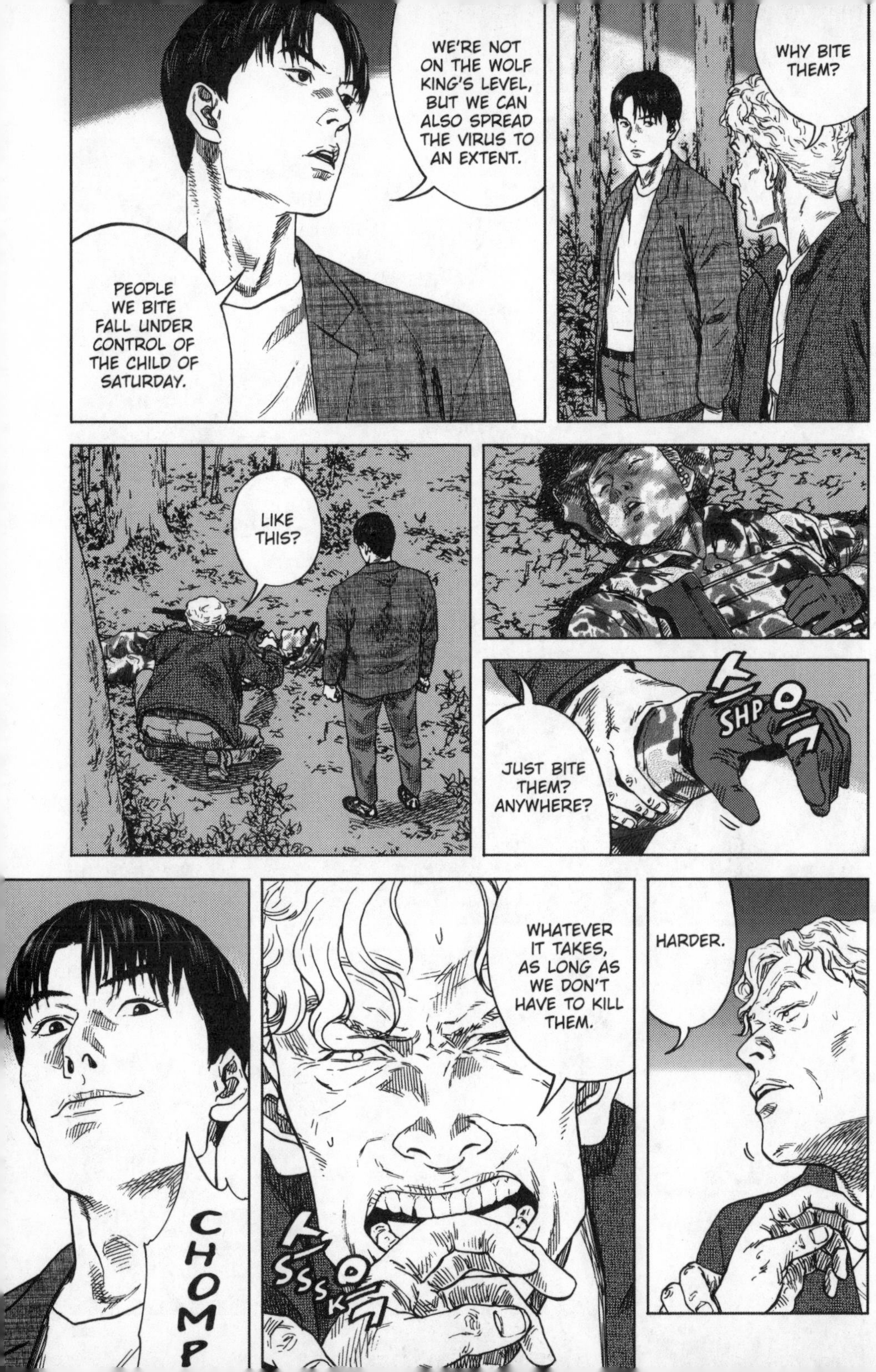
WHY BITE THEM?
WE'RE NOT ON THE WOLF KING'S LEVEL, BUT WE CAN ALSO SPREAD THE VIRUS TO AN EXTENT.
PEOPLE WE BITE FALL UNDER CONTROL OF THE CHILD OF SATURDAY.
SHP
JUST BITE THEM? ANYWHERE?
LIKE THIS?
HARDER.
WHATEVER IT TAKES, AS LONG AS WE DON'T HAVE TO KILL THEM.
SSSK
CHOMP

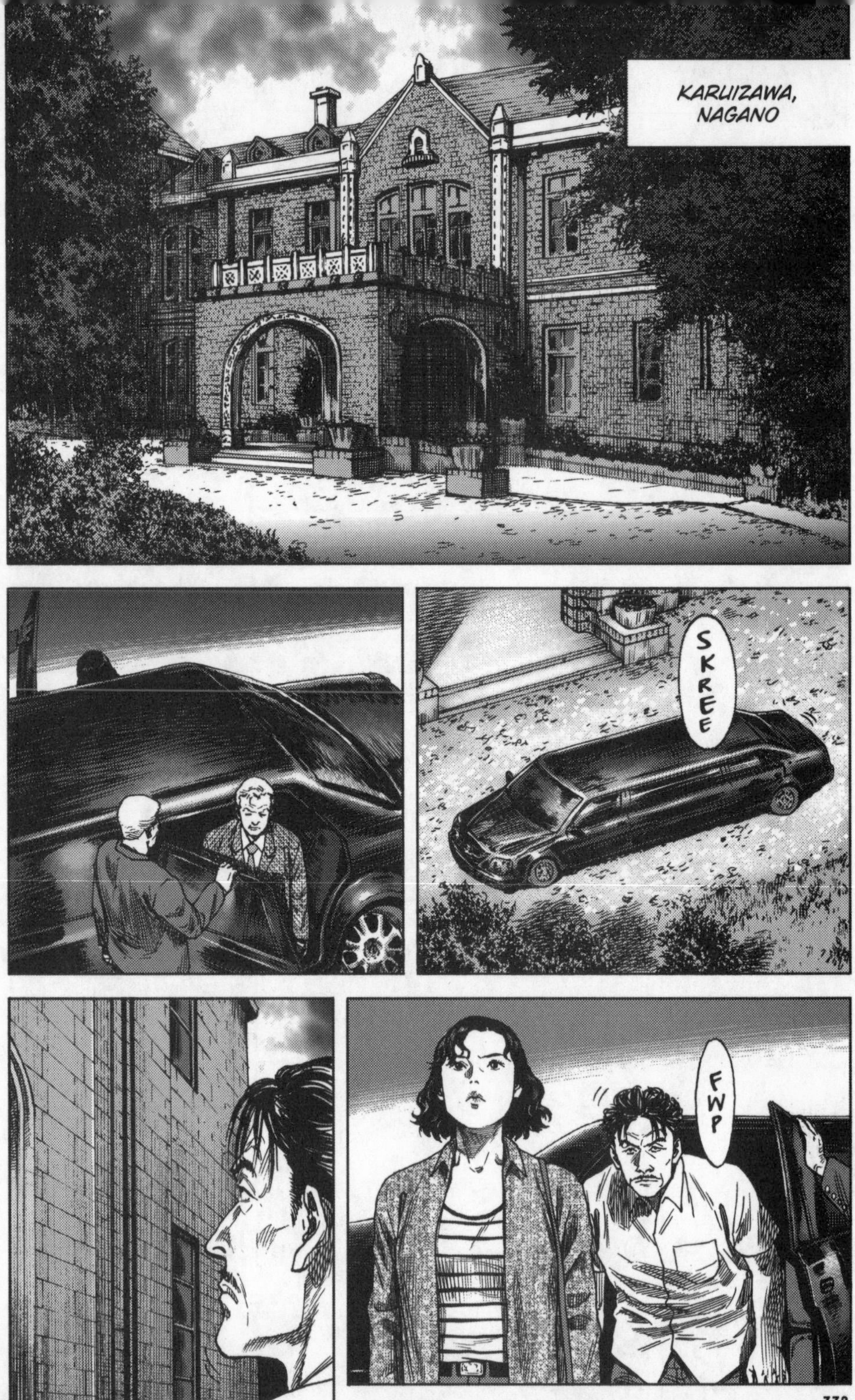
KARUIZAWA, NAGANO
SKREE
FWP

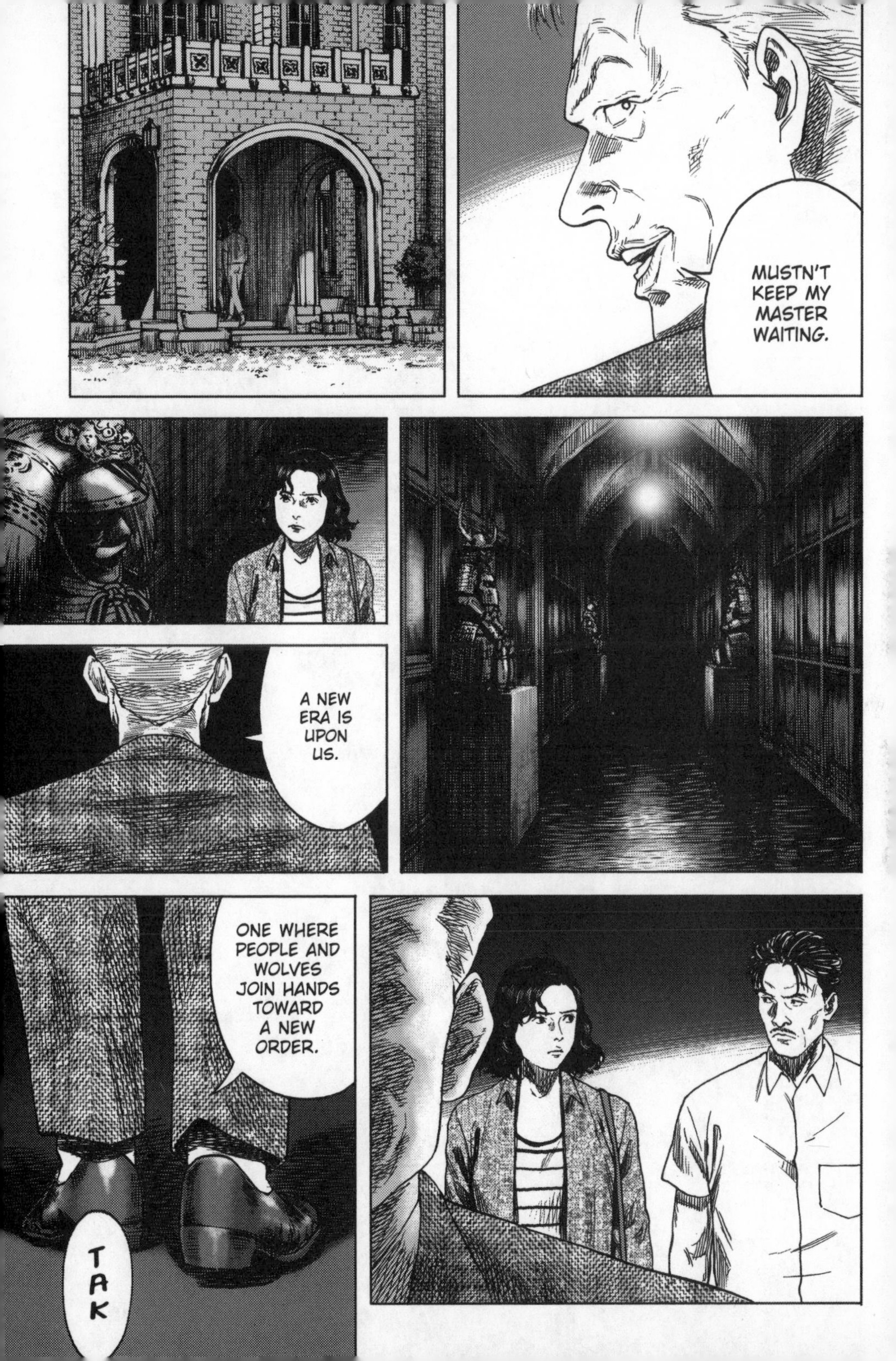
MUSTN'T KEEP MY MASTER WAITING.
A NEW ERA IS UPON US.
ONE WHERE PEOPLE AND WOLVES JOIN HANDS TOWARD A NEW ORDER.
TAK

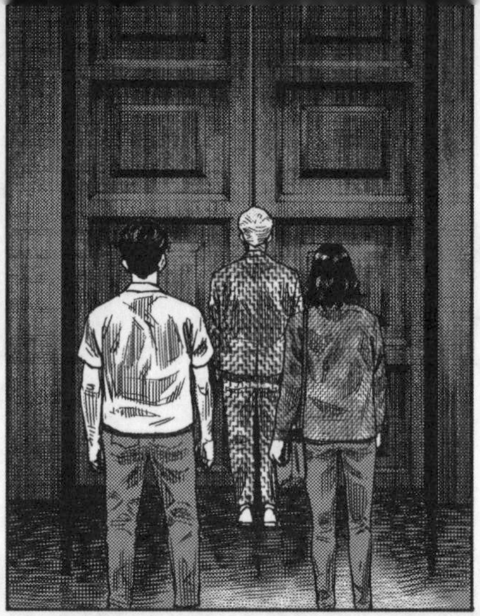

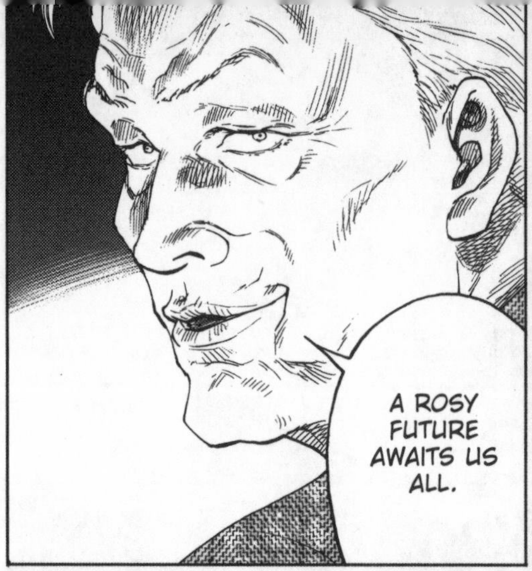
A ROSY FUTURE AWAITS US ALL.

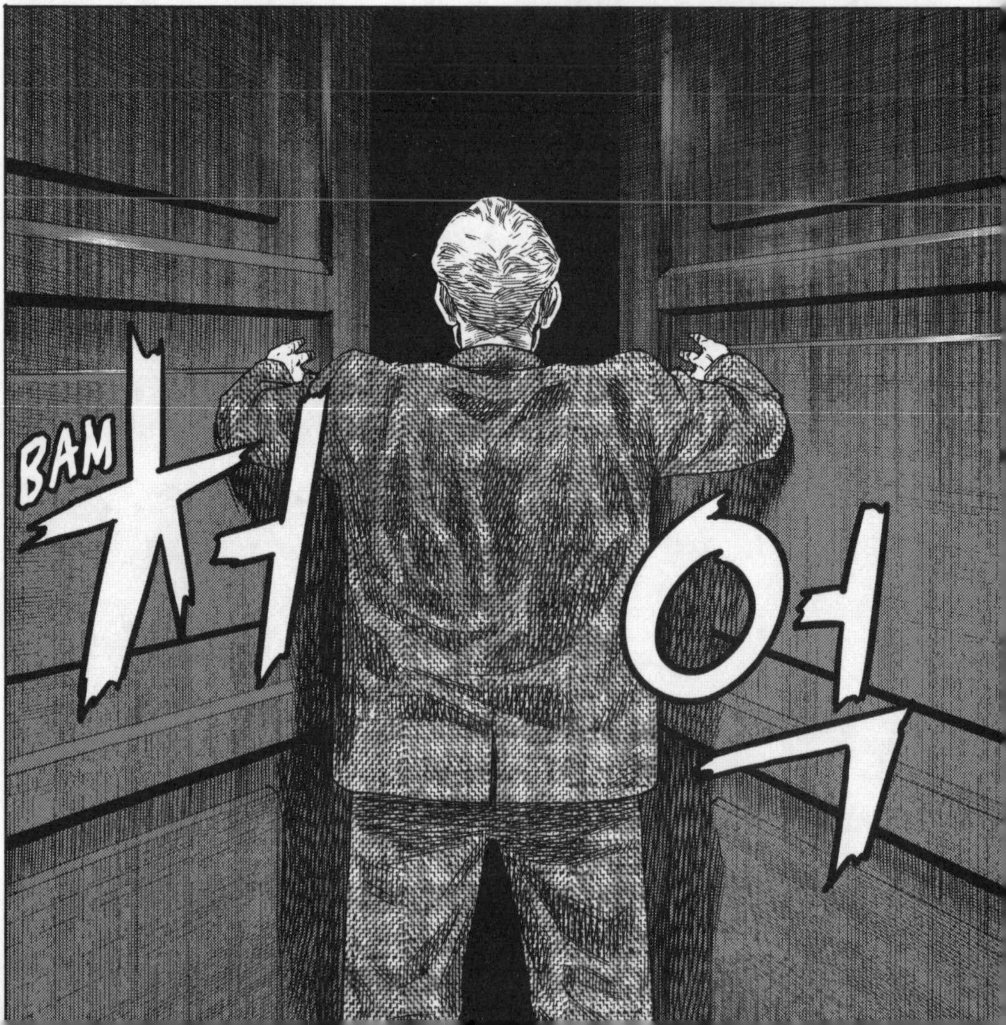
BAM

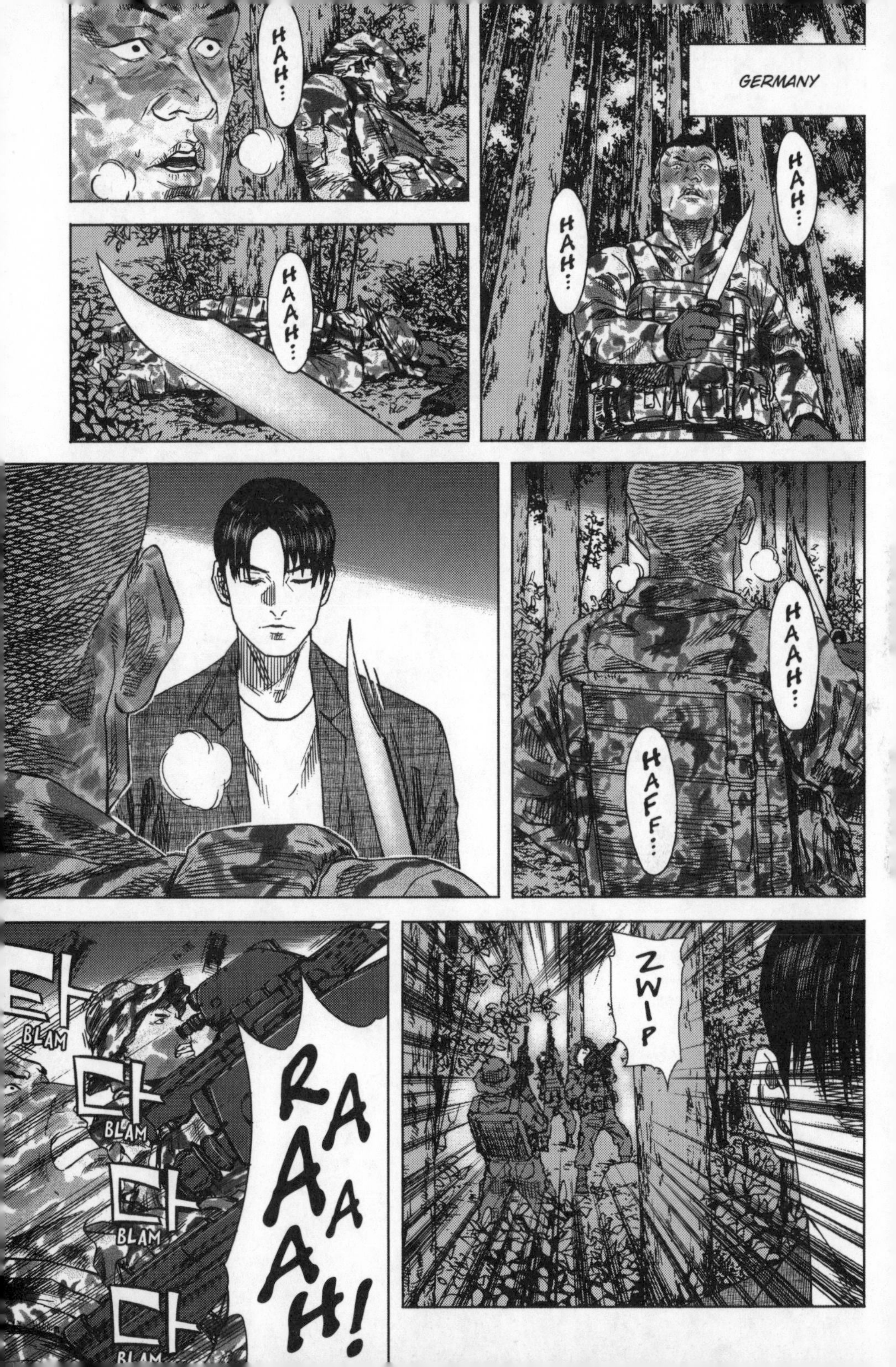
GERMANY
HAH...
HAH...
HAH...
HAAAH...
HAAAH...
HAFF...
ZWIP
타
BLAM
다
BLAM
다
BLAM
다
RAAAAH!

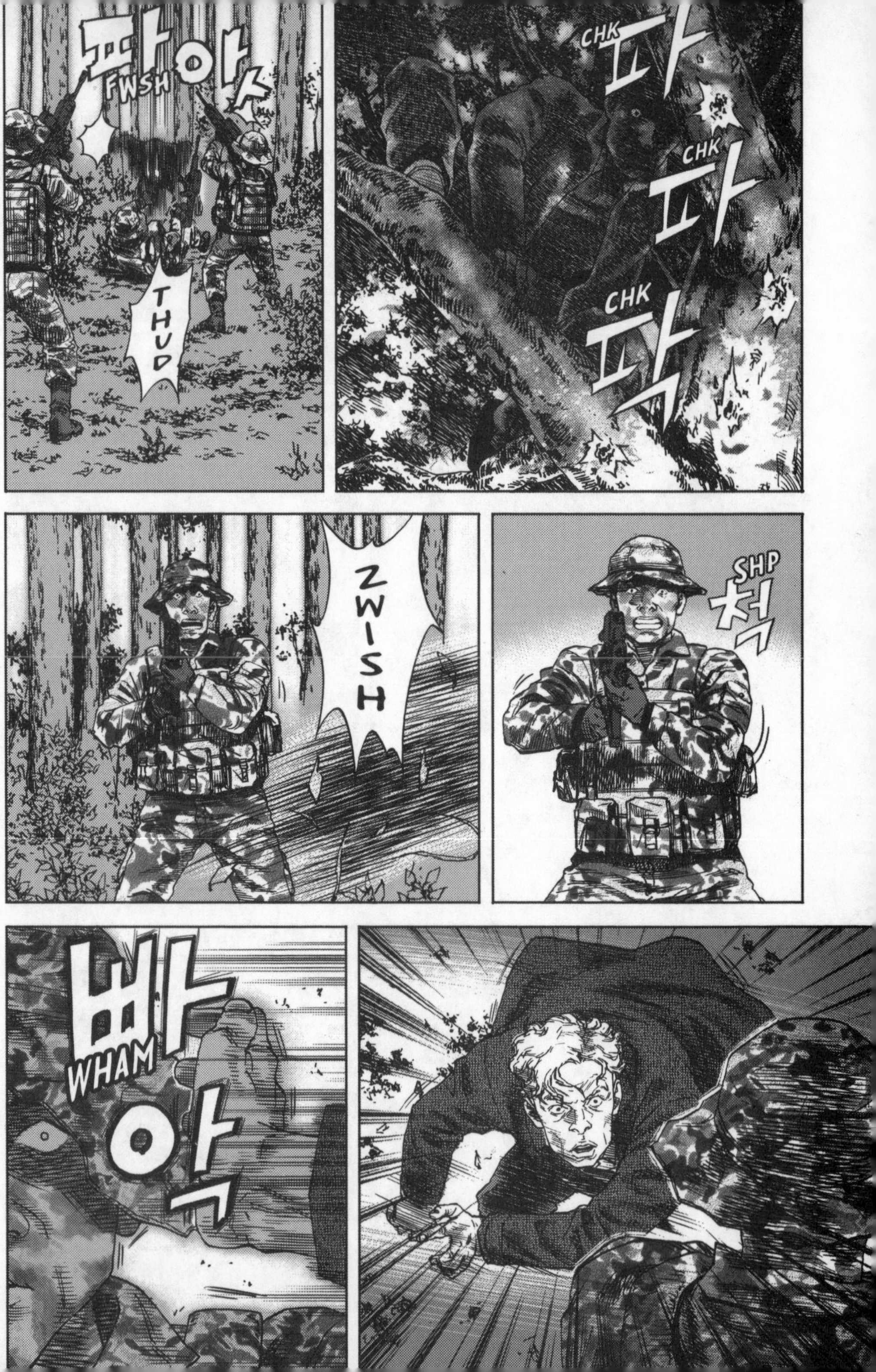
CHK
파
CHK
파
CHK
팍
FWSH
파아악
THUD
SHP
척
ZWISH
WHAM
빠악

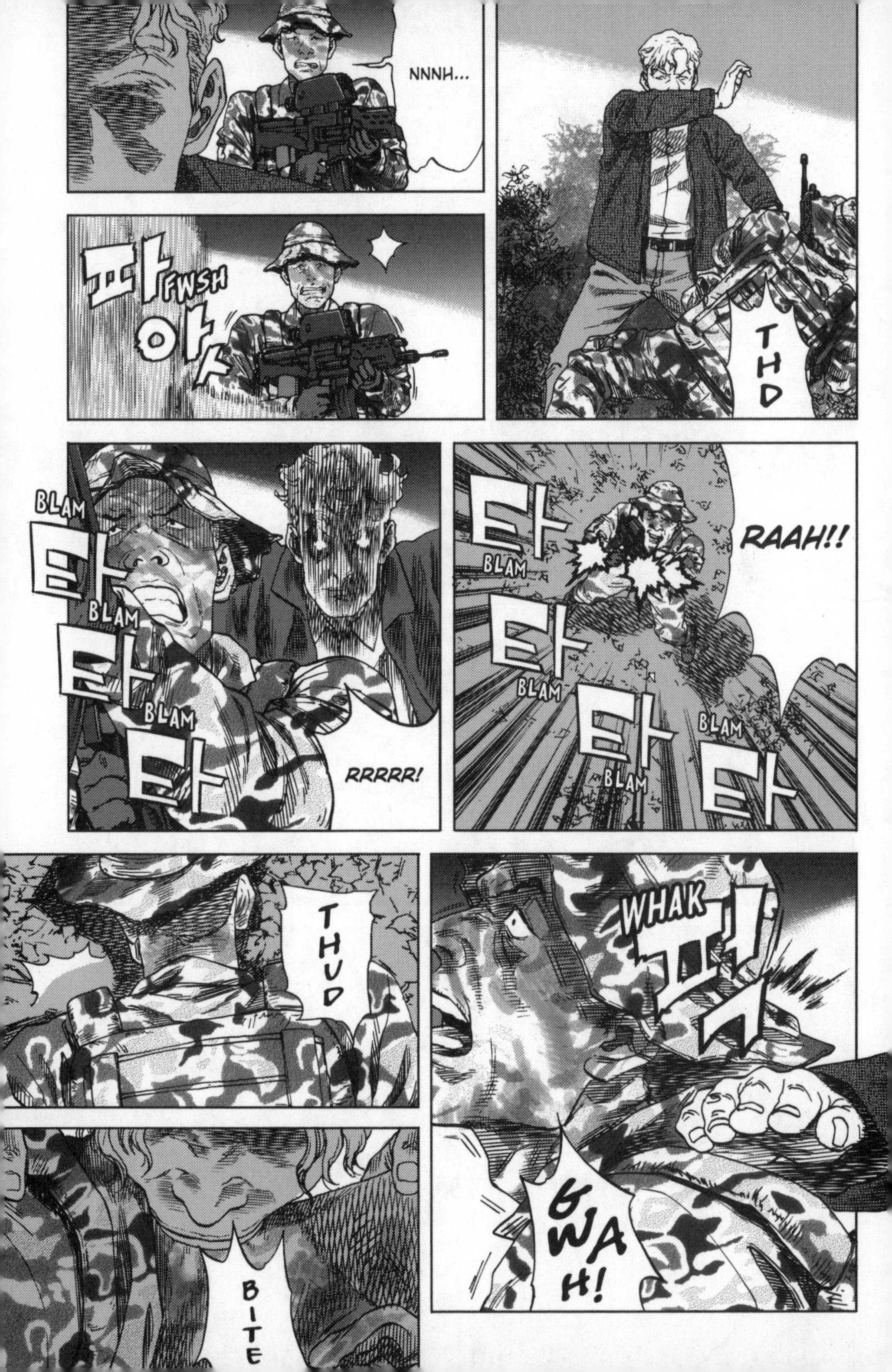
THD
NNNH...
파아
FWSH
RAAH!!
타 BLAM
타 BLAM
타 BLAM
타 BLAM
타
BLAM
타 BLAM
타 BLAM
타
RRRRR!
WHAK
퍽
UWAH!
THUD
BITE

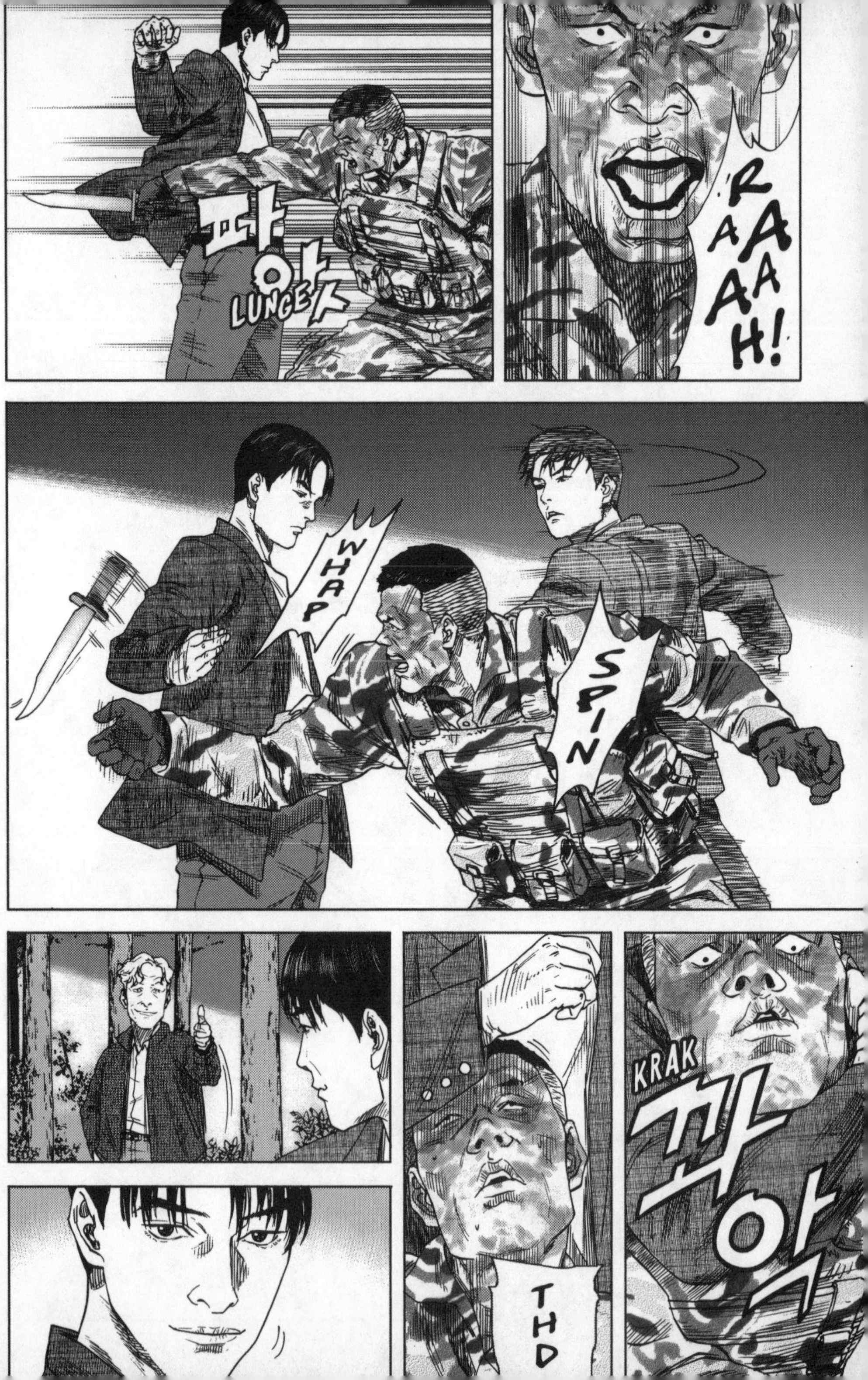
RAAAAH!
파앗
LUNGE
SPIN
WHAP
KRAK
까악
THD

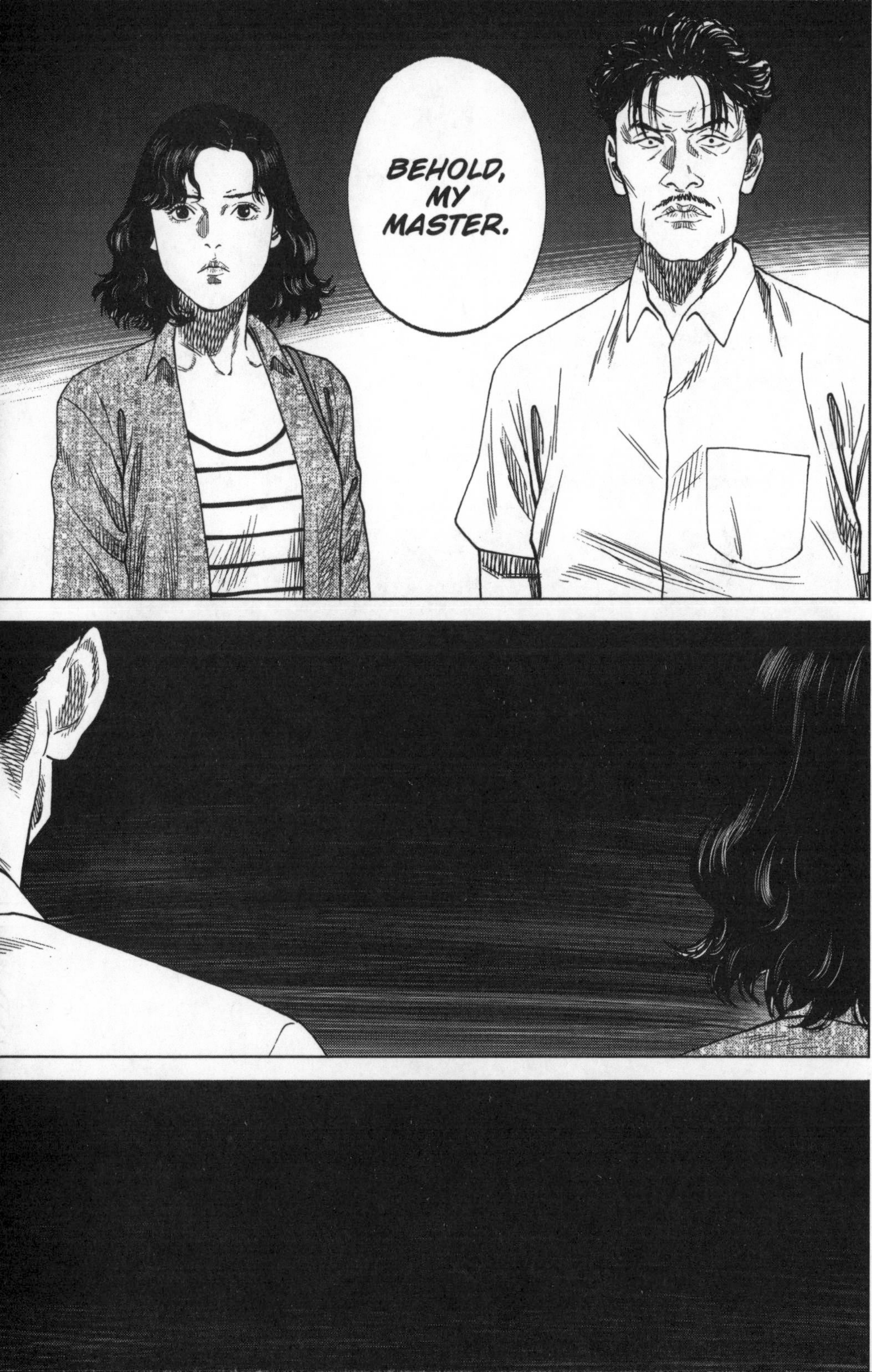
BEHOLD, MY MASTER.

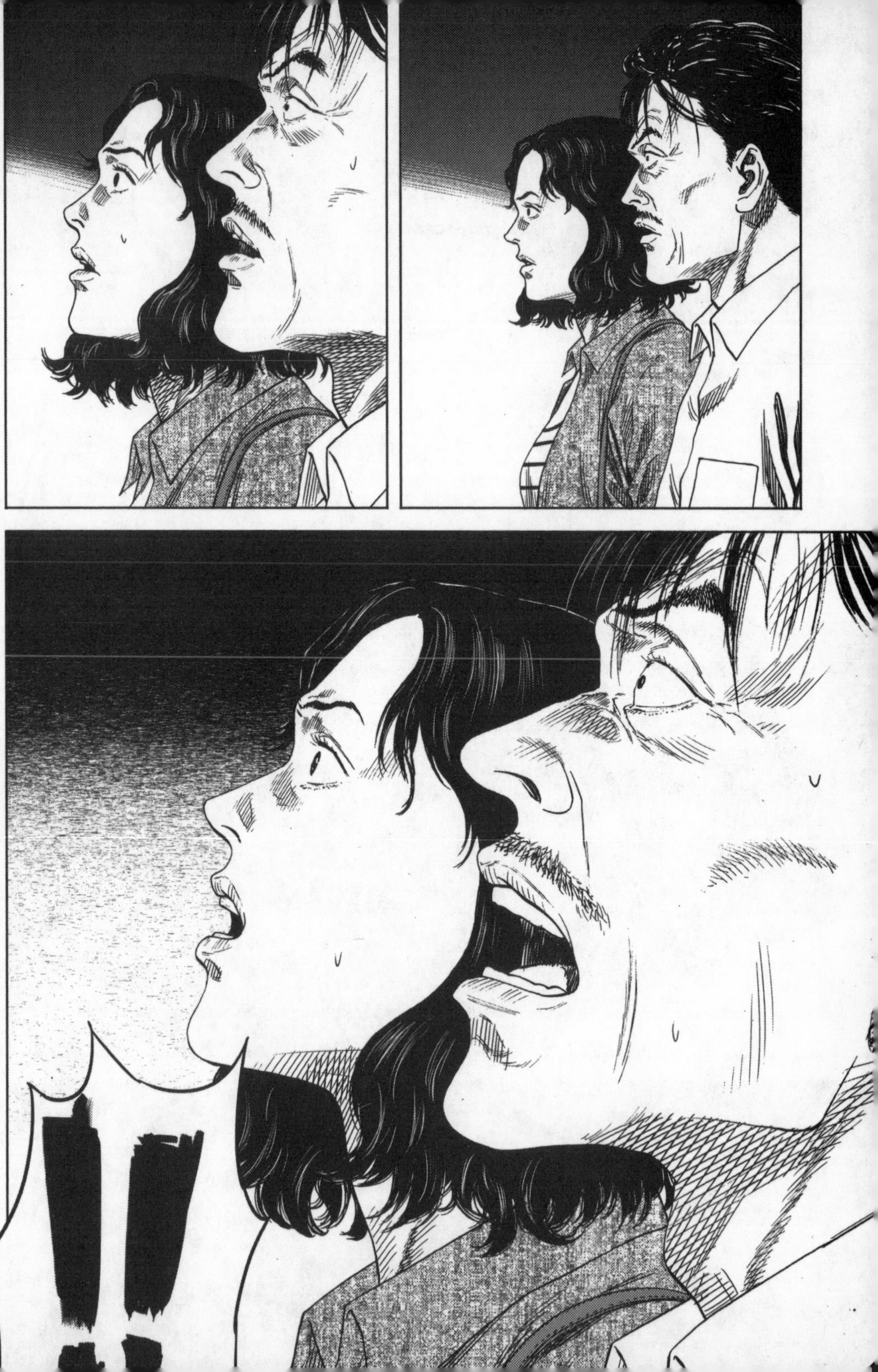
!!

KING OF EDEN

KING OF EDEN

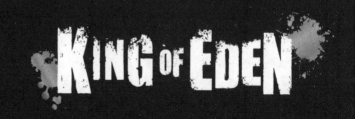

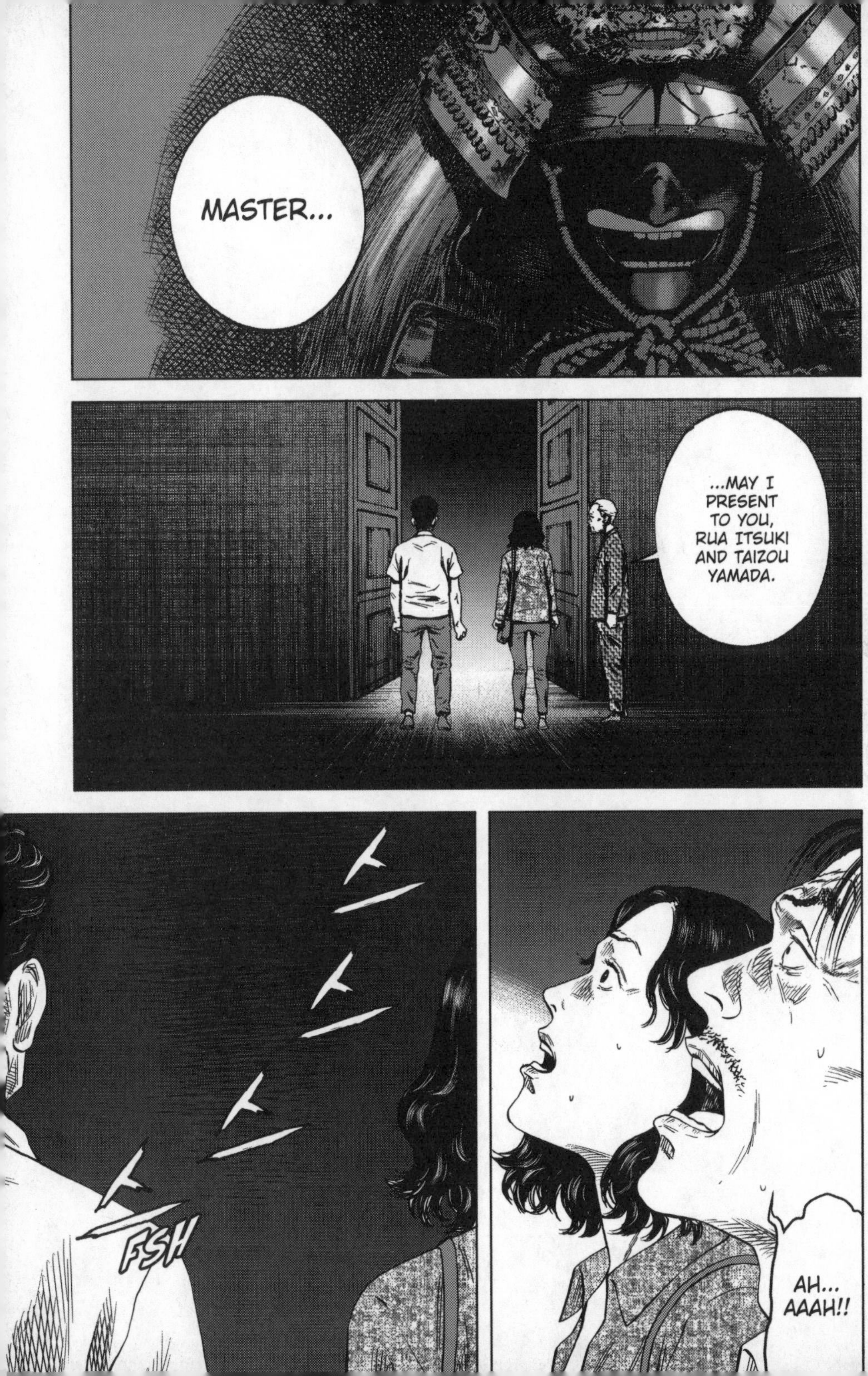
MASTER...
...MAY I PRESENT TO YOU, RUA ITSUKI AND TAIZOU YAMADA.
AH... AAAH!!
FSH

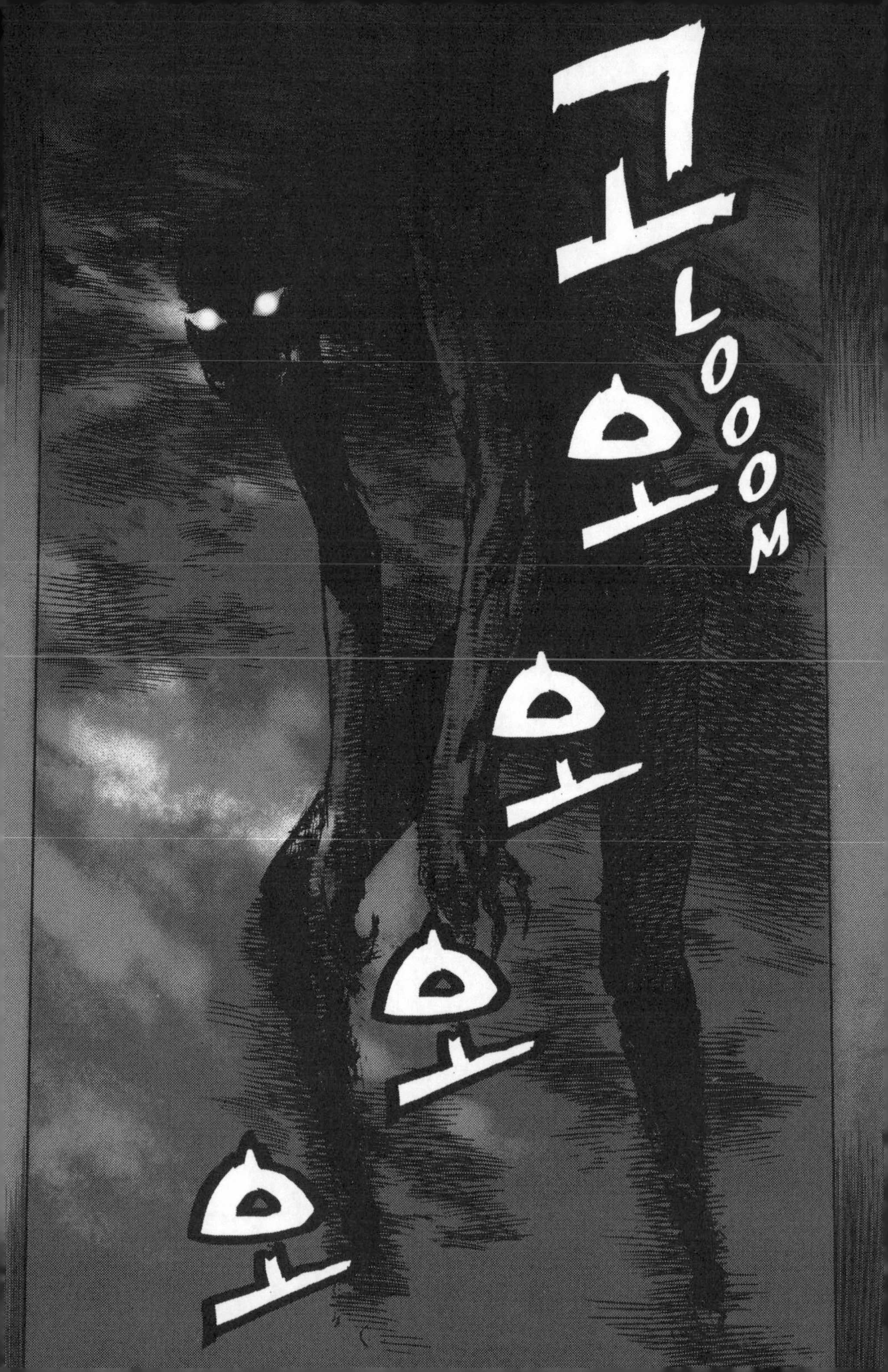

고오오오
LOOOOM

AH...
AH...
AHHH...

AAAA-
AAAA-
AAH...

P-P-P-
PLEASE
FORGIVE
ME.

I-I-I
WOULDN'T
WANNA GO UP
AGAINST YOU,
NOT FOR ALL
THE MONEY IN
THE WORLD.

SO
PLEASE,
LET ME
LIVE!

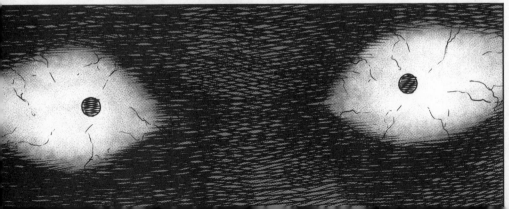

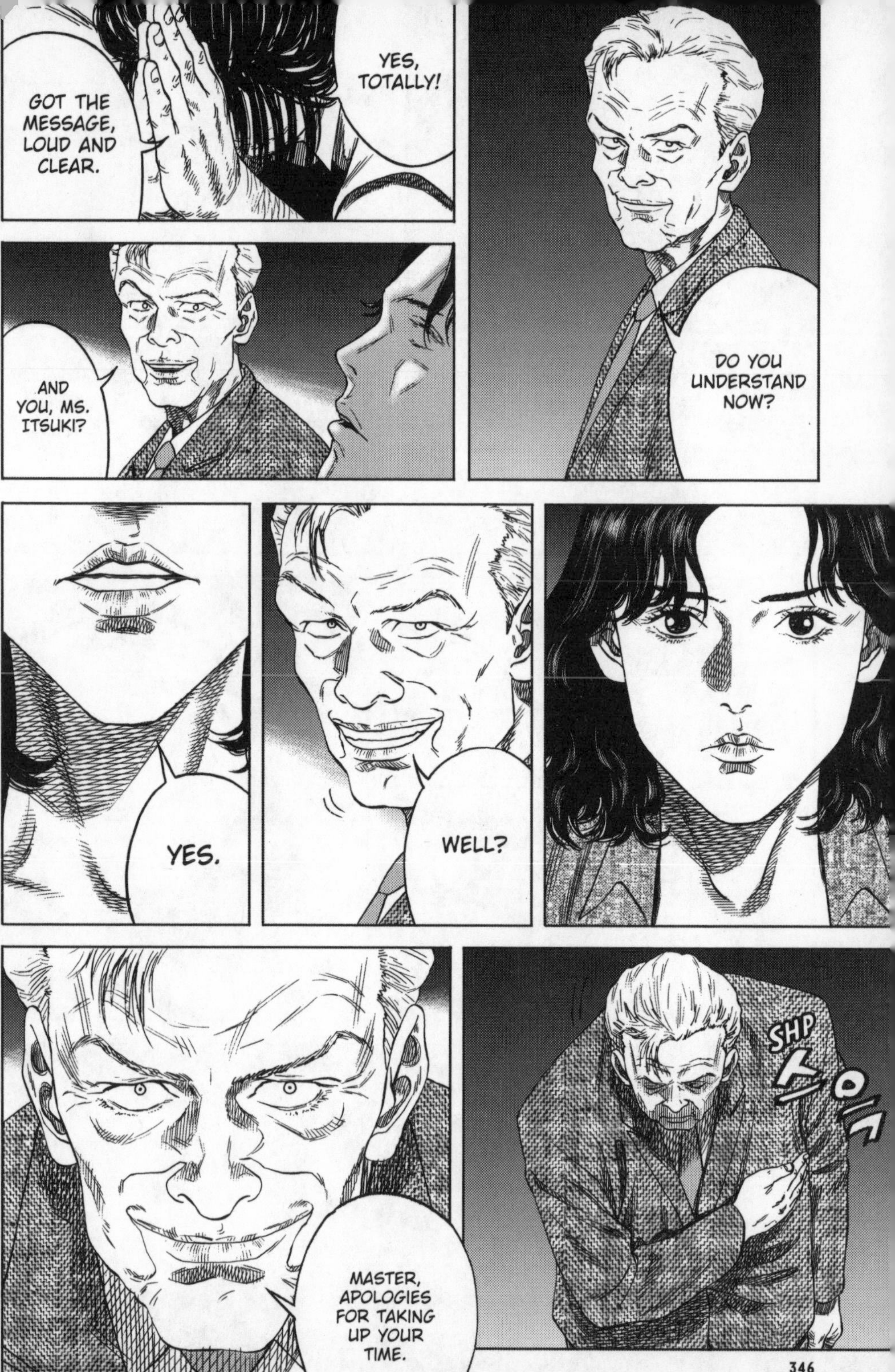
DO YOU UNDERSTAND NOW?
YES, TOTALLY!
GOT THE MESSAGE, LOUD AND CLEAR.
AND YOU, MS. ITSUKI?
WELL?
YES.
SHP
MASTER, APOLOGIES FOR TAKING UP YOUR TIME.

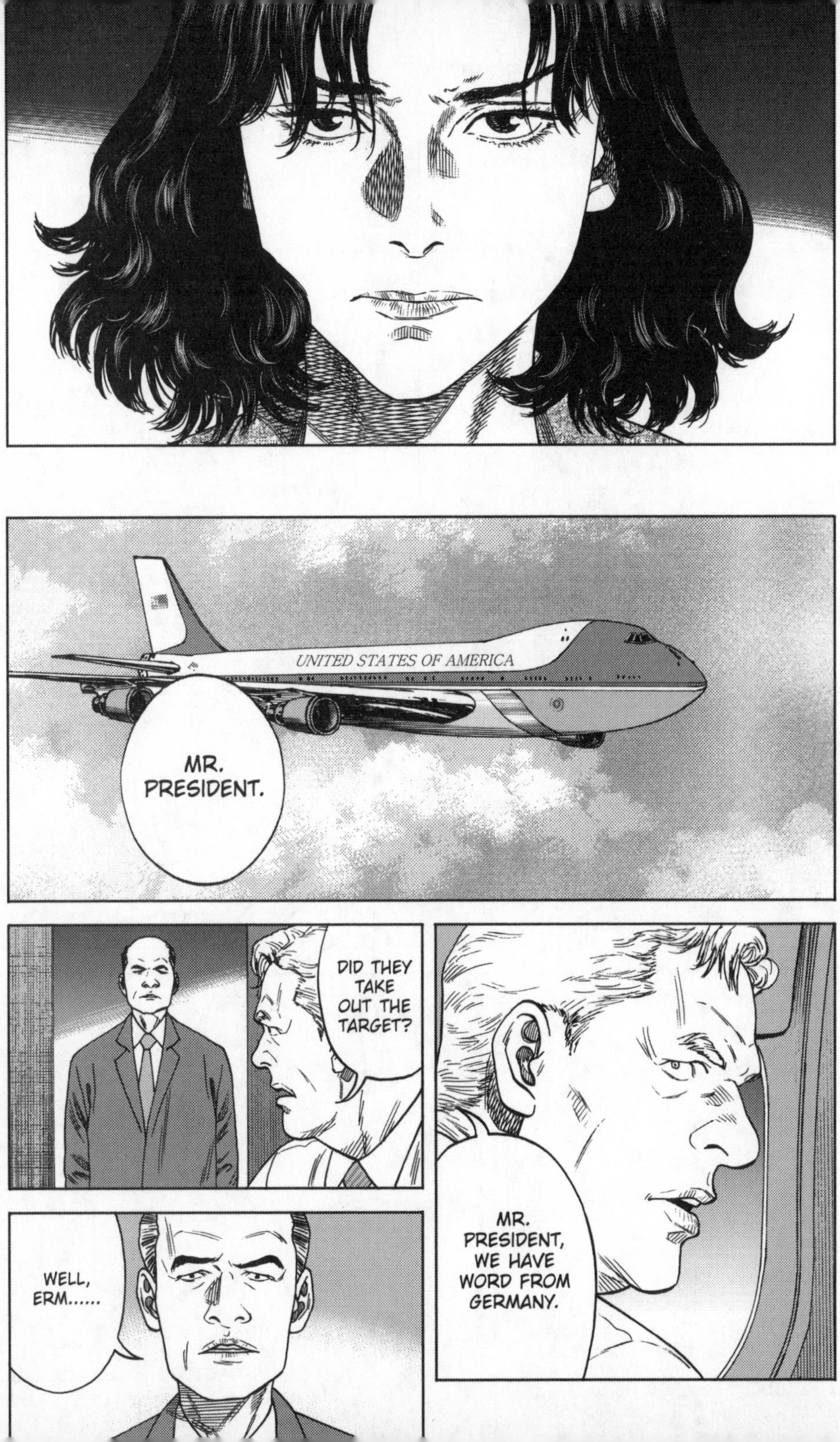
UNITED STATES OF AMERICA
MR. PRESIDENT.
MR. PRESIDENT, WE HAVE WORD FROM GERMANY.
DID THEY TAKE OUT THE TARGET?
WELL, ERM......

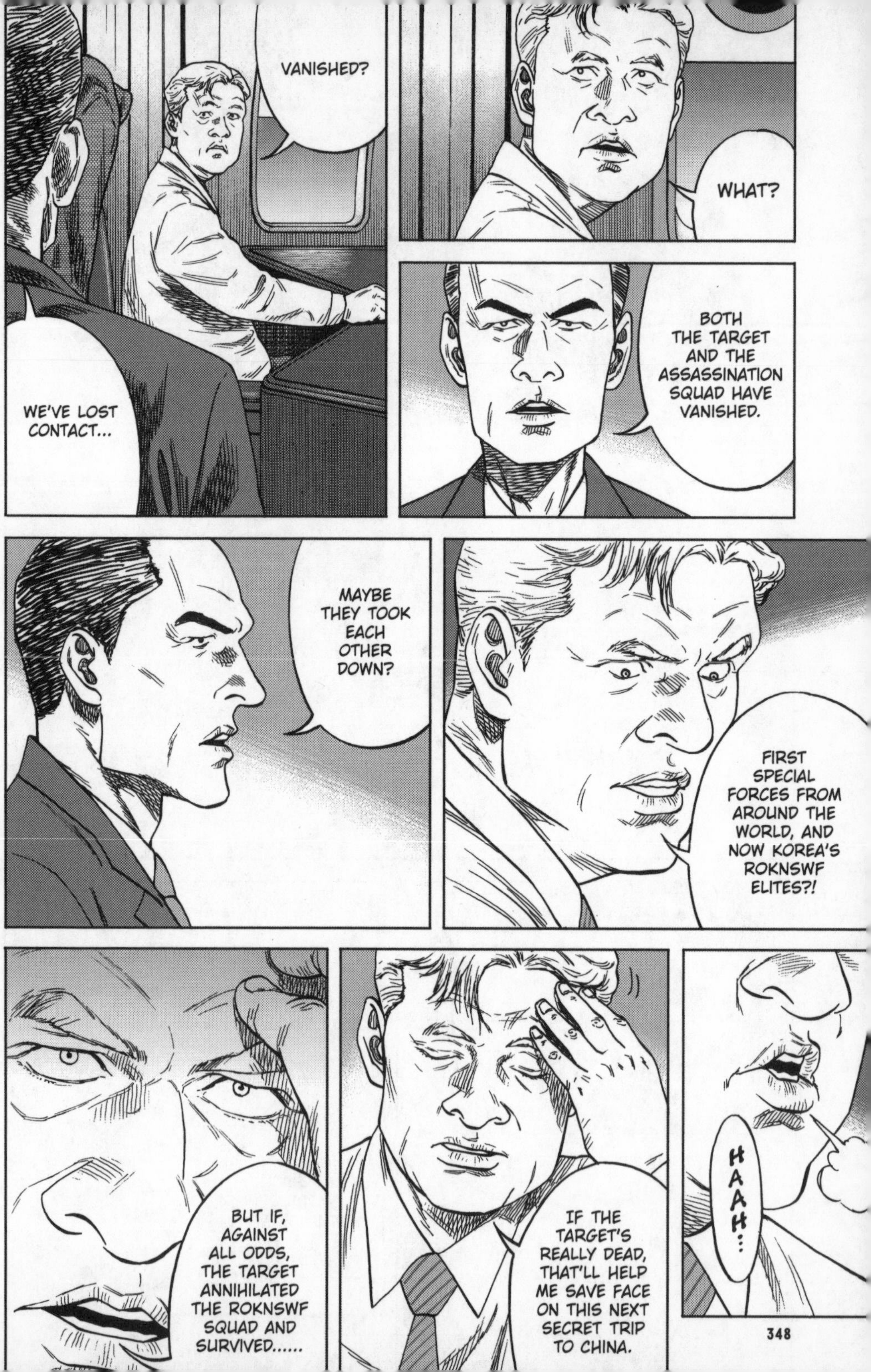
WHAT?
BOTH THE TARGET AND THE ASSASSINATION SQUAD HAVE VANISHED.
VANISHED?
WE'VE LOST CONTACT...
FIRST SPECIAL FORCES FROM AROUND THE WORLD, AND NOW KOREA'S ROKNSWF ELITES?!
MAYBE THEY TOOK EACH OTHER DOWN?
HAAAH...
IF THE TARGET'S REALLY DEAD, THAT'LL HELP ME SAVE FACE ON THIS NEXT SECRET TRIP TO CHINA.
BUT IF, AGAINST ALL ODDS, THE TARGET ANNIHILATED THE ROKNSWF SQUAD AND SURVIVED......

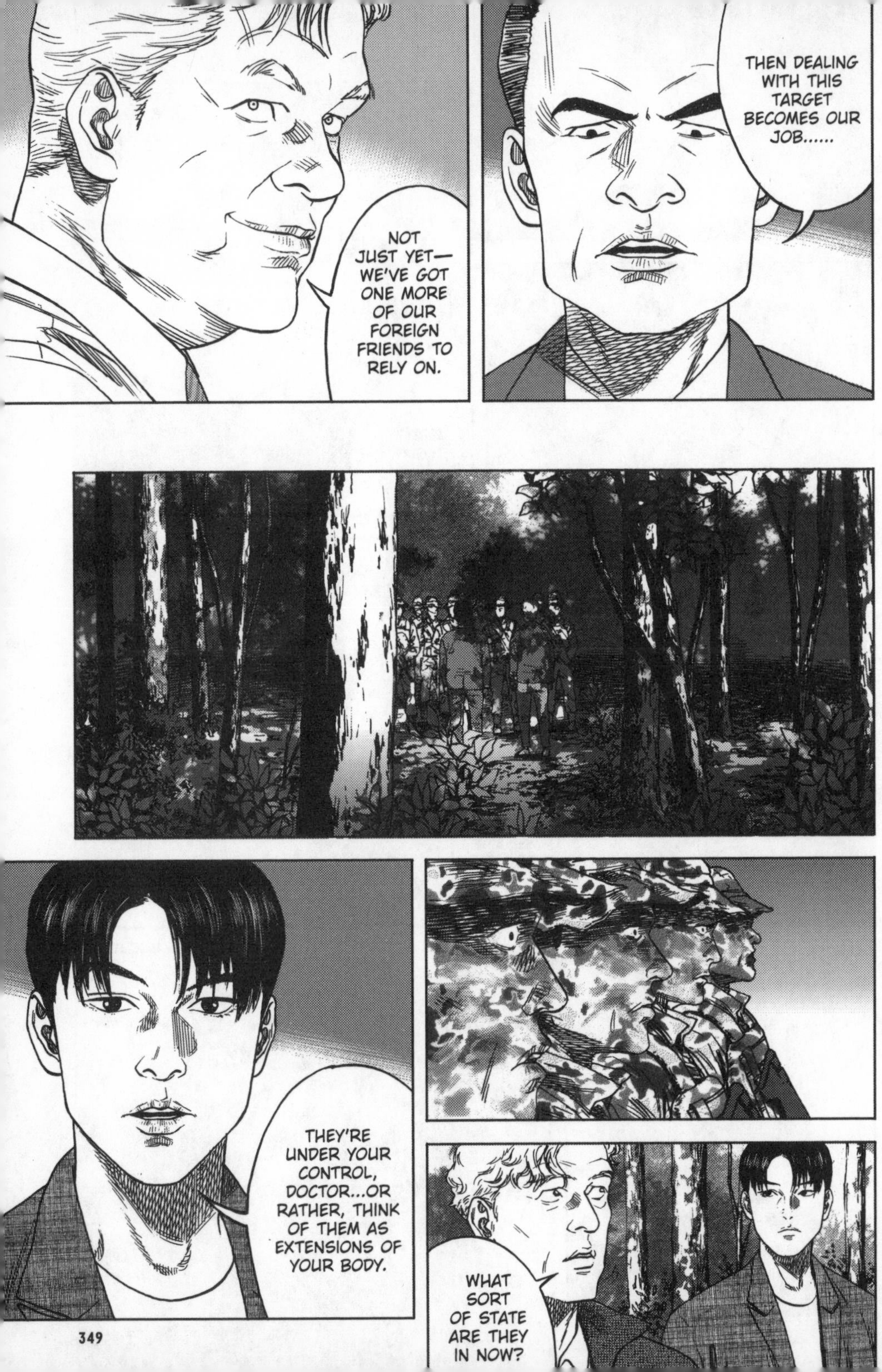
THEN DEALING WITH THIS TARGET BECOMES OUR JOB......
NOT JUST YET—WE'VE GOT ONE MORE OF OUR FOREIGN FRIENDS TO RELY ON.
WHAT SORT OF STATE ARE THEY IN NOW?
THEY'RE UNDER YOUR CONTROL, DOCTOR...OR RATHER, THINK OF THEM AS EXTENSIONS OF YOUR BODY.

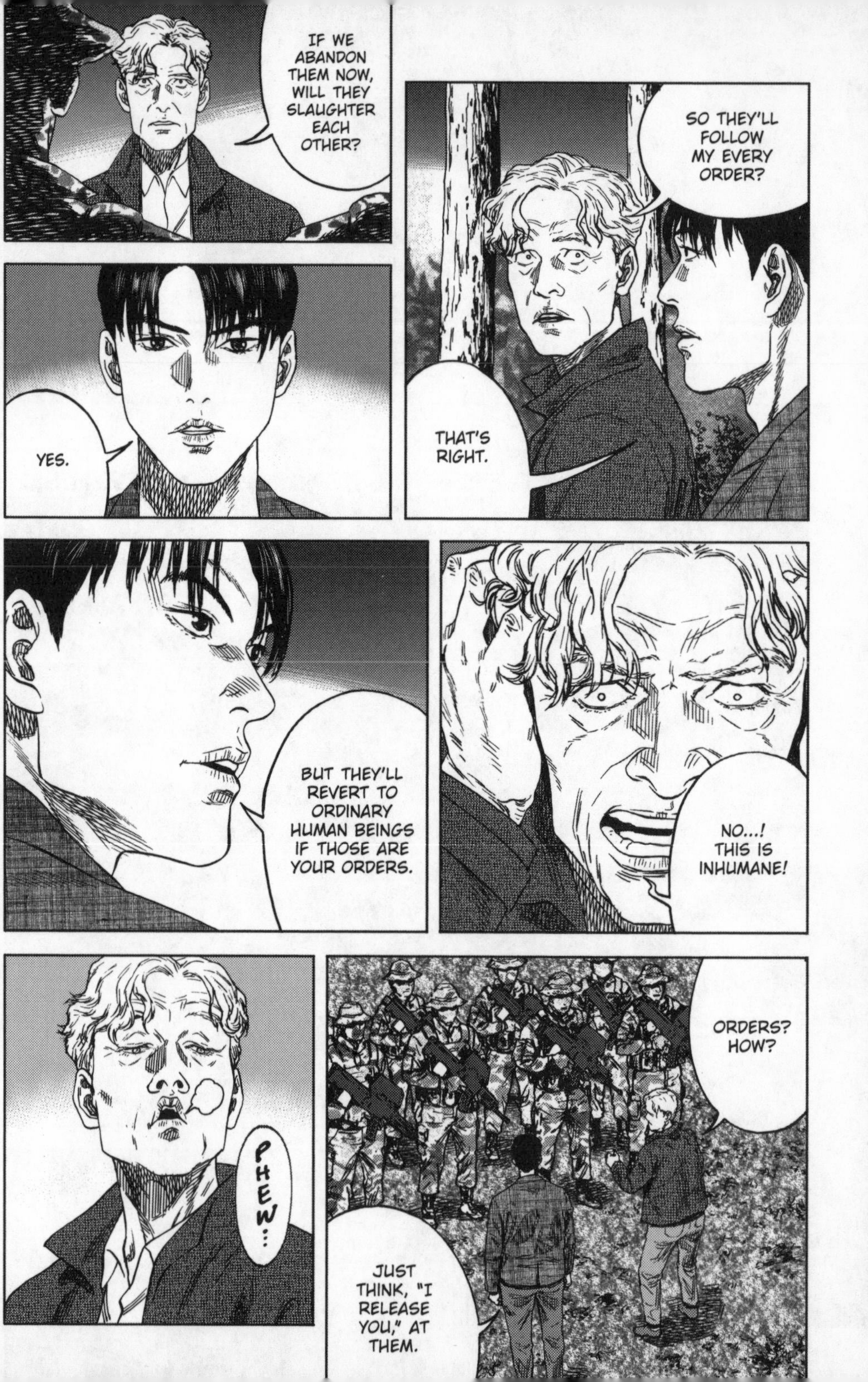
SO THEY'LL FOLLOW MY EVERY ORDER?
THAT'S RIGHT.
IF WE ABANDON THEM NOW, WILL THEY SLAUGHTER EACH OTHER?
YES.
NO...! THIS IS INHUMANE!
BUT THEY'LL REVERT TO ORDINARY HUMAN BEINGS IF THOSE ARE YOUR ORDERS.
ORDERS? HOW?
JUST THINK, "I RELEASE YOU," AT THEM.
PHEW...

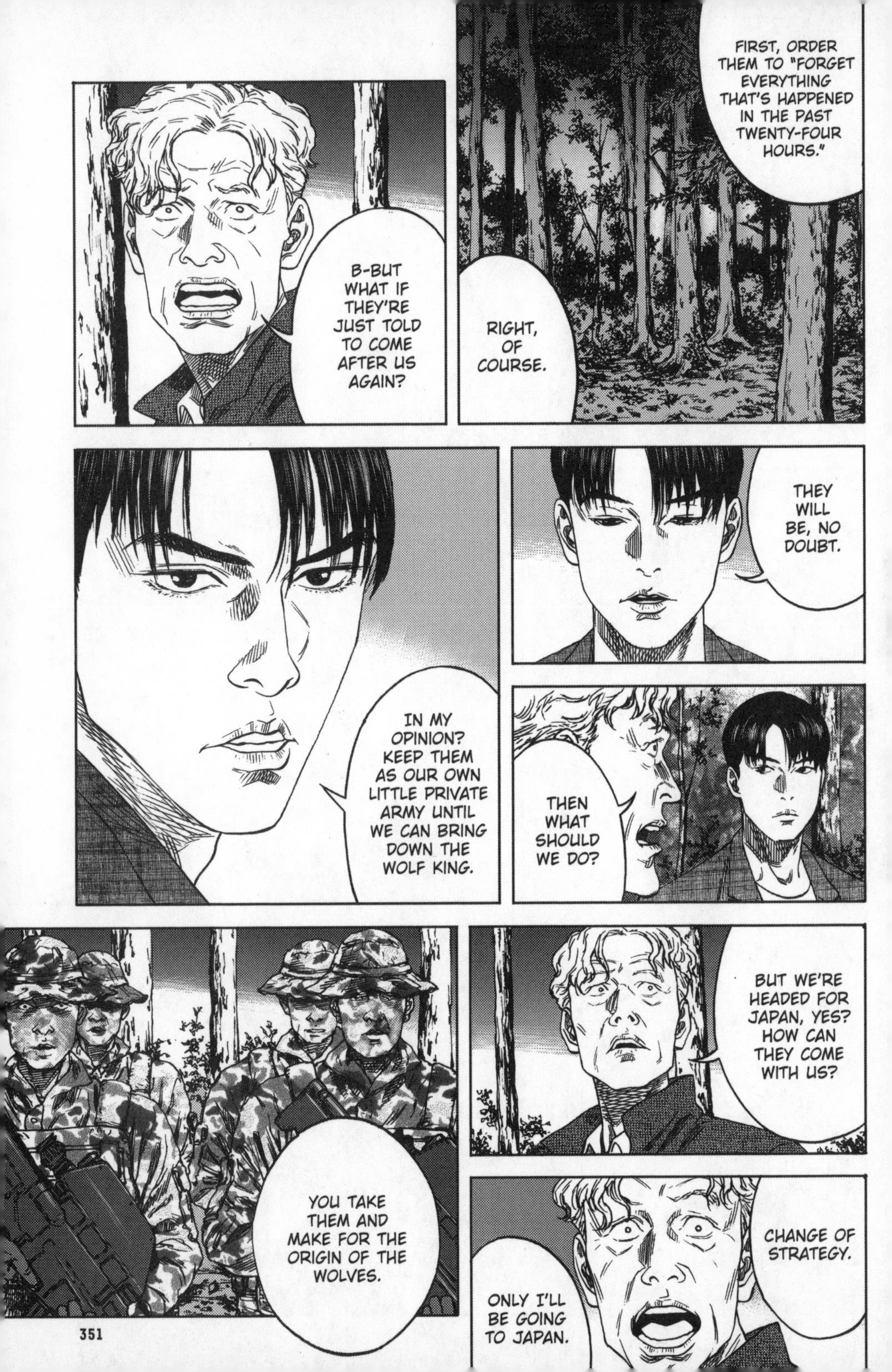

FIRST, ORDER THEM TO "FORGET EVERYTHING THAT'S HAPPENED IN THE PAST TWENTY-FOUR HOURS."
RIGHT, OF COURSE.
B-BUT WHAT IF THEY'RE JUST TOLD TO COME AFTER US AGAIN?
THEY WILL BE, NO DOUBT.
THEN WHAT SHOULD WE DO?
IN MY OPINION? KEEP THEM AS OUR OWN LITTLE PRIVATE ARMY UNTIL WE CAN BRING DOWN THE WOLF KING.
BUT WE'RE HEADED FOR JAPAN, YES? HOW CAN THEY COME WITH US?
CHANGE OF STRATEGY.
ONLY I'LL BE GOING TO JAPAN.
YOU TAKE THEM AND MAKE FOR THE ORIGIN OF THE WOLVES.

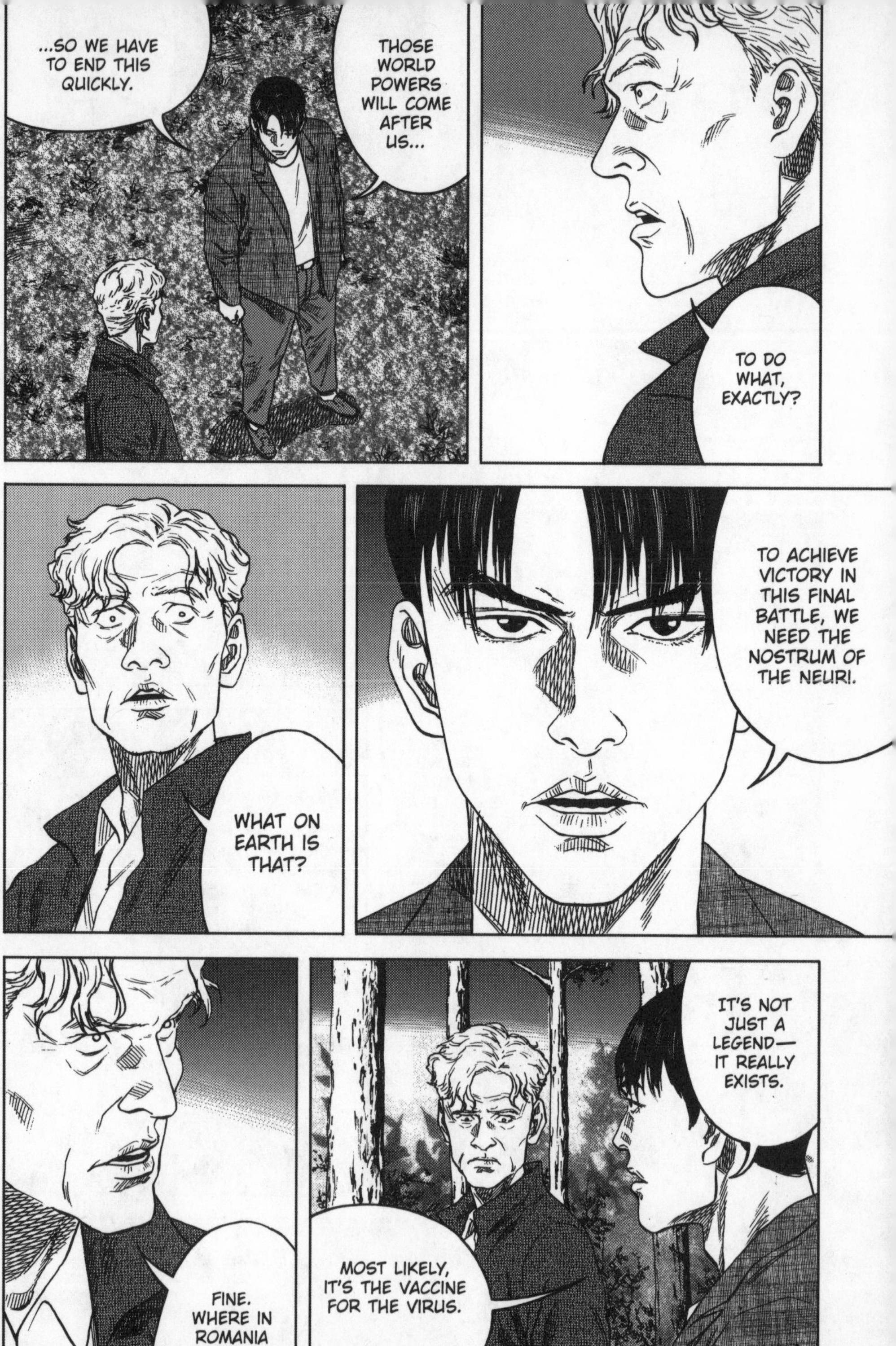
TO DO WHAT, EXACTLY?
THOSE WORLD POWERS WILL COME AFTER US...
...SO WE HAVE TO END THIS QUICKLY.
TO ACHIEVE VICTORY IN THIS FINAL BATTLE, WE NEED THE NOSTRUM OF THE NEURI.
WHAT ON EARTH IS THAT?
IT'S NOT JUST A LEGEND—IT REALLY EXISTS.
MOST LIKELY, IT'S THE VACCINE FOR THE VIRUS.
FINE. WHERE IN ROMANIA SHOULD I SEARCH?

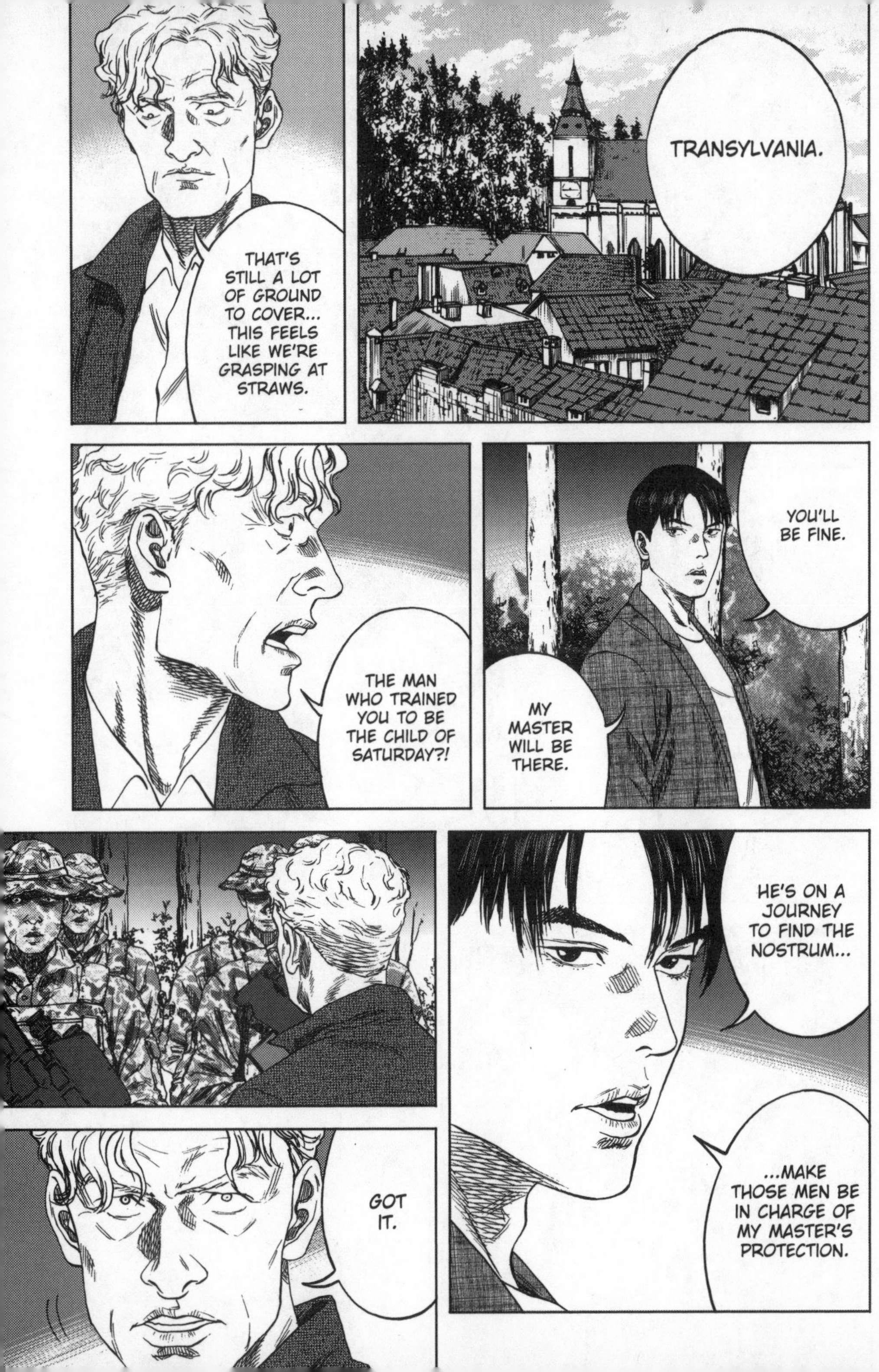
TRANSYLVANIA.
THAT'S STILL A LOT OF GROUND TO COVER... THIS FEELS LIKE WE'RE GRASPING AT STRAWS.
YOU'LL BE FINE.
MY MASTER WILL BE THERE.
THE MAN WHO TRAINED YOU TO BE THE CHILD OF SATURDAY?!
HE'S ON A JOURNEY TO FIND THE NOSTRUM...
...MAKE THOSE MEN BE IN CHARGE OF MY MASTER'S PROTECTION.
GOT IT.

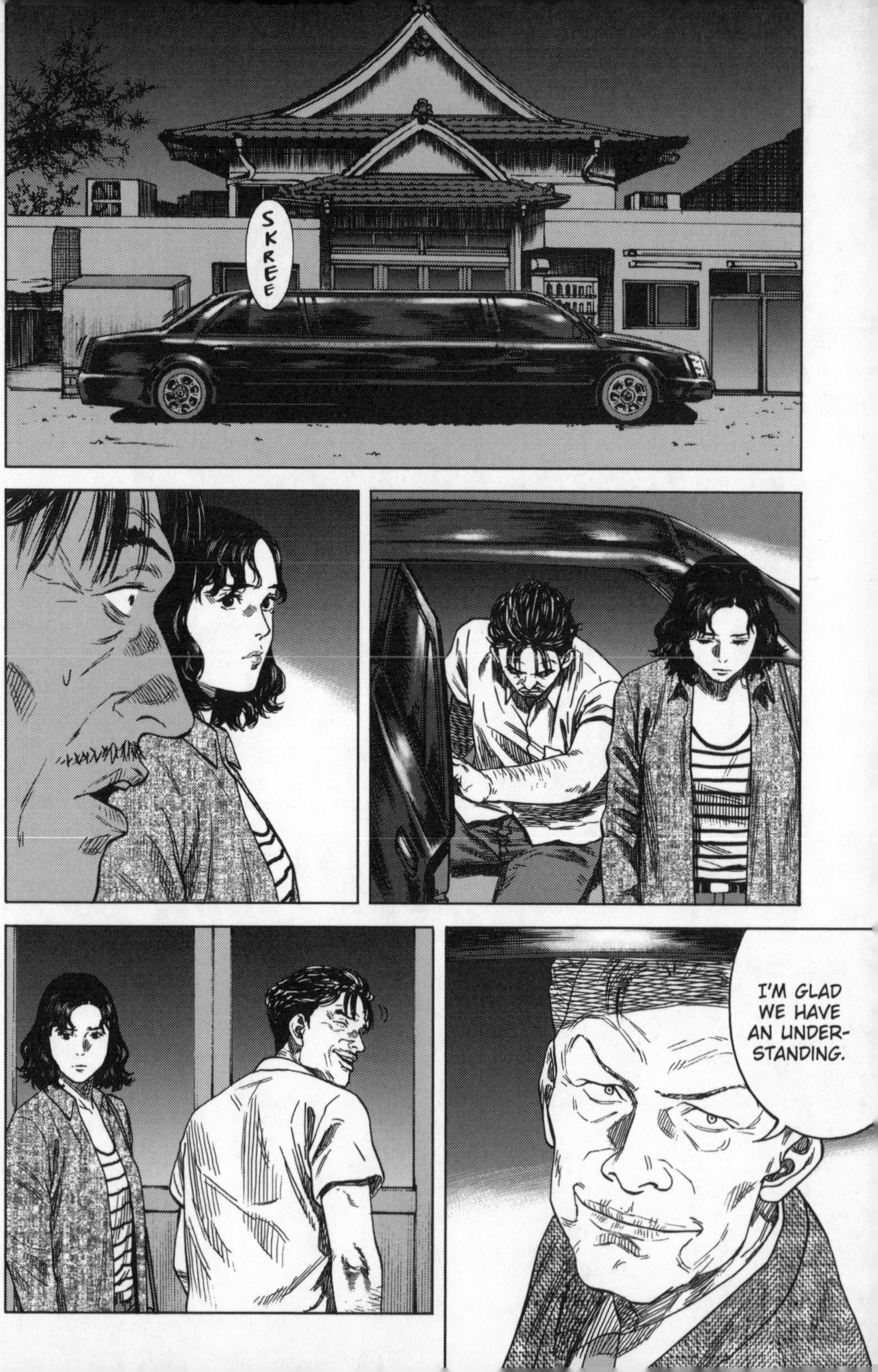
SKREE
I'M GLAD WE HAVE AN UNDER-STANDING.

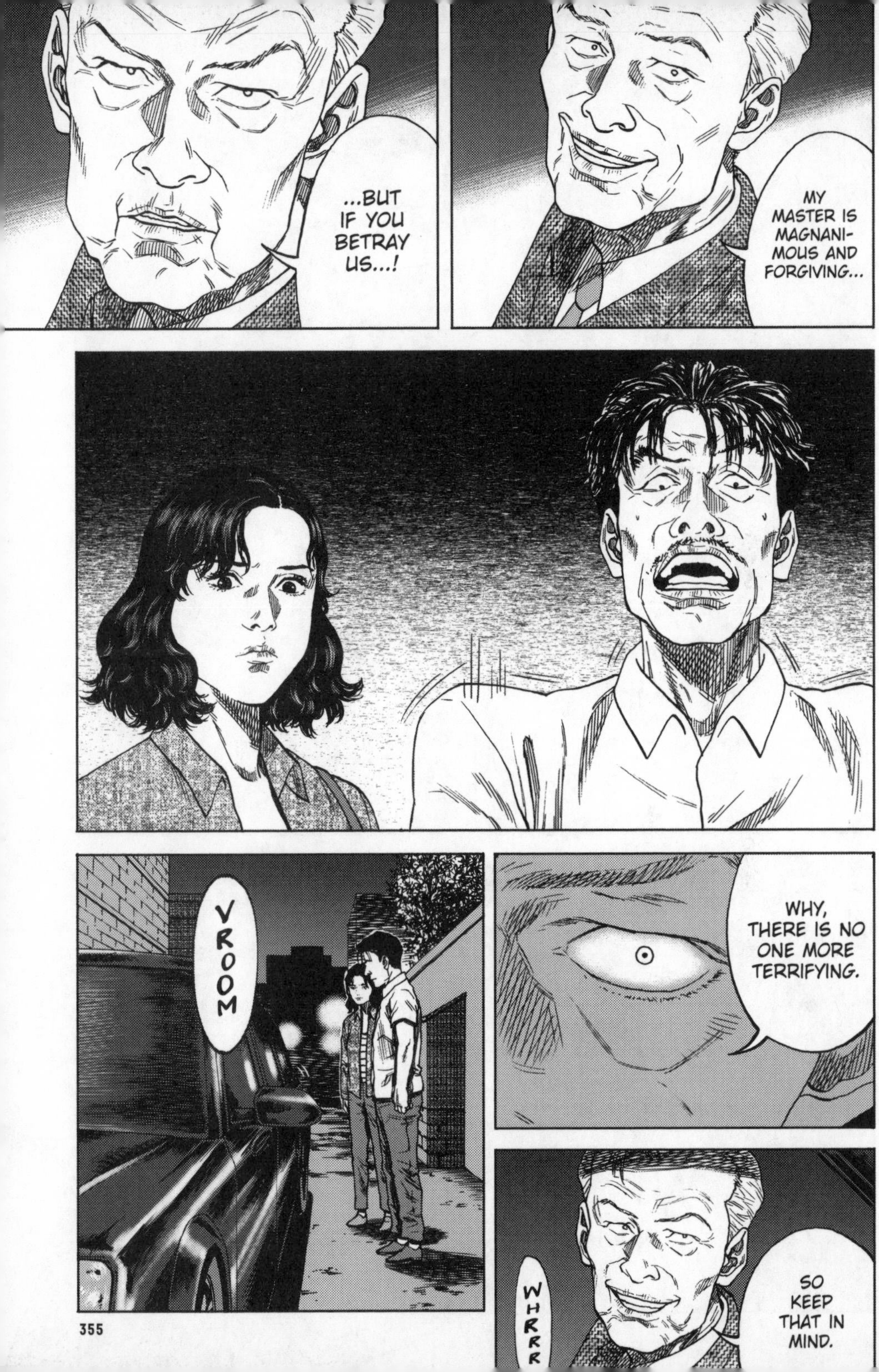
MY MASTER IS MAGNANI-MOUS AND FORGIVING...
...BUT IF YOU BETRAY US...!
WHY, THERE IS NO ONE MORE TERRIFYING.
SO KEEP THAT IN MIND.
WHRRR
VROOM

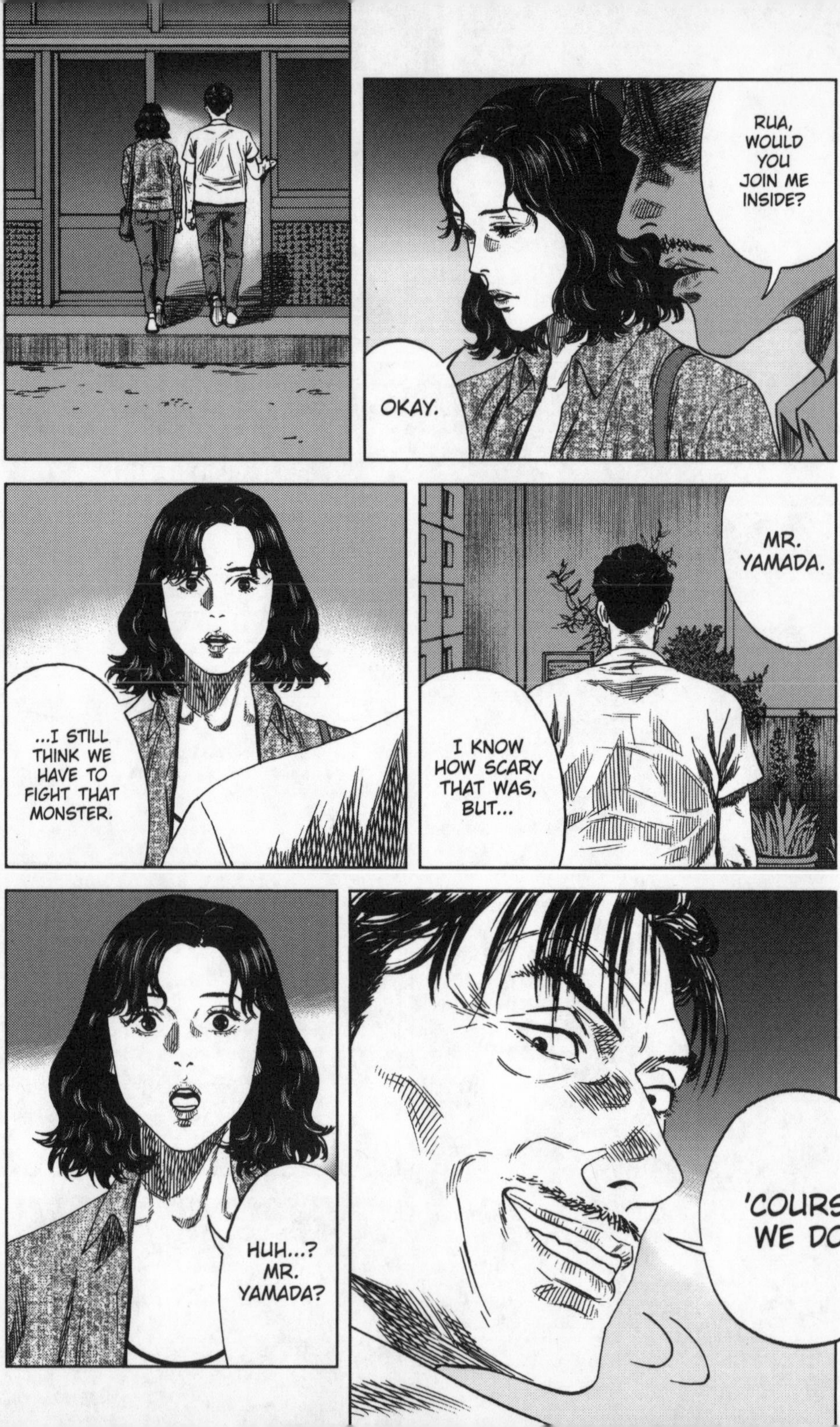
RUA, WOULD YOU JOIN ME INSIDE?
OKAY.
MR. YAMADA.
I KNOW HOW SCARY THAT WAS, BUT...
...I STILL THINK WE HAVE TO FIGHT THAT MONSTER.
'COURSE WE DO.
HUH...? MR. YAMADA?

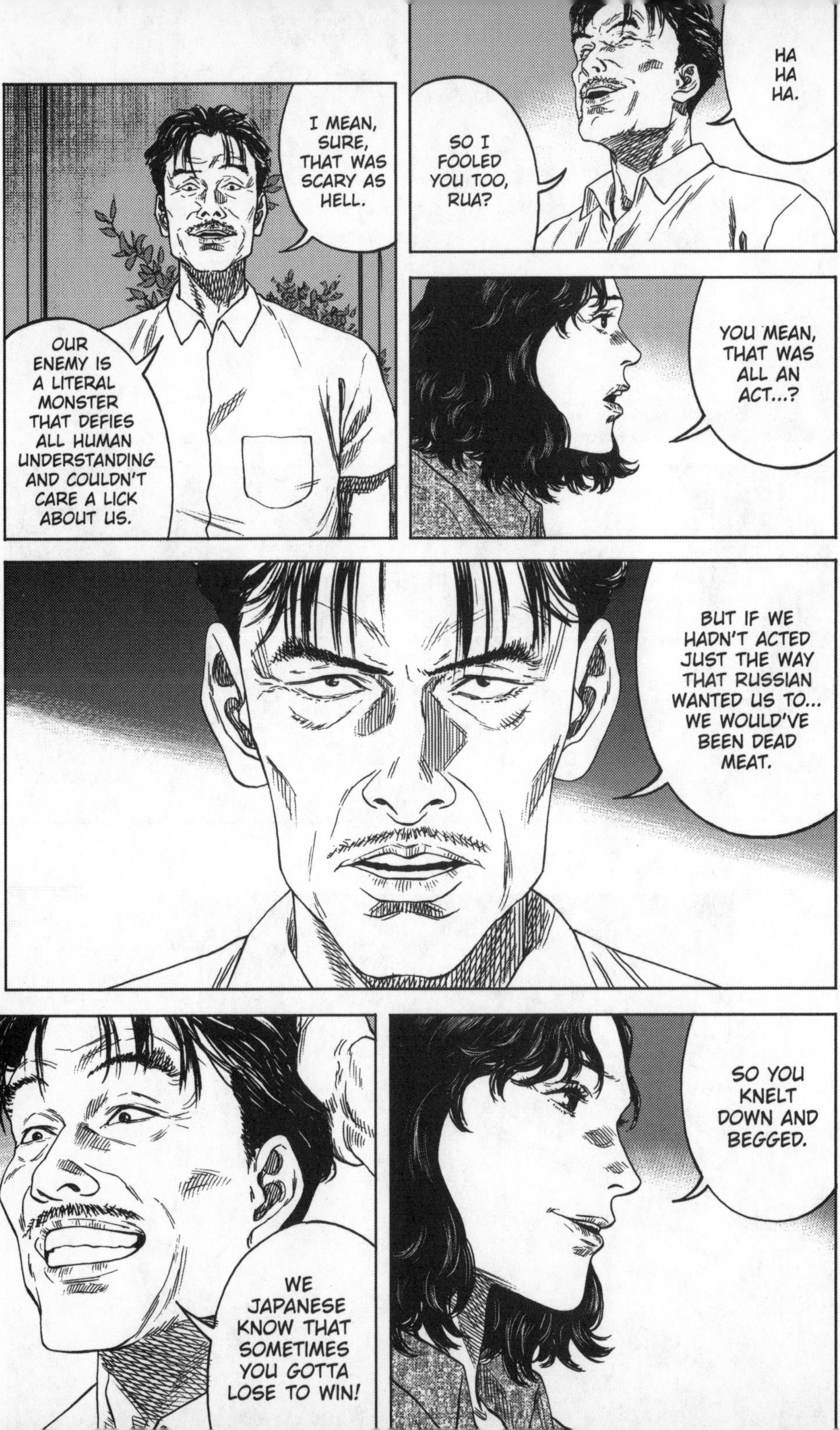

HA HA HA.
SO I FOOLED YOU TOO, RUA?
YOU MEAN, THAT WAS ALL AN ACT...?
I MEAN, SURE, THAT WAS SCARY AS HELL.
OUR ENEMY IS A LITERAL MONSTER THAT DEFIES ALL HUMAN UNDERSTANDING AND COULDN'T CARE A LICK ABOUT US.
BUT IF WE HADN'T ACTED JUST THE WAY THAT RUSSIAN WANTED US TO... WE WOULD'VE BEEN DEAD MEAT.
SO YOU KNELT DOWN AND BEGGED.
WE JAPANESE KNOW THAT SOMETIMES YOU GOTTA LOSE TO WIN!

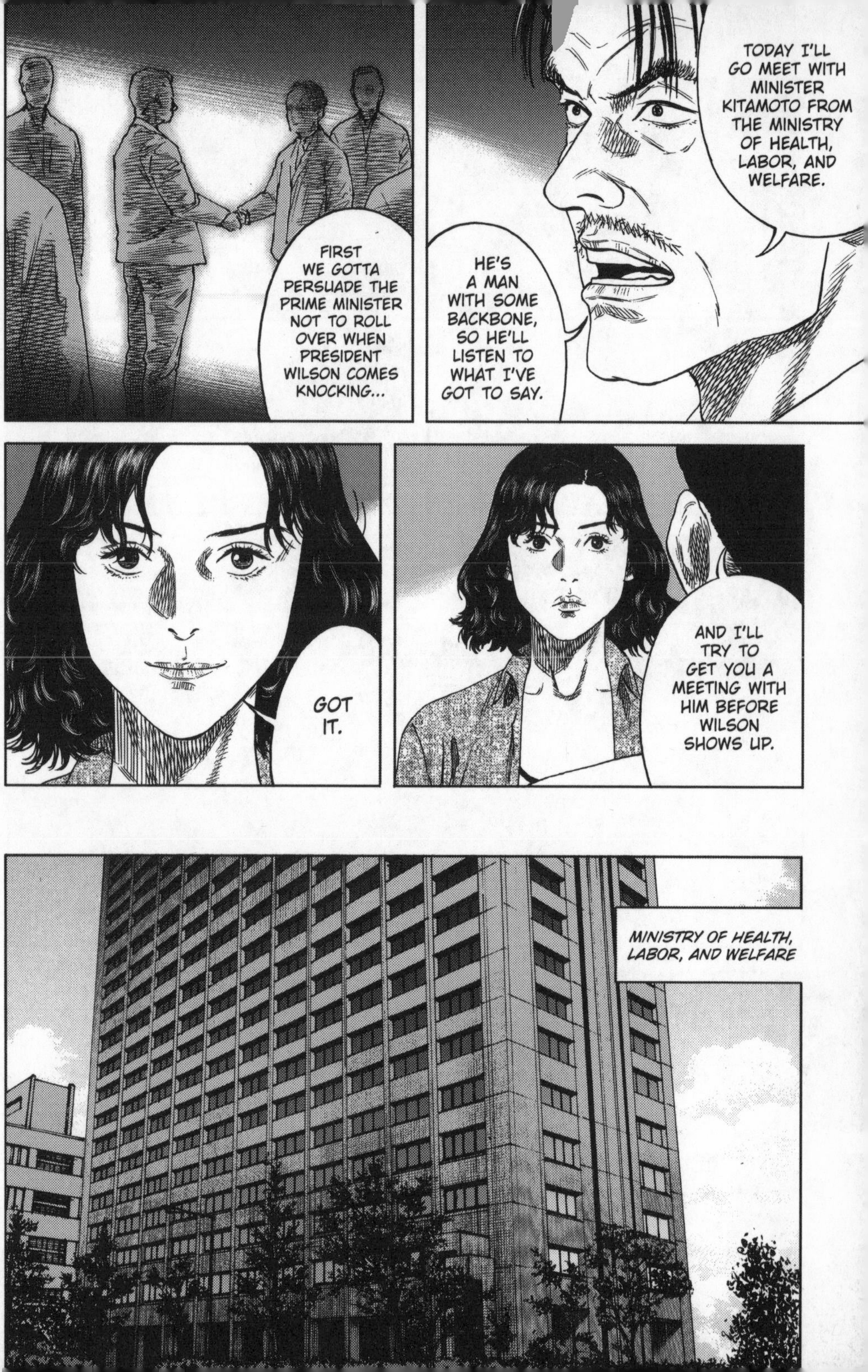
TODAY I'LL GO MEET WITH MINISTER KITAMOTO FROM THE MINISTRY OF HEALTH, LABOR, AND WELFARE.
HE'S A MAN WITH SOME BACKBONE, SO HE'LL LISTEN TO WHAT I'VE GOT TO SAY.
FIRST WE GOTTA PERSUADE THE PRIME MINISTER NOT TO ROLL OVER WHEN PRESIDENT WILSON COMES KNOCKING...
AND I'LL TRY TO GET YOU A MEETING WITH HIM BEFORE WILSON SHOWS UP.
GOT IT.
MINISTRY OF HEALTH, LABOR, AND WELFARE

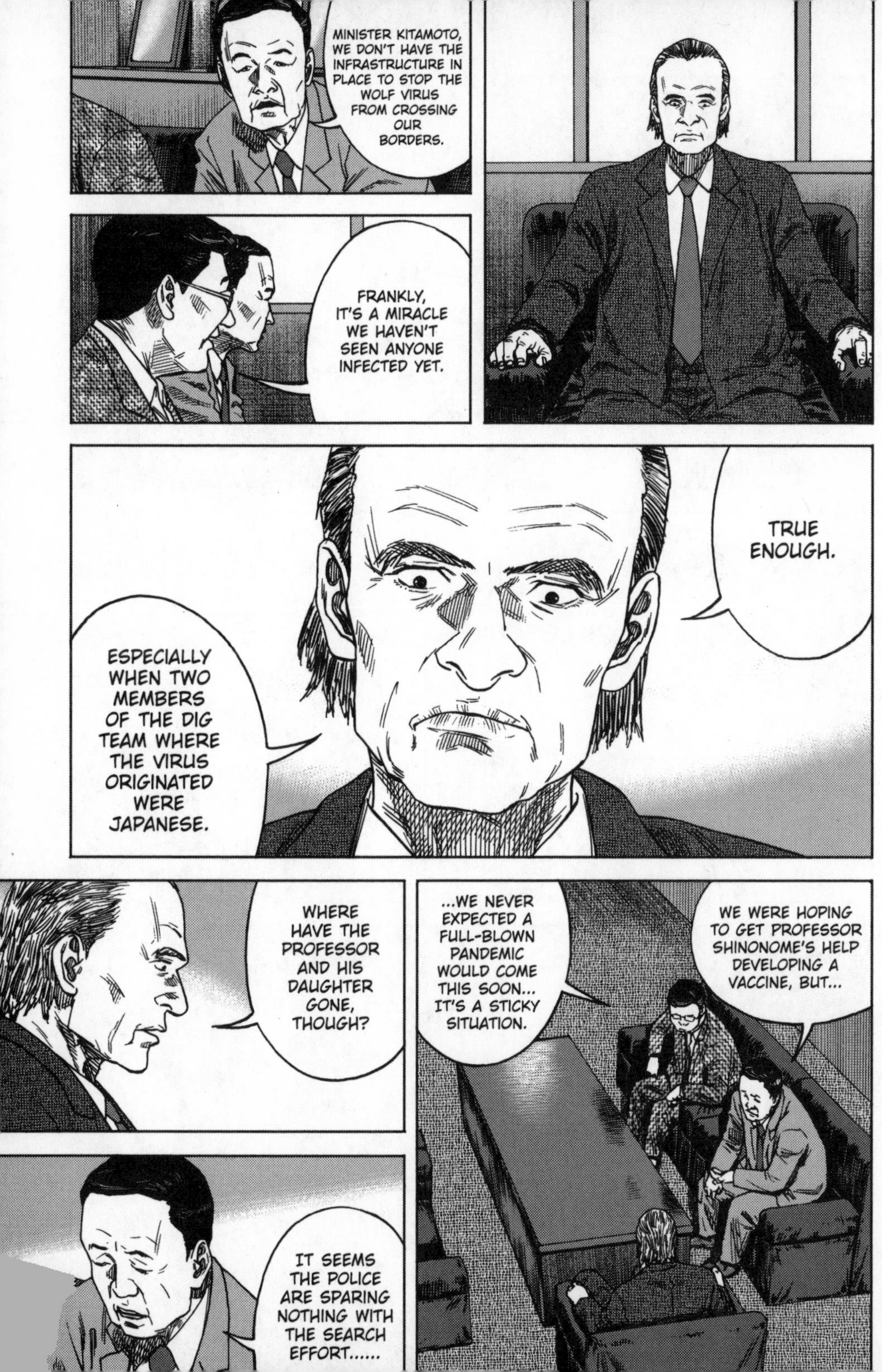
MINISTER KITAMOTO, WE DON'T HAVE THE INFRASTRUCTURE IN PLACE TO STOP THE WOLF VIRUS FROM CROSSING OUR BORDERS.
FRANKLY, IT'S A MIRACLE WE HAVEN'T SEEN ANYONE INFECTED YET.
TRUE ENOUGH.
ESPECIALLY WHEN TWO MEMBERS OF THE DIG TEAM WHERE THE VIRUS ORIGINATED WERE JAPANESE.
WE WERE HOPING TO GET PROFESSOR SHINONOME'S HELP DEVELOPING A VACCINE, BUT...
...WE NEVER EXPECTED A FULL-BLOWN PANDEMIC WOULD COME THIS SOON... IT'S A STICKY SITUATION.
WHERE HAVE THE PROFESSOR AND HIS DAUGHTER GONE, THOUGH?
IT SEEMS THE POLICE ARE SPARING NOTHING WITH THE SEARCH EFFORT......

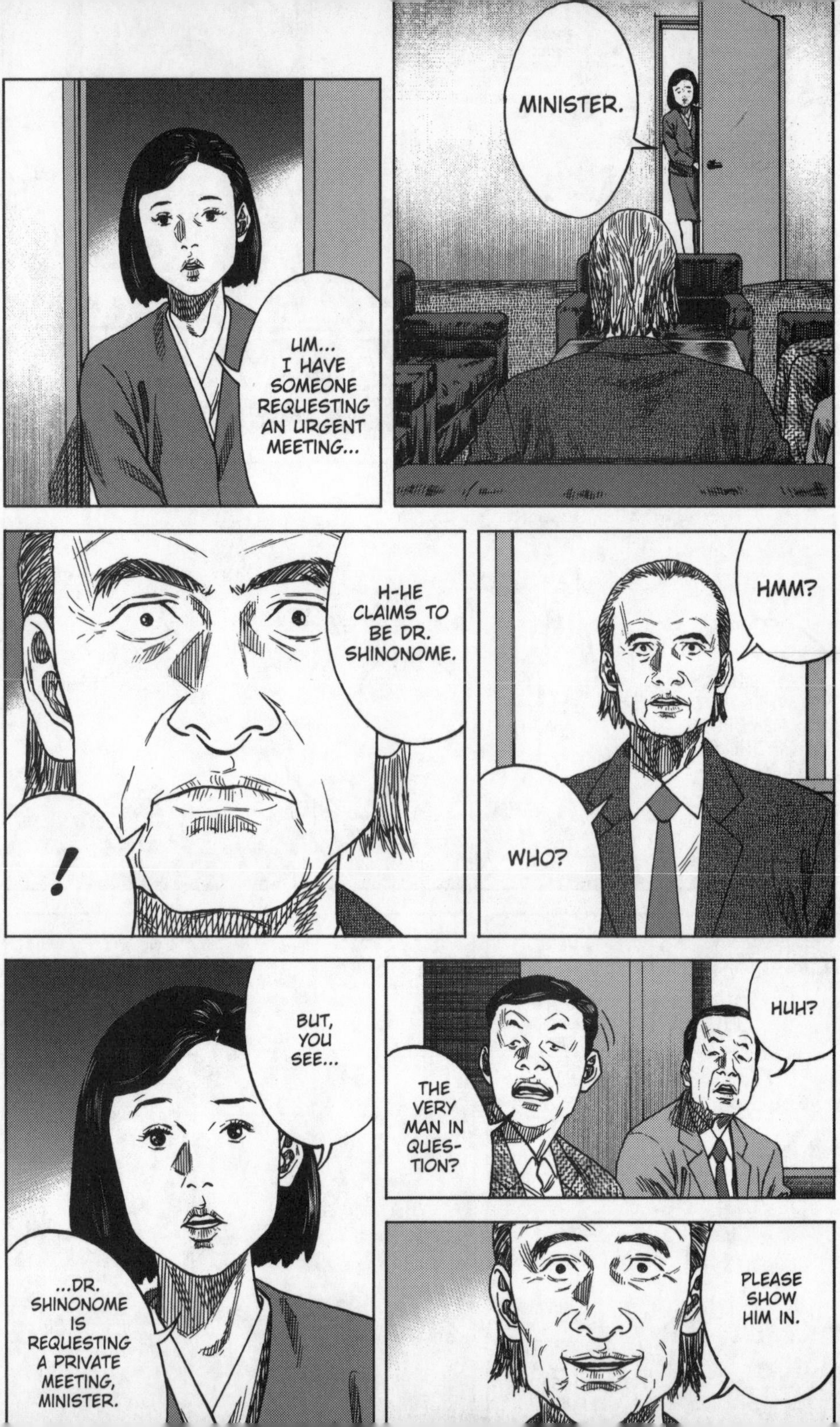
MINISTER.
UM... I HAVE SOMEONE REQUESTING AN URGENT MEETING...
HMM?
WHO?
H-HE CLAIMS TO BE DR. SHINONOME.
!
HUH?
THE VERY MAN IN QUES-TION?
PLEASE SHOW HIM IN.
BUT, YOU SEE...
...DR. SHINONOME IS REQUESTING A PRIVATE MEETING, MINISTER.

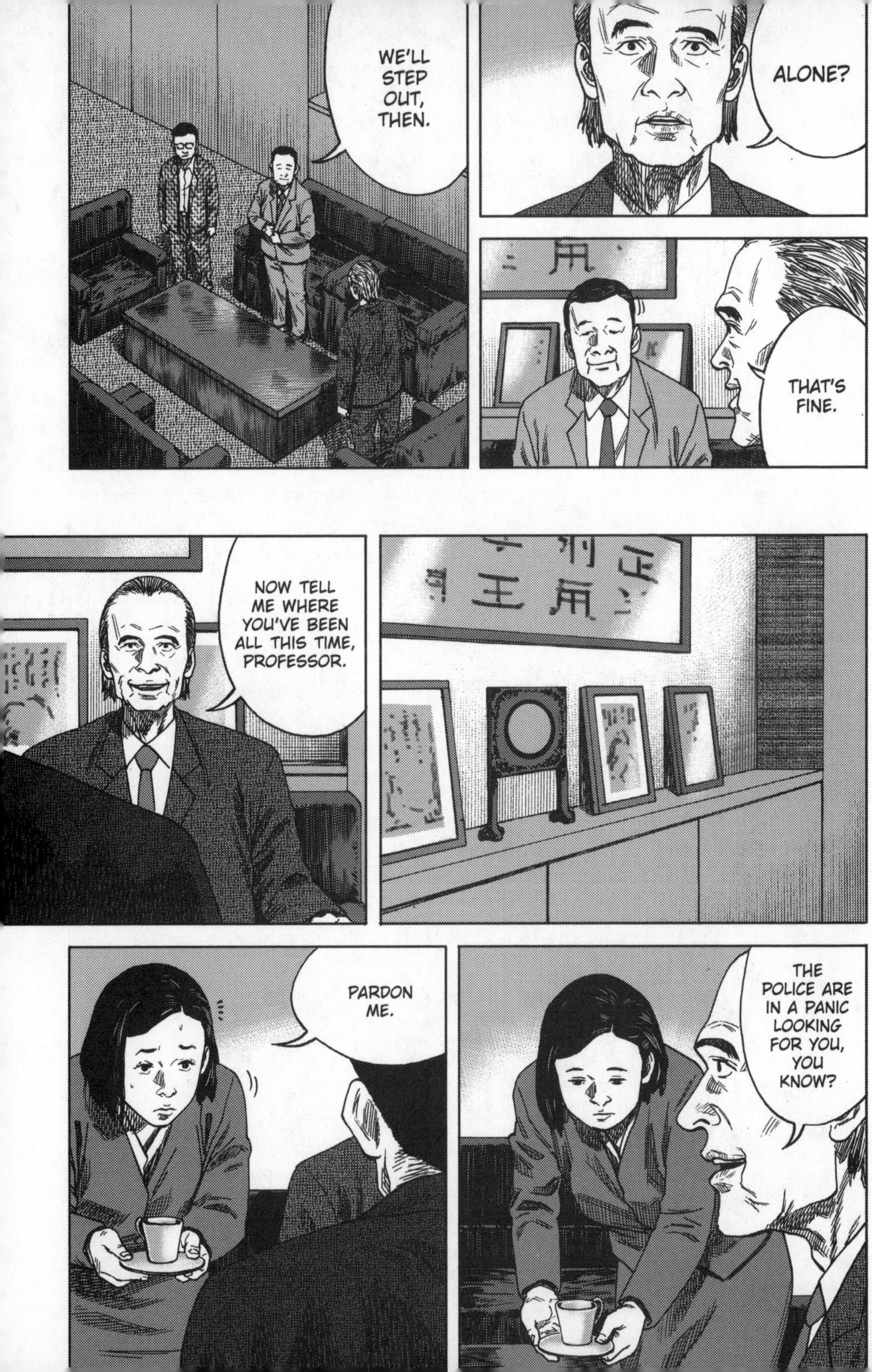
ALONE?
THAT'S FINE.
WE'LL STEP OUT, THEN.
NOW TELL ME WHERE YOU'VE BEEN ALL THIS TIME, PROFESSOR.
THE POLICE ARE IN A PANIC LOOKING FOR YOU, YOU KNOW?
PARDON ME.

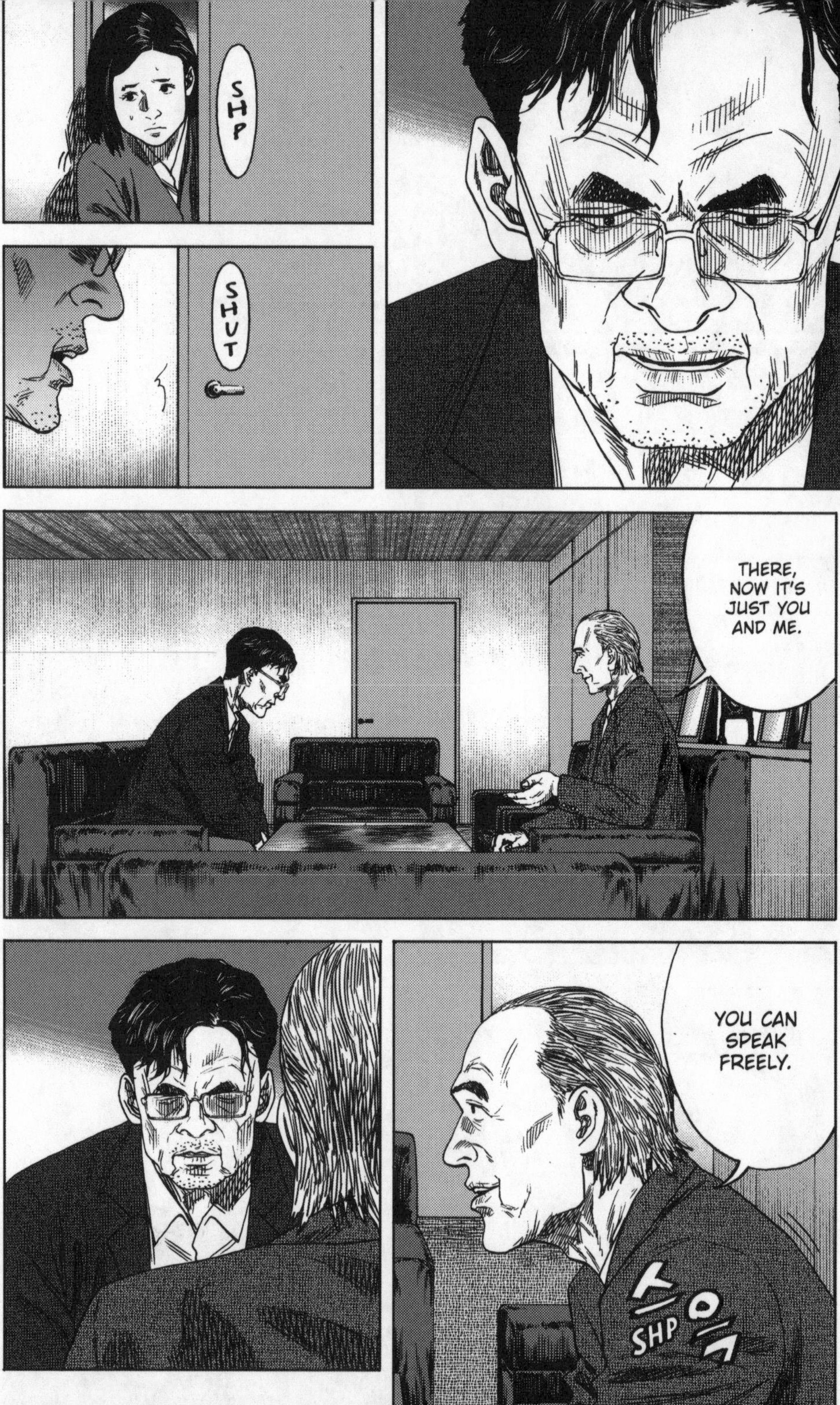
SHP
SHUT
THERE, NOW IT'S JUST YOU AND ME.
YOU CAN SPEAK FREELY.
SHP

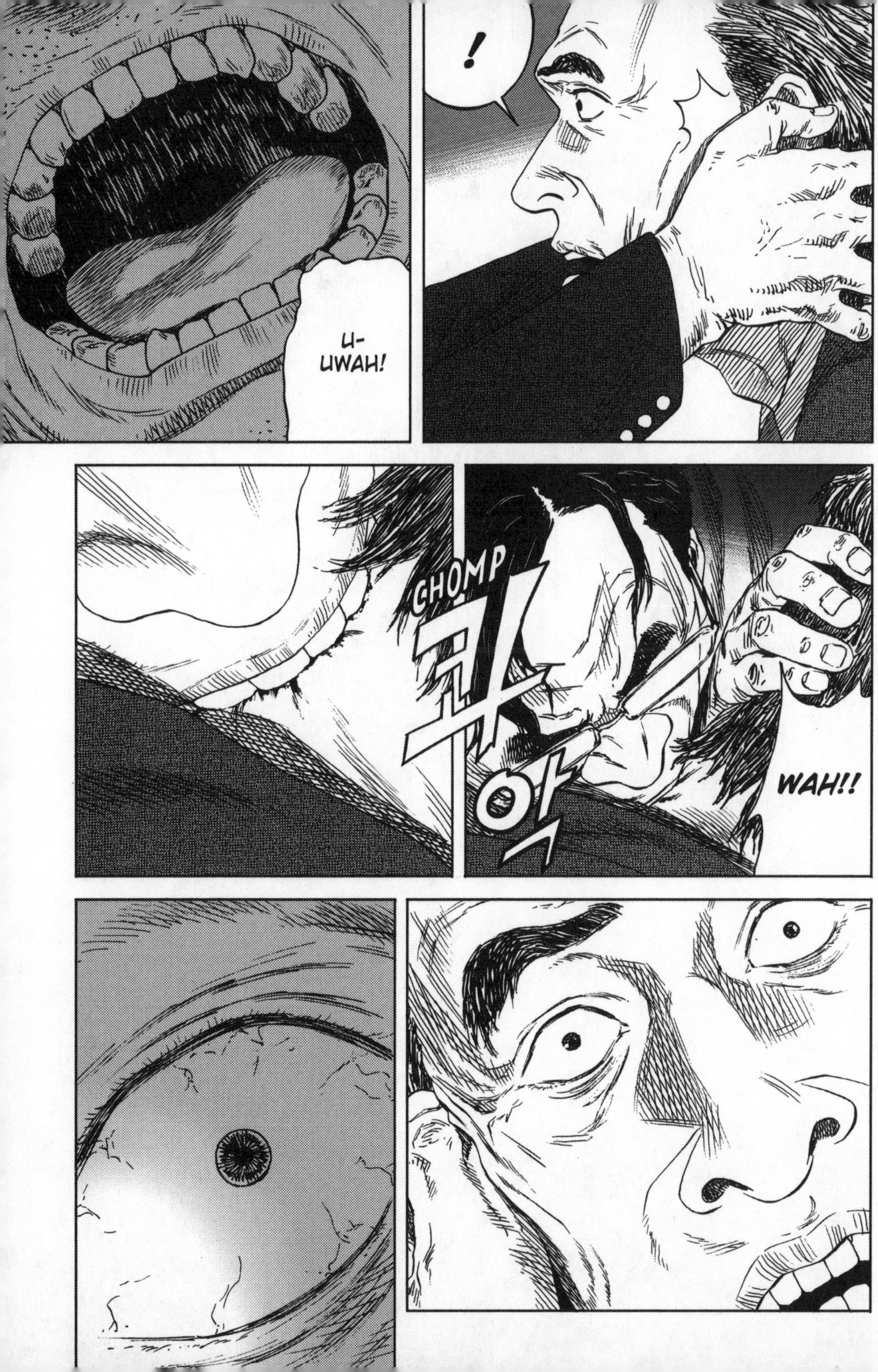
!
U-UWAH!
CHOMP
콰악
WAH!!

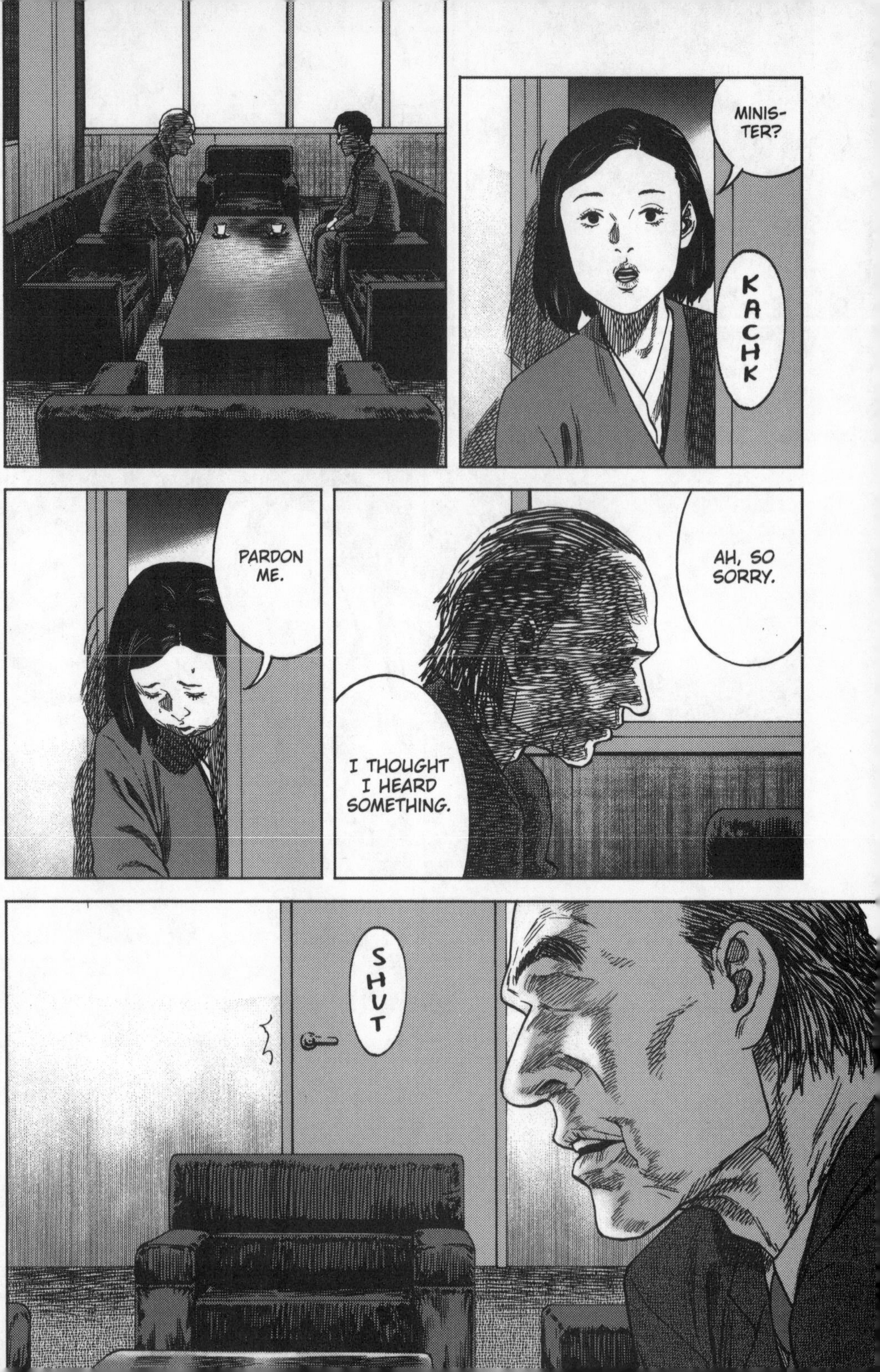
MINIS-
TER?
KACHK
AH, SO
SORRY.
I THOUGHT
I HEARD
SOMETHING.
PARDON
ME.
SHUT

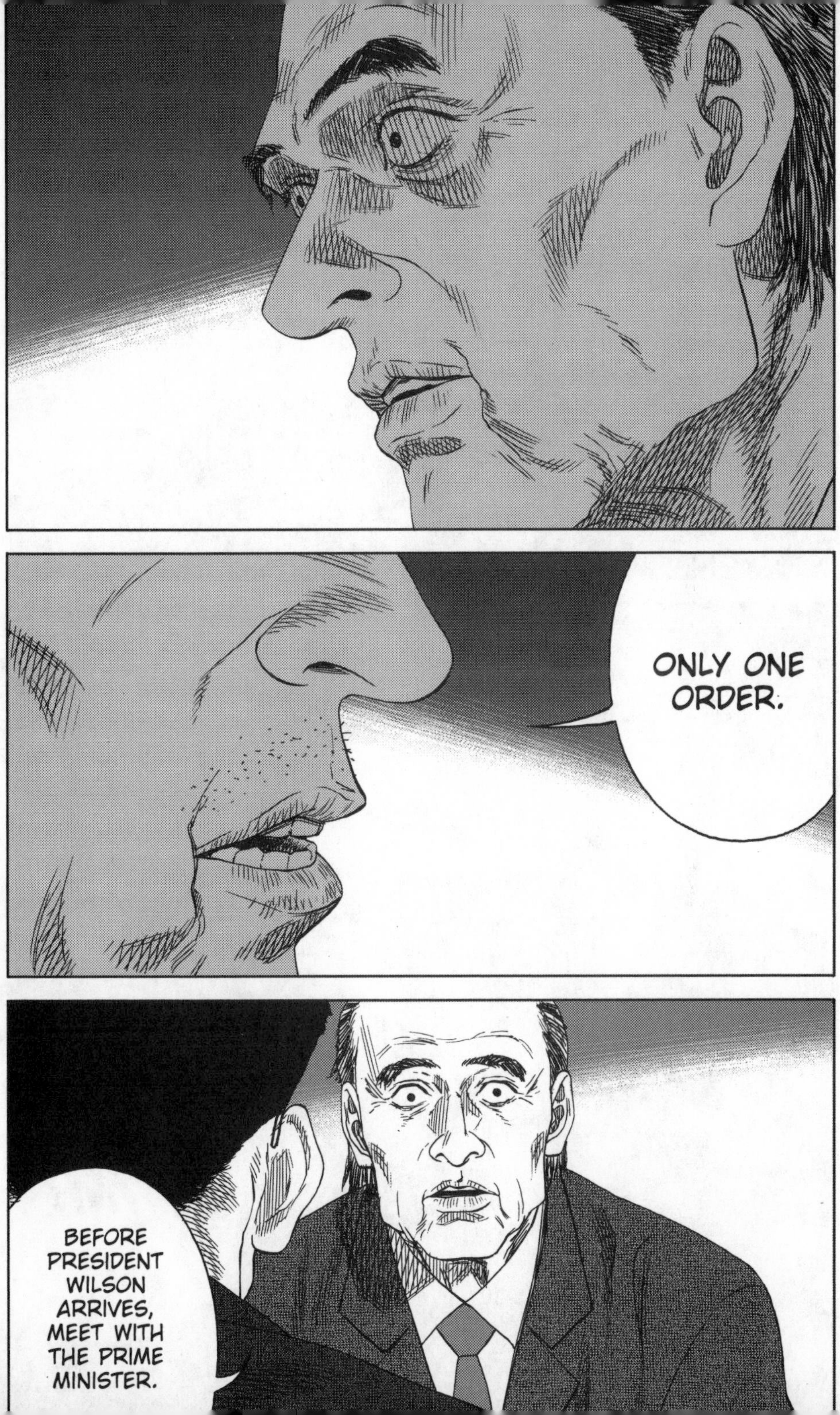
ONLY ONE ORDER.
BEFORE PRESIDENT WILSON ARRIVES, MEET WITH THE PRIME MINISTER.

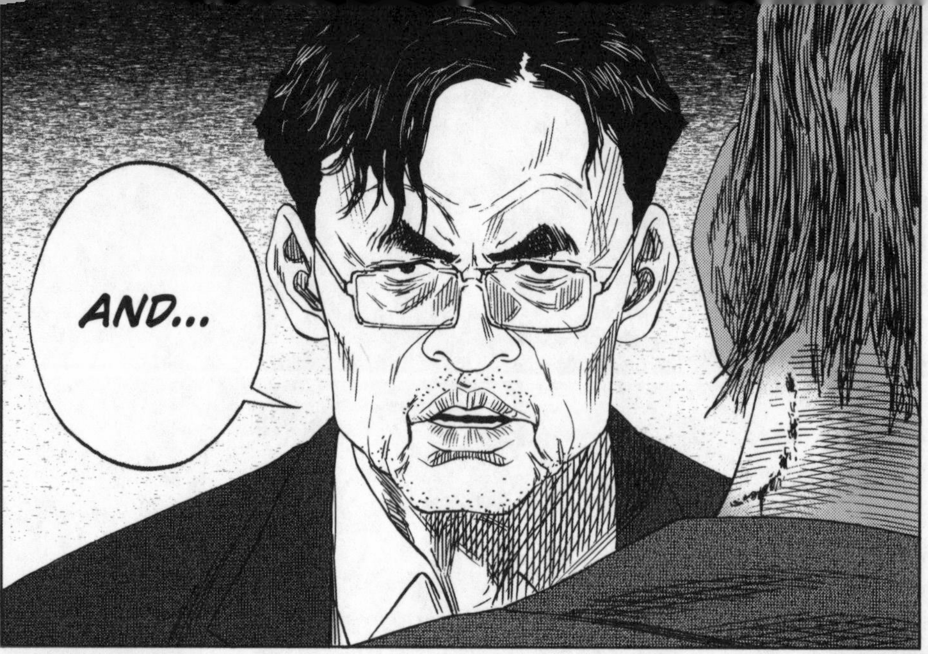
AND...

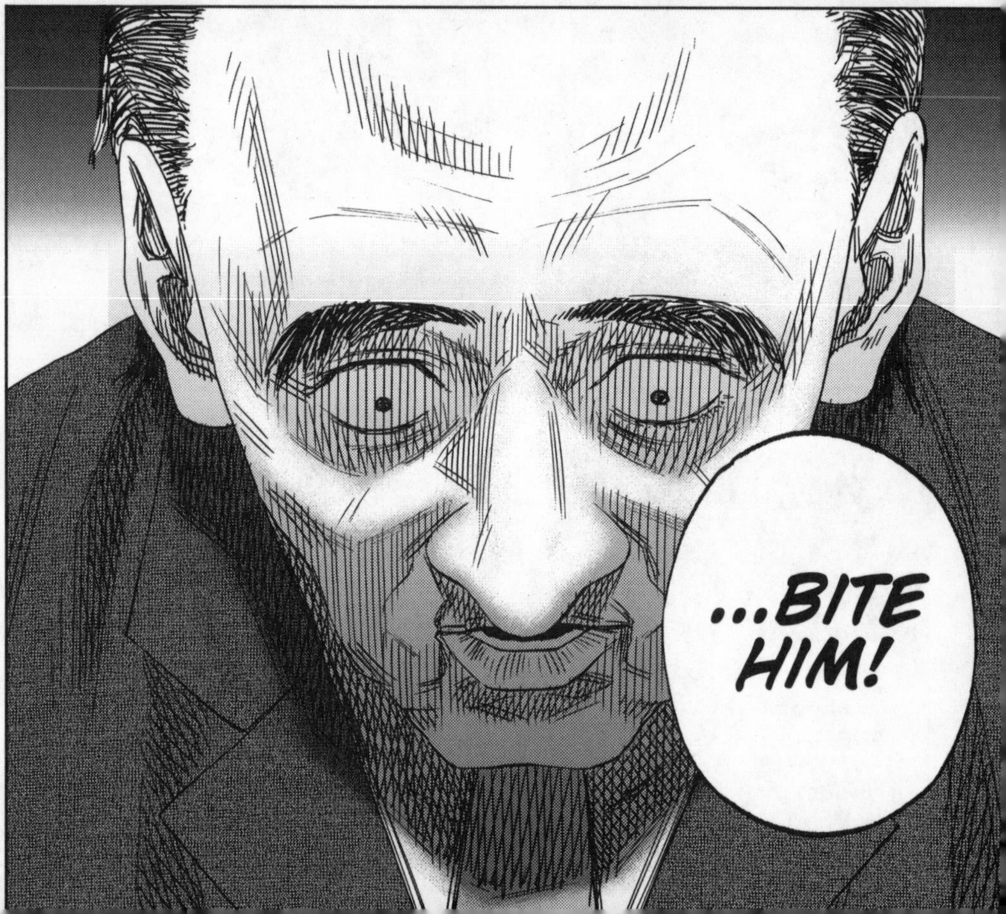
...BITE HIM!

KING OF EDEN

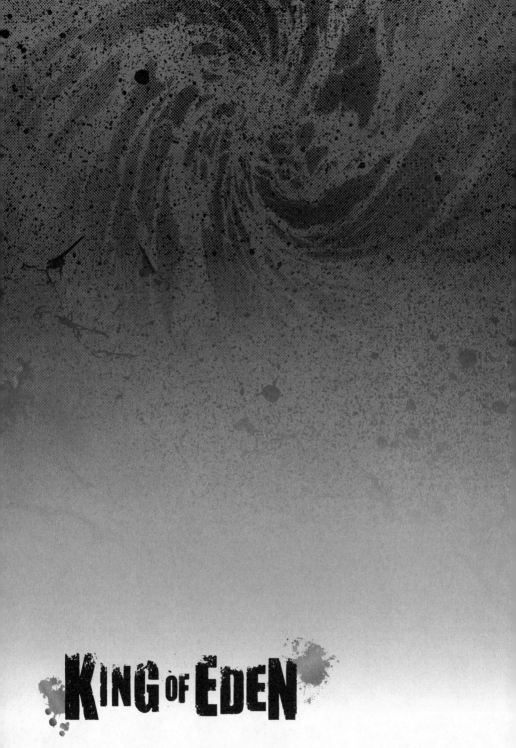

KING OF EDEN

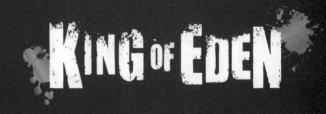

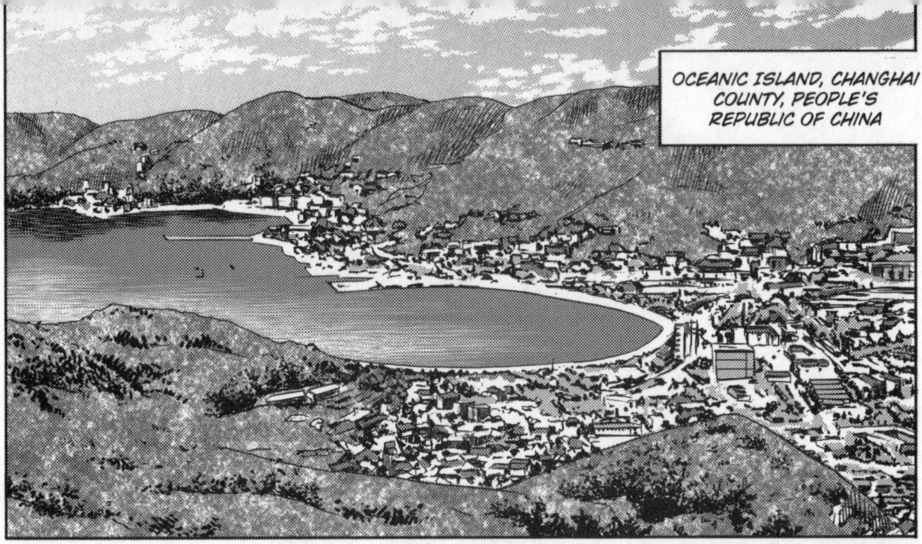
OCEANIC ISLAND, CHANGHAI COUNTY, PEOPLE'S REPUBLIC OF CHINA
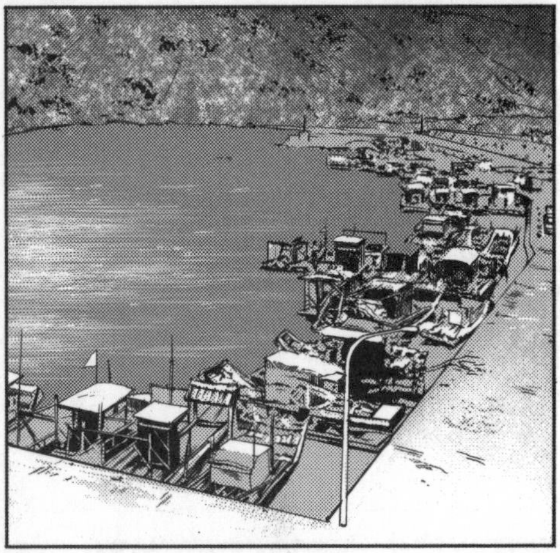
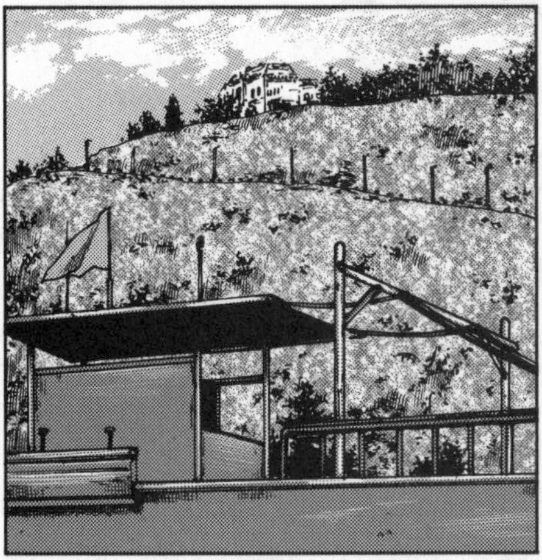
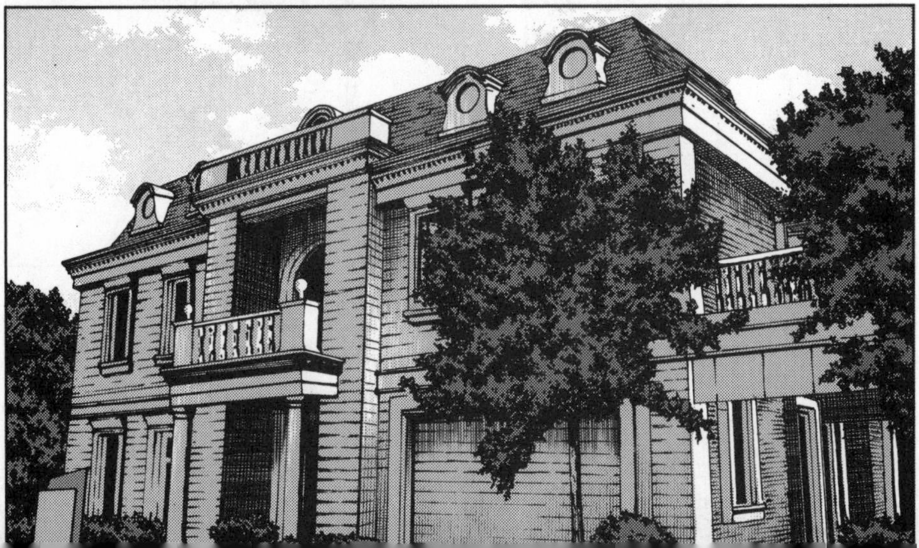

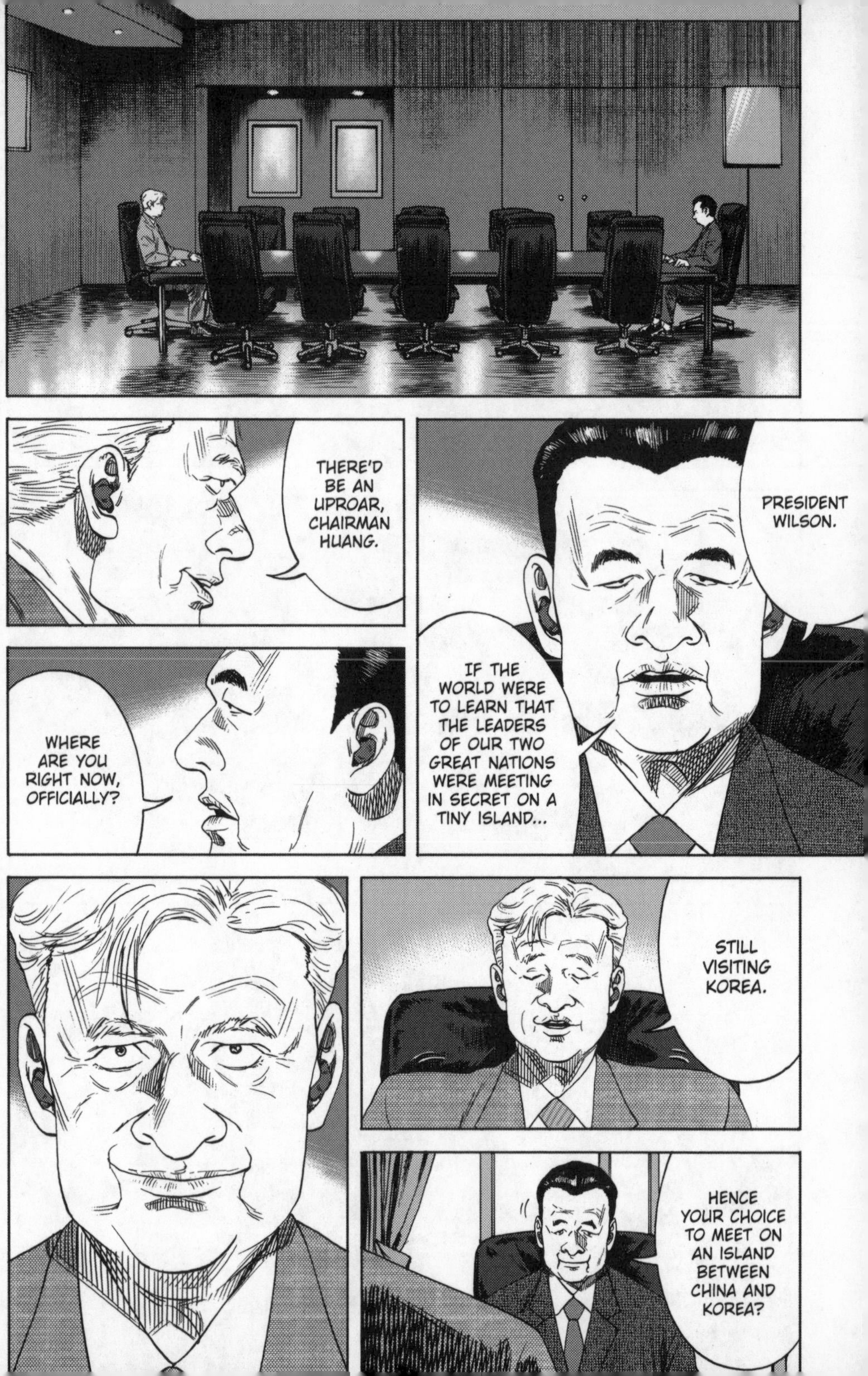
PRESIDENT WILSON.
IF THE WORLD WERE TO LEARN THAT THE LEADERS OF OUR TWO GREAT NATIONS WERE MEETING IN SECRET ON A TINY ISLAND...
THERE'D BE AN UPROAR, CHAIRMAN HUANG.
WHERE ARE YOU RIGHT NOW, OFFICIALLY?
STILL VISITING KOREA.
HENCE YOUR CHOICE TO MEET ON AN ISLAND BETWEEN CHINA AND KOREA?

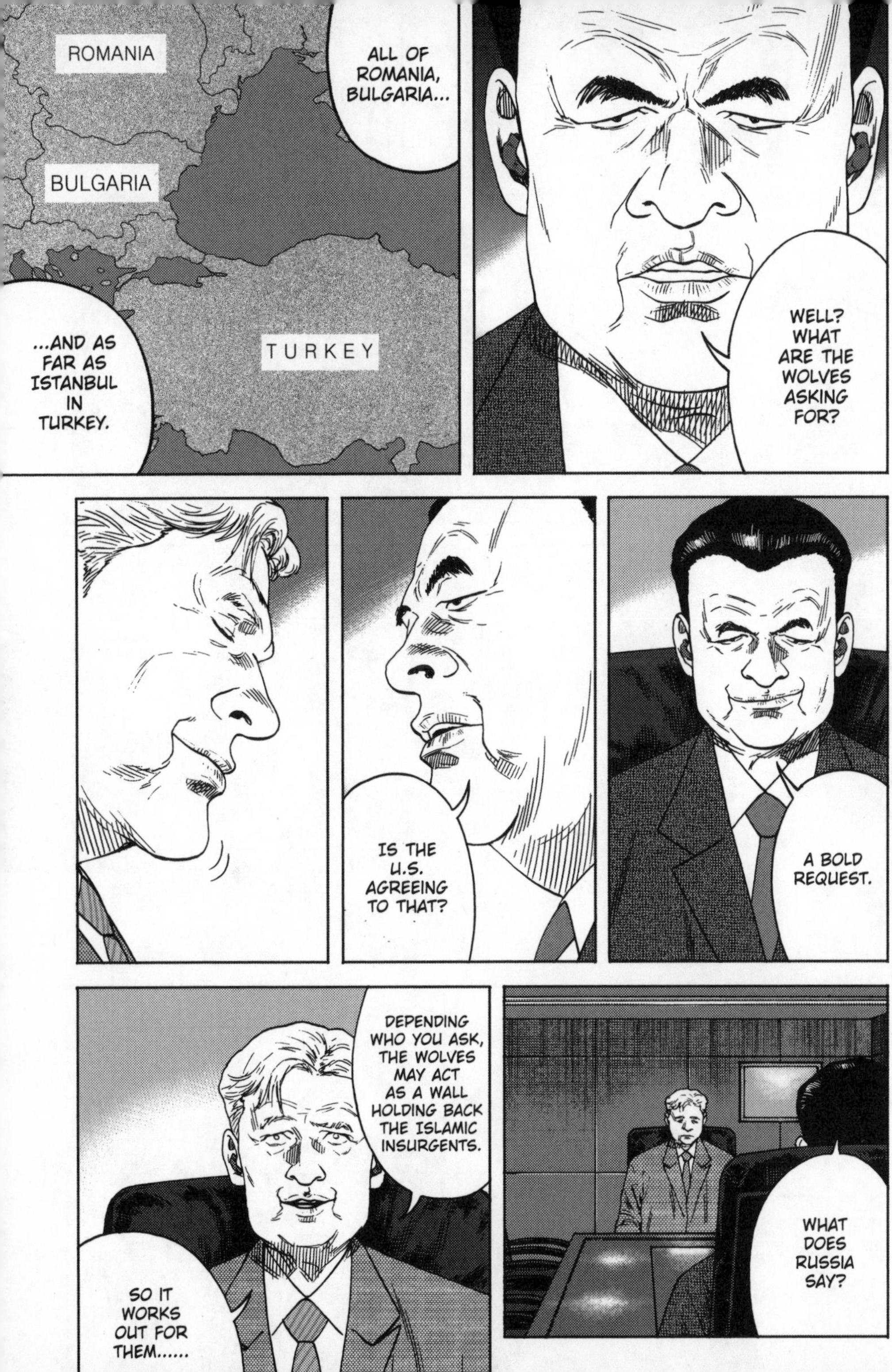

WELL? WHAT ARE THE WOLVES ASKING FOR?
ALL OF ROMANIA, BULGARIA...
ROMANIA
BULGARIA
TURKEY
...AND AS FAR AS ISTANBUL IN TURKEY.
A BOLD REQUEST.
IS THE U.S. AGREEING TO THAT?
WHAT DOES RUSSIA SAY?
DEPENDING WHO YOU ASK, THE WOLVES MAY ACT AS A WALL HOLDING BACK THE ISLAMIC INSURGENTS.
SO IT WORKS OUT FOR THEM......

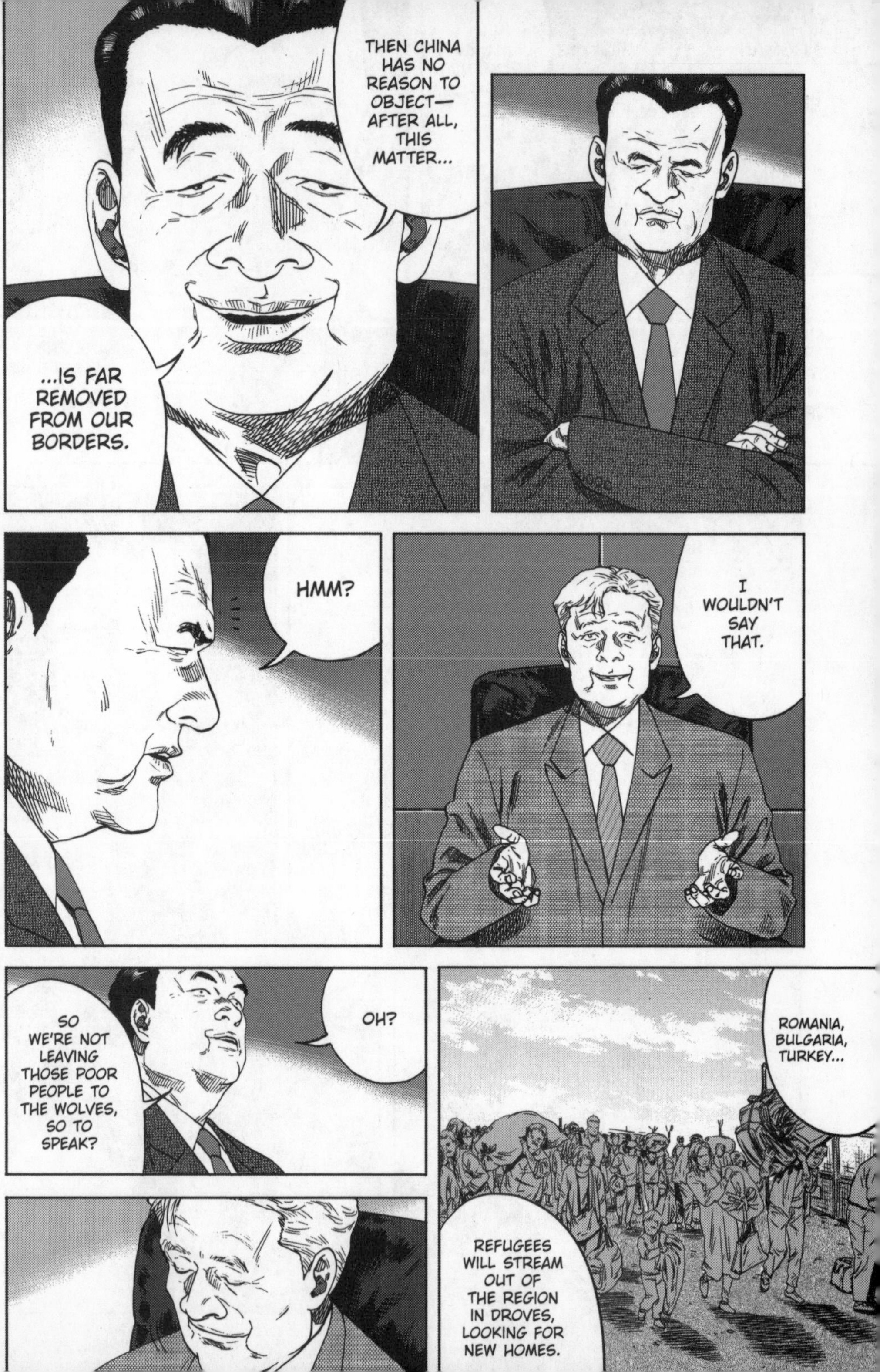

THEN CHINA HAS NO REASON TO OBJECT— AFTER ALL, THIS MATTER...
...IS FAR REMOVED FROM OUR BORDERS.
I WOULDN'T SAY THAT.
HMM?
ROMANIA, BULGARIA, TURKEY...
REFUGEES WILL STREAM OUT OF THE REGION IN DROVES, LOOKING FOR NEW HOMES.
OH?
SO WE'RE NOT LEAVING THOSE POOR PEOPLE TO THE WOLVES, SO TO SPEAK?

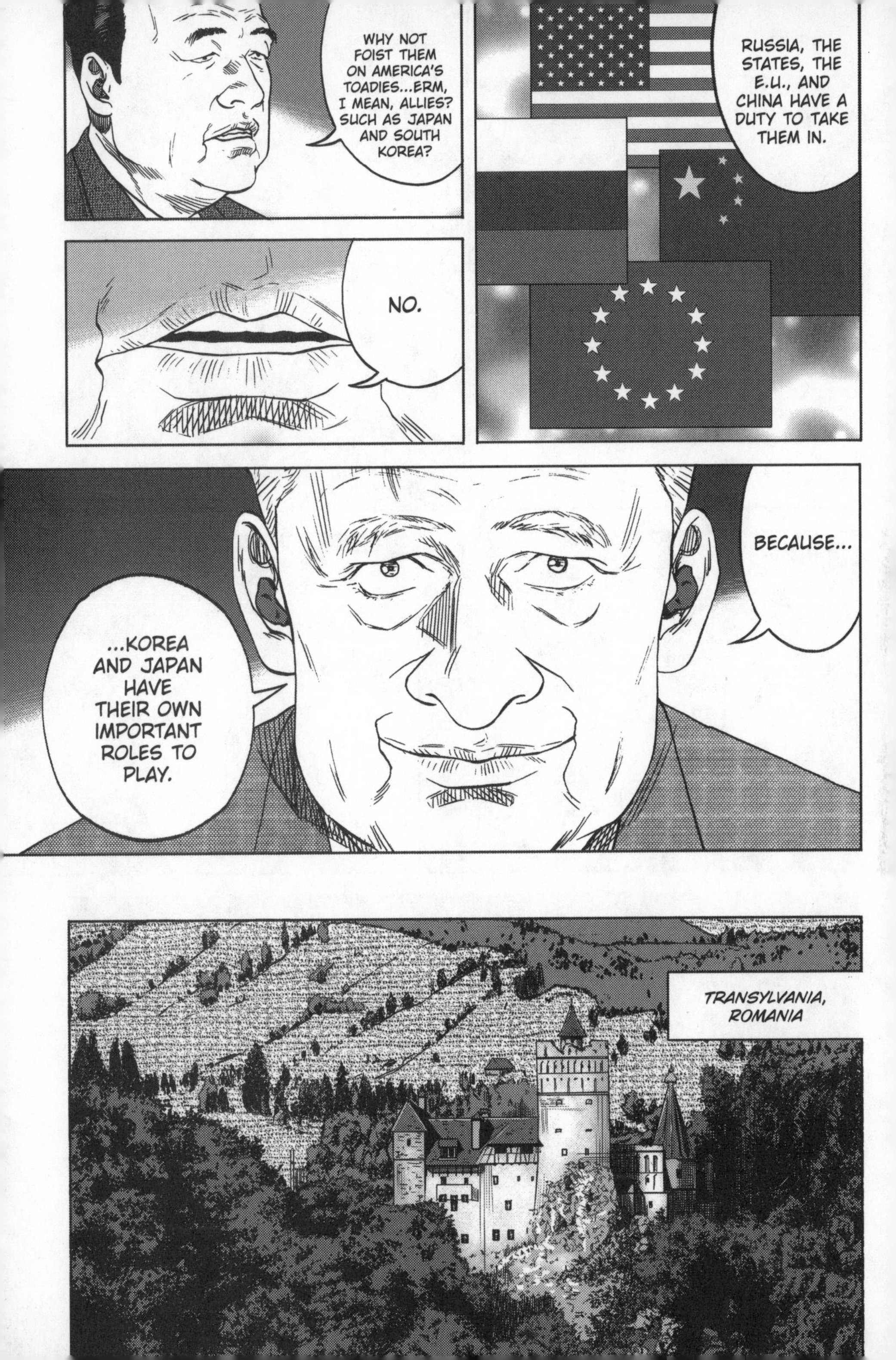

RUSSIA, THE STATES, THE E.U., AND CHINA HAVE A DUTY TO TAKE THEM IN.
WHY NOT FOIST THEM ON AMERICA'S TOADIES...ERM, I MEAN, ALLIES? SUCH AS JAPAN AND SOUTH KOREA?
NO.
BECAUSE...
...KOREA AND JAPAN HAVE THEIR OWN IMPORTANT ROLES TO PLAY.
TRANSYLVANIA, ROMANIA

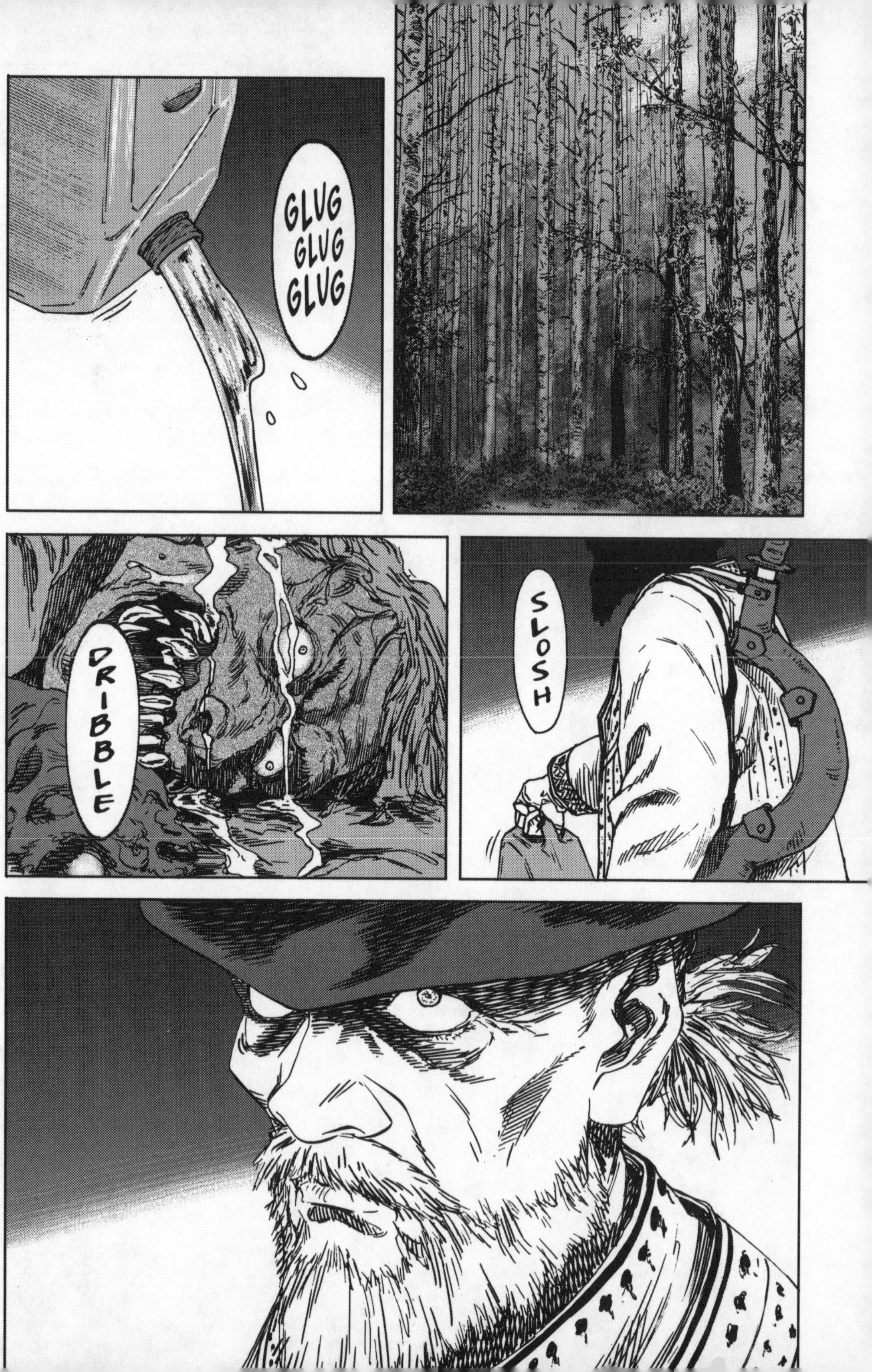
GLUG GLUG GLUG
SLOSH
DRIBBLE

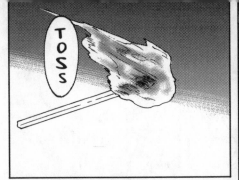

TOSS

BLAZE

DOWNRIGHT BAFFLING...

BLAAAZE

THAT THE WOLF KING WOULD BE SO FAR OFF IN ASIA...

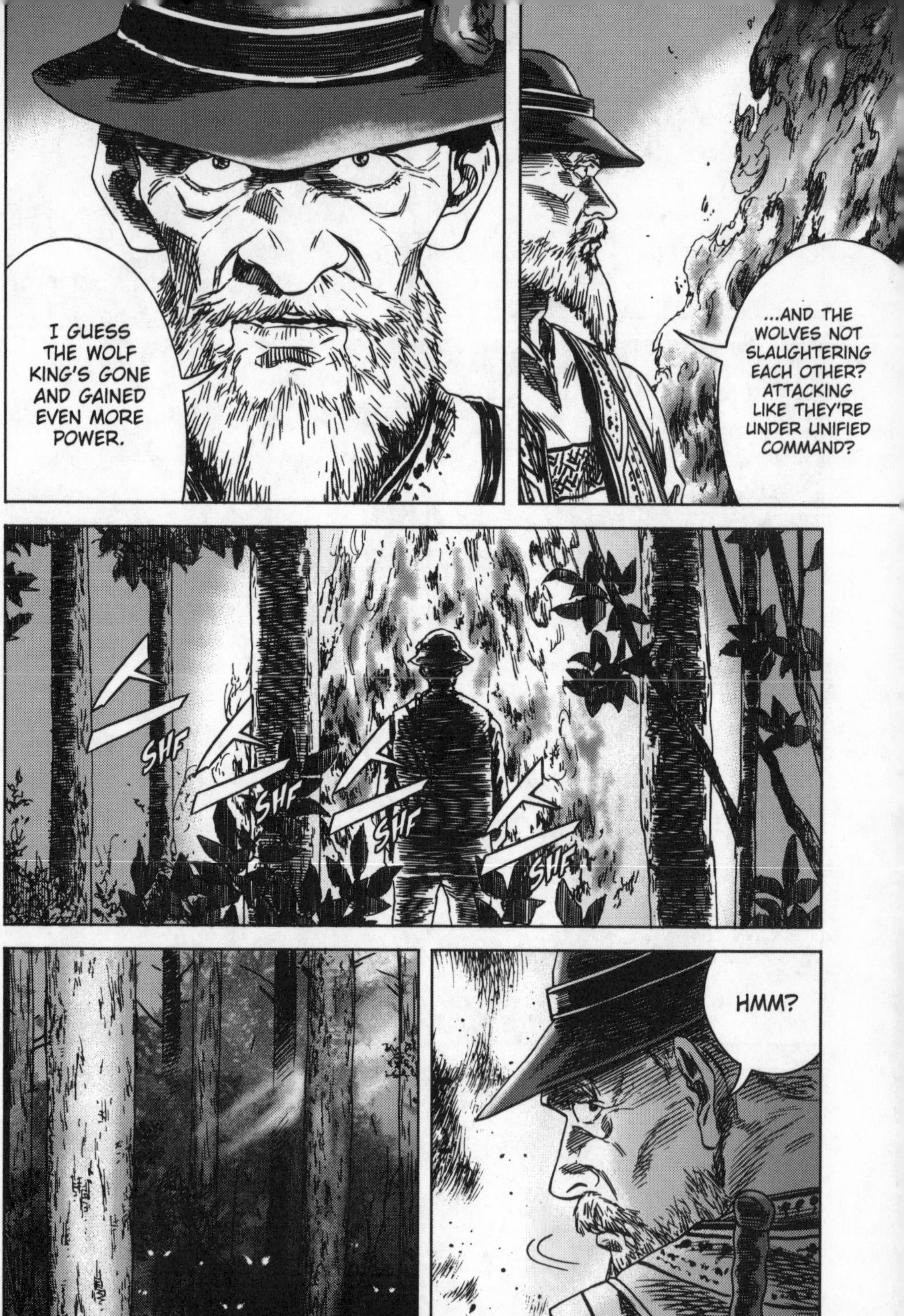
...AND THE WOLVES NOT SLAUGHTERING EACH OTHER? ATTACKING LIKE THEY'RE UNDER UNIFIED COMMAND?
I GUESS THE WOLF KING'S GONE AND GAINED EVEN MORE POWER.
SHF
SHF
SHF
SHF
HMM?

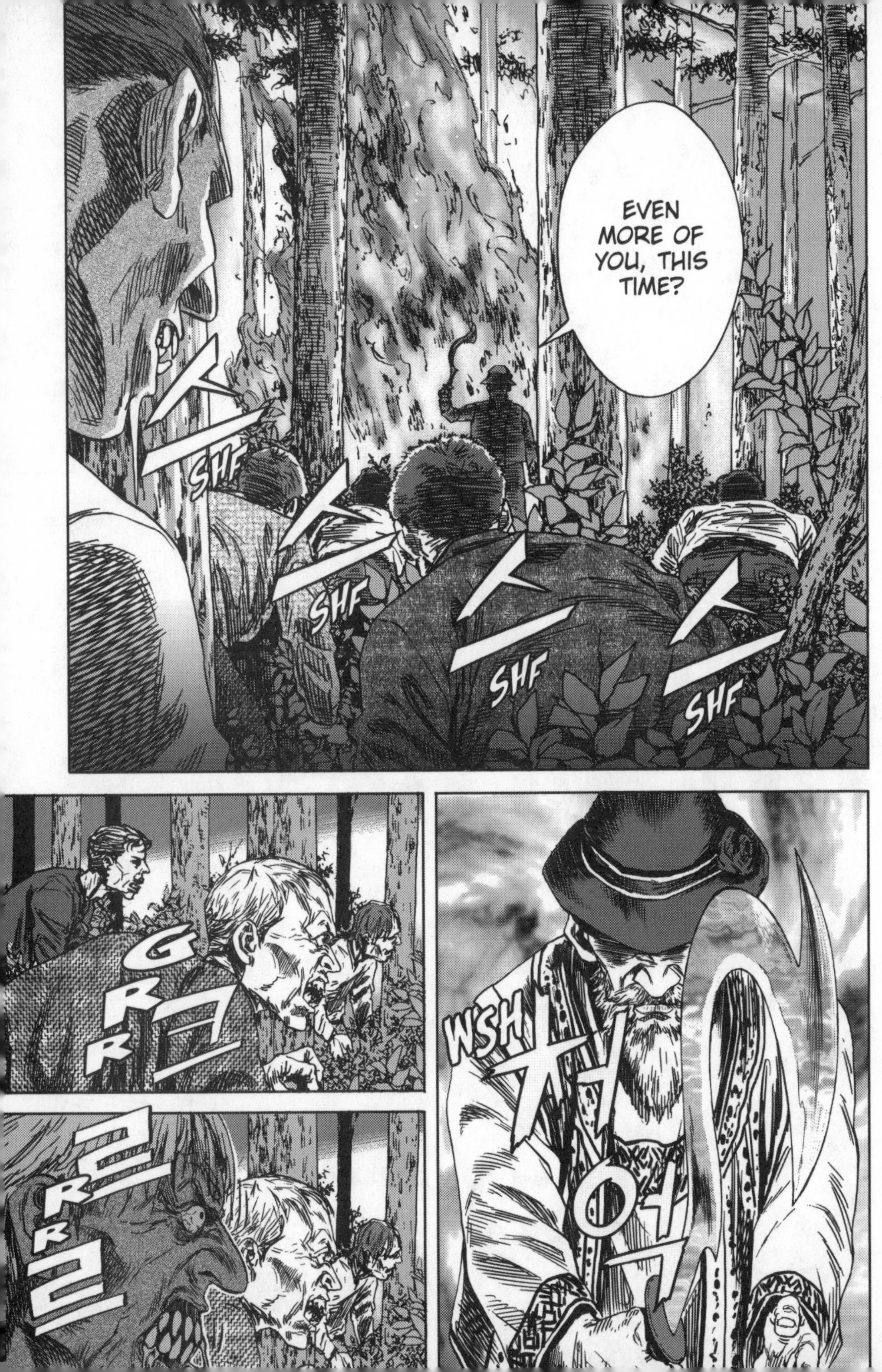
EVEN MORE OF YOU, THIS TIME?
SHF
SHF
SHF
SHF
WSH
GRR
RR

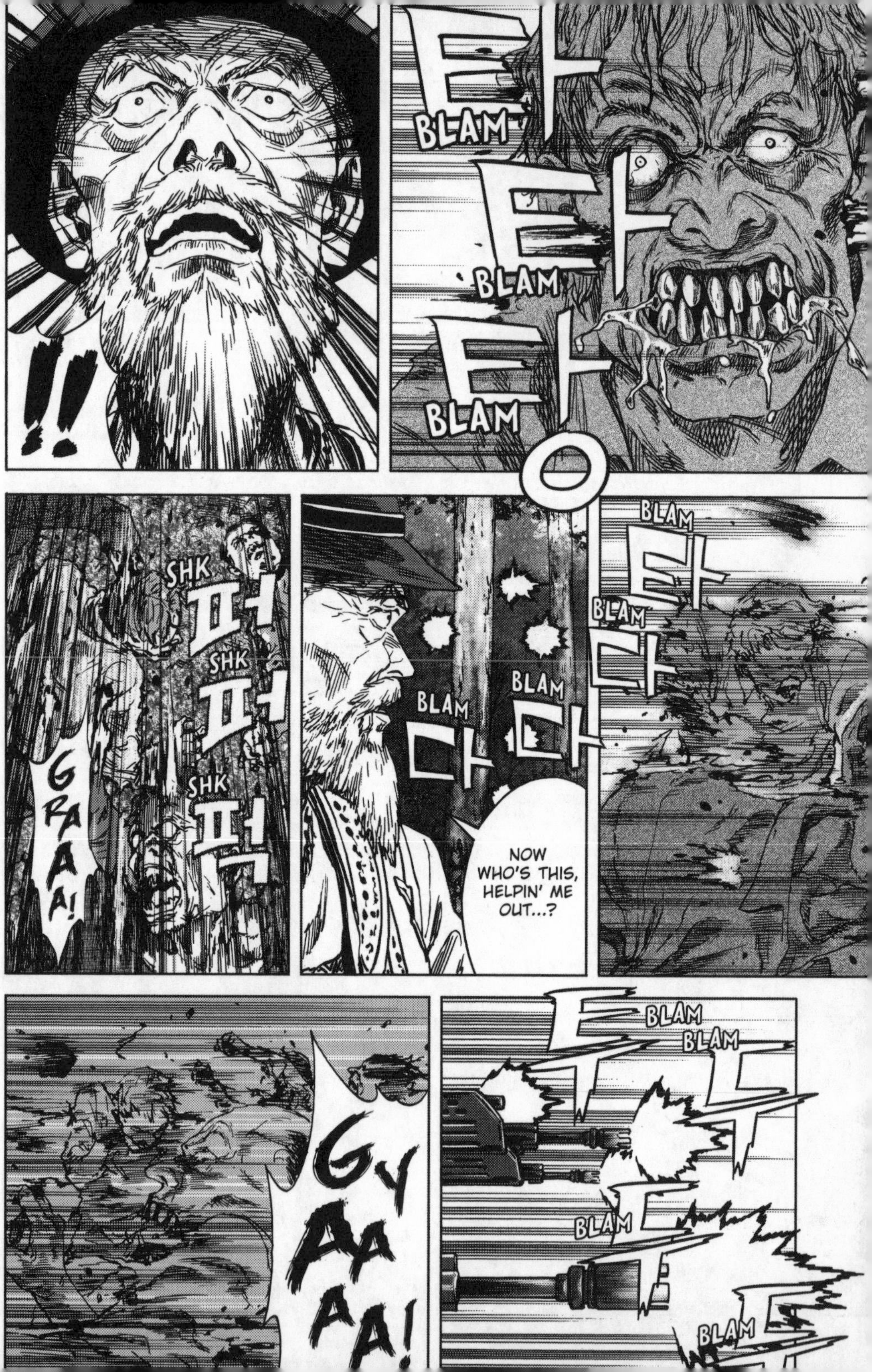
BLAM
BLAM
BLAM
!!
BLAM
BLAM
BLAM
BLAM
NOW WHO'S THIS, HELPIN' ME OUT...?
SHK
SHK
SHK
GRAAA!
BLAM
BLAM
BLAM
BLAM
GYAAAA!

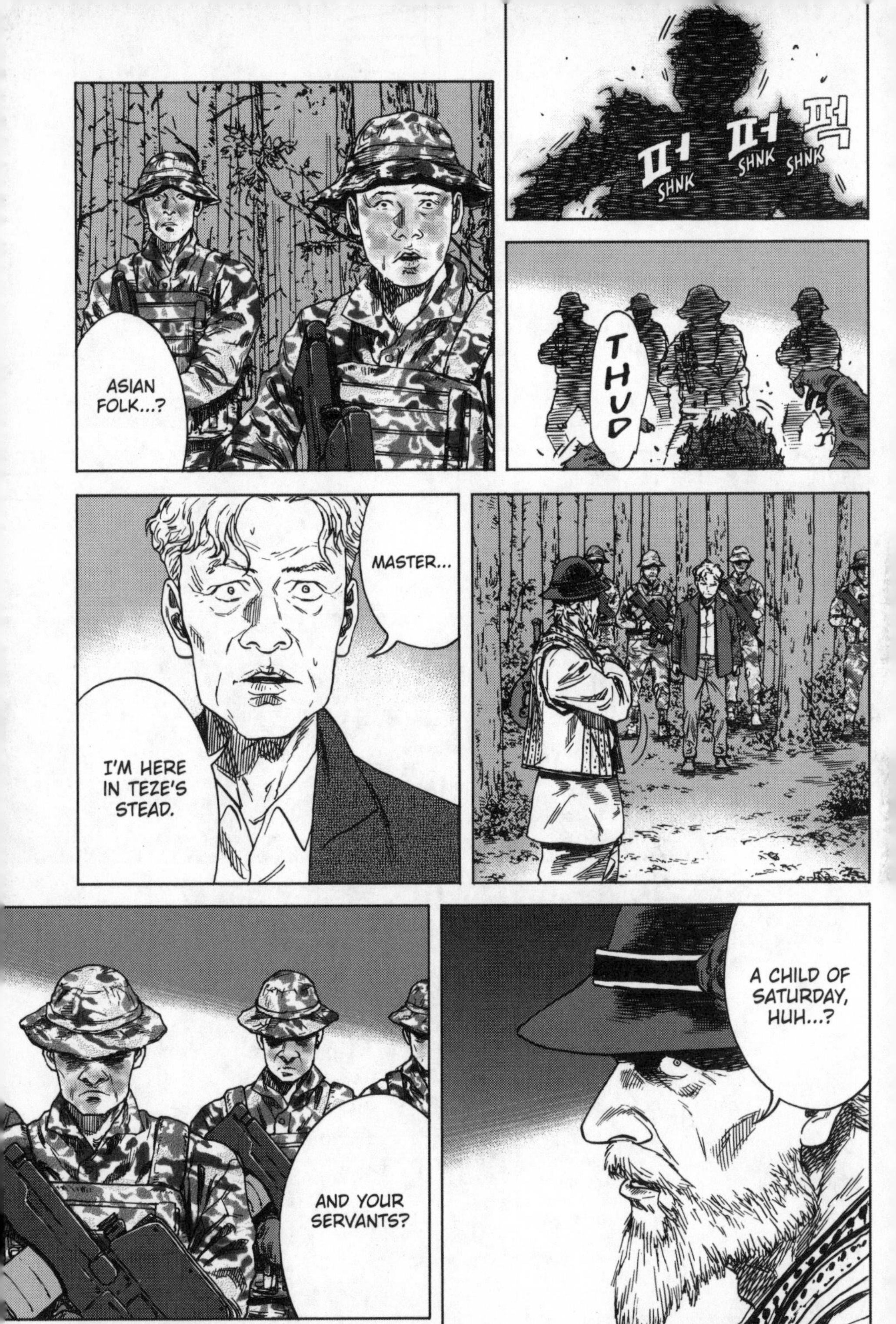
퍼 퍼 퍽
SHNK SHNK SHNK
THUD
ASIAN FOLK...?
MASTER...
I'M HERE IN TEZE'S STEAD.
A CHILD OF SATURDAY, HUH...?
AND YOUR SERVANTS?

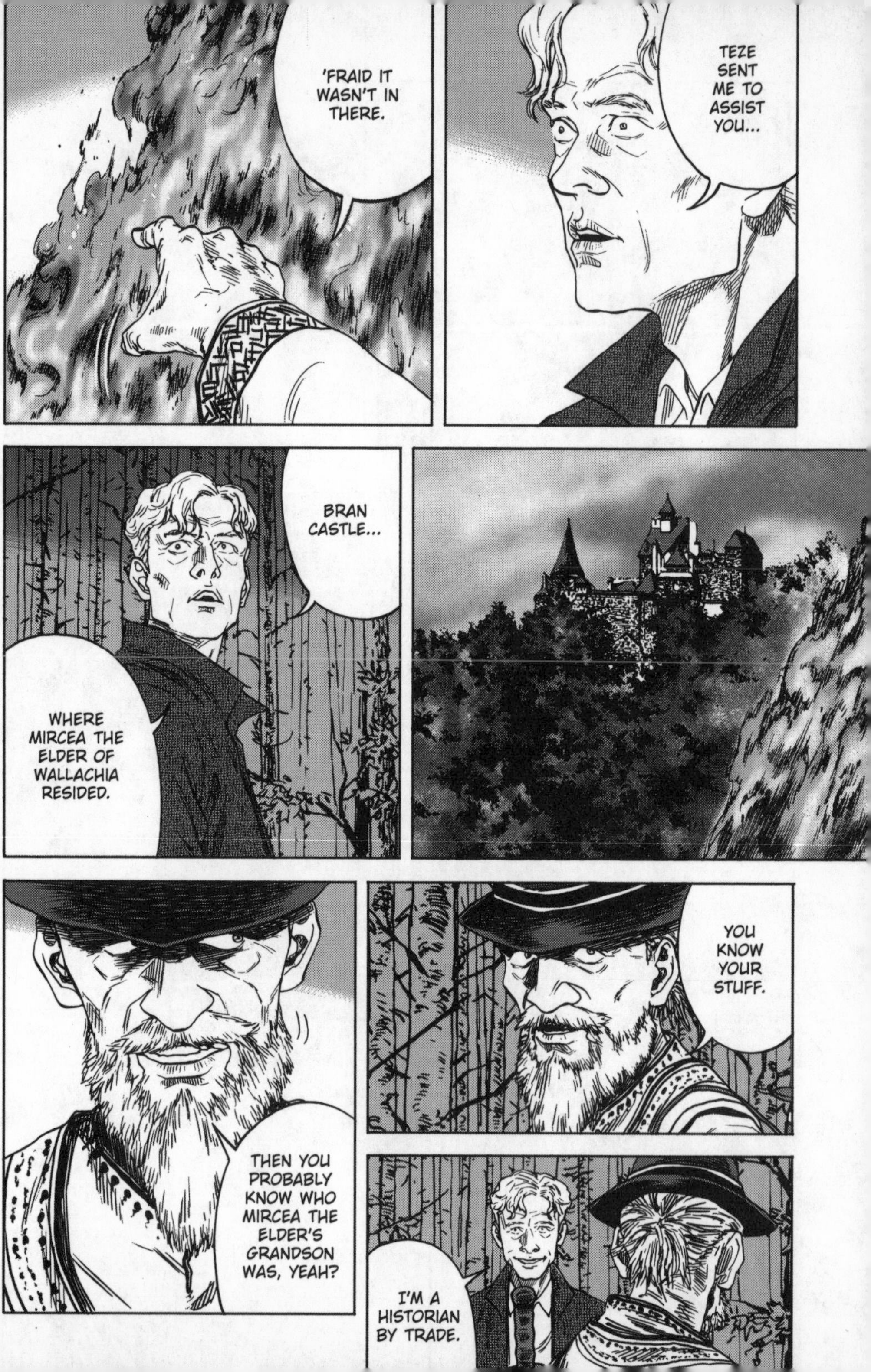
TEZE SENT ME TO ASSIST YOU...
'FRAID IT WASN'T IN THERE.
BRAN CASTLE...
WHERE MIRCEA THE ELDER OF WALLACHIA RESIDED.
YOU KNOW YOUR STUFF.
I'M A HISTORIAN BY TRADE.
THEN YOU PROBABLY KNOW WHO MIRCEA THE ELDER'S GRANDSON WAS, YEAH?

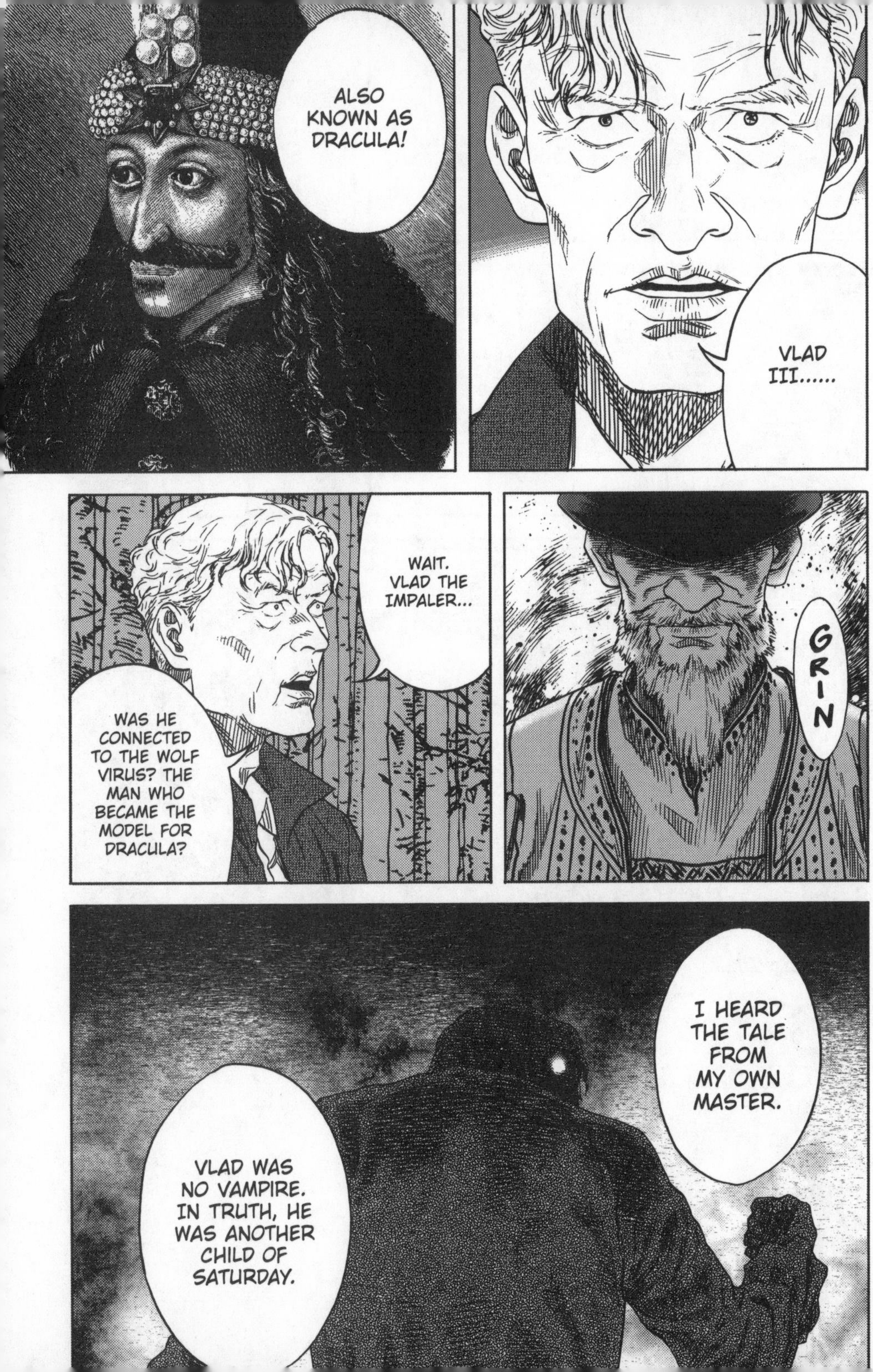
VLAD III......
ALSO KNOWN AS DRACULA!
GRIN
WAIT. VLAD THE IMPALER...
WAS HE CONNECTED TO THE WOLF VIRUS? THE MAN WHO BECAME THE MODEL FOR DRACULA?
I HEARD THE TALE FROM MY OWN MASTER.
VLAD WAS NO VAMPIRE. IN TRUTH, HE WAS ANOTHER CHILD OF SATURDAY.

?!

VLAD III'S GREATEST SIN WAS TURNING SCORES OF HIS SERVANTS INTO WOLVES.

!

THEN HE MANIPULATED THOSE SERVANTS INTO SLAUGHTERING THE FORCES OF OTTOMAN TURKEY.

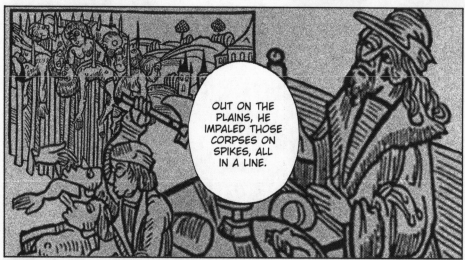

OUT ON THE PLAINS, HE IMPALED THOSE CORPSES ON SPIKES, ALL IN A LINE.

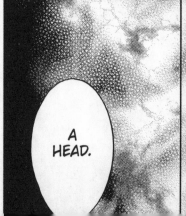

A HEAD.

WHAT WERE YOU HOPING TO FIND AT DRACULA'S CASTLE, THEN?

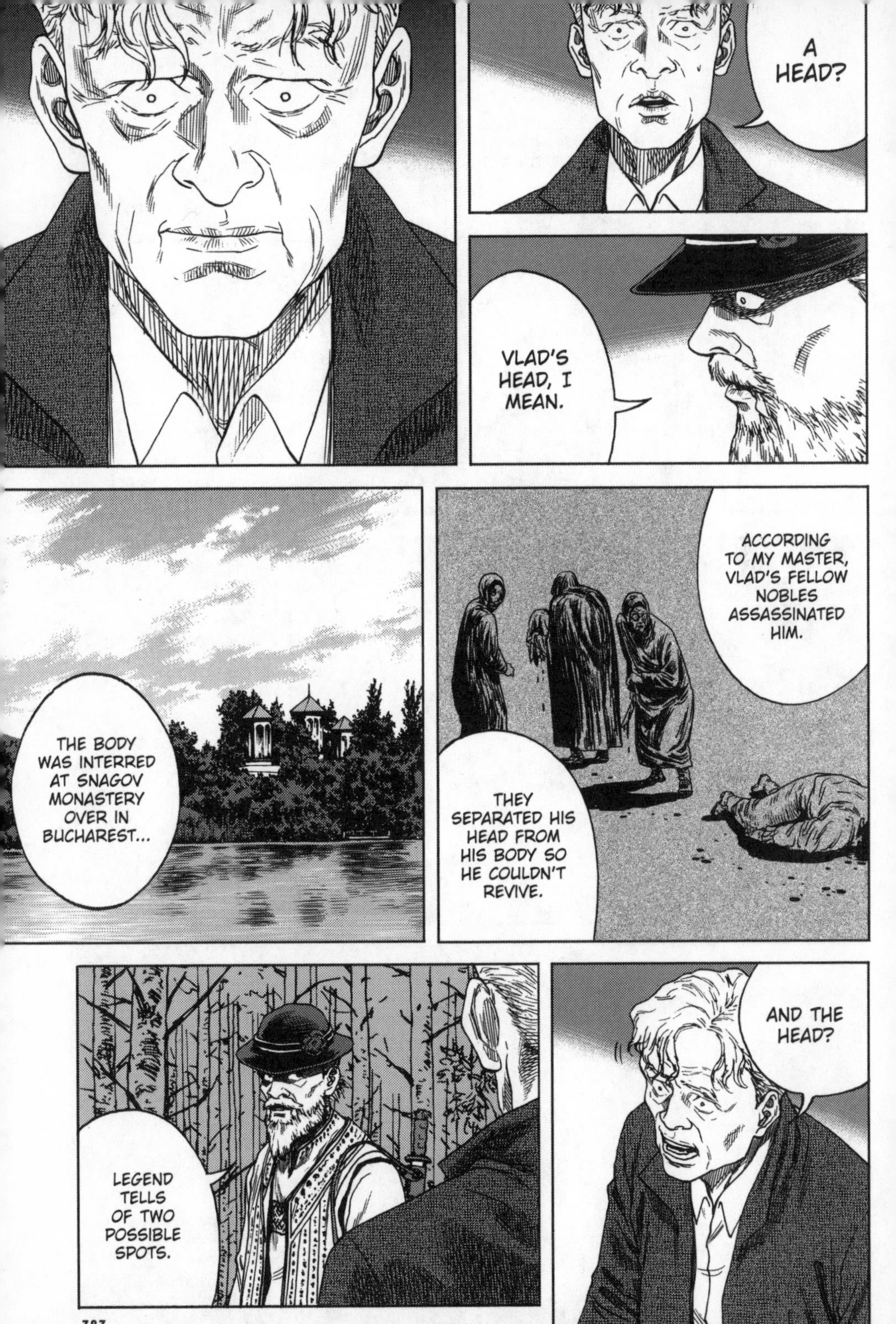
A HEAD?
VLAD'S HEAD, I MEAN.
ACCORDING TO MY MASTER, VLAD'S FELLOW NOBLES ASSASSINATED HIM.
THEY SEPARATED HIS HEAD FROM HIS BODY SO HE COULDN'T REVIVE.
THE BODY WAS INTERRED AT SNAGOV MONASTERY OVER IN BUCHAREST...
AND THE HEAD?
LEGEND TELLS OF TWO POSSIBLE SPOTS.

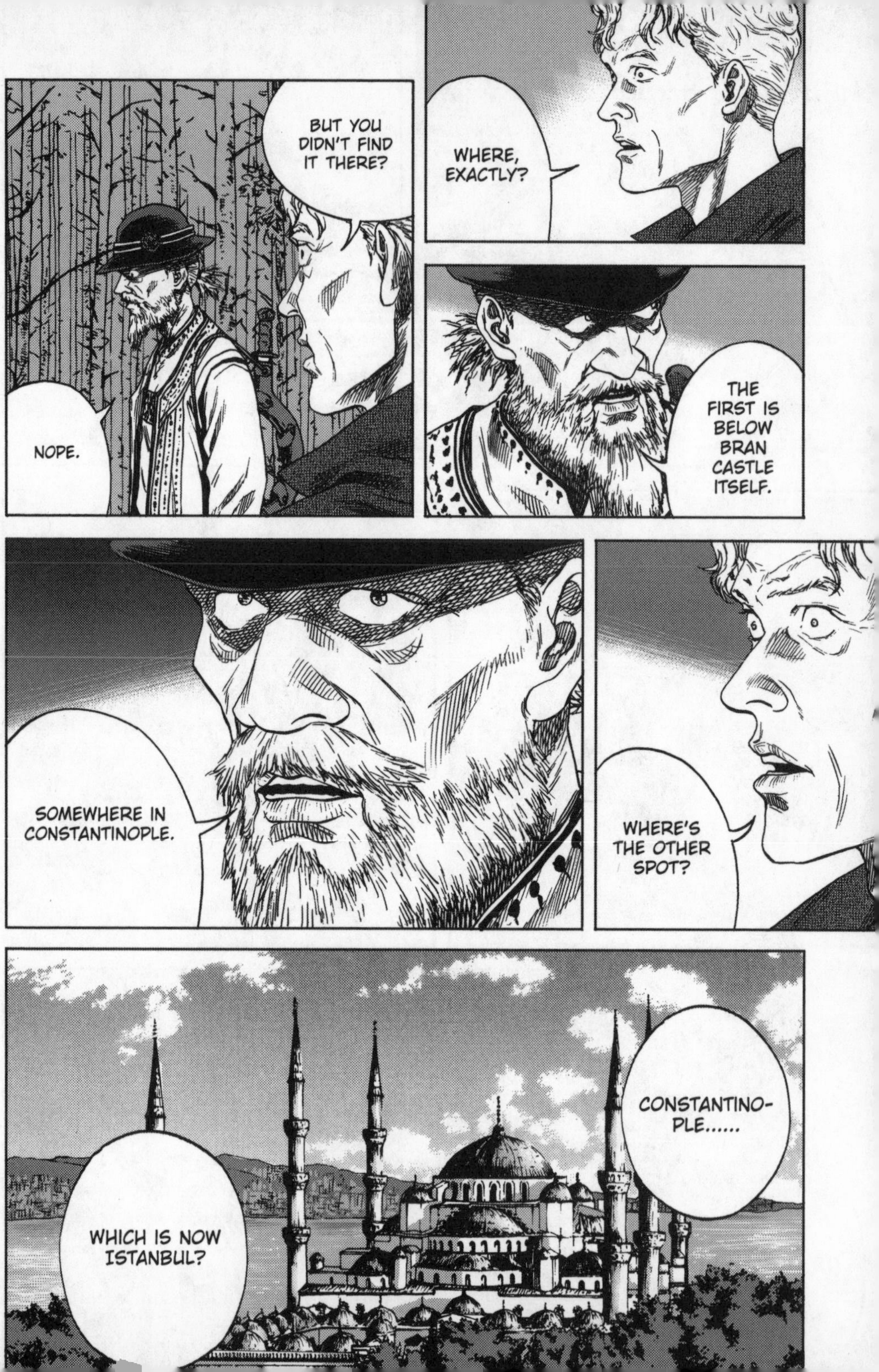
WHERE, EXACTLY?
THE FIRST IS BELOW BRAN CASTLE ITSELF.
BUT YOU DIDN'T FIND IT THERE?
NOPE.
WHERE'S THE OTHER SPOT?
SOMEWHERE IN CONSTANTINOPLE.
CONSTANTINO-PLE......
WHICH IS NOW ISTANBUL?

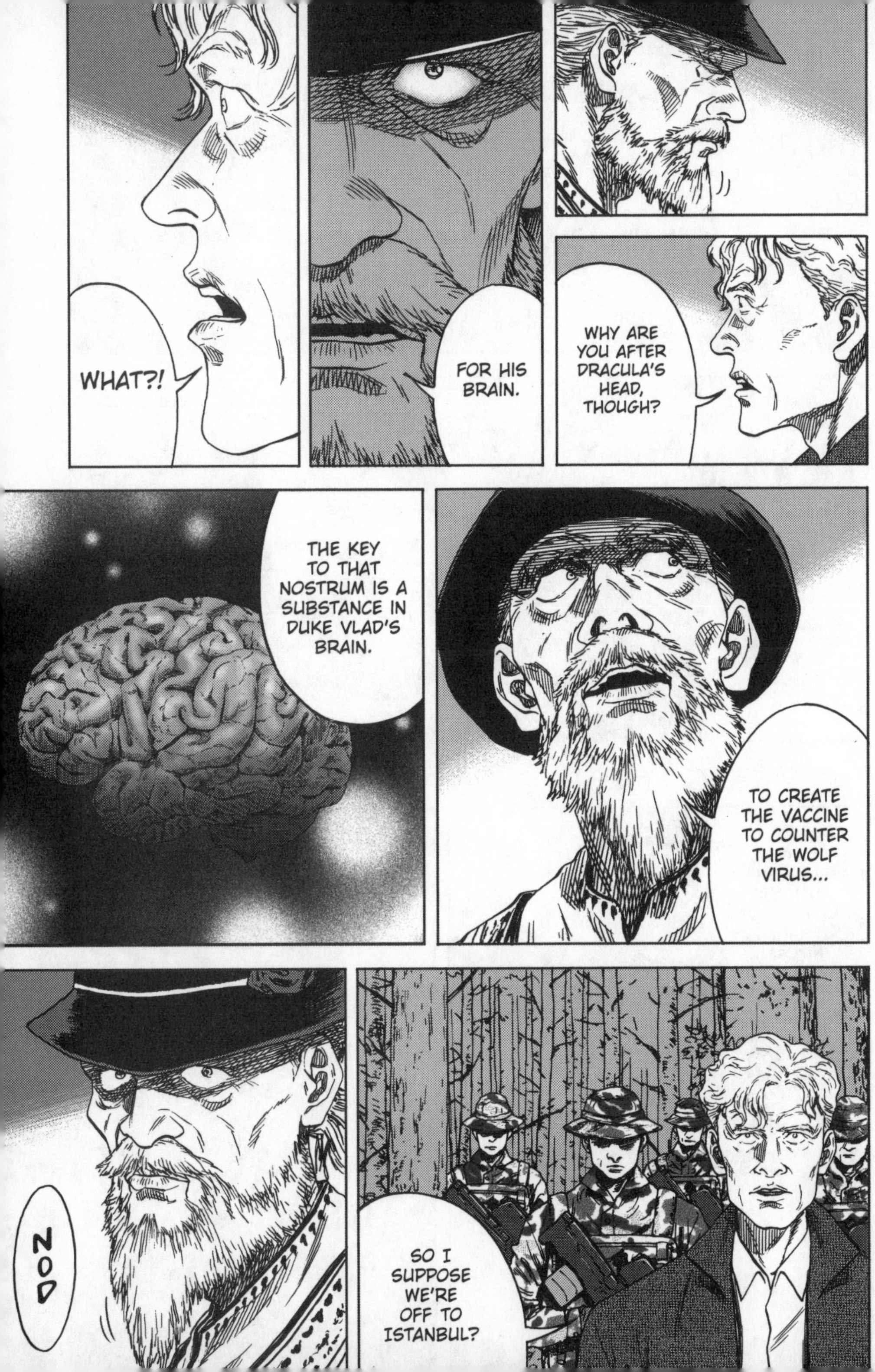
WHY ARE YOU AFTER DRACULA'S HEAD, THOUGH?
FOR HIS BRAIN.
WHAT?!
TO CREATE THE VACCINE TO COUNTER THE WOLF VIRUS...
THE KEY TO THAT NOSTRUM IS A SUBSTANCE IN DUKE VLAD'S BRAIN.
SO I SUPPOSE WE'RE OFF TO ISTANBUL?
NOD

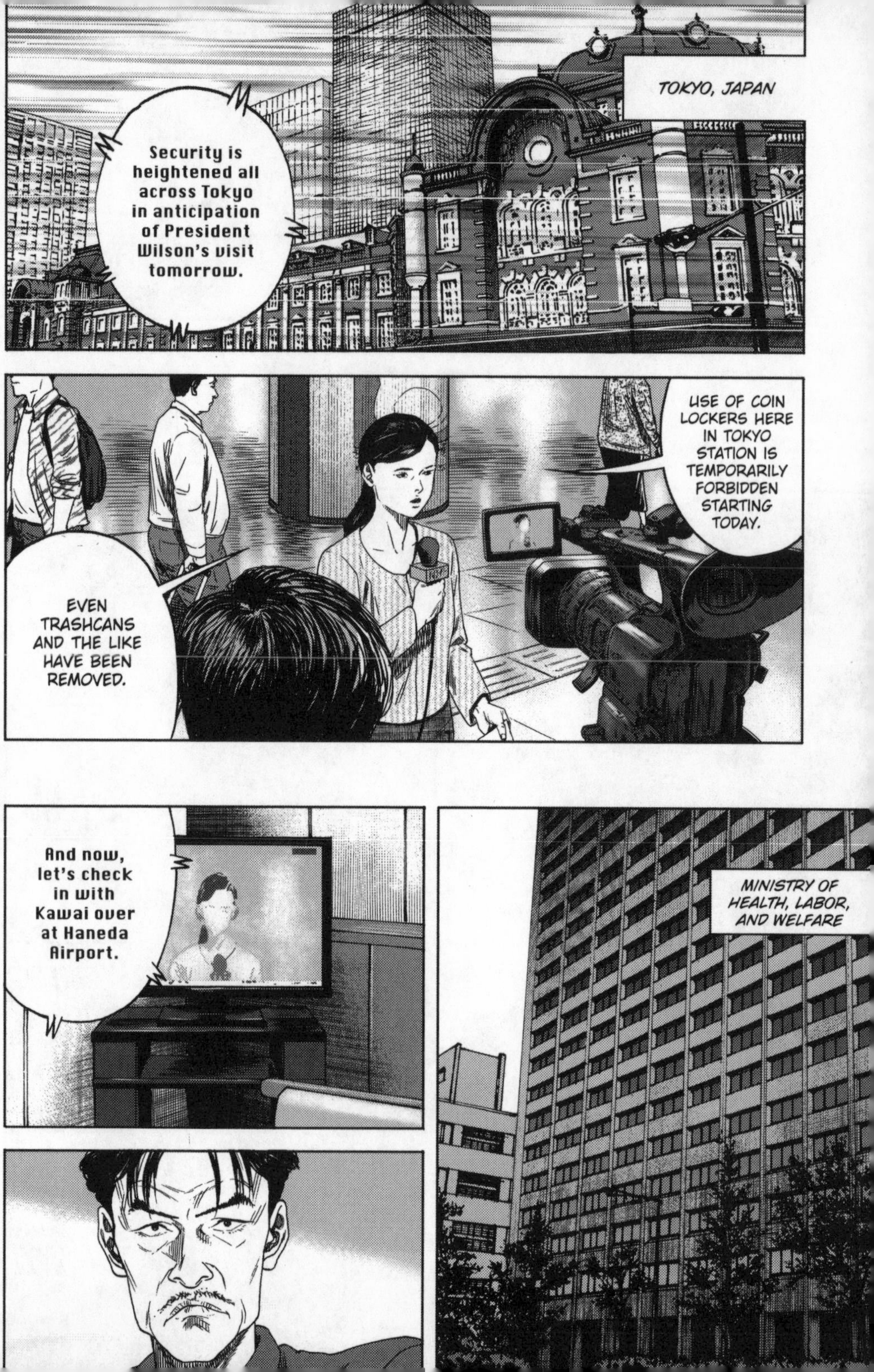
TOKYO, JAPAN
Security is heightened all across Tokyo in anticipation of President Wilson's visit tomorrow.
USE OF COIN LOCKERS HERE IN TOKYO STATION IS TEMPORARILY FORBIDDEN STARTING TODAY.
EVEN TRASHCANS AND THE LIKE HAVE BEEN REMOVED.
MINISTRY OF HEALTH, LABOR, AND WELFARE
And now, let's check in with Kawai over at Haneda Airport.

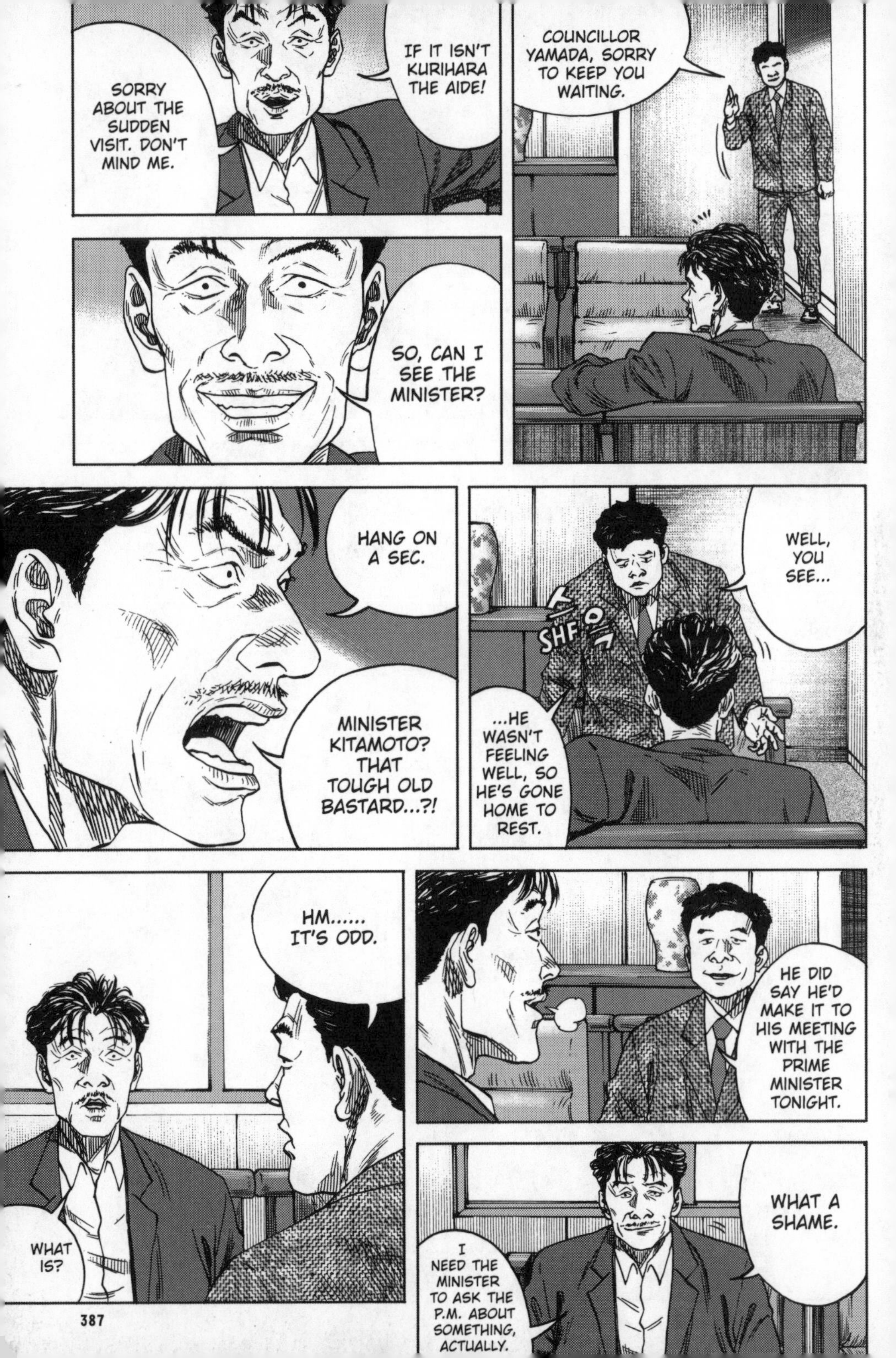
COUNCILLOR YAMADA, SORRY TO KEEP YOU WAITING.
IF IT ISN'T KURIHARA THE AIDE!
SORRY ABOUT THE SUDDEN VISIT. DON'T MIND ME.
SO, CAN I SEE THE MINISTER?
WELL, YOU SEE...
SHF
...HE WASN'T FEELING WELL, SO HE'S GONE HOME TO REST.
HANG ON A SEC.
MINISTER KITAMOTO? THAT TOUGH OLD BASTARD...?!
HE DID SAY HE'D MAKE IT TO HIS MEETING WITH THE PRIME MINISTER TONIGHT.
WHAT A SHAME.
I NEED THE MINISTER TO ASK THE P.M. ABOUT SOMETHING, ACTUALLY.
HM...... IT'S ODD.
WHAT IS?

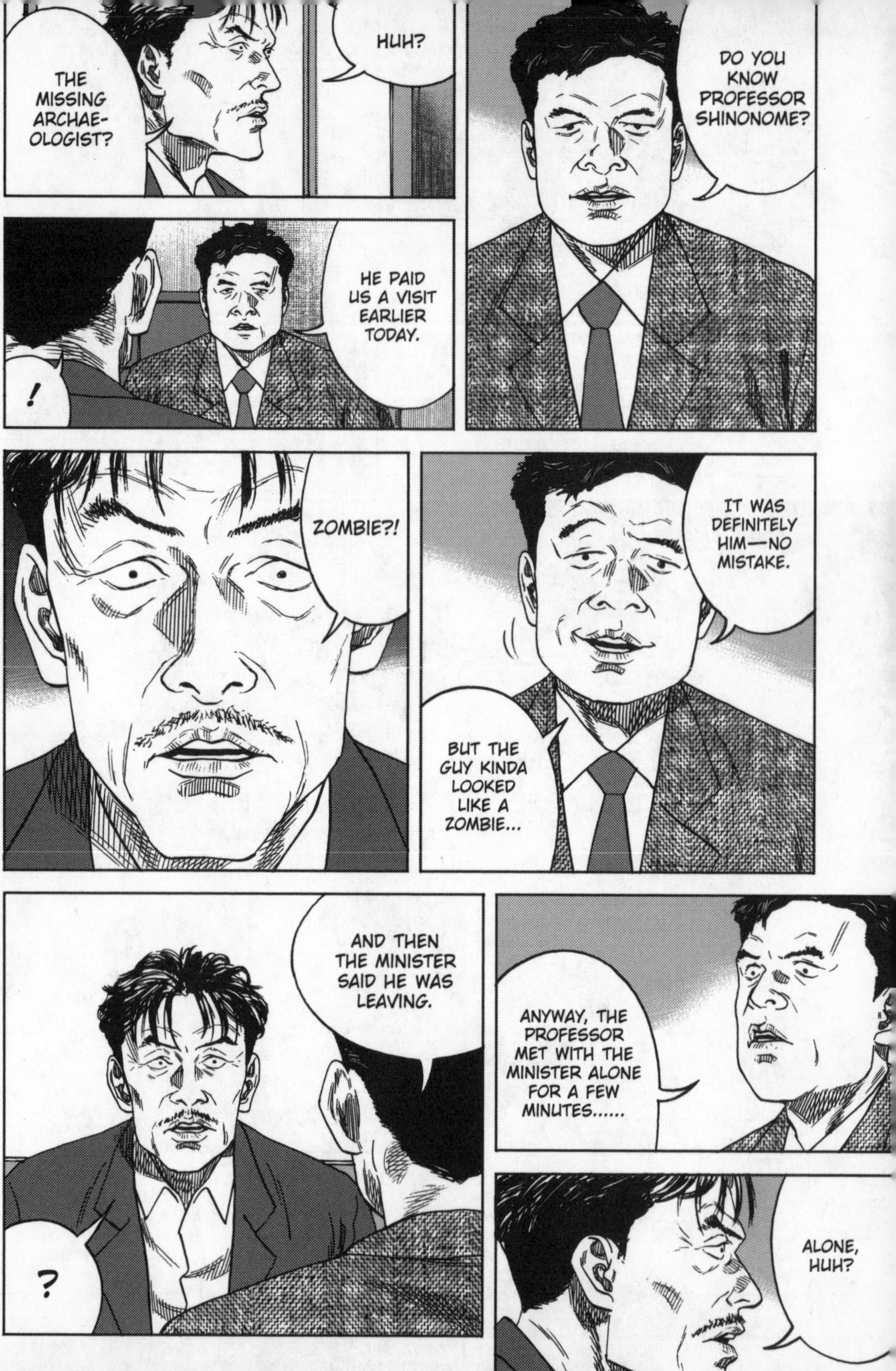
DO YOU KNOW PROFESSOR SHINONOME?
HUH?
THE MISSING ARCHAEOLOGIST?
HE PAID US A VISIT EARLIER TODAY.
!
IT WAS DEFINITELY HIM—NO MISTAKE.
BUT THE GUY KINDA LOOKED LIKE A ZOMBIE...
ZOMBIE?!
ANYWAY, THE PROFESSOR MET WITH THE MINISTER ALONE FOR A FEW MINUTES......
ALONE, HUH?
AND THEN THE MINISTER SAID HE WAS LEAVING.
?

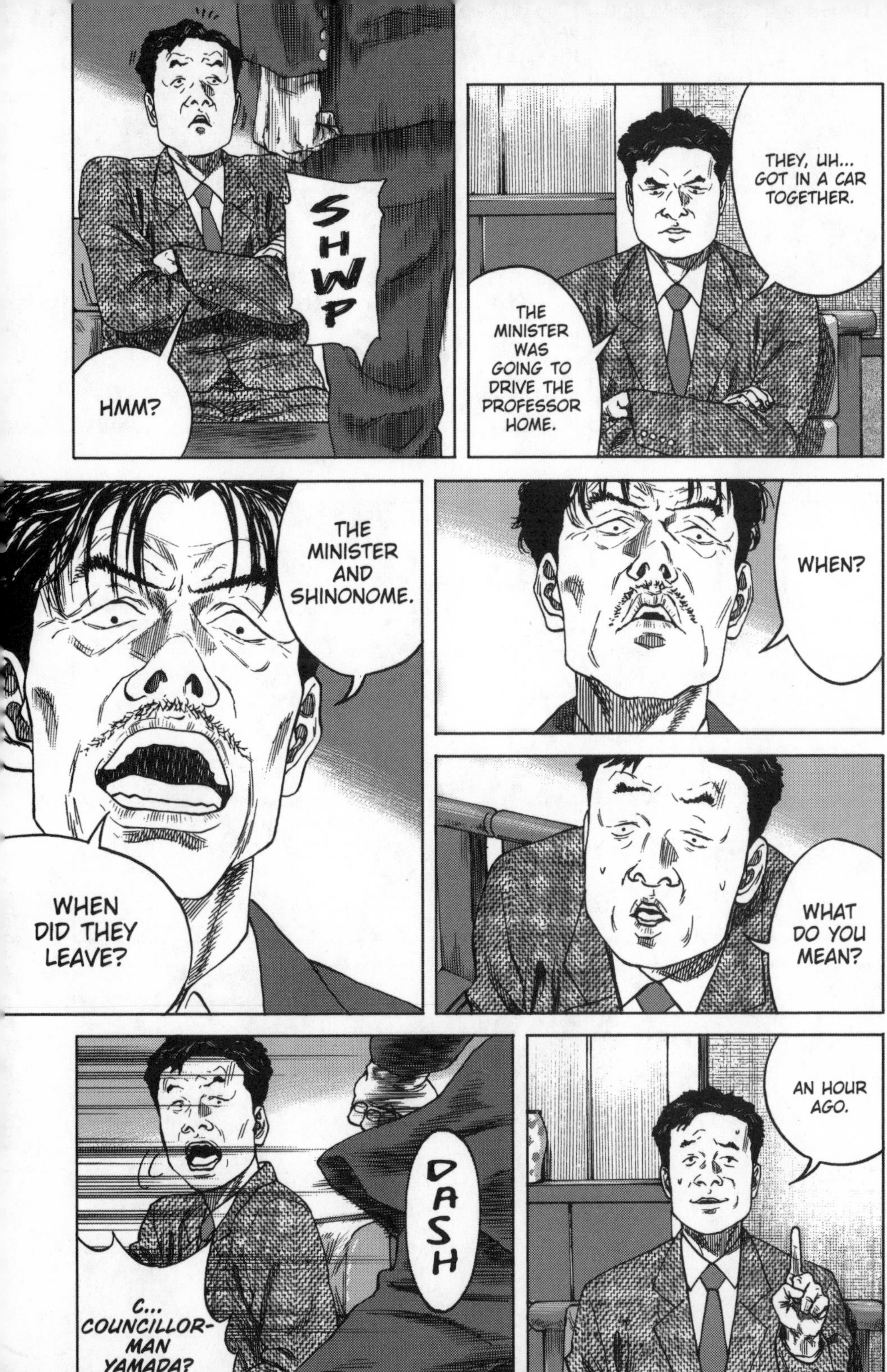

THEY, UH... GOT IN A CAR TOGETHER.
THE MINISTER WAS GOING TO DRIVE THE PROFESSOR HOME.
SHWP
HMM?
WHEN?
WHAT DO YOU MEAN?
THE MINISTER AND SHINONOME.
WHEN DID THEY LEAVE?
AN HOUR AGO.
DASH
C... COUNCILLOR-MAN YAMADA?

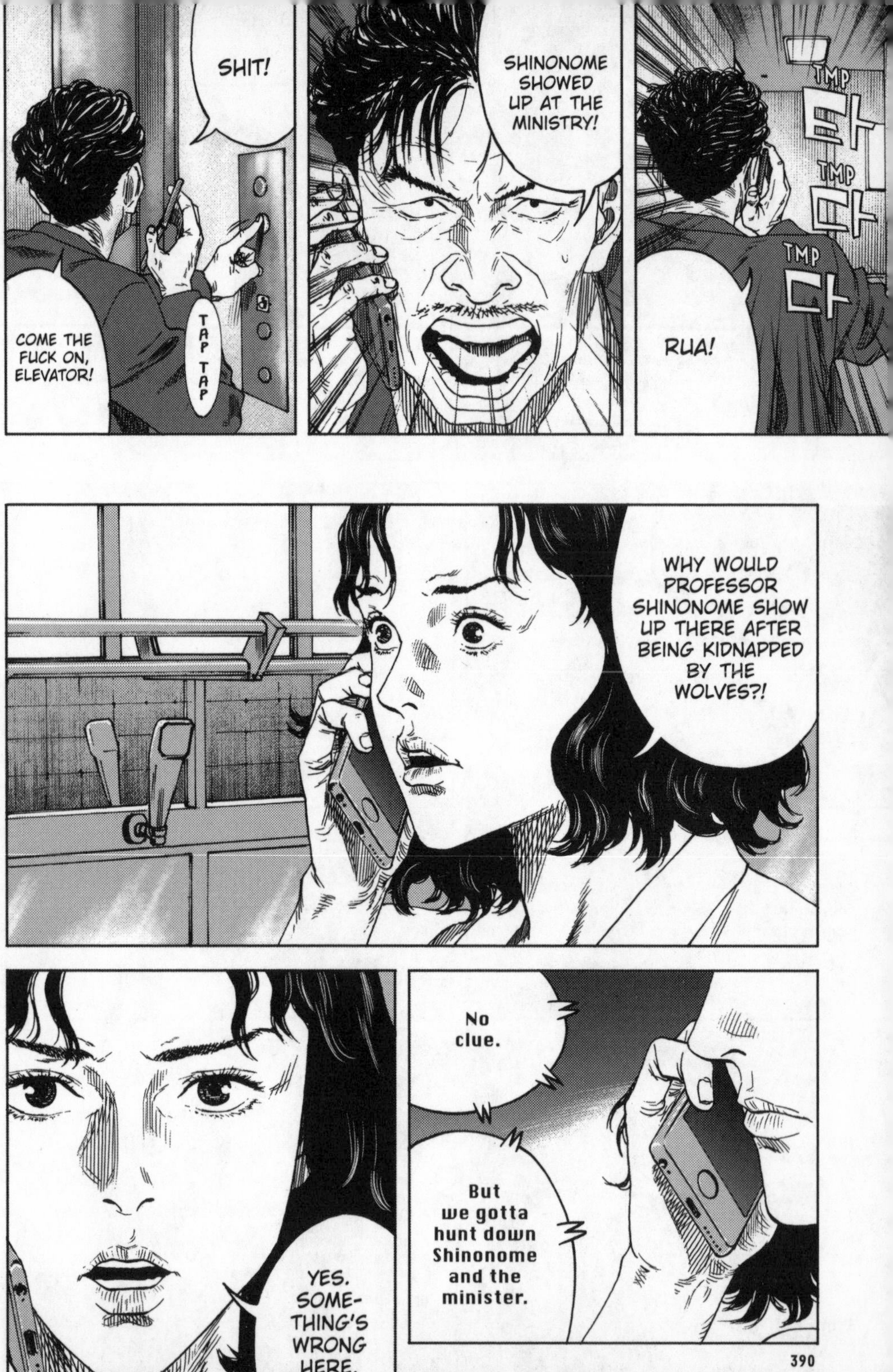
TMP 타
TMP 다
TMP 다
RUA!
SHINONOME SHOWED UP AT THE MINISTRY!
SHIT!
TAP TAP
COME THE FUCK ON, ELEVATOR!
WHY WOULD PROFESSOR SHINONOME SHOW UP THERE AFTER BEING KIDNAPPED BY THE WOLVES?!
No clue.
But we gotta hunt down Shinonome and the minister.
YES. SOME-THING'S WRONG HERE.

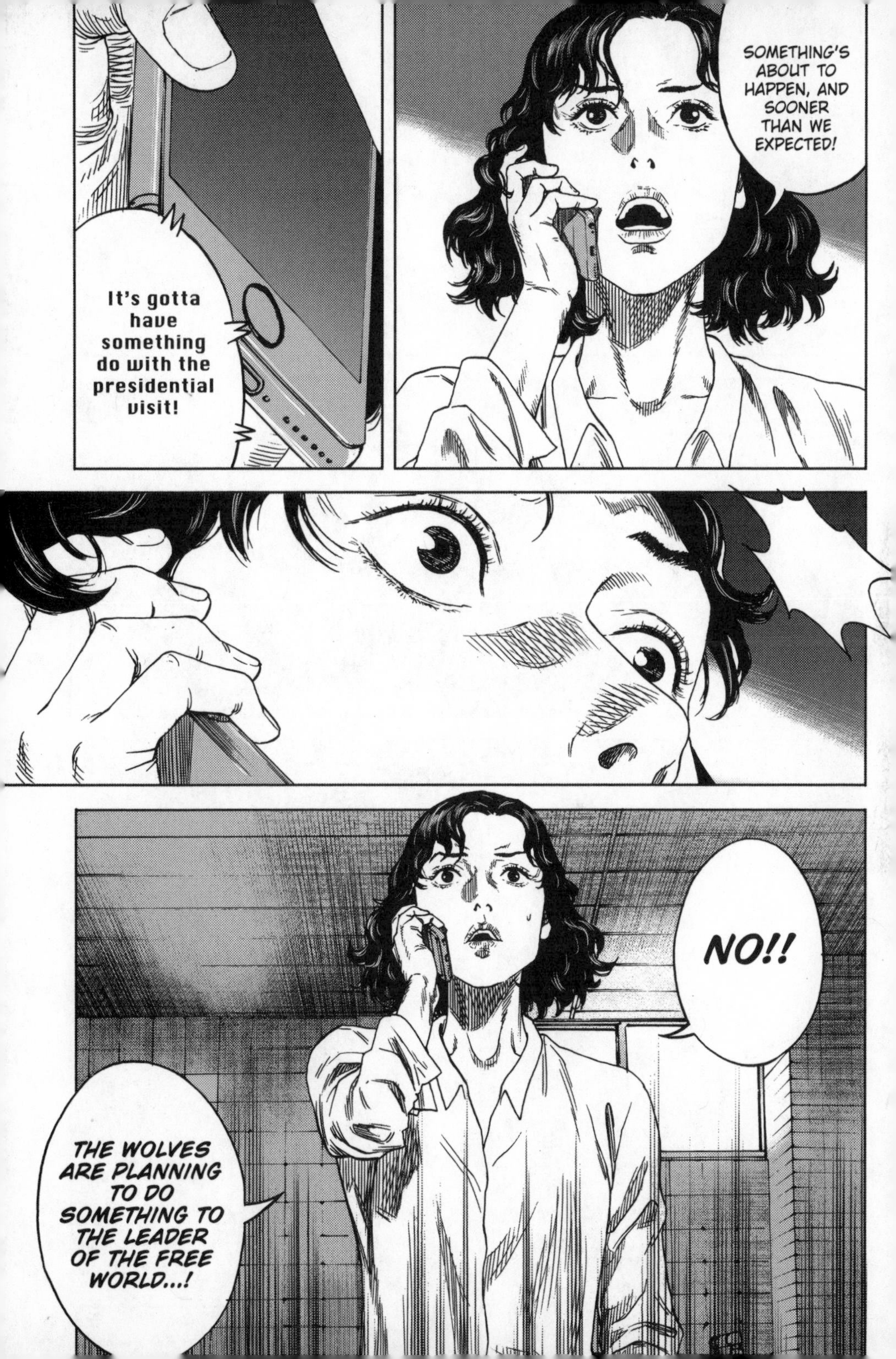
SOMETHING'S ABOUT TO HAPPEN, AND SOONER THAN WE EXPECTED!
It's gotta have something do with the presidential visit!
NO!!
THE WOLVES ARE PLANNING TO DO SOMETHING TO THE LEADER OF THE FREE WORLD...!

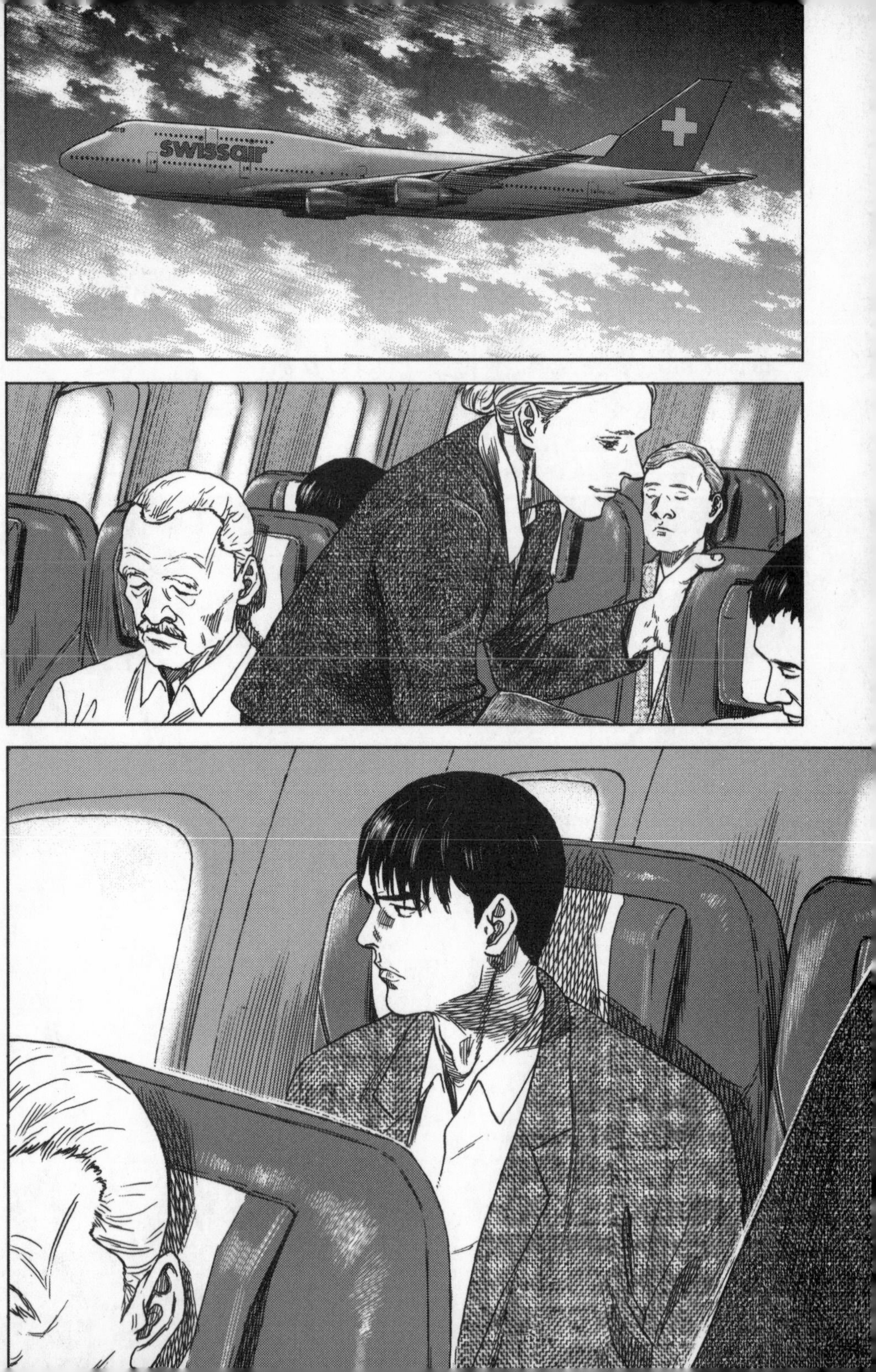
swissair

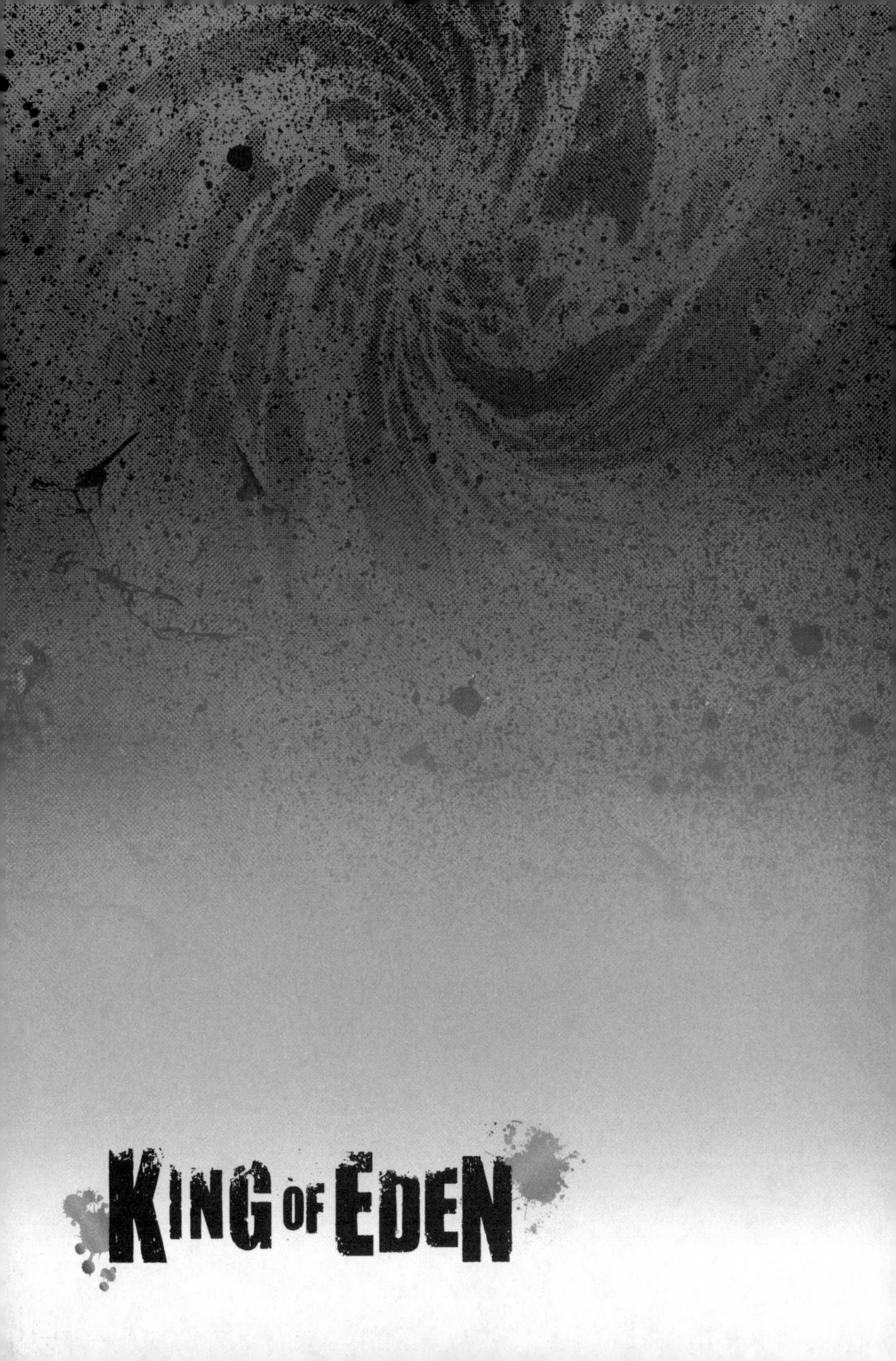
KING OF EDEN

KING OF EDEN

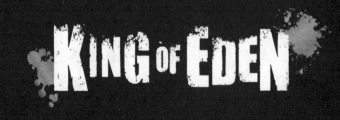

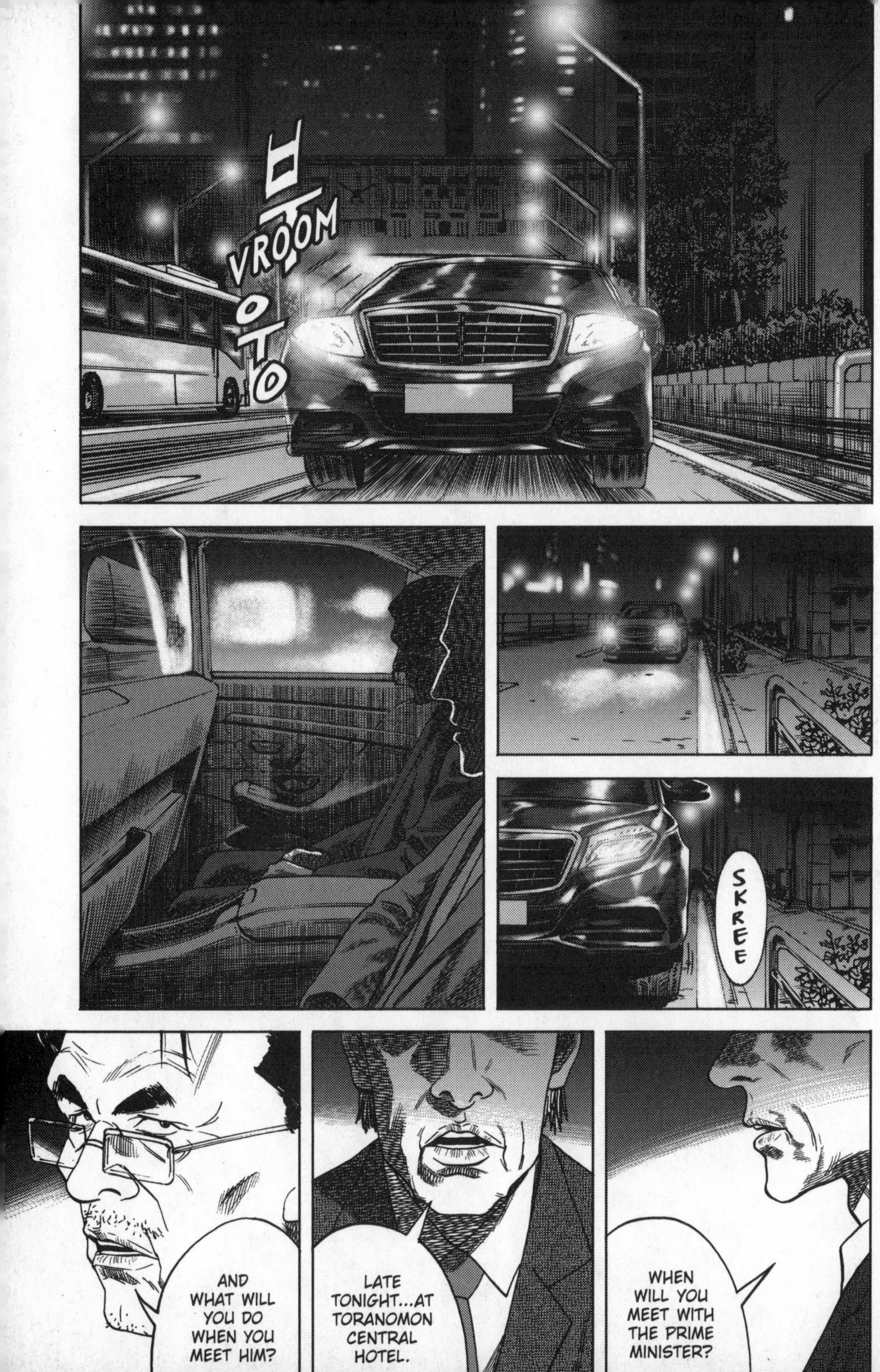
VROOM
OTO
SKREE
WHEN WILL YOU MEET WITH THE PRIME MINISTER?
LATE TONIGHT...AT TORANOMON CENTRAL HOTEL.
AND WHAT WILL YOU DO WHEN YOU MEET HIM?

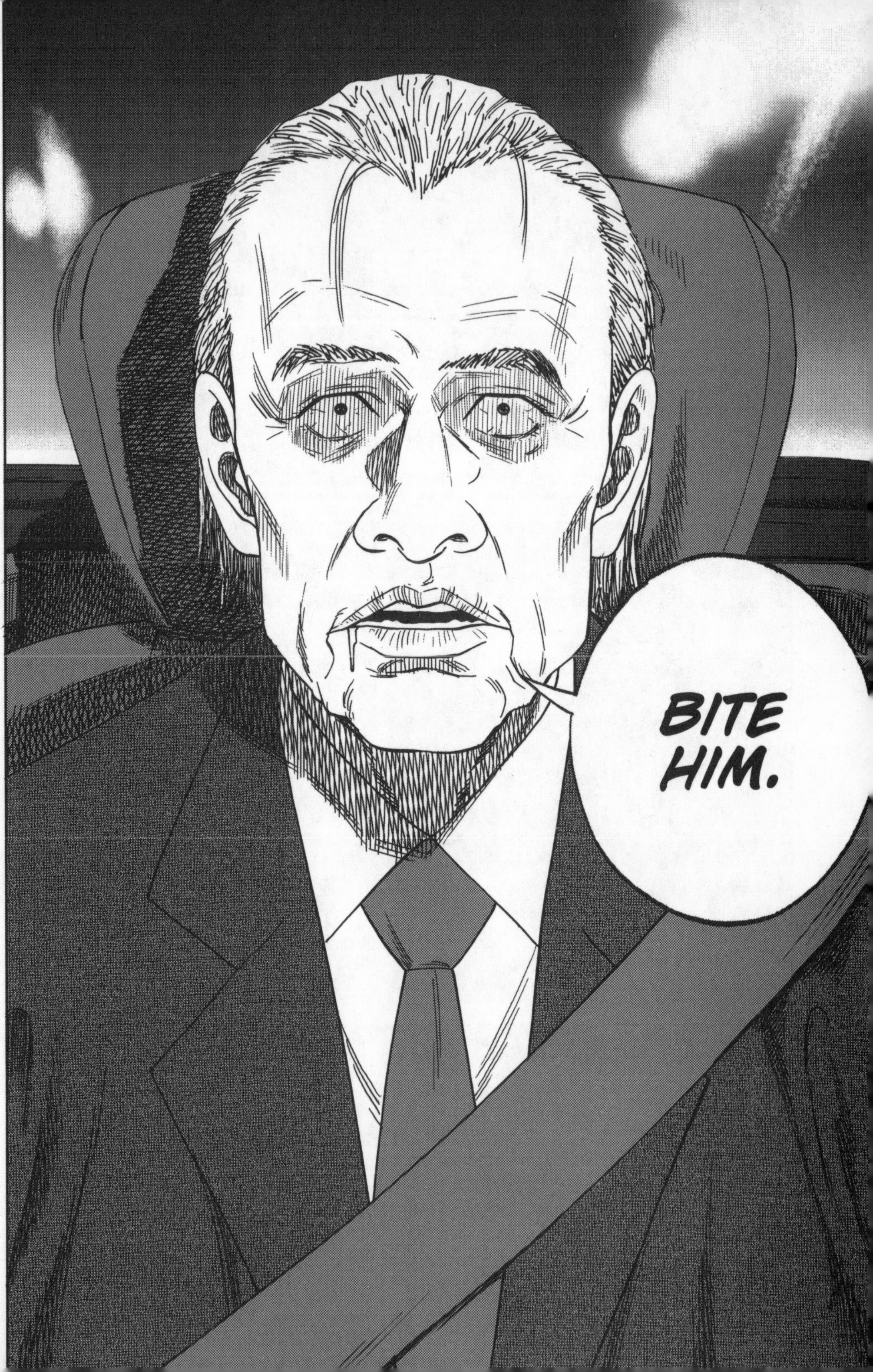
BITE HIM.

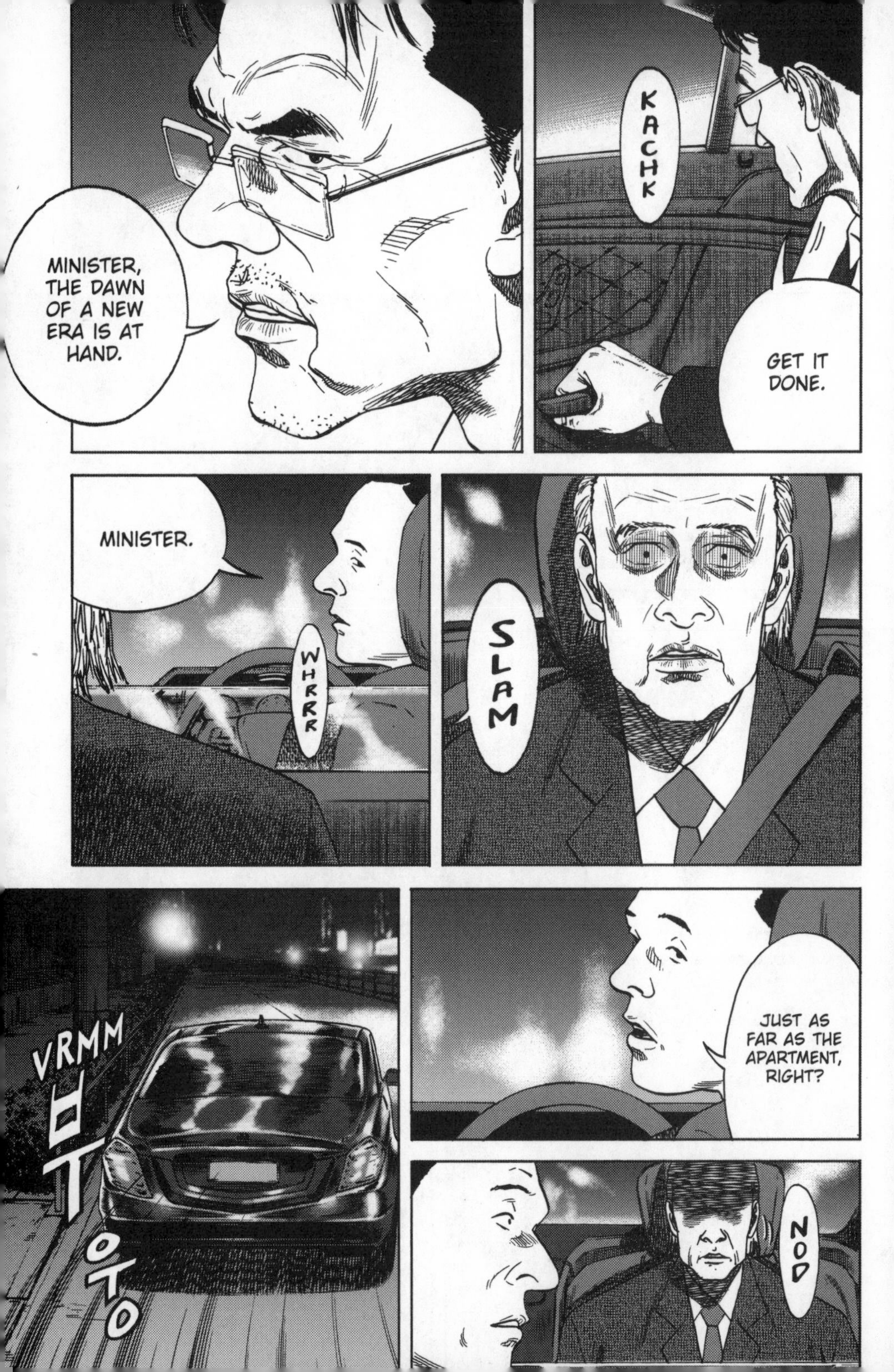
KACHK
GET IT DONE.
MINISTER, THE DAWN OF A NEW ERA IS AT HAND.
SLAM
MINISTER.
WHRRR
JUST AS FAR AS THE APARTMENT, RIGHT?
NOD
VRMM
OTO

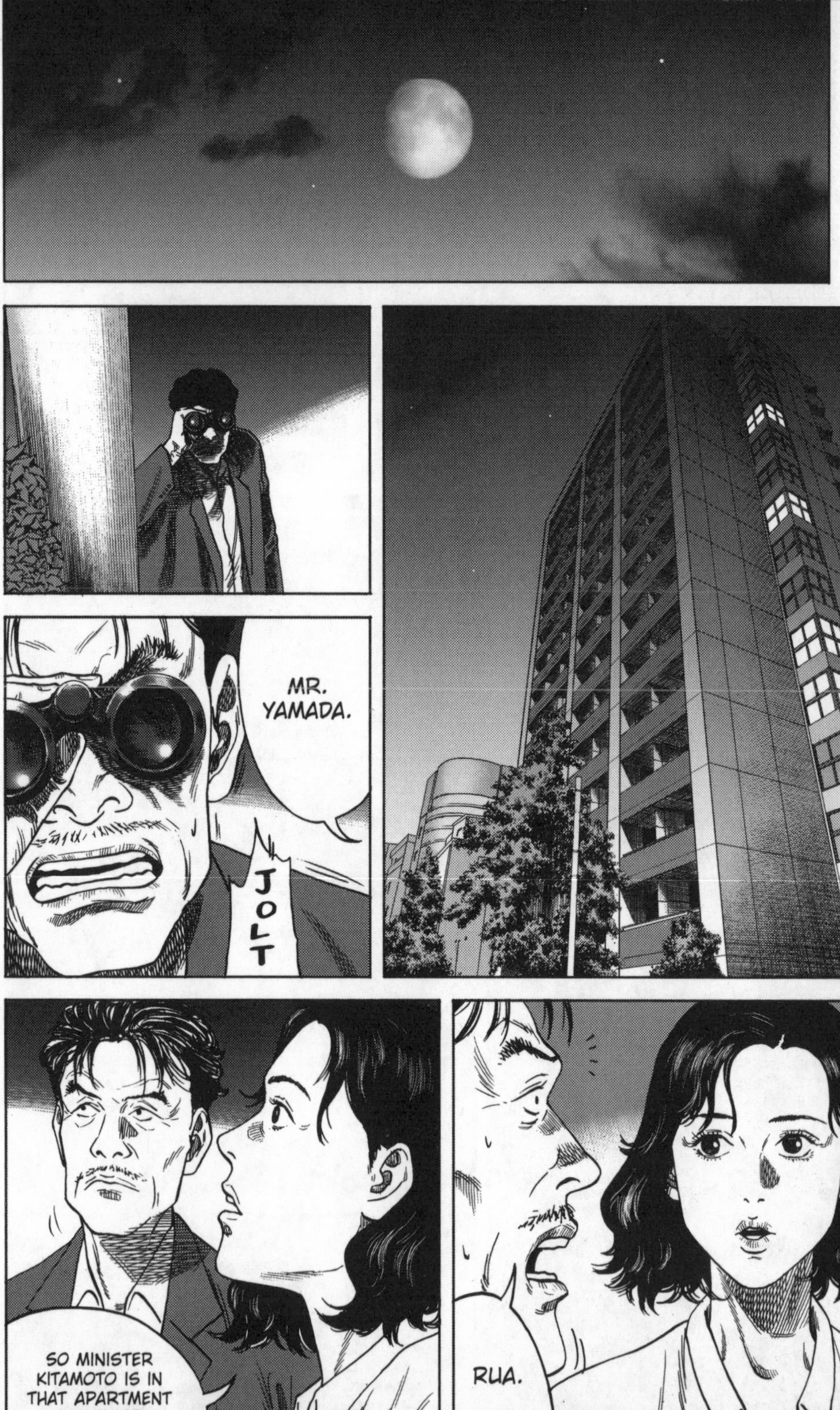
MR. YAMADA.
JOLT
RUA.
SO MINISTER KITAMOTO IS IN THAT APARTMENT BUILDING?

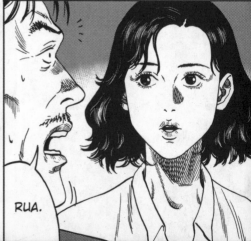

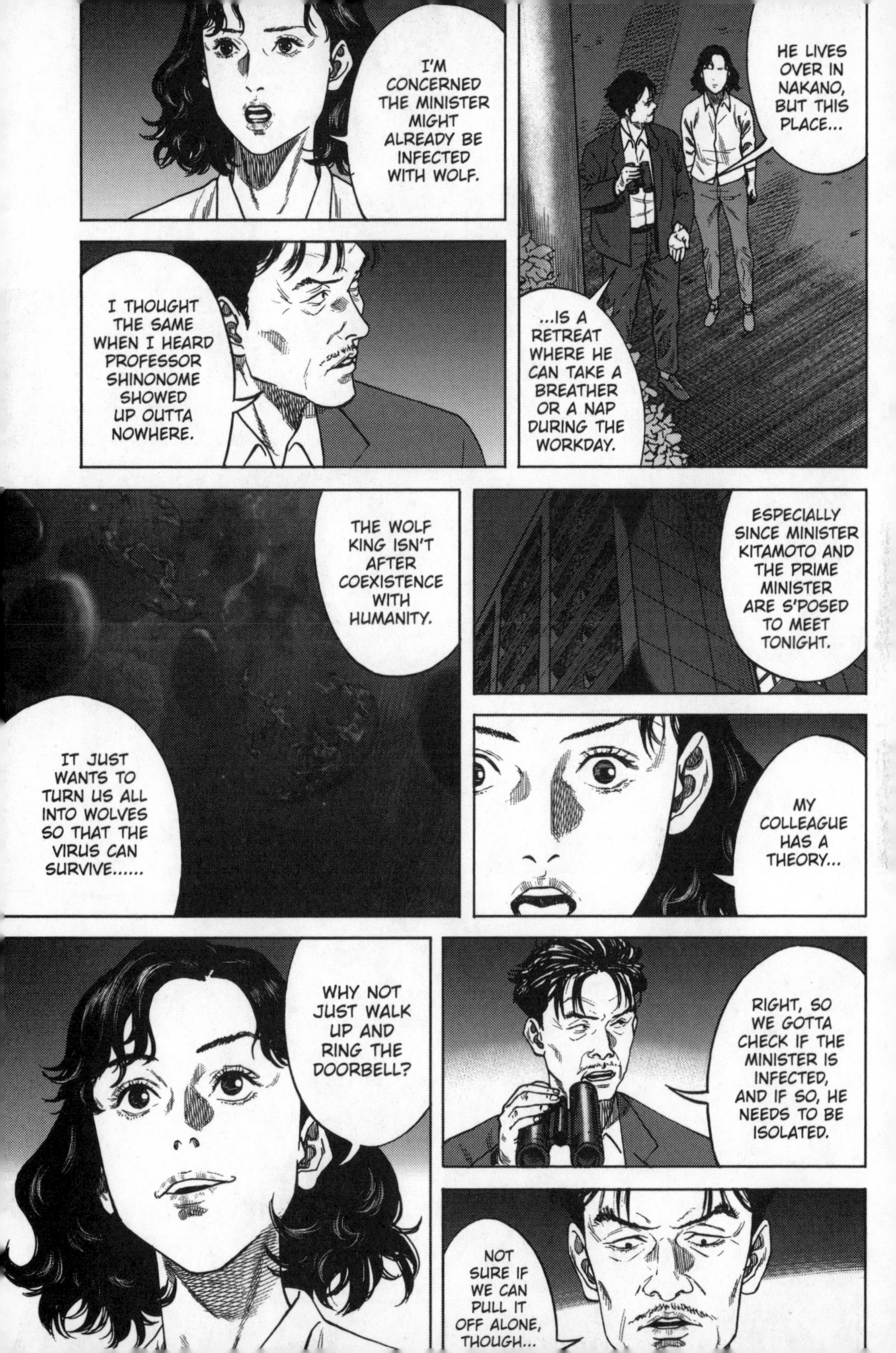
HE LIVES OVER IN NAKANO, BUT THIS PLACE...
...IS A RETREAT WHERE HE CAN TAKE A BREATHER OR A NAP DURING THE WORKDAY.
I'M CONCERNED THE MINISTER MIGHT ALREADY BE INFECTED WITH WOLF.
I THOUGHT THE SAME WHEN I HEARD PROFESSOR SHINONOME SHOWED UP OUTTA NOWHERE.
ESPECIALLY SINCE MINISTER KITAMOTO AND THE PRIME MINISTER ARE S'POSED TO MEET TONIGHT.
MY COLLEAGUE HAS A THEORY...
THE WOLF KING ISN'T AFTER COEXISTENCE WITH HUMANITY.
IT JUST WANTS TO TURN US ALL INTO WOLVES SO THAT THE VIRUS CAN SURVIVE......
RIGHT, SO WE GOTTA CHECK IF THE MINISTER IS INFECTED, AND IF SO, HE NEEDS TO BE ISOLATED.
NOT SURE IF WE CAN PULL IT OFF ALONE, THOUGH...
WHY NOT JUST WALK UP AND RING THE DOORBELL?

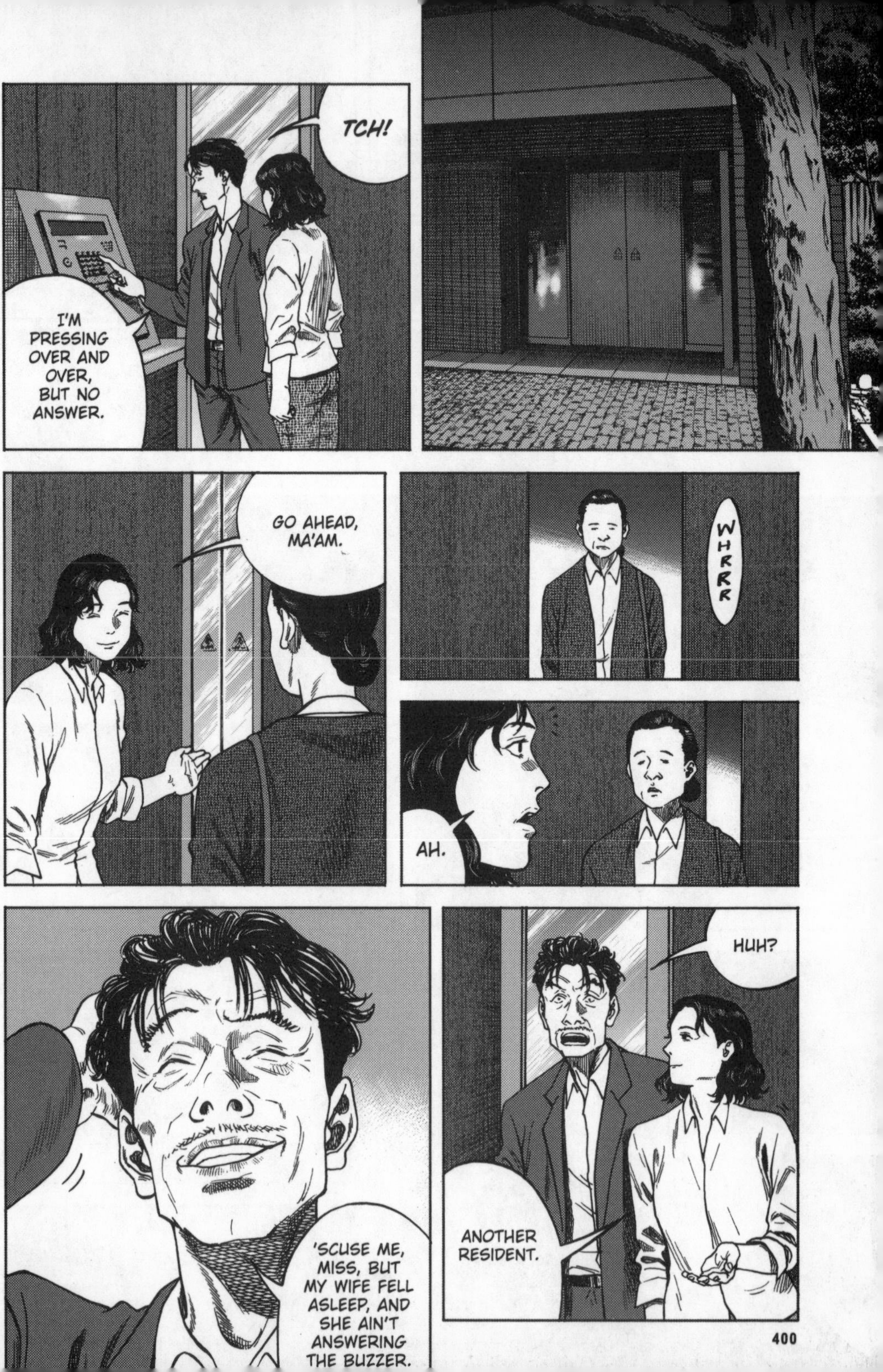
TCH!
I'M PRESSING OVER AND OVER, BUT NO ANSWER.
WHRRR
AH.
GO AHEAD, MA'AM.
HUH?
ANOTHER RESIDENT.
'SCUSE ME, MISS, BUT MY WIFE FELL ASLEEP, AND SHE AIN'T ANSWERING THE BUZZER.

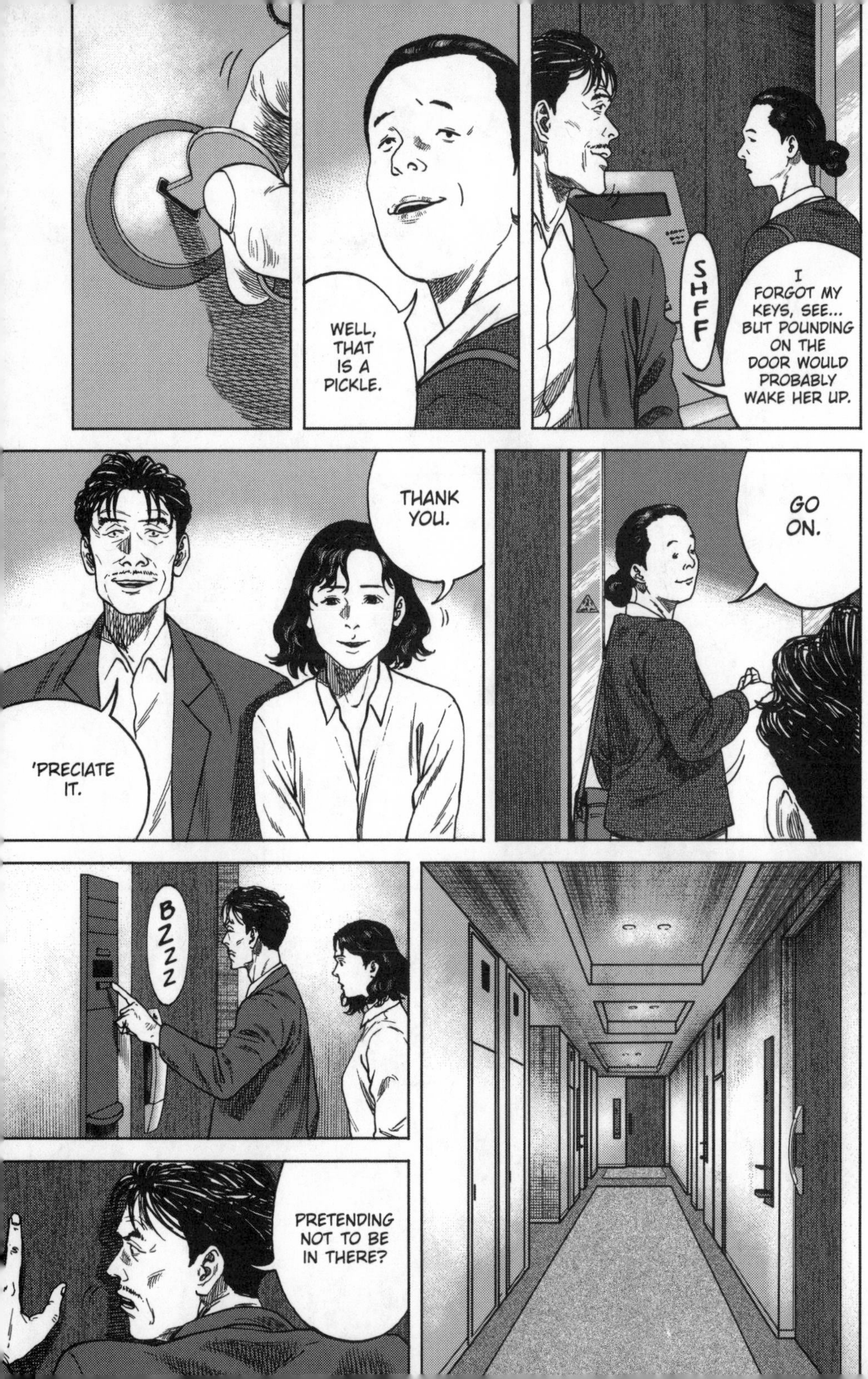
I FORGOT MY KEYS, SEE... BUT POUNDING ON THE DOOR WOULD PROBABLY WAKE HER UP.
SHFF
WELL, THAT IS A PICKLE.
GO ON.
THANK YOU.
'PRECIATE IT.
BZZZ
PRETENDING NOT TO BE IN THERE?

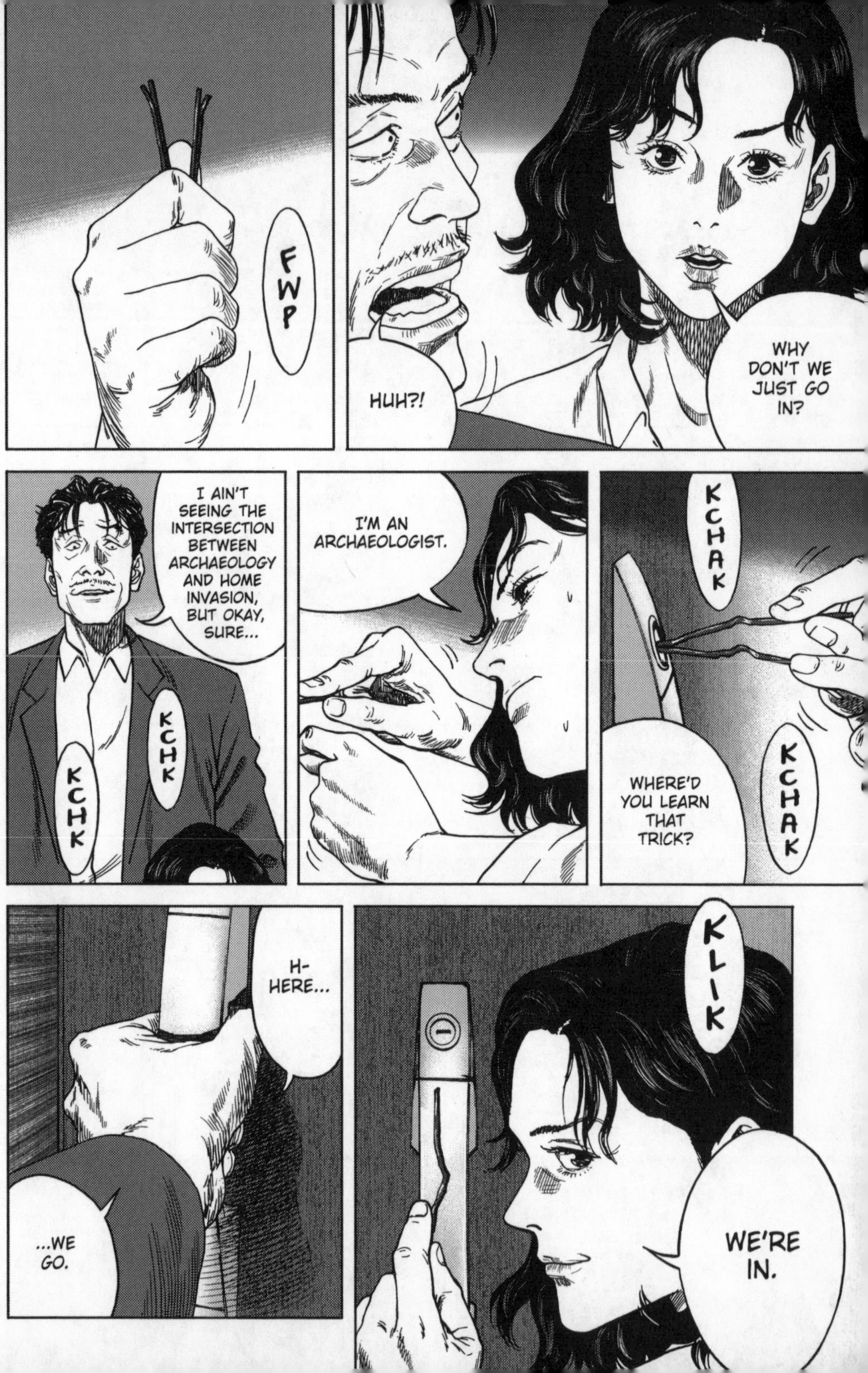
WHY DON'T WE JUST GO IN?
HUH?!
FWP
KCHAK
WHERE'D YOU LEARN THAT TRICK?
KCHAK
I'M AN ARCHAEOLOGIST.
I AIN'T SEEING THE INTERSECTION BETWEEN ARCHAEOLOGY AND HOME INVASION, BUT OKAY, SURE...
KCHK
KCHK
KLIK
WE'RE IN.
H- HERE...
...WE GO.

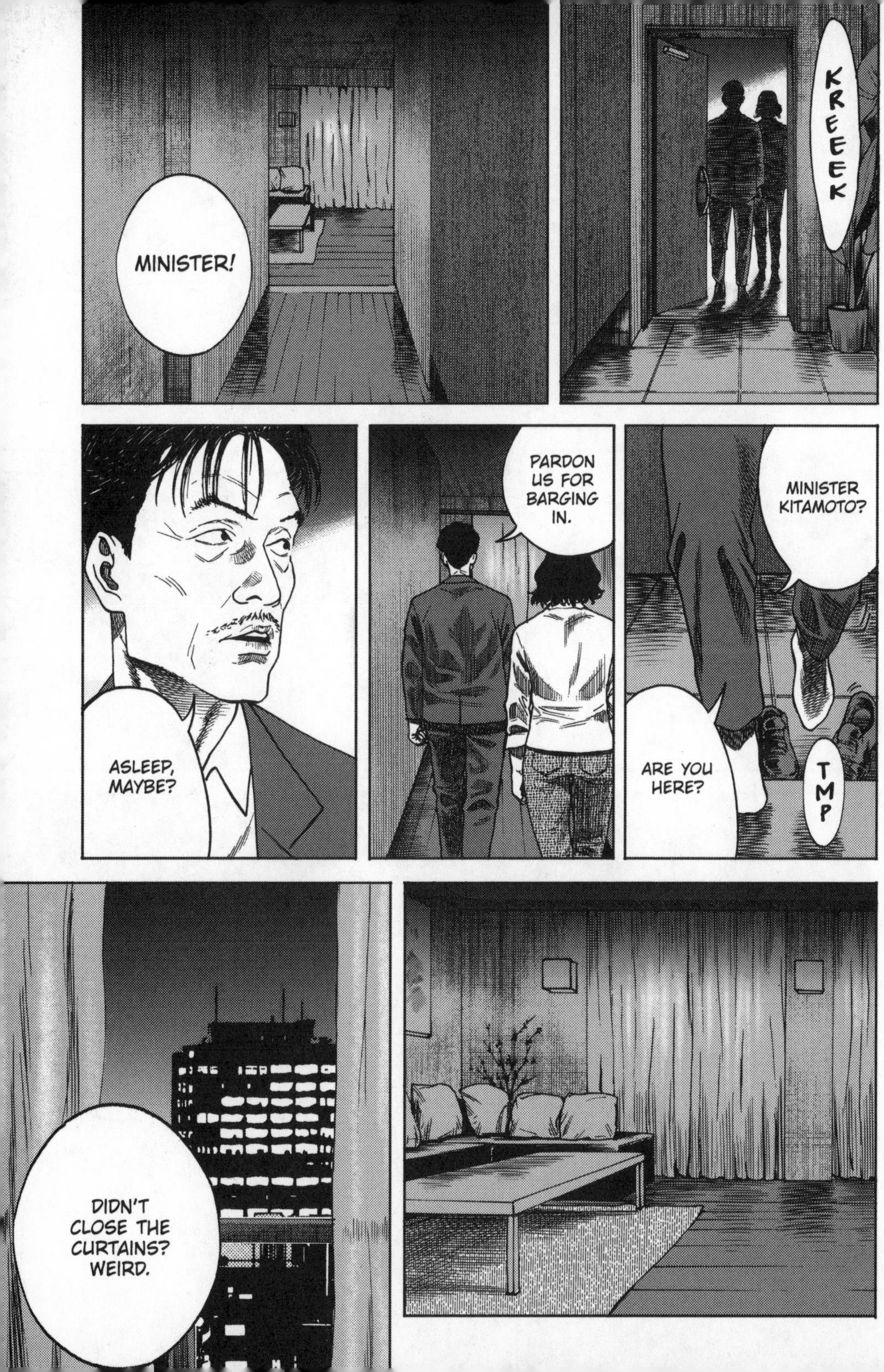
KREEEK
MINISTER!
MINISTER KITAMOTO?
ARE YOU HERE?
TMP
PARDON US FOR BARGING IN.
ASLEEP, MAYBE?
DIDN'T CLOSE THE CURTAINS? WEIRD.

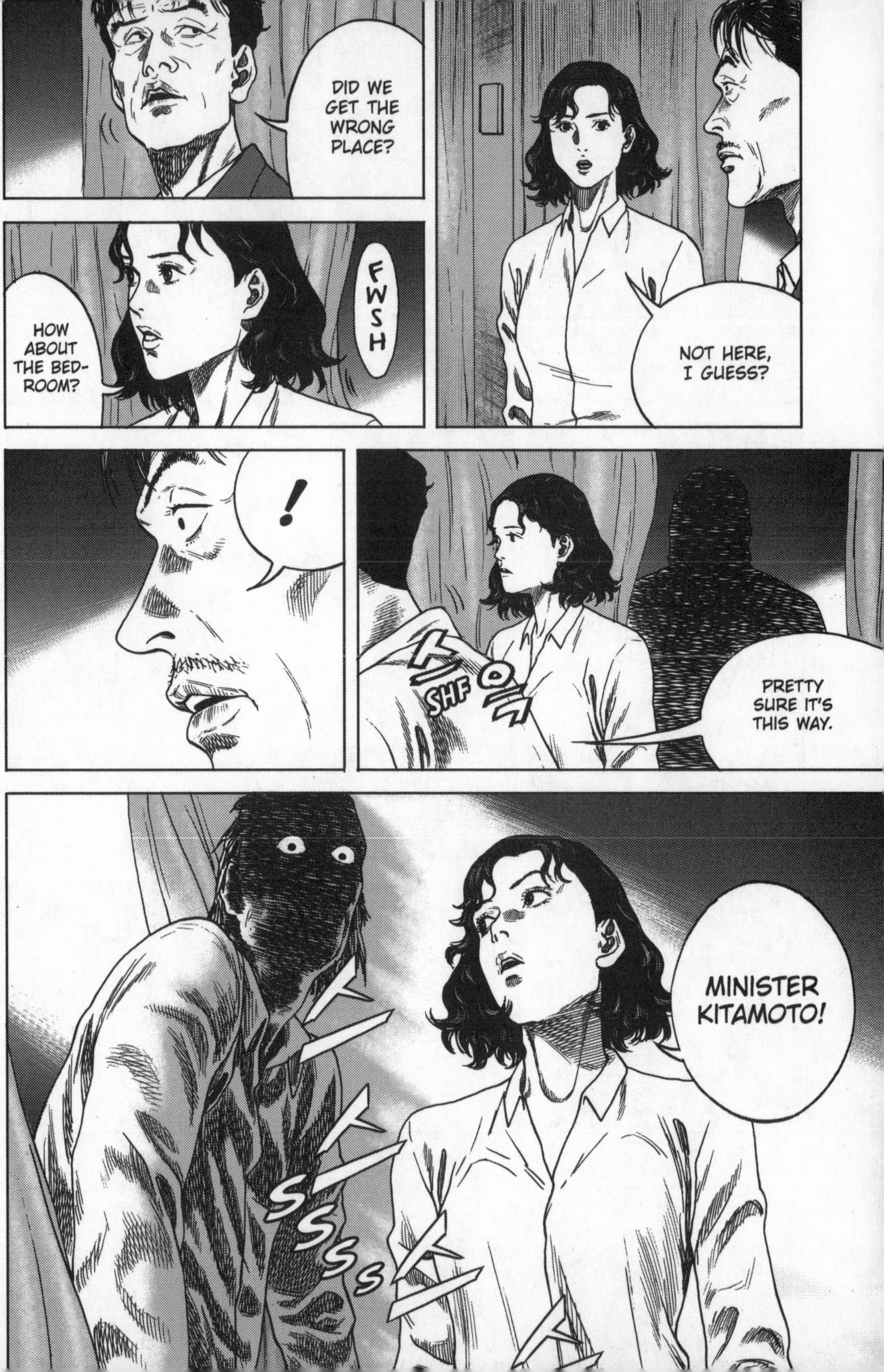
NOT HERE, I GUESS?
DID WE GET THE WRONG PLACE?
FWSH
HOW ABOUT THE BED-ROOM?
SHF
PRETTY SURE IT'S THIS WAY.
!
MINISTER KITAMOTO!
SSSSS

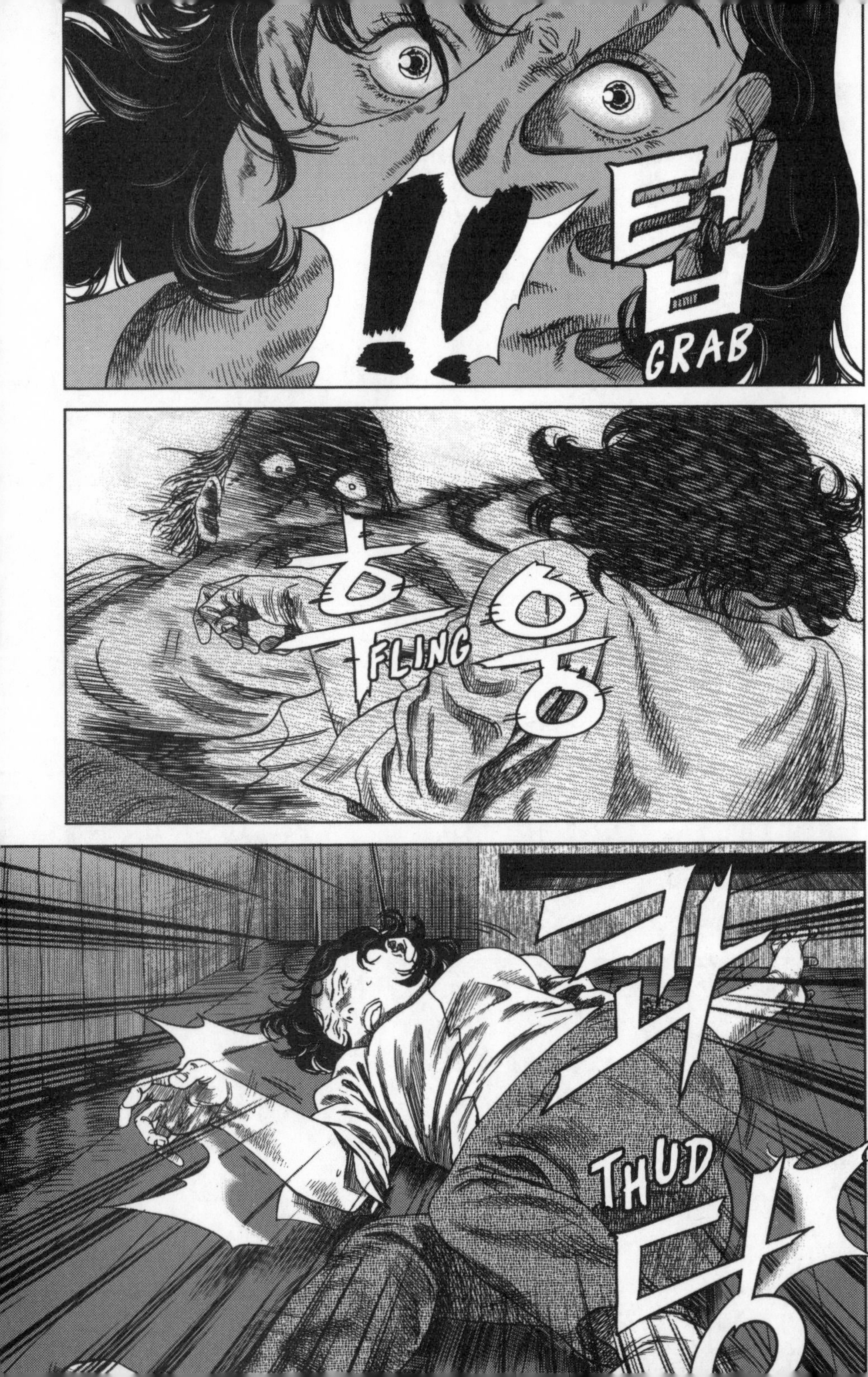
!!
텁
GRAB
후웅
FLING
커당
THUD

M-M-M-MINISTER KITAMOTO?

IT'S ME, Y-YAMADA.

UWAAAA!

UM, SORRY FOR DROPPING BY UNINVITED...

TWITCH

UMM, YOU *WANT TO CHANGE?*

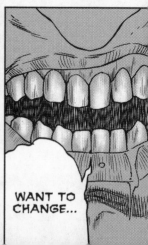

WANT TO CHANGE...

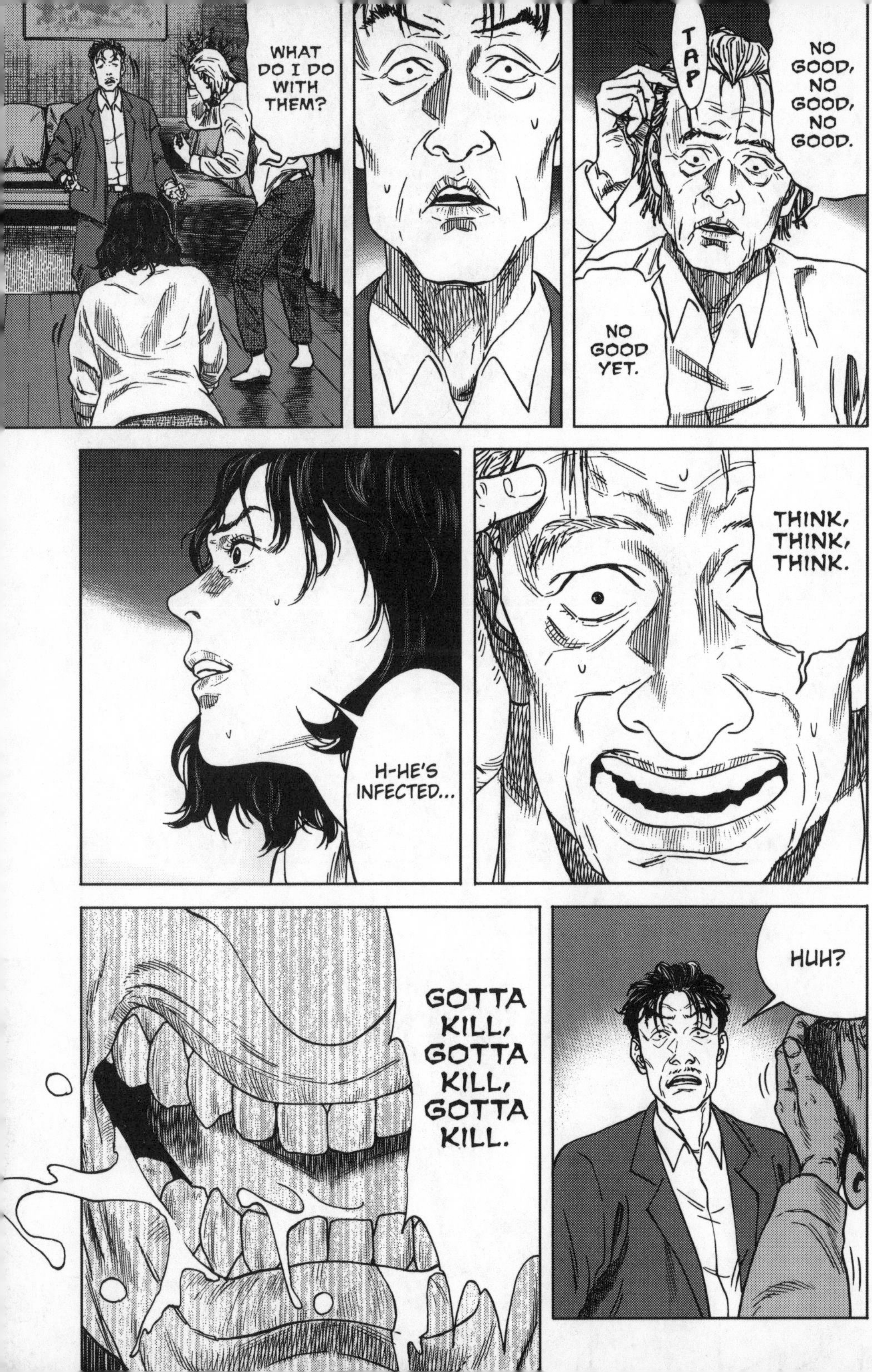
TAP
NO GOOD, NO GOOD, NO GOOD.
NO GOOD YET.
WHAT DO I DO WITH THEM?
THINK, THINK, THINK.
H-HE'S INFECTED...
HUH?
GOTTA KILL, GOTTA KILL, GOTTA KILL.

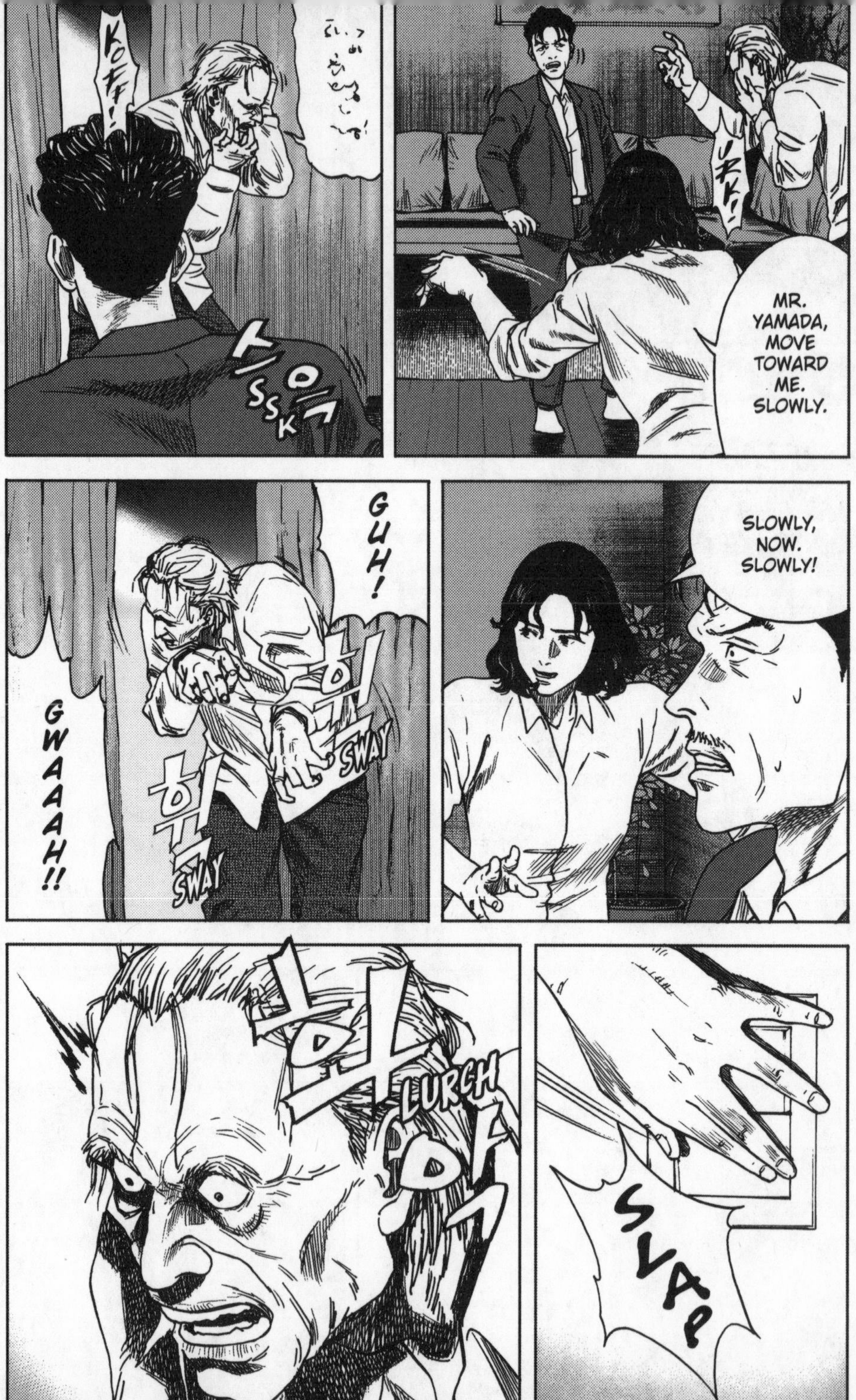
URK!
MR. YAMADA, MOVE TOWARD ME. SLOWLY.
KOFF!
SSK
SLOWLY, NOW. SLOWLY!
GUH!
SWAY
SWAY
GWAAAAH!!
SNAP
LURCH

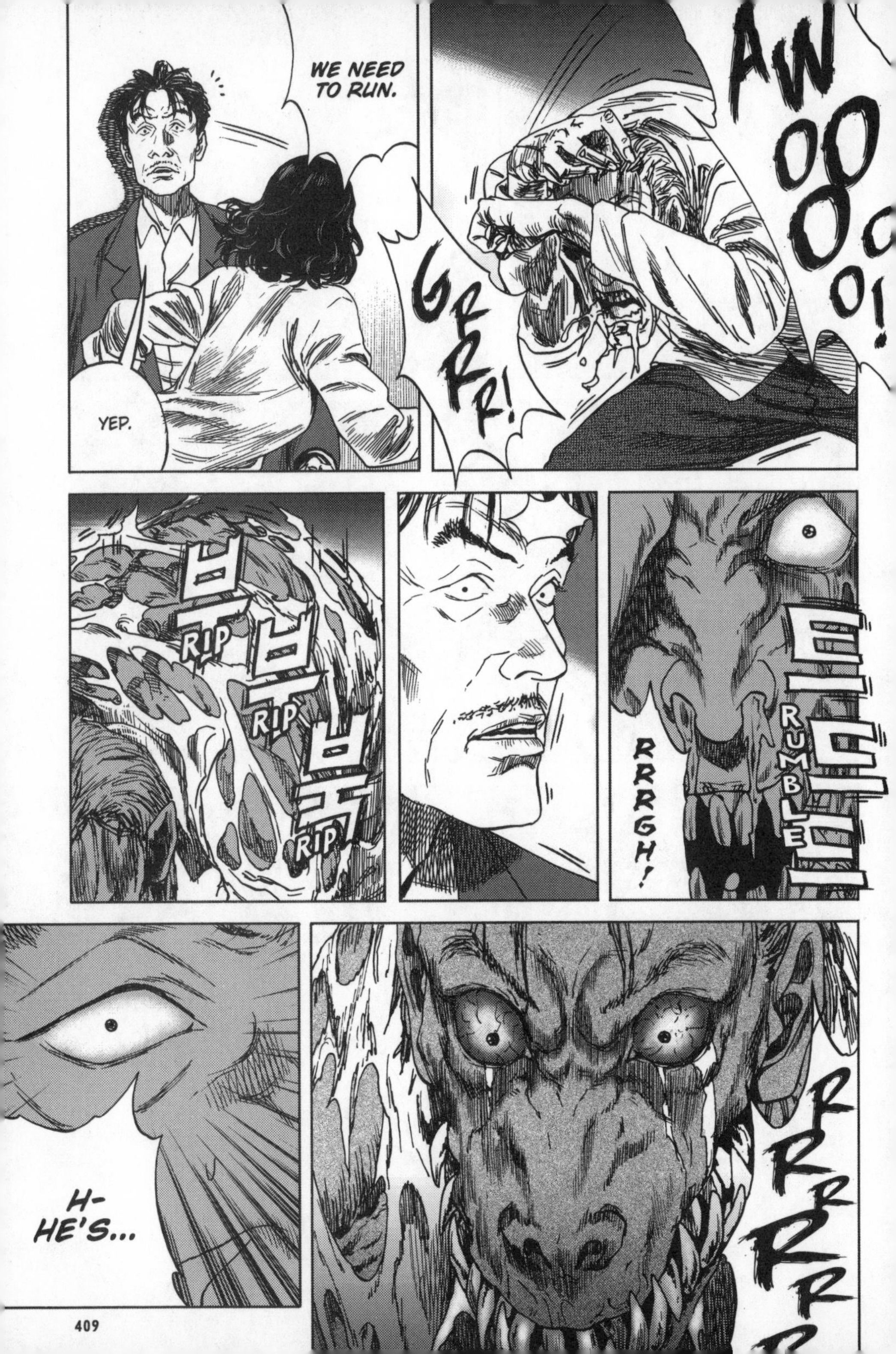
AWOOOOO!
GRRR!
WE NEED TO RUN.
YEP.
RUMBLE
RRRGH!
RIP
RIP
RIP
RRRRRR
H-
HE'S...

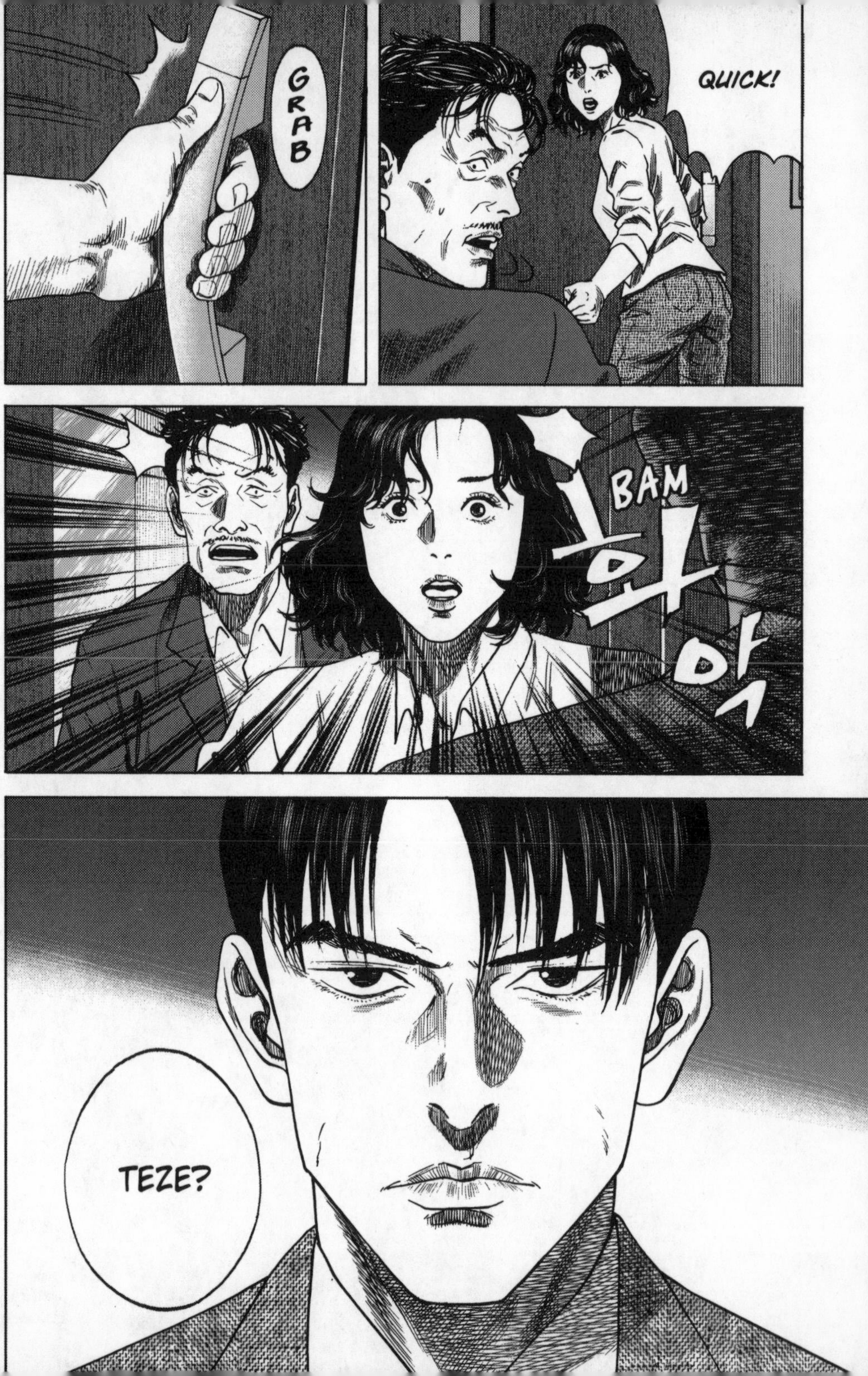
QUICK!
GRAB
BAM
TEZE?

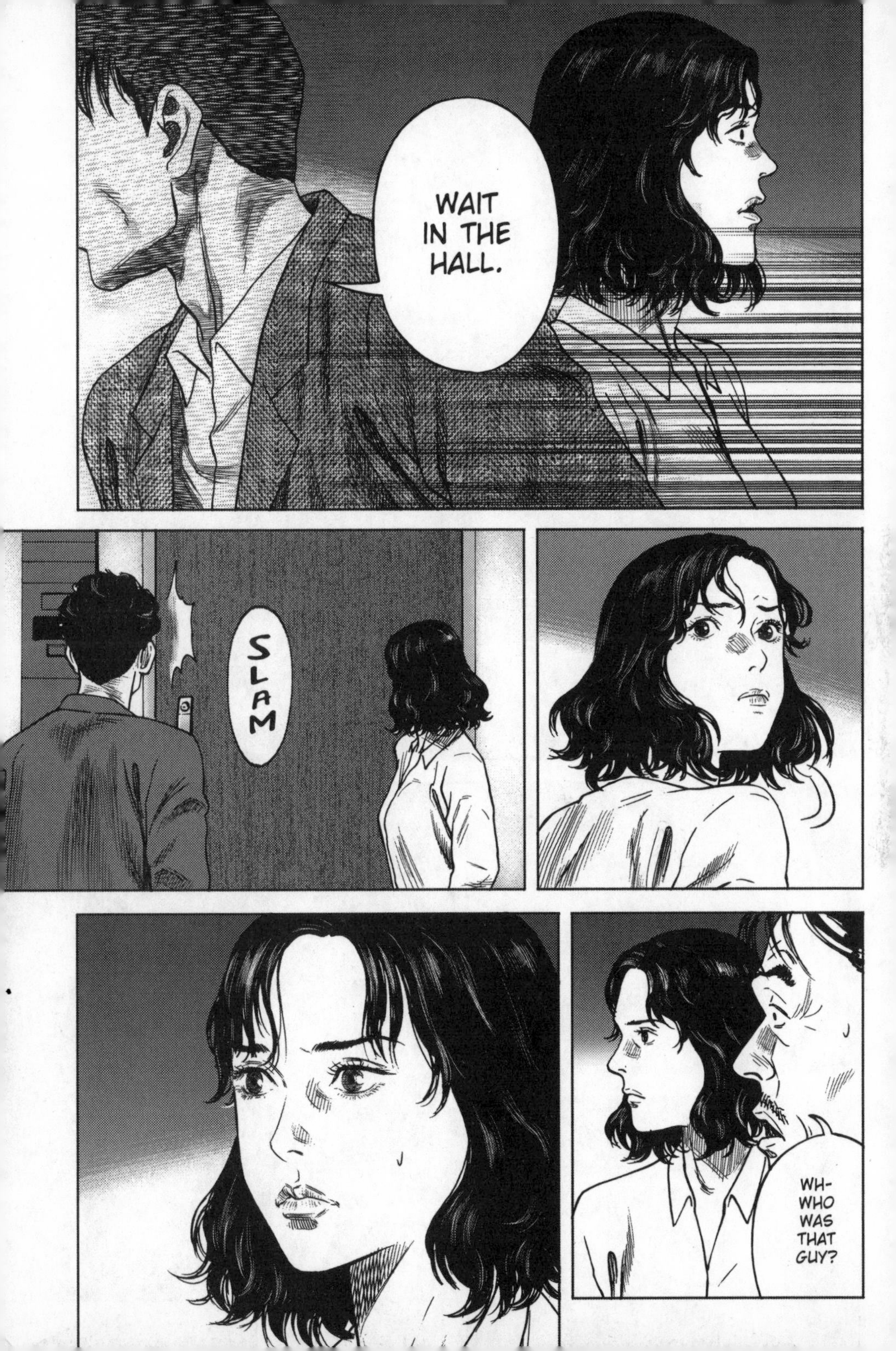
WAIT IN THE HALL.
SLAM
WH- WHO WAS THAT GUY?

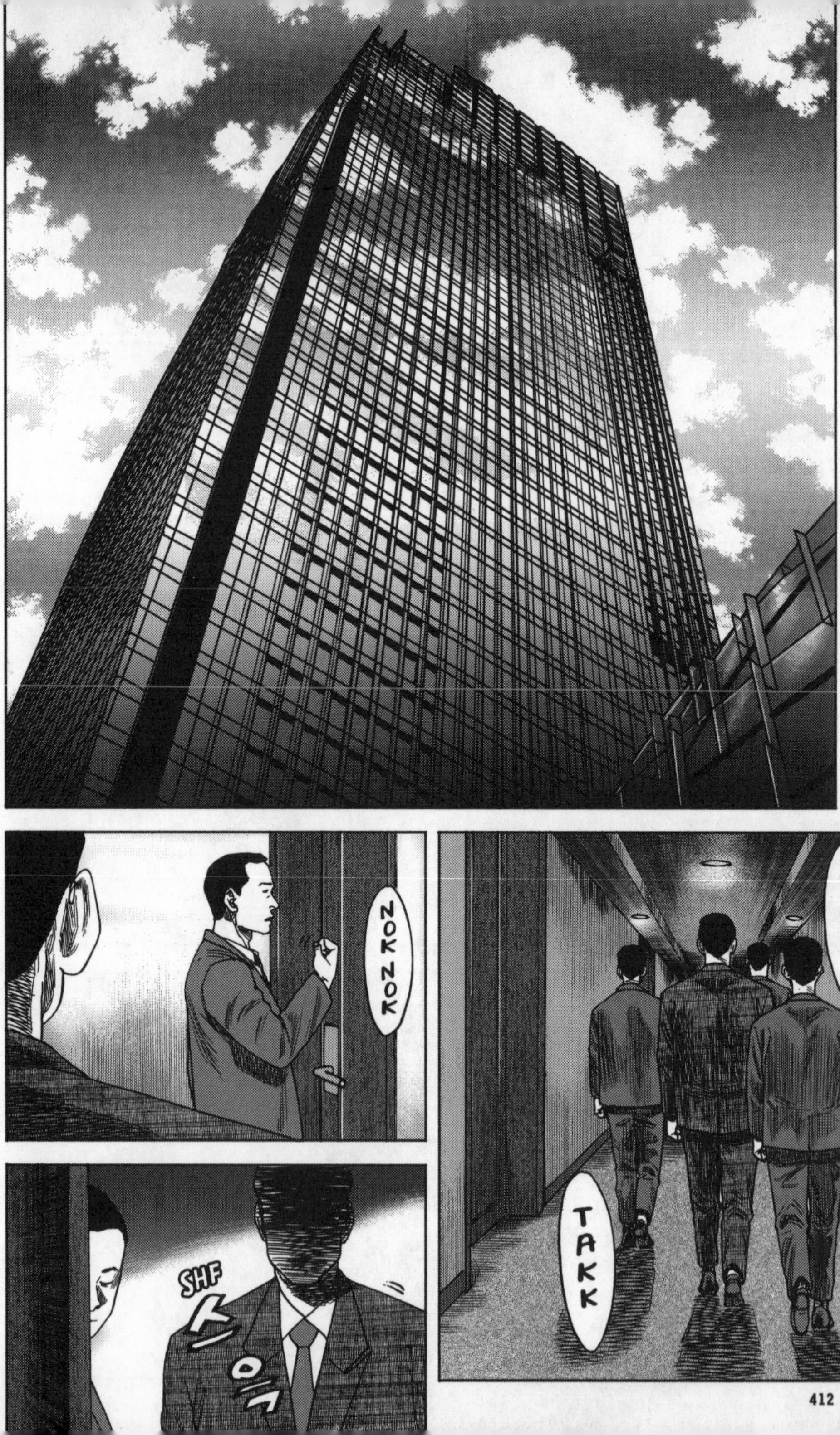
TAKK
TAKK
NOK NOK
SHF

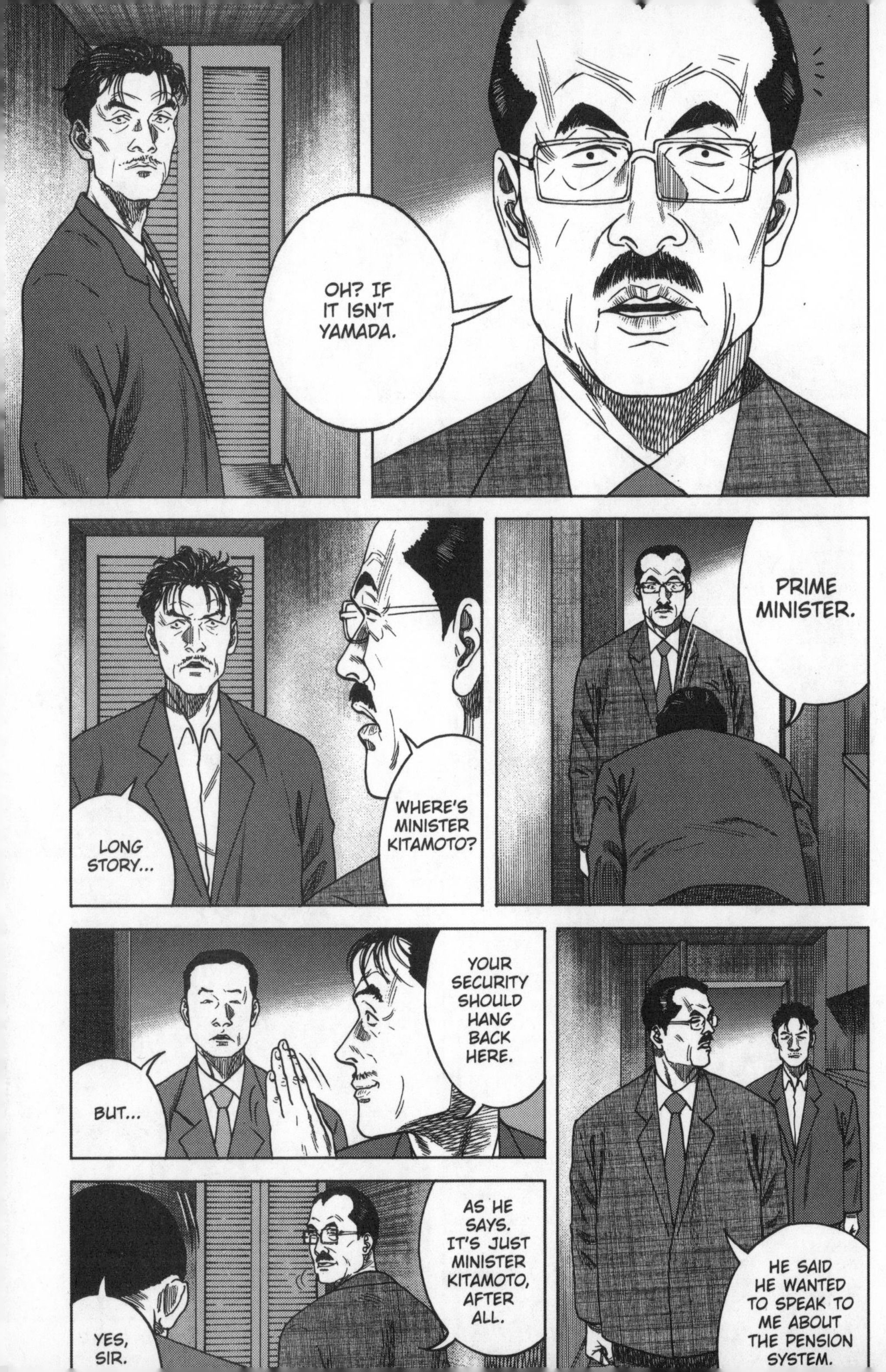
OH? IF IT ISN'T YAMADA.
PRIME MINISTER.
WHERE'S MINISTER KITAMOTO?
LONG STORY...
HE SAID HE WANTED TO SPEAK TO ME ABOUT THE PENSION SYSTEM.
YOUR SECURITY SHOULD HANG BACK HERE.
BUT...
AS HE SAYS. IT'S JUST MINISTER KITAMOTO, AFTER ALL.
YES, SIR.

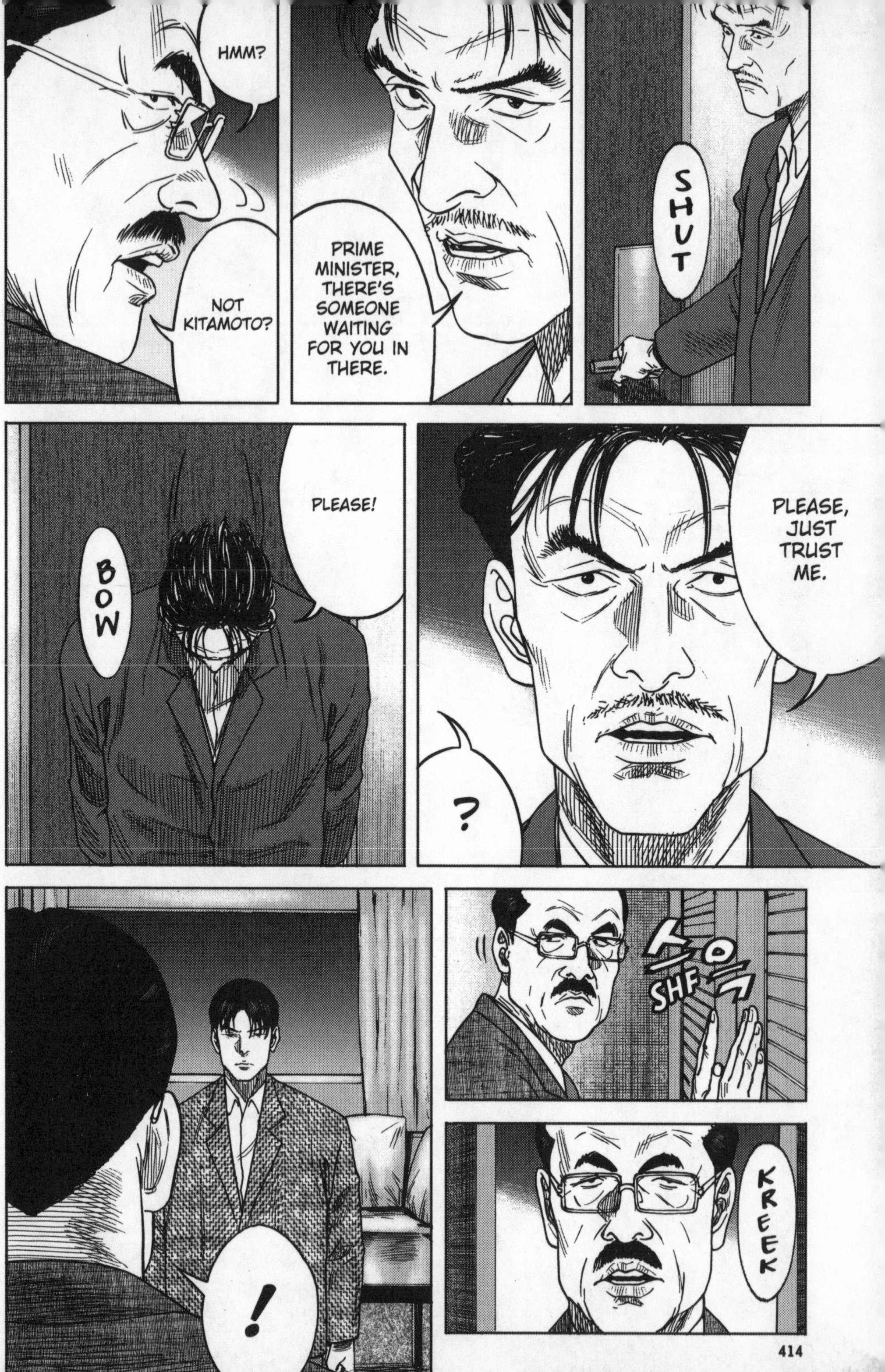
SHUT
PRIME MINISTER, THERE'S SOMEONE WAITING FOR YOU IN THERE.
HMM?
NOT KITAMOTO?
PLEASE, JUST TRUST ME.
?
PLEASE!
BOW
SHF
KREEK
!

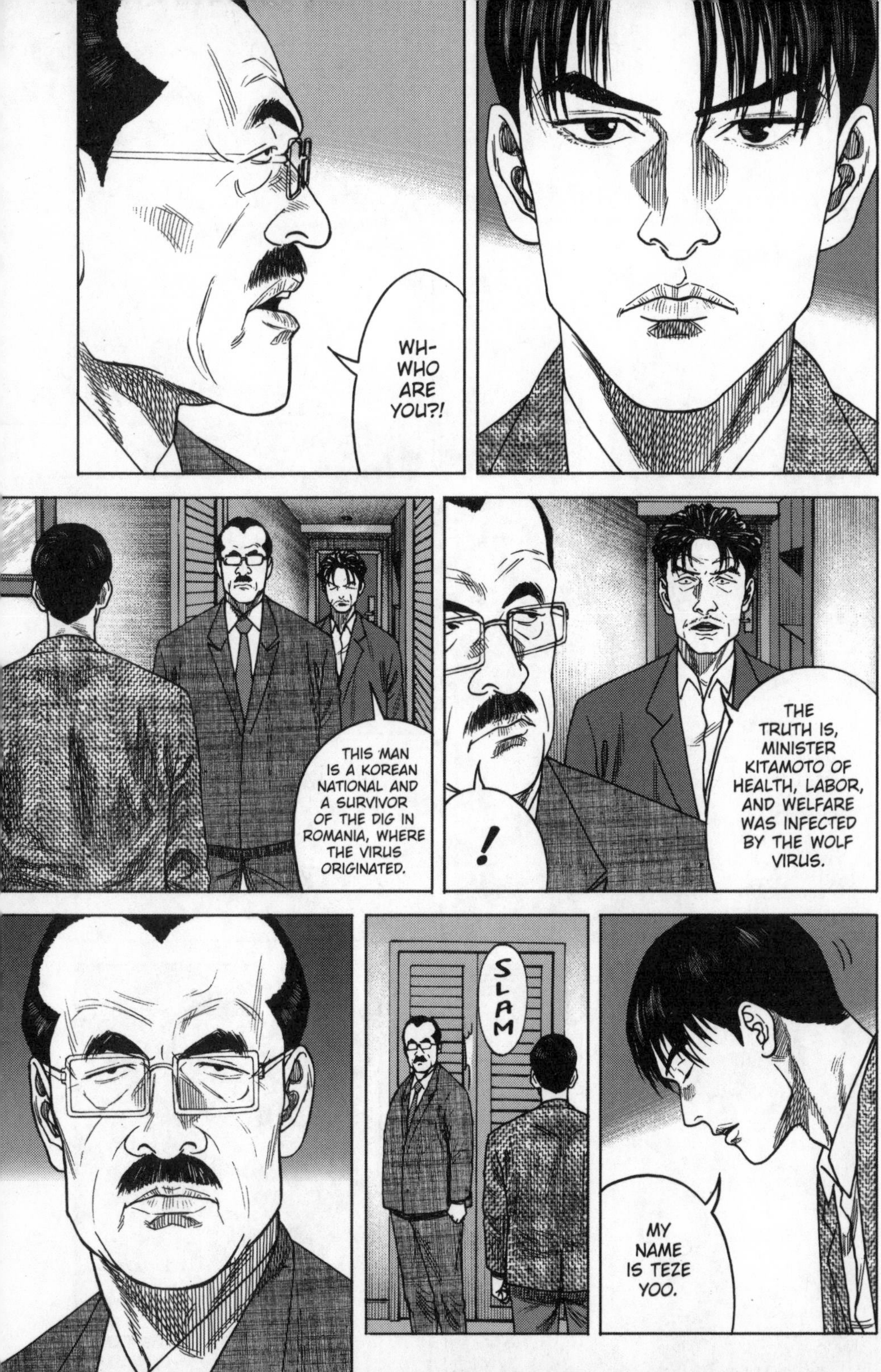
WH- WHO ARE YOU?!
THE TRUTH IS, MINISTER KITAMOTO OF HEALTH, LABOR, AND WELFARE WAS INFECTED BY THE WOLF VIRUS.
!
THIS MAN IS A KOREAN NATIONAL AND A SURVIVOR OF THE DIG IN ROMANIA, WHERE THE VIRUS ORIGINATED.
MY NAME IS TEZE YOO.
SLAM

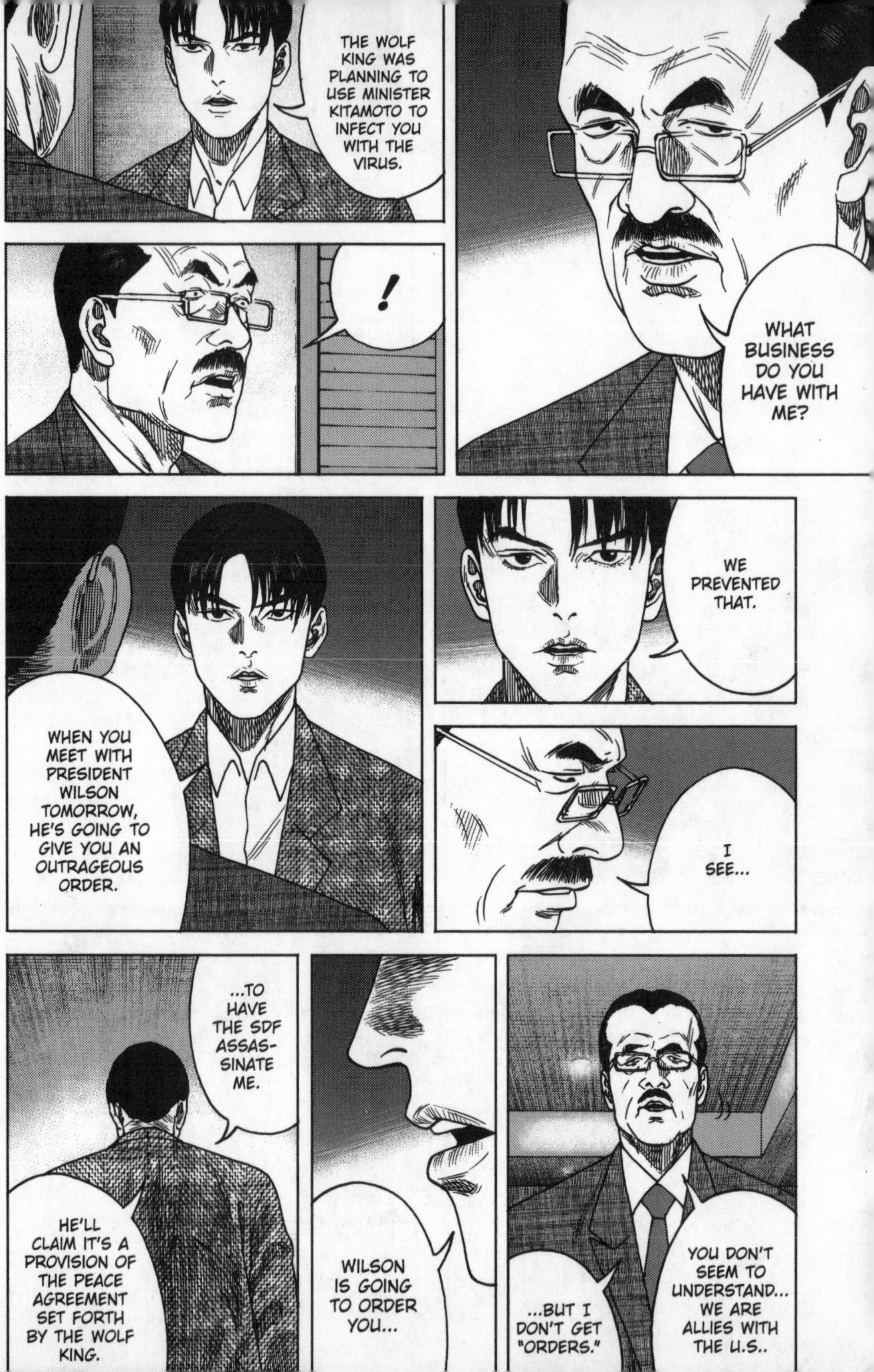
WHAT BUSINESS DO YOU HAVE WITH ME?
THE WOLF KING WAS PLANNING TO USE MINISTER KITAMOTO TO INFECT YOU WITH THE VIRUS.
!
WE PREVENTED THAT.
I SEE...
WHEN YOU MEET WITH PRESIDENT WILSON TOMORROW, HE'S GOING TO GIVE YOU AN OUTRAGEOUS ORDER.
YOU DON'T SEEM TO UNDERSTAND... WE ARE ALLIES WITH THE U.S..
...BUT I DON'T GET "ORDERS."
WILSON IS GOING TO ORDER YOU...
...TO HAVE THE SDF ASSAS-SINATE ME.
HE'LL CLAIM IT'S A PROVISION OF THE PEACE AGREEMENT SET FORTH BY THE WOLF KING.

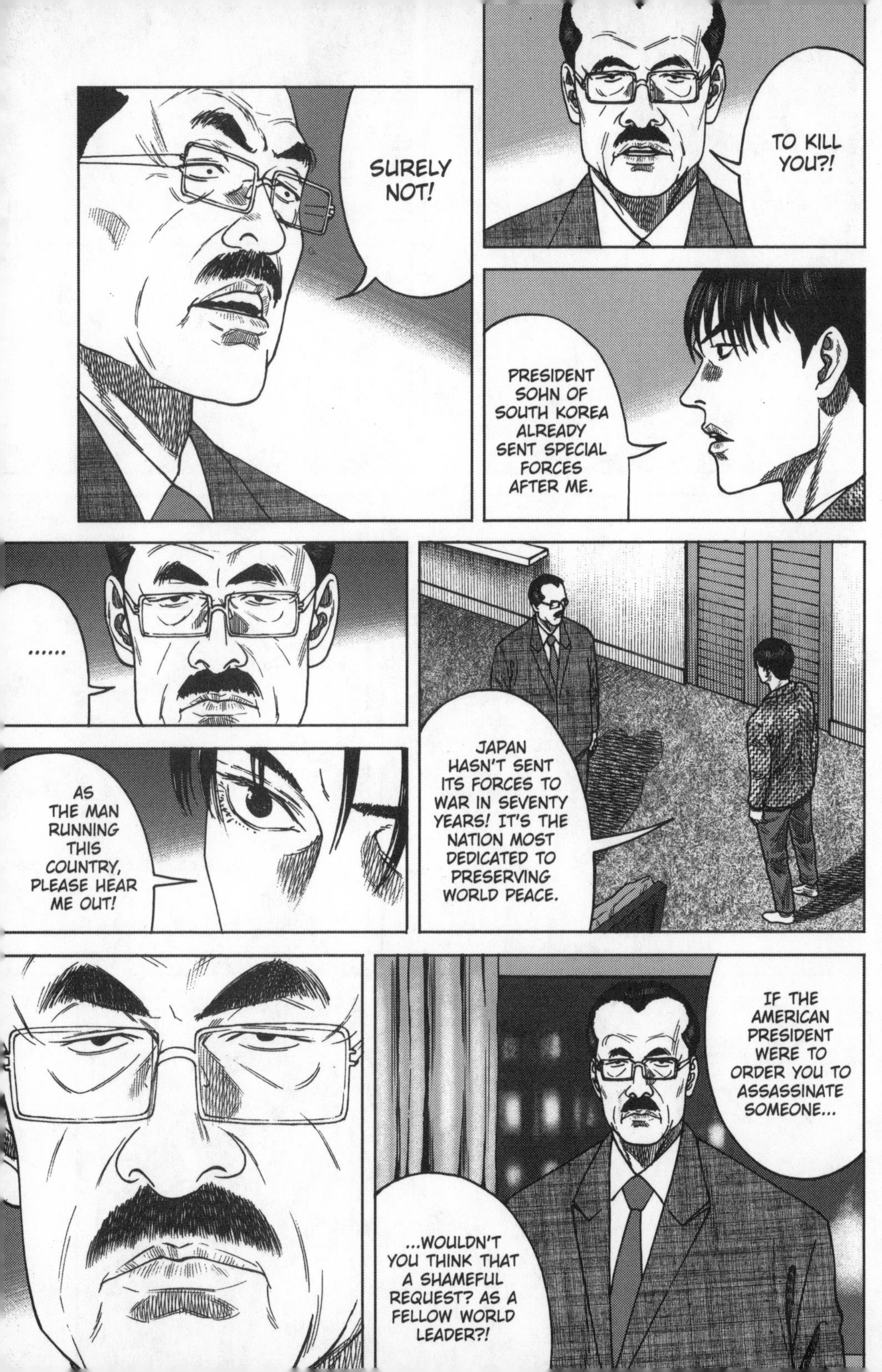

TO KILL YOU?!
PRESIDENT SOHN OF SOUTH KOREA ALREADY SENT SPECIAL FORCES AFTER ME.
SURELY NOT!
JAPAN HASN'T SENT ITS FORCES TO WAR IN SEVENTY YEARS! IT'S THE NATION MOST DEDICATED TO PRESERVING WORLD PEACE.
......
AS THE MAN RUNNING THIS COUNTRY, PLEASE HEAR ME OUT!
IF THE AMERICAN PRESIDENT WERE TO ORDER YOU TO ASSASSINATE SOMEONE...
...WOULDN'T YOU THINK THAT A SHAMEFUL REQUEST? AS A FELLOW WORLD LEADER?!

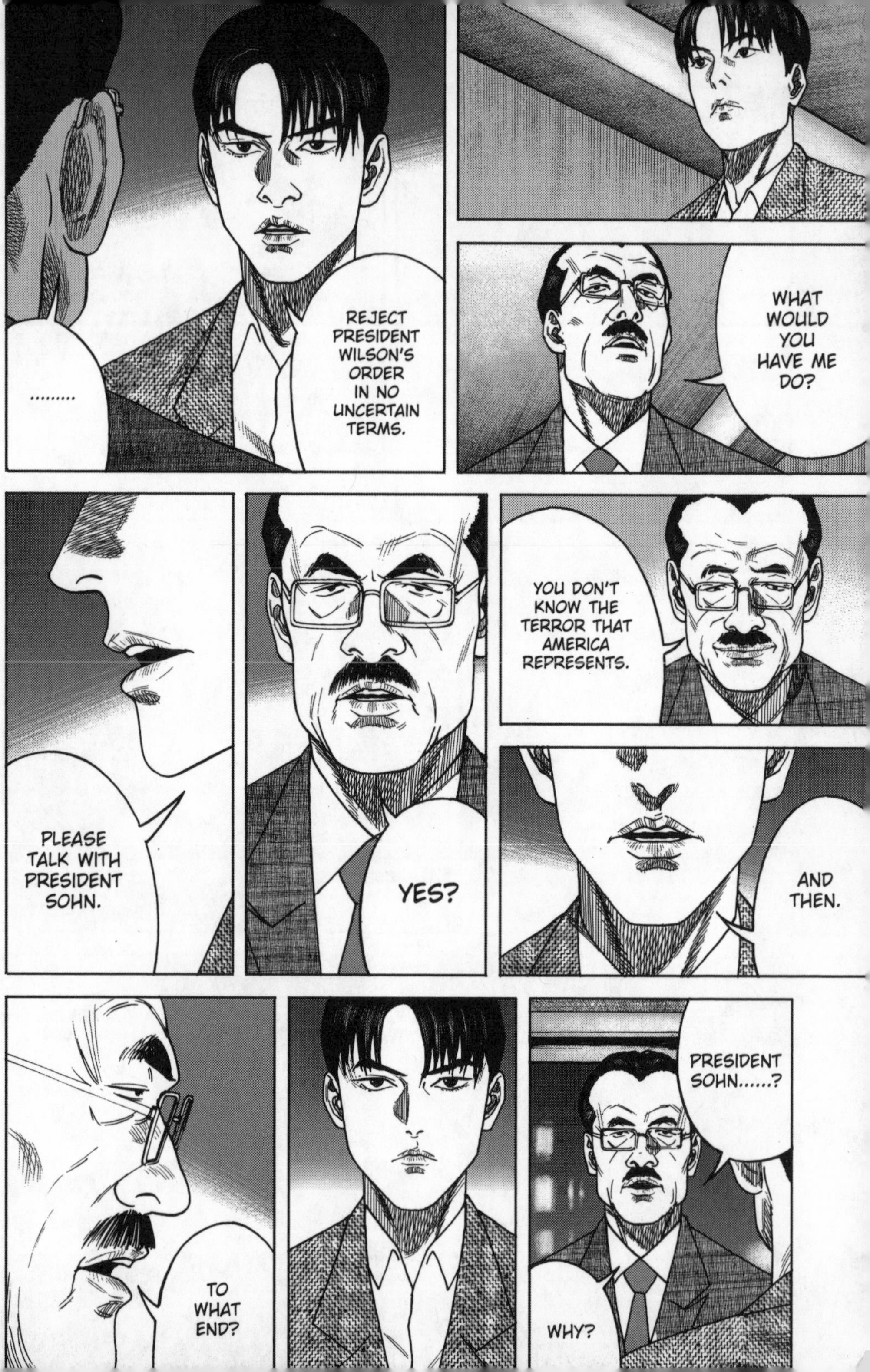

WHAT WOULD YOU HAVE ME DO?
REJECT PRESIDENT WILSON'S ORDER IN NO UNCERTAIN TERMS.
....
YOU DON'T KNOW THE TERROR THAT AMERICA REPRESENTS.
AND THEN.
YES?
PLEASE TALK WITH PRESIDENT SOHN.
PRESIDENT SOHN......?
WHY?
TO WHAT END?

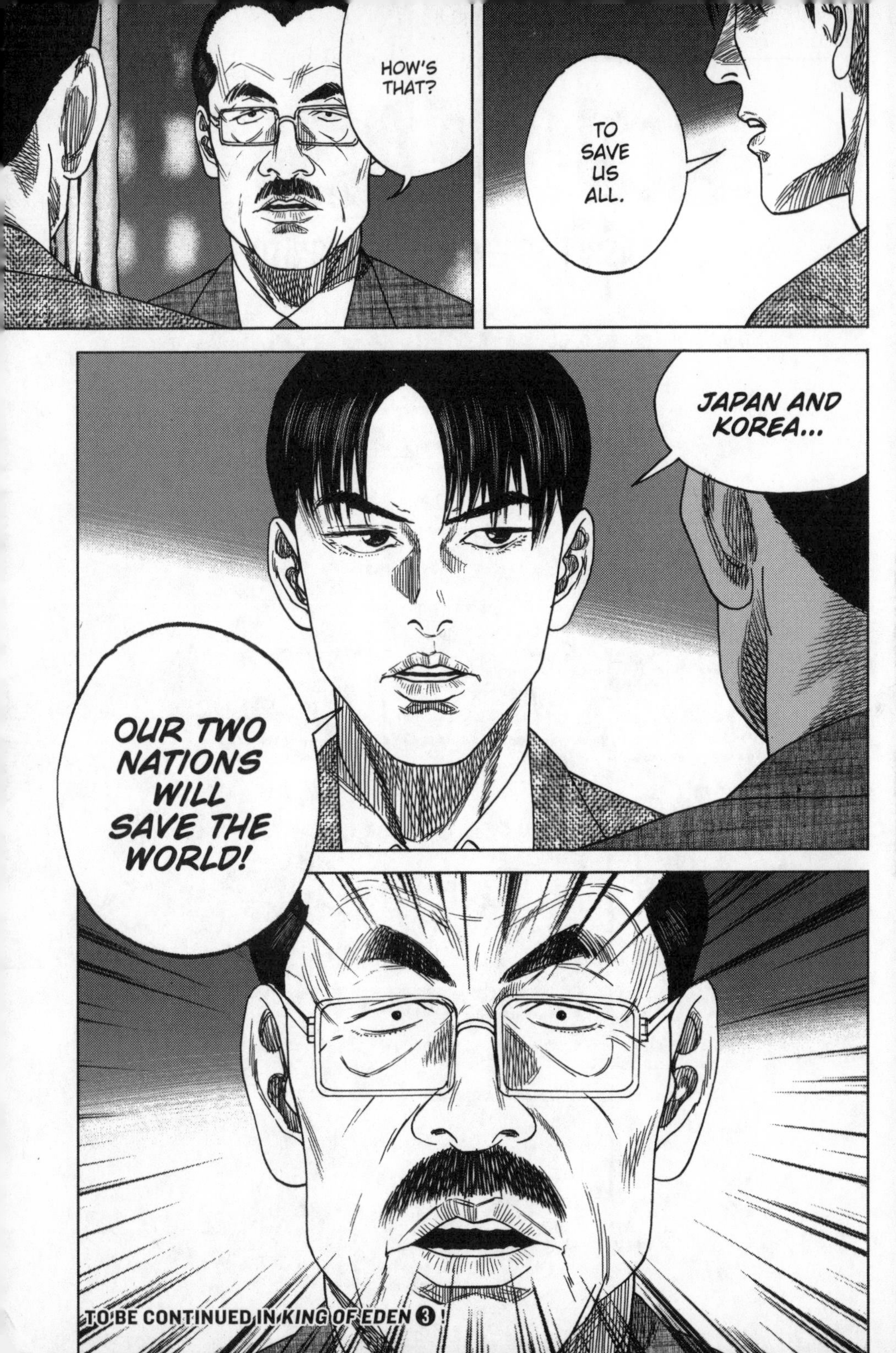
TO SAVE US ALL.
HOW'S THAT?
JAPAN AND KOREA...
OUR TWO NATIONS WILL SAVE THE WORLD!
TO BE CONTINUED IN KING OF EDEN 3 !

KING OF EDEN 02

Story by **TAKASHI NAGASAKI**   Art by **IGNITO**

Translation: **CALEB D. COOK**   Lettering: **ABIGAIL BLACKMAN**

KING OF EDEN Volume 2
© 2016 Takashi Nagasaki
© 2016 Ignito
All rights reserved.
First published in Korea in 2016 by Haksan Publishing Co., Ltd.
English translation rights arranged with Haksan Publishing Co., Ltd.

English translation © 2020 by Yen Press, LLC

Yen Press
150 West 30th Street, 19th Floor
New York, NY 10001

Visit us at yenpress.com
facebook.com/yenpress
twitter.com/yenpress
yenpress.tumblr.com
instagram.com/yenpress

First Yen Press Edition: December 2020

Yen Press is an imprint of Yen Press, LLC.
The Yen Press name and logo are trademarks of Yen Press, LLC.

The publisher is not responsible for websites (or their content) that are not owned by the publisher.

Library of Congress Control Number 2020936432

ISBNs: 978-1-9753-1294-7 (paperback)
        978-1-9753-1293-0 (ebook)

10 9 8 7 6 5 4 3 2 1

WOR

Printed in the United States of America